READER'S DIGEST CONDENSED BOOKS

READER'S DIGEST ASSOCIATION (CANADA) LTD.
215 Redfern Ave., Montreal, Que. H3Z 2V9

Editor: Deirdre Gilbert
Associate Editor: Anita Winterberg
Design: Andrée Payette
Production Manager: Holger Lorenzen

© 1996 The Reader's Digest Association, Inc. (except *OSCAR: The True Story of a Husky*)
© 1996 The Reader's Digest Association (Canada) Ltd.
© 1992 Reader's Digest (Australia) Pty Ltd.

ISBN 0-88850-394-6

FIRST EDITION
PRINTED IN THE U.S.A.

Reader's Digest Condensed Books

In this volume

COME TO GRIEF
by Dick Francis

What sort of madman would creep about in the dead of night injuring prize racehorses? That's what Sid Halley, private investigator, wants to know. To Sid's dismay, the early clues lead straight to a longtime friend, Ellis Quint—the scion of a prominent family, an adored TV personality. Surely, he couldn't be guilty. Or could he? Spurred on by suspicion, Halley is catapulted into an investigation he fears will cost him friendships—and maybe his life. / Page 7

COMING HOME
by Rosamunde Pilcher

It was a golden time, that summer of 1939. With her parents abroad, young Judith Dunbar was welcomed into the carefree world of the Carey-Lewis family. At their opulent estate on England's Cornish coast, her life was suddenly filled with a gaiety and love she'd never known. But all too soon the winds of war scatter friends and lovers alike, leaving Judith to hope that those dear to her will one day come home again. An enthralling novel from one of today's best-loved storytellers. / Page 143

OSCAR
The True Story of a Husky
by Commander Nils Lied

Many old Antarctic hands recall
careening across the snow and ice
on a creaking wooden sled behind
a team of huskies as one of their
most pleasurable and enduring
memories. But as the years
have passed, the excited howling
of the explorers' dogs has all but
disappeared, replaced now by
the roar of the internal combustion
engine. In this portrait of Oscar,
most famous and best loved
of all Antarctic huskies, Nils Lied
gives a fascinating insight into
life on a vast but little-known
continent in an earlier era of high
adventure. / Page 379

THAT CAMDEN SUMMER
by LaVyrle Spencer

Camden, Maine, is all a-whisper.
After eighteen years Roberta Jewett
has returned to her hometown with
three daughters…and *without*
her husband! Divorce is virtually
unheard of in 1916, and folks bristle
at Roberta's free-spirited ways.
All she really wants is to raise her
girls in peace, without anyone else's
help, thank you very much. But as
the town's hostility grows, she
discovers that going it alone can get
her into serious trouble. And
listening to her heart might just
be the only way out. / Page 457

GRIEF
Dick Francis

It seems incredible, but someone has been injuring valuable thoroughbred ponies all across Britain, leaving them crippled and maimed. Who in his right mind would do such a thing? Sid Halley, a street-tough P.I., thinks he knows. The question is, will he live long enough to prove his case?

1

I HAD this friend, you see, that everyone loved.

(My name is Sid Halley.)

I had this friend that everyone loved, and I put him on trial.

The trouble with working as an investigator, as I had been doing for approaching five years, was that occasionally one turned up facts that surprised and appalled and smashed peaceful lives forever.

It had taken days of inner distress for me to decide to act on what I'd learned. Miserably, by then, I'd suffered through disbelief, through denial, through anger and at length through acceptance—all the stages of grief. I grieved for the man I'd known, for the man I *thought* I'd known, who had all along been a façade. I grieved for the loss of a friendship, for a man who still looked the same but was different, alien, despicable. I could much more easily have grieved for him dead.

The turmoil I'd felt in private had on public disclosure become universal. The press, jumping instinctively and strongly to his defense, had given me, as his accuser, a severely rough time. On racecourses, where I chiefly worked, longtime acquaintances had turned their backs. Love, support and comfort poured out towards my friend. Disbelief and denial and anger prevailed; acceptance lay a long way ahead. Meanwhile, I, not he, was the target for hatred. It would pass, I knew. One had simply to endure it, and wait.

On the morning set for the opening of his trial, my friend's mother killed herself. The news was brought to the Law Courts in

Reading, where I, a witness for the prosecution, waited alone in a side room to be called. One of the court officials came to give me the suicide information and to say that the judge had adjourned the day's proceedings.

"Poor woman!" I exclaimed, truly horrified. But the official's own sympathies were with the accused. He eyed me without favor and said I should return the following morning.

I left the room and walked slowly along the corridor towards the exit. I was fielded on the way by a senior lawyer, who drew me aside. "His mother took a room in a hotel and jumped from the sixteenth floor," he said without preamble. "She left a note saying she couldn't bear the future. What are your thoughts, Sid?"

I looked at the dark, intelligent eyes of Davis Tatum, a clumsy fat man with a lean, agile brain. "Perhaps he'll change his plea."

He half smiled. "You're in the wrong job."

I continued to the outside world to catch a train and then a taxi home.

Ginnie Quint, I thought, traveling through London. Poor, poor Ginnie Quint, choosing death in preference to the everlasting agony of her son's disgrace.

The taxi stopped outside the house in Pont Square, off Cadogan Square, where I lived on the second floor, with a balcony overlooking the central railed garden. As usual the square was quiet, with little passing traffic and only a few people on foot. An early October wind shook the dying leaves on the lime trees, floating a few of them to the ground like soft yellow snowflakes.

I climbed out of the cab and paid the driver. As I turned towards my front steps, a man who was quietly walking past sprang at me in fury and tried to brain me with a long metal bar.

I moved quickly enough to catch its weight on my shoulder, not my head, then fielded a second brutal blow with my right forearm. He was screaming at me, half demented. I seized his wrist, rolled the bulk of his body backwards over my leg and sent him sprawling. He yelled—cursing, incoherent, threatening to kill.

The taxi still stood there, its driver staring wide-mouthed. I yanked open the door and stumbled in. "Drive," I said urgently. "Drive."

"But—"

"Go *on*. Before he finds his feet and breaks your windows."

He closed his mouth and meshed his gears and wavered along the road. "Look," he said, protesting, "I didn't see nothing. I'm on my way home. D'you want me to drop you off at the police?"

"Just drive," I said, my heart thudding.

"Well . . . but where to?"

Good question. I could think of only one place to go. My haven in many past troubles. "Paddington," I said.

"The hospital, d'you mean?"

"No. The trains."

"But you've just come from there!"

"Yes, but please go back."

He rocked round in a U-turn and set off for Paddington Station, where he assured me again that he hadn't seen nothing nor heard nothing neither.

I simply paid him and let him go, and if I memorized his cab-licensing number, it was out of habit, not expectation.

As part of my normal equipment I wore a mobile phone on my belt, and walking slowly into the airy terminus, I called the man I trusted most in the world, my ex-wife's father, Rear Admiral Charles Roland, retired, in Aynsford, near Oxford. To my distinct relief he answered at the second ring.

"Charles," I said, my voice cracking a bit, "may I . . . visit?"

"Of course," he said. "Use the side door. It's not locked."

I smiled, reassured by his brevity. An undemonstrative man, he gave me nevertheless a consciousness that he cared what happened to me and would proffer rocklike support if I needed it. Like I needed it at the moment.

It was past four when the country taxi decanted me at Charles's vast old house at Aynsford and I walked into the pile I really thought of as home, the one constant in my life.

Charles occupied the large leather armchair in his small "ward-room" off the drawing room, where we always sat when we were alone. It was there that he kept his desk, his collection of fishing flies, his nautical books, his racks of priceless old orchestral recordings. It was there on the dark green walls that he'd hung photographs of the ships he'd commanded and of shipmates, and there, also, that he'd positioned a painting of me as a jockey riding over a fence at Cheltenham racecourse, a picture that summed up every ounce of vigor needed for race riding.

11

"Hullo," I said.

He spent all of five seconds looking me over. "You look thin. It's this bloody case. Weren't you supposed to be in court today?"

"It was adjourned until tomorrow."

"Get a drink," he said. An order, not an invitation.

I walked obediently to a tray on the table and looked assessingly at its decanters. I doubted if I could pour. Then I glanced up at my picture. In those days, six years ago, I'd had two hands. In those days I'd been steeplechasing's champion jockey. A nightmare fall had resulted in a horse's sharp hoof half ripping off my left hand and rendering it useless, the end of that career and the slow, lingering birth of another, as a detective. I'd spent two years pining for what I'd lost, and drifted, rudderless, like a wreck that didn't quite sink but was unseaworthy all the same. I was ashamed of those years. At the end of them, a ruthless villain had smashed beyond mending the remains of the useless hand and had galvanized me into a resurrection of the spirit, and provided the impetus for me to seek a myoelectric false hand. It worked on nerve impulses from my truncated forearm and looked realistic.

My present problem was that I couldn't move its thumb far enough from its fingers to grasp a heavy cut-glass decanter, and my right hand since the attack wasn't working too well, either. I gave up and sat in an old gold brocade armchair nearby.

"What's the matter?" Charles asked abruptly. "Why did you come? Why don't you pour a drink?"

After a moment I said dully, knowing it would hurt him, "Ginnie Quint killed herself this morning."

"What?"

"This morning. She jumped from a hotel window."

His fine-boned face went stiff. Charles had known Ginnie Quint for thirty or more years and had been fond of her and had been a guest in her house often.

Powerful memories lived in my mind also. Memories of a motherly woman, inoffensively rich, working generously for several charities and glowing in reflected glory from her famous, good-looking, successful only child, the one everyone loved.

Her son, Ellis, that I had put on trial.

The last time I'd seen Ginnie, she'd glared at me with incredulous contempt, demanding to know how I could *possibly* seek to destroy the golden Ellis, who counted me his friend, who trusted me. She rejected the guilt possibility absolutely, as did almost everyone. Even Charles, at first, had said doubtfully, "Sid, are you *sure?*"

After the first bombshell—a proposed solution to a crime that had had half the country baying for blood (but not *Ellis's* blood; that was unthinkable)—there had been his remand into custody (a *scandal;* he should be let out *immediately* on bail), and then a sudden press silence while the sub judice law came into effect.

Under British sub judice law no case might be publicly discussed between the remand and the trial. Uninformed public opinion had consequently stuck at the Ellis-is-innocent stage, and I'd had nearly three months, now, of obloquy.

Ellis Quint, you see, was a Young Lochinvar. Once champion amateur jump jockey, he had flashed onto television screens like a comet—brilliant, able, the ultimate chat-show host that raised the nation's happiness level, the shining star to whom everyone, from tiara to baseball cap, responded. Manufacturers fell over themselves to tempt him to endorse their products, and half the kids in England strode about in jockey-type riding boots. And it was this paragon that I sought to eradicate.

No one seemed to blame the tabloid columnist who'd written, "The once revered Sid Halley, green with envy, tries to tear down a talent he hasn't a prayer of matching." Or "A spiteful little man trying to compensate for his own inadequacies."

The telephone at my waist buzzed suddenly, and I answered.

"Sid—Sid—" The woman on the other end was crying. I'd heard her cry often.

"Are you at home?" I asked.

"No. In the hospital."

"Tell me the number, and I'll phone straight back." To Charles I said, "May I use your phone?"

He waved a hand permissively towards his desk, and I called Linda Ferns back. She was trying not to cry. "Sid, Rachel's worse. She's asking for you. Can you come?"

"How bad is she?"

"Her temperature keeps going up—" A sob stopped her.

Dear God. Nine-year-old Rachel Ferns lay in a hospital a hundred and fifty miles away. Ill to death this time, it seemed.

I explained where I was. "I have to be in court tomorrow morn-

13

ing, but I'll come as soon as I get out. Promise her. Tell Rachel I'll be there tomorrow. Tell her I'll bring six wigs and an angelfish."

I put down the receiver. Charles said, "The child?"

"It sounds as if she's dying."

"You knew it was inevitable."

"It doesn't make it any easier." I sat down again slowly. "I would go tonight if it would save her life, but I—" I stopped, knowing no one could.

Charles said, "What else is there—that you haven't told me?"

I looked at him.

"I know you too well, Sid," he said. "You didn't come all this way to tell me about Ginnie. You could have done that by phone."

I shifted in the chair. "Gordon Quint tried to kill me," I said.

Gordon Quint was Ginnie's husband. Ellis was their son.

It struck Charles silent, and it took a great deal to do that.

After a while I said, "When they adjourned the trial, I went home. Gordon was waiting in Pont Square—with an iron bar." I swallowed. "He aimed for my head, but I ducked and it hit my shoulder. He tried again. I used judo to tumble him onto his back, and all the while he was screaming that I'd killed Ginnie. He was half mad, raving, really. Said I'd destroyed his family. Swore I'd die for it. I don't think he knew what he was saying."

Charles said dazedly, "So what did you do?"

"The taxi was still there, so . . . er . . . I got back into it."

"You got back— But what about Gordon?"

"I left him lying on the pavement, screaming revenge. I . . . er . . . I don't think I'll go home tonight, if I can stay here."

Charles said faintly, "Of course you can stay. You told me once that this was your home. Believe it."

I did. Aynsford offered respite. I would go back soon enough to defuse Gordon Quint. I would swear an oath in court and tear a man to shreds. I would hug Linda Ferns and, if I was in time, make Rachel laugh. But for this one night I would sleep soundly in Charles's house and let the well of mental stamina refill.

Charles said, "Did Gordon . . . er . . . hurt you, with his bar?"

I sighed. "I think he's cracked a bone in my arm."

His gaze flew instantly to the left arm—the plastic job.

"No," I said. "The other one."

Aghast, he said, "Your *right* arm?"

14

"Well, yeah. But only the ulna, which is on the little-finger side of the arm. The radius will act as a natural splint."

"But *Sid*—"

"Don't *worry*, Charles. It'll heal. I broke the same bone worse when I was racing."

"But you had two hands then."

"Yes, I did. So would you pick up that damned heavy brandy decanter and slosh half a pint of anesthetic into a glass?"

Wordlessly he got to his feet and complied. Afterwards he said, "So the taxi driver was a witness."

"The taxi driver is a don't-get-involved man. But look," I said reasonably, "what would you have me do? Prosecute? Gordon Quint is not your average murderer. Besides, he's your friend, and I, too, have eaten in his house. But he hates me for attacking Ellis, the light of his life, and he'd not long learned that his adored wife had killed herself because she couldn't bear what lies ahead. So how do you think he feels?" I paused. "I'm just glad he didn't succeed in smashing my brains in—for *his* sake as well as my own."

Charles shook his head resignedly, and we sat in companionable silence. I drank brandy, and the knots of tension relaxed in my stomach, but I felt the effects of the iron bar from neck to fingers. So why didn't I give up chasing the deadlier crooks? I'd stopped asking myself why I did it. Clearly there was a need for what I could do. I had more offers of work than I could accept.

Most jobs took less than a week, particularly those that involved looking into someone's credit. Trainers paid me to assure that if they bought expensive two-year-olds for new owners, they wouldn't be left with a mountain of debt. I'd saved people from confidence tricksters, and I'd uncovered absconding debtors, thieves and imaginative felons of all sorts. People had sobbed on my shoulders from joy and deliverance; others had threatened and battered to make me quit. Linda Ferns would hug me and Gordon Quint hate me. So why didn't I quit? I didn't know the answer.

The mobile phone buzzed, and I answered it.

"Sid, this is Davis Tatum. I've news for you." Tatum was a lawyer in the same firm as the prosecutor in Ellis's case.

"Give me your number, and I'll call you back."

"Oh? Oh, okay." He gave his number, and as before, I used Charles's phone to call.

15

"Sid," said Tatum, "Quint is changing his plea from not guilty to guilty by reason of diminished responsibility. Seems his mother's demonstration of no confidence in his innocence has had its effect." He chuckled. "The trial will be adjourned for a week, so you don't have to turn up tomorrow."

"Good."

"But I hope you will. There's a job for you."

"What sort of job?"

"Investigating, what else? Can we meet privately?"

"All right," I said. "How about five o'clock in the upstairs bar of Le Meridien restaurant in Piccadilly?"

"Good. But where are you? The press are looking for you."

"They can wait a day. See you tomorrow."

I replaced Charles's receiver. He looked at the mobile instrument I'd laid on the table and asked the obvious question: "Why do you ring them back? Why don't you just talk?"

"Well," I said, "someone is listening to this gadget."

"Listening?"

I explained about the insecurity of open radio transmission, which allowed anyone clever and expert to hear what they shouldn't.

Charles said, "How do you know someone's listening to you?"

"A lot of small things people know that I haven't told them."

"Who is it?"

"I don't know. Someone has also accessed my computer."

He said with slight impatience, "Computers are beyond me."

"I've had to learn," I said. "A bit different from scudding over hurdles. . . . I wish I was still racing."

"I know. But if you were, you'd be coming to the end of it now—at thirty-four—wouldn't you?"

I nodded. Thirty-five loomed.

"You're of more use to more people the way you are."

Charles had said once that I was like a brick wall when things were bad, that I shut out the world and retreated into myself. Jenny, my loved and lost wife, had said she couldn't live with it. She'd wanted me to give up race riding and become a softer-shelled person, and when I wouldn't—or couldn't—we had shaken acridly apart. She had recently remarried, this time to a safe, uncomplicated fellow with a knighthood. The unhappy Mrs. Halley was now serenely Lady Wingham. A photograph of her with

16

the beaming Sir Anthony stood in a silver frame on Charles's desk.

"How's Jenny?" I asked politely.

"Fine," Charles answered. "He's a bore, after you."

"You can't say such things."

"I can say what I bloody well like in my own house."

In harmony and mutual regard we passed the evening, disturbed only by five more calls on my mobile phone, all demanding to speak with Sid Halley. I said each time, "This is an answering service. Leave your number, and we'll pass on your message."

All of the callers, it seemed, worked for newspapers, a fact that particularly left me frowning. I told Charles, "This number's not in any directory. I give it only to people I'm working for. So how do half the London papers know it?"

"How will you find out?" Charles asked.

"Um . . . engage Sid Halley to look into it, I daresay."

Charles laughed. I felt uneasy. Someone had been listening on that number, and now someone had broadcast it. It wasn't that my phone conversations were excessively secret—I'd started the semi-exclusive client number so that the machine didn't buzz unnecessarily at awkward moments—but now I had a sense that someone was crowding me. Assaulting me electronically. *Stalking.*

I went to bed early and found that Charles's longtime house-keeper, Mrs. Cross, had as usual left warm welcoming lights on in my room and had put out fresh pajamas and fluffy towels. A pity the day's troubles couldn't be as easily cosseted into oblivion.

I undressed and brushed my teeth and eased off the artificial hand. My left arm ended uselessly four inches below the elbow—a familiar punctuation, but still a sort of bereavement.

My right arm now twinged violently at every use.

Damn the lot, I thought.

2

THE morning brought little improvement.

Waking to a couple of faulty arms, I telephoned London from Charles's secure number and talked to my friend at Teledrive, a car-hire firm I sometimes used when I wanted to keep away from

17

prying eyes. "Bob?" I said. "I need to get from northwest of Oxford to Kent, Canterbury. There'll be a couple of stops on the way and, sometime this afternoon, a return to London. Can you do it?"

"Give me the address," he said briefly. "We're on our way."

I joined Charles in the dining room for breakfast. He held a newspaper account of Ginnie Quint's death. " 'Friends say she appeared depressed about her son's forthcoming trial,' " he said, reading aloud. " 'Her husband, Gordon, was unavailable for comment.' In other words, the press couldn't find him."

Ordeal by newsprint, I thought. The latter-day torture.

"Seriously, Sid," Charles said, "take care."

"Sure." I sorted through the flurry of impressions I'd gathered in the brief seconds of violence in Pont Square. "I don't know where Ginnie was when she jumped," I said, "but I don't think Gordon was with her. I mean, when he leaped at me, he was wearing workday clothes: mud on his boots, old tweed jacket. He hadn't been staying in any sixteen-story hotel. And the metal bar he hit me with . . . it was a five-foot iron fence post, the sort you thread wire through for fencing. I'd say he was at home in Berkshire, working, when he was told about Ginnie."

I told Charles I'd engaged Teledrive to pick me up.

"Is Mrs. Ferns paying you?" Charles neutrally asked.

"Not anymore."

"Who is, exactly?" He liked me to make a profit. I did, but he seldom believed it.

"I don't starve," I said. "Have you ever tried three or four eggs whipped up in mushroom soup? Instant mushroom omelette, not at all bad."

"Disgusting," Charles said.

"You get a different perspective, living alone."

"You need a new wife," Charles said. "What about that girl who used to share a flat with Jenny? I thought you and she were having an affair."

No one had affairs anymore. Charles's words were half a century out of date. But though the terms might now be different, the meaning was eternal.

"A summer picnic," I said. "The frosts of winter killed it off."

The car arrived. I thanked Charles for his sanctuary. "Anytime," he said.

We parted as usual without physically touching. Eye contact said it all. Getting the driver to thread his way through the maze of shopping dead ends in the town of Kingston, in Surrey, I acquired six party wigs from a carnival store and an angelfish in a plastic tub from a pet shop; and, thus armed, arrived eventually at the children's cancer ward that held Rachel Ferns. Linda greeted me with glittering tears. In one of those unpredictable quirks that made leukemia a roller coaster of hope and despair, Rachel was marginally better, awake, and pleased at my arrival.

"Did you bring the angelfish?" she demanded by way of greeting.

I held up the plastic bucket. Linda took it and removed the lid. Inside, the shining black-and-silver fish swam vigorously.

"I'm going to call him Sid," Rachel said.

She'd been a lively, pretty child according to photographs. Now she was all huge eyes in a bald head, and frighteningly frail.

When her mother first called me to investigate an attack on Rachel's pony, the illness had been in remission. Rachel had become special to me, and I'd given her a fishtank complete with lights, plants, Gothic castle and brilliant tropical inhabitants. Rachel had spent hours getting to know her new friends. Half the fish were called Sid. The tank stood in the Fernses' sitting room at home, and it seemed uncertain now whether Rachel would see the new Sid among his mates.

It was there, in the comfortable room with its unaggressively expensive modern sofas, glass-topped tables and stained-glass Tiffany lamps, that I had first met my clients Linda and Rachel Ferns.

Linda Ferns, on the telephone, had begged me to come. Five or six ponies in the district had been attacked by vandals, and one of the ponies belonged to Rachel. The police hadn't found the vandals, and her daughter was very distressed and having terrible nightmares. Would I *please* come? "I've heard you're my only hope."

I mentioned my fee. "Anything," she said.

She hadn't told me then that Rachel was ill unto death.

When I met the huge-eyed, bald-headed child, she shook hands with me gravely. "Are you really Sid Halley?" she asked.

I nodded.

"Mum said you'd come. Daddy said you didn't work for kids."

19

"I do sometimes."

"My hair is growing," she said, and I could see thin blond fuzz just showing over the pale scalp.

"I'm glad."

She nodded. "Quite often I wear a wig, but they itch. Do you mind if I don't?"

"Not in the least."

"I have leukemia," she said calmly.

"I see."

She studied my face, a child old beyond her age. "You will find out who killed Silverboy, won't you?" she said.

"I'll try," I said. "How did he die?"

"I'll tell you," Linda interrupted. "Rachel, you take Pegotty into the garden and push him round to see the flowers."

Pegotty was a contented-looking baby strapped into a buggy. Rachel pushed him outside and could presently be seen through the window giving him a close-up acquaintance with an azalea.

Linda watched. "She needs a bone marrow transplant," she said, trying to suppress sobs. "But no match to her has been found."

I said inadequately, "I'm sorry."

"Her father and I are divorced," Linda said without bitterness.

"Yes," I said.

"A bunch of vandals," Linda continued in a sudden fury, "maimed a lot of ponies in this area. Kids found their ponies *mutilated*." She blinked. "Three ponies around here were blinded. Rachel was terribly upset. All the children were. And the police couldn't find who'd done it."

"Was Silverboy blinded?" I asked.

"No, it was worse. For Rachel, it was worse. She found him out in the paddock. . . ." Linda wiped her eyes. "She wanted to sleep in a makeshift stable—a lean-to, really—with Silverboy, and I wouldn't let her. She was too ill. I know she thinks Silverboy would be alive if I'd let her sleep out there."

"What happened to him?" I asked neutrally.

Linda shook her head, unable still to tell me. She was a pretty woman in a conventional thirty-something way: trim figure, short fair hair—all the beauty tips come to admirable life. Only a dullness in the eyes spoke of the strains assailing her.

"She went out," she said eventually, "to see that his water trough was filled and not frozen over. It was bitter cold—February—and she came running back screaming, *screaming.* . . ."

I waited. She finally said starkly, "Rachel found his *foot.*"

There was a moment of utter stillness, an echo of the stunned disbelief of that dreadful morning.

"It was in all the papers," Linda said.

I nodded. I'd read about the blinded Kent ponies, hadn't realized that one had lost a foot. "I've found out since you telephoned," I said, "that round the country, not just here in Kent, there have been another half a dozen or so attacks on ponies and horses in fields."

She said unhappily, "I did see a paragraph about a horse in Lancashire, but I threw the paper away so that Rachel wouldn't read it. Every time anything reminds her of Silverboy, she has a whole week of nightmares. She wakes up sobbing. She comes into my bed, crying. Please, please find out why . . . find out *who.*"

"If you kept any newspaper accounts about the attacks on Silverboy and other ponies, I'd like to see them," I said.

She left the room and returned with a small blue suitcase. "Everything's in here," she said, "including a tape of a TV program Rachel was in." She blinked against tears. "It was actually the only good thing that happened. Ellis Quint talked with the children, and he was utterly sweet with them. So kind. Rachel loved him."

"I know him. If anyone could comfort the children, he could."

I took the case with its burden of many small tragedies back with me to London and spent indignant hours reading accounts of a degree of vandalism that must have been mind-destroying when discovered by loving children.

I hadn't seen the program when it was broadcast. The twenty-minute videotape, dated in March, showed Ellis Quint at his best, the gentle healer of unbearable sorrows, the sensible, caring commentator urging the police to treat these crimes with the seriousness given to murders. How good he was, I thought, at pitching his responses exactly right. He put his arms around Rachel and talked to her without sentimentality, not mentioning until the end of the program, when the children were offscreen, that the loss of her pony was just one more intolerable blow in a life already full of burdens.

21

For that program Rachel had worn a blond wig that gave her back her pre-chemotherapy looks. Ellis, as a final dramatic effect, had shown for a few seconds a photo of her bald and vulnerable— an ending poignant to devastation.

We had been close friends for years, Ellis and I. We had ridden against each other in races, he as a charismatic amateur, I as a dedicated pro, but both with the inner fire that made hurtling over large jumps on semiwild half-ton horses at thirty miles an hour seem wholly reasonable.

Meeting him at the races, as I often did, I asked if he'd learned any more about the mutilated Kent ponies.

"My dear old Sid," he said, smiling. "It's June now. That was months ago, wasn't it? You know what television's like. Insatiably hungry. If there were any more discoveries, I would have been told and I would have done a follow-up, but I've heard nothing."

I said, "Rachel Ferns still has nightmares."

"Poor little kid."

"She said you were very kind."

"Well . . ." He made a self-deprecating movement of his head. "It isn't so very difficult. Actually, that program did marvels for my ratings."

AMONG the newspapers Linda Ferns had given me, a London daily, the *Pump*, had stirred up the most disgust, and after about six phone calls I ran to earth the man who'd practically burned holes in the page with the heat of his prose—Kevin Mills, the *Pump*'s chief bleeding-heart reporter.

"A drink?" he said to my invitation. "Don't see why not."

We met in a pub (nice anonymous surroundings), and he told me he'd personally been down to Kent. He'd interviewed all the children and their parents, and also a lady who ran the local Pony Club, and he'd pestered the police until they'd thrown him out.

"Zilch," he said, downing a double gin and tonic. "No one saw a thing. All those ponies were out in fields, and all of them were attacked sometime between sunset and dawn."

"Always in the dark," I said.

He shook his head. "The attacks were all on fine nights, near the full moon. One poor little girl found her pony's foot near his water trough. Ellis Quint did a brilliant TV program about it. That pony was the last one in Kent, as far as I know. The police think it was a bunch of local thugs who got scared off by the fuss. And people stopped turning ponies out into unguarded fields."

I ordered him another double. He was middle-aged, half bald, doing nicely as to paunch. After he'd wiped an untidy mustache on the back of his hand, I asked him about the later, copycat attacks on thoroughbreds in other places, not Kent.

"Copycat?" he repeated. "So they say."

"But?" I prompted.

He drank, thought it over, confided, "The others are not in bunches, like Kent. As far as I know, there were about five very young horses—foals and yearlings. None of them were mares, and none of them was blinded. But . . ." He hesitated, sure of his facts, I thought, but not of how I would react to them.

"Go on."

"See, three others were two-year-olds, and all of those had a foot off." I felt the same revulsion that I saw in his face. "One was in March," he said, "one in April, one last month. Always on moonlit nights."

"But why haven't you written about it?"

"I get sent to major disasters," he said. "Air crashes, accidents, murders. Some nutter driving around chopping off a horse's foot now and again is not priority. But if there's another one this month, I'll give it both barrels. Now don't you go feeding this to other papers. I want my scoop."

"Silence," I promised, "if . . ."

He asked suspiciously, "If what?"

"If you could give me a list of the people whose thoroughbreds have been damaged."

He said cautiously, "It'll cost you."

"Done," I said, and we agreed both on a fee and on my giving him first chance at any story I might come up with.

He fulfilled his commitment that same afternoon by sending a motorbike courier bearing a sealed brown envelope containing the names and vague addresses of the owners of vandalized thorough-breds. I set off by car to visit them.

Four days later, when I returned to Linda Ferns's house, I had heard enough about man's inhumanity to horses to last me for life. But except for the three two-year-olds and Rachel's pony, the inju-

23

ries inflicted, including a hacked-off muzzle, were without pattern. It was the severed feet that were connected.

"I came across his foot by the water trough in the field," one woman said. "Just the *foot*. Tell you the truth, I brought up my breakfast." She swallowed. "He wasn't anywhere near his foot—the off-fore foot, it was. He'd wandered away on three legs, and he was eating, as if nothing had happened."

"What did you do?" I asked.

"I called the vet. He came. He gave *me* a tranquilizer."

"Was the colt insured?" I asked.

There had been no insurance. They had bred the two-year-old themselves and had been going to race him later in the year. They had been to the Cheltenham races and had backed the winner of the Gold Cup. A great day, and the very next morning . . .

I asked her for the vet's address and went to see him.

"How was the foot taken off?" I asked.

He wrinkled his forehead. "I don't rightly know. It was neat. Just the one cut, fast and clean. That was all. And the colt was calm—let me walk right up to him."

"Was it done with an axe?"

He hesitated. "I'd say more like a machete. But whoever did it was used to handling horses. That colt was loose, though wearing a head-collar."

The police had found no culprit. They'd had a report of a blue Land Rover driving away along the lane from the colt's field, but Land Rovers were two a penny in the countryside. Case not closed, but also not being actively investigated.

I drove northwards to Lancashire, into a gale of anger. Big, blustery and impressively furious, a large-scale farmer let loose his roaring sense of injustice. "Best colt I ever owned," he bellowed. "And he was *fast,* I'll tell you. He was going to Newmarket the next week." He mentioned a prestigious trainer who I knew wouldn't have accepted rubbish. "And then the damn police asked if I'd killed him for the insurance. He wasn't insured. I told them to bug off." Then words failed him. I'd met many people unjustly accused of setting fires, battering children, stealing, and I knew the vocal vibrations of truly outraged innocence. I was sure he had not taken the foot off his own colt and told him so. Some of his anger abated into surprise. "So you *believe* me?"

"I sure do." I nodded. "The point is, who knew you'd bought a fine fast colt that you had at your farm in a field?"

"Who knew? Half the county knew. I'd been boasting about him at Aintree the day before the Grand National. I was at one of those sponsors' lunch things—Topline Foods it was—and the colt was fine. It was the night after the National that the colt was got at."

He showed me photographs of the severed foot, the off fore, cut just below the fetlock. The pictures jolted. It didn't help that I'd seen my own left wrist in much the same condition. I said, "What was your vet's opinion?"

"Same as mine."

I went to see the vet. One chop, he said. Only one.

"What weapon?"

He didn't know.

I pressed onwards to Yorkshire, where barely a month earlier, at the time of the York Spring Meeting, a dark brown two-year-old colt had been deprived of his off-fore foot on a moonlit night. One chop. No insurance. Angry owners. No clues.

These owners, a stiff-upper-lip couple, asked me insistently, "Why would anyone do such a pointlessly wicked thing?"

I had no answer.

The wife said, "We had such a lovely week. Every year we have people to stay for the York Spring Meeting—such fun, you see— and this year dear Ellis Quint was one of our guests. He was filming for one of his television programs at the races, so we were all invited behind the scenes and enjoyed it so. And then, the very night after all our guests had left, well . . ."

"That colt was so beautiful," she said, "and he was going into training soon. All our guests had admired him."

The husband said with difficulty, "Jenkins—our groom—found the foot by the gate, beside the water trough."

His wife went on. "Jenkins told us that Ellis had done a program a few months ago about a pony's foot being cut off and the children being so devastated. So we wrote to Ellis about our colt, and he phoned at once to say how awful for us. There wasn't anything he could do, of course, except sympathize."

"No," I agreed, and I felt only the faintest twitch of surprise that Ellis hadn't mentioned the York colt when I'd been talking to him less than a week earlier about Rachel Ferns.

25

3

BACK in London, I met Kevin Mills for lunch.
"It's time for both barrels," I said.

He swigged a double gin. "What have you discovered?"

I outlined the rest of the pattern, beyond what he'd told me about two-year-olds and moonlit nights. A single chop from something like a machete, always to the off-fore foot, always near a water trough, always after a major local race meeting. And no insurance.

"And this Saturday," I said levelly, "we have the Derby."

Mills put his glass down slowly, frowning, thinking. "Tell you what. It's worth a *warning*. I'll get the message into the paper somewhere. 'Don't leave two-year-old colts unguarded in open fields during and after Epsom.' I don't think I can do more than that."

"It might be enough."

"Yeah. *If* all the owners of colts read the *Pump*."

"It will be the talk of the racecourse. I'll arrange that."

Mills went away to write his column, and I traveled on to Kent to report to Linda.

"I don't think the thugs that mutilated ponies round here had anything to do with Silverboy," I told her.

Linda protested. "But there couldn't be *two* lots of vandals."

"I think there were."

We sat by the sitting-room window again, watching Rachel push Pegotty in his buggy around the lawn. "I'd do anything to save her," Linda said. "The doctor said that if she'd had several siblings, one of them might have had the right tissue type. Joe—Rachel's father—is half Asian. It seems harder to find a match. Joe donated sperm, and I had the baby by artificial insemination. But he doesn't match Rachel." She gulped. "So I have Pegotty—he's Peter, but we call him Pegotty—and we still can't find a match for Rachel."

"I'm so sorry," I said.

She nodded. "Go and talk to Rachel. She likes you."

I went into the garden, and Rachel and I sat side by side on a bench, like old buddies. I apologized for not yet finding Silverboy's attacker.

"But you will, won't you?"

"I hope so," I said.

She nodded. "I told Daddy I was sure you would. He says some-one chopped your hand off, just like Silverboy." She regarded me gravely, awaiting confirmation.

"Er," I said, unnerved, "not exactly like Silverboy. Does it matter to you?"

"Yes," she said. "I was thinking about it in bed last night. I have awful dreams. I tried to stay awake because I didn't want to go to sleep and dream about you having your hand chopped off."

She was trying to be calm, but I could feel hysteria near the surface; so, stifling my own reluctance to talk about it, I gave her an abbreviated account of what had happened.

"I was a jockey," I began, "and one day my horse fell in a race, and while I was on the ground, another horse landed straight on my wrist and . . . um . . . tore it apart. It got stitched up, but I couldn't use my hand much. I had to stop being a jockey and start doing what I do now—finding out things."

She nodded.

"Well, I found out something that an extremely nasty man didn't want me to know, and he . . . er . . . he hurt my bad wrist so much the doctors couldn't fix it, so they decided that I'd be better off with a useful plastic hand instead of the useless old one."

"So he didn't really . . . not *really* chop it off."

"No. So don't waste dreams on it."

She smiled with quiet relief and put her hand down delicately but without hesitation on the plastic skin of the replacement.

"It isn't *warm*," she said with surprise.

"Well, it isn't cold, either."

She laughed with uncomplicated fun. "How does it work?"

"I tell it what to do," I said simply. "I send a message from my brain down my arm saying 'open thumb from fingers,' or 'close thumb,' to grip things; and the messages reach very sensitive termi-nals called electrodes, which are inside the plastic and against my skin." I paused. "My real arm ends about there." I pointed. "The electrodes feel my muscles trying to move. That's how it works."

"Do electrodes work on electricity? I mean, you're not plugged into the wall or anything?"

"Clever girl!" I said. "There's a special battery that slots into the outside, and I charge up the battery on a charger, which is plugged into the wall."

She looked at me assessingly. "It must be pretty useful to have that hand. Ellis Quint told Daddy you can't tell it's plastic unless you touch it."

I asked, surprised, "Does your daddy know Ellis Quint?"

She nodded. "He helped Daddy buy Silverboy. He was really sorry when he found out that's who he was doing the program about."

"Yes, he would be."

"I wish," she said, looking at my hand, "that Silverboy could have had a new foot with electrodes and a battery." She rubbed her own fingers over the plastic ones.

I said, "Will you show me where you kept Silverboy?"

She drew back, then said, "If I can hold your hand."

"Of course." I stood up and held out my real hand.

"No. I mean, can I hold this hand that you can't feel?"

It seemed to matter to her that I wasn't whole, that I would understand someone ill, without hair. I said lightly, "You can hold which hand you like."

She nodded, then pushed Pegotty into the house and matter-of-factly told Linda she was taking me to see where Silverboy had lived. Linda gave me a wild look but let us go, so the bald-headed child and the one-handed man walked in odd companionship down a short lane to the field at its end.

The field was a lush paddock of little more than an acre. A pipe with a tap stood next to the galvanized water trough.

"His foot was by the trough," she said jerkily. "I mean, you could see *blood* . . . and white bones."

"Don't talk about it." I pulled her with me back along the lane, afraid I should never have asked her to show me.

She gripped my unfeeling hand in both of hers. "It's all right when I'm awake," she said. "I don't like going to sleep."

The desperation of that statement had to be addressed. I stopped walking and said, "I don't usually tell anyone this, but I still have bad dreams about my hand. I dream I'm still a jockey. I dream about my smashed wrist. Rotten dreams can't be helped. They're awful when they happen, but one does wake up."

"And then you have leukemia . . . or a plastic arm."

28

"Life's a bugger," I said.

She put her hand over her mouth, and in a fast release of tension, she giggled. "Mum won't let me say that."

"Say it into your pillow."

"Do you?"

"Pretty often."

We went on into the house, and Rachel again pushed Pegotty into the garden. I stayed in the sitting room with Linda.

"Was she all right?" Linda asked anxiously.

"She's a very brave child," I said. "Linda, did you hear anything at all the night Silverboy was attacked? Any car engines?"

"Everyone asks that. I'd have said if I had. The police think the thugs stopped their car in the road and walked down the lane to the field."

"Could they have seen Silverboy from the road?"

"Yes. The police say they must have been out looking for un-guarded ponies like Silverboy. Why don't you ask them?"

"If you believed the police, you wouldn't have asked me for help."

"Joe says calling you in is a waste of money," she confessed.

"Ah. I can stop right now, if you like."

"No. Yes. I don't *know*." Undecided, she said, "Rachel dreams that Silverboy is standing in the field in the moonlight. He's *shining*, she says. And a dark mass of monsters oozes down the lane— oozes is what she says—to kill him. She runs to warn him but can't get through the monsters. They clutch at her like cobwebs. They reach Silverboy and smother his light, and all his hair falls out, and she wakes up screaming. It's always the same nightmare. I thought if you could find out who cut off Silverboy's foot, the monsters would have names and faces and Rachel would stop thinking they're lumps that ooze and won't let her through."

After a pause I said, "Give me another week."

She turned away sharply and, crossing to a desk, wrote me a check. I looked at the amount. "That's more than we agreed on."

"Whatever Joe says, I want you to go on trying."

I gave her tentatively a small kiss on the cheek. She smiled.

I drove back to London thinking of the cynical old ex-policeman who had taught me the basics of investigation. "There are two cardinal rules in this trade," he said. "One, never believe everything a client tells you. And two, never never get emotionally involved with your client." Which was all very well, except when your client was a bright, truthful nine-year-old fighting a losing battle against a rising tide of lymphoblasts.

I BOUGHT a take-out curry on the way home and ate it before spending the evening on overdue paperwork: detailed accounts of what I'd done on behalf of clients, itemized bills supported by receipts. I almost always played fair, even with clients I didn't like. Investigators had been known to charge for seven days' work when, with a little application, they could have finished the job in three. I didn't want that sort of reputation. Speed succeeded in my new occupation as essentially as in my old.

My pleasant (and, frankly, expensive) apartment consisted of a bathroom and kitchen and three other rooms: bedroom, big sunny sitting room, and a third, smaller room that I used as an office. I had no secretary or helper. No one read the secrets I uncovered except the client and me, and whatever the client did with the information he'd paid for was his or her own business.

I typed a report on my word processor, using a computer system that wasn't connected to any phone line. That way no one could tap into it. As an added precaution against thieves, I used unbreakable passwords. It was my second computer system that could theoretically be accessed—the one connected by modem to the big wide world of universal information. Any snooper was welcome to anything found there.

My cynical mentor had said, "If you use random passwords and change them weekly, you should be safe while you're actually working on something, but once you've finished, put a backup copy in a bank vault and wipe the office computer clean. Never forget that people you are investigating may go to violent lengths to stop you."

He had been right about that.

I had told Rachel about my own bad dreams, but I could never describe how vivid and liquefying they could be. That night, after falling asleep, I descended into a familiar dungeon.

It was always the same. It was a big dark place, and some people were coming to cut off both my hands. *Both.*

They were making me wait, but they would come. There would be agony, humiliation, helplessness—and no way out.

I semi-awoke in shaking, sweating, heart-thudding terror, then realized with flooding relief that I was safe in my own bed. I slid back into sleep, and the whole appalling nightmare cycled again.

I forced myself to wake up properly, to get out of bed, put on a robe and sit in the sitting room with all the lights on.

I looked at the space where a left hand had once been, and I looked at the strong whole right hand and acknowledged that often I could not repress stabs of savage, petrifying fear that one day it would indeed be both. The trick was not to let the fear rule my life.

It was pointless to reflect that I'd brought the terrors on myself. I had chosen to be a jockey, chosen to go after violent crooks, was even now actively hunting someone who knew how to cut off a horse's foot with one chop. I had to be mentally deranged.

But then, there were people like Rachel Ferns.

Much of my torment could have been avoided but for my own obstinate nature. But that child had had her hair fall out and had found her beloved pony's foot, and none of that was her fault. No nine-year-old mind could sleep sweetly under such assaults.

Oh, Rachel, I thought, I would dream your nightmares for you if I could.

IN THE morning I made a chart of the four similar cases. Across the top I wrote, "Ferns," "Cheltenham," "Aintree," "York," and down the left-hand column I entered, "date," "name of owner," "racing program," "motive" and, finally, "who knew of victim's availability?"

I phoned Kevin Mills. "Sid," he said heartily. "The warning will be in the paper tomorrow."

"Great," I said, "but could you get something that would raise all sorts of reverberations if I asked for it myself?"

"Such as what?"

"Such as Topline Foods' guest list for the lunch they gave at Aintree the day before the National."

He said, "What are you up to?"

"The scoop is still yours. Exclusive."

"I don't know why I trust you."

"It pays off," I said, smiling, and he put down his receiver with a crash, but I knew he would do what I asked.

It was Friday. At Epsom they would be running the Coronation Cup and also the Oaks, the fillies' equivalent of the Derby.

Racecourses still drew me as if I were tethered to them with bungee elastic, but before setting out, I telephoned the woman whose colt's foot had been amputated after the Cheltenham Gold Cup.

"Would you mind a few more questions?"

"Not if you can catch the villains."

"Well, was the two-year-old alone in his field?"

"Yes, he was. In the paddock nearest to the house."

"And," I said neutrally, "how many people knew about him?"

"All our friends knew. We were excited about his prospects and had been asking around about trainers at Cheltenham. I'm sure you know you're in the Hall of Fame there."

"It's an honor," I said. "They gave me an engraved glass goblet."

"Well, we were looking at the exhibit on your life when dear Ellis Quint stopped to chat."

Oh, *hell,* I thought.

Her warm smile was audible. "We've known Ellis for years, of course. So he called in at our house for a drink on his way home after the Gold Cup. Such a *lovely* day." She sighed. "And then those *villains* . . . You will catch them, won't you, Sid?"

"If I can," I said.

I drove to Epsom Downs, spirits as gray as the sodden skies. The bars were crowded. I went up on the stands and watched the two-year-olds, those thousand-pound bodies, swoop down at speeds near forty miles an hour on spindly forelegs scarcely thicker than a man's wrist.

Horses had very fast instincts for danger and were easily scared. Young horses seldom stood still. Yet one chop had done the job each time. *Why* had those poor animals stood quietly while the deed was done?

I drifted around pleasurably for the rest of the day, slept thankfully without nightmares and found on a dry and sunny Derby Day that my friendly *Pump* reporter had really done his stuff.

"Lock up your colts," he directed in the paper, and he outlined in succinct paragraphs the similarities in "the affair of the four severed fetlocks" and pointed out that on that very night after the Derby—the biggest race of all—there would be moonlight enough for flashlights to be unnecessary. "And if," he finished with a flourish, "you should spy anyone creeping through the fields armed with a machete, phone ex-jockey turned gumshoe Sid Halley, who can be reached via the *Pump*'s special hot line. Phone the *Pump!* Save the colts! Halley to the rescue!"

I NEEDN'T have worried about spreading the message on the racecourse. No one spoke to me about anything else all afternoon.

I phoned the *Pump* myself and was told that Mills had gone to a train crash—sorry.

"So how are you rerouting calls about colts to me?" I asked. "I didn't arrange this."

"As Kevin isn't available, we're rerouting all Halley hot line calls to . . ." The number read out was my own!

Hell's bells, I thought. He could have warned me.

I watched the Derby with inattention. An outsider won. Later Ellis teased me about the piece in the *Pump*. "Hot Line Halley," he said, clapping me on the shoulder, deeply friendly and wiping out in a flash the doubts I'd been having about him. "It's an extraordinary coincidence, Sid, but I actually *saw* one of those colts. I was staying with some chums for the York meeting, and after we'd gone, someone vandalized their colt."

"The really puzzling thing is motive," I said. "I went to see all the owners. None of the colts was insured. Nor was Rachel Ferns's pony."

"Does insurance really take the place of racing? All this sounds a pretty dull life for you, after what we used to do."

"Does television replace it for you?"

"Not a hope." He laughed. "Danger is addictive, wouldn't you say? I get bloody bored sometimes with being a chat-show celebrity. Don't you ache for speed?"

"Every day," I said.

"You're about the only person who understands me. No one else can see that fame's no substitute for danger. Well, good luck, Hot Line," Ellis said.

It was the owners of two-year-old colts that had the good luck. My telephone rang nonstop all that night, but the calls were all from people jumping at shadows. The moonlight shone on quiet fields, and no two-year-old thoroughbred or pony lost a foot.

In the days that followed, interest and expectation dimmed and died. It was twelve days after the Derby, on the last night of the Royal Ascot meeting, that the screaming heebie-jeebies reawoke.

4

O N THE Monday after the Derby, Kevin Mills faxed me the list of guests entertained by Topline Foods before the Grand National. It was the top of the list that did the psychological damage. "Guest of honor," it announced, "Ellis Quint."

All the doubts I'd banished came roaring back. Back, too, came self-ridicule. It was *stupid* to give any weight to a coincidence. All the same, I got my chart out, and in very small letters, as if to physically diminish the implication, I wrote in each "who knew of victim's availability?" space the unthinkable words, "Ellis Quint."

The "motive" boxes still remained empty, though. I wrote, "self-gratification," but it seemed too weak. Insanity? Psychosis? No. Impossible. It didn't fit the Ellis I knew. Not the man I'd raced against and laughed with and had deemed a close friend for years. One couldn't know someone that well and yet not know them at all. Could one?

Relentless thoughts kept me awake all night, and in the morning I sent Linda Ferns's check back to her. "I've got no further," I wrote. "I'm exceedingly sorry."

"Dear Sid," Linda wrote back. "Keep the money. I know you'll find the thugs one day. I don't know what you said to Rachel, but she hasn't had any bad dreams since you came last week. For that alone I would pay you double. Affectionately, Linda Ferns."

I put the check in a pending file, caught up with paperwork and attended my usual judo training session.

The judo I practiced was the subtle art of self-defense, the shifting of balance that used an attacker's own momentum to overcome him. With the built-in drawbacks of half an arm, a light frame and a height of about five feet seven, my overall requirement was not physical domination but survival.

I did the routines absentmindedly. Ellis wouldn't leave my thoughts.

I was wrong. Of *course* I was wrong. Ellis's face was universally known. He wouldn't risk being seen sneaking around fields at night armed with anything like a machete.

34

But he was bored with celebrity. Fame was no substitute for danger, he'd said. Everything he had was not enough.

All the same . . . *he couldn't.*

In the second week after the Derby I went to the four days of the Royal Ascot meeting. Ellis was there, of course, and sought me out.

"How's it going, Hot Line?"

"The hot line is silent."

"There you are, then. You've frightened your foot merchant off."

"Forever, I hope."

"What if he can't help it?" Ellis said.

I turned my head, looked in his eyes. "I'll catch him."

He smiled and looked away. "Everyone knows you're a whiz at that sort of thing, but I'll bet you—"

"Don't," I interrupted. "Don't bet on it. It's bad luck."

Someone came up to his other elbow, claiming his attention, and he was drawn away. I couldn't believe that he told me *why.*

What if he can't help it?

Could compulsion lead to cruel, senseless acts? Yes, it could.

But not in Ellis. No, *not* in Ellis.

At five thirty in the morning the day after the Ascot Gold Cup, I sleepily answered my telephone to hear a high, agitated female voice saying, "I want to reach Sid Halley."

"This is Sid Halley," I said, pushing myself up to sitting and squinting at the clock. "How can I help you?"

"We have a colt with a foot off," she said.

After a breath-catching second I said, "Your name and address?"

She gave them—"Betty Bracken, Manor House, Combe Bassett, Berkshire"—stumbling on the words as if she couldn't remember. Then she said jerkily, "But why? Why our colt?"

"I'll be there in an hour," I said.

What if he can't help it?

Let it not be Ellis, I thought.

I made the eighty-mile trip to Berkshire in record time. It was a lovely June morning, fine and fresh, as I curled through the gates, cruised to a stop and walked through the open front doors to loud voices and a general gnashing of teeth. The woman who'd phoned rushed up to me. "Sid Halley? Thank heaven."

There were two uniformed policemen in the room, and a crowd

35

of what later proved to be family members, neighbors and ramblers, along with half a dozen dogs.

"Where's the colt?" I asked the woman.

"In the field. The vet's there." She led me at once through back passages reminiscent of those of Aynsford, of those of any house built with servants in mind. We passed a gun room and a mudroom and emerged at last through a rear door into a yard inhabited by trash cans. From there we hurried along a hedge-bordered path to a metal-railing gate. Finally, before us was a lane full of vehicles and about ten people leaning on paddock fencing.

My guide was tall, thin, fluttery, about fifty, dressed in old cord trousers and a drab olive sweater. I had the impression that she was a woman to whom looks mattered little. But she was deferred to. The men leaning on the fence rails straightened and all but touched their forelocks. "Morning, Mrs. Bracken." She nodded and ushered me through the gate.

In the field stood two more men, a masculine-looking woman and a colt with three feet. One of the men, tall and white-haired, came forward. "Now, Mrs. Bracken, it's time to put your poor boy out of his misery. And you'll be Sid Halley, I suppose," he said with a strong Scottish accent. We shook hands.

I walked over to the colt and found him wearing a head-collar, with a rope halter held familiarly by the woman. He watched me with calm, bright eyes, unafraid. I stroked his nose, talking quietly. He moved his head upward against the pressure. I stroked his neck. His skin was dry: no pain, no fear, no distress.

I squatted down for a close look at the colt's off fore. The severed end had been sliced through as cleanly as if a practiced chef had used a disjointing knife.

"Well?" the Scotsman challenged.

I stood up. "Where's his foot?"

"Over yon, behind the water trough." As I turned, he added, "I put it there, out of sight. It was they ramblers that came to it first."

"Ramblers?"

Mrs. Bracken explained. "One Saturday every June the local rambling clubs turn out in force to walk the footpaths in this part of the country, to keep them legally open for the public. They gather soon after dawn, while it is still cool, and set off across my land first. They hammered on my door about five fifteen."

I walked over to the water trough to look at the foot. There were horse-feed nuts scattered everywhere. There was a light shoe on the hoof, the sort fitted to youngsters to protect their forefeet in the field. I hadn't seen other severed feet. The reality moved me to fury and to grief.

I unclipped the mobile phone from my belt and called a veterinary surgeon friend in Lambourn, twelve miles away. Bill Ruskin and I had worked on other, earlier puzzles together. "Bill?" I said. "This is Sid Halley."

"Go to sleep," he said.

"Wake up. It's six fifty, and I'm in Berkshire with the severed off-fore hoof of a two-year-old colt."

"Jeez." He woke up fast.

"I want you to look at it. What do you advise?"

"How long has it been off? Any chance of sewing it back on?"

"It's been off at least three hours, I'd say."

"What shape is the colt in generally?" he asked.

"Quiet. No visible pain."

"See if the owner'll have the colt shipped over here."

Mrs. Bracken gaped at the suggestion and said, "Yes," faintly.

Bill said, "Find a sterile surgical dressing for the leg. Wrap the foot in another dressing and a plastic bag, and pack it in a bucket of ice cubes. Where shall I send the horse ambulance?"

I explained where I was, and added, "There's a vet here urging to put the colt down. Use honey-tongued diplomacy."

"Put him on."

I handed my phone to the vet. The Scot scowled. Bill talked.

"Very well," the Scot said frostily, finally, and set about enclosing the raw leg in a surgical dressing and wrapping up the foot.

Mrs. Bracken said simply, "I didn't want to lose him. It's worth a try."

Mrs. Bracken and I returned to the house, which still rang with noise. I asked one of the policemen to shoo the crowd out. Soon the large drawing room was inhabited by five humans, three dogs and a clutter of used cups. Mrs. Bracken drifted around picking up cups from one place, only to put them down in another. She looked at me vaguely. "I paid a quarter of a million for that colt."

"Is he insured?"

"No. I don't insure my jewelry, either."

She looked round the room. Five people sat on easy chairs, offering no help. "Would someone make tea?" she asked.

No one moved.

"Mm," I said. "Well . . . er . . . who is everybody?"

"Goodness, yes. Rude of me. That's my husband." Her gaze fell affectionately on an old bald man who looked as if he had no comprehension of anything. "He's deaf, the dear man."

"I see."

"And that's my aunt, who mostly lives here." The aunt was also old and proved unhelpful.

"Our tenants." Mrs. Bracken indicated a stolid couple. "They live in part of the house. And my nephew."

Even her normal good manners couldn't keep the irritation from her voice at this last identification. The nephew was a teenager with a loose mouth and an attitude problem. He was staring at me intensely, almost, I thought fleetingly, as if he wanted to tell me something by telepathy.

I turned to Mrs. Bracken. "If you tell me where the kitchen is, I'll make you some tea."

"But you've only one hand."

I said, "I can't climb Everest, but I can sure make tea."

A streak of humor began to banish the morning's shock from her eyes. "I'll come with you," she said.

The kitchen, like the whole house, had been built on a grand scale. Without difficulties we made a pot of tea and sat at the well-scrubbed old wooden central table to drink it from mugs.

"You're not what I expected," she said. "You're *cozy*."

I liked her—couldn't help it.

She went on. "You're not like my brother said. I'm afraid I didn't explain that it is my brother who is out in the field with the vet. It was he who said I should phone you. He didn't say you were cozy; he said you were flint. I should have introduced you, but you can see how things are. Actually, I rely on him dreadfully."

"Is he," I asked neutrally, "your nephew's father?"

"Goodness, no. Jonathan is my sister's son. Fifteen. He got into trouble—expelled from school, on probation. My sister was at her wits' end, so I said he could come here for a bit." She looked suddenly aghast. "You don't think *he* had anything to do with the colt?"

"No, no. What trouble did he get into? Drugs?"

She sighed, shaking her head. "He was with two other boys. They stole a car and crashed it. Joyriding, they called it. Stealing, that's what it was. And Jonathan isn't repentant. Really, he can be a *pig*."

I drank hot tea and asked, "Is it well known hereabouts that you have this great colt in that field?"

She nodded. "Eva, who looks after him, talks of nothing else. All the village knows. That's why there are so many people here."

"And your friends?" I prompted. "Who among them came here in person to admire the colt?"

She was far from stupid, and also vehement. "No one who came here could *possibly* have done this! People like Lord and Lady Dexter? Gordon and Ginnie Quint? Darling Ellis? Of course not!"

"Of course not," I said. Ellis.

We finished the tea and went back to the drawing room. Jonathan stared at me again, and to test my own impression, I jerked my head in the direction of the door, walking that way. He stood and followed me to the front door and onto the drive. "You want to tell me something, don't you?" I said.

"I don't know. Why do you think so?"

I'd seen that bursting-at-the-seams expression too often to mistake it. He knew something that he ought to tell. I said, guessing, "Were you awake before four o'clock?"

He didn't answer, so I tried again. "You hate to be helpful, is that it? No one is going to catch you behaving well—that sort of thing? Tell me what you know. I'll give you as bad a press as you want. Your obstructive reputation will remain intact."

He glared at me. I waited.

"She'd kill me," he said. "Aunt Betty has these effing stupid rules. Be back in the house at night by eleven thirty."

"And last night," I suggested, "you weren't?"

"I got probation," he said. "Did she tell you?"

"Yeah."

"If she knew I went out again, I could get youth custody."

"If she turned you in, you mean?"

He nodded. "But to cut a foot off a horse . . ."

Perhaps he had a better nature somewhere after all. Stealing cars was okay; maiming racehorses wasn't.

"If I fix it with your aunt, will you tell me?" I asked.

39

"Make her promise not to tell Uncle Archie, her brother. He's worse. He's Establishment, man."

I made no promises. I said, "Just spill the beans. Last night you were coming back from the village. . . . When, exactly?"

"It was dark. Just before dawn. I was *running*. Aunt Betty lets the dogs out before six."

I thought, and asked, "Did you see any ramblers?"

"No. It was earlier than them."

"So who was it that you saw?"

"Not a who—what." He paused and reassessed his position. "I didn't go to the village," he said. "I'll deny it."

"You were restless. Unable to sleep. You went for a walk."

He said, "Yeah, that's it," with relief.

"And you saw?"

"A Land Rover."

"That's not so extraordinary, in the country."

"No, but it wasn't Aunt Betty's. It was blue, not green. It was in the lane near the gate into the field. I ran into it in the dark."

"Was it facing you, or did you run into the back of it?"

"Facing."

"What part of it did you touch?"

"The hood." Then he added, as if surprised by the extent of his memory, "It was quite hot."

"Did you see a number plate?"

"Not a chance. I wasn't hanging about for things like that."

"Was there no one inside?"

"I looked in fast, on the way past. No people, just machinery."

"What sort of machinery?"

"How do I know? It had handles sticking up. Like a lawn mower."

"How about an ignition key?"

"Hey!" It was a protest of hurt feelings. "I don't take every car I see. Not alone—ever."

"There's no fun in it if you're alone?"

"Not so much."

"So there *was* a key in the ignition?"

"I suppose so. Yeah."

"Think, then. Was there a key ring?"

He said unwillingly, "It was a bunch of keys. They had a little silver horseshoe dangling from them on a little chain."

"Now go back a bit to when you put your hand on the hood. You must have been looking at the windshield. Was there a tax disk on it?"

"It must have done, mustn't it?" he said.

"Anything else? Like, say, a sticker saying 'Save the Tigers'? Shut your eyes and think," I urged him. "You're running. You don't want to be seen. You nearly collide with a Land Rover. Your face is quite near the windshield—"

"There was a red dragon," he interrupted. "A red circle with a dragon in it. One of those transparent transfers that stick to glass."

"Great," I said. "Anything else?"

He gave it concentrated thought but came up with nothing more.

"I'm nothing to do with the police," I said, "and I won't spoil your probation, and I won't give you away to your aunt, but I'd like to write down what you've told me, and if you agree that I've got it right, will you sign it?"

"Hey. I don't know. I don't know why I told you."

"It might matter a lot, and I'd like to find this bugger."

"So would I." He meant it. Perhaps there was hope for him yet.

He turned on his heel and went rapidly into the house, not wanting to be seen in even semi-reputable company, I assumed. I followed more slowly. He had not returned to the drawing room, where the tenants still sat stolidly, the difficult old aunt complained about being woken carly, the deaf husband said "Eh?" at frequent intervals and Betty Bracken sat looking into space. Only the dogs, lying down, resting their heads on their front paws, seemed sane.

I said to Mrs. Bracken, "Do you by any chance have a typewriter?"

"There's one in the office," she said incuriously. "I'll show you." She rose and led me to a small, tidy back room. "Help yourself."

I sat at the typewriter and put in the date. Then I wrote:

> Finding it difficult to sleep, I went for a walk at about three thirty in the morning. In the lane near the paddock gate I passed a blue Land Rover. I did not look at the number plate. The engine was still hot when I touched the hood in passing. There was a key in the ignition on a ring with a silver horseshoe. There was no one in the vehicle. There was some sort of equipment behind the front seat. On the windshield I observed a small transfer of a red dragon in a red circle. I went past the vehicle and returned to the house.

41

I left the little office in search of Jonathan, running him to earth in the kitchen. He paused over breakfast cereal, spoon in air, while he read what I'd written. Wordlessly I held a ballpoint pen out to him. He hesitated, shrugged and signed with a flourish. He seemed actually pleased with his civic-mindedness.

Back in the drawing room, I asked where Mrs. Bracken had gone. The aunt, the tenants and the deaf husband made no reply. Negotiating the hinterland passage and the dustbin yard again, I arrived back at the field to find Mrs. Bracken, the fence leaners, and the Scots vet and her brother watching the arrival of the horse ambulance, a narrow, low-slung trailer pulled by a Land Rover. There was a driver and a groom used to handling sick and injured horses. The poor colt made a painful-looking stagger up a gentle ramp into the stall.

"Oh, *dear*," Mrs. Bracken whispered. "How could they?"

I shook my head. Rachel's pony and four prized colts. How could *anyone?*

The vet patted Betty Bracken on the arm, claimed his car from among the vehicles in the lane and drove away.

I unclipped my mobile phone and got through to someone at the *Pump,* who forwarded my call to an irate Kevin Mills at home.

"Where the devil are you?" he yelled. "All anyone gets on the hot line is your answering machine, saying you'll call back."

I explained.

"It's supposed to be my day off," he grumbled. "Can you meet me in the pub? Five o'clock?"

"Make it seven," I suggested.

"It's no longer a *Pump* exclusive, I suppose you realize?" he demanded. "But give me the inside edge, will you, buddy?"

"It's yours."

I closed my phone and warned Betty Bracken to expect the media.

"Oh, no!"

"Your colt is one too many."

"Archie!" She turned beseechingly to her brother for help.

"My dear Betty," he said, "if you can't bear to face the press, simply don't be here."

"But . . ." she wavered.

"I shouldn't waste time," I said.

42

The brother gave me an appraising glance. He himself was of medium height, lean, gray in color, a man to get lost in a crowd. His eyes alone were notable: brown, bright and *aware*. I had an uncomfortable feeling that he knew a good deal about me.

"We haven't actually met," he said to me civilly. "I'm Betty's brother, Archie Kirk."

I said, "How do you do," and I shook his hand.

5

THE lady of the manor refused to leave without her husband, and the uncomprehending old man, still saying "Eh?" was helped with great solicitude through the front door and to Archie Kirk's ancient Daimler. Betty spooned her beloved into the back seat and folded herself in beside him, patting him gently. Archie Kirk took his place behind the wheel as natural commander in chief and drove away, leaving for me the single short parting remark "Let me know."

I nodded automatically. Let him know *what?* Whatever I learned, I presumed.

I looked but couldn't find Jonathan, so I just had to trust that his boorishness would keep him well away from any inquisitive reporters. I wanted, if I could, to find the Land Rover he'd seen before its driver learned there was a need for concealment. The first thing, though, was the colt himself.

My Mercedes, milk-coffee colored, stood out front, and I set off for Lambourn, wondering what to do concerning the police. They did not, in general, approve of freelance investigators like myself, especially if working on something they felt belonged to them alone. I stepped gingerly around their sensitive areas, and also those of racing's own security services, run by the Jockey Club and the British Horseracing Board.

With the Jockey Club, I fluctuated between flavor of the month and anathema, according to who currently reigned as senior steward. With the police, collaboration depended very much on the individual I reached. The police force as a whole was divided into autonomous districts, like the Thames Valley Police, who solved crimes in their own area but might not take much notice outside.

Approaching Lambourn, I became aware of a knocking in the car and pulled over to the side with gloomy thoughts of broken shock absorbers. But after the car stopped, the knocking continued. With awakening awareness I climbed out and opened the trunk.

Jonathan lay curled in the luggage space, assaulting the milk-coffee bodywork with his shoe.

"What the hell are you doing there?" I demanded.

He looked at his shoe. Silly question. I rephrased it. "Get out."

He maneuvered himself out onto the road and walked to the locked passenger door with no attempt at apology. I slammed the trunk lid and returned to the driver's seat. I lowered the window a little and shouted, "It's only three miles to Lambourn."

"No. Hey! You can't leave me here!"

Want to bet, I thought, and set off along the deserted road. I saw him in the rearview mirror, running after me determinedly. I drove slowly, but faster than he could run. He went on running nevertheless.

After nearly a mile a curve in the road took me out of his sight. I stopped. He came around the bend, saw my car and put on a spurt, racing toward me. Resignedly I unlocked the passenger door, and he climbed in. I noted with interest that he was hardly out of breath.

Jonathan's haircut, I thought as he settled into his seat, shouted his adolescent insecurity, his desire to shock or at least to be noticed. He had bleached haphazard streaks into his hair. Straight and thick, the mop was parted in the center with a wing curving down to each cheek. From one ear around to the other ear the hair had been sliced off in a straight line. Below the line his scalp was shaved. To me it looked ugly, but then, I wasn't fifteen.

I asked Jonathan, "Have you remembered something else?"

"No, not really."

"Then why did you stow away?"

"Come on, man, give me a break. What am I supposed to do all day in that graveyard of a house?" He had a point.

"Tell me about your uncle," I said.

"What about him?"

"For starters, what does he do?"

44

"He works for the government. Some sort of civil servant. Dead boring."

Boring, I reflected, was the last adjective I would have applied to what I'd seen in Archie Kirk's eyes. "Where does he live?" I asked.

"A couple of miles from Aunt Betty."

Reaching Lambourn, I took the turn that led to the equine hospital. They were just unloading the colt from the ambulance.

I said to Jonathan, "If you want to wait half an hour for me, fine. Otherwise you're on your own. But if you try stealing a car, I'll personally see you lose your probation."

He glowered at me. I went across to where Bill Ruskin, in a white coat, was watching his patient's arrival. He said, "Hello, Sid," absentmindedly, then collected the bucket containing the foot and led the way into his laboratory.

Unwrapping the foot, he stood it on the bench and looked at it assessingly. "A clean job. Probably the colt hardly felt it."

"How was it done?" I asked.

"Hm." He considered. "There's no other point on the leg that you could amputate a foot without using a saw. I doubt if a single swipe with a heavy knife would achieve this precision."

I nodded.

"Yes, well, I think we might be looking at some kind of heavy shears. But how did he get the colt to stand still?"

"There were horse nuts on the ground."

He nodded morosely. "Slimeball. Even if I can reattach the foot, the colt will never race."

"His owner knows that. She wants to save his life."

"I'll get on with anesthetizing the colt now." He shook his head. "The foot's been off too long. I don't hold out much hope. But I'll give it a try."

"Phone my mobile." I gave him the number. "Anytime."

"See you, Sid. And catch the bugger."

I returned to my car to find Jonathan jogging around with excitement. "What's up?" I asked.

"That Land Rover that pulled the trailer with the colt—"

"What about it?"

"It had a red dragon on the windshield!"

"What? But you said a blue—"

"Yeah, yeah, it wasn't the Land Rover I saw in the lane, but it definitely had a red dragon transfer on it. Not exactly the same, I don't think, but I saw it close to before they drove off, and it has letters in it." His voice held triumph.

"Go on, then," I said. "What letters?"

"Aren't you going to say 'well done'?"

"Well done. What letters?"

"E.S.M. They were cut out of the red circle."

I returned to the hospital to find Bill and asked him where he'd bought his Land Rover.

"Our local garage got it for us from a firm in Oxford."

"What's the name of the firm?"

He thought briefly. "English Sporting Motors. Ask for Roger Brook."

The morning seemed to have gone on forever, but it was still before eleven o'clock when I talked to Roger Brook—tubby, smooth and self-important—in the sales office of English Sporting Motors.

It appeared that the red dragon transfers were slightly different each year. Brook showed Jonathan past and present dragon logos, and Jonathan with certainty picked the one that had been, Brook said, that of the year before last.

"Great," I said with satisfaction. "How many blue Land Rovers did you sell in that year? I mean, what are the names of the buyers?"

Roger Brook pursed his lips and shook his head. Not the firm's policy to give out information about its customers.

I said ruefully, "I don't want to bother the police."

"Well . . ."

"And of course there would be a fee for your trouble."

A fee was respectable, where a bribe wasn't. In the course of life I disbursed a lot of fees.

Roger Brook with dignity took his reward, and Jonathan and I left with the names and addresses of two hundred and eleven purchasers of blue Land Rovers a little back in time. One of the vehicles had been delivered to Twyford Lower Farms Ltd.

I knew Twyford Lower Farms. It was owned by Gordon Quint.

Noon, Saturday. I sat in my parked car outside English Sporting Motors, while Jonathan fidgeted beside me. "Go and get some lunch and be back here in twenty minutes," I said.

He had no money. I gave him some. "Twenty minutes."

He promised nothing, but returned with three minutes to spare.

I spent his absence deciding what to do, and when he slid in beside me, I set off again for Combe Bassett.

"Where are we going?"

"To see your Aunt Betty."

"But hey! She's not at home. She's at Archie's."

"Then we'll go to Archie's. You can show me the way."

He didn't like it but made no attempt to jump ship. We arrived in due course outside a house an eighth the size of the manor. It was frankly modern and not at all what I'd expected.

I got out of the car and pressed the doorbell. The woman who answered was small and wore a sleeveless sundress.

"Er . . ." I said to her inquiring face, "Archie Kirk?"

Her gaze lengthened beyond me to include Jonathan in my car, a sight that pinched her mouth and jumped her to an instant wrong conclusion. She whirled away and returned with Archie, who said repressively, "What is *he* doing here?"

"Can you spare me half an hour?" I asked.

"What's Jonathan done?"

"He's been extraordinarily helpful. I need your advice."

"Helpful!"

"Yes. Could you hold your disapproval in abeyance for half an hour while I explain?"

He gave me an intense inspection, the brown eyes sharp and knowing. Decision arrived there plainly. "Come in," he said.

"Jonathan's afraid of you," I told him. "Could I ask you to invite him in and not give him the normal tongue-lashing?"

"No one speaks to me like this." He was, however, only mildly affronted.

I smiled at his eyes. "That's because they know you. But I met you only this morning."

"And," he said, "I've heard about your lightning judgments."

Archie Kirk asked Jonathan into the house. Jonathan complied, even if reluctantly.

In a middle-sized sitting room Betty Bracken, her husband and the small woman who'd answered my ring were sitting in armchairs drinking coffee. The room's overall impression was of old oak and books, a room for dark winter evenings and lamps and log fires, not fitted to the dazzle of June. None of the three faces turned towards us could have looked welcoming to the difficult boy.

48

The small woman, introducing herself as Archie's wife, offered me coffee. "And . . . er . . . Jonathan? Coca-Cola?"

Jonathan, as if reprieved, followed her to the kitchen, and I told Betty Bracken that her colt was being operated on and she should have news soon. She was pathetically pleased.

I said casually to Archie, "Can I talk to you in private?" and without question he said, "This way," and transferred us to an adjacent room—his study—again all dark oak and books.

"What is it?" he asked.

"I need a policeman."

He gave me a long glance and waved me to a chair. I told him about Jonathan's night walk (harmless version) and about our tracing the Land Rover. I said that I knew where the Land Rover might now be, but that to get a search warrant to examine it, I needed a cooperative policeman—one that would neither brush me off nor do the police work sloppily. "I thought you might know someone," I finished. "This whole thing depends on crawling up to the machine-gun nest on one's belly, so to speak."

He sat back in his chair, thinking, then picked up the phone. "Norman, this is Archie Kirk."

Whoever Norman was, it seemed he was unwilling.

"It's extremely important," Archie said.

Norman apparently capitulated, but with protest.

"You had better be right," Archie said to me, disconnecting.

"Who is he?"

"Detective Inspector Norman Picton, Thames Valley Police."

"Brilliant," I said.

"He's off-duty. He's on the gravel-pit lake. He's a clever and ambitious young man. And I," he added with a glimmer, "am a magistrate and may sign a search warrant myself if he can clear it with his superintendent."

He rendered me speechless, which quietly amused him.

"You didn't know?" he asked.

I shook my head and found my voice. "Jonathan said you were a civil servant."

"That, too," he agreed. "How did you get that boorish young man to talk?"

"Er . . ." I said, "what is Inspector Picton doing on the lake?"

"Waterskiing," Archie said.

49

THERE WERE SPEEDBOATS, children, wet suits, picnics. I parked my car alongside Archie's. We had agreed to bring both so that I could go on to London, with Archie ferrying Jonathan back to the Brackens'. Jonathan hadn't warmed to the plan, but had ungraciously accompanied me as the lesser horror than spending the afternoon mooching aimlessly around Archie's aunt-infested house.

On the shortish journey from Archie's house he had asked three moody questions, two of which I answered.

First: "How come you get so much done so quickly?"

No answer possible.

Second: "Did you ever steal anything?"

"Chocolate bars," I said.

And third: "Do you mind having only one hand?"

I said coldly, "Yes."

He glanced at me with surprise. I supposed he wasn't old enough to know it was a question one shouldn't ask, but then, perhaps he would have asked it anyway.

When we climbed out of the car, he looked around, not with a sneer, but with interest. I said, "Can you swim?"

"Do me a favor."

"Then go jump in the lake."

"Go to hell," he said, and actually laughed.

Archie had meanwhile discovered that one of the figures scudding over the shining water was the man we'd come to see. We waited a fair while until a large presence in a blue wet suit let go of the rope pulling him and skied free and gracefully to a landing. He stepped off his skis grinning, knowing he'd shown off his considerable skill, and wetly shook Archie's hand.

"Sorry to keep you waiting," he said with easy authority, "but I reckoned once you got here, I'd have had it for the day."

Archie said formally, "Norman, this is Sid Halley."

I shook his hand, and I received the sort of slow, searching inspection I'd had from Archie. "Well," he said, "I'll get dressed."

He was back in five minutes, clad now in jeans and sneakers. "Right," he said to me. "Give."

"Er . . ." I hesitated. "Would it be possible for Mr. Kirk's nephew Jonathan to go for a ride in a speedboat?"

Both he and Archie looked over at Jonathan, lolling unprepossessingly against my car. Jonathan did himself no favors, I thought. Self-destruction was rampant in every tilt of the anti-authority haircut.

"He doesn't deserve a speedboat ride," said Archie.

"I don't want him to overhear what I'm saying."

"That's different," Norman Picton decided. "I'll fix it."

Jonathan ungraciously allowed himself to be driven around the lake by Norman's wife. We watched the boat race past with a roar, Jonathan's streaky mop blown back in the wind.

"There's a lot of good in him," I said mildly. Both men shook their heads.

I said, "Try this on for size," giving them Jonathan's signed statement to read—Picton first, Archie after.

Archie said in disbelief, "He never talks. He wouldn't have said all this."

"I asked him questions," I explained. "Those are his answers. And we wouldn't know of the Land Rover's presence in the lane or its probable owner except for him."

"What exactly is the search warrant for?" Picton asked. "One can't get search warrants without good cause."

"Well," I said, "Jonathan put his hand on the hood of a vehicle parked near the field where Betty Bracken's colt lost his foot. If you search a certain Land Rover and find his handprint, would that prove that you'd found the right wheels?"

Picton said, "Yes."

"I think," I said, "that it would be a good idea to fingerprint that hood before it rains, don't you?"

"Where is it?" Picton asked tersely.

I produced the English Sporting Motors list and pointed. "There," I said. "That one."

"But you're quite wrong," Archie said. "I've been a guest there. They're friends of Betty's."

"And of mine," I said.

He listened to the bleakness I could hear in my own voice.

"Who are we talking about?" Picton asked.

"Gordon Quint," Archie said. "It's rubbish."

"Who is Gordon Quint?" Picton asked.

"The father of Ellis Quint," Archie said.

"Ah." Picton nodded. "But the fact that Twyford Lower Farms Limited owned a blue Land Rover of the relevant year isn't enough," he objected. "We must have good reason to believe it was that one and no other that we are looking for."

Archie said thoughtfully, "Search warrants have been issued on flimsier grounds before."

He and Picton walked away from me, the professionals putting distance between themselves and Sid Public. If they refused to follow the trail, I thought, it would be a relief, on the whole, and I'd be off the hook. But there could be another month and another colt.

They came back, asking why I linked the Quint name to the deed. I described the entries on my chart. "Not conclusive," Archie said, and I agreed.

Picton repeated what I'd just said: "Rachel's pony was bought on the advice of Ellis Quint?"

I said, "And Ellis did a broadcast about the pony losing his foot."

They didn't want to believe it any more than I did. There was a fairly long, indeterminate silence.

Jonathan came back looking uncomplicatedly happy from his fast laps round the lake, and Norman Picton asked if he would like to try skiing itself, not just a ride in the boat.

Jonathan, on the point of enthusiastically saying "Yes," remembered his cultivated disagreeableness and said, "I don't mind."

Picton said cheerfully, "My wife will drive. My son will watch the rope. We'll find you some swimming trunks and a wet suit."

He led Jonathan away. Archie watched inscrutably.

"Give him a chance," I murmured. "Give him a challenge."

"Pack him off to the colonies to make a man of him?"

"Scoff," I said with a smile. "But long ago it often worked. He's bright, bored and not yet a totally confirmed delinquent."

Picton returned, saying, "The boy will stay here until I get back. We'll take two cars—mine and Mr. Halley's. In that way he can go on to London when he wants. We'll leave your car here, Archie. Is that all right?"

Archie said he didn't trust Jonathan not to steal it.

"He doesn't think stealing's fun without his pals," I said.

Archie stared. "That boy never says *anything.*"

He locked his car and climbed in beside me, and we followed Norman into Newbury, to his official place of work.

I sat in my car outside the police station while Archie and Picton arranged the backups: photographer, fingerprinter, the detective

52

constable to be Inspector Picton's note-taking assistant. I wished I were anywhere else, engaged on any other mission.

Archie and Picton came out of the police station followed by their purposeful troop. Archie, sliding in beside me, said the search warrant was signed, the superintendent had given the expedition his blessing, and off we could go to the Twyford Lower Farms.

I sat without moving, without starting the car.

"What's the matter?" Archie demanded.

I said with pain, "Ellis is my friend."

6

GINNIE Quint was gardening in a large straw hat and gloves in front of the comfortable main house of Twyford Lower Farms.

"Hello, dear Sid!" She greeted me warmly, standing up, holding the dirty gloves wide and putting her soft cheek forward for a kiss. "What a nice surprise. But Ellis isn't here."

She looked over my shoulder to where the Picton contingent were erupting from their transport. "Who are your friends, dear?" Then she saw Archie Kirk. "My dear man. How nice to see you."

Norman Picton, carrying none of Archie's or my social-history baggage, came rather brutally to the point.

"I'm Detective Inspector Picton, madam, Thames Valley Police. I have a warrant to inspect your blue Land Rover."

Bewildered, Ginnie said, "Sid . . . Archie. What's this about?"

"It's possible," I said unhappily, "that someone borrowed your Land Rover last night and . . . er . . . committed a crime."

"Could I see the Land Rover, please, madam?" Picton insisted.

"It's in the farmyard. I'll get my husband to show you."

The scene inexorably unwound. Gordon, steaming out of the house to take charge, could do nothing but protest in the face of a properly executed search warrant. The police went about their business, photographing, fingerprinting. Every stage was carefully documented.

The two sticking-up handles Jonathan had noted behind the front seat were, in fact, those of a light lawn mower. There were also tools; iron posts for fencing; a bag of horse-feed nuts; a rolled leather apron, like those used by farriers; a heavy four-pronged fork; and a large knife like a machete, wrapped in sacking.

The knife was clean, sharp and oiled.

Gordon, questioned, growled that the knife was for clearing ditches, thinning woodland, small jobs around the fields.

There was a second, longer bundle of sacking lying beneath the fencing posts. Norman Picton drew it out and unwrapped it.

"Lopping shears," Gordon pronounced. "For lopping off small tree branches. Have to keep young trees pruned, you know." He took them up to show how they worked. The act of parting the long handles widely away from each other opened heavy metal jaws at the far end—sharp, oiled jaws wide enough to grip a branch three inches thick. With a quick motion Gordon pulled the handles towards each other, and the metal jaws closed with a snap.

I felt faintly sick.

Archie walked away speechlessly, and Gordon, not understanding, walked after him, saying, puzzled, "Archie! What is it?"

Picton said to me, "Well?"

"Well," I said, swallowing, "what if you examined those shears—the hinge—and found one drop of blood or one hair?"

"So these shears fit the bill?"

I nodded faintly. "Lopping shears. Oh, Lord."

Picton and I walked in the wake of Archie and Gordon, returning to Ginnie in front of the house.

"I don't understand," Ginnie was saying. "You say the Land Rover may have been taken for use in a crime? What crime?"

Gordon jumped in without waiting for Picton to explain. "It's always for robbery. Where did the thieves take it?"

Instead of answering, Picton asked if it was Gordon Quint's habit to leave the ignition key in the Land Rover.

"Of course not," Gordon said, affronted.

"If you did by any chance leave the key available, would it have been on a key ring with a silver horseshoe?"

"Oh, no," Ginnie said guilelessly. "That's Ellis's key ring."

I DROVE Archie Kirk back to Newbury. "There's no doubt that it was the Quint Land Rover in my sister's lane," he said. "But there's no proof that Ellis himself was anywhere near."

"No," I agreed. "No one saw him."

"Did Norman ask you to write a report?"

"Yes."

"He'll give your report and Jonathan's statement to the prosecution, along with his own findings. After that, it's up to them."

"Mm."

At the police station, saying good-bye, Archie said, "Sid, I do have some idea of what you're facing. I just wanted you to know."

"I . . . er . . . thanks," I said. "If you wait a minute, I'll phone the equine hospital and find out how the colt is doing."

The news was moderate.

"I've done my absolute best," Bill reported, "and, bar infection, the foot could technically stay in place. But no promises, mind."

"You're brilliant," I said.

He chuckled. "It's nice to be appreciated."

I said, "A policeman will come and collect some of the colt's hair and blood."

"Good. Catch the bugger," he said.

I REACHED the pub half an hour late for my appointment with Kevin, and he wasn't there. Without regret I mooched tiredly to the bar and bought a whisky.

A woman's voice at my side said, "Are you Sid Halley?"

I turned reluctantly. She had shining black shoulder-length hair, bright, light blue eyes and dark red lipstick, sharply edged. Naturally unblemished skin had been given a matte porcelain powdering. Black eyebrows and eyelashes gave her face strong definition, an impression her manner reinforced. She wore black clothes in June. I found it impossible to guess her age from her face, but her manicured hands said no more than thirty.

"I'm India Cathcart, from the *Pump*," she said. "My colleague Kevin Mills has been called away to a rape."

"Oh," I said vaguely, but I knew her by name and reputation. She was a major columnist, a ruthless interviewer, a pitiless exposer of pathetic human secrets. She was also funny, and I, like every *Pump* addict, avidly read her stuff and laughed even as I winced. I did not, however, aim to be her quarry.

"I came to pick up our exclusive," she said.

"Ah. Fraid there isn't one."

"But you said—"

"I hoped," I agreed.

"We tried to reach you. Where have you been all day?"

"With friends," I said.

"I went to Combe Bassett. What did I find? No colt, with or without feet. No Sid Halley. No sobbing colt owner. I find some batty old fusspot who says everyone went to Archie's house."

I gazed at her with a benign expression.

"So," continued India Cathcart with visible disgust, "I go to the house of a Mr. Archibald Kirk, and what do I find *there*? I find about five other newspapermen, sundry photographers, a Mrs. Archibald Kirk and a deaf old gent saying 'Eh?' "

She looked past me to the bartender. "Mineral water and lemon, please." She paid for her own drink as a matter of course.

"You're not playing fair," she said, judging me over the rim of her glass. "It was the *Pump*'s hot line that sent you to Combe Bassett. Kevin says you pay your debts. So pay."

"The hot line was his idea. Not a bad one, except for all the false alarms. But there's nothing I can tell you this evening."

"Not can't. Won't."

"It's often the same thing."

"Spare me the philosophy." Then she said, "Are you married?"

"Divorced."

"Children?"

I shook my head. "How about you?"

She was more used to asking questions than answering. There was perceptible hesitation before she said, "The same."

I drank my Scotch. I said, "Tell Kevin I'm very sorry I can't give him his inside edge. Tell him I'll talk to him on Monday."

"Not good enough."

"No, well . . . I can't do more." I put my empty glass on the bar. "Good-bye."

"Wait." She gave me a straight stare, one that saw no need to make points in a battle that had been won by the generation before her. She said, "My expense account would run to two dinners."

"Your restaurant or mine?" I said, smiling.

We ate in a brightly lit, crowded, black-mirrored restaurant that was clearly the in-place for the in-crowd. India's choice. India's habitat. As we followed a lisping young greeter to a central, noteworthy table, she trailed me behind her like a comet's tail (Halley's?) while introducing me to no one.

From long habit I ordered things that could reasonably be dealt with one-handed: watercress mousse, then duck curry with baked plantains. India had baby eggplants with pesto and crisped frogs' legs that she ate uninhibitedly with her fingers.

The best thing about the restaurant was that the decibel level made private conversation impossible. "So," India raised her voice, "how much was the colt worth?"

"No one knows," I said.

"Kevin told me it cost a quarter of a million."

"What it cost and what it was worth are different. It might have won the Derby. It might have been worth millions. No one knows."

"Do you always play word games?"

"Quite often." I nodded. "Like you do."

"Where did you go to school?"

"Ask Kevin," I said, smiling.

"Kevin's told me things about you that you wouldn't want me to know."

"Like what?"

"Like it's easy to be taken in by your peaceful front. Like you having tungsten where other people have nerves. Like you being touchy about losing a hand. That's for starters."

I'd throttle Kevin, I thought. I said, "How are the frogs' legs?"

"Muscular."

"Never mind," I said. "You have sharp teeth."

Her mind quite visibly changed gears from patronizing to uncertain, and I began to like her.

Risky to like her, of course.

After the curry and the frogs we drank black coffee and spent a pause or two in eye-contact appraisal. In the way one does, I wondered what she looked like in bed. And in the way that one doesn't cuddle up to a potential cobra, I made no flicker of an attempt to find out.

She paid for our meal, as promised, and I offered her a lift home.

"Thanks. But there's a bus." I didn't press it.

We parted on the sidewalk outside the restaurant. No kiss. No handshake. A nod from her. Then she turned and walked away, and I had no faith at all in her mercy.

ON SUNDAY MORNING I reopened the small blue suitcase Linda had lent me and reread the clippings' about the maimed Kent ponies. Then I replayed the videotape of the program Ellis had made of the child owners, watching it with a different perspective.

There on the screen his good-looking face was filled with compassion and outrage. Blinding ponies, cutting off a pony's foot, he said, those were crimes akin to murder.

Ellis, I thought, how *could* you?

What if he can't help it?

His instinct for staging was infallible. He had the children sitting around on hay bales in a tack room, dressed in riding breeches and black riding hats. Several of them were in tears. He himself sat on the floor among them—casual in a dark open-necked jogging suit, a peaked cap pushed back on his head, sunglasses in pocket—helping them cope with grief.

There were phrases he had used when talking straight to the camera that had brought the children's horrors disturbingly to life: "pierced empty sockets, their eyesight running down their cheeks," and "a purebred silver pony, proud and shining in the moonlight."

A silver pony shining in the moonlight. Rachel's nightmare.

In the moonlight. Ellis had *seen* the pony in the moonlight.

I played the tape again, listening with my eyes shut, undistracted by his familiar face or Rachel's. He said, "A silver pony trotting trustfully across the field, lured by a handful of horse nuts."

He shouldn't have known that. And the Fernses hadn't fed the pony on nuts. The agent of destruction had brought them.

In the afternoon I wrote a long, detailed report for Norman. Early next morning, as he had requested, I drove to the Newbury police station and delivered it into his own hands. He informed me, disgustedly, that as Ellis Quint lived in the Metropolitan area, the Thames Valley Police could not pursue the inquiry.

"I thought these divisions were being done away with."

"Everything takes time."

I left him to sort out his problems and set off for Kent. On the way, wanting to give Rachel Ferns a cheering-up present, I stopped in Kingston and walked round looking for inspiration. A windowful of tumbling puppies made me pause. I went into the pet shop, but emerged with a fishtank, water weeds, Gothic castle, lights, fish food and three buckets of tropical fish.

Rachel was waiting by the gate.

"You're half an hour late," she accused.

"Have you heard of the M25?"

"*Everyone* makes that motorway an excuse."

"Well, sorry."

Her bald head was still a shock. Apart from that, she looked well, her cheeks full and rounded by steroids. She wore a loose sundress and clumpy sneakers on sticklike legs. It was crazy to love someone else's child so comprehensively, yet for the first time ever I felt the idea of fatherhood take a grip.

Jenny had refused to have children on the grounds that any racing day could leave her a widow, and at the time I hadn't cared one way or another. If ever I married again, I thought, following Rachel into the house, I would want a daughter.

Linda gave me a bright, bright smile, a pecking kiss and the offer of a gin and tonic while she fixed us some pasta for our lunch.

"How are things?" I asked.

"Happy. Rachel was out waiting for you two hours ago. I don't know what you've done to her. But you said you'd got news for me."

"Later. After lunch. And I've brought Rachel a present."

The fishtank after lunch was the ultimate success. Rachel was enthralled. The vivid fish swam through the Gothic ruins, the water weeds rose and swelled, the lights and bubbles did their stuff. Rachel sprinkled fish food and watched her new friends eat. Her pale face glowed. Linda came with me into the garden.

"Any news about a transplant?" I asked.

"It would have been the first thing I'd told you."

We sat on the bench. The roses bloomed. It was a beautiful day, heartbreaking.

Linda said tearfully, "In acute lymphoblastic leukemia, which is what Rachel's got, chemotherapy causes remission more than ninety percent of the time. In seven out of ten children, the remission lasts—" She stopped.

"And it has come back in Rachel?"

"Oh, Sid, the disease came back in Rachel after less than two years. They reestablished her in remission again, but I know they don't suggest transplants unless they have to, because only about half of them are successful. They can do so much nowadays. One day they may cure everybody. But oh . . . oh . . ."

59

I put my arm around her shoulders and waited until the weeping passed. Then I told her I'd discovered who had maimed and destroyed Silverboy. "You're not going to like it," I said, "and it might be best if you can prevent Rachel from finding out."

Linda looked at me fearfully. "I've *wanted* her to know who killed Silverboy. That's what I'm paying you for."

"I don't want your money. Linda . . . I'm so very sorry . . . but it was Ellis Quint himself who cut off Silverboy's foot."

She sprang to her feet, immediate anger filling her. "How can you say such a thing?" she demanded. "He couldn't possibly!"

I stood up also. "Linda—"

"Don't say anything. I won't listen. I *won't*. You're crazy. Of course I'm not going to tell Rachel what you've accused him of, because you're *wrong*. So please . . . *go*. Just go."

"Linda, listen."

"No!"

I said, "Ellis has been my own friend for years. This is terrible for me, too."

She put her hands over her ears, screaming, "Go away. Go away."

I touched her shoulder. She jerked away. After a minute I said, "Phone me, then," and went back into the house.

Rachel was on her knees, peering into the wet little world. "I have to go now," I told her.

"Good-bye." She looked at the fish, not turning, sure I would come back. It was a temporary farewell, between friends.

"Bye," I said, and drove ruefully to London, knowing that Linda's rejection was only the first of many.

In Pont Square the telephone was ringing when I opened my front door, and continued to ring while I poured water and ice from a jug in the refrigerator, and continued to ring while I drank it, and continued to ring while I changed the battery in my left hand.

In the end, I picked up the receiver.

"Where have you been?" Norman Picton's voice filled my ear. "Ellis Quint is in custody," he said.

"He's *what?*"

"Well, he's sort of in custody. He's in hospital, under guard."

"Norman," I said, disoriented, "start at the beginning."

"Right. This morning two plainclothes officers of the Metropolitan Police went to his flat intending to interview him. He came out

60

of the building before they reached the main entrance, so, knowing him by sight, they approached him and identified themselves. At which point"—Picton cleared his throat—"at which point Mr. Ellis Quint pushed one of the officers away so forcefully that the officer overbalanced into the roadway and was struck by a passing car. Mr. Quint himself then ran into the path of traffic and was struck a glancing blow by a bus. Mr. Quint was dazed. He was taken to hospital, where he is in a secure room while investigations proceed."

I said, "Are you reading that from a written account?"

"That's so."

"How about an interpretation in your own earthy words?"

"I'm at work. I'm not alone."

"Okay," I said. "Did Ellis panic, or did he think he was being mugged?"

Picton half laughed. "I'd say the first. His lawyers will say the second. But d'you know what? When they emptied his pockets at the hospital, they found a packet of cash—and his passport."

I sighed. "How's the officer he pushed?"

"Broken leg. He was lucky."

"And when Ellis's daze wears off?"

"It'll be up to the Met. They can legally hold him for one day while they frame a charge. I'd say that's a toss-up. With the clout he can muster, he'll be out in hours."

"What did you do with my report?"

"It went to the proper authorities."

"Thanks for phoning," I said.

"Keep in touch." An order, it sounded like.

7

THE week got worse, alleviated only by a letter from Linda on Thursday morning. It said:

I'm sorry I talked to you as I did. I still cannot believe that Ellis Quint would cut off Silverboy's foot.

Anyway, it was very nice of you to bring the fishtank for Rachel. I can't tear her away from it. She keeps asking when you will come

61

back, and I don't like to tell her you won't. So if you'll visit us again,
I will not say any more about your being wrong about Ellis. I ask
you for Rachel.

I wrote back thanking her for her letter, accepting her invitation
and saying I would phone her soon.

The following Tuesday, Ellis was charged with "actual bodily
harm" for having inadvertently pushed "an assailant" into the path
of potential danger and was set free "pending inquiries."

Disillusioned, Norman Picton reported, "The only approxi-
mately good thing is that they confiscated his passport. His lawyers,
of course, are screeching that it's a scandal."

"Where's Ellis now?"

"Look to your back, Sid."

On Wednesday, Ellis was quietly arrested and spent the night in
custody. On Thursday morning he was charged with severing the
foot of a colt: the off-fore foot of a two-year-old thoroughbred
owned by Mrs. Elizabeth Bracken of Combe Bassett Manor. To the
fury of most of the nation the magistrates remanded him to custody for another seven days, a precaution usually applied to those
accused of murder.

Norman Picton phoned me privately on my home number.

"I'm not telling you this, understand," he said. "It would mean
my job."

"I hear you," I said. "I won't talk."

"No," he said, "that, I believe. I looked up the transcript of the
trial of that man that smashed off your hand. You didn't tell *him*
what he wanted to know, did you?"

"No . . . well . . . everyone's a fool sometimes."

"Some fool. Anyway, the reason why Ellis Quint is remanded for
seven days is because after his arrest he tried to hang himself in his
cell with his tie."

"He didn't!"

"No one took his belt or tie away, because of who he was. No one
in the station believed the charge. There's all hell going on now. No
one's telling anyone outside anything on pain of death, so Sid—"

"I promise," I said.

"They'll remand him next week for another seven days, partly to
stop him committing suicide and partly because . . ." He faltered.

"I *promise*," I said again.

"Well, there's horse blood in the hinges of the shears, and horse blood and hairs in the sacking. They've taken samples from the colt for DNA testing. The results will be back next week."

"Does Ellis know?"

"I imagine that's why he tried the quick way out. Incidentally, the simple knot he tied slid undone because the tie was pure silk."

"Norman—"

"I keep forgetting he's your friend. Anyway, his lawyers are demanding proof that Ellis himself was ever at Combe Bassett by night. They know we would have to drop the case if they can come up with a trustable alibi for any of the other amputations, but so far they haven't managed it. It's early days, though. They'll dig and dig. You can bet on it."

"Yeah."

"People in the force are already saying you're off your rocker. They say Ellis is too well known, that wherever he went, he would be recognized. Therefore if no one recognized him, that in itself is proof he wasn't there."

"Mm," I said. "I've been thinking about that. Do you have time off at the weekend?"

"Not this weekend, no. Monday, do you?"

"I'll see if I can fix something up with Archie . . . and Jonathan. Where can I reach you?"

"Police station. Say you're John Paul Jones."

KEVIN Mills dominated the front page of the *Pump* on Friday— a respite from the sexual indiscretions of a Cabinet minister but a demolition job on me. "The *Pump*," he reminded readers, "had set up a hot line to Sid Halley to report attacks on colts. The *Pump* disclaimed all responsibility for Sid Halley's now ludicrously fingering Ellis Quint as the demon responsible for torturing defenseless horses. Quint, whose devotion to thoroughbreds stretches back to his career as the country's top amateur race rider, the popular hero in the ancient tradition of gentlemen sportsmen . . ."

More of the same.

"See also, Analysis, page 10, and India Cathcart, page 15."

I read the leader column: "Should an ex-jockey be allowed free rein as pseudo-sleuth? (Answer: No, of course not.)" And then, dredging deep for steel, I finally turned to India Cathcart's piece:

> Sid Halley, smugly accustomed to acclaim as a champion, in short time lost his career, his wife and his left hand, and then watched his friend soar to super-celebrity status, all the things that he considered should be his. Who does this pathetic little man think he's kidding? He's no Ellis Quint. He's a has-been with an ego problem, out to ruin what he envies.

The *Pump*, Cathcart went on, would not let that happen. Sid Halley was a beetle the *Pump* would exterminate.

Damn and blast her, I thought, and for the first time in eighteen years got drunk.

On Saturday morning, groaning around the apartment with a headache, I found a message in my fax machine, a handwritten scrawl from Kevin Mills: "Sid, sorry, but you asked for it."

Most of Sunday, voices on my answering machine delivered angry opinions. Two calls relieved the gloom. One from Charles Roland: "Sid, if you're in trouble, there's always Aynsford." And a second from Archie Kirk: "I'm at home. Norman Picton says you want me."

Two men with cool, dispassionate minds, I thought gratefully. They would listen before condemning. I phoned back to Charles, who seemed relieved I sounded sane.

"I'm all right," I said.

"Are you sure, Sid?"

"Positive."

"Sid, come—anytime," Charles said.

I phoned Archie and asked if Jonathan was still staying with Betty Bracken. Archie said, "I've been talking to Norman. Jonathan is now addicted to waterskiing and spends every day at the lake. Betty is paying hundreds and says it's worth it to get him out of the house. He'll be at the lake tomorrow. Shall we all meet there?"

We agreed on a time, and when we arrived the next day, Jonathan was out on the water, a flying figure in a scarlet wet suit. He went up a ramp, flew, turned a somersault in the air and landed smoothly on two skis.

"*That*," Archie said in disbelief, "is *Jonathan?*"

"He's a natural," Norman said. "And fearless."

Archie and I watched Jonathan ski confidently up the sloping landing place with almost as much panache as Norman himself.

Jonathan grinned. He looked blazingly *happy.*

I took a soft sports bag out of my car and held it out to him, asking him to take it with him to the dressing rooms.

"Hi," he said. "Okay." He took the bag and walked off barefoot, carrying his skis.

"Incredible," Archie said. "But he can't ski through life."

"It's a start," Norman said.

After a few minutes we were approached by a figure in a dark tracksuit and running shoes, a navy baseball cap and sunglasses, and carrying a sheet of paper. He stopped within fifteen feet of us.

"Yes?" Norman asked, puzzled, as to a stranger.

I said, "Take off the cap and the glasses."

He took them off. Jonathan's streaky hair shook forward into its normal startling shape, and his eyes stared at my face. I gave him a slight jerk of the head, and he came the last few paces and handed the paper to Norman, who read aloud what I'd written on it.

"Jonathan, this is an experiment. Please put on these clothes, the baseball cap peak forward, hiding your face. Wear the sunglasses. Bring this paper. Walk towards me, stop a few feet away, and don't speak. Okay?

Thanks,
Sid"

Norman lowered the paper, looked at Jonathan and said blankly, "Oh, hell."

"Is that the lot?" Jonathan asked me.

"Brilliant," I said, and he walked off to change.

"He looked totally different," Archie commented, still amazed.

I said to Norman, "Did you look at the tape of Ellis's program that I put in with my report?"

"Yes, I did."

"When Ellis was sitting on the floor with those children," I said, "he was wearing a dark tracksuit, open at the neck. He had a peaked cap pushed back on his head. He looked boyish. He had a pair of sunglasses tucked into a breast pocket."

After a silence Norman said, "But he wouldn't wear those clothes on television if he'd worn them to mutilate the Ferns pony."

"Oh, yes he would. It would deeply amuse him. There's nothing gives him more buzz than taking risks."

"A baseball cap," Archie said thoughtfully, "entirely changes the shape of someone's head."

I nodded. "A baseball cap and a pair of running shorts can reduce any man of stature to anonymity."

"We'll never prove it," Norman said.

Jonathan slouched back in his own clothes, his habitual half sneer firmly in place. Archie's exasperation with him returned.

"This is not the road to Damascus," I murmured.

"Damn you, Sid." Archie glared and then laughed.

"What are you talking about?" Norman asked.

"St. Paul's conversion on the road to Damascus happened like a thunderclap," Archie explained. "Sid's telling me not to look for instant miracles by the gravel-pit lake."

I DROVE back to London. My answering machine had so many messages that it had run out of recording tape. Among the general abuse were three separate calls from the owners of the other colt victims, echoing Linda Ferns's immovable conviction.

The lady from Cheltenham: "Ellis is absolutely innocent. I'm sorry, Sid, but you're not welcome here anymore."

The angry Lancashire farmer: "You're a moron, do you know that? Why don't you give up trying to be Sherlock Holmes."

The lady from York: "Dear Ellis! He's worth ten of you."

I switched off the critical voices, but they went on reverberating in my brain. I'd known it would be bad, but why the urge to bang my head against the wall? Because I didn't have tungsten nerves, whatever anyone thought.

The press more or less followed the *Pump*'s lead. Pictures of Ellis—handsome, confident—smiled from newsstands everywhere. Trial by media found Ellis the wronged and innocent hero, Sid Halley the twisted, jealous cur snapping at his heels.

Tuesday was much the same. On Wednesday, Ellis appeared again before magistrates, who that time set him free on bail.

Norman phoned. "It was fixed beforehand. Two minutes in court. Different time than posted. The press arrived after it was over. Ellis greeted them, free, smiling broadly."

"Damn."

"His lawyers have done their stuff. It's rubbish to think the well-balanced personality intended to kill himself—his tie got caught somehow, but he managed to free it. The policeman he pushed failed to identify himself adequately and is now walking about comfortably in a cast. The colt Ellis is accused of attacking is alive and recovering well. As bail is granted in cases of manslaughter, it is unnecessary to detain Ellis Quint any longer on far lesser charges. So he's walked."

"Is he still to be tried?"

"So far. His lawyers have asked for an early trial date so that he can put this unpleasantness behind him. He will plead not guilty, of course. And I think there's a heavyweight maneuvering somewhere in this case."

"A heavyweight? Who?"

"Don't know. It's just a feeling. Since our reports—yours and mine—reached the prosecution, there's been a new factor. Not exactly a cover-up; more a redirection. Someone with muscle is trying to get you thoroughly, and *malignantly,* discredited."

"Thanks a bunch."

"Sid, seriously, look out for yourself."

As IF nothing had happened, Ellis resumed his television program and began making jokes about Sid Halley. "Sid Halley? That friend of mine! Have you heard that he comes from Halifax? Halley facts—he makes them up."

Hilarious.

When I went to the races, which I didn't do as often as earlier, people either turned their backs or laughed, and I wasn't sure which I disliked more.

Ellis behaved as if there were never going to be a trial, as if awkward details like Land Rovers, lopping shears and confirmed matching DNA tests tying the shears to the Bracken colt were never going to surface once the sub judice silence ended.

July came in with a deluge that flooded rivers, and no colt was attacked at the time of the full moon, perhaps because the nights were wet and windy and black with clouds.

The press finally lost interest in trashing Sid Halley, and Ellis Quint's show wrapped up for the summer break. I went down to Kent a couple of times, taking new fish for Rachel. Neither Linda nor I mentioned Ellis. She hugged me good-bye each time and asked when I would be coming back. Rachel, she said, had had no more nightmares. They were a thing of the past.

August came and left quietly. No colts were attacked. The hot line went cold. India Cathcart busied herself with a Cabinet member's mistress.

Then, in September, one dew-laden early fall Saturday morning after a calm moonlit night, a colt was discovered with a foot off.

There were no hot line calls from the *Pump,* but Norman Picton scorched the wires. "Have you heard? It was a yearling colt this time. Apparently there aren't many two-year-olds in the fields just now. The yearling belonged to some people near Northampton. They're frantic. Their vet put the colt down. But get this. Ellis Quint's lawyers have already claimed he has an alibi."

I stood in silence in my sitting room.

"Sid?"

"Mm."

"You'll have to break that alibi. Otherwise, it will break *you.*"

"Can you find out from the Northampton Police what his alibi actually is?"

"Piece of cake. I'll phone you back."

I put down the receiver and went over to the window. The little square looked peaceful and safe, the railed garden a tree-dappled haven where generations of privileged children had run and played. I'd spent my own childhood in Liverpool's back streets, my father dead and my mother fighting cancer. I in no way regretted the contrast in origins. I had learned self-sufficiency and survival there.

Norman phoned back later in the morning. "Your friend," he said, "reportedly spent the night at a private dance in Shropshire, roughly a hundred miles to the northwest of the colt. Endless friends will testify to his presence, including his hostess, a duchess. It was a dance given to celebrate the twenty-first birthday of the heir."

"Damn."

"Sid," Norman's voice said, "do you realize the trial is due to start two weeks from Monday?"

"I do realize."

"Then get a move on with this alibi."

"Yes, sir, Detective Inspector."

He laughed. "Put the bugger back behind bars."

ON TUESDAY, I WENT TO SEE THE Shropshire duchess, for whom I had ridden winners in my former life. She even had a painting of me on her favorite horse, but I was no longer her favorite jockey.

"Yes, of *course* Ellis was here all night," she confirmed. Short, thin and at first unwelcoming, she led me through the armor-dotted entrance hall of her drafty old house to the sitting room.

"I cannot *believe,* Sid," she said, "that you've accused Ellis of something so disgusting. You and he have been friends for years."

"But he *was* here?" I asked.

"All night. It was five or later when everyone started to leave. The band was playing still. We'd all had breakfast. . . ."

"When did the dance start?" I asked.

"*Start?* The invitations were for ten. But you know how people are. It was eleven or midnight before most people came. We had the fireworks at three thirty because rain was forecast for later, but it was fine all night, thank goodness."

"Did Ellis say good night when he left?"

"My dear Sid, there were over three hundred people here."

"So you don't actually remember when Ellis left?"

"The last I saw of him, he was dancing an eightsome with that gawky Raven girl. Do drop it, Sid. I'm seeing you now for old times' sake, but you're not doing yourself any good, are you?"

"Probably not."

She patted my hand. "I'll always *know* you, at the races."

"Thank you," I said.

I WENT to Northampton to see a Miss Richardson and a Mrs. Bethany, joint owners of the Windward Stud Farm, home of the latest colt victim, and to my dismay found Ginnie Quint there as well.

All three women were in the stud farm's office. Miss Richardson was a tall, bulky figure in tweed jacket, worn cord trousers and wiry gray short-cropped curls. Mrs. Bethany, a smaller, less powerful version of Miss Richardson, was reputedly the one who stayed up at night when the mares were foaling.

Ginnie Quint, sitting behind one of the desks, leaped furiously to her feet the instant I appeared in the doorway and poured over me a concentration of verbal volcanic lava. "He *trusted* you. He would have *died* for you."

I said absolutely nothing. I sensed Miss Richardson and Mrs. Bethany listening in astonishment, not knowing who I was nor what I'd done to deserve such an onslaught.

"You're going to go into court and try to send your best friend to prison. You're not fit to live." Emotion twisted her gentle features into ugliness. Her words came out spitting.

As there was no hope of Ginnie's listening to anything I might say, I unhappily but pragmatically turned to retreat, intending to return another day to talk to the owners of the farm. But I found my way barred by two policemen.

"Sergeant Smith reporting, madam," one of them said to Miss Richardson.

She nodded. "Yes, Sergeant?"

"We've found an object hidden in one of the hedges round the field where your horse was done in."

No one objected to my presence, so I remained in the office, quiet and riveted.

Sergeant Smith held a long, narrow bundle. "Could you tell us, madam, if this belongs to you?"

"What is it?" Miss Richardson asked.

The sergeant lifted back the filthy cloth to reveal a pair of lopping shears.

Miss Richardson and Mrs. Bethany stared at them unmoved. Ginnie Quint turned slowly white and fainted.

71

8

So HERE we were in October, with the leaves weeping yellowly from the trees.

Here I was, perching on the end of Rachel Ferns's bed, wearing a huge, fluffy orange clown wig and a red bulbous nose, making sick children laugh while feeling far from merry inside.

"Have you hurt your arm?" Rachel asked conversationally.

"Banged it," I said.

She nodded. Linda looked surprised. Rachel said, "When things hurt, it shows in people's eyes."

She knew too much about pain for a nine-year-old. I said, "I'd better go before I tire you."

She smiled, not demurring. She, like the children wearing the other wigs I'd brought, had very short bursts of stamina. I took off the clown wig and nose and kissed her good-bye.

"You'll come back?"

"Of course."

She sighed contentedly, knowing I would. Linda walked with me from the ward to the hospital door. I put my arms around her.

"Rachel asks for you all the time," she said. "Joe cuddles her and cries. She cuddles him, trying to comfort him. She's her daddy's little girl. She loves him. But you—you're her friend. You make her laugh, not cry. It's you she asks for all the time, not Joe."

"I'll always come if I can."

She went back into the hospital, and I rode dispiritedly back to London in a Teledrive car. Though I had more than an hour to spare, I decided against Pont Square and took the sharp memory of Gordon Quint's attack straight to the restaurant in Piccadilly where I'd agreed to meet the lawyer Davis Tatum. I sat upstairs at a bar table to wait.

Tatum arrived late and out of breath from having apparently walked up the stairs instead of waiting for the elevator. He wheezed as he lowered his six-foot three-inch bulk into the chair opposite.

He was a case of an extremely agile mind in a totally unsuitable body. There were large cheeks, double chins, fat-lidded eyes and a neck like a weight lifter's. A charcoal pin-striped suit strained over a copious belly. Except in the brain box, nature had dealt him a sad hand.

"First of all," he said, "I have some bad news. Ellis Quint has retracted his guilty plea."

"*Retracted!*" I exclaimed. "How can one retract a confession?"

"Easily." He sighed. "Quint says he was upset yesterday about his mother's death, and what he said about feeling guilty was misinterpreted. In other words, his lawyers know you have so far not been able to break his alibi for the night that last colt was attacked, and they think they can therefore get the Bracken colt charge dismissed, despite the Land Rover and circumstantial evidence. I regret to tell you they are likely to succeed."

He didn't have to tell me that my reputation would never recover if Ellis emerged with his intact.

His eyes glimmered behind the folds of fat. "I saw the report that you sent to the prosecution. I told a friend it had surprised me, both by its thoroughness and by your deductions and conclusions. He said I shouldn't be surprised. He said you'd had the whole top echelon of the Jockey Club hanging on your every word when you cleared up two major racing messes for them."

"A year last May," I said. "Is that what he meant?"

"I expect so. The job I'd like you to do might need an assistant. He said you had an assistant then."

"Chico Barnes. He got married," I said briefly. "His wife doesn't like what I do, so he's given it up. He teaches judo—gives me a lesson most weeks, but I can't ask him for any other sort of help."

"Pity."

"Yes. He was good. Great company and bright."

"And he got *deterred*. That's why he gave it up."

I went, internally, very still. I said, "What do you mean?"

"I heard," he said, his gaze steady on my face, "that he got beaten with some sort of thin chain to deter him from helping you. To deter him from all detection. And it worked." Davis Tatum leaned back in his chair, which creaked under his weight.

"I heard," he said, "that the same treatment was doled out to you, and in the course of things the Jockey Club mandarins made you take your shirt off. They said they had never seen anything like it. The whole of your upper body was black with bruising, and

73

there were vicious red weals all over you. And that you'd calmly explained to them how and why you'd been attacked and who had arranged it. You got one of their big shots chucked out."

"Who told you all that?"

"One hears things."

I thought in unprintable curses. The six men who'd seen me that day with my shirt off had agreed never to talk about it. They'd wanted to keep to themselves the villainy I'd found within their own walls, and nothing had been more welcome to me than that silence. It had been bad enough at the time. I didn't want continually to be reminded.

"Who told you?"

"I gave my word."

"One of the Jockey Club?"

"I gave my word. If you'd given your word, would *you* tell *me*?"

"No."

He nodded. "That's what I was told. I asked around about you."

Tatum twisted in his seat to call the barman. "Tanqueray and tonic, please. And for you, Sid?"

"Scotch. A lot of water."

The barman brought the glasses, setting them out.

"Health," Davis Tatum toasted, raising his gin.

"Survival," I responded, and drank to both.

He put down his glass and came finally to the point. "I need someone who is clever, unafraid and able to think fast in a crisis."

I smiled. "No one's like that. What's the job?"

He waited while four businessmen arrived and sank into monetary conversation at the table farthest from where we sat.

"Do you know who I mean by Owen Yorkshire?" Tatum asked.

"Owen Yorkshire." I rolled the name around in memory and came up with only doubts. "Does he own a horse or two?"

"He does. He also owns Topline Foods."

"Topline—as in sponsored race at Aintree? As in Ellis Quint, guest of honor at the Topline lunch the day before the Grand National?"

"That's the fellow."

"And the inquiry?"

"Find out if he's manipulating the Quint case to his own private advantage, and why."

I said, "I did hear that there's a heavyweight abroad. But why me? Why not the police? Or the old-boy internet?"

"Because you include silence in what you sell."

"I'm expensive," I said. "Who's paying?"

"The fees will come through me."

"In case you're wondering," I said, "when it comes to Ellis Quint, I gave the client's money back, in order to be able to stop him myself. I have to tell you that you'd run that risk."

He leaned forward and extended his pudgy hand.

"We'll shake on it," he said, and grasped my palm with a firmness that sent a shock wave fizzing clear up to my shoulder.

"What's the matter?" he said, sensing it.

"Nothing. Will you give me your assurance that you won't tell anyone about that Jockey Club business?"

"But it's to your credit."

"It's a private thing. I don't like fuss."

"You have my assurance." He looked at me thoughtfully. "Sid, where it really counts, you are respected."

There was a drift of flowery scent behind me, and a young woman tweaked a chair round to join our table, looking triumphant.

"Well, well, well," she said. "Mr. Davis Tatum and Sid Halley. What a surprise."

I said, to Davis Tatum's mystified face, "This is Miss India Cathcart, who writes for the *Pump*. If you say nothing, you'll find yourself quoted repeating things you never thought, and if you say anything at all, you'll wish you hadn't."

Tatum opened his mouth indignantly, and I shook my head. He stared at me, then with a complete change of manner said in smooth, lawyerly detachment, "Miss Cathcart, why are you here?"

"Why? To see you, of course."

"But why?"

She looked from him to me and back again, her appearance just as I remembered it: flawless porcelain skin, light blue eyes, cleanly outlined mouth, black shining hair. She wore brown and red, with amber beads.

She said, "Isn't it improper for a colleague of the crown prosecutor to be seen talking to one of the witnesses?"

"No, it isn't," Tatum said.

"India," I said, "Mr. Tatum is not the prosecutor in any case where I am a witness, and we may talk about anything we care to."

"Did you tell her we were meeting here?" Tatum asked me.

"Of course not," I said.

"Then how—why, Miss Cathcart, are you here?"

"The paper sent me."

"The *Pump* told you we'd be here?" Tatum asked.

"My editor said to come and see. And he was right."

"Mm," I said. "Interesting."

India said to me, "Kevin says you went to school in Liverpool."

Tatum, puzzled, asked, "What did you say?"

She explained, "Sid wouldn't tell me where he went to school, so I found out." She looked at me accusingly. "You don't sound like Liverpool. You sound more like Eton. How come?"

"I'm a mimic," I said.

If she really wanted to, she could find out also that between the ages of sixteen and twenty-one I'd been more or less adopted by a Newmarket trainer (who *had* been to Eton), who made me into a good jockey and by his example taught me how to speak, how to behave and how to manage the money I earned. He'd been already old then, and he died. I often thought of him.

"Kevin told me you were a slum child," India said.

"Slum is an attitude, not a place. Where did your editor get the idea that you might find us here?"

"He didn't say. It doesn't matter."

"It is of the essence," Tatum said.

"It's interesting," I said, "because to begin with, it was the *Pump* that worked up the greatest head of steam about the mutilations. But the minute I linked Ellis Quint to them, the *Pump* changed direction and started tearing me apart. I can surely ask, India, why do you write about me so ferociously? Is it that you do so many hatchet jobs that you can't do anything else?"

She looked uncomfortable. "My editor gives me guidelines."

"You mean he tells you what to write?"

"Yes. No."

"Which?"

She looked from me to Tatum and back. "He edits my piece to align it with overall policy."

I said nothing. Tatum said with gravitas, "If I read any lies or innuendos about my having improperly talked to Sid Halley about the forthcoming Quint trial, I will sue you personally for defamation, Miss Cathcart, and I will ask for punitive damages."

I felt almost sorry for her. She stood up, her eyes wide.

"Say we weren't here," I said.

I couldn't read her expression. She headed for the stairs.

Tatum said, "But how did she—or her paper—know we would be here?"

I asked, "Do you feed your appointments into a computer?"

He frowned. "My secretary does. We have a system that can tell where all the partners are. I told her I was coming here, but not who I was meeting. That still doesn't explain . . ."

I sighed. "Yesterday evening you phoned my mobile number."

"Yes, and you phoned me back."

"Someone's been listening on my mobile phone's frequency."

"But you called me back. They heard almost nothing."

"You gave your name. How secure is your office computer?"

"We change passwords every three months."

"There are people who crack passwords just for the fun of it. Someone has accessed my own computer during the past month. A combination of my mobile phone and your office computer must have come up with the *possibility* that your appointment was with me. Someone in the *Pump* did it. So they sent India along to find out, and here we are. And because they succeeded, we now know they tried."

"It's incredible."

"Who runs the *Pump*? Who sets the policy?"

Tatum said thoughtfully, "The editor is George Godbar. The proprietor's Lord Tilepit."

"Any connection with Ellis Quint?"

He shook his head. "Not that I know of."

"I think I'd better find out."

Davis Tatum smiled.

I left the restaurant in a taxi. Although it seemed unlikely that Gordon Quint would still be hanging about Pont Square with murderous feelings, I had the taxi make two reconnoitering passes around the railed central garden.

All seemed quiet. I paid the driver, walked without incident up the steps to the front door and let myself into the haven of home.

I retrieved a few envelopes from the letter box and found a page

77

in my fax. It seemed a long time since I'd left, but it had been only the previous morning.

My cracked arm hurt. Well, it would. The best way, always, to minimize woes was to concentrate on something else. I phoned the handy acquaintance who had set up my computers for me.

"Doug," I said, "someone is listening in on my mobile."

He sniffed. "So you want to know how to stop it?"

"You're dead right."

"Ditch your analog mobile. They have radio signals that can be listened to. Get a digital."

"Teach me."

"The signal sent to a digital telephone," he said, "is not one signal, as in analog, but is eight simultaneous signals, each transmitting one eighth of what you hear. It is impossible for anyone to decode them, except the receiving mobile."

"So," I said, fascinated, "where do I get one?"

"Try Harrods," he said.

"*Harrods?*"

"Or anywhere else that sells phones."

Amused and grateful, I hung up. I opened my mail and checked the fax. The fax, being most accessible, got looked at first.

A handwritten message read simply, "Phone me," and gave a long number. The writing was Kevin Mills's, but the fax machine he'd sent it from was anonymously not the *Pump*'s.

I phoned the number given, which would have connected me to a mobile, and got only the instruction, "Please try later."

There were a dozen messages I didn't much want on my answering machine and a piece of information I *definitely* didn't want, in a large brown envelope from Shropshire.

The envelope contained a copy of a glossy county magazine, one I'd sent for, as I'd been told it included lengthy coverage, including a complete guest list, of the heir to the dukedom's coming-of-age dance. Among the four pages of pictures was one of a spectacular burst of fireworks. And there in a group of heaven-gazing spectators, there in white tuxedo, there unmistakably stood Ellis Quint.

My heart sank. The fireworks had started at three thirty. At three thirty, when the moon was high, Ellis had been a hundred miles northwest of the Windward Stud Farm's yearling.

So, I thought, he had to have taken the colt's foot off early. Say

78

by one o'clock. He could then have arrived for the fireworks by three thirty. I'd found no one who'd seen him *arrive*, but several who swore to his presence at five fifteen, when he had helped the heir to climb onto a table to make a drunken speech. The heir had poured a bottle of champagne over Ellis's head. Everyone remembered *that*. Ellis could not have driven back to Northampton before dawn.

For two whole days the previous week I'd traipsed round Shropshire, handed on from grand house to grander, asking the same two questions (according to sex): Did you dance with Ellis Quint? Or, did you drink or eat with him? The answers at first had been freely given, but as time went on, news of my mission spread before me until I was progressively met by hostile faces and frankly closed doors. Shropshire was solid Ellis country. They were not going to say that they didn't know when he'd arrived.

In the end, I returned to the duchess's front gates and from there drove as fast as prudence allowed to the Windward Stud Farm, timing the journey at two hours and five minutes. I'd proved nothing except that Ellis had had time.

Enough time was not enough.

As always before gathering at such dances, the guests had given and attended dinner parties both locally and farther away. No one that I'd asked had entertained Ellis at dinner.

No dinner was not enough.

I went through the guest list, crossing off the people I'd seen. There were still far more than half unconsulted. I hadn't the time or, to be frank, the appetite to locate and question all the guests, even if they would answer. There must have been people—local people—helping with the parking of cars that night. Chico would have chatted people up in the local pubs and found out if any of the car parkers remembered Ellis's arrival. Chico was good at pubs.

The police might have done it, but they wouldn't. The death of a colt still didn't count like murder.

The police.

I phoned Norman Picton's police-station number and gave my name as John Paul Jones. He came on the line in a good humor and listened to me without protest.

"Er . . ." I began, "I was at Windward Stud Farm when the police found the lopping shears in the hedge."

79

"Yes, you told me."

"Well, I've been thinking. Those shears weren't wrapped in sacking, like the ones we took from the Quints."

"No. And the shears weren't the same, either. The ones at Northampton are a newer model, one sold everywhere in garden centers. The problem is that Ellis Quint hasn't been reported as buying any, not in the Northamptonshire police district nor ours."

"Is there any chance," I asked, "of my looking again at the material used for wrapping the shears? The cloth might tell us where the shears came from. *Which* garden center, do you see?"

"I'll see if they've done that already."

"Thanks, Norman."

"Thank Archie. He drives me to help you."

"Does he?"

He heard my surprise. "Archie has *influence*," he said, "and I do what the magistrate tells me."

When he'd gone off the line, I tried Kevin Mills again and reached the same electronic voice: "Please try later."

After that I sat in an armchair while the daylight faded and the lights came on in the peaceful square. I thought of Ellis and the wasteland he had made of my year. I thought of Rachel Ferns and Silverboy and lymphoblasts. I thought of the press and especially the *Pump* and India Cathcart and the orchestrated months of vilification.

I thought for a long time about Archie Kirk, who had drawn me to Combe Bassett and given me Norman Picton. I wondered if it had been from Archie that Norman had developed a belief in a heavy presence behind the scenes. I wondered if it could possibly be Archie who had prompted Davis Tatum to engage me to find that heavyweight. I wondered if it could possibly have been Archie who told Davis Tatum about my run-in with the bad hat at the Jockey Club, and if so, how did *he* know?

I thought about Gordon Quint's rage and the practical difficulties his fencing post had inflicted. I thought of Ginnie Quint's despair. I thought of the colts and their chopped-off feet.

When I went to bed, I dreamed the same old nightmare.

Both hands.

I awoke sweating.

Damn it all to hell.

9

IN THE morning I went across London to Companies House, which held the records of public and private companies. Topline Foods, I learned, was an old company recently taken over by new investors. The chief shareholder and managing director was Owen Yorkshire. There were fifteen nonexecutive directors, of whom one was Lord Tilepit. It was located at Frodsham, Cheshire. The product of the company was foodstuffs for animals.

I traveled home (safely) and phoned Archie, who was, his wife reported, at work. "I'll give him a message when he gets back."

I tried Kevin Mills and this time nearly got my eardrums perforated. "At last!"

"I've tried you a dozen times," I said.

"If you're in Pont Square, can I see you? I'm not far away."

He was at my door in less than ten minutes.

"This is *nice*," he said, looking around. "Not what I expected."

There was a Sheraton writing desk and buttoned brocade chairs and a couple of modern wood inlaid tables. The overall colors were grayish blue—soft and restful. The only intruder was an ancient slot machine that worked on tokens.

I always left a few tokens haphazardly nearby. Kevin picked one up, fed it into the slot and pulled the handle. The wheels clattered and clunked. He got two cherries and a lemon.

"What wins the jackpot?" he asked.

"Three horses with jockeys jumping fences."

He looked at me sharply.

"It used to be bells. That was boring, so I changed it."

The machine was addictive. Kevin played throughout our conversation, but the nearest he came was two horses and a pear.

"The trial has started, Sid," he said, "so give us the scoop."

"The trial's only technically started. You know very well I can't tell you a thing. Why did the *Pump* stop helping the colt owners and shaft me instead?"

"Policy," he said, concentrating hard on the machine. Two bananas and a blackberry.

"Whose policy?"

"The public wants demolition. They gobble up spite."

"Yes, but—"

"Look, Sid," he said, playing the machine fast, "now and then we get a *request,* such as 'lean hard on Sid Halley.' We get the word from on high—and don't ask *who* on high. I don't know. None of us likes it, but we have a choice: Go along or go somewhere else."

"And India Cathcart?" I asked.

He pulled the lever. Two lemons and a jumping horse came to rest in a row. "India," he said, "for some reason didn't want to trash you. Her editor squeezed the poison out of her drop by drop for that first piece. In the end, he wrote most of it himself. She was furious, but she couldn't do anything about it."

I was more pleased than I would have expected. "What about the continued stab wounds almost every week?"

"I guess she goes along with policy. She has to eat."

"Is it George Godbar's policy?"

"The big white chief himself? Yes, you could say the editor of the paper has the final say."

"And Lord Tilepit?"

Mills gave me an amused glance. Two pears and a lemon. "He's not a hands-on proprietor. We hardly know he's alive."

"Does he give the overall policy to George Godbar?"

"Probably. Why do I get the idea that *you* are interviewing *me?*"

"I cannot imagine. What do you know about Owen Yorkshire?"

"Who's he?" A horse, a demon and some cherries.

"Quite likely a friend of Lord Tilepit."

He banged the slot machine. "The bloody thing hates me."

"It has no soul," I said. I fed in a stray token myself and pulled the handle. Three horses. Life's little irony.

Kevin Mills took his paunch, his mustache and his disgruntlement off to his word processor, and I again phoned Norman.

"My colleagues now think John Paul Jones is a snitch," he said. "What is it this time?"

"Do you have any of those horse nuts I collected from Betty Bracken's field, and the ones from the Land Rover?"

"Yes. They're identical in composition."

"Then could you find out if they were manufactured by Topline Foods Limited, of Frodsham in Cheshire?"

After a short silence he said cautiously, "Why does it matter?"

"You know you told me you thought there might be a heavyweight somewhere behind the scenes? I've been asked to find out."

"Jeez," he said. "Who asked you? Archie Kirk?"

"Not so far as I know."

"Huh!" He sounded unconvinced. "I'll go this far. If you get me some authenticated Topline nuts, I'll see if I can run a check on them to find out if they match the ones we have."

"I'll get some Topline nuts, but they probably won't match."

"Why not?"

"The balance of ingredients will have changed. Every batch will have its own profile, so to speak."

"What interests you in Topline Foods?" Norman asked, but I didn't answer. "All right. You can't tell me now. I hate amateur detectives." He sighed heavily. "I've got your piece of that Northampton material."

"You're *brilliant*," I said. "Where can I meet you?"

"Come to the lake at five o'clock. I'm picking up the boat to take it home for winter storage. Okay?"

"I'll be there."

I phoned the hospital in Canterbury. Rachel, the ward sister told me, was "resting comfortably."

I spent the afternoon exchanging my old vulnerable analog mobile for a digital model. From my apartment I then phoned Miss Richardson at the stud farm, who said vehemently that no, I certainly might *not* call on her again. The Quints were dear friends, and it was all my fault that Ginnie had killed herself.

I called Miss Richardson's vet to ask how long he thought the foot had been off when the colt was found at seven o'clock. All he could say was that neither the colt's leg nor the severed foot showed signs of recent bleeding. Miss Richardson had insisted he put the colt out of his misery immediately, and he had done so.

The wound had been clean: one chop. The vet said he was surprised a yearling would have stood still long enough for shears to be applied. Yes, he confirmed, the colt had been lightly shod, and yes, there had been horse nuts scattered around, but Miss Richardson often gave her horses nuts as a supplement to grass.

After that I had to get to the lake. I experimentally flexed and clenched my right hand. Sharp protests. I resorted to ibuprofen and drove to the lake wishing Chico were around to do it.

Norman had loaded his boat halfway onto its trailer. "Give me a hand, will you? Pull when I lift."

I looked at the job and said briefly that I couldn't.

"You only need one hand for pulling."

I told him about Gordon Quint's attack. Predictably, he said I should make an official complaint.

"No," I said. "This is unofficial, and ends right here."

He went off to fetch a friend to help him and then busied himself with wrapping and stowing his powerful outboard.

I said, "What first gave you the feeling that there was some heavyweight meandering behind the scenes?"

"First?" He went on working while he thought. "I expect it was because one minute I was putting together an ordinary case—even if Ellis Quint's fame made it newsworthy—and the next I was being leaned on to find some reason to drop it.

"No one has entirely given in to the pressure," he pointed out. "The case against Ellis Quint has not been dropped. True, it's now in a ropy state. You yourself have been discredited to the point where you're almost a liability to the prosecution."

In effect, I thought, I'd been commissioned by Davis Tatum to find out who had campaigned to defeat me.

Norman backed his car up to the boat trailer and hitched them together. Then he unlocked the glove compartment of the car and handed me a plastic bag. "One strip of dirty rag," he said cheerfully. "It's got some sort of pattern in it, but no garden-center name or anything."

"I don't have high hopes," I said, "but frankly, just now every straw's worth clutching."

"How far can I trust you?" he asked.

"I thought we'd discussed this already."

"That was months ago." Then he made a decision and handed me a business-size brown envelope. "It's a copy of the analysis done on the horse nuts," he said. "Read it and shred it."

"Okay. And thanks."

I held the envelope and plastic bag together and knew I couldn't take such trust lightly.

"I've been thinking," I said. "Do you remember, way back in June, when we took those things out of the Land Rover?"

"Of course I remember."

"There was a farrier's apron. We didn't take that, did we?"

He frowned. "No. What's significant about it?"

I said, "It's odd that the colts should stand still long enough for the shears to close round the ankle, even with head-collars and those nuts. But horses have an acute sense of smell, and all those colts had shoes on—I checked—and they would have known the smell of a blacksmith's apron. I think Ellis might have worn that apron to reassure the colts. They may have thought he was the man who shod them. They would have *trusted* him. He could have lifted an ankle and gripped it with the shears. It's how I'd get a two-year-old to let me near his legs."

"Then as far as I'm concerned," he said, "that's how it was done."

We said good-bye, and he drove off with a wave. I returned to my car to make the short journey to the home of Archie Kirk.

He had returned from work. He took me into his sitting room. "How's things?" he asked. "Whisky?"

I nodded. "A lot of water."

He indicated chairs, and we sat.

"Will you answer some questions?" I said.

"It depends what they are."

I drank some whisky and let my muscles relax. "For a start, what do you do?" I said.

"I'm a civil servant."

"That's not . . . well . . . specific."

With his glass halfway to his lips he said, "Start at the other end."

I smiled. "Then . . . do you know Davis Tatum?"

After a pause he answered, "Yes."

It seemed to me he was growing wary. I said, "How's Jonathan?"

He laughed. "I hear you play chess," he said. "I hear you're a whiz at misdirection."

I played chess only with Charles at Aynsford, and not often. "Do you know my ex–father-in-law, Charles Roland?" I asked.

With a glimmer he said, "I've talked to him on the telephone."

At least he hadn't lied to me, I thought, and if he hadn't lied, he'd given me a fairly firm path to follow.

"I checked on the colt," I said. "The foot stayed on."

Archie nodded. "Betty's delighted. The colt is permanently lame, but they're going to see if he's any good for stud."

Archie's sweet wife came in and asked if I would stay to dinner;

she could easily cook extra. I thanked her but stood up to go. Archie came out to my car with me.

He said, "I work in a small, unacknowledged department set up to foretell the probable outcome of any high political appointment. We also predict the consequences of pieces of proposed legislation. We are always on the lookout for exceptional independent investigators with no allegiances. They're hard to find. We think you're one."

I stood beside my car in the dying light, looking into the extraordinary eyes. I said, "Archie, I'll work for you to the limit as long as I'm sure you're not sending me into a danger that you know exists but are not telling me about."

He took a deep breath but gave no assurances.

He was still standing on his gravel as I drove out through his gates. A true civil servant, I thought ruefully. No positive assurances could ever be given, because the rules could at any time be changed under one's feet. I drove north to Charles's house and found him in the wardroom. He made no reference to the fact that it was the second time in three days that I had sought his sanctuary. He merely pointed to the gold brocade chair and poured brandy for me without asking. I sat and drank and looked gratefully at the restraint of this man who'd commanded ships and was now my only anchor.

"How's the arm?" he asked briefly, and I said lightly, "Sore."

He nodded and waited. After a longish pause I said, "Do you know a man called Archibald Kirk?"

"No, I don't think so."

"He says he talked to you on the telephone. It was months ago, I think. He may have been asking you about me. Sort of checking up, like a reference. You probably told him that I play chess."

He said, "I've been asked several times about your character and ability. I always say, if they're looking for an investigator, they couldn't do better. Why do you ask about this Archibald Church?"

"Kirk," I said. "Do you remember coming with me to the Jockey Club? The day we got the head of the security section sacked?"

"I could hardly forget it, could I?"

"You didn't tell Archie Kirk about it, did you?"

"Of course not. I gave you my word *never* to talk about it."

"Someone has," I said morosely. I thought a bit and asked, "Do you know a lawyer called Davis Tatum?"

"I know *of* him. Never met him."

"You'd like him. You'd like Archie, too." I paused and went on. "They both know about that day at the Jockey Club."

"But Sid, does it matter?"

"Davis Tatum and, I'm sure, Archie have engaged me to find out who is moving behind the scenes to get the Quint trial quashed. Tatum made a point of telling me that he knew all about the mandarins insisting I take off my shirt, and why. I think he and Archie are trying to reassure themselves that if they ask me to do something dangerous, I'll do it."

He gave me a long, slow look. Finally he said, "And will you?"

I sighed. "Probably."

"What sort of danger?"

"I don't think they know. But realistically, if someone has an overwhelming reason for preventing Ellis's trial from ever starting, who is the person standing chiefly in the way?"

"You."

"Yes. So they're asking me to find out if anyone might be motivated enough to ensure my permanent removal from the scene."

He sat as if frozen.

I sighed. "Davis Tatum gave me a name—Owen Yorkshire. He owns a firm called Topline Foods, which sponsored a lunch at Aintree the day before the Grand National. Ellis Quint was guest of honor. Also among the guests was a man called Lord Tilepit, who is both on the board of Topline Foods and the proprietor of the *Pump,* which has been busy mocking me for months. And so," I said finally, "I'll go and see what Owen Yorkshire and Lord Tilepit are up to, and if I don't come back, you can kick up a stink."

"Don't do it, Sid."

"But if I don't, Ellis will walk out laughing and my standing in the world will be down the tubes forever, if you see what I mean."

After a while he said, "I do vaguely remember talking to this Archie fellow. He asked about your *brains.* He said he knew about your physical resilience. Odd choice of words—I remember them now. I told him you played a wily game of chess. And it's true, you do. But it was a long time ago. Before all this happened."

I nodded. "He already knew a lot about me when he got his sister to phone at five thirty in the morning to tell me about her colt."

"So that's who he is? Mrs. Bracken's brother?"

"Yeah." I drank brandy and said, "If you're ever talking to Sir

Thomas Ullaston, would you mind asking him if he told Archie Kirk or Davis Tatum about that morning in the Jockey Club?"

Sir Thomas Ullaston had been senior steward at the time and had conducted the proceedings that led to the removal of the head of the security section, who had arranged for Chico and me to be thoroughly deterred from investigating anything ever again. As far as I was concerned, it was all past history, and I most emphatically wanted it to remain so.

Charles said he would ask Sir Thomas.

"Ask him not to let the *Pump* get hold of it."

Charles contemplated that possibility with about as much horror as I did myself.

The doorbell rang distantly, and Charles frowned at his watch. "Who can that be? It's almost eight o'clock."

We soon found out. An ultrafamiliar voice called, "Daddy?" and an ultrafamiliar figure appeared in the doorway. Jenny—my some-time wife, my still embittered wife.

Smothering my dismay, I stood up, and Charles also.

"Jenny," Charles said, advancing to greet her. "What a lovely surprise."

She turned her cheek toward him coolly, as always, and said, "We were passing." She looked at me without much emotion and said, "We didn't know *you* were here until I saw your car outside."

I took the few steps between us and gave her the sort of cheek-to-cheek salutation she'd bestowed on Charles.

"You look thin," she observed.

She, I thought, looked as beautiful as always, but there was nothing to be gained by saying so. I didn't want her to sneer at me. She could hurt me with words whenever she tried.

Her handsome new husband had followed her into the room, apologizing for having appeared without warning.

"My dear fellow, anytime," Charles assured him.

Charles poured drinks and suggested dinner. Anthony Wingham waffled a grateful refusal. He and Charles made small talk until they'd exhausted the weather. Into a sudden silence Jenny said, "Well, Sid, you've got yourself into a proper mess this time. Ellis Quint! The papers pestered me, too. I suppose you know?"

I unwillingly nodded.

"That reporter from the *Pump*," Jenny complained. "India

Cathcart. She wanted to know all about you and about our divorce. Do you know what she wrote? She wrote that I'd told her that quite apart from being crippled, you weren't man enough for me."

"I read it," I said briefly.

"Did you? And did you like it? Did you like that, Sid?"

I didn't reply. It was Charles who fiercely protested. "Jenny! Don't."

Her face suddenly softened, all the spite dissolving, revealing the gentle girl I'd married. The transformation happened in a flash, like prison bars falling away. Her liberation, I thought, had come at last.

"I didn't say that," she told me. "I really didn't. She made it up."

I swallowed, finding the old Jenny harder to handle than her scorn. "What *did* you say?" I asked.

"Well, I . . . I told her," Jenny said, "that whatever she wrote, she wouldn't smash Sid, because no one had ever managed it. I told her that he never showed his feelings and that steel was putty compared to him and that I couldn't live with it."

Charles and I had heard her say that before. It was Anthony who looked surprised. He inspected my harmless-looking self from his superior height and obviously thought she had got me wrong.

"India Cathcart didn't believe Jenny, either," I told him.

"What?"

"He reads minds, too," Jenny said, putting down her glass. "Anthony, darling, we'll go now. Okay?" To her father she said, "Sorry it's such a short visit," and to me, "India Cathcart is a witch."

I kissed Jenny's cheek. "I still love you," I said quietly.

She looked briefly into my eyes. "I told her the truth."

"I know."

"Don't let her break you."

"No."

"Well," she said brightly, loudly, "good-bye, Sid."

She looked happy. She laughed. I ached for the days when we'd met, when she looked like that always, but one could never go back. "Good-bye, Jenny," I said.

Charles, uncomprehending, went to see them off and came back frowning. "She tears you to pieces," he said. "*I* can't stand it. Why don't you ever fight back?"

"Look what I did to her."

"She knew what she was marrying."

"I don't think she did. It isn't always easy, being married to a jockey."

"You forgive her too much. And then, do you know what she said when she was leaving? I don't understand her. She gave me a hug, not a dutiful peck on the cheek, and said, 'Take care of Sid.'"

I felt instantly liquefied inside, close to tears.

"Sid . . ."

I shook my head. "We've made our peace," I said.

"When?"

"Just now. The old Jenny came back. She's free of me. She felt free quite suddenly, so she'll have no more need to . . . to tear me to pieces, as you put it."

He said, "I hope so," but looked unconvinced.

Later as we ate companionably together, I discovered that even though his daughter might no longer despise or torment me, what I perversely felt wasn't relief, but loss.

10

I LEFT Aynsford for London next morning, and I took my strip of rag to the laundry, where they fed it twice through the dry-cleaning cycle. What emerged was basically light turquoise in color, with a pattern of green, brown and salmon pink, and black stains that had stayed obstinately in place.

I consulted an interior decorator and learned that my rag was silk, an expensive fabric, with the pattern woven in, not printed. It appeared to be the work of a solitary weaver. "Try Saul Marcus in West London," the decorator suggested.

I found Saul Marcus in white-bearded person in an airy artist's studio near Chiswick, where he created fabric patterns. He looked with interest at my rag but shook his head. "It might be Patricia Huxford's work," he said at length. "She does—or did—work like this sometimes. I don't know of anyone else."

"Where would I find her?"

"Sussex. Somewhere like that."

"Thank you very much."

Returning to Pont Square, I looked in the Sussex phone books, then tried directory inquiries, the central computerized number finder. An impersonal voice told me that the number of Patricia Huxford, Chichester, West Sussex, was unlisted. My arm ached, and while I was unenthusiastically thinking of driving the roughly seventy miles to Chichester, Charles phoned.

"I've been talking to Thomas Ullaston," he said. "I thought you'd like to know."

"Yes," I agreed with interest. "What did he say?"

"Thomas didn't deny that he'd told someone about that morning, but he assured me it was a man of utmost probity. I asked if it was Archibald Kirk, and he *gasped*. He said Kirk sought him out because he wanted to know how good an investigator you were. It seems it's hard to find good independent investigators they can trust. Thomas told Kirk to trust *you* and found himself telling about that chain and those awful marks."

"Yeah," I said, "go on."

"Thomas told Kirk that with your jockey constitution and physical resilience—he said physical resilience, Thomas did, so that's exactly where Kirk got that phrase from—you'd shaken off the whole thing as if it had never happened."

"Yes," I said, which wasn't entirely true.

Charles chuckled. "Thomas said he wouldn't want young master Halley on his tail if he'd been a crook."

Young master Halley found himself pleased.

"Sid . . . be careful."

I smiled as I assured him I would. Be careful was hopeless advice to a jockey, and at heart I was as much out to win as ever.

On my way to the car, I bought some robust adhesive bandage and, with my right forearm firmly strapped and a sufficient application of ibuprofen, drove to the public library in Chichester and asked to see the electoral roll. I found Patricia Huxford within fifteen minutes: "Bravo House, Lowell."

Hallelujah.

I followed my road map to the village of Lowell and found Bravo House, a small converted church, with a herd of cars and vans outside. As people seemed to be walking in and out of the high west door, I walked in, too. I had arrived, it was clear, at the end of a photographic session for a glossy magazine.

A small woman in an astonishing dress was descending from a

sort of throne that had been built on a platform where the old transepts crossed the nave. Spotlights were being switched off, and photographers were dismantling equipment. There were effusive thanks in the air and the overall glow of a job done well.

I waited, looking about me, discovering the changes from church to modern house. The window glass, high up, was clear, not colored. The stone-flagged nave had rugs, no pews, and comfortable modern sofas pushed back against the walls to accommodate the crowds. Nothing had been done to spoil the sweep of the vaulted ceiling and soaring stone arches.

The media flock drifted down the nave and left. Patricia Huxford waved them off, closed her heavy door and, turning, was surprised to find me still inside.

"So sorry," she said, and began to open the door again.

"I'm not with the photographers," I said. "I came to ask you about something else."

"I'm tired," she said. "I must ask you to go."

"You look beautiful," I told her, "and it will only take a minute." I brought my scrap of rag out and showed it to her. "If you are Patricia Huxford, did you weave this?"

"Trish," she said absently. "I'm called Trish." She looked at the strip of silk and then at my face. "What's your name?" she asked.

"John Sidney."

John Sidney. My real two first names, the ones my young mother had habitually used. And I used John Sidney in my job whenever I didn't want to be known to be Sid Halley. After the past months of all-too-public drubbing I wasn't sure that Sid Halley would get me anything anywhere but a swift heave-ho.

Trish Huxford, somewhere in her middle to late forties, was pretty, blond, small-framed and cheerful. Bright, observant eyes looked over my gray business suit and unthreatening manner: my usual working confidence-inspiring exterior. I saw her relax.

The amazing dress she had worn for the magazine photographs was utterly simple, hanging heavy and straight from her shoulders, floor-length and sleeveless, with a soft ruffled frill around her neck. It was the cloth of the dress that staggered: It *shimmered.*

"Did you weave your dress?" I asked.

"Of course."

"I've never seen anything like it."

"No, you wouldn't, not nowadays. Where did you come from?"

"London. Saul Marcus suggested you might know who wove my strip of silk."

"Saul! How is he?"

"He has a white beard," I said. "He seemed fine."

"I haven't seen him for years. Will you make me some tea? I don't want marks on this dress."

I smiled. "I'm quite good at tea."

She led the way past the throne and around a white-painted screen into what had once probably been a vestry and was now a small kitchen. "Mugs and tea are on that shelf," she said.

I half filled her electric kettle and plugged it in, and she spent the time walking around, watching the miraculous effect of her dress.

Intrigued, waiting for the water to boil, I asked, "What is it made of?"

"What do you think?"

"Er, it looks like . . . well . . . gold."

She laughed. "Quite right. Gold, silver thread and silk. Normally I wear jeans and an old smock. Today is playacting."

"And magnificent," I said as I filled the mugs.

She nodded. "No one, these days, makes cloth of gold."

"It's breathtaking," I said.

"You know something?" She drank some tea. "You're the only person who's seen this dress who hasn't asked how much it cost."

"I did wonder."

"And I'm not telling. Give me your strip of silk."

I took her empty mug and handed her the rag. She smoothed her fingers over it. "I made quite a lot of this at one time." She paused, then said abruptly, "Come along." We went this time through a door in another partition and found ourselves in her workroom.

There were three looms, all bearing work in progress. There was also a business section with filing cabinets.

"I make fabrics you can't buy anywhere else," she said. "Most of it goes to the Middle East." She walked towards the largest of the three looms, a monster that rose in steps to double our height.

"I made your sample on this," she said. "It's a Jacquard loom. Nowadays almost no one outside the Middle East thinks the beauty of this weave is worth the expense, but once, I used to make quite a lot of it to order for castles and great houses in England."

I said neutrally, "Would you know who this piece was for?"

"My dear man, no. But I probably still have the records. Why do you want to know?"

"I was given the strip and asked to find its origin."

She opened cupboard doors to reveal ranks of box files, and ran her fingers along the labels on the spines until she came to one that her expression announced as possible. She lifted the box file from the shelf. Inside were stiff pages, samples of fabric stapled to them, with details of fibers, dates and purchasers' names.

She turned the pages slowly. "That's the one!" she exclaimed suddenly. "I wove it almost thirty years ago as a hanging for a four-poster bed."

I asked without much expectation, "Who for?"

"It says here a Mrs. Gordon Quint."

Ginnie? *Ginnie* had owned the material?

"It must have been this one commission," Trish Huxford said. "I don't think I made these colors for anyone else." She looked at the stains disfiguring the strip I'd brought. "What a pity. I think of my fabrics as going on forever. They could easily last two hundred years. I love the idea of leaving something beautiful in the world. I expect you think I'm a sentimental old bag."

"I think you're splendid," I said truthfully.

She closed the file and put it back on the shelf, asking, "Does Mrs. Quint want some more of this fabric, do you think?"

"I don't know," I said.

ON THE drive back to London I pulled off the road to phone Davis Tatum at his home number.

He was in and wanting to know what I'd done for him so far.

"Tomorrow," I said, "I'll visit Topline Foods. Who did you get Owen Yorkshire's name from?"

"I can't tell you."

"Do you mean you promised not to, or you don't know?"

"I mean, just go and take a look."

I said, "Sir Thomas Ullaston told Archie Kirk about that little matter at the Jockey Club, and Archie Kirk told *you*. So did the name Owen Yorkshire come to you from Archie Kirk?"

"Blast," he said.

"I like to know what I'm getting into."

After a pause he said, "Owen Yorkshire has been seen twice in the boardroom of the *Pump.* We don't know why."

"Thank you," I said.

"Is that enough?"

"To be going on with, yes. Oh, and my mobile phone is now safe. No more leaks. See you later."

I drove on to London and left the car, as I normally did, in a large public underground garage near Pont Square. Then I walked along the alleyway between tall houses that led into the opposite side of the square from my flat. I came to a dead stop when I saw that the streetlight outside my window was not lit.

There were two locked gates into the central garden, one opposite the path I was on, and one on the far side, opposite my house. Standing in shadow, I got out the resident-allocated key, went quietly across the road and unlocked the near gate.

Nothing moved. I eased the gate open, slid through and closed it. No squeaks. I moved slowly from patch to patch of shaded cover. Near the far side I stopped. I stood with my back to a tree, waiting.

And then I saw him.

In a car parked by one of the few meters was, unmistakably, Gordon Quint. He was looking straight ahead, waiting for me to arrive by road or pavement.

I retreated, frankly scared, expecting him to see my movement, but nothing happened. From tree to tree I regained the far gate, eased through it, crossed the road and walked back to my car and sat in it, not exactly trembling, but nonetheless stirred up. So much, I thought, for Davis Tatum's myth of a clever, unafraid investigator.

I kept in the car an overnight bag containing the personality-change clothes I'd got Jonathan to wear: dark two-piece tracksuit (trousers and zip-up jacket) and sneakers and a baseball cap. The bag also contained a long-sleeved open-necked shirt, two or three charged-up batteries for my hand, and a battery charger, to make sure. Habitually around my waist I wore a belt with a zipped pocket big enough for a credit card and money.

I sat in the car considering the matter of distance and ulnas. Frodsham, the home of Topline Foods, was near Liverpool, over two hundred miles away. I had already driven a hundred and fifty to Chichester and back. I'd never missed Chico so much.

I resignedly set off northwards. It was an easy three-hour drive normally. I drove for only one, then stopped at a motel to eat and sleep, and in the morning wheeled on again, trying to ignore both the obstinately slow-mending fracture and India Cathcart's column in the copy of the *Pump* that I'd bought from the motel's newsstand.

Most of her page concerned yet another politician caught with his trousers at half-mast, but the far-right column said:

> Sid Halley, illegitimate by-blow of a nineteen-year-old window cleaner and a packer in a biscuit factory, ran amok as a brat in the slums of Liverpool. Nothing wrong with that! But this same Sid Halley now puts on airs of middle-class gentility. A flat in Chelsea? Sheraton furniture? Posh accent? Go back to your roots, lad. No wonder Ellis Quint thinks you're funny.
>
> The slum background explains Halley's envy. The chip on the shoulder grows every day. Now we know why.
>
> The Halley polish is all a sham, just like his plastic left hand.

Why did it so bloody *hurt?* I thought.

My father had been killed in a fall eight months before my birth and a few days before he was to marry my eighteen-year-old mother. She'd done her best as a single parent in hopeless surroundings. *Give us a kiss, John Sidney.* I hadn't ever run amok. I'd been a quiet child, mostly. *Have you been fighting again, John Sidney?* She hadn't liked me fighting, though one had to sometimes, or be bullied.

And when she knew she was dying, she'd taken me to Newmarket and left me with the king of trainers to be made into a jockey, as I'd always wanted. So I couldn't possibly go back to my Liverpool "roots." I had no sense of ever having grown any there.

I had never envied Ellis Quint. I'd always liked him. I'd been a better jockey than he, and we'd both known it. If anything, the envy had been the other way around. But it was useless to protest.

My mobile phone buzzed. I answered it.

"Kevin Mills," a familiar voice said. "Where are you? I tried your apartment. Have you seen today's *Pump* yet?"

"Yes."

"India didn't write it," he said. "She filled that space with some paragraphs on sexual stress, and they were edited out."

"Then you wrote it yourself," I said. "You're the only person on the *Pump* who's seen my Sheraton desk."

"Blast you. Where are you?"

"Going back to Liverpool."

"Sid, look, I'm sorry."

"Policy?"

He didn't answer.

"No one's listening to this phone anymore. You can say what you like."

"Jeez." He laughed. "That didn't take you long." He paused. "You might not believe it, but most of us on the *Pump* don't like what we've been doing to you."

"Rise up and rebel," I suggested dryly.

"We have to eat," he said. "Listen, the paper's received a lot of letters from readers complaining that we're not giving you a fair deal."

"How many is a lot?"

"Two hundred or so. Believe me, that's a *lot*. But we're not allowed to print any."

I said with interest, "Who says so?"

"The editor, Godbar himself, and he doesn't like it, either, but the policy is coming from the very top."

"Tilepit?"

"Are you *sure* this phone's not bugged?"

"You're safe."

"You've had a mauling, Sid, and you don't deserve it. Yes, it's Tilepit. The proprietor himself."

"Well, thanks."

He said, "Did Ellis Quint *really* cut off those feet?"

I smiled ruefully. "The jury will decide."

"Sid, look here," he protested, "you *owe* me!"

"Life's a bugger," I said.

11

NINE o'clock Friday morning I drove into the town of Frodsham and asked for Topline Foods.

Near the river, I was told—the Mersey.

The historic docks of Liverpool's Mersey waterfront had long been silent, but at Frodsham there was a riverside vantage point with, away to the north, some still working docks at Runcorn. One of those docks was occupied by Topline Foods.

I'd stopped the car where I could see the sweep of river with the seagulls swooping and the stiff breeze tautening flags at the horizontal. I stood in the cold, smelling the salt and the mud.

Were these roots? I'd always loved wide skies, but it was the wide sky of the racecourse at Newmarket that I thought of as home. When I was a boy, there'd been no wide skies, only narrow streets.

The day after my mother died, I'd ridden my first winner, and that evening I'd got drunk for the first and only time until the arrest of Ellis Quint. Stirring and getting back into the car, I wondered where to find all those tungsten nerves I was supposed to have.

I'd better simply get on with it, I thought.

I drove down from the vantage point, located the Topline Foods factory and passed through its twelve-foot-high open gates. There was a guard in a gatehouse, who paid me no attention.

I parked at the end of one of many rows of cars and decided on a clothing compromise of suit trousers, zipped-up tracksuit top, white shirt, no tie, ordinary shoes. No threat to anybody.

The factory, built around three sides of the big central area, consisted of loading bays with semitrailers backed into them, a vast main building and a new-looking office block. I ambled across to the office building and shouldered open a heavy glass door that led into a large entrance hall—and found that the security arrangements were all inside.

Behind a desk sat a purposeful-looking middle-aged woman in a green jumper. Flanking her were two men in navy-blue security-guard suits with Topline Foods insignia on their breast pockets.

"Name, please," said the green jumper. "State your business."

She had a distinct Liverpool accent. With the same inflection in my own voice, I told her that my name was John Sidney and I had come "to see if you made some horse nuts." I paused. "Like," I lamely finished, dredging up the idiom.

"Of course we make horse nuts. It's our business."

"Yes," I told her earnestly, "but this farmer, like, he asked me to see if it was you that made some horse nuts that someone had given him, that were very good for his young horse, but he was given them loose and not in a bag, and all he has is a list of what's in them. He'll be a big customer if these are the nuts he's looking for."

She was bored by the rigmarole, but she lifted a telephone and repeated a shortened version of my improbable tale. She inspected me from head to foot. "Couldn't hurt a fly," she reported.

She put down the receiver. "Miss Rowse will be down to help you. Raise your hands."

"Eh?"

"Raise your hands, please."

Surprised, I did as I was told. One of the security guards patted me down, missing the false hand and the cracked bone.

Green jumper wrote "John Sidney" onto a clip-on identity card, and I clipped it dutifully on. "Wait by the elevator," she said.

I waited.

The doors finally parted to reveal a teenage girl with wispy fair hair: Miss Rowse. We rode the elevator to the third floor.

She smiled and led me down a newly carpeted passage to a comfortable office conspicuously labeled CUSTOMER RELATIONS. "Come in," Miss Rowse said proudly. "Please sit down."

I looked around. "Nice office," I said. "Have you been here long?" (Guileless Liverpool accent, just like hers.)

"I'm new this week. You're my second inquiry."

No wonder, I thought, she'd let me in.

I said, "Are all the offices as plush as this?"

"Yes," she said. "Mr. Yorkshire, he likes things nice."

"Is he the boss?"

"The chief executive officer." She nodded. The words sounded stiff and unfamiliar, as if she'd only just learned them.

"Topline Foods must be doing all right to have rich new offices like these," I said admiringly.

"They've got TV cameras coming tomorrow to set up for Monday. They brought dozens of potted plants round this morning. Ever so keen on publicity, Mr. Yorkshire is, Mrs. Dove says. Mrs. Dove, she's my boss really. She's office manager."

"The plants do make it nice and homey," I said. "Which TV company, do you know?"

She shook her head. "All the Liverpool big noises are coming to a reception on Monday. The TV cameras are going all over the factory."

An older and more cautious woman came in, revealing herself to be Mrs. Dove. Middle-aged and personally secure, I thought.

Status, ability and experience all combining in priceless efficiency.

"Can I help?" she asked. "Marsha dear, I thought we'd agreed you would always come to me for advice."

"Miss Rowse has been really helpful," I said. "She's going to find someone to answer my question. Perhaps you could yourself?"

Mrs. Dove (gray hair pinned high under a flat black bow, high heels, customer-relations neat satin shirt) listened with slowly glazing eyes to my tale of the nutty farmer.

"You need our Willy Parrott," she said when she could insert a comment. "Come with me."

I waggled conspiratorial fingers at Marsha Rowse and followed Mrs. Dove's busy back view along the expensive passage with mostly empty offices on each side. She continued through a thick fire door at the end, to emerge on a gallery around an atrium in the main factory building, where the nuts came from.

Rising from the ground, level almost to the gallery, were huge mixing vats, all with paddles circulating. The sounds were an amalgam of whir, rattle and slurp. The air bore fine particles of cereal dust. It looked and smelled rather like a brewery, I thought.

Mrs. Dove passed me on to a man in brown overalls, who inspected my dark clothes and asked if I wanted to be covered in fallout. "Not particularly," I said.

He raised patient eyebrows and gestured to me to follow him down an iron staircase and along another gallery to a little cubbyhole office. I commented on the contrast from the office building.

"Fancy fiddle-faddle," he said. "That's for the cameras. This is where the work is done."

"I can see that," I told him admiringly.

"Now, lad," he said, looking me up and down, unimpressed, "what is it you want?"

He wasn't going to be taken in by the farmer twaddle. I explained in a shorter version and produced Picton's analysis of the nuts from Combe Bassett and the Land Rover and asked if it was a Topline formula. He read the list of ingredients: wheat, oat feed, rye grass, molasses, salt, vitamins. . . .

"Where did you get this?" he asked.

"From a farmer, like I told you."

"The list isn't complete. It doesn't give percentages. I can't possibly match it to any of our products. But your farmer couldn't do better than our Sweetfield mix. It contains everything on your list."

"Are other people's cubes much different?"

"There aren't many manufacturers. We're perhaps fourth on the league table, but after this advertisement campaign we expect that to zoom up. The new management aims for the top." He smiled. "Owen Yorkshire's brought the old place back to life."

I thanked him for his time. Very interesting job, I told him. Obviously he ran the department that mattered most.

He took the compliment as his due and offered to let me tag along with him while he went to his next task, checking a new shipment of wheat. I accepted with an enthusiasm that pleased him.

He gave me a set of overlarge brown overalls and told me to clip the identity card on the outside, like his own. "Security is vital," he said to me. "Owen's stepped it all up. Our competitors wouldn't be above adding foreign substances to the mix. That would put us out of business."

I gave him an impressed look.

We walked along the gallery and came to another fire door, which he lugged open. "All internal doors are locked at night now, and there's a watchman with a dog." He stopped at a place from which we could see bags traveling along on an endless belt of bag-size ledges. "I expect you saw the two security men in the entrance hall?"

"They frisked me." I grinned. "Going a bit far, I thought."

"They're Owen's private bodyguards," Willy Parrott said with a mixture of awe and approval. "They're real hard men from Liverpool. Owen says he needs them in case the competitors try to get rid of him the old-fashioned way."

I frowned disbelievingly. "Competitors don't kill people."

"Owen says he's taking no risks, because he definitely is trying to put other firms out of business."

He led the way down some nearby concrete stairs and through another heavy door, and I realized we were on ground level. "You don't need to go back upstairs to get out," he said. "There's a door out to the yard just down here."

I thanked him for showing me around, but while I was in midsentence, he looked over my shoulder and his face changed completely from man in charge to subservient subject.

I turned to see what had caused this transformation and found it

101

to be not a royal person, but a large man in white overalls accompanied by several anxious blue-clad attendants.

"Morning, Willy," the man said. "Everything going well?"

"Yes, Owen. Fine."

"Good. Has the Canadian wheat come up from the docks?"

"They're unloading it now, Owen."

"Good. We should have a talk about future plans. Come up to my new office at four this afternoon."

"Yes, Owen."

The eyes of the businessman glanced my way incuriously. I was wearing brown overalls and an identity card and looked like an employee. Willy didn't attempt to explain my presence, for which I was grateful. Willy was almost on his knees in reverence.

Owen Yorkshire was, without doubt, impressive. Easily over six feet tall, he was large but not fat. Luxuriant, closely waving hair spilled over his collar, with the beginnings of gray in the lacquered wings sweeping back from above his ears. It was a hairstyle that in its way made as emphatic a statement as Jonathan's. Yorkshire intended not only to rule but to be remembered. His accent was not quite Liverpool and not at all London, but powerful, his voice unmistakably an instrument of dominance.

Willie said, "Yes, Owen," several more times; then Yorkshire and his satellites swept onwards, Willy looking after him.

"Do you work tomorrow?" I asked. "Is the factory open on Saturdays?"

He reluctantly removed his gaze from the Yorkshire back view and began to think I'd been there too long. "We're opening on Saturdays from next week," he said. "Tomorrow they're making more advertising films, and on Monday, too. Off you go, then, lad. Leave the overalls and identity tag back at the entrance."

I thanked him again and, still in the brown overalls, went out into the central yard, now clogged with vans and truckloads of television and advertising people. The television contingent were from Liverpool. The advertisement makers, according to the identification on their vans, were from Intramind Imaging (Manchester) Ltd.

I went up to one of the Intramind drivers. "You must have an exciting job," I said enviously. "Do you see all those film stars?"

He sneered. "We make advertising films, mate. Sure, sometimes we get big names, but mostly they're endorsing things."

"What sort of things?"

"Sports gear, often. Shoes, golf clubs."

"And horse cubes?"

He didn't mind a bit of showing off. He said, "They've got a lot of top jockeys lined up to endorse the horse nuts."

"Have they?" I asked interestedly. "Why not trainers?"

"It's the jockeys the public know by their faces."

He didn't, I saw gratefully, even begin to recognize my own face.

I walked to my car and made an uneventful exit through the tall, unchecked gates. Odd, I thought, that the security-paranoid Yorkshire didn't have a gate bristling with electronic barriers and ominous name gatherers. The only reason I could think of was that he didn't *want* name takers recording every visit.

I stopped in a public car park, took off the brown overalls and decided to go to Manchester.

INTRAMIND Imaging proved to be a much bigger outfit than I'd pictured. I shed the tracksuit top and the Liverpool accent and approached the reception desk in suit, tie and business aura.

"I've come from Topline Foods," I said. "I'd like to talk to whoever is in charge of their account."

If one pretended sufficient authority, I'd found, doors got opened, and so it was at Intramind Imaging. A Mr. Gross would see me. An electric door latch buzzed me into an inner hallway.

Mr. Gross was "third door on the left." The door had his name on it: Nick Gross. He wore a black satin shirt, long hair and a gold earring. Stuck in a time warp of departing youth, I thought.

"You're making advertising films for Topline," I said.

"So what? If you're another of their whining accountants, it isn't our fault you haven't been able to use those films you spent millions on. They're all brilliant stuff—the best. So you creep back to your Mr. Yorkshire and tell him if he wants his jockey series, he has to send us a check every week. Tell him not to forget that in ads the magic is in the *cutting*, and the cutting comes *last*. No check, no cutting. And that means no campaign. Got it?"

"Yes."

"Right. Off you trot, then."

I meekly removed myself but, walking as if I belonged there, went down a passage between increasingly technical departments.

I came to an open door and could see a screen showing familiar pieces of an ad campaign currently collecting critical acclaim. There were bursts of fast action as short as three seconds followed by longer intervals of black.

A man walked into my sight and saw me standing there.

"Yes?" he said. "Do you want something?"

"Is that," I said, "one of the mountain bike ads?"

"It will be when I cut it together. Who are you, exactly?"

"From Topline Foods. I came to see Nick Gross."

"Ah." There was a world of comprehension in the monosyllable. He was younger than Nick Gross and not so mock rock star in dress. I asked him, "Did you work on the Topline ads?"

"No, thank heaven. A colleague did. All that cabbage spent and eight months of award-worthy brilliant work sitting idle in cans on the shelves. And all because some twisted little pipsqueak gets the star attraction arrested for something he didn't do."

I held my breath, but he had no flicker of an idea what the pipsqueak looked like. I said I'd better be going, and he nodded vaguely. No one paid me any attention on the way out.

I DROVE into the center of Manchester and anonymously booked into a spacious room in the Crown Plaza Hotel. Tatum might have a fit over the expense, but I wanted a shower, room service and cosseting.

I phoned Tatum's home and got an answering machine. I asked him to call back to my mobile number and then phoned Intramind and asked a few general questions that I hadn't thought of in my brief career on the spot as a Topline employee. Were advertising campaigns originally recorded on film, I wanted to know, and could the public buy copies. I was told that Intramind usually used film, and no, the public could not buy copies. The finished film would be transferred onto broadcast-quality videotape, known as Betacam. These tapes belonged to the clients.

"Thanks very much," I said politely, grateful for knowledge.

Davis Tatum phoned soon after. "Sid," he said, "where are you?"

"Manchester."

"Any progress?"

"Some," I said. "Tomorrow evening—would you be able to go to Archie Kirk's house?"

"I should think so, if it's important. What time?"

"Could you arrange that with him? About six o'clock, I should think. I'll arrive there sometime myself. Don't know when."

With a touch of complaint he said, "It sounds a bit vague."

I thought I'd better not tell him that with burglary, times tended to be approximate.

12

I PHONED the *Pump*, asking for India Cathcart. Silly me. She was never in on Fridays. "Tell her Sid Halley would like to talk to her," I said, and gave the switchboard operator my mobile number.

I sat for a good while planning what I would do the next day. If all else failed, I would try Plan B—escape with skin intact.

I had some food sent up. At ten fifteen my mobile buzzed.

"Sid?" India said nervously.

"Hello."

"Don't say anything. I'll cry if you say anything." After a pause she said, "Sid! Are you there?"

"Yes. But I don't want you to cry, so I'm not saying anything."

"Oh." It was half a choke, half a laugh. "How can you be so— so *civilized?*"

"With enormous difficulty," I said. "Are you busy Sunday evening? Your restaurant or mine?"

She said disbelievingly, "Are you asking me out to dinner?"

"Well," I said, "it's not a proposal of marriage. Just food."

"How can you *laugh?*"

"Why are you called India?" I asked.

"I was conceived there. What has that got to do with anything?"

"I just wondered," I said. "Lord Tilepit—have you met him?"

"Yes." She sounded a bit bewildered. "He comes to the office party at Christmas. He shakes everyone's hand."

"What's he like?"

"Do you mean to look at?"

"For a start."

"Fairly tall. Light brown hair." A pause, then, "Your restaurant." I smiled. Her quick mind could reel in a tarpon.

"Lord Tilepit," I said. "Could anyone be physically in awe of him?"

"No." It was clear that she thought the idea laughable.

"So his leverage is all economic. Is there anyone *he* is in awe of?"

"I don't know. Why do you ask?"

"That man has spent four months directing his newspaper to ruin me," I said. "You must allow I have an interest."

"But you aren't ruined. You don't sound in the least ruined. And anyway, your ex-wife said it was impossible."

She silenced me.

She said, "Your ex-wife's still in love with you."

"No, not anymore."

"I'm an expert on ex-wives," India said. "Your Jenny said she couldn't live in your purgatory, but when I suggested you were a selfish brute, she defended you like a tigress. Do you still love *her?*"

I found a calm voice. "I regret a lot, but it's over. She has a better husband, and she's happy. What about *your* ex?"

"I fell for his looks. It turned out he wanted an admiration machine in an apron. End of story."

Smiling to myself, I said, "May I have your phone number?"

She said, "Yes," and gave it.

"Kensington Place restaurant. Eight o'clock."

"I'll be there."

I USUALLY took off my false hand at bedtime and replaced it after showering in the morning. Putting it on was a matter of talcum powder, getting the angle right and pushing hard.

Even after three years, whatever lighthearted front I might now achieve in public, in private the management of amputation still took a positive effort of the get-on-with-it ethos.

I'd charged up two batteries overnight, so I started the new day, Saturday, with a fresh battery in the hand and a spare in my pocket. I wore the tracksuit, white shirt and the dark sneakers. Into my overnight bag I packed the battery charger and my other clothes. In my belt I carried money and a credit card, and in my pocket six keys on a ring that bore also a miniature flashlight. Three of the keys were variously for my car and the entry doors of my flat. The other three would, between them, open any ordinary lock.

I checked out of the hotel and found the way back to Frodsham, parking within sight of the Topline wire-mesh gates. As before, the gates were open and no one going in or out was challenged.

At eleven o'clock the film crews arrived, disgorging film cameras (Intramind Imaging), a television camera (local station) and dozens of people looking purposeful, with heavy equipment and chest-hugged clipboards. I put on the brown overalls and identity badge and drove unhesitatingly through the gates, stopping near the unloading bays. Then I walked straight past the few Saturday hands, saying "Morning" as if I belonged.

Inside, I walked up the stairs and along the gallery leading to Willy Parrott's office. The paddles were silent in the vats. There were cameras being positioned below, with Owen Yorkshire himself directing the director, his authoritative voice telling the experts their job.

He was too busy to look up. I went on along the gallery, coming to the fire door that led up the flight of metal stairs. The fire doors were locked at night but open by day, Willy had said. Thankful, I reached the plush carpet of the offices and a door announcing OFFICE MANAGER, A. DOVE.

Mrs. Dove's door was locked twice: an old-looking mortise and a new knob with a keyhole in the center. These were locks I liked.

I went to work. Once inside, I relocked the door so that anyone outside trying it for security would find it as it should be. If anyone came with keys, I would have warning enough to hide.

Mrs. Dove's cote was large and comfortable. There were the routine office machines—fax, copier, calculator—and, on the desk, a computer. There were multiple filing cabinets and a tall white-painted cupboard that was locked.

The filing cabinets were a waste of time. What they offered was the entirely respectable basis of next year's audit. After investigating the desk drawers, which held only stationery, I switched on the computer, pressing the buttons for LIST FILES and ENTER. Scrolls of file names appeared, and I tried one at random: "Aintree." Onto the screen came details of the lunch given the day before the Grand National: guest list, menu, a summary of the speeches.

Nothing I could find seemed any more secret. I switched the computer off and turned my lock pickers to the tall white cupboard. The feeling of time running out, however irrational, shortened my breath and made me hurry.

Inside the white cupboard I found a second computer. I

switched it on, pressed LIST FILES again, and this time found myself looking not at individual subjects, but at directories, each of which contained file names, such as "Formula A." What I had come across were the more private records, some very secret.

In quick succession I highlighted the directories and brought them to the screen until one baldly listed "Quint"; but no amount of button pressing got me any further.

Think.

The reason I couldn't get the Quint information onto the screen must be because it wasn't in the computer.

Okay? Okay. So where was it?

On the shelf above the computer stood a row of box files, numbers 1 to 9, but not one labeled QUINT. Inside number 1 were several letters referring to loans made to Topline, and also a blue floppy disk. I fed the disk into the computer. On the screen I got a single word: "Password?"

Password? Heaven knew. I looked into the box files one by one and came to QUINT in number 6. There were three floppies in there.

I fed in the first.

"Password?"

Second and third disks—"Password?"

Damn, I thought.

Searching for anything helpful, I lifted down a heavy white cardboard box that filled the rest of the shelf. In it was a row of videotapes double the ordinary width. The label on one said BROADCAST-QUALITY VIDEOTAPE, BETACAM. Under that was the legend QUINT SERIES. 15 X 30 SECS. I saw that all of the labels were the same.

These double-sized tapes needed a special tape player not available in Mrs. Dove's office. I could, of course, simply put one of them inside my jacket and walk out with it. I could take all the "Password?" disks. If I did, I was (a) stealing, (b) in danger of being found carrying the goods, (c) making it impossible for any information they held to be used in a later legal inquiry. I would steal the information if I could, but not the software.

Someone tried to open the door.

There was no time to restore the room to normal. I could only speed to where I would be hidden by the door when it swung inward. Plan B meant simply running.

The knob turned again and rattled, but nothing else happened.

Whoever was outside had presumably been either keyless or reassured; in either case, it played havoc with my breathing.

Oddly, the pumping adrenaline brought me my computer answer, which was, if I couldn't bring the contents of a floppy disk to the screen, I could transfer it whole to *another* computer, one that would give me all the time I needed to crack the password or to get help from people who could.

Alongside the computer was a telephone cable, unattached, and I snapped it into the socket on the computer, thereby connecting Mrs. Dove's modem to the worldwide Internet. Then I tapped in my own Pont Square phone number and transferred the three QUINT disks from box number 6 to my own computer in London and, for good measure, another disk from box 3, identified as TILEPIT.

I knew of no way of transferring the Betacam tapes. I looked through the papers in the QUINT box and made a photocopy of one page—a list of racecourses—folding it and hiding it in the zipped pocket of my belt. Finally, I closed down the computer, checked that the box files and tapes were as they should be, relocked the cupboard, then gently opened the door to the passage.

Silence.

Breathing out with relief, I relocked Mrs. Dove's door and went down the fire stairs to the ground-floor entrance hall.

One step into the lobby proved one step too far. Something hit my head, and one of the beefy bodyguards flung a sort of strap round my body, effectively pinning my upper arms to my sides.

I plunged about a bit and got another crack on the head, which left me barely able to think. I was aware of being in the elevator, aware of having my ankles strapped together and of being dragged ignominiously over some carpet and dropped into a chair. "Tie him up," a voice said, and another strap tightened across my chest, so that when the temporary mist cleared, I woke to a state of near physical immobility.

The voice belonged to Owen Yorkshire. He said, "Well done. Go back downstairs and don't let anyone up here."

The door closed behind the bodyguards. We were in Owen Yorkshire's office, and the Yorkshire confronting me was very angry, disbelieving and, I would have said, frightened.

"What are you doing here?" he demanded, bellowing.

His voice echoed in the quiet room. His big body loomed over me, his big head close to mine. All his features, I thought, were slightly oversized: big nose, big eyes, square jaw, big mouth. The collar-length black wavy hair with its gray-touched wings seemed to vibrate with vigor. I would have put his age at about forty.

"Answer!" he yelled. "What are you doing here?"

I didn't reply. He snatched up from his desk a heavy fifteen-inch-long silvery wrench and made as if to hit my head with it, then threw it back down disgustedly.

He went abruptly out of the room, returning with two people: Mrs. Dove and a man, a stranger. Both exclaimed in surprise at the sight of my trussed self.

"Do you know who this is?" Yorkshire demanded furiously.

The man shook his head, mystified. Mrs. Dove, frowning, said to me, "Weren't you here yesterday? Something about a farmer?"

"This," Yorkshire said with scorn, "is Sid Halley." The man's face stiffened. "*This*, Verney," Yorkshire went on with biting sarcasm, "is the feeble creature you've spent months thundering on about. And Ellis said he was dangerous! Just look at him! All those big guns to frighten a mouse."

Verney *Tilepit*. I'd looked him up in *Burke's Peerage*. Verney Tilepit, third baron, age forty-two, a director of Topline Foods, proprietor—by inheritance—of the *Pump*.

Verney Tilepit's grandfather had been one of the old, roistering, powerful opinion makers who'd had governments dancing to their tune. The third baron had surfaced after years of quiescence, primarily, it seemed, to discredit a minor investigator. Policy! His bewildered grandfather would have been speechless.

He was fairly tall, as India had said, and he had brown hair. The flicking glance I gave him took in small features bunched in the middle of his face, small sandy mustache, large, light-framed glasses. Nothing physically threatening. Perhaps I felt the same disappointment in my adversary as he plainly did about me.

"How do you know he's Sid Halley?" Mrs. Dove asked.

Owen Yorkshire said disgustedly, "One of the TV crew knows him. He'd filmed him often."

Owen Yorkshire picked up the telephone, pressed numbers, waited and forcefully spoke.

"Get over here quickly," he said. "We have a crisis." He slammed down the receiver and stared at me balefully. "What are you

110

doing here?" He picked up the wrench again. "Answer!" he yelled.

I did manage an answer of sorts. I spoke to Tilepit directly in a weak, mock-respectful tone. "I came to see you, sir."

Tilepit said, "What for?" and "What made you think I would be here?"

"Someone told me you were a director of Topline Foods, so I came here to ask you to stop your paper telling lies about me."

Tilepit didn't know how to answer such naïveté. Yorkshire properly considered it barely credible. He spoke to Mrs. Dove. "Go down and make sure he hasn't been in your office."

"I locked it when I left last night, Owen."

"Go and look," he said. "And check that cupboard."

Mrs. Dove was gone a fair time, during which I worried more and more anxiously that I'd left something slightly out of place. I breathed slowly, trying not to sweat.

When she finally came back, she said, "The TV crews are leaving. Everything's ready for Monday. And, oh, the man from Intramind Imaging says they want a check."

"What about the office?"

"The office is all right." She was unconcerned. "It was all locked. Just as I left it."

"And the cupboard?" Yorkshire insisted.

"Locked." She thought he was overreacting. I was concerned only to show no relief.

"What are you going to do with him?" she asked, indicating me. "You can't keep him here. The TV crew downstairs know he's here. They want to interview him. What shall I say?"

Yorkshire with black humor said, "Tell them he's tied up."

She wasn't amused. She said, "I'll say he went out the back way. And I'll be off, too. I'll be here by eight Monday morning." She looked at me calmly and spoke to Yorkshire. "Let him go," she said unemotionally. "What harm can he do?"

NEITHER of these two men, I thought, listening to them, was a full-blown criminal. Not yet. Yorkshire was near the brink.

He still held the heavy adjustable wrench, slapping its head occasionally against his palm, as if it helped his thoughts.

"Please untie me," I said.

Tilepit might have done it. He clearly was unused to—and disturbed by—even this level of violence. But Yorkshire said, "We wait."

He opened a desk drawer and drew out, bizarrely, a jar of pickles. Dumping the wrench temporarily, he unscrewed the lid, pulled out a green finger and crunched it with large white teeth.

"Pickle?" he offered Tilepit. The baron averted his nose.

Yorkshire, shrugging, chewed uninhibitedly and went back to slapping his palm with the wrench.

"I'll be missed," I said mildly, "if you keep me much longer."

"Let him go," Tilepit said with a touch of impatience. "He's right. We can't keep him here indefinitely."

"We wait," Yorkshire said heavily, fishing out another pickle, and to the accompaniment of noisy munching, we waited.

The door opened finally behind me, and both Yorkshire and Tilepit looked welcoming and relieved. I didn't. The newcomer, who came around in front of me blankly, was Ellis Quint.

Ellis, in open-necked white shirt; Ellis, handsome, macho, vibrating with showmanship; Ellis, the nation's darling.

"What's Halley doing here?" he demanded, sounding alarmed.

"He was wandering about," Yorkshire said, pointing a pickle at me. "I had him brought up here."

Tilepit announced, "Halley says he came to ask me to stop the *Pump*'s campaign against him."

Ellis said positively, "He wouldn't have done that."

"Why not?" Yorkshire asked. "Look at him. He's a wimp."

"A *wimp!*"

Despite my precarious position, I smiled involuntarily at the incredulity in Ellis's voice. I saw the same private smile on his face: the acknowledgment of brotherhood, of shared experience, of injuries taken lightly, of indescribable triumphs. Whatever we were now, we had once been more than brothers. The past—our past—remained.

The smiles died. Ellis said, "This *wimp* could ruin us all." He put his face close to mine. "Still the same old Sid, aren't you? Cunning. Nerveless. Win at all costs. But you'll not get me into court, Sid. You haven't been able to break my Shropshire alibi, and my lawyers say that without that, the prosecution won't have a chance. You'll have destroyed your own reputation, not mine."

It seemed to me as if the cruel hidden side of Ellis suddenly took over. He put his hands on the hard shell of my left forearm and raised it until my elbow formed a right angle. The tight straps round my upper arms and chest prevented me from doing anything to stop him.

Ellis peeled back the brown overall sleeve and the blue one underneath. He pulled my shirtsleeve back and looked at the plastic skin underneath. "I know something about that hand," he said. "I got a brochure on purpose." He felt up my arm until he came to the top of the textured glove that gave the hand an appearance of life. He rolled it down as far as the wrist. Then, with concentration, he pulled it off finger by finger, exposing the mechanics.

Ellis smiled.

He put his own strong right hand on my electrical left and pressed and twisted, and then, when the works clicked free, unscrewed the hand in several turns until it came right off.

Ellis looked into my eyes as at a feast. "Well?" he said.

"Damn you to hell."

He smiled and let the unscrewed hand fall onto the carpet.

13

TILEPIT looked shocked enough to vomit, but Yorkshire laughed. Ellis said to him sharply, "It's not funny. Everything that has gone wrong is because of *him*, and don't you forget it."

Yorkshire protested, "But he's only—"

"Don't say *only*," Ellis interrupted, his voice hard and loud. "Don't you understand it yet? What do you think he's doing here? What does he know? He's not going to tell you. I *know* him. His nickname's Tungsten Carbide—that's the hardest of all metals. We've got to decide what to do with him. How many people know he's here?"

"My bodyguards," Yorkshire said. "They brought him up."

It was Lord Tilepit who gave him the real bad news. "A TV crew told Owen that Sid Halley was in the building."

"A *TV crew!*"

"They wanted to interview him. Mrs. Dove said she would tell them he'd gone."

"Mrs. Dove! Did she see him tied in that chair?"

"Yes," Tilepit said faintly.

"You stupid . . ." Words failed Ellis, but for only a few short seconds. "Then," he said flatly, "you can't kill him here."

"*Kill* him?" Tilepit couldn't believe what he'd heard. "I'm not— Are you talking about murder?"

"Oh, yes, my lord," I said dryly, "they are. With Your Lordship behind bars as an accessory. You'll love it in the slammer."

I'd meant only to get Tilepit to see the enormity of what Ellis was proposing, but in doing so, I'd unleashed Yorkshire's rage. He kicked my unscrewed hand with such force that it crashed against the wall. Then, realizing the wrench was still in his hand, he swung it at my head.

I saw the murderous intention in his face but couldn't avoid the blow. The heavy wrench connected with my cheekbone.

"I said *not here*," Ellis shouted. "Do you want his blood and brains all over your carpet? Too many people know he came here. When he doesn't turn up, you'll get the police in here looking for him. Find something to stop him bleeding. One drop of his blood here, you're looking at twenty-five years."

Yorkshire, bewildered by Ellis's attack, turned sullen. Tilepit tentatively produced a handkerchief embroidered with a coronet, which Ellis pressed on my cheek until the worst of the bleeding stopped. Then he snatched the wrench away from Yorkshire and they both went out of the office, leaving Tilepit alone with me.

"How did you get yourself into this mess?" I asked.

No answer.

"It must have seemed pretty harmless," I said, "just to use your paper to ridicule someone. Well, it *is* going to cost you."

"I can't do anything." He was worried, unhappy, helpless.

"Untie me," I said with urgency.

He dithered, and inevitably, the opportunity passed. Ellis and Yorkshire came back, and neither would meet my eyes.

Bad sign.

Ellis, looking at his watch, said, "We wait."

"What for?" Tilepit asked uncertainly.

Yorkshire said, to Ellis's irritation, "The TV people are on the point of leaving. Everyone will be gone in fifteen minutes."

Tilepit looked at me, his anxieties showing plainly. "Let Halley go," he begged.

114

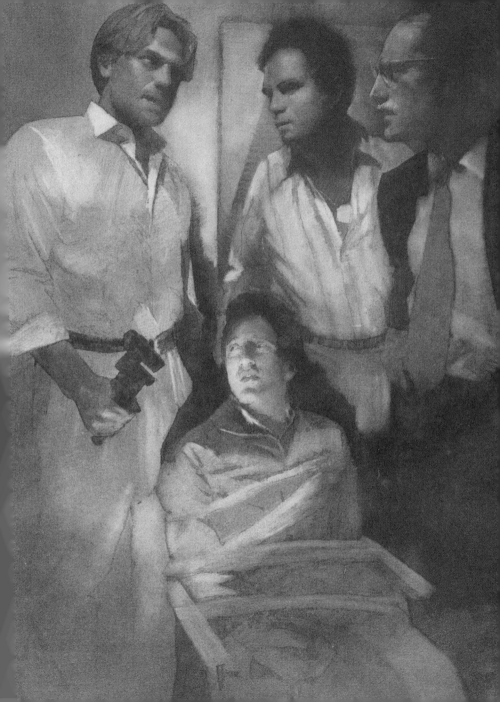

Ellis said comfortingly, "Sure, in a while."

Ellis still held the wrench. Could *he* personally kill *me,* I wondered, to save himself? He wanted to get even, but *kill?* I didn't know.

He walked around to my right-hand side. Time stood still.

Without warning he bashed the wrench across my knuckles. In the moment of utter numbness that resulted, he slid the wrench onto my wrist and tightened the screw until the jaws squeezed the upper and lower sides of my wrist together, compressing blood vessels, nerves and ligaments, bearing down on the bones inside.

I said, "Ellis," in protest. For the few seconds that he looked into my face, his expression was flooded with awareness . . . and shame. Then he seemed to go into a kind of trance, as if the clench of forged steel jaws on a wrist were the only reality.

I thought, If the wrench had been lopping shears, the whole devastating nightmare would have come true. I shut my mind to it, made it cold. Sweated, all the same.

I thought, What I see in his face is the full-blown addiction. Not the cruel satisfaction he could get from unscrewing a false hand, but the sinful fulfillment of cutting off a live hoof.

I glanced very briefly at Yorkshire and Tilepit and saw their frozen, bottomless astonishment, and I realized that until that moment of revelation they hadn't wholly believed in Ellis's guilt.

I said, "Ellis," sharply, not from anger or even fear, but in disbelief that he could do what he was doing, in a lament for the old Ellis.

He got the screw to tighten another notch. My wrist hurt. Somewhere up my arm, the ulna grumbled.

I yelled at him. "Ellis!" And again, "Ellis!"

He straightened, looking vaguely down at the heavy wrench. He tied it to the arm of the chair with a strap and went over to the window, not speaking, but not rational, either.

I tried to dislodge myself from the wrench, but the grip was too tight. My hand was pale blue and gray. If the damage went on too long, the hand could be lost.

Both hands. Oh, God. Oh, *God.*

"Ellis," I said yet again, but in a lower voice this time—a plea for him to return to the old self.

I waited. Tilepit cleared his throat in embarrassment. Yorkshire, as if in unconscious humor, crunched a pickle. Minutes passed.

Ellis left the window and crossed with bouncing steps to the chair where I sat. He looked into my face and enjoyed what he could undoubtedly see there. He undid the wrench with violent jerks and dropped it onto the desk.

No one said anything. Ellis seemed euphoric, high, as if unable to control his exhilaration.

I got stabbing pins and needles in my fingers and was thankful for it. My hand felt dreadful but turned slowly yellowish pink.

Ellis, coming down slightly, looked at his watch. He plucked the cosmetic glove for the false hand off the desk and shoved it inside my shirt. With a theatrical flourish he zipped up the front of my tracksuit to keep his gift from falling out.

He looked at his watch again. Then he went across the room, picked up the unscrewed hand and slapped it into my living palm. There was a powerful impression that he was making sure no trace of Sid Halley remained in the room.

He undid my restraints. "Screw the hand back on," he said.

Perhaps because they had bent from being kicked or perhaps because my real hand was almost useless, the screw threads wouldn't mesh. After three half-turns they stuck. The hand looked reattached but wouldn't work.

"Stand up," Ellis said.

"You're letting him go!" Tilepit exclaimed, relieved.

"Of course," Ellis said. Yorkshire was smiling.

"Put your hands behind your back," Ellis told me.

I did so, and he strapped my wrists tightly together.

"This way." He pulled me to the door and into the passage. Looking back, I saw Yorkshire put his hand on the telephone.

Ellis pressed the call button for the elevator, and the door opened immediately. "Get in," he said.

I looked at his unsmiling face. Expressionless. I stepped into the elevator, and he leaned in quickly and pressed the button for the ground floor, then jumped back. The door closed between us. The elevator began its short journey down.

To tie together the wrists of a man who could unscrew one of them was an exercise in futility. All the same, the crossed threads and my fumbling fingers gave me trouble and some severe moments of panic before the hand slipped free. The elevator had already reached its destination by the time I'd shed the tying strap.

I put the mechanical hand deep into my right tracksuit trousers

117

pocket. Surreal, I grimly thought. The long sleeve of brown overalls covered the void where it belonged.

The two blue-clad bodyguards were missing from the lobby. They were outside, busily positioning a Topline van. A van, I understood, for a journey to an unmarked grave.

Ellis had given me a chance. He'd sent me down thirty seconds too soon. At least I had the answer to the question, which was no, he wouldn't personally kill me. Taking a couple of deep breaths, I shot out through the doors and sprinted not for my car, but toward the open gates.

There was a shout from one of the blue figures. To my dismay the gatekeeper came to unwelcome life, barring my exit.

I ran straight at him. He wasn't expecting my left foot to knock aside the inside of his knee or for my back to bend and curl like a cannonball into his stomach. He fell over backwards, and I was on my way before he struggled to his knees.

I stumbled out onto the road. In one direction lay houses, so I staggered that way. Better cover. I needed cover before anyone chased me in the Topline van.

I chose one house with no life showing and walked unsteadily up the path to the back garden. I emerged into the next street and began to think about where I was going and what I looked like. Brown overalls. Yorkshire would be looking for brown overalls. I took them off and dumped them in a brown-looking hedge.

Taking off the overalls revealed the nonexistence of a left hand. I put the pink exposed end of arm, with its bare electrical contacts, into my left-hand jacket pocket and walked, not ran, up the street. I hadn't the strength to run.

There was a boy in the distance coming towards me on Roller-blade skates and wearing not the ubiquitous baseball cap, but a striped woolen hat. That would do, I thought. I fumbled some money out of the zip pocket in my belt and stood in his way.

He tried to avoid me until he saw the money in my hand.

"Sell me your hat," I suggested. "For the money."

He snatched the money and aimed to skate away, but I stuck out a foot and tripped him. He gave me some choice swear words but also the hat, throwing it at me.

I put it on and slouched along towards the road that crossed the end of the residential street and saw the Topline Foods van roll past. Whatever they were looking for, it didn't seem to be a dark tracksuit with a striped woolen hat.

Plan B: Run away. Okay.

Plan C: Where to?

I reached the end of the houses and turned left into a street that offered a possible refuge: a place selling ice cream. I was barely through the door when outside the window my own Mercedes went past, Ellis driving.

Jonathan, it seemed, wasn't alone in his car-stealing skill.

"What do you want?" a thin young woman asked, bored.

"Er . . . that one," I said, pointing at random.

"Cup or cone? Large or small?"

"Cone. Small." I felt disoriented, far from reality. I paid for the ice cream and licked it, and it tasted of almonds.

"You've cut your face," she said.

"I ran into a tree."

There were tables with people sitting at them, mostly adolescent groups. I sat down away from the window and within ten minutes saw the Topline van pass twice more and my own car, once. Tremors ran in my muscles. Fear or overexertion or both.

There was a men's room at the back of the shop. I went in there when I'd finished the ice cream and looked at my reflection in the mirror over the sink. The cut along my left cheekbone had congealed into a thick, blackening line. Dampening a paper towel, I dabbed at the mess, trying to remove the clotted blood without starting new bleeding, but making only a partial improvement.

Locked in a cubicle, I had another try at screwing my wandering hand into place and this time at length got it properly aligned and fastened, but it still wouldn't work. Wretchedly depressed, I fished out its glove and with difficulty, because of no talcum and an enfeebled right hand, pulled it into a semblance of reality.

Damn Ellis, I thought mordantly.

Never mind. Get on with it.

I went out and walked along the street. The Topline Foods van rolled past quite slowly, driven by one of the security guards, who was intently scanning the other side of the road.

I came to a bus shelter with several people waiting. I added myself and stood with my back to the road. Five long minutes later my Mercedes pulled up on the far side of the road with a white Rolls-Royce behind it. Ellis stepped out of my car, and Yorkshire out of the Rolls. They conferred together, furiously stabbing the air, pointing up and down the street. I bent my head and prayed to remain unspotted.

The bus came, and I surged on with the others, resisting the temptation to look out the window until the bus was traveling again. I saw with relief that the two men were still talking.

I had no idea where the bus was going. Who cared? Distance was all I needed. I'd paid to go to the end of the line.

The end of the line proved to be the railway depot in Runcorn, halfway to Liverpool, going north when I needed to go south.

I got off the bus and went to the depot. There was no Mercedes, no Rolls-Royce, no Topline Foods van in sight, which didn't mean they wouldn't think of buses and trains eventually. The depot didn't feel safe. There was a train to Liverpool due in four minutes, I learned, so I bought a ticket and caught it.

The feeling of unreality continued. At the Liverpool depot, I read the timetable for trains going south. An express to London, I thought, then backtrack to Reading and get a taxi to Archie Kirk's.

No express for hours. What else, then?

The incredible words took a time to penetrate: Liverpool to Bournemouth, departing at three ten p.m. A slow train, meandering south, with many stops on the way. One of them was *Reading.*

I sprinted, using the last shreds of strength. It was already, according to the big depot clock, three oh seven. Whistles were blowing when I stumbled into the last car in the train. I had no ticket and little breath, but a marvelous feeling of escape. That feeling lasted only until the first stop, which I discovered with horror to be Runcorn. Square one, where I'd started. All fear came flooding back.

Nothing happened. The train quietly rolled onwards. Out on the platform a Topline Foods security guard was speaking into a hand-held telephone and shaking his head.

IT TOOK four hours. In that time the screwed-tight wires of tension slackened to manageable. It grew dark. The train clanked and swayed into realms of night. Life felt suspended.

There were plenty of taxis at Reading. I traveled in one to Archie Kirk's and rang the bell. He came himself to open the door.

"Hello," I said.

He stood there staring, then said awkwardly, "We'd almost given you up." He led the way into his sitting room.

There were four of them: Davis Tatum, Norman Picton, Archie himself, and Charles. I had no idea what I looked like, but what I saw on their faces was shock.

"Sid," Charles said, standing up. He insisted I take his place in a comfortable chair and himself perched on a hard one.

"You've cut your face," Norman Picton said.

I also ached more or less all over. My head felt heavy and my hand was swollen and sore. On the bright side, I was alive and home—safe. I was *not* at this point going to faint.

"Sid!" Charles said sharply, putting out a hand.

"Oh . . . yes. Well, I went to Topline Foods." I shifted in my chair and took a grip on things.

Archie said, "Take your time," but sounded as if he didn't mean it.

I smiled. I said, "Owen Yorkshire was there. So was Lord Tilepit. So was Ellis Quint."

"Quint!" Davis Tatum exclaimed.

"Mm. Well, you asked me to find out if there was a heavyweight lumbering about behind the Quint business, and the answer is yes, but it is Ellis himself."

"But he's a playboy," Tatum protested. "What about the big man, Yorkshire?" Tatum's own bulk quivered. "One hears his name."

I nodded. "Owen Yorkshire is a heavyweight in the making."

"What do you mean?"

"Yorkshire's on the edge. Incipient megalomania. He has an uncontrolled desire to be a tycoon. He's built an office block fit for a major industry—before building the industry. He's publicity mad. He plans to take over the whole horse-feed nuts industry. He employs at least two bodyguards who will murder to order, because he fears his competitors will assassinate him, which is paranoia." I paused, then said, "And he is *desperate* to save Ellis Quint's reputation."

Archie asked, "Why?" slowly.

"Because," I said, "he has spent a colossal amount on an advertising campaign featuring Ellis, and if Ellis is found guilty of cutting off a horse's foot, that campaign can't be shown."

"But a few advertisements can't have cost that much," Archie objected.

"With megalomania," I said, "you don't make a few advertisements. You engage an expensive, highly prestigious firm—in this case Intramind Imaging of Manchester—and you travel the world."

With clumsy fingers I took from my belt the folded copy of the paper in the QUINT box file in Mrs. Dove's office. It contained a list of the world's major racecourses—fifteen altogether. "They filmed a thirty-second commercial in each place."

They all understood.

"Those commercials are reported to be brilliant," I said, "and Ellis himself wants them shown as much as Yorkshire does."

"Have you seen them?" Davis asked.

"No, I haven't." I explained about the special Betacam tapes.

Norman Picton, with his policeman's mind, asked, "Where were the tapes? Where did you get that list of racecourses?"

I said without emotion, "In an office at Topline Foods."

He gave me a narrow inspection.

"My car is still somewhere in Frodsham," I told him. "Could someone look for it?" I gave him its registration number.

"Why did you leave it?" he asked.

"Er . . . I was running away at the time." For all that I tried to say it lightly, the grim reality reached them.

"Well," I sighed, "I'd invaded Yorkshire's territory. He found me there. It gave him the opportunity to get rid of the person most likely to send Ellis to jail. I accepted that possibility when I went there, but like you, I wanted to know what was causing trouble behind the scenes. And it is the money spent on those ads." I paused. "Yorkshire and Ellis set out to discredit me so that nothing I said would get Ellis convicted. They used Tilepit because he owned the *Pump*. They persuaded him that Ellis was innocent and that I was all that the *Pump* has maintained. Lord Tilepit was duped by Ellis, and so also was Yorkshire himself."

"How, Sid?" Davis asked.

"Ellis dazzles people. To Yorkshire he was a step up the ladder. Today they planned to wipe me out of the way. Yorkshire would have done it himself in reckless anger. Ellis stopped him, but left it to chance that the bodyguards might do it. But I escaped them. Yorkshire now knows Ellis is guilty, but he cares only to be able to show that brilliant ad campaign and make himself a big man, with the power to bring mayors to his doorstep. If Yorkshire isn't stopped, he'll be manipulating more than the *Pump*. He's the sort of man you get in the kitchens of political clout."

After a moment Archie asked, "So how do we stop him?"

I shifted in the chair. "I can, possibly, give you the tools."

"What tools?"

"His secret files. You can take it from there."

"But," Archie said blankly, "where are these files?"

"In my computer in London." I explained the Internet transfer. Charles looked the most shocked, Archie the least.

Archie said, "If I ask you, will you work for me another time?"

I looked into the knowing eyes and nodded.

14

I WENT home to Aynsford with Charles.

It had been a long evening. All four men had wanted details, which I found as intolerable to describe as to live through.

I didn't tell them about Ellis's games with my hands. I didn't know how to explain to them that for a jockey his hands were at the heart of his skill: One *talked* to a horse through one's hands. Ellis knew what the loss of a hand had meant to me, and that day he'd been punishing me in the severest way he could think of for trying to strip him of what *he* now valued most: universal acclaim.

I didn't know how to make them understand that to him the severing of a horse's foot had become a drug more addictive than any substance invented, that the risk and the power were intoxicating, that I'd been lucky he'd had only a wrench to use on me.

I told them only about Yorkshire's cutting my face. I told them about the escape by judo and the boy on Rollerblade skates and the ice-cream cone and catching the bus within sight of Yorkshire and Ellis. I made it sound almost funny.

Davis asked about Ellis's Shropshire alibi. I explained that I hadn't had time to find out when he had arrived at the dance. "It's a matter of asking the people who parked the cars," I said.

"There isn't much time," Davis pointed out. "Sid, couldn't you do it tomorrow?"

Tomorrow—Sunday. On Monday, the trial.

123

Archie said firmly, "No, Sid can't. There's a limit—"

Archie's doorbell rang. His wife had left to spend the evening with her sister-in-law, Betty Bracken, so he went to the summons and came back with a displeased expression, followed by Jonathan.

The rebel wings of hair were much shorter. The yellow streaks had all but grown out. There were no shaved areas of scalp.

"I came to see you," he said. "The aunts said you were here."

I said, "How did you get here from Combe Bassett?"

"Ran."

He was not in the least out of breath.

"Can you ride a motorbike?" I asked.

"Do me a favor! But what for?"

"To go to Shropshire," I said.

I was predictably drowned by protests, but I explained to Jonathan what was needed. "Find someone—anyone—who saw Ellis Quint arrive at the dance. Find the people who parked the cars."

Out of my belt I took all the money I had left, and gave it to him. "I want receipts," I said. "Bring me paper. A signed statement from a witness. It's all got to be solid."

"Is this," he asked slowly, "some sort of test?"

"Yes."

"Okay."

"Don't stay longer than a day," I said. "Don't forget, you may be asked to give evidence this week at the trial."

"As if I could forget." He gave me a wide smile and departed.

"You *can't*," Archie said to me emphatically. "He's—he's—"

"He's bright," I said. "He's observant. He's athletic. Let's see how he does in Shropshire. I need a new Chico."

"But Jonathan steals cars."

"An ability to steal cars," I said with humor, "is in my eyes an asset. Let's see how he does tomorrow with this alibi. If he learns nothing, I'll go myself on Monday."

"That will be too late," Davis said.

"Not if you get your colleague to ask for one more day's adjournment. And don't let him back down. Tell him to insist on prosecuting. Then, if we can't break Ellis's alibi, get him to argue that the Northampton colt was a copycat crime."

I stood up, feeling a shade fragile. Archie came out into the hall with Charles and me and offered his hand in farewell. Charles shook warmly. Archie lifted my wrist and looked at the swelling and the deep bruising that was already crimson and black.

"No explanation?" Archie asked. I shook my head.

"Stone walls tell more," Charles informed him calmly.

On the drive to Aynsford, Charles asked, "How *did* you hurt your hand?"

I sighed. "Ellis had a go at it."

"Ellis?"

"Mm. If he'd had shears instead of a wrench, I would now have no hands. For heaven's sake, keep your eyes on the road."

"But *Sid*—"

"Don't *fuss,* Charles. There'll be no lasting harm." I paused. "If he'd wanted to kill me today, he could have done it, but instead he gave me a chance to escape."

He drove on to Aynsford in silence. Braking outside the door, he said regretfully, "If you and Ellis hadn't been such friends . . . No wonder poor Ginnie couldn't stand it."

Charles saw the muscles stiffen in my face. "What is it, Sid?"

"I . . . I may have made a wrong assumption."

"What assumption?"

"Mm?" I said vaguely. "Have to think."

"Then think in bed," he said lightly. "It's late."

I thought for half the night.

AT AYNSFORD I kept duplicates of all the things I'd lost in my car—battery charger, razor, clothes—all except the mobile phone. The no-car situation was solved again by Teledrive, which came to pick me up on Sunday morning.

To Charles's restrained suggestion that I pass the day resting, I replied that I was going to see Rachel Ferns. Charles nodded.

RACHEL, Linda told me on the telephone, was home from the hospital for the day. "Do come," she begged. "Rachel needs you."

Rachel herself looked bloodless. In the five days since I'd seen her, the bluish shadows under her eyes had deepened and she had lost weight, so that the big eyes gave her the look of an exotic bird.

Linda hugged me in the kitchen. "There's good news," she said. "They've found a donor."

"But that's *marvelous.*" Like a sunburst of hope, I thought.

125

She poured two drinks, and we clinked to the future.

Rachel was half sitting, half lying on a small sofa that had been repositioned in the sitting room so that she could look into the fish-tank. I sat beside her and asked how she felt.

"Did my mum tell you about the transplant?" she said.

"Terrific news."

"I might be able to run again."

Running must have at that point seemed as distant as the moon.

Rachel said, "I begged to come home to see the fishes. I have to go back tonight, though. I hoped you would come today."

"You knew I would come."

Linda made steamy rice with bits of chicken and shrimp for lunch, which we all ate with spoons, and then returned to the only important subject. "The donor is a ninety percent match," she said. "You never get a hundred percent, even from siblings. Ninety percent is great."

"They're going to put me into a sort of bubble," Rachel said.

Linda cleared the plates and asked if I would stay with Rachel while she looked to Pegotty. When she'd gone, Rachel and I sat on the sofa. She cuddled by my right arm but held my other hand—the plastic one—pulling it across her.

After a long pause she said, "Are you afraid of dying?"

Another pause. "Sometimes," I said. "Are you?"

"Yes, but I can't tell Mummy. I don't like her crying. What's dying like?"

"I don't know. Like going to sleep, I should think."

"It's funny to think of not being here," Rachel said. "I mean, to think of being a *space*."

"The transplant will work. You'll be running by Christmas."

She said, "Do you know what I'll be thinking, lying there in the bubble feeling awfully sick?"

"What?"

"Life's a bugger."

I hugged her, but gently. "You'll do fine."

"Tell me how to be brave."

What a question, I thought. I said, "When you're feeling awfully sick, think about something you like doing. You won't feel as bad if you don't think about how bad you feel."

She thought it over. "Is that what *you* do?"

"It's what I do if something hurts, yes. It does work."

"What if nothing hurts yet, but you're going into something scary?"

"Well . . . it's all right to be frightened. No one can help it. Just don't let being frightened stop you."

"I'm going into the bubble tomorrow," Rachel murmured. "I don't want to cry when they put me in there."

"Make the bubble your palace," I said. "It's to keep you safe from infection—safe from dragons. You won't cry."

She snuggled against me, happier, I hoped. I loved her incredibly. Rachel would run again. She *had* to.

PATIENT Teledrive got me back to London with time to spare before meeting India for dinner. The restaurant called Kensington Place was near the northern end of Church Street, the famous road of antique shops. Teledrive left me on the northwest corner, where I dawdled awhile, looking in the brightly lit windows of Waterstone's bookshop, wondering if Rachel would be able to hear the store's children's audiotapes in her bubble.

A large number of young Japanese men and women were milling around, armed with cameras, taking flash pictures of one another. They bowed to me politely. I bowed unenthusiastically in return.

We all waited. They bowed some more. At length one of the young women shyly produced a photograph, which she held out to me. I found I was looking at a mass wedding of about ten happy couples in formal suits and Western bridal gowns. Raising my head from the photo, I was met by twenty smiles.

I smiled back. The shy young woman retrieved her photo, nodded her head towards her companions and clearly told me that they were all on their honeymoon. More smiles all round. More bows. One of the men held out his camera to me and asked—I gathered—if I would photograph them all as a group.

I took the camera, and they arranged themselves in pairs.

Click. Flash. All the newlyweds beamed.

I was presented, one by one, with nine more cameras. Nine more bows. I took nine more photos. Flash. Flash. Group euphoria.

I left the happy couples and walked fifty yards down Church Street towards the restaurant. There was a narrow side street beside it, and opposite, on the other side of the street, a small recessed area with a patch of scrubby grass and a slatted park bench. I would sit there, I decided, and watch for India. The restaurant was directly opposite the bench.

I crossed Church Street. I was turning to sit when I heard a bang and felt a searing flash of pain across my back and into my right upper arm. The impact knocked me sprawling on the bench, half lying, half sitting. I thought incredulously, I've been *shot*.

Gordon Quint walked out of the shadows of the side street and came across the street towards me carrying a handgun. He was coming inexorably to finish what he'd started, and he appeared not to care if anyone saw him.

I didn't seem to have the strength to get up and run away.

Gordon looked like a farmer from Berkshire, not an obsessed murderer. He wore a checked shirt and a tie and a tweed jacket. He was a middle-aged pillar of the community, a judge and jury, and a hangman—a raw, primitive, walking act of revenge.

He stopped in front of me and aimed at my chest. "This is for Ginnie," he said. His voice was hoarse.

I was silent. I wanted to stand. Couldn't manage it.

"Say something!" he shouted. I looked not at his gun, but at his eyes.

Gordon stared at my face. He didn't blink, didn't waver.

Now, I thought frozenly. It's going to be *now*.

A voice was shouting in the road, urgent, frantic, coming nearer, far too late. "Dad!"

Ellis. Ellis . . . running across the road, waving an iron fencing post and shouting, "Dad, don't! Don't do it."

Gordon could hear Ellis shouting, but the demented hatred simply hardened in his face. His arm straightened until his gun was a bare yard from my chest.

Perhaps I won't feel it, I thought.

Ellis swung the iron post with two hands and all his strength and hit his father on the side of the head.

The gun went off. The bullet hissed past my ear and slammed into a shopwindow behind me. There were razor splinters of glass and flashes of light and shouting and confusion everywhere.

Gordon fell unconscious facedown on the scrubby patch of grass, his gun beneath him. My blood ran into a widening pool below the slats of the bench. Ellis stood for an eternity of seconds holding the fencing post and staring at my eyes as if he could see into my soul, as if he would show me his.

Then he dropped the post and went away at a slow run, loping across Church Street and down the side road into the shadows. No one tried to stop him. People thought he was going to bring help.

I was suddenly surrounded by worried Japanese faces. I lost account of time. A police car arrived, lights flashing. An ambulance made an entrance.

A young woman pushed through the growing crowd, yelling that she was from the press. India. India . . . come to dinner.

"Sorry," I said.

"*Sid* . . ." Horror in her voice and a sort of despair.

"Tell Kevin Mills . . ." I said. My mouth was dry from loss of blood. She bent her head down to mine to hear. I said, "Those Japanese people took photos. I saw the flashes. Tell him to . . . get the photos . . . and he can have . . . his exclusive."

15

INDIA wasn't a newspaperwoman for nothing. The front page of Monday's *Pump* bore the moderately accurate headline SHOT IN THE BACK, with, underneath, a picture of Gordon Quint aiming his gun unequivocally at my heart.

Kevin had gone to town also, acknowledging that the long campaign of denigration of me had been a mistake. There had been twenty Japanese eyewitnesses to the shooting. Kevin, armed with an interpreter, had got the story right. And Gordon Quint, though still unconscious, would in due course be "helping the police with their inquiries." Kevin observed that Ellis Quint's whereabouts were unknown.

Inside the paper there were more pictures. One showed Ellis, arms and fence post raised, on the point of striking his father.

I read the *Pump* while sitting upright in a high bed in a small white side room in Hammersmith Hospital, alone except for a constant stream of doctors, nurses, police, and people with clipboards. The surgeon who'd dealt with my punctures told me the bullet had plowed along a rib and in and out of the arm. There was muscle damage, but with physiotherapy the arm should be almost as good as new. I had an arm . . . and a hand . . . and a life.

In the afternoon Archie Kirk and Norman Picton argued themselves past the NO VISITORS sign on the door.

"The Frodsham police found your car," Norman said, "but I'm afraid it's been stripped. It's up on bricks—no wheels."

Poor old car. It had been insured, though, for a fortune.

"Is there any news of Ellis?" I asked. "Or of Gordon?"

"Gordon Quint," Norman said in a policeman's voice, "was, as of an hour ago, still unconscious in a secure police facility. No one is predicting when he'll wake up, but as soon as he can understand, he'll be charged with attempted murder."

"And Ellis?" I asked.

Archie said, "No one knows where he is."

"What happened this morning," I asked, "about the trial?"

"Adjourned. Ellis Quint's bail is rescinded, as he didn't turn up. A warrant for his arrest has been issued."

"And Jonathan," I asked. "Did he go to Shropshire?"

"Yes," Norman said heavily. "And he found the car parkers."

"Good boy," I said.

"It's *not* so good." The car parkers had signed a statement saying that Ellis Quint arrived at the dance at about eleven thirty. They remembered not only because of who he was but because he had offered them his autograph. They knew it was before midnight because their employment as car parkers had ended then.

"It's a solid alibi," Norman observed gloomily. "He was in Shropshire when the Northampton yearling was attacked."

"Mm."

"You don't seem disappointed, Sid," Archie said, puzzled.

"I think," I said, "that you should phone Davis Tatum. I want him to make sure the prosecutors don't give up on the trial."

"You told him that on Saturday." He was humoring me, I thought.

"I'm not light-headed from bullets, Archie, if that's what you think. Since Saturday I've worked a few things out, and they are not as they may seem."

"What things?"

"Ellis's alibi, for one."

"But Sid—"

130

"Listen," I said, "this isn't all that easy to say, but I have to explain that *I* am not as I seem. Most people look at me and see a harmless person—not big, not tall, no threat to anyone. I'm not complaining. In fact, I choose to be like that because people then *talk* to me, which is necessary in my job.

"But Ellis knows me better. It was Ellis who years ago gave me the nickname Tungsten Carbide, because I wasn't easy to . . . intimidate. And all this summer Ellis has been afraid of me. That's why he got Tilepit to set his paper onto me. He wanted to defeat me by ridicule."

I paused. Neither of them said a word.

I went on. "Ellis is not what he seems, either. Everyone thinks him a playboy, a delightful entertainer. But he's not only that. He's a strong, purposeful man with enormous skills of manipulation. You and Davis can't believe that it is Ellis himself who is the heavyweight, not Yorkshire, but Ellis and I both know it. Ellis has manipulated everyone—Yorkshire, Tilepit, the *Pump,* public opinion and also his lawyers."

Archie said, "So why aren't you disappointed that Ellis's Shropshire alibi can't be broken?"

"Because Ellis set it up that way."

"How do you mean?"

"He made for himself a positively unbreakable alibi in Shropshire to invalidate the whole Combe Bassett case. The supposition was that if Ellis couldn't have done one attack, then he hadn't done the other, and the case against him would be withdrawn. So he got someone else to go to Northampton."

"But *who would,* Sid?" Archie asked.

"Gordon. His father."

Archie and Norman both stiffened. "He *couldn't,*" Archie said.

"He did."

"But *Sid—*"

"I know," I sighed. "You, Charles and I have all been guests in his house. But he shot me last night. See it in the *Pump.*"

Archie said weakly, "But that doesn't mean—"

"I'll explain," I said. My skin was sweating. It came and went a bit, now and then. An affronted body, letting me know.

They waited. I said, "Gordon and Ginnie Quint gloried in their wonderful son, whom I accused of a revolting crime. Ginnie stead-

131

fastly believed in his innocence. But Gordon, faced with all the evidence we gathered from his Land Rover, must have come to acknowledge that the unthinkable was true."

Archie nodded.

I went on. "Ellis's persecution of me didn't work; I was still *there*. The trial was drawing nearer, and I was going to describe in court, with the public listening, just how Ellis could have cut off the foot of Betty's colt. The outcome of the trial wasn't the point. The evidence would have convinced enough people of his guilt to destroy forever the shining-knight persona. And Topline Foods couldn't have used those diamond-plated ads."

I took a deep couple of lungfuls of air. I was talking too much. I didn't feel well. Not enough oxygen; not enough blood.

I said, "The idea of the Shropshire alibi probably came when Ellis was invited to the dance. They saw it as a way to stop the trial. You have to remember that Gordon is a farmer. He's used to the idea of the death of animals being profitable. I daresay that the death of one insignificant yearling was as nothing to him when set beside the saving of his son."

Archie and Norman listened as if not breathing.

"Ellis is many things, but he's not a murderer. In spite of several opportunities, he hasn't let me be killed."

"But Gordon all but succeeded," Norman pointed out.

"Yes," I agreed, "but that wasn't to help Ellis."

"What was it, then?"

I'm too tired, I thought, but I'd better finish it. I said to Norman, "You remember that piece of rag you gave me?"

"What rag?" Archie asked.

Norman outlined for him the discovery at Northampton of the lopping shears wrapped in dirty material.

"The local police brought the shears into the stud farm's office while I was there. The farm's owners were there, and so was Ginnie Quint, who was a friend of theirs. Ginnie said how much she despised me for falsely accusing her son, my *friend*. Then she watched the policeman unwrap the shears, and quite slowly she went white . . . and fainted."

"The sight of the shears," Norman said, nodding.

"It was the sight of the material."

"How do you mean?"

132

"Because that filthy old cloth had once been part of some bed hangings. They were woven by a Patricia Huxford near Chichester. She looked up her records and found that that fabric had been made nearly thirty years ago—exclusively—for Ginnie Quint."

Archie and Norman both stared.

"Ginnie recognized the material," I said. "Not only that, she knew that Ellis had been in Shropshire the night Miss Richardson's colt was done, and she understood that only one other person could have wrapped lopping shears in that unique fabric. Ginnie realized that *Gordon* had maimed the yearling, and she fainted."

Archie and Norman looked shocked.

I sighed. "I didn't understand that until night before last, when everything sort of *clicked*. But now I think it wasn't just because of Ellis's terrible guilt that Ginnie killed herself but because it was Gordon's guilt as well. It was too much to bear."

I paused briefly and went on. "Ginnie's suicide sent Gordon berserk. He blamed me for having destroyed his family. Last night, in the actual moment the picture in the *Pump* was taken, he was telling me the bullets were for Ginnie. It was my life for hers."

The white room was silent.

LATER in the day I phoned the hospital in Canterbury and spoke to the ward sister.

"How is Rachel?" I asked.

"Mr. Halley! But I thought—I mean, are you—"

"I'm absolutely okay," I assured her. "How's Rachel?"

"You know that she's a very sick little girl, but we're all hopeful of the transplant."

"Did she go into the bubble?"

"Yes, very bravely. She says it's her palace and she's its queen."

"Give her my love. I'll make it there by Thursday."

"I'll tell her."

KEVIN Mills and India came to visit before ten o'clock the following morning, on their way to work.

I was again sitting up in bed but by then felt much healthier. In spite of my protests, my mending arm was still held immobile in a swaddle of splint and bandages. Give it another day's rest, I'd been told. All very well, except that the nurses had been too busy that

133

morning to reunite me with my left hand. I felt naked without it, and could do nothing for myself, not even scratch my nose.

Kevin and India came in looking embarrassed and said far too brightly how glad they were to see me awake and recovering.

I smiled. "My dear children, I'm not a complete fool."

"Look, mate . . ." Kevin's voice faded. He wouldn't meet my eyes.

I said, "Who told Gordon Quint where to find me?"

Neither of them answered.

"India," I pointed out, "you were the only person who knew."

"Sid!" She was anguished, as she had been in Church Street when she'd found me shot, and she wouldn't look at my face, either.

Kevin smoothed his mustache. "It wasn't her fault."

"Yours, then?"

"You're not a fool," Kevin said. "You've guessed what happened. Otherwise you'd be flinging us out of here right now."

"Correct."

"The turmoil started Sunday morning at our editorial meeting. I mean, George Godbar was in a positive *lather* about reversing policy on S. Halley," Kevin said.

"The boss had leaned on him?"

"*Leaned!* There was panic. Our lord the proprietor wanted you bought off."

"How nice," I said.

"He'd suggested ten thousand smackers, George said. Try ten million, I said. George called for copies of everything the *Pump* has published about you since June. Such *poison*," Kevin said. "Seeing it all together like that. I mean, it silenced the whole meeting, and it takes a lot to do that."

India still wouldn't meet my eyes and wouldn't sit down.

"Sit," I said mildly. She perched uneasily. "If we make another dinner date," I said, "don't tell anyone."

"Oh, Sid."

"She didn't mean to get you *shot*," Kevin protested. "The Tilepit wanted you found. The *Pump*'s lawyer had passed each piece week by week as just on the safe side of actionable, but at the meeting, when he read the whole file at once, he was *sweating*, Sid. He said the *Pump* should settle out of court for whatever you ask."

"How did Gordon Quint find me?" I asked again.

"George begged us all to find you, to say the *Pump* would confer sainthood immediately and fatten your bank balance, and I phoned India on the off chance. She said not to worry, she would tell you herself; and I asked her how . . . and where. There didn't seem to be any harm in it."

"And you told George Godbar?" I said. "And he told Lord Tilepit? And *he* told Ellis, I suppose."

Kevin said, "George phoned Ellis's father, looking for Ellis. He told Gordon where you'd be if Ellis wanted to find you."

Round and round in circles, and the bullets come out here.

I sighed again. I was lucky to be alive. I would settle for that. I also wondered how much I would get out of the *Pump*. Only enough, I decided, to keep His Lordship grateful.

"There you are, then, Sid." Kevin was ready to go. "Makes us even, right?"

"Even." I nodded.

India stood up as if to follow him. "Stay a bit," I suggested.

India watched Kevin go. Her face looked softer. At that hour in the morning she hadn't yet put on the sharply outlined lipstick nor the matte porcelain makeup. This was the essential India I was seeing. How different, I wondered, was the inner spirit from the cutting brain of her column.

She came over to my left side and looked at the plastic hand lying on the locker next to my bed.

"How does it work?" she asked.

I explained about the electrodes, as I had for Rachel.

She looked at the immobilized right arm and at the left hand on the locker, and she demanded, "Why don't you put this on? You'd be better with it on, obviously."

"A nurse will do it when she can."

"Let *me* do it," India said.

"No."

"Because you're too bloody *proud?*"

Because it's too private, I thought.

I was wearing one of those dreadful hospital gowns that fasten at the back. A white flap covered my left shoulder, upper arm, elbow and the short piece of forearm. Tentatively India turned back the flap. "You hate it, don't you?" she said.

"Yes."

"I would hate it, too."

I can't bear this, I thought. I can bear Ellis unscrewing my hand and mocking me. I can't bear love.

India picked up the electric hand. "What do I do?" she asked.

I said with difficulty, "Talcum powder."

"Oh." She picked up the white tinful of comfort for babies. "In the arm, or on you?"

"On me."

She sprinkled powder on my forearm and smoothed it over my skin. Her touch sent a shiver right down to my toes.

"And now?" she asked anxiously.

"Now hold it so that I can put my arm into it."

She concentrated. I put my forearm into the socket. "Turn the thumb towards you a bit. Not too far. That's right. Now push up while I push down."

"Like that?" She was trembling.

"Like that," I said. The arm gripped where it was designed to.

I sent the messages. We both watched the hand open and close.

India abruptly left my side and picked up her purse.

"Don't go," I said.

"If I don't go, I'll cry."

I thought that might make two of us. The touch of her fingers on the skin of my forearm had been a caress more intimate than any act of sex. I felt shaky. I felt more moved than ever in my life.

"Come back," I said.

She came nearer. I stretched out my left arm and fastened the hand on her wrist.

She looked at it. I tugged, and she took the last step to my side.

She saw quite clearly what I intended and bent her mouth to mine as if it were not the first time, as if it were natural.

A pact, I thought.

A beginning.

TIME drifted when she'd gone.

At midday a nurse burst into my quiet room. "Don't you have your television on? You're on it."

She switched on knobs, and there was my face on the screen, with a newsreader saying, "Sid Halley is recovering in hospital." There was film of me in racing colors, taken years ago after winning

136

the Grand National. Then the news slid to drought and intractable famine.

The nurse said, "Wait," and twiddled more knobs. An announcer intoned, "Police today found the body of Ellis Quint in his car, deep in New Forest, Hampshire. . . ."

Frozen, I heard, as if from a distance, "Foul play is not suspected." On the screen was the rear view of a white car.

"This is a sad ending," the announcer said, appearing at least to show genuine regret, "to a fairy-tale life. Ellis Quint will be remembered as the dashing amateur steeplechase jockey whose courage and gallantry inspired a whole generation. In recent months he has been troubled by accusations of cruelty to animals from his long-time colleague and supposed friend, Sid Halley. Quint was due to appear in court yesterday to refute those charges."

There was a montage of Ellis winning races and wowing a chat-show audience. The nurse indignantly switched off the set. "They didn't say anything about your being shot," she said crossly.

"Never mind."

The reputation Ellis had manufactured for me couldn't be reversed in a night. Slowly perhaps. Perhaps never.

Ellis was dead.

I sat in the quiet white room.

Ellis was *dead*.

AN HOUR later a hospital porter brought me a letter that had been left at the hospital's reception desk and overlooked until now.

When he'd gone, I held the envelope in the pincer fingers and tore it open with my teeth.

The letter was from Ellis, his handwriting strong with life. It said:

> Sid, I know where you are. I followed the ambulance. If you are reading this, you are alive and I am dead. I didn't think you would catch me. I should have known you would.
>
> I did that old pony to make a good program. Terrific story. I needed a good one. My ratings were slipping.
>
> Then I lusted to do it again. The danger. The risk, the difficulty. And that scrunch. I can't describe it. It gives me an ecstasy like nothing else. Cocaine is for kids. Sex is nothing. The scrunch of bones is a million-volt orgasm.

137

And then there's you. I know all you fear is helplessness. I know you. I wanted to make you helpless in Owen Yorkshire's office, but all you did was sit there watching your hand turn blue. I could feel you willing me to be my real self, but my real self wanted to hear your wristbones crunch. I wanted you to crumble.

And then suddenly I was glad you weren't sobbing and whining, and I was proud of you, and I felt happy and higher than a kite. And I didn't want you to die, not like that. Not because of me.

I see now what I've done. What infinite damage.

My father did that last colt. I talked him into it.

It's cost my mother's life. If my father lives, they'll lock him up for trying to kill you. They should have let me hang, back in June when I tried with my tie.

The letter ended there except for three words much lower down the page:

You win, Sid.

The sheet of paper lay on the white bedclothes. No one else would see those words, I thought.

I remembered Rachel saying how odd it would be to be dead. To be a *space*.

The whole white room was a space.

Good and evil, he had been my friend. An enemy, but finally a friend.

I had the win, but there was no one standing in the stirrups to share it with.

Regret, loss, acceptance and relief—I felt them all.

I grieved for Ellis Quint.

DICK FRANCIS

With the publication of *Come to Grief*, author Dick Francis has thirty-four best-selling novels to his credit. That is not only an impressive literary record but one that follows a long and distinguished career as a champion jockey in Britain. With such world-class achievements behind him, Francis might be forgiven if, at age seventy-five, he decided to relax for a while. (He and his wife, Mary, live in the Caribbean, so what could be easier?) But to the delight of his legions of fans, Francis still writes a mystery a year and still tries, as he says, "to make every book better than the last one."

In the case of *Come to Grief* he managed that nicely. But he had some unusual assistance along the way. During an auction to raise money for needy children, the British Broadcasting Corporation invited people to bid on "Things That Money Can't Buy." Among the offerings—a chance "to have one's name used as a character in Dick Francis's next book." The results were satisfactory all around. The lucky winner, Patricia Huxford, got to appear in *Come to Grief* (as a weaver), the needy children got a handsome contribution, and the busy author had to come up with one less name for a character.

COMING HOME
Rosamunde Pilcher

Rosamunde Pilcher

Coming Home

Welcome to Nancherrow, a beautiful estate on the sun-washed coast of Cornwall. It is a magical place of deep woods, rocky coves, and sparkling sea.

Here Judith Dunbar, young and alone, finds a home with the aristocratic Carey-Lewis family and their fun-loving circle of friends.

But on the horizon loom the dark clouds of a war that will forever alter the landscape of their lives.

A spellbinding saga of loves lost and found—and of a special place that no reader will ever forget.

PART I

❧ *1935* ❧

THE Porthkerris Council School stood halfway up the steep hill which climbed from the heart of the little town to the empty moors beyond. It was a solid Victorian edifice, built of granite blocks, surrounded by a tall wrought-iron fence, and presented a forbidding face to the world. But on this late afternoon in December it stood fairly ablaze with light, and from its doors streamed a flood of excited children, jostling and giggling and uttering shrieks of cheerful abuse at each other before finally dispersing and setting off for home.

It was the end of the winter term, and there had been a school Christmas party. Singing games had been played and relay races won, and the children had eaten a tea of saffron buns and fizzy lemonade. Finally they had lined up and one by one had shaken the headmaster by the hand and been given a bag of sweets.

Gradually the noisy outflux of children was reduced to a trickle. Last of all, as the school clock chimed a quarter to five, there came through the open door two girls—Judith Dunbar and Heather Warren, both fourteen years old, both dressed in navy-blue coats and rubber boots, and with woolen hats pulled down over their ears. Judith was fair, with two stubby pigtails, freckles, and pale blue eyes; while Heather had inherited her coloring from her father and, through him, back over the generations, from some Spanish sailor washed ashore on the Cornish coast after the destruction of the Armada. And so her skin was olive, her hair raven black, and her eyes dark and bright.

They were the last to depart because Judith was leaving Porthkerris School forever and had had to say good-bye to all the teachers. But finally they were on their way through the gates. The overcast day had slipped early into darkness, and a thin drizzle fell, shimmering against glowing streetlamps. They began to walk, descending into the town. Judith sighed. "Well, that's it. I never thought I'd feel sad to leave any school, but I do now."

"It's not going to be the same without you."

"It's not going to be the same without you either. But you're lucky, because at least you've still got friends. I've got to start all over, brand-new, trying to find someone I like at St. Ursula's. And I have to wear that uniform."

Heather's silence was sympathetic. At Porthkerris everybody wore their own cheerful clothes, but St. Ursula's was a private school. The girls wore green tweed overcoats, and hats and thick stockings guaranteed to make even the prettiest totally plain. But worst of all was the prospect of boarding. The Warrens were an intensely close family, and Heather could not imagine a worse fate than to be torn from her parents and her two brothers. It didn't matter that St. Ursula's was in Penzance, only ten miles away. Ten miles was forever if you had to live away from Mum and Dad.

However, poor Judith had no choice. Her father worked in Colombo, in Ceylon, and for four years Judith, her mother, and her little sister had lived apart from him. Now Mrs. Dunbar and Jess were returning to Ceylon, and Judith was being left behind, with little idea of when she would see her mother again.

Heather cast about for something cheerful to say. "There'll be holidays."

"With Aunt *Louise*."

"But at least you'll still be here, living in Penmarron. As it is, you can come over, and we'll go down to the beach. Or go to the pictures."

"It would be a sort of escape."

"Oh, you," Heather said. "You make it sound like going to prison. What's your aunt's house like?"

"It's quite big, right up at the top of the golf course. I've got her best spare room, and there's even room for my desk."

"Sounds all right to me. Don't know why you're making such a fuss."

"It's just not *home*. And it's so bleak and windy. The house is called Windyridge, and no wonder. There always seems to be a gale blowing at Aunt Louise's windows."

"Some spooky."

"The other thing is, it's so far from everywhere, and the nearest bus stop's two miles away. And Aunt Louise won't have time to drive me around, because she's always playing golf."

"What you need is a bike. Then you could go wherever you wanted. It's only three miles to Porthkerris over the top road."

"You are brilliant. I never thought of a bike."

"Get your mother to give you one for Christmas."

"I've already asked for a jersey for Christmas. A polo-neck."

"Well, ask for a bike as well. She can scarcely say no, going away, and not knowing when she's going to see you again."

But Judith only said, "I'll see."

They walked on, passing the fish-and-chips shop, bright with cheerful light. The smell from the open door was mouthwatering.

"This aunt of yours—Forrester. Your mother's sister, is she?"

"No. My father's. She lived in India with her husband. He's dead now, and she lives alone."

Their conversation had brought them down the hill to the center of the town and the parting of their ways. Heather would carry on in the direction of the harbor, down cobbled lanes to the square granite house where the Warren family lived over Mr. Warren's grocery shop, and Judith would climb another hill and head for the railway station.

They stood in the soaking drizzle beneath the streetlamp and faced each other. "I suppose it's good-bye, then," said Heather. "You can write to me. And ring the shop if you want to leave a message. Like coming over when it's holidays."

"I'll do that."

They had been friends for four years. It was a poignant moment. Abruptly Heather leaned forward and planted a kiss on Judith's rain-damp cheek. Then she turned and went running down the street. Judith, feeling bereft, continued on her way, climbing the narrow pavement between small shops brightly decorated for Christmas. The wind came in gusts, bringing the sound of breakers booming up on the beach below.

At the top of the hill she paused to lean her elbows on a low granite wall. She saw the blurred jumble of houses slipping away down to the dark harbor. The red and green riding lights of fishing boats were reflected in the inky water, and far out, the lighthouse flashed its warning to passing ships.

She shivered. Too cold to stand here. She began to run, her book bag thumping against her side; came to a flight of granite steps; and hurtled down them to the railway station. The little branchline train was waiting at the platform.

Traveling to school in the little train was going to be one of the things that she was really going to miss, because the line ran for three miles along a spectacular stretch of coast: cliffs and deep cuttings, bays and beaches, and then the sand dunes and the huge lonely beach, which she had come to think of as her own.

Sometimes when people learned that Judith had no father, because he was on the other side of the world working for a prestigious shipping company called Wilson-McKinnon, they were sorry for her. How awful to be without a father. But as with the children of every British India family, she had always known that long separations were inevitable.

Judith had been born in Ceylon and lived there until she was ten. During that time Colombo was home—the spacious bungalow on the Galle Road, with a verdant tropical garden, and always a fresh breeze blowing in off the ocean. But inevitably, the day came when they had to say good-bye to the house and the garden. And to Dad. It was not until after the three-week ocean voyage had been made, and she and her mother were back in England, that Judith was let into the secret that there was a new baby on the way.

Because they had no establishment of their own, Aunt Louise, prompted by her brother, Bruce, had taken matters into her own hands, located Riverview House, and leased it as a furnished let. Soon after they took up residence, Jess was born. And now the time had come for Molly Dunbar to return to Colombo. Jess, at four years of age, was going with her, and Judith was remaining behind in Cornwall. She envied them dreadfully.

At fourteen Judith reckoned that she was mature enough to have really important decisions—those that were going to affect *her*— shared and discussed. But Mummy never discussed. She simply told.

I have had a letter from your father, and Jess and I are going to have to go back to Colombo. Which had been a bit of a bombshell.

But worse. *We have decided that you should go to St. Ursula's as a boarder. It's all arranged for the January term.* As though she were a sort of parcel or a dog being put into a kennel.

But what about the holidays?

You'll stay with Aunt Louise. She's very kindly said that she'll take care of you, and be your guardian while we're abroad.

Which was, perhaps, most daunting of all. During their sojourn in Penmarron, Aunt Louise had never been anything but kind. It was just that she was all wrong. Old—at least fifty—and faintly intimidating; not cozy in the least. And Windyridge was an old person's house, orderly and quiet. Two sisters, Edna and Hilda by name, who worked for her as cook and house parlormaid, were equally elderly, not a bit like darling Phyllis, who did everything for them all at Riverview House but still found time to play, and read fortunes with tea leaves.

They would probably spend Christmas Day with Aunt Louise. They would go to church, and then there would be roast goose for lunch, and afterwards a brisk walk over the golf course. Not very exciting. Christmas ought to be as it was in books and on Christmas cards, but it never was. Mummy wasn't much good at decorating with holly or dressing a tree. In fact, she wasn't really much good at anything like that. As for St. Ursula's, Judith hadn't even been to see the school, nor to meet the probably terrifying headmistress, Miss Catto.

The train was slowing down. It ground to a hissing halt, and she collected her bag and stepped out onto the platform. The tiny station stood opposite the bottom gate of the Riverview House garden. She went through the waiting room and emerged into an unlit lane. She crossed the road, opened the gate, and went up the steeply sloping path. At the top, the house loomed before her, with curtained windows glowing in friendly fashion. The ornamental lantern over the front door had been turned on, and in its light she saw an alien car parked on the gravel. Aunt Louise, come, no doubt, for tea.

A big black Rover. Solid and dependable. But any person who ventured onto the narrow roads of Penmarron had reason to be wary of its appearance. Aunt Louise, regular churchgoer and pillar of the golf club, underwent a sort of personality change the moment she got behind the wheel, roaring around blind corners at fifty miles an hour, the heel of her hand on the horn.

Judith did not want, instantly, to be faced by Aunt Louise. She made her way around to the back door, through the scullery, and so into the kitchen. Here she found Jess sitting at the scrubbed table with her crayons and coloring book, and Phyllis, in her muslin apron, dealing with a pile of ironing.

Phyllis smiled. "Hello. What are you doing, sneaking in the back way?" She was a bony girl, pale, with mousy hair, but had the sweetest disposition of any person Judith had ever known.

"I saw Aunt Louise's car."

"That's no reason. Have a good party, did you?"

"Yes." She delved into her coat pocket. "Here, Jess," and she gave her little sister her bag of sweets.

Jess looked at them. "What are they?" She was a beautiful child, chubby and silver blond, but dreadfully spoiled and babyish.

"Sweets, of course, silly." Judith pulled off her coat and hat. "I didn't know Aunt Louise was coming for tea."

"Telephoned, she did, about two o'clock," Phyllis said. "And your aunt Biddy called this morning."

Judith perked up. Aunt Biddy was Mummy's own sister and a favorite of Judith's. "What did she want?"

"I wasn't eavesdropping, was I? You'll have to ask your mum. You'd better go in. There's scones if you're hungry."

With some reluctance Judith left the snug companionship of the kitchen and crossed the hall. From the sitting room came the low murmur of voices. She opened the door.

They sat, Molly Dunbar and her sister-in-law, Louise Forrester, on either side of the hearth, with a tea table set up between them. This had been laid with a linen cloth and a plate of hot scones spread with cream and strawberry jam. A coal fire flickered in the grate. Because Riverview House was a furnished let, it was not specially well appointed. But Molly had brought from Ceylon her favorite bits and pieces, and these were set about the place: ornaments in jade and ivory and red lacquer, and family photographs in silver frames.

"You'll have such a lot to do," Aunt Louise was saying. "If I can help . . ." She leaned forward to place her cup and saucer on the table and glanced towards the door. "Well, look who's here."

Molly turned. "Judith. I thought perhaps you'd missed the train."

"No. I've been talking to Phyllis." She closed the door and crossed the room to kiss Aunt Louise's proffered cheek. Aunt Louise accepted this but made no move to kiss Judith in return.

She was not one to show emotion. She sat there, a well-built woman in her early fifties, with surprisingly elegant legs and narrow feet in polished chestnut brogues. She wore a tweed coat and skirt, and her short gray hair was deeply marcel waved.

A handsome woman but, if old sepia photographs were to be believed, never beautiful. Indeed, when she was twenty-three and still unspoken for, her parents had packed her off to India to stay with army relations. There she met Jack Forrester, a major in the Bengal Rifles. They shared a love for tennis and the golf at which Louise excelled. It was a sound marriage, and when Jack retired, they returned to England and settled in Penmarron to be near the golf course. Most fine days saw them out together on the fairways. After Jack died, every day still saw Louise out on the golf course.

Now she asked Judith, "How did the Christmas party go?"

"It was all right. There were saffron buns"—Judith eyed the tea table—"but I'm still hungry."

"Well, we've left plenty," said Molly. Judith pulled up a low stool and reached for a plate and a scone.

"Did you say good-bye to all your friends?"

"Yes. And then I walked down the hill with Heather—"

"Who is Heather?" asked Aunt Louise.

"Heather Warren. She's my special friend."

"You know," said Molly, "Mr. Warren, the grocer in Porth-kerris."

"*Oh!*" Aunt Louise raised her eyebrows. "The dashing Spaniard. Such a good-looking man."

She was obviously in a good mood. Judith decided that this was the right moment to broach the subject of the bicycle.

"Actually, Heather had the most frightfully good idea—that I ought to have a bicycle."

"A *bicycle?*" Molly said.

"Mummy, you sound as though I'm asking for a car or a pony. I think it's a really good idea. Windyridge is miles to the bus stop. With a bicycle I can get myself about; Aunt Louise won't have to drive me. *Then* she can get on with her golf."

Aunt Louise gave a snort of laughter. "You've certainly thought of everything."

Molly found her voice. "But Judith, isn't a bicycle dreadfully expensive? And we have so many other things to buy. The clothes list for St. Ursula's is yards long."

"I thought you could give it to me for Christmas."

"But I've already got your Christmas present. Besides, you'll have to go on the main roads. You might have an accident."

Here Aunt Louise intervened. "Oh, Molly, don't fuss. What harm can the child come to? I'll stand you a bicycle, Judith."

"Really? Aunt Louise, you are a brick. When can we buy it?"

"What about Christmas Eve?"

Molly said faintly, "Oh, no."

Louise frowned. "What's the matter *now?*" Judith thought Aunt Louise was often impatient with Molly, treating her more like an idiot girl than a sister-in-law. "Thought of more objections?"

"No. . . . It's just that we won't be here. I haven't told you, Louise." She turned to Judith. "Aunt Biddy rang. She's asked us to spend Christmas with them in Plymouth. You and me and Jess."

Christmas with Aunt Biddy! "What did you *say?*" Judith asked.

"I said we would."

If Aunt Louise hadn't been there, Judith would have jumped up and down and danced around the room in her excitement.

"In that case," Aunt Louise said, "we'll buy the bicycle after Christmas. In fact, I was going to ask you all to spend Christmas with me, but it looks as though Biddy's saved me the trouble."

"Oh, Louise, I'm sorry. Now I feel I've let you down."

"Rubbish. Better for us all to have a bit of a change. Will Biddy's boy be there?"

"Ned? Unfortunately, no. He's going to Zermatt to ski with some of his term at Dartmouth Naval College."

Aunt Louise raised her eyebrows, not approving of extravagant gallivanting. She thought Biddy spoiled her only child quite appallingly. "Pity," was all she said. "He would have been a companion for Judith."

"Aunt Louise, Ned's sixteen! He wouldn't take any notice of me at all. I expect I shall enjoy myself much more without him there."

"You're probably right. And, knowing Biddy, you'll have a high old time. When she was here last summer, I found her in your garden sunbathing in a two-piece bathing suit. Flesh pink. She might just as well have been naked."

"She's always very up to date." Molly felt moved to stand up for her flighty sister, however feebly. "What will you do for Christmas, Louise? I do hope you won't feel abandoned."

"Heavens, no. I'll maybe ask Billy Fawcett over for a drink and then we'll go down to the club for lunch." Judith had a mental picture of all the golfers, in their knickerbockers and stout shoes, pulling crackers and donning paper hats. "And then perhaps have a rubber or two of bridge."

Molly frowned. "Billy Fawcett? I don't think I know him."

"No. You wouldn't. Old friend from the Quetta days. Retired now, and thought he'd give Cornwall a try. He's rented a bungalow down my road. Keen golfer, so I've put him up for the club."

"That's nice for you, Louise, having an old friend nearby. And a golfer too. Not that you're ever short a partner."

But Louise was not about to commit herself. "It depends," she said, "on what sort of handicap he gets." She looked at her watch. "Heavens, is that the time?" She pulled herself out of her chair, and Molly and Judith rose to their feet. "Tell Phyllis, a delicious tea. If I don't see you before Christmas, Molly, have a ripping time. And Judith, we'll buy the bicycle at the half-term holidays."

❧ *1936* ❧

*T*HE black morning was so cold that, slowly waking, Judith felt as if her nose were frozen to her face. She reached to turn on the bedside light. Her new clock—from Uncle Bob, and one of her best presents—said seven forty-five. It was the last day. She felt a bit depressed. Their Christmas holiday was over, and they were going home.

The room in which she lay was in the attic of Aunt Biddy's house. Judith preferred this room, with its sloping ceilings and dormer window and flowery cretonne curtains. But the meager heating of the rooms below did not penetrate the space.

A short time before Christmas the temperature had dropped alarmingly, just as the Dunbars traveled up-country. Alighting at Plymouth had been a bit like arriving in Siberia, with driving showers of sleet. Which was unfortunate, because Aunt Biddy and Uncle

Bob lived in what had to be the coldest house in Christendom. The house went with Uncle Bob's job, which was captain in charge of the Royal Naval Engineering College at Keyham.

Despite the freezing cold, this had been a truly magical Christmas. Biddy, who never did things by halves, had dressed the entire house. Her Christmas tree, standing in the hall and filling it with lights and drifting tinsel and the smell of spruce, was the most magnificent that Judith had ever seen. Other rooms were just as festive, with swags of holly and ribbon, and in the dining room and drawing room great coal fires burned nonstop.

And there had been so much to do, so much going on all the time. Luncheon and dinner parties, with dancing to the gramophone, and friends kept dropping in for tea or for drinks.

Being with Uncle Bob was the undoubted highspot of the holiday. Judith had never known that fathers could be so interesting, so funny. In his study he had shown her his photograph albums and let her play records on his gramophone. He had introduced her to classical music, and she felt as if she were being transported into another land. They had all gone ice-skating, and it was he who had helped her around the rink until she found what he called her sea legs. And at parties he introduced her to guests, just as though she were a grown-up.

Dad, although dear and missed, had never been such fun. Admitting this to herself, Judith had felt a bit guilty, because over the last couple of weeks she had scarcely thought of him. It was not easy to go on missing a person when life had been lived without him for so long.

The new clock now pointed to eight o'clock. Time to get up. She flung back the covers, hopped out of bed, and, as swiftly as she could, got dressed and packed her suitcase. Breakfast would be waiting, and she was hungry.

BIDDY Somerville sat at the end of her dining-room table, drank black coffee, and tried to ignore the fact that she had a slight headache. Bob sat at the other end of the table, hidden from her by the opened pages of *The Times*. He was fully dressed in uniform because his seasonal leave was over and today he returned to work. The rest of their little house party had not yet appeared.

They were leaving today, and Biddy found herself feeling quite sorry that the time had come to say good-bye. Molly was Biddy's only sister, and there was no knowing when they would see each other again. As well, Biddy felt a bit guilty; she hadn't done enough for the Dunbars during their last four years here. Finally she had asked them over for the holidays.

The fact that she had little in common with her sister, and scarcely knew the two girls, had rendered her not too hopeful as to the outcome. But it had all been a surprising success. Molly, it was true, had wilted from time to time, defeated by the social whirl, and Jess was a spoiled brat, dreadfully indulged. But Judith had proved a real eye-opener, the sort of girl Biddy would have liked as a daughter of her own—entertaining herself if necessary, and enthusiastic about any diversion. She was also, Biddy thought, extraordinarily pretty . . . or would be in a few years. The rapport she had struck up with Bob was a bonus. He liked her for her good manners and the way she spoke up and looked you in the eye; but as well, there was a natural attraction, a father-daughter relationship that both of them had missed out on.

Perhaps they should have had daughters. But there was only Ned, packed off to prep school when he was eight and then to Dartmouth Naval College. The years flew by so fast. Now he was sixteen, and soon he'd be done with his studies and sent to sea. Be grown up. Get married. Produce a family of his own. Biddy sighed. Being a grandmother did not appeal to her.

Bob lowered his paper, folded it, and slapped it down on the table. "Time I was off." He pushed back his chair and stood up, a tall and squarely built man, his bulk made yet more impressive by the dark, double-breasted, gold-buttoned naval jacket. His face, clean-shaven and craggy, was shadowed by bushy eyebrows, and his thick hair, iron gray, lay smooth on his head.

He looked at the empty table. "What time is their train?"

"This afternoon. It's the *Cornish Riviera.*"

"I don't think I can make it. Say good-bye for me. Say good-bye to Judith."

"You'll miss her."

"I . . ." A man who did not show his emotions, he searched for words. "I don't like her being abandoned. Left on her own."

"She won't be on her own. Louise is there."

"She needs more than Louise is able to offer. Maybe you could ask her here for a few days. Judith, I mean. During the holidays. Or would that be an awful bore for you?"

"No, not at all. I'll suggest it."

He came to drop a kiss on the top of her unruly head. "See you this evening, then."

"Bye, darling."

He went. She finished her coffee and poured another. Then she leafed through her mail. There was a letter from Devon, where her father was the incumbent of a tiny parish and her mother had struggled all her life with genteel poverty. It was a miracle, thought Biddy, that she and Molly had managed to escape the vicarage in which they had been brought up.

For neither had been prepared for life. Neither had trained as a nurse, nor gone to university, nor learned how to type. If Molly hadn't been invited to that tennis party with the Luscombes and there met Bruce Dunbar, home on his first long leave from Colombo and searching desperately for a wife, heaven alone knew what might have happened to the poor girl. A lifetime of spinsterhood, probably.

Biddy was different. From an early age she saw clearly that if she was going to have any sort of life, she was going to have to take care of herself. At school her best friend was the daughter of a naval commander, living in a large house near Dartmouth. As well, the girl had brothers. Biddy decided this was fertile ground, and managed to wangle an invitation to stay for the weekend. She was, as she had every intention of being, a social success. She was attractive, with long legs and bright dark eyes and a mop of curly brown hair, and she had a sure instinct as to when to be polite, when to be charming, how to flirt with men. Her careless lifestyle earned her something of a reputation, and at nineteen she enjoyed the dubious fame of being engaged to two young navy men at the same time, swapping rings as their different ships came into port. But when she was twenty-one, she had married serious Bob Somerville, and had never regretted it.

They had had good times, for she loved to travel and was never unwilling to pull up stakes and join Bob wherever he was sent. Two years in Malta had been the best, but none of it had been bad. No, she had been very fortunate.

The clock on the dining-room mantelpiece struck half past eight, and Biddy scooped up Bob's newspaper. It did not make cheerful reading. Spain seemed headed for a civil war, Herr Hitler was making noisy speeches about the remilitarization of the Rhineland, and Mussolini boasted of his growing naval strength in the Mediterranean. It was all a bit frightening, and she tried not to think about Ned, committed to the Royal Navy, ripe for combat. Then the door opened and Molly came in.

Biddy was not yet dressed. She had a housecoat pulled on over her nightgown. And so Molly's appearance, neatly turned out, engendered a sisterly dart of irritation.

"I'm sorry I'm late," Molly said.

"Not late at all. Did you sleep well?"

"Not really. I was up and down all night. Jess had dreadful nightmares. She's still asleep, poor pet. Judith's not appeared either?"

"She's probably packing. She'll turn up in a moment. Get something to eat."

Molly went to the sideboard, lifted the lid of the sausage dish, and hesitated. Biddy raised her eyebrows. "Not hungry?"

"Not really. I'll have a bit of toast."

Molly Dunbar's claim to beauty lay in her extraordinarily girlish appearance—the fluffy fair hair, the rounded cheeks, the eyes which reflected a sort of bewildered innocence. Men were apt to find this charming, because it made them feel protective. Now, however, Biddy experienced a certain concern. There were dark shadows beneath Molly's eyes, and her cheeks were unusually pale.

"Are you feeling all right?"

She poured coffee. "Oh, I don't know. It's all the things that have to be done when I get home. Organizing everything—closing the house, trying to help Phyllis find a new job, and catching the boat back to Colombo. I'd put it all out of my mind while I was here with you. Now I've got to start being sensible again." She hesitated and then said quite violently, "The awful thing is that right now I think I'd give anything not to be going. I hate leaving Judith. I hate us all being torn apart."

Her voice cracked. For a dreadful moment Biddy feared that she was about to burst into tears. "Oh, Molly, you're just tired. Not sleeping. It makes one depressed."

"Yes." Molly sighed, but at least she wasn't weeping. She drank coffee, laid down her cup. "But still I can't help wishing that Bruce worked in London or Birmingham or *anywhere,* so that we could live in England and be together. I know you think I'm being silly."

"No, I do understand. When Bob and I went to Malta, I simply hated leaving Ned. But there it is. We can't be everywhere at once. The thing to be certain about is that you're leaving Judith at a school that is caring. You're happy with the school?"

"Oh, yes. Even if I hadn't been going back to Ceylon, I think I should have sent Judith to St. Ursula's. The Porthkerris School has been excellent academically, but the children there are a pretty mixed bunch. It doesn't *lead* anywhere, does it? Socially, I mean."

Biddy had to laugh. "Honestly, Molly, you always were the most appalling snob."

"I'm not a snob. But people matter."

"Yes, they certainly do."

"What are you getting at now?"

"Louise. I wouldn't want to spend my holidays with her."

This threw Molly into a state of instant agitation. "Oh, Biddy, *please* don't start interfering and raising objections. It's all been arranged, and there's nothing to be said."

"Who said I was going to raise objections?" Biddy asked, and immediately started raising them. "She's such a tough old bird. So boring with her endless golf and her bridge games."

"Actually, she's very kind. She's been a tower of strength to me. But most important, she's reliable. She'll give Judith security."

"Perhaps Judith needs more than security."

"Such as?"

"Emotional space, freedom to grow in her own direction. She'll soon be fifteen. She'll need to spread wings. You don't want her to be shut away and bored stiff."

"It doesn't matter now. It's too late. She's going to Louise."

Biddy managed to control her rising impatience. "But wouldn't it be fun for her to come to us from time to time? No, don't look so horrified; it was Bob's idea. It would be a nice break for her."

"I—I don't want to upset Louise . . . rock the boat. Oh, please understand, Biddy. Perhaps later on."

"There may not be a later on."

"What do you mean?" Molly demanded in evident alarm.

"Read the papers. Bob doesn't trust Herr Hitler further than he could throw him. And the same goes for fat old Mussolini."

"You mean"—Molly swallowed—"a war?"

"Oh, I don't know. But I don't think we should fritter around with our private lives, because, perhaps very soon, we won't have any. You think I'm a bad influence on Judith, I suppose. All those wicked parties and young lieutenants coming to call. That's it, isn't it? You might as well admit it."

"It isn't that! You know it isn't."

It had turned into a proper row, with both of them raising their voices.

"Let's just forget it." And with this, Biddy, exasperated, reached for *The Times,* snapped its pages open, and retreated behind it.

Silence. Molly, quite shattered by the awfulness of everything, sat in a state of trembling agitation. Finally she pushed back the cuff of her cardigan and looked at her watch.

"Where is Judith?" She stood abruptly and went to the door to call for her tardy daughter. But Judith was already there, just across the hall, sitting at the foot of the staircase.

"What *are* you doing?"

"Tying my shoelace."

She did not meet her mother's eyes, and Molly realized that her daughter had been there for some time and had heard every word of the acrimonious and regrettable exchange.

It was Jess who came to her rescue. "Mummy." Molly looked up and saw her younger child peering at her through the banister rail. Jess, still in her nightdress and with her curls awry. "Mummy!"

"I'm coming, darling." She crossed the hall and went upstairs.

Judith waited until she was gone, then went into the dining room. Aunt Biddy looked at her bleakly. "Oh, dear. Sorry about that."

"It's all right." Judith was not used to having grown-ups apologize to her. She got herself a sausage and sat down.

After a bit, "Did you hear it all?" Aunt Biddy asked.

"Most of it. I shall be all right with Aunt Louise, you know."

"I know that. It isn't that I'm worried about your well-being, just the fact that quite possibly it won't be much fun."

Judith said, "I've never had proper grown-up fun before. Not before this Christmas. I would love to come back." Judith picked up her knife and fork and cut the sausage in two. "If I came to visit, would you still be in this house?"

"I don't know. Keyham's a two-year appointment, and we're due to move this summer. Bob wants to go back to sea. If he does, I shall try to buy a little house of our own. We've always lived in quarters, but it would be nice to have a permanent base. I thought Devon."

Judith popped a bit of sausage into her mouth and chewed thoughtfully. "What I really hate," she admitted at last, "is being treated as though I were the same age as Jess. I'm never *asked* about things or *told* about things. If I hadn't heard you shouting at each other, I should never have known that you'd asked me to stay with you."

"I know. But you mustn't be too hard on your mother. At the moment she's in a state of upheaval, and who can blame her if she does start twittering around like a wet hen?" She laughed and was rewarded by the beginnings of a smile from Judith.

"Now"—Biddy got to her feet—"I can hear your mother and Jess on their way downstairs. I must go and put some clothes on."

Before she reached the door, Molly and Jess had come into the room, Jess now dressed in a little smock and white socks. Biddy paused to drop an airy kiss onto Molly's cheek. "Don't bother about a thing," she said, which was the nearest she could get to an apology; then she was gone, running up the stairs to her bedroom.

AND so the quarrel was swept away. Judith was relieved that the air was clear between her mother and aunt, and it was only when they were at the station, waiting for the *Riviera,* that she had time to regret the absence of Uncle Bob. She wanted to thank him for so much, and thanks were never the same written in a letter.

Her feet were frozen. She tried to stamp some life into them, while Aunt Biddy and Mother chatted and Jess sat on the edge of a trolley, swinging her legs and hugging her "Golly," a revolting toy she took with her everywhere.

And then something really good happened. Aunt Biddy stopped chattering and said, "Oh, look. There's Bob."

Judith swung around. Frozen feet were forgotten. There he was, a huge, unmistakable figure coming down the platform, with a great grin on his craggy features.

"Had a moment or two to spare, decided to come and see our little party on board." He looked down at Judith. "I couldn't let you go without saying good-bye properly."

160

She beamed up at him. She said, "I'm glad you came. I wanted to thank you for everything. Especially for the clock."

"You'll have to remember to wind it." Then Uncle Bob cocked his head, listening. "I think that's the train now."

And indeed the railway lines were humming, and Judith saw the huge green-and-black engine surge into view. It crept alongside the platform and, with a hiss of steam, stopped, dead on time.

The porter heaved their suitcases on board and went in search of seats. Uncle Bob, with seamanlike thoroughness, followed him to make sure the job was done in a proper fashion. Molly, panicking slightly, lifted Jess into her arms and hopped up into the train, and had to lean down to kiss her sister good-bye.

"We've had a wonderful Christmas. Wave good-bye to Aunt Biddy, Jess."

Jess, still clutching Golly, flapped a little white-furred paw.

Aunt Biddy turned to Judith. "Good-bye, dear child. You've been a little brick." She stooped and kissed her. "Don't forget. I'm always here. Up you get, now."

On board, Judith gave a final wave and then plunged down the corridor after the others. A compartment had been found containing only one young man, who sat, with an open book on his knee, while the porter piled luggage in the racks over his head. When all was stowed, Uncle Bob tipped the porter and sent him on his way.

"You must go," Judith told him, "or the train will move, and you'll be caught."

He smiled down at her. "It's never happened yet. Good-bye, Judith." Then he was gone. A moment later the train began to move. They were on their way.

The other occupant of the carriage sat by the door, and so they settled themselves in the window seats. It was very warm, so gloves and coats were removed and stowed in the rack. Jess knelt on the prickly plush and pressed her nose against the smutty window. Judith sat opposite, and her mother sank down beside Jess. She began to fan her face with her hand.

"Goodness, it's hot," she said to nobody in particular. "I wonder . . ." Now she was addressing the young man whose privacy they had disturbed. He looked up from his book, and she smiled disarmingly. "Would you mind if we opened the window a chink?"

"Of course." He was very polite. He laid aside his book and

moved to the window. Judith tucked her legs out of the way and watched as he let the window down an inch. "How's that?"

"Perfect."

He went back to his seat and picked up his book again. Covertly Judith studied him. His book looked large and dull, and she wondered why it so absorbed his interest; he did not strike her as a studious type, being broad-shouldered and solidly built. Quite fit, she decided. He was dressed in corduroys and a tweed jacket, and draped around his neck was a long, striped woolen scarf. He had hair that was no particular color, neither fair nor brown, and it looked as though it needed a good cut. He wore horn-rimmed spectacles, and there was a deep cleft in the middle of his chin. She wondered how old he was and decided about twenty-five. But she hadn't much experience of young men, and it was hard to be sure.

She turned back to the window. In a moment they would be going over the Saltash Bridge, and she didn't want to miss the sight of all the naval men-of-war at anchor in the harbor. But Jess was already bored, and she began scrambling down off the seat in order to scramble up again. Her shoe kicked Judith's shin painfully.

"Oh, sit *still*, Jess."

Jess responded by flinging Golly at her sister and howling.

"Oh, *Judith*." Mother took Jess on her knee and then apologized to the young man. "I'm sorry. We've disturbed your peace."

He looked up from his book and smiled. It was a particularly charming smile, revealing even white teeth, and it lit up his plain features, so that suddenly he was almost good-looking.

"Not at all," he reassured her.

"Have you come from London?" Molly asked.

She was obviously in a conversational mood. The young man closed his book. "Yes. I was working over Christmas and the New Year. I'm taking my holiday now."

"Goodness, what a shame. Fancy having to work over Christmas. What do you do?"

Judith thought she was being rather nosy, but the young man looked quite happy to talk. "I'm a houseman at St. Thomas's."

"Oh, a *doctor!*"

Judith thought he looked much too young to be a doctor, but it explained the reason for his heavy book. He was probably studying some obscure disease.

"Not a very amusing Christmas for you. Now you're going home?"

"Yes. To Truro. My parents live there."

"We're going farther than that. We've been staying with my sister and her husband. He's a captain at the Engineering College."

It sounded a little as though she were bragging. To divert attention, Judith said, "Here's the bridge coming now."

To her surprise the young man seemed as excited about this as she was. "I must have a look," he said, and he came to stand beside her, steadying himself with a hand on the window's edge. He smiled down at her, and she saw that his eyes were neither brown nor green, but speckled, like a trout. "It's too good to miss, isn't it?"

The wheels were slowing. The iron girders clanked past, and far below gleamed cold winter water, crammed with sleek gray cruisers and destroyers and pinnaces, all flying the white ensign.

She said, "I think it's a special bridge."

"Brunel's masterpiece. Brunel designed it for the Great Western Railway. The wonder of the day. Still wonderful, for that matter."

They fell silent. He stayed there until the train had crossed the bridge and steamed into Saltash, on the Cornish side of the Tamar, and then he went back to his seat and picked up his book again.

Judith, gazing out into the gathering twilight, decided that, after all, it had not been such a bad day. It had started a bit gloomily, with her mother and Aunt Biddy having that terrible row, but out of it had come the knowledge that Aunt Biddy and Uncle Bob actually liked her enough to want to have her to stay again. Another good thing had been Uncle Bob's appearing at the station to see them off. And finally, talking to the young doctor. It occurred to her that he was the sort of person one would like to have as a brother.

Eventually the train steamed into Truro, and their fellow passenger stood and said good-bye. Through the window Judith watched him make his way down the lamplit platform. Then he was gone.

After that, it was a bit dull, but there wasn't far to go. At the Porthkerris junction, crossing to the other platform, Judith felt the wind blowing in from the sea, and although it was cold, it was no longer frosty, but soft and damp. They piled into the small train, and minutes later they were piling out again onto the platform at Penmarron Halt.

Jess had fallen asleep, and Molly had to carry her across the dark road and up the shadowed path. As they came to the house, the door opened and Phyllis was there to welcome them.

"Look who's here, turned up like a lot of bad pennies." She hurried down the steps. "Here, give me the child, madam. You must be exhausted. Now come along, let's get you all in. There's a nice fire in the sitting room and a boiled fowl for your supper."

Phyllis, decided Molly, really was a treasure, and life without her was never going to be the same. Once Phyllis had imparted a bit of village gossip, she bore Jess upstairs to bathe and feed her and put her to bed. Judith followed, chattering. "I got a clock from Uncle Bob, Phyllis. It's in a leather case. . . ."

With the journey behind her Molly all at once felt totally exhausted. She took off her fur coat and slung it over the banister. Then she gathered up the mail on the hall table and went into the sitting room. The coal fire burned brightly, and she stood in front of it and leafed through her letters. There was one from Bruce, but first she would pour herself a large whisky and soda. Settled in her chair by the fire, she took a delicious, warming mouthful, then reached for her husband's letter.

IN HER bedroom, Judith unpacked her night things, then her Christmas loot. She laid her gifts out on her desk, and once Phyllis had finished with Jess, she came in to have a look.

"Yours was the best gift, Phyllis. It was kind of you."

"At least you won't come asking me for scissors all the time. And thank you for the bath salts. I like Evening in Paris best."

Phyllis had to inspect everything else and marvel at its splendor. "Feel that jumper. So soft. And the little clock! No excuse for being late for breakfast now. What did you get from your dad?"

"I asked for a cedarwood box, but it hasn't arrived yet."

"Oh, well, it'll come." Phyllis settled herself on the bed. "Now"—she was agog with curiosity—"tell me what you did."

So Judith told her—all about Aunt Biddy's house, and about skating, and about Uncle Bob and his gramophone, and about the parties and the Christmas tree and the decorations.

"Aw." Phyllis let out a sigh of envy. "It sounds *lovely*."

Judith was sure that Phyllis's Christmas had been a fairly thin one. Phyllis, whose father was a tin miner out St. Just way, was the eldest of five children, and how they all squeezed into their tiny stone house was a conundrum.

"What did *you* do, Phyllis? Did you get a Christmas present?"

"Yes. A blouse from Mum and a box of hankies from Cyril."

Cyril Eddy was Phyllis's young man, another tin miner. She and Cyril didn't see much of each other, because St. Just was so far away, but she kept a photograph of him in her bedroom.

"What did you give him?"

"A collar for his whippet. He was some pleased." A coy expression came into her face. "You meet any nice young men, did you?"

"Oh, Phyllis, of course not. Aunt Biddy's friends are grown up. Except on the last night two young lieutenants came in after dinner for a drink. But," she added, "they were far too busy being amused by Aunt Biddy to look at me."

"That's your age. Couple of years, you'll have boys round you like flies round a honeypot." Phyllis smiled. "You never fancy a boy?"

"I don't know any. Except . . ." She hesitated.

"Go on. Tell Phyllis."

"There was this man on the train. A young doctor. He was really nice. I wouldn't mind meeting somebody like that."

"Perhaps you will."

"Not at St. Ursula's."

"You don't go to a place like that to meet boys. You go to get educated. And don't turn up your nose at that. I had to leave school to go into service. I can't do much more than read and write. By the time you're done, you'll be passing exams and winning prizes."

"I suppose you didn't have time to look for another job?"

"Didn't have the heart, somehow. Never mind. Madam said she'd help, give me a good reference." She stopped short. "That's funny. She hasn't come up for her bath. Go down like a good girl and tell her the bathroom's empty." She rose. "I'd better see to the potatoes."

When she was gone, Judith combed her hair and ran downstairs to the sitting room. "Mummy, Phyllis says that if you want to—"

She got no further. Something was terribly wrong. Her mother sat in her armchair by the fire, her face stricken with despair and made swollen by weeping. On the floor at her feet were the pages of a letter.

"Mummy!" She rushed to her mother's side. "Whatever is it?"

165

"Oh, *Judith.* It's a letter from Dad. I can't bear it."

"What's happened to him?"

"Nothing." Molly dabbed at her face with a sodden handker-chief. "It's just that . . . we're not staying in Colombo. He's got a new job. We have to go to Singapore."

"But why does that make you cry?"

"Because it's *another* move. As soon as I get to Colombo, we've got to pack up and go on again. To somewhere strange. And I shan't know anybody. And I'm so tired, and there's so—"

Her tears flowed anew. Judith kissed her, feeling almost as dis-traught as her weeping mother. Which wouldn't do at all. One of them had to be strong, or everything was going to fall to pieces. She took a deep breath or two and composed herself.

Molly had gathered the letter up off the floor. "Oh, dear, I am sorry. I don't know what came over me."

Judith sat down on the fireside stool. "May I read the letter?"

"Of course." She handed it over.

Dearest Molly,

By the time you get this, Christmas will be over. I hope you and the girls had an enjoyable time. I have fairly momentous news. The chairman called me into his office yesterday and told me that they want me to move to Singapore, as company manager for Wilson-McKinnon. It is a promotion, and I hope you will be as pleased as I am. The new job does not commence until the month after you and Jess arrive here, so the three of us will sail to Singapore to-gether. I know you will miss Colombo, as I will, but we shall travel together, and be together when we set up in our new home.

Judith did not need to read any more. She folded the pages and gave them to her mother. "It sounds quite exciting."

"I don't *want* to be excited. I want a *home,* not moving all the time. And everybody telling me I do things all wrong."

"But you *don't!*"

Molly blew her nose, and smiled a bit sheepishly. She said, "I'm sorry about this morning. That silly row. About Biddy asking you to stay and me being so uncooperative. It's just that Louise, well, she doesn't approve of Biddy, and it just seemed another complication to deal with. Perhaps I didn't handle it very well."

Judith said, "I don't mind about any of that."

"And I feel so guilty, because I have made plans for you without discussing them. School and Aunt Louise. And now there's so much to do." She was off again. "I haven't even bought your uniform."

She was so fraught that Judith felt, all at once, enormously protective. She said, "I'll help. We'll do it together. As for that awful school uniform, why don't we get it tomorrow. We'll go to Medways, in Penzance. We'll take the car, and we won't come back until we've got every single thing."

Molly looked instantly more cheerful. She said, "All right. We'll leave Jess with Phyllis, and we'll have lunch at the Mitre Hotel, for a treat."

"And then we'll drive to St. Ursula's and look at the place. Now I'll go and tell Phyllis that we're ready to eat."

Her mother leaned forward and kissed her. "Thank you. You've made me feel quite different."

MOLLY opened her eyes at half past seven. It was scarcely light, but she felt refreshed, ready for whatever the day had to bring.

Which was shopping for the school uniform. She got out of bed and went to draw back the curtains. The sky was clear. Perhaps, Molly thought, it would turn into one of those days that spring steals from a Cornish winter. She would keep it whole, separate, an entity on its own, a single day spent with her elder daughter. Remembered, it would be sharp-edged and vivid, like a photograph.

Over breakfast she spooned boiled egg into Jess's mouth and broke the news that she was to be abandoned for the day.

Jess said, "I don't want to." Her bottom lip stuck out like a shelf.

"Of course you do. You and Phyllis can take Golly for a walk and buy fruit gums."

"Don't *want* to." Tears poured down Jess's face, and her mouth went square. Judith said, "Oh, now she's off." But just then Phyllis came in with hot toast in a rack and said, "What's all this, then?" She scooped the howling Jess up into her arms and bore her firmly out of the room. By the time she reached the kitchen, the wails had started to subside.

"Thank goodness," said Judith.

Half an hour later they were ready to go, Molly armed with the school's clothes list and her handbag and checkbook. They let themselves out the door, and Molly, a tentative driver, climbed

167

gingerly behind the wheel of the little Austin Seven. Judith got in beside her, and they set off. It took a while for Molly to get her nerve up, but she finally achieved a speed of thirty miles an hour.

Before long the sea came into view, a pearly blue in the thin morning sunshine, and they saw the great sweep of Mounts Bay. Then the road ran on between the railway line and sloping farmland, and Penzance lay ahead, the harbor busy with fishing boats.

In town, they parked the car in the Greenmarket and headed for Medways, an old-fashioned, somber shop, with plate-glass windows displaying outdoor wear—tweeds, woolens, hats, and raincoats for both ladies and gentlemen. Inside, all was fitted in dark wood, and smelled of rubber waterproofs and fusty assistants. The children's department was on the second floor, with long, polished counters and tall windows. An elderly assistant who approached them wore a sad black dress and walked as though her feet hurt.

"Good morning, madam. Want some help, do you?"

"Yes, we do." Molly fished in her bag for the clothes list. "The St. Ursula's uniform. For my daughter."

Two bentwood chairs were produced, and Molly, drawing off her gloves, settled down.

"Where would you like to begin, madam?"

"At the top of the list, I think. One green tweed overcoat."

"Lovely material, the overcoats are. And I'll bring the jacket and skirt as well. For Sundays, they are. For church."

Judith, sitting down, found her attention caught by something on the other side of the department—a second mother and her daughter also shopping together. Their shop lady was young and jolly-looking, and a lot of chat and laughter seemed to be taking place. Which was extraordinary, because they too were buying the entire St. Ursula's uniform, and piles of garments, most in that deadly bottle green, were being packed into large boxes and tied up with string.

"I could have them delivered, Mrs. Carey-Lewis."

"No. We'll take them. I've got the car. I'll just need some kindly body to help me down."

"I'll fetch young Will from the stockroom."

Judith saw that the girl across the room was probably about thirteen, very thin, and long-legged and flat-chested as a boy. She wore scuffed sandals and knee stockings, a pleated tartan skirt, and a dreadfully shabby navy-blue sweater that looked as though it had once belonged to some large male relation. But she was sensationally pretty, with a long, slender neck and curly dark hair cut quite short. Her eyes, beneath strong dark brows, were violet-blue, her skin the color of honey, and when she smiled, it was a wicked urchin's grin.

She sat leaning her elbows on the counter, her spindly legs wound around the legs of the chair. Ungraceful and yet not graceless, because there was such overweening confidence about her that one knew instinctively that nobody, in all her life, had ever told her that she was clumsy, or stupid, or dull.

The last knot was tied, the string cut with scissors. "How will you be paying this morning, Mrs. Carey-Lewis?"

"Oh, put it on my account. That's the simplest."

"*Mummy!* You know Pops said you had to pay right away, because you always throw bills into the wastepaper basket."

Much laughter all round. "Darling, you mustn't give my secrets away."

Mrs. Carey-Lewis's voice was deep and ripe with amusement, and it was difficult to come to terms with the fact that she was anybody's mother. She looked like a film star or a glamorous older sister. Fine-boned and slender, her face was made up to porcelain paleness, with arched eyebrows and a scarlet mouth. Her hair was corn gold and silky straight, cut in a simple bob that had nothing to do with fashion and everything to do with style. She wore—and this was particularly outré—gray flannel trousers. Slacks, they were called. Over her shoulders was a short brown fur jacket. A red-tipped hand dangled by her side, holding the loop of a scarlet leather leash, the other end of which was attached to a motionless, furry, cream-colored cushion.

"Well, that's it." She slid her arms into the sleeves of her jacket and, in doing so, dropped the leash. "Come along, darling, we'll go and have coffee, and I'll buy you an ice cream, or something."

The furry cushion on the floor came to life, pulled itself onto four velvety feet, and turned towards Judith. It shook itself and then proceeded with much dignity across the carpet towards her, trailing the red leash like a royal train.

A dog. Judith adored dogs but had never been allowed one. A Pekingese. Irresistible. She slid from the chair and crouched to greet him. "Hello." She laid her hand on the soft domed head, and it was like stroking cashmere.

"Pekoe! What are you up to?" His mistress came after him, and Judith straightened up. Mrs. Carey-Lewis stooped and picked up the leash, and Judith caught a drift of her perfume—sweet and heavy as the scent of remembered flowers in the gardens of Colombo. "Thank you for being kind to him. Do you like Pekes?"

"I like all dogs."

"He's very special. A lion dog. Aren't you, my darling?"

Her eyes were mesmerizing, so brilliantly blue and unblinking that Judith could only stare. Mrs. Carey-Lewis smiled, as though understanding, and turned to go, moving away like a queen, with her dog and her daughter and the shop assistant, beneath the pile of boxes, forming a procession behind her. As she passed Molly, she paused.

"Are you kitting your child up for St. Ursula's as well?"

Molly, caught unawares, seemed taken aback. "Yes. Yes, I am."

"Have you *ever*, in *all* your life, seen so many hideous garments?" She was laughing. She raised her arm in a vague gesture of farewell and led her little party down the stairs.

They watched her go. For a moment nobody said anything. Their departure left behind an extraordinary vacuum, as though a light had been turned off or the sun lost behind a cloud. It occurred to Judith that this probably always happened when Mrs. Carey-Lewis walked out of a room. She took her glamour with her and left only the humdrum behind.

Molly cleared her throat. "Who was that?"

"That's Mrs. Carey-Lewis, of Nancherrow," said the lady in the sad black dress. "Out beyond Rosemullion, on the Lands End Road. It's a lovely place, right on the sea."

"And is that her daughter?"

"Yes. That's Loveday. Her baby. She's got two other children, but they're nearly grown up. A girl and a boy."

Loveday. She was called Loveday Carey-Lewis. It was a marvelous name. You couldn't miss with a name like that.

"Is she going to St. Ursula's as a boarder?" Judith asked.

"Weekly boarder, I believe. Going home on weekends. Apparently Colonel and Mrs. Carey-Lewis sent her to a school in Hampshire, but she ran away. Got herself home on the train and said she wasn't going back, because she missed Cornwall. So they're sending her to St. Ursula's instead."

"She sounds," said Molly, "a little spoilt."

"Being the baby, she's had her own way all her life."

"Yes." Molly looked a bit uncomfortable. "I see. . . . Now Judith, go into the fitting room and try on this gym tunic."

By eleven o'clock they were done with Medways, and the piles of uniform were folded and boxed. For them there was no offer to carry their purchases to their car. And so, laden like a couple of packhorses, they went back to the Austin.

They were by no means finished. Still the shoe shop to visit and the sports shop. And the saddler for an attaché case. Another trip to the car, another unloading of parcels. By now it was half past twelve, so they walked down Chapel Street to the Mitre and there lunched splendidly on roast beef, and for pudding there was apple charlotte and Cornish cream.

Afterwards they drove to the other side of town. At the top of a hill they came to a pair of gates. A sign said ST. URSULA'S SCHOOL. They turned in through the gates and onto a driveway bordered by stands of rhododendron. The house stood at the end, with a gravel sweep in front of the imposing front door. It was holiday time, and there didn't seem to be anybody about.

"Do you think we should ring?" Molly asked.

"Let's don't," Judith said. She saw that the main part of the house was quite old, with stone windowsills and Virginia creeper clambering up granite walls. Beyond this original building lay a modern wing with, at the far end, a stone archway leading into a small quadrangle.

They walked, their footsteps crunching on the gravel, from time to time pausing to peer through windows. A classroom—desks with lids and inkwells and a chalky blackboard; farther on, a science laboratory, with counters and Bunsen burners.

"Let's explore the garden," Judith said.

Which they did, following a wandering path through shrubberies. After a bit they came upon a cobbled sun-trap with a bench, and it seemed a good place to sit for a moment. They faced a view of the bay, a glimpse of the sea, framed by eucalyptus trees.

Molly leaned back, turned her face up to the sun, closed her eyes. She said, "What do you think?"

"It's a beautiful garden."

Molly opened her eyes and smiled. "Is that a comfort?"

"If you have to be shut up somewhere, it helps if it's beautiful."

"Oh, don't say that. It makes me feel as though I were abandoning you in some sort of prison. And I don't want to leave you anywhere. I want to take you with me."

"I'll be all right."

"If—if you want to go to Biddy at any time, you can, you know. I'll speak to Louise. All I really want is for you to be happy."

"I do too, but it doesn't always happen."

"You must make it happen."

"So must you. You mustn't be in such a state about going to Singapore. You'll probably love it. It's like going to some party. The ones you dread very often turn out to be the best fun of all."

"Yes," Molly sighed. "I have to think of it as an adventure."

A vapor, too fine to be called a cloud, drifted over the face of the sun. Judith shivered. "I'm getting cold. Let's move."

They strolled back to the Austin and set off for home. It had been a good day, Molly decided. Not just because they had achieved so much but because it had been done so companionably. Somehow she had crossed a difficult bridge in the relationship with her elder daughter. Perhaps she had left it rather late, but at least it was done.

OVER the following days at Riverview House there seemed to be crates and boxes everywhere. Molly found another position for Phyllis, in Porthkerris, and spent much time on the telephone, speaking to the shipping company, the passport office, the bank, Louise, and her sister Biddy.

"What was that about?" Judith asked, coming in on the tail end of one conversation.

"Oh, I think I've fixed everything. After I've taken you to St. Ursula's, I'll close this house, and Jess and I will spend the last night with Louise. She's promised to drive us to the station in her car."

The station carrier arrived at the front door with his horse and cart, and onto this were roped securely Judith's desk and other possessions to be transported to Aunt Louise's house. Judith watched the cart's departure, bumping up the road to travel the three miles to Windyridge. Then the man who ran the village filling station made an offer for the Austin Seven, and it was sold.

"How are you going to take me to St. Ursula's?" Judith asked.

"We'll order a taxi. And it can bring Jess and me home again."

"I don't actually want Jess to come. She'll just be a nuisance. Cry or something. And if she cries, then you will, and me too."

"Oh, Judith. It seems a little unfair."

"I think it's kind. Anyway, I don't suppose she'll even notice."

But Jess was not a stupid child, and she witnessed the dismemberment of her home with considerable alarm. Familiar objects disappeared; packing cases stood in the hall. Her doll's house, her hobbyhorse, there one day, were gone the next. Only Golly was left. She had no idea what was happening; only she liked none of it.

On the last day, they had lunch in the kitchen, the four of them sitting around Phyllis's scrubbed table. Afterwards Jess was given a tiny packet of fruit gums, which occupied her attention while her mother and Judith disappeared upstairs.

Phyllis was in the scullery, scouring saucepans, when Jess saw the strange black car turn in at the gate. Cheeks bulging with sweets, she went to tell Phyllis, who dried her hands. "That'll be the taxi."

Jess went with her into the hall, and they let the man into the house. Luggage was piled at the foot of the stairs—the brass-bound trunk, suitcases and bags, and Judith's new attaché case. He went to and fro, manhandling everything out to his taxi. Jess stood and stared.

And then Mummy and Judith came downstairs, and Mummy had her coat and hat on, and Judith was wearing a green suit that Jess had never seen before. It was so frighteningly strange that Jess burst into hysterical weeping, clinging to her mother's coat.

It was Judith who stepped forward and picked her up and hugged her very tight, and Jess put her arms around Judith's neck and sobbed, "Where you *going?*"

Judith had never imagined anything so dreadful would happen. "Oh, Jess, it'll be all right. Mummy will be back very quickly."

"I want to *come.*"

Her weight was sweet, the fat little arms and legs unbearably soft and dear. She smelled of soap, and her hair was silky as floss. It was no use recalling all the times that Judith had been cross with her. All that was important was that they were saying good-bye and that Judith loved her. She pressed kisses onto Jess's cheeks.

"You mustn't cry," she implored. "I'll write you letters, and you must send me lovely drawings and pictures. And just think. When I see you again, you'll be eight years old and nearly as tall as I am." Judith kissed her again and then handed her to Phyllis.

"You take care of Golly, now. Good-bye, Phyllis. I'll write."

They embraced, but Phyllis couldn't give Judith much of a cuddle, because of having her arms full of Jess. And she didn't seem to be able to say anything much except "Good luck."

They all trooped out of the house. Her mother dropped a kiss on Jess's damp cheek. "I'll be back," she promised, "in a little while. You be a good girl to Phyllis." Then they got into the taxi.

"Wave good-bye, Jess," Phyllis told her, and the taxi went crunching away over the gravel. They saw Judith's face pressed against the back window, and Judith was waving too, until the taxi trundled out of sight.

Halfway to Penzance, Judith announced that she wanted their good-byes to be quick. She could manage, she said. She did not want her mother to go into the school with her.

And so it only took moments. A porter dealt with her trunk and her suitcases. There were other children there in their green uniforms, and all at once Judith was one of them. Molly looked into her face and saw there the promise of a beauty which would be evident when they were together again. They kissed and hugged, promised to write, and then Judith was gone, walking away, up the steps and through the open door. She never looked back.

THE head girl of St. Ursula's was a strapping creature named Deirdre Ledingham, who took her responsibilities with great seriousness: ringing bells, escorting the long, straggly line of girls, weekly, to church, and each day standing behind a large oak table in the Main Hall handing out the mail.

"Emily Backhouse. Joan Betworthy."

A large, heavy parcel, plastered in foreign stamps. "Judith Dunbar?"

"She's not here," somebody said.

"Well, someone fetch her. Who's in her dorm?"

"I am."

The girl who had spoken, Deirdre saw, was Loveday Carey-Lewis. She frowned. She had decided that this newcomer was cheeky, altogether too big for her boots, and a small penance seemed to be in order. "No, you'd better take it to her. And it's jolly heavy, so mind you don't drop it."

Loveday moved forward, gathered up the enormous parcel, and set off up the wide staircase, headed for the dormitories. Her burden became heavier with each step. What on earth could be in it? She reached the landing, went to the door of her dormitory, and staggered in.

Judith was there, washing ink off her hands in the single basin which the six girls in the dorm shared. "I've found you," said Loveday, and she tipped the parcel onto Judith's bed and collapsed beside it.

Her unexpected appearance, bouncing in like a jack-in-the-box, caused Judith to be overcome by a painful shyness. From that moment in Medways when she had first set eyes on the Carey-Lewis mother and daughter, she had thought Loveday fascinating and longed to get to know her. But during their first few weeks at St. Ursula's, Loveday had totally ignored her presence, leaving Judith with the sad conviction that she was such a nonentity that Loveday did not even recognize her. Now she was here.

"You weren't at Letters. Deirdre told me to bring you this. It weighs a ton. Do come and open it; I want to know what's inside."

Judith reached for a towel. "I think it's a Christmas present."

"Christmas present! But it's February."

"I know. It's taken ages." She joined Loveday on the bed, the impressive package between them. She saw the stamps and smiled. "It's come from Ceylon. My father works there."

"What about your mother? Where is she?"

"She's just gone back to be with him. She's taken my little sister, Jess, with her."

"You mean you're all *alone?* Goodness, that's awful. I didn't know. When I saw you in the shop—"

"So you *did* see me?"

"Yes, of course. Do you think I'm blind?"

"No. It's just that you didn't talk to me. I thought perhaps you hadn't recognized me."

"Well, you haven't talked to *me*," Loveday mocked, her vivid face alight with amusement. "Anyway, we're talking now." She laid her hand on the parcel. "Do open it. I'm bursting to see what's inside. And hurry. Or it'll be the lunch bell, and we'll have to go."

But Judith couldn't open the present in a hurry. She had waited so long for the cedarwood box, and now it was here, and she wanted to keep the excitement going and, once it was open, to examine every detail of her new possession.

"There's no time now. I'll do it later. We'll open it together. We'll change quickly for supper, and then we'll have heaps of time. And it'll be something lovely to look forward to all afternoon."

"Oh, all right." Loveday was persuaded, but obviously against her will. "How you can be so strong-minded I can't imagine."

"It just makes it last longer."

"Have you got a photo of your dad?" Loveday's eyes moved to Judith's white-painted chest of drawers, identical to the other five around the dormitory.

"Yes." She reached for it and handed it to Loveday.

"He looks quite nice. And is this your mother? Yes, of course, I recognize her. Would you like to see my photographs?"

"Oh, yes, please."

They got up from the bed and went to Loveday's end of the dormitory. The school rule was that you were allowed two photographs, but Loveday had about six.

"This is Mummy, all dressed up in her white fox furs. And this is Pops. . . . Isn't he heaven? And Tiger, his Labrador. And this is my sister, Athena, and my brother, Edward."

Judith had never imagined anyone could have such a handsome, beautiful, and glamorous lot of relations, all looking as though they had stepped from the pages of some society magazine. "How old is Athena?"

"She's eighteen. She had her London season last year and then went off to Switzerland to learn French. She's still there."

"What will she do when she comes back?"

"Stay in London probably. Mummy's got a little house in Cadogan Mews. Athena's got strings of boyfriends, and she's always going away for the weekend and things."

It sounded an enviable existence. "She looks like a film star," Judith said a little wistfully. "And your brother?"

"Edward? He's sixteen. He's at Harrow."

The building was suddenly rent by the clangor of the lunch bell. "Oh, bother," said Judith. "We'd better go. Later we'll open the parcel together."

After that, it felt as if the whole color and shape of the day had miraculously changed. First the overtures of friendship with Loveday Carey-Lewis, and there was still the ceremonial unwrapping of the box to look forward to. Then, at lunch, it wasn't prunes and custard—which she hated—for pudding, but vanilla sponge with syrup, which was a treat. Then she got eight out of ten for her French verb test, and when it was time for games, she even enjoyed the hockey, whacking the leather ball with effortless precision.

And then it was tea, and then prep, and, at last, time to change for supper. She fled upstairs, two at a time, to the dormitory, drew the white cotton curtains of her cubicle, and tore off her clothes. She managed to grab a bathroom before anyone else got there, but even so, by the time she returned to the dormitory, Loveday was waiting, sitting on Judith's bed, dressed in the drab green gabardine frock with white linen collar and cuffs which was their regulation garb for evenings.

"Gosh, you've been quick!" Judith exclaimed.

"Hurry up. I've got my nail scissors here to cut the string."

Judith flung on her dress, tied her hair back with a ribbon, and was ready. She cut the string, then had to pick away at the coarse stitches with which the heavy outer wrapping had been sewn into place. Then there was a thick wadding of newspaper covered with strange Eastern characters. Everything smelled spicy and foreign. The last wrapping was shiny white paper. This was torn away and, at last, the Christmas gift revealed. They sat and gazed at it.

"It's divine," Loveday breathed.

It was indeed more splendid than Judith had dared to hope. The wood was the color of honey, smooth as satin and intricately carved. Its ornamental latch was silver, embossed in a flowerlike design, and a Chinese lock slipped into this like a little padlock. The key was fastened by a strip of glued paper to the lid of the box. With it Judith opened the padlock, and then she raised the lid, to reveal two miniature chests of drawers. The scent of cedar filled the air. Loveday said, "Did you *know* it was going to be like this?"

"Something like this. My mother had one in Colombo. But it wasn't nearly as lovely." She opened one of the little drawers. It slid smoothly, revealing a gleaming red lacquer finish within.

"What a place to keep your treasures! Goodness, you're lucky. Let's close it up again, and then I can have a go with the key. . . ."

They might have played with it forever had not Matron come bouncing into the dormitory. She heard their voices and flung back the cubicle curtains. Startled, they looked up to see her glaring at them. "What are you two doing, whispering away? You know you're not allowed in cubicles together."

Judith opened her mouth to apologize, but Loveday, not frightened of anybody, said, "Look, Matron, isn't it gorgeous? Judith got it from her father in Ceylon. Oh, do look. It's got darling little drawers." She opened one to show Matron in such a beguiling manner that Matron's fury abated, and she even took a step forward to peer through her spectacles at the object.

"I must say," she admitted, "that's a pretty thing, but where on earth are you going to keep it, Judith? There's no space in your locker."

"I suppose I could take it to Aunt Louise's at half term."

"Haven't *you* got somewhere safe, Matron?" Loveday cajoled. "In a sickroom cupboard, maybe? Just for the time being?"

"Well, I'll see. Meanwhile, clear up that mess before the supper bell goes. And back you go to your own cubicle, Loveday."

"Thank you, Matron." Loveday smiled sweetly, and Matron turned and stalked off. They kept straight faces until she was out of earshot, and then dissolved into giggles.

MATRON took the box and put it in the bottom of the first-aid cupboard. That Sunday, Judith wrote to thank her father. On Wednesday of the following week, when she presented herself to collect her mail, she was told by Deirdre Ledingham that Miss Catto wanted to see her right away.

Judith's heart dropped. Eyes turned towards her, filled with awe, as though she had done something dreadfully wicked. She did a quick dig-around in her conscience and came up with nothing. No running in the corridor; no talking after lights. Judith, terrified, went off.

Miss Catto, the headmistress, was an ever present influence in the school. Her study, on the ground floor, was the holy of holies, the center of everything that went on. She was held in much respect, and when she made an entrance, black academic gown flowing behind her, at prayers or meals in the dining room, the entire school fell silent and rose to its collective feet.

Miss Catto's study stood at the end of a long corridor. Dry-mouthed, Judith rapped on the door and heard "Come in."

Miss Catto sat behind her desk. "Oh, Judith. Come, sit down."

Judith closed the door and went into the room and sat down. It was a bright morning, the study flooded with sunlight. There was a jug of wild primroses on Miss Catto's desk.

"Stop looking so agonized, Judith. I just want to have a word." She leaned back in the chair. "How are you getting on?"

"All right, thank you, Miss Catto."

For all her elevated position Miss Catto was comparatively young—not yet forty—with a fresh complexion and clear blue eyes. She smiled. "Have you heard from your mother?"

"Yes. I got a letter that was posted in Gibraltar."

"I'm glad. Now, you seem to have made friends with Loveday Carey-Lewis?"

Did Miss Catto miss nothing? "Yes."

"What's happened is that Mrs. Carey-Lewis phoned me. Love-day wants to take you home for a weekend. Would you like to go?"

"Like to?" Judith could scarcely believe her ears. "Oh, Miss Catto, I'd love to."

"You must understand that it's a great privilege, because officially half term is the only weekend that boarders are allowed away. But in the circumstances I think it might be good for you."

"Oh, thank you."

"You'll go with Loveday on Saturday morning. I'll telephone your aunt Louise. As your legal guardian, she must know. So . . ." Her smile was a dismissal. She rose to her feet, and Judith scrambled to hers. "I'll let Mrs. Carey-Lewis know. Off you go, now."

"Yes, Miss Catto, and thank you so much."

She ran Loveday to earth in her classroom, waiting for the luncheon bell. "You beast, Loveday! You brute!"

But Loveday saw her rosy, ecstatic face and shrieked with glee. "She said *yes!*" They clung to each other, leaped up and down in a wild dance of delight. "I never thought she would."

"But you never told me that you'd asked your mother."

"I promised I wouldn't, because we were afraid Miss Catto would refuse permission. And I've nearly burst keeping it secret. Oh, I can't wait. . . . What are you suddenly looking so gloomy about?"

"I've just remembered. I haven't any home clothes. All my things are at Aunt Louise's."

"Oh, heavens, that doesn't matter. You can borrow Athena's."

There was no time for more, as the bell began to clang.

"The best thing about going home," said Loveday in her loud and carrying voice, "is that there are no bloody bells," which earned her an order mark from her shocked form prefect and reduced Loveday to her usual state of disrespectful giggles.

AT TEN o'clock in the morning they were both packed and ready to leave. They had even rescued the cedarwood box from a disapproving Matron. With Judith carrying her new treasure, and Loveday an overnight bag in each hand, out the door they went.

It was a wonderful day, cold and windy, with great white clouds scudding across the starch-blue sky. The car was already there, with Mrs. Carey-Lewis behind the wheel. It was a new Bentley, navy-blue, and Mrs. Carey-Lewis had let the top down.

She raised an arm as they appeared. "There you are, darlings."

"Mummy, this is Judith."

"Hello, Judith. Lovely to see you. Heavens, that box looks heavy. Put it all on the back seat. Now, everybody settled?" She switched on the ignition, the engine purred, and they were off.

Judith settled back in the padded leather seat and heaved a great, secret sigh of pleasure. As they swept out through the school gates, Loveday chattered. "We decided at the last moment to bring the box, and Matron was livid, wasn't she, Judith? I don't think she likes us much. Mummy, who's home this weekend? Anybody exciting?"

"Not really. Only Tommy Mortimer, down from London."

"Oho! Tommy Mortimer. He's Mummy's boyfriend," Loveday explained to Judith. "He brings her gorgeous chocolates."

"Oh, Loveday, you are ridiculous." But her mother didn't sound annoyed, simply amused. "You mustn't believe a word this child says, Judith, but you've probably found that out already."

"It's true! Athena says he's been swooning over you for years; that's why he never married. Have you had a letter from Athena?"

"Oh, darling, you know she's hopeless at letters. But we did have a scrawl from Edward to tell us that he's in the second pair for rackets. And Jeremy Wells turned up this morning. He and Pops and Tommy have disappeared into the woods to shoot pigeons."

"Jeremy. Oh, good. I haven't seen him for ages." To Judith she said, "He used to be Edward's tutor when Edward was trying to get into Harrow. And sort of an old boyfriend of Athena's when she was sixteen. His father is our doctor. Pops simply loves Jeremy."

Judith was beginning to be a bit nervous. So many people and so much going on, and all so worldly, so alien to anything she had ever experienced. She hoped that during the next two days she would not commit some gauche social blunder and so embarrass everybody, especially herself. As for Loveday, she had never heard any child speak to her mother in such a way, gossiping as though they were contemporaries, teasing her about a boyfriend. Tommy Mortimer. He, more than anybody, was a source of wonder. The mothers Judith knew simply did not have boyfriends. It was, Judith decided, all going to be extremely interesting.

By now they had left the town behind them, driven through a small fishing village, and climbed a steep hill onto the empty country which lay beyond. The narrow road wound and twisted, following the contours of meandering drystone walls, the boundaries of random farms, the buildings of which could be glimpsed, low-roofed and ancient, huddled against the wind. Gentle hills swept down to the cliffs and the dazzling sun-speckled sea. It was very different from the other side of Cornwall. Judith said, "It's so beautiful."

Mrs. Carey-Lewis smiled. "It's not far from Penmarron. Nowhere in Cornwall is very far from anywhere else."

"It is if you haven't got a car."

"Didn't your mother have a car?"

"Yes. An Austin Seven. But she wasn't very fond of driving it."

"What is the point of having a car," Loveday asked, "if you never drive?"

Judith felt that perhaps she had been disloyal and should now stick up for her absent mother. "Well, it's better than being like my aunt Louise, who drives her Rover at about a hundred miles an hour. My mother used to dread going anywhere with her."

"I think I should too," said Mrs. Carey-Lewis. She fell silent for a moment and then, "What do you call your mother?" Which was, thought Judith, a fairly odd question.

"Mummy."

"And what are you going to call me?"

181

"Mrs. Carey-Lewis."

"Very right and proper too. But I simply hate being called Mrs. Carey-Lewis. I always think people are talking to my mother-in-law." Judith could think of absolutely nothing to say to this, but Mrs. Carey-Lewis just went on talking. "I really like being called Diana." She turned her head to smile at Judith. "So let's start as we mean to go on. Say my name now, aloud."

"Diana."

"Shout it to the world."

"Diana!"

"Much better. Now all together . . ."

"Diana!"

Their voices were blown away by the wind. The road, a gray ribbon, wound ahead of them, and they were all laughing.

After another ten miles or so they were in a district of running streams and deep wooded valleys. Rosemullion lay ahead, a cluster of whitewashed cottages, a pub, and an ancient church and graveyard. Then the road climbed steeply again, and at the crest of the hill it leveled off and the impressive gateway came into view—curved walls enclosing tall wrought-iron gates which stood open and framed a long, wooded driveway, winding out of sight. Diana changed gears, and the Bentley swung in through the entrance.

"This is it. Nancherrow," she said.

As the road wound on, never seeming to reach anywhere, Judith fell silent. Everything was a bit overpowering. She began to suspect that Nancherrow was not a house at all, but a castle. "It's such a long drive," she finally said.

Diana laughed. "Yes. The old house burnt down in 1910. My father-in-law built another—larger and much more convenient. Just the most wonderful home that we all adore."

At last the road turned a final corner, and the house stood revealed. It was of local granite, slate-roofed like any traditional farmhouse, with long windows on the two floors and a line of dormer windows above these. Its eastern wall was smothered with clematis and climbing roses, and all about stretched green lawns and ornamental flower beds. At the front of the house these lawns took the form of terraces, with flights of stone steps. In the distance could be glimpsed the blue horizon and the sea.

For all its splendor it wasn't frightening in any way. From that first moment Judith fell in love with Nancherrow and immediately felt that she understood Loveday much better. Now she knew exactly why Loveday had run away from school in Hampshire and found her way back to this magical place.

The Bentley drew to a halt outside the front door. They piled out, gathering up possessions, and filed indoors, Judith, loaded with her cedarwood box, bringing up the rear. Up stone steps they went, through a flagged porch and then inner glassed doors, to the central hallway. It all seemed enormous, but despite the generous proportions, the immediate impression was of a family house, friendly and unpretentious, and Judith at once felt at home.

The walls of the hallway were paneled in wood, and polished floors were scattered with worn Persian rugs. The wide staircase, thickly carpeted, rose in three straight flights to the upper landing. In the middle of the central hall was a round pedestal table, on which stood a tureen with white narcissi. As well, a worn leather visitors book, a dog lead or two, a stack of mail. Opposite the staircase was a fireplace, the mantelpiece much carved and ornamented.

As Judith stared about her, Diana paused at the table. "Off you go, then, Loveday, and take care of Judith. I think Mary's in the nursery. The men are coming in for lunch at one, so don't be late." And with that, she picked up her letters and was on her way, walking down the long, wide hallway furnished with antique furniture and ornate mirrors.

"Come on. Let's find Mary Millyway. She's my old nanny."

Loveday headed up the stairs, lugging their overnight bags. Judith followed with her box. At the top of the stairs was another long passage. Loveday broke into a run. "Mary!"

"Here I am, pet!"

Judith had little experience of English nannies or nurseries. Consequently, she entered the Nancherrow nursery with a certain trepidation, which was instantly dispelled. For this was a large, sun-filled sitting room, with a great bay window and a view of the garden and that distant sparkling horizon. It had bookcases, sofas and chairs with flowery slipcovers, and a round table covered with a blue cloth. Other delights stood all about: cheerful pictures, a radio, a fireplace, a basket of knitting. The only concessions to nursery life were a battered rocking horse and an ironing board.

This board was set up, and at it Mary Millyway had been hard at work. "Well, here you are." Mary set down her iron and opened her arms to Loveday, who flung herself into them for a huge hug. "There's my wicked baby." Releasing Loveday, Mary said, "So this is your friend. What's this you've brought with you?"

"It's my cedarwood box."

"It looks as though it weighs a ton. Put it on the table, for goodness' sake." Which Judith gratefully did.

Loveday explained. "We wanted to show it to Mummy. Judith got it for her Christmas. This is Judith, Mary."

Mary Millyway. A tall and rawboned Cornishwoman no more than thirty-five, with coarse fair hair and a freckled face, and wearing a gray tweed skirt and a white cotton blouse.

"Hello, Judith. You look older than I thought you'd be."

"I'm fourteen."

"She's in a form above me," Loveday explained, "but we're in the same dormitory. And Mary, she hasn't got any home clothes, and mine will be too small for her. Is there something of Athena's she can borrow? Something she doesn't want anymore."

"Certainly is. Never known such a girl for wearing things once and then throwing them away. I'll tell you what"—Mary picked up her iron again—"you take Judith and show her where she's sleeping. The pink room at the end of the passage. And when I've finished my ironing, I'll see what I can find."

"All right." Loveday grinned at Judith. "Come on," and she was off. Judith, pausing only to grab up her bag, had to run to keep up. At the far end the passage took a turn to the right, and another rambling wing was revealed. Here Loveday paused.

"It's all so big," Judith said in wonder.

"It has to be because there are always people coming to stay. This is the guest wing." As she went ahead, Loveday opened and closed doors. "This is the blue room. Tommy Mortimer's usually in here. And this is the big double room. And then it's you."

They had reached the last door, and like every other room in this delectable house, it was paneled in wood. It had two windows, hung in a chintz of toile de Jouy. The carpet was pink, and there was a high brass bed and a huge Victorian wardrobe.

"Do you like it?"

"It's lovely."

Judith saw a skirted dressing table with a triple mirror, and a proper armchair with pink cushions.

"And this is your bathroom."

Quite overwhelming. She went to inspect it and saw the black-and-white-checked floor, the huge bath, immense white towels.

Loveday returned to the bedroom to fling wide the window. "And this is your view, but you have to peer a bit to see the sea."

Judith joined her, and they stood side by side, leaning on the stone sill and feeling the wind on their faces. Below them was a large cobbled courtyard, in the middle of which stood a dovecote. White pigeons flew about, to fill the air with their satisfied cooing. Beyond the courtyard was a road and then mown grass, rolling away to a line of trees.

Judith leaned out a little farther. "Is that a stable?"

"No. You can't see the stables from here. But I'll take you after lunch to meet my pony, Tinkerbell. You can ride her if you like."

"I've never ridden a horse," Judith admitted, not admitting at the same time that she was frightened of horses.

"Tinkerbell's adorable, and she never bites or bucks." Loveday paused. "It's Saturday, so maybe Walter will be there."

"Who's Walter?"

"Walter Mudge. His father farms Lidgey—that's the home farm. Walter's really nice. He's sixteen. He sometimes comes at week-ends to muck out the horses and help the gardener." Abruptly Loveday withdrew her head. "I'm getting cold. Come on. Let's do your unpacking."

There wasn't very much to unpack. When they had finished, Loveday kicked the empty bag under the bed. "Now let's go see if Mary dug up something for you to wear. If I don't get out of this horrible uniform soon, I'm going to start screaming."

And she was out of the room and off again, racing away back to the nursery as though defying every school rule that had been drummed into her wayward head.

They found Mary kneeling in front of a tall armoire, with the deep bottom drawer opened and various garments set around her.

Loveday couldn't wait. "What have you found? Mary, this is a new jersey. Athena got it last hols. What's it doing in this drawer?"

"You may well ask. She caught the elbow on a bit of barbed wire. I mended it, but would she wear it? Not her, the little madam."

"Here . . ." Loveday tossed it to Judith, who caught it, and it was like catching thistledown, so weightless and soft was the wool. Cashmere. And holly red, one of her favorite colors.

"Now, here's a nice gingham blouse. And a pair of shorts." The shorts were navy flannel, pleated like a little skirt.

Loveday approved. "Those'll do, won't they, Judith? Go put them on, because I want to show you everything else."

Back in her bedroom, Judith laid the shorts, the jersey, and the blouse ceremoniously on the bed, for in truth she felt a bit as though she were about to change for a party. Everything about this house had a party feel to it. She took off her uniform and, savoring the novelty, dressed in Athena Carey-Lewis's castoffs. She brushed her hair, tying it back with a fresh navy-blue ribbon, and inspected herself in the long mirror set in the wardrobe door. And it was amazing, because she looked so different. Another girl, almost grown up. She could not help smiling.

The door burst open. "Are you ready?" Loveday demanded. "Goodness, you look nice. It must be something to do with Athena. She always looks sensational. Now let's explore the house, and then you'll know your way around."

Which they duly did. Loveday had pulled on a disreputable pair of jodhpurs, which were already too short for her skinny shins, and a shapeless sweater of dark purple, which had darns in the elbows.

"You've seen the guest wing, so we'll start with Mummy's room."

"Are we allowed?"

"Oh, yes. She doesn't mind, provided we don't fiddle and squirt all her scent." She opened the door and pranced ahead of Judith. "Isn't it gorgeous?"

Wordless, Judith gazed about. She had never seen such a bedroom. The walls were pale, neither white nor pink nor peach. There were thick swagged draperies smothered in roses, and inside these a drift of filmy white curtains. The wide bed was draped in the same filmy white, with a canopy over it, so that it looked like a bed in which a princess might sleep.

A thought occurred to Judith about the sweet-scented, flowery bedroom. "Where does your father put his things?"

"Oh, Pops has got his own bedroom because he snores and keeps everybody awake. Come on, I'll show you more."

After a tour of the other family bedrooms they went downstairs.

Judith was beginning to feel a bit bemused, but Loveday was inexhaustible.

"This is Pops's study. And in here the billiard room; sometimes the men come here after dinner and play. And the dining room, all laid for lunch, as you can see. Come and meet Mrs. Nettlebed."

"Who's that?"

"Our cook, and she's married to Mr. Nettlebed, our butler. They have a little flat over the garage."

A butler. It was all becoming grander and grander.

And so they came at last to the kitchen. This was the same as most Cornish kitchens, except that it was much larger. There was the familiar rack for airing clothes, hoisted high to the ceiling, the dresser loaded with china, the table in the middle of the floor.

At this stood Mrs. Nettlebed, arranging bits of glacé fruit onto the top of a trifle. She was a small, dumpy lady in a white apron and cap. When Loveday burst in, Mrs. Nettlebed's round cheeks bunched up into a besotted expression of pure delight. Loveday, it was instantly obvious, was her treasure and her joy.

"My dear life. There's my baby!" She held her sticky hands wide and leaned forward for the kiss which Loveday pressed upon her cheek. "Look at you! Soon be taller than me. This is your friend?"

"She's called Judith."

"Pleased to meet you, Judith. Come for the weekend? Up to high jinks you'll be with this little tinker."

"What's for lunch, Mrs. Nettlebed?"

"Shooter's stew and boiled cabbage. I just heard the men in the yard. Shouldn't be more than ten minutes."

"Ten minutes." Loveday made a face. "I'm starving. Come on, Judith. Let's go and find Mummy."

They found Diana in the drawing room, curled up in the corner of a vast cream sofa, reading a novel. She raised her head to smile. "Darlings, there you are. What do you want to drink?"

A mirrored table stood against one wall, neatly arranged with bottles and glasses. Loveday went to inspect its offerings. She said, "I really feel like Orange Corona, but there isn't any."

"That dreadful stuff that turns your mouth orange? Ring for Nettlebed, and we'll find out if he has a bottle tucked away."

Loveday pressed a bell in the wall above the table. Diana asked Judith, "What do you think of my darling house?"

"It's beautiful. But I'm not sure that this room isn't the nicest of all." With a parquet floor scattered with rugs, it was filled with sunlight and exotic hothouse blooms, all purple and white and fuchsia. The curtains and slipcovers were cream brocade, the sofas and chairs filled with cushions in pale greens and pinks and blues.

Judith longed to take in every detail so that if she never came again to this house, she would be able to keep a perfect picture of it in her mind.

The door behind them quietly opened and a deep voice was heard. "You rang, madam?"

Mr. Nettlebed. Loveday had not prepared Judith for his awesome appearance. He was tall, white-haired, and quite handsome in a gloomy way. Judith wondered how anybody plucked up the nerve to ask him to do anything, let alone give him an order.

"Oh, Nettlebed, thank you," said Diana. "Loveday wants some Orange Corona. Would you see if there is any in the pantry?"

"Certainly," said Nettlebed. "I shall go and ascertain."

He went, closing the door behind him. Loveday grimaced. "He's a pompous old—"

"*Loveday,*" Diana interrupted. Her voice had turned icy.

Judith felt awkward, but Loveday was undismayed. She went to lean over the back of the sofa, her curly dark head almost touching her mother's sleek golden one. "What are you reading?"

"A novel."

"What's it about?"

"Love. Unhappy love."

"I thought all love was happy."

"Oh, darling. Not every woman is lucky." She reached for her drink, a little triangular cocktail glass filled with silvery liquid. As she took a sip, the door of the drawing room opened once more.

"Pops!" Loveday left her mother's side and fled into his arms.

"Hello, my baby." They hugged and kissed, he stooping to her. "We've missed you." He ruffled her hair, smiling down at his youngest child as though she were the most precious creature on earth. So loved was Loveday by everybody that Judith found it hard not to feel a small pang of envy.

"Diana"—he crossed over to kiss his wife—"are we late?"

She tilted her head to smile up into his face. "Not at all. Did you have a good morning?"

"Splendid. Tommy's on his way, and Jeremy's cleaning my gun for me."

Standing on the sidelines, Judith assumed a bland expression, hiding her shock at his appearance. For Colonel Carey-Lewis was so much older than in the photo she had seen that he looked more like Diana's father than her husband. True, he held himself with the stance of a soldier, but his hair was white, his nose long and beaky, and his eyes, deep in his lined face, were the faded blue of some ancient countryman. He was tall and spare, dressed in venerable tweeds and moleskin knickerbockers.

He turned to Judith. "And you must be Loveday's friend?"

She looked up into his eyes and saw them both watchful and kindly. Then he smiled. "How very pleasant that you could come," he said, and they shook hands formally. She realized instinctively that he was just as shy as she felt. This made her like him very much.

At this moment they were interrupted by the appearance of a second gentleman, with, hard on his heels, Nettlebed, who bore a bottle of Orange Corona on a silver salver.

"Diana, are we all in disgrace for taking so long?"

"Oh, darling Tommy, don't be silly. Have a good morning?"

"Great fun." Tommy Mortimer stood for an instant rubbing his hands together, as though grateful to be out of the cold. He too was dressed for shooting, in elegant tweeds and a canary-colored waistcoat. His face was boyish and good-humored, his whole manner theatrical. "Here I am," it seemed to say. "Now we can all start having a wonderful time."

He crossed the room to drop a kiss on Diana's cheek, then turned to Loveday. "Hello there, wicked one! Got a kiss for your honorary uncle? How's school? Have they turned you into a lady yet?"

"Oh, Tommy, don't ask such stupid questions. This is Judith Dunbar, and this, ta-ra, ta-ra, is Tommy Mortimer."

Tommy laughed, amused by her impudence. The Colonel by now had had enough of formalities. It was time for a drink. Nettlebed poured a dry martini for Mr. Mortimer, beer for the Colonel, Orange Corona for the girls. Tommy came to sit on the sofa beside Diana, with an arm gracefully disposed along the back of the cushions. Judith wondered if he was an actor.

As she sipped her Orange Corona, she did not notice the last member of the shooting party enter the room. A much younger man, bespectacled, dressed in corduroys and a hefty sweater, he paused just inside the door. Judith looked up and saw him watching her. For an instant they stared, and then he smiled. "It is you, isn't it? The girl on the train?"

He came across the room to her side. Judith was so delighted that she was unable to speak, so she simply nodded.

"What an extraordinary coincidence. Are you Loveday's friend?"

She smiled and nodded again. "I'm Judith Dunbar."

"Jeremy Wells."

"Jeremy!" From the sofa, Diana had spied him. "You must have tiptoed in. Are you introducing yourself to Judith?"

He laughed. "I don't need to. We've already met. On the train."

Everybody was suitably amazed by the coincidence and wanted to hear all the details. How they had shared the compartment and gazed from the Saltash Bridge at the naval men-of-war.

"How's your little sister?" Jeremy asked.

"She's gone. Back to Colombo with my mother. And then they're moving to Singapore. My father's got a new job."

"Will you be joining them?"

"No. Not for years."

It was lovely. It was like being a grown-up—dressed in Athena's clothes, and sipping a drink, and having everybody delighted because she had a friend of her own. She remembered telling Phyllis about him and saying, *I wouldn't mind meeting someone like that.* And now he was here. Now she knew him properly. It had really happened.

From the hall, the gong for luncheon rang out. Diana handed the empty glass to Tommy Mortimer, rose to her feet, and led the way to the dining room. The Colonel said, "Judith, you must tell me more about how you and Jeremy came to meet."

THE Colonel sat at the head of the long dining table, with Loveday and Judith placed on either side. Diana was at the far end, with Tommy on her left and Jeremy at her right. Mary Millyway, who had appeared as they all settled down, had taken her seat and was talking to Jeremy—whom she had obviously known forever—being brought up to date on his work at the hospital.

The meal was delicious. The stew was dark and rich, with a winy sauce, and the cabbage, lightly dusted with grated nutmeg, was green and sweet. Nettlebed, having handed around the platters, had withdrawn, soft-footed, from the room. Judith was relieved to see him go. His chilling presence was enough to make anybody knock over a glass of water.

Now, however, she was beginning to enjoy herself. The Colonel was being very courteous and hostly, and making her feel at home.

The bell was rung for Nettlebed to return, and the pudding was served. Syrup tart and bottled plums and Cornish cream. The Colonel now turned his attention to Loveday, who had a great deal to tell him about the iniquities of school, the impossibility of learning algebra, and the hatefulness of Matron.

Judith spooned cream over her syrup tart and heard Tommy Mortimer and Diana laying plans for London—for the Chelsea Flower Show, and Wimbledon and Henley and Ascot.

All at once Diana became aware of Judith. She smiled. "I'm sorry. We're being boring. And this is your day. Tell me, what do you want to do this afternoon?" She raised her voice slightly. "What does everybody want to do this afternoon?"

Loveday said, "I want to ride Tinkerbell."

"Darling, what about Judith? Perhaps it would be kind to do something that she wants to do."

"I don't mind," Judith said, fearing some sort of argument, but Loveday didn't seem to care about arguments or rows.

"Oh, Mummy, I really want to ride Tinkerbell. And it's not good for her not being regularly exercised."

"I don't want you going out on your own."

"She won't be on her own," the Colonel told her. "Young Walter's down at the stables this afternoon. I'll send word to him to have the horses saddled up and ready."

Down the table he indulgently regarded his wife. "How are you going to spend the rest of the day? I've letters to write."

"Oh, Tommy and I are all arranged for. I've asked the Parker-Browns over for bridge. But that still doesn't solve the problem of our guest."

Judith felt dreadfully embarrassed, a tiresome nuisance. Then Jeremy Wells said, "Why don't I do something with Judith? We'll all go down to the stables, and she and I will take the dogs on to the cove." He smiled at Judith, and she was filled with gratitude,

because he had come so easily to her rescue. "Would you like to do that?"

"Yes, I'd love it."

Diana beamed. "Well, isn't that splendid? Everything settled. Judith, you'll adore the cove, our own little beach. Now, why don't we go to the drawing room and have coffee."

The two girls stayed in the dining room to help Mary and Nettlebed clear the table and then went upstairs to prepare for their expeditions. Mary produced extra pullovers for them, and Loveday's jodhpur boots, her string gloves, her hard hat, and a crop. "Off with you," she said. "And when you get back, I'll have tea ready here."

Like puppies escaping, they galloped downstairs to the drawing room. Loveday opened the door. "Jeremy! We're ready."

"I'll meet you in the gun room. In one minute."

They went on their way. The back passage led to the gun room, which smelled pleasantly of linseed oil and old mackintoshes and

dog. Tiger was there, ready for a bit of exercise. He was a huge black Labrador, with a tail that wagged like a piston.

"Hello, darling Tiger. Are you going to come for a lovely walk?"

"Of course he is," said Jeremy, coming in with Pekoe.

Loveday said, "Come on, then. Walter will be waiting."

The stables lay a little way from the house, screened from sight by a coppice of young oak trees. They approached the yard, where two mounts were saddled up and tethered to iron rings set in the wall: Tinkerbell, and Ranger, the Colonel's hunter. Tinkerbell was a charming little gray pony, but Ranger was a great bay, seeming, to the wary Judith, the size of an elephant.

A young man stood with the animals, tightening the girth strap of the little gray. "Hello, Walter," Loveday called. "You're all ready!"

"Mr. Nettlebed sent word." He ducked his head at Jeremy. "Hello, Jeremy. Didn't know you were down. Coming out with us?"

"No, not today. We're going to the cove. This is Loveday's friend, Judith Dunbar."

Walter nodded at Judith. He said, "Hello."

He was an extraordinarily good-looking young man—slim and dark and sunburned as a Gypsy, with black hair that covered his head in curls and eyes dark as coffee beans. He wore corduroy breeches, a thick shirt striped in blue, and a leather waistcoat. He made Judith think of Heathcliff in *Wuthering Heights*, and she could see why Loveday was so keen to go riding. Even Judith could understand the lure of the horse if one was to have the dashing companionship of Walter Mudge.

Judith and Jeremy stood and watched them mount. Walter swung himself up into the saddle with an effortless grace that suggested that he might, just slightly, be showing off.

"Have fun," Judith told Loveday.

She raised her crop. "You too."

As hoofs clattered across the yard, Judith asked, "Where will they go?"

"Probably up to the moor. Come on. It's too cold to stand."

They went the way that the riders had taken and then turned off to the right, where the path sloped down through the gardens. The dogs shot ahead and were soon lost to view. "They won't get lost, will they?" Judith, feeling responsible for their well-being, was anxious, but Jeremy reassured her. "They know this walk as well as anybody. By the time we've reached the cove, they'll be there."

He led the way and she followed, along a winding graveled path which led in the direction of the sea. The formal lawns and flower beds were left behind them as they passed through a small wrought-iron gate. Then the path narrowed and plunged downwards into a jungle of semitropical vegetation—camellias, lush thickets of bamboo, and tall-stemmed palms. A stream appeared from the undergrowth of ivy and moss and fern, and tumbled its way down a rocky bed. The path where they walked crossed and recrossed the stream by means of ornamental wooden bridges, contrived in designs that were vaguely Oriental. Once over the last bridge, Jeremy paused, waiting for Judith to catch up. "Now we come to the tunnel."

He set off once more. She saw that, ahead, the sloping path plunged into a cavern of gunnera, that prickly stemmed plant with leaves large as umbrellas. Judith had seen gunnera growing before, but never in such daunting profusion, and it took a small effort of courage to duck her head and follow her guide into the tunnel. It was like being underwater, so damp was everything, so aqueous and green.

Moments later they emerged from the primeval gloom and stood once more in the bright winter afternoon. The air was sweet with the tang of seaweed, and she knew that they were close to the beach. With some care they scrambled down rough-hewn steps into a disused stone quarry. On the far side of the quarry, a grassy bank sloped up to a wooden gate. They climbed the bank and then the gate, and jumped down onto the tarmac of a narrow farm road. On the far side of this was a drystone wall, and then, finally, there were the low cliffs and the sea—intensely blue, flecked with white-caps.

The cliffs were not steep, and a turfy track led down to the rocks and a curving sickle of white sand. Gulls hung screaming overhead, and waves thundered up onto the shore. As Jeremy had promised, the dogs were already there. Otherwise there was no living soul to be seen.

"Does anybody ever come here?" Judith asked.

"No. I think most people don't even realize that the cove exists."

Jeremy climbed down to a wide shelf of rock overhanging the sand, and she followed. He smiled at her. "It's such a perfect place. This rock is where we have picnics. Why don't we sit down for a moment."

Which they did, shifting about to find a perch on the hard rock. And Judith was warmed by the dazzling sunshine and by the easy presence of her companion.

She said, "I am glad you brought me to see it. But I hope you don't feel that you had to. I'm very good at doing things on my own."

"I'm sure you are. But don't worry. I wanted to come. I like it here." He sat with his elbows resting on his knees, squinting out to sea through his spectacles.

They fell silent. Judith thought of Loveday and Walter, probably cantering over the moors, but the tiny twinge of envy she had known was gone. Better to be here, and with this nice man.

After a bit she said, "You know it all so well here, don't you? I mean Nancherrow. As though it were your own home."

Jeremy leaned back on his elbows. "I've been coming here for years. I got to know the Carey-Lewises because of my father being their family doctor. Then as I grew older, the Colonel sort of took me under his wing, began to ask me to shoot with him, which was immensely kind."

"And Athena and Edward? Are they your friends too?"

"They're a good deal younger than me, but yes. When Athena was first going to dances, I used to be given the responsibility of being her partner—not that she ever danced with me, but I was considered reliable enough to get her home in one piece."

"She's very beautiful, isn't she?"

"Ravishing. Like her mother. Men fall about her like ninepins."

"And Edward?"

"Edward I got to know very well, because when I was a medical student, I was perpetually short of cash, so the Colonel offered me a holiday job. I suppose you'd call it being a tutor. Edward needed extra coaching to get into Harrow. So I spent a good deal of time around and about."

"I see why you seem to be part of the family."

"One becomes absorbed. And you? Had you any idea what to expect when you were invited to Nancherrow?"

"Not really."

"The first impression is something of an experience. But I don't think you've been overwhelmed."

"No." She thought about this. "But only because they're all so nice. If they weren't, it would be a bit frightening. I mean, butlers and ponies and nannies. Is Colonel Carey-Lewis frightfully rich?"

"The money is Diana's. She was the only child of an immensely wealthy gentleman called Lord Awliscombe. When he died, she was well provided for."

Diana, it seemed, had been blessed with everything. "She must have had a very special fairy godmother. To be so beautiful and wealthy and charming. And still so young."

"She was only seventeen when she married Edgar. He's much older than Diana, of course, but adored her all her life and finally won her. And it's been a great marriage."

"If he loves her so, doesn't he mind about Tommy Mortimer?"

Jeremy laughed. "Do you think he should mind?"

She was embarrassed, as though she had sounded like some dreadful prig. "No, it just seems . . ." She floundered. "I won-dered if he was an actor."

"All those expansive gestures and the mellifluous voice? An easy mistake to make. No. He's a jeweler. His family owns Mortimer's, in Regent Street. His great cry is that he loves only Diana, but I think he enjoys being a bachelor and playing the field. He looks after Diana when she disappears up to London, and he comes down here when he feels in need of a spot of fresh air."

It was still difficult to understand. "Doesn't the Colonel *mind?*"

"I don't think so. They've worked out their own lives. Diana has this little mews house in London, and she needs to escape to the city from time to time. Edgar hates London. *His* life is Nancherrow and the farm and the estate. A busy man."

At this juncture the dogs, having had enough of sand and sea, came scrabbling up over the rocks. At the same time, the wind turned cold. The time had come to move on.

They got back to the house by five o'clock. "Mary'll be expecting us, with her kettle on the boil," Jeremy said. "I want to wash my hands. I'll meet you in the nursery."

Judith went upstairs to her room. But it felt different now. She was returning to Nancherrow, not seeing it for the first time. She pulled off the cashmere sweater and went into the bathroom to wash her hands with scented soap. Then she brushed her hair and tied it neatly back. Her face in the mirror was rosy with exercise and fresh air. She turned off the light and went in search of tea.

Jeremy was already there, sitting at the table with Mary and Loveday and buttering himself a hot scone. The fire was blazing, and the curtains were drawn against the darkening evening. "Did you love the cove, Judith?" Loveday asked.

"It was beautiful. And did you have a good ride?"

Yes, Loveday said. She had had a perfect afternoon, with plenty of adventure. Tinkerbell had jumped a four-barred gate, and Ranger had been spooked by a sack blowing on a thorn hedge, but Walter had been brilliant and managed to calm him down again. And on the top of the moor they had galloped for miles, and it had all been absolute heaven, and she couldn't wait to go out with Walter again.

Jeremy leaned back in his chair and stretched. "If I don't go now, I shan't be home in time for supper." He pulled himself to his feet, and as he did so, the door opened and Diana appeared.

"Well, here you all are, gorging. Jeremy, you look as though you're about to leave us."

"I'm afraid so. Thank you for the lunch and everything." He said his good-byes to everyone, went to the door, and was gone.

Diana came to settle herself on the sofa. "Judith, what about that beautiful box you brought with you? You promised you'd show it to me. Bring it over here, and we'll look at it now."

And so the next ten minutes or so were spent in Judith's displaying the charms of the cedarwood box. Diana was gratifyingly enchanted, opening and shutting the tiny drawers. "Where are you going to keep it?"

"I suppose at Aunt Louise's. I'll take it at half term."

"Why don't you leave it here," Diana said. "In your bedroom. So every time you come to stay, it will be waiting for you."

"*Here?* But . . ." She was going to be invited to return. That was all she could think.

"And you must bring some clothes and leave them here as well, just as though this were your other home. Then you won't have to wander around in Athena's castoffs."

"I've loved wearing them. I've never had a cashmere pullover."

"Then we'll hang it in your cupboard. The beginning of your Nancherrow wardrobe."

It was Sunday morning. On the other side of the village of Rosemullion, Lavinia Boscawen lay in her downy double bed and watched the night sky lighten with the dawn. The curtains were drawn back as far as they could go because she had always believed the outdoors, with its scents and sounds, was too precious to be shut away.

The curtains were very old—not as old as Mrs. Boscawen herself, but as old as the nearly fifty years she had lived in the Dower House. Sunshine and wear had faded and shredded them. No matter. Once they had been pretty, and she had chosen and loved them. They would see her out.

This morning it was not raining. For that she was grateful. Although at eighty-five she had stopped striding up and down to the village, it was still pleasant to be able to spend an hour or two pottering about in the garden.

Today her nephew Edgar and dear Diana were coming for luncheon, bringing Loveday and Tommy Mortimer and Loveday's school friend. It would be interesting to discover what sort of a girl that naughty, wayward child would choose to bring home for the weekend.

For luncheon there would be a pair of ducklings, fresh vegetables, a lemon soufflé, and bottled nectarines. The luncheon would mean a lot of work for Isobel.

Isobel. In old age Lavinia had very few worries. But Isobel *was* a bit of a worry. Ten years younger than Lavinia, she was getting beyond all the cooking and the caring which had been her life for forty years. Yet whenever Lavinia brought the conversation around to the subject of Isobel's retirement, Isobel would become huffy and hurt.

Downstairs a door opened and shut. Lavinia stirred on her piled linen pillows and turned to reach for spectacles on the bedside table. She looked at the time: seven thirty. She could hear the stairs creak, footsteps across the landing. A cursory knock, and Isobel appeared bearing on a tray Lavinia's early morning glass of hot water, in which floated a slice of lemon.

Isobel said, "Morning. Some cold it is." She set down the tray on the table. Her hands were gnarled and reddened, and her frizzy gray hair was scraped back into a bun.

"Oh, thank you, Isobel." Then on impulse Lavinia said, "I do hope you're not going to have to do too much today. Perhaps we should stop having luncheon parties."

"Now don't start that again." Isobel fussily tugged at the curtains. "Anyway, it's all on the road. Table laid, all the vegetables done. Like a fried egg for your breakfast?"

"Thank you. That would be a treat."

Isobel departed. Her footsteps faded, treading cautiously down the staircase. Lavinia drank her hot lemon water, thought about the lunch party, and decided that she would wear her new blue dress.

LOVEDAY's behavior that morning made it clear that Great-aunt Lavinia was one of the few people—perhaps the only person— capable of exerting any influence on her wayward personality. She dressed without the slightest objection in the clothes which Mary Millyway had set out for her—a checked woolen dress with shining white collar and cuffs, white kneesocks, and black patent leather shoes.

Finding Loveday in the nursery, having her hair brushed by

Mary and looking so unusually smart, Judith started to worry about her own appearance. "I can't go out for luncheon in *shorts,* can I?" she appealed to Mary. "And I don't want to wear a uniform."

"I'll find you a nice skirt, and I'll polish up your shoes for you. Then you'll be bright as a new penny."

The skirt, purloined from Athena's cupboard, was a tartan kilt. Mary wrapped it around Judith's waist and fixed the leather straps. "There. Perfect." She smiled. "Lovely, you look. As though you wouldn't call the king your cousin."

By the time the nursery party put in its appearance at breakfast, the others were already there. Diana wore a pale gray flannel coat and skirt, so immaculately cut that it rendered her slender as a wand. The Colonel and Tommy Mortimer were equally formal, wearing suits with waistcoats.

Later in the morning they drove to Rosemullion, all five of them in the Colonel's Daimler, to attend services at the tiny church. Afterwards he decided they would leave the car and walk to their luncheon engagement.

They took the narrow, winding road up the hill from the village. Tall stone walls stood on either side. In ten minutes, rather breathless, they reached their destination, an open gateway in the wall on the right, where a narrow drive curved away between neat hedges of escallonia.

The little party followed the drive. And then the Dower House stood before them. It was not large, but possessed a dignity that at once impressed. A square house, tucked into the shelter of the hill, whitewashed, with Gothic windows, a gray slate roof, and a stone porch smothered in clematis.

As they approached, an elderly woman emerged onto the porch.

"Good morning, Isobel."

"Morning, Mrs. Carey-Lewis. Lovely, isn't it, but chilly yet. Come along in. Take your coats, shall I?"

Judith, unbuttoning her school coat, looked covertly about her. The Dower House was like stepping back in time. So old—certainly pre-Victorian—so perfectly proportioned, so quiet that over the murmur of voices the slow tocking of the grandfather clock was clearly audible. The hallway was flagged in slate and laid with rugs, and an airy circular staircase rose from this, curving up beneath a Gothic window.

Diana led the way through an opened door into the drawing room. "Aunt Lavinia!" Her voice was warm with genuine pleasure. "You are a saint to tolerate such an invasion."

As Lavinia Boscawen greeted her guests, Judith hung back, not because she was shy, but because there was so much to look at. A pale room, flooded with sunshine which streamed through tall windows. Soft pinks and creams and greens. A long bookcase crammed with leather-bound volumes, an ornate Venetian mirror over the mantelpiece. In the grate a small coal fire flickered, and the sunshine sparked into rainbow brilliance the faceted drops of a crystal chandelier.

"Judith."

She realized with a start that Diana had said her name.

"Come and say how do you do. Aunt Lavinia, this is Loveday's friend, Judith Dunbar."

Mrs. Boscawen waited, sitting very upright in a chair, her blue woolen dress flowing to her ankles. She was old. Wonderfully old. Her cheeks were netted with wrinkles, but her faded blue eyes sparked with interest.

"My dear." She took Judith's hand in her own. "How delightful that you were able to come. Not very exciting perhaps, but I do love meeting new friends. Now come and find somewhere to sit. Edgar, will you see that everybody has a sherry. We've ten minutes before Isobel rings her gong. Diana, my dear, what news of Athena?"

At the base of the windows was a long cushion. With attention elsewhere Judith went to kneel upon it, to look out over the deep, roofed veranda to the sloping garden. At the foot of the lawn stood a coppice of Monterey pines and, beyond it, the distant blue line of the sea. It was as though they had all been magically transported to some Italian villa high above the Mediterranean.

"Do you like gardens?" Again the old lady was addressing her.

"I like this one especially," Judith told her.

"You are a child after my own heart. After luncheon we shall put on coats and go out and look around."

"*I'm* not going to," Loveday interrupted. "It's far too cold."

"I don't suppose anyone else will want to," Aunt Lavinia observed gently. "But that won't stop Judith and me enjoying a walk. We can get to know each other. Ah, my sherry. Thank you, Edgar." She raised her glass. "And thank you all, so much, for being here."

201

Judith sat with her back to the window and reached to take a tumbler of lemonade from the Colonel. Opposite, Loveday caught her eye and broke into a wicked grin. Judith's heart, all at once, brimmed with affection for her. And gratitude too, because Loveday had already shared so much with her, and now, because of Loveday, she was here.

AUNT Lavinia had not forgotten her promise and, when lunch was over, brought Judith out of doors for a little tour. She had put on a pair of stout gardening boots and an immense tweed cape. An ebony cane kept her steady and was useful for pointing.

"As you can see, my land slopes all the way down the hill. When we came here, I wanted a garden in compartments, each with its own character. So we planted escallonia and privet hedges and trained the gateways into arches. You see?" They passed beneath the first archway. "My rose garden. All old-fashioned roses."

"How long have you lived here?"

Aunt Lavinia paused, and Judith decided that it was pleasant to be in the company of a grown-up who seemed to be in no hurry and happy to chat. "Nearly fifty years now. But my home, when I was a child, was Nancherrow, and this was the Dower House for Nancherrow. My grandmother lived here when she was as old as I am. We rented it for years, and when my husband retired, we were able to buy it. We were very happy here. Now. . . Next we come to the children's garden. Has Loveday told you about the Hut?"

Judith, bewildered, shook her head.

"No, I don't suppose she would. The Hut was never hers the way it was Athena's and Edward's. They used to spend whole days here and, when they were older, were allowed to sleep out—so much more fun than a tent, don't you think? Come along."

She led the way, down a flight of stone steps into a little orchard of apple and pear trees. Across the orchard, tucked in a sheltered corner, stood the Hut. It was like a log cabin, with a shingle roof and two windows on either side of a blue door. At the front was a porch with wooden steps and a fretwork rail. It wasn't a child-size house, but a proper place, where grown-ups could come and go without ducking their heads.

Judith said, "Who comes here now?"

Aunt Lavinia laughed. "No one, really. But I keep it aired, and each year it gets a good coat of creosote. Here's the key. Go and open the door."

Judith went ahead, ducking beneath the branches of apple trees, and so up the two steps to the porch. She opened the door. Inside, she saw two bunks, one on either side beneath the slope of the roof; a table and two chairs; a rag rug. The windows were hung with blue-checked curtains, and there were blue blankets and cushions on the bunks. Above her head a hurricane lamp hung from a hook. She imagined the Hut in darkness, with the lamp lit and the blue curtains drawn, and the thought occurred to her, rather sadly, that perhaps at fourteen she should be too old for such innocent joys.

"So what do you think of it?"

Judith turned, and Aunt Lavinia stood in the open doorway.

"Perfect."

"I thought you would be charmed." The old lady peered about her. "Poor little house. It needs company. We need babies, don't we? A new generation." She smiled. "Perhaps it's time to return. I am glad you are Loveday's friend. I think you are a good influence."

It was the half-term holidays, and Judith was spending them with Aunt Louise at Windyridge. Sitting in her bedroom at her desk, she chewed her pen as she grappled with a dilemma. She loved her parents but was wise to their shortcomings. Which made it difficult to tell them about Nancherrow, simply because it had all been so unbelievably wonderful, and they themselves had never enjoyed such a glamorous lifestyle. They did not have friends with large houses, who took luxury and ease for granted. So if she went into elaborate detail about the grandeur of Nancherrow, perhaps it would seem as though Judith were somehow criticizing their own simple way of life. And the last thing she wanted to do was to distress them.

Then inspiration struck: Jeremy Wells, the young doctor on the train, putting in such an unexpected appearance and giving up his afternoon to show Judith the cove. With him to write about, the letter would be easy. She started off, the words flying across the paper.

She thought of sunny Nancherrow, wishing she were there with Loveday instead of at Aunt Louise's soulless house, with only her aunt and the cook and the housemaid for company.

There had been much gloom in the dormitory that Friday morning in early March when they awoke to dismal weather. At ten o'clock the boarders streamed out to the various waiting cars. Aunt Louise was there in her old Rover. On the journey through the rain, sitting beside Aunt Louise as she had clashed her gears and pressed hard upon the accelerator, Judith had closed her eyes and expected instant death. But somehow they had reached Penmarron, and Windyridge, the house rearing up through swirling mist.

Hilda, the maid, had come to the door to help carry suitcases upstairs, and Judith followed her. Staring out of her bedroom window now, she tried to think of cheerful things. The new bicycle, to be bought in Porthkerris. Four days of freedom from school. She would telephone Heather and make some plans.

Over lunch, which was chops and stewed apples, Aunt Louise showed interest in the visit that Judith had paid to the Carey-Lewises, and asked about the garden.

"It's full of lovely things. There are hydrangeas all the way up the drive. And camellias and things. And they've got their own little beach."

After lunch they drove to the Porthkerris bicycle shop. They agreed on a dark green Raleigh with a black saddle, three speeds, and its own pump for blowing up the tires. The rain had, obligingly, stopped, and when they returned to Windyridge, Aunt Louise watched Judith mount the bike and do a couple of turns around the path which circled the lawn.

"Well," said Aunt Louise, "and how's that?"

"It's absolutely perfect. Oh, thank you, Aunt Louise." Hanging on to the handlebars, she planted a kiss on Aunt Louise's unreceptive cheek. "I'm going for a ride now. Round the village."

"Off you go, then. Enjoy yourself." And with that, she went indoors to her knitting.

IT WAS heaven, like flying. Spinning down the hill and through the village, she sailed past the shops, the post office, and the pub, and cycled on. The air was sweet, and the tires of the bicycle skimmed over the bumps and puddles, and she felt as though she could have traveled to the ends of the earth.

But the afternoon was fading, and it was time to head for home. The road ran uphill, with fields on one side and the golf links on the other. Pedaling furiously, she discovered that it was much steeper than she had imagined. Alongside the clubhouse, she dismounted, resigning herself to pushing the bicycle.

"Hello there." Judith stopped and turned to see who had called. A man was coming through the clubhouse gate. He was dressed for golf, in baggy plus fours and a yellow pullover, and wore a tweed cap at a rakish angle. "You must be Judith."

"Yes, I am," said Judith without any idea who he could be.

"Your aunt told me you'd be here for the weekend." He had a florid complexion, a mustache, and a pair of bright and knowing blue eyes. "I'm Colonel Fawcett. Billy Fawcett. Old friend of Louise's, from India. Now I'm her next-door neighbor."

Recognition dawned. "Oh, yes. She told Mummy and me about you. You were a friend of Uncle Jack's."

"That's right. Same regiment." He eyed the bicycle. "That's a handsome piece of kit. Walking, are you? I'll walk with you, if I may."

It was rather annoying to have her solitude disturbed, but she said, "Yes, of course," and they set off, talking in a polite but stilted fashion. At the gate of Windyridge she paused, expecting him to say his good-byes. But Colonel Fawcett made great play of pushing back the cuff of his pullover and squinting at his wristwatch.

"Quarter past five. Well, I've a few moments to spare, so why don't I come in with you and pay my respects to Louise?"

Judith could think up no objection to this. And so together they went up the graveled path. At the front door, "I have to put my bicycle in the garage," she told him.

"Don't worry. I'll let myself in," and without even knocking, he opened the door and went inside.

Left alone, Judith made a private grimace at his retreating back. She did not approve of his high-handed behavior. But perhaps Aunt Louise was fond of him and did not object to his bursting in uninvited. Thoughtfully she wheeled the bicycle into the garage.

In the sitting room she found him already settled by the fire, looking as though he had been there forever. Aunt Louise had poured him a drink and picked up her knitting.

"And how are you going to spend your weekend, Louise?" He had taken his first large mouthful, cradling the glass in his stubby fingers. "Made plans?"

"I'm playing golf on Sunday with Polly and John Richards, and a friend they've got staying."

"So how are you going to spend your day?" Billy Fawcett cocked an eye at Judith.

"I'll probably visit a friend in Porthkerris."

"Can't have you kicking your heels on your own. Always available if you need a bit of company." Judith pretended not to hear this. She was not certain if she liked Colonel Fawcett.

He laid down his tumbler and reached into his pocket for a cigarette. He lit up, and Judith saw that his fingers were stained with tobacco. His mustache looked a bit frizzled too.

"How about a visit to the pictures?" he suddenly suggested. "They're showing *Top Hat* at the Porthkerris cinema. Fred Astaire and Ginger Rogers. Why don't you let me take you both. Tomorrow evening. My treat, of course."

Aunt Louise seemed a bit taken aback. Perhaps this was the first time that Billy Fawcett had offered to pay for anything.

"That's very good of you, Billy. What about you, Judith? Or perhaps you've already seen it?"

Judith had been wanting to see *Top Hat* for ages. But she would have preferred to go with Heather; together they could have swooned contentedly over the glamorous pair gliding over the dance floor. It wouldn't be quite the same with Aunt Louise and Billy Fawcett.

"No. I haven't seen it."

"Would you like to go?" asked Aunt Louise.

"Yes." There wasn't much else to say. "Yes, I'd love it."

"Splendid." Billy Fawcett slapped his tweeded knee. "When shall we go? Six-o'clock show? I'm afraid you'll have to be the chauffeur, Louise. My old banger's coughing a bit."

"Very well. If you come here, we'll all go together. It's very kind of you."

"A pleasure. Two lovely ladies to escort." He reached for his tumbler, drained the whisky, and sat on, empty glass in his hand.

Aunt Louise raised her eyebrows. "The other half, Billy?"

"Well." He gazed into the empty glass, as though surprised to see it in such a sad state. "Well, if you insist."

"Help yourself."

So he heaved himself to his feet and went to the drink tray. Watching him, Judith thought he looked quite frighteningly at home. She wondered about his bungalow and decided it was probably cheerless and cold. Perhaps he was dreadfully poor. Perhaps that was why he seemed to be insinuating himself into Aunt Louise's well-ordered life. Perhaps, horror of horrors, he was *courting* Aunt Louise, with marriage in mind.

Judith decided to forget her instinctive fears. Aunt Louise was far too sensible to make any rash commitment. But the idea, once planted, had taken root, and there was no way of ignoring it.

THE next morning she rang Heather.

"Judith! What are you doing?"

"It's half-term weekend. I'm with Aunt Louise. I wondered if I could see you tomorrow. Could I come over?"

"Oh, darn it. We're going up Bodmin for the weekend to visit my gran. We're leaving in about five minutes. I didn't know you'd be home. What's school like? Made any friends?"

"Yes. It's not bad."

"And your mum? Had a letter yet?"

"Yes. Lots. And they're all right, and Jess is all right."

"Look, I'll see you Easter holidays. Ring me up and we'll fix something. I've got to go, Judith. Dad's tooting the horn. Don't forget. Ring me."

"I won't."

She went, feeling flat, to tell Aunt Louise the bad news.

"Oh, dear. Never mind. With a bit of luck, tomorrow will be fine and dry, and you can go out on your bicycle. Perhaps up to Veglos Hill. All the wild primroses are out up there. You can bring me back the first bunch of the season."

"Yes. I suppose so." But it was still disappointing.

Billy Fawcett presented himself at the door at half past four. They piled into the Rover, Billy in the front with Aunt Louise. On the way, Billy turned in his seat to grin at Judith, and she saw his yellowed teeth and his twinkling eyes. "How about tomorrow? Get hold of your chum?"

Judith looked out the window and pretended not to hear, praying the subject would be dropped. But Aunt Louise let spill the beans. "Unfortunately, Heather's away."

Billy Fawcett eyed Judith. "So you'll have to fill in your own time, eh? Well, if you need a bit of company, I'm just down the road."

He turned to face ahead once more, and Judith, rude as Loveday, put out her tongue at the back of his head.

They came coasting down the hill into town. Aunt Louise parked the car, and they crossed to the cinema. Billy Fawcett lined up at the ticket office to pay for the seats, while Aunt Louise and Judith gazed at the shiny black-and-white photographs which advertised the film. A thrill of anticipation shivered down Judith's spine, but Aunt Louise only sniffed. "I do hope it's not going to be *silly*."

The inside of the cinema was cramped and stuffy. Judith was about to edge her way into a row, but Billy Fawcett intervened. "Ladies first, Judith. Let's see your aunt comfortably settled." Which meant that Judith sat between them.

The lights dimmed. They watched trailers for the next show. Then there was the news—Herr Hitler strutting around, reviewing some parade. And then, at last, *Top Hat.*

"Thank goodness," said Aunt Louise. "I thought it was never going to start."

But Judith hardly heard her. Settled deep in her seat, her eyes glued to the screen, she was caught up in the sight and sound of the story being told. And before long, there was Fred Astaire on a stage, tapping and juggling his cane. The plot thickened, and he met Ginger Rogers and pursued her, and sang, "Isn't This a Lovely Day to Be Caught in the Rain?" and then they danced together.

It was at this juncture that Judith became aware that Billy Fawcett was restless, shifting around. She changed her position slightly, to give his legs more space and, as she did so, felt something on her knee. The something was Billy Fawcett's hand, which stayed there, heavy and uncomfortably warm.

The shock of this destroyed all concentration. She continued to stare at the screen, but saw nothing as she grappled with this alarming crisis. What was she meant to do? Did he know that his hand was on her knee? Did he perhaps think it rested on the narrow arm which divided the cramped velvet seats? Should she tell him?

But then his fingers tightened and gripped, and she knew that his intrusion was no accident. His hand moved higher, up her thigh. In the darkness she sat in terrified horror, wondering where he would stop and how she could possibly alert Aunt Louise.

Up on the screen something amusing had taken place. The audi-

ence burst into peals of laughter. Under cover of this sound Judith
pretended she had dropped something, slid out of her seat, and
landed on her knees, jammed between the two rows of seats.

"What on earth," Aunt Louise demanded, "are you doing?"

"I've lost my barrette."

"Leave it, then, and we'll find it at the end of the film."

"Shh! Quiet!" came a furious whisper from the row behind.

"Sorry." With some difficulty she wriggled back into her seat,
this time squeezed so close to Aunt Louise that the armrest dug
into her rib cage. Surely now he would leave her alone.

But no. Another five minutes and the hand was there again.
Fondling, moving, creeping upward. . . .

She sprang to her feet.

Aunt Louise became exasperated. "Judith, for heaven's *sake*."

"I have to go to the lavatory," Judith hissed. "Let me by."

"Shh! Other people are watching. Do you mind being quiet?"

"Sorry."

She went clambering over Aunt Louise's knees and the knees of
all the other irritated people in their row. She sped up the dark aisle
and at the back found the ladies' cloakroom, and went in and sat,
and nearly cried with disgust and despair. That horrible man. Why
did he have to touch her? The idea of going back into the cinema
gave her the shivers. She just wanted to go home and never, ever
have to see him again.

She had thought Billy Fawcett rather pathetic and ridiculous.
Now she felt ridiculous too, and demeaned as well. So demeaned
that she knew she could never bring herself to tell Aunt Louise
what had happened. The mere idea of looking her in the eye and
saying "Billy Fawcett tried to put his hand up my knickers" was
enough to make her burn with shame.

One thing was for sure: She would go back into the cinema and
would not budge until Aunt Louise took Judith's seat beside Billy
Fawcett and let Judith take her own place. She would stand and
argue until Aunt Louise was forced, out of sheer embarrassment, to
do as Judith insisted. Billy Fawcett was *her* friend, and she could
jolly well sit next to him.

THE March sky, which had been clear, with a brilliant full moon,
suddenly darkened, and a wind sprang up from nowhere, howling

about the house on the hill. She lay in bed, terrified, and stared at the square space of the window, waiting for what was inevitably going to happen. Over the sound of the wind, she heard footsteps on the gravel and then a thump as the top of a wooden ladder was set against the windowsill. She lay still. There was nothing else to do. He was coming, with his manically twinkling eyes and his hot and fumbling fingers. And then his head came over the windowsill, and he was smiling.

Billy Fawcett.

Judith sat up in bed and screamed, but it was daylight now, she was awake, and the terrible image mercifully faded. There was only her own window and the morning light beyond.

A dream. Her heart thudded like a drum. She was trembling. And the dream was gone, but the problem of Billy Fawcett remained.

She thought about facing Aunt Louise over breakfast. Aunt Louise had been very good about the disaster at the cinema, saying no word until she and Judith were back at Windyridge alone.

After the film was finished, they had piled into the Rover and returned to Penmarron, Billy Fawcett keeping up a perky conversation all the way. As they approached the gates of Windyridge, he said, "Drop me here, Louise my dear, and I'll make my own way home. Splendid of you to drive us."

"We enjoyed ourselves, Billy. Didn't we, Judith?" The car halted, and he clambered out. "Thank you for our treat."

"A pleasure, my dear. Bye, Judith." And he had the effrontery to wink at her. Then he was on his way.

At the house, Aunt Louise had not been really angry, simply at a loss to know what on earth had got into Judith. "Hopping about like that, and all the fuss about sitting in *my* seat."

Which was all quite reasonable. Judith apologized. "I am sorry about everything."

"I was quite enjoying the film too. I didn't think I would, but it was amusing."

"I thought it was funny too," Judith fibbed. In fact, she couldn't remember anything about it at all.

The row, it seemed, was over. Aunt Louise led the way into the dining room, where Edna had left them a cold mutton supper.

But Judith was not hungry. "You all right?" Aunt Louise asked. "You look dreadfully pale. Why don't you pop off to bed."

Now, the morning after, Judith felt not only tired but grubby. Contaminated by the unspeakable Billy Fawcett and his prowling hand. She flung back the rumpled sheets and went across the landing to have a bath and wash her hair. Then, feeling marginally better, she put on clean clothes and went downstairs.

Aunt Louise, dressed for golf, was sipping coffee, cheerfully looking forward to her game. "How did you sleep? Did you dream of Fred Astaire?"

"No. No, I didn't." Judith helped herself to bacon and eggs.

Her aunt glanced at the window. "It looks quite a promising day. Do you want to go off on your bicycle, or is there something else you'd like to do?"

"No. I think I *will* go up Veglos and look for primroses for you."

"I'll get Edna to make a sandwich and pack it in a haversack. And maybe a bottle of ginger beer. She and Hilda are off at ten today."

Later, brogued and wearing a beret, and with her clubs stowed on the back seat of the Rover, Aunt Louise departed for the club. In the kitchen, Judith's picnic had been assembled on the table. The specter of Billy Fawcett, lurking just down the road, meant that there was no time to hang about. With the haversack slung across her shoulder, Judith let herself out the back door, wheeled her bicycle out of the garage, and sped away.

It was a bit like escaping. Furtive, swift, and secret. But the awful thing was that as long as Billy Fawcett was around, this was how it was going to be.

THE following afternoon Aunt Louise drove Judith back to St. Ursula's, dressed once more in school uniform. So much for the midterm break, Judith thought.

"Hope you've enjoyed yourself."

"Very much, thank you. I really like my bike."

"I'll keep an eye on it for you."

Judith couldn't think of anything else to say, because the bike was really the only good thing about the weekend. All she wanted now was to get back to the familiar surroundings of school.

DEIRDRE Ledingham opened the library door. She said, "So *there* you are."

Judith looked up. It was an afternoon in late March, and she had come to the library to do some reading for an English literature essay.

"Miss Catto wants to see you in her study. Better not keep her waiting," she added bossily.

After that first interview Judith was no longer terrified of Miss Catto. Now, having neatened herself up and only slightly apprehensive, she went to the study.

Miss Catto was there, behind her desk, just as before. "Judith! Come and sit down."

She complied, and Miss Catto came straight to the point. "The reason I sent for you has nothing to do with school. I am afraid it is going to come as something of a shock, so I want you to prepare yourself. It's your aunt Louise. . . ."

Judith stopped listening. She knew instantly what Miss Catto was about to tell her. Aunt Louise was going to marry Billy Fawcett. The palms of her hands went clammy, and the blood drained from her cheeks. The nightmare was going to come true.

Miss Catto's voice continued. Judith tried to concentrate on what her headmistress was saying. Something about last night. ". . . driving home from a bridge game at about eleven o'clock . . ."

The truth dawned. She was talking about Aunt Louise and her car. Nothing to do with Billy Fawcett.

". . . an accident. A terrible collision." Miss Catto paused. "Are you all right, Judith? You understand what I'm trying to tell you?"

She nodded. Aunt Louise had had a car smash. That was it. Aunt Louise driving too fast, as always. "She's all right?"

"Oh, Judith, no. I'm afraid she's not. She was killed instantly."

Judith stared at Miss Catto, her face filled with defiant disbelief, because she knew that something so violent and final simply couldn't be true. And then saw the compassion in Miss Catto's eyes and knew that it was.

Dead. Aunt Louise. She heard herself take a deep breath that sounded like a shudder. She said calmly, "Where did it happen?"

"Up on the road that goes over the moor. A truck had broken down, been abandoned. No light. She drove into the back of it."

Aunt Louise driving home in the darkness. "Who told you?"

"Mr. Baines. He's your aunt's solicitor in Penzance. I believe he has sent your father a telegram. He will, naturally, follow this up with a letter. And I will write to your mother."

"But what about Edna and Hilda?" For the first time real distress sounded in Judith's voice. "Aunt Louise's cook and her housemaid . . . They'll be terribly upset."

"Yes, I'm afraid they are. The local constable broke the sad news. They have decided to stay in your aunt's house for the time being."

Judith said, "Will there be a funeral?"

"Yes, of course. And I shall come with you."

"I've never been to a funeral."

Miss Catto rose to her feet, crossed to the window, and gazed out. "Funerals are a part of death, Judith, as death is part of life. That is a desolate thing for someone of your age to come to terms with, but you're not alone. I am here to help you through it. You are being very brave, but don't feel constrained. Don't be afraid to cry."

But tears, with their easing, had never seemed further away.

"I'm all right."

"Good girl. I think it would be nice to have a cup of tea. Would you like that?"

Judith nodded. Miss Catto rang for a housemaid, then settled herself in an armchair by the hearth. She said, "I only met your aunt a couple of times, but I liked her so much. There was no nonsense about her. I felt quite at ease knowing you were in her charge."

Which brought the conversation to the vital question. Judith made her voice as casual as she could. "Where will I go now?"

"We must talk about that."

"I have Aunt Biddy."

"Of course. Mrs. Somerville, in Plymouth. Your mother gave me the address and telephone number. I will contact her."

A knock sounded on the door, and one of the housemaids put her head into the room. "Oh, Edith, could you bring us a tea tray?"

The girl withdrew, and Miss Catto continued. "Would you like to spend your holidays with your aunt Biddy?"

"Yes. I love her and Uncle Bob. They're really nice and fun."

"Well, we'll work something out. Just remember that you are surrounded by friends. Now come and sit here by the fire."

Sunday, 5th April 1936

Dear Mummy and Dad,

I know that you have got telegrams and that Miss Catto and Mr. Baines are both writing to you. It was dreadfully sad about Aunt

Louise and I shall miss her very much, because she was so kind.

As for me, please don't worry. I could have gone to Aunt Biddy for the Easter holidays, but she is very occupied just now with a new house which she has bought in Devon and she's taking care of her parents, who have both been ill. But I am sure that I can stay with the Warrens in Porthkerris for a bit. And then I can go to Aunt Biddy in the summer.

The funeral was last Thursday. Mr. Baines came in his car and took Miss Catto and me. The service was in Penmarron Church and there were lots of people there and a great many flowers everywhere.

Here Judith became stuck. Memories of the funeral were blurry. Known faces had swum into her vision from time to time; it was hard to put names to them. But Billy Fawcett had been there. She had spied him standing at the back of the church looking at her, and with a new courage bolstered by the presence of her headmistress, she met his eye and stared him down. Before he turned away, she saw on his face an expression of pure hatred.

He was not amongst the mourners at the graveside, and for this small mercy Judith felt grateful. But his was a recurring specter, still haunting her dreams. Shivering in the wind, she had wished that it was *he* they were about to inter in this grave and not Aunt Louise. It was all so dreadfully unfair. Why should Aunt Louise be snatched away to eternity while that gruesome old groper lived on?

But no time for brooding, because she had to finish her letter.

Tomorrow afternoon Mr. Baines is coming to school and I have to see him to talk about what he calls family affairs. I suppose to do with school and things, but have no idea what this means.

MR. BAINES had established himself behind Miss Catto's desk and littered it with a lot of documents. He was a very tall man, with brindled hair and enormous horn-rimmed spectacles. In his tweed suit and checked shirt he looked the very epitome of a successful country solicitor. Mr. Baines, on the day of the funeral, had been extremely kind. Now he came out from behind the desk and brought forward a chair for her. Then he returned once more to his papers.

"First I want to set your mind at rest about Edna and Hilda. I have found a position for them with an old client of mine who lives up near Truro. A single lady, pleasant working conditions." He smiled.

"Oh, thank you." Judith felt most grateful. "It sounds absolutely perfect."

Mr. Baines opened a folder. "Now, down to business. Before she died, your aunt drew up a comprehensive will. Generous annuities have been arranged for Hilda and Edna. Everything else, her entire estate, she has left to you."

Judith gazed at him. "It sounds an awful lot."

"It is a lot," said Mr. Baines gently.

"But . . ." Mr. Baines was being very patient, watching her. "Why me? Why not Dad? He's her brother."

"Your father has a sound job, a career, and future security. And your aunt Louise was very fond of you. She saw, I think, a great potential. She wanted you to have the freedom to be your own person and to make your own choices."

"But . . . I see." It sounded overwhelming. Worrying, even.

"She has left you her house and everything in it. And most important, her capital investments."

"But what would I do with her house?"

"I think it should be put on the market and the resultant sum of money invested." He leaned forward, his arms on the desk. "You have to understand that your aunt Louise was a *very* wealthy lady. She has left you substantially provided for."

It was all very puzzling. "The Dunbars were never rich. Mummy and Dad were forever talking about economizing."

"Mrs. Forrester's fortune was not Dunbar money. Jack Forrester was a man of considerable private means. Everything he had he left to his wife. Your aunt. She, in turn, hands it on to you."

"It's hard to imagine, exactly, what it all means." She frowned.

"It means security and independence for the rest of your life. You will always be in control of your own affairs, able to handle them just as you see fit. Does the prospect alarm you?"

"A bit."

"Don't be alarmed. For the time being, the inheritance will be administered by trustees. I shall be one of them, and I thought we should ask Captain Somerville to join the team."

215

"Uncle Bob?" Mr. Baines had done his homework. "Yes."

"I'll get something drawn up. And meantime, I'll arrange an allowance for you. You'll need to buy clothes, books, all the small expenditures that parents or guardians normally deal with."

"Thank you very much."

"You'll be able to go shopping. I'm sure there must be something that you've been yearning for."

"Well, I'm saving up for a gramophone, but I haven't got far."

"You can buy a gramophone," Mr. Baines told her. "And a stack of records. Perhaps there is something of Mrs. Forrester's that you would like to keep?"

"No." Judith had her desk, her books, her bicycle. And her cedarwood box at Nancherrow. "No. There's nothing I want."

"Right." He started to gather together his documents. "That's it, then. We'll have another meeting, and I'll fill in any details—"

At this moment the door opened, and they were joined by Miss Catto. "Not interrupting, am I? Given you enough time?"

Judith rose to her feet. Mr. Baines too stood, towering over the pair of them. "Plenty of time. And thank you for letting us have the use of your study."

He packed his briefcase and came around from behind the desk. "Good-bye, then, Judith." He beamed benevolently down on her and loped from the room.

She turned to face her headmistress. There was a moment's pause, and then Miss Catto said, "Well? How does it feel to know that financial security so simplifies life?"

"I never knew Aunt Louise was wealthy."

"It was one of her greatest assets—a total lack of pretension. And I think your aunt has paid you a great compliment."

"Mr. Baines says I can buy a gramophone. And a collection of records like Uncle Bob's."

She smiled at that. "I have more news for you. I have had a long chat on the telephone with Mrs. Carey-Lewis. She was deeply distressed to hear about Mrs. Forrester's death. And she says that of course you must go to Nancherrow for the Easter holidays." She paused. "You look astonished. Are you pleased?"

"*Yes.*" Nancherrow. A month at Nancherrow with the Carey-Lewises. It was like being offered a holiday in paradise, unthought of and unimagined. "I . . . Yes, I would like to go."

"Then I'll accept, conditionally, on your behalf. I must get your mother's permission. But I can send a cable."

"I'm sure she'll say yes. But all my things are at Aunt Louise's house."

"That can be taken care of. Mrs. Carey-Lewis told me that you already have your own bedroom at Nancherrow, and there is plenty of room for everything."

"I don't know how anybody can be so kind."

"People are kind. There's just one more thing to remember: To talk of money, the excess or lack of it, is vulgar to the extreme. One either boasts or whines, and neither makes for good conversation. Do you understand what I am saying?"

"Yes, Miss Catto."

"Good girl. Now, I've got history essays to correct, and you must be on your way."

SHE walked out of the study thinking of Nancherrow, and the best was knowing that she was going to stay for the whole of the Easter holidays. She would go back to the pink bedroom, where the window looked down onto the courtyard and the doves and where her cedarwood box awaited her. And she would wear Athena's clothes and become once more that other person. The strange thing was that she felt like that other person even now, because everything, already, was different.

She thought about Aunt Louise and tried to feel grateful, though sad, but was incapable of feeling anything very much. She thought about being very wealthy. So what did she want above all else? A car? A house? Roots perhaps. A home and a family and a place to go to that was forever. Belonging. Not just staying with the Carey-Lewises, or Aunt Biddy, or even the cheerful Warrens. But all the money in the world couldn't buy roots. She knew that.

She tried to sort out the momentous confusion of the day. Maybe for now it was simply going to have to be a case of taking one thing at a time. Easter holidays and then back to school. School for four years and, after that, with a bit of luck, a voyage to Singapore. The family once more—Mummy and Dad and Jess. After Singapore perhaps England again. Oxford or Cambridge.

She found herself yawning. She was weary. Tired of being a grown-up, with all a grown-up's decisions and dilemmas. She wanted Loveday. To giggle and whisper with and to concoct plans for their time together at Nancherrow.

Saturday, 11th April

Dear Mummy and Dad,

Thank you for sending the cable to Miss Catto and saying that I can spend Easter with the Carey-Lewises. This is the first day of the holidays and it's ten thirty in the morning, and someone from Nancherrow is going to come and collect me at eleven. The reason I didn't go home yesterday, with Loveday, is because Mr. Baines wanted to take me shopping in Truro to buy a gramophone.

"Judith!" Matron, in her usual bossy fluster. "For heaven's sake, what are you doing? The Nancherrow car is here, and they're waiting. They've got your luggage. Now hurry up."

Judith sprang to her feet, gathering up the pages of her letter and bundling them into her attaché case. By the time she had pulled on her coat and jammed on her hat, Matron was on her way, a bustle of starched apron, down the corridor.

Outside, it was a beautiful morning, with a blue sky and sailing clouds. Judith's luggage had already been stowed, and beside the car, leaning against the hood and yarning companionably, stood two male figures. One was Palmer, the Nancherrow gardener and chauffeur. The other was a stranger, young and blond, dressed in a white polo-necked pullover and a pair of corduroys. When he saw Judith and Matron emerge through the door, he came across the drive to meet them. "Hello there." He held out his hand. "You're Judith. How do you do. I'm Edward."

Loveday's brother. He had his mother's blue eyes, and strong, chunky features. Though full-grown and broad-shouldered, he still wore the youthful face of a boy—tanned and very smooth and fresh-complexioned—and his friendly grin was a flash of even, white teeth. Despite the informality of his clothes, his appearance was so glamorously adult that Judith wished she had taken time to comb her hair.

Politely, she shook his hand. "Hello."

"We're early, I know, but we've got some things to do in Penzance. Now, are you ready?"

"Yes, of course."

"Thank you for finding her, Matron." Edward smoothly took

charge, ushering Judith into the car with a touch of his hand on her back. As they rolled down the drive between the rhododendrons, Judith settled herself in her seat and pulled off her hat.

"Sorry it's us come to fetch you, but Pops has got some meeting or other, and Ma's taken Loveday to a pony-club rally." A lock of fair hair fell across his forehead, and he put up his hand to push it back. "Do you like horses?"

"Not particularly."

"Thank heavens. One in the family's quite enough. I personally could never be doing with them. One end bites, the other end kicks, and they're uncomfortable in the middle. Anyway, that's why Palmer and I are here. You know Palmer, don't you?"

"I've seen him at Nancherrow. I don't think we've ever been introduced."

"That's all right," said Palmer over his shoulder. "I know all about you. Coming to stay for a bit? That'll be nice."

"In another month," Edward explained, "I'd have fetched you myself, because I'll be driving by then. I mean, officially. I drive around Nancherrow, but I'm not able to go out onto the main road until I'm seventeen. Incidentally, I've got to go to Medways to get measured for a new tweed. Do you mind hanging around for a bit?"

"No." In fact, she felt quite pleased, because hanging around meant time spent in the company of this engaging young man.

"It won't take long. And Pops said I could give you lunch at the Mitre, but it's such a stuffy old place." He leaned forward. "Palmer, what's that pub called in Lower Lane?"

"You can't take the young lady into a pub. She's underage."

"We can pretend she's older."

"Not in that uniform."

Edward looked at Judith. She hoped that she wouldn't blush. He said, "No, I suppose not. Well, we'll find somewhere splendid that isn't the Mitre."

Judith said nothing to this. The Mitre had always been her idea of a really special place to be taken for lunch. But now, it seemed, it was stuffy, and Edward had more lively ideas. Wherever they went, she hoped she would be able to deal with it all, and order the right sort of drink, and not drop her napkin. Despite these private anxieties, it was impossible not to feel rather excited.

By now they were in the middle of the town, heading towards the

219

Greenmarket. "This is perfect, Palmer. Drop us here. And perhaps pick us up in a couple of hours."

He leaned across Judith and opened the door. She got out, and he followed, and they walked together down the sunny, crowded pavement in the direction of Medways.

It was funny coming back. The same gloomy interior, high-collared assistants. But different. Because last time she had come here, she had been with her mother, both of them feeling their way into a new life. On that day, she had seen Diana and Loveday Carey-Lewis for the first time and been dazzled by them. And here she was, a few months later, strolling casually into the shop with Loveday's glorious elder brother. Circumstances had taken over her life.

"Good morning, Edward." The tailor had emerged from some dim back room, with his tape measure slung around his neck.

"Morning, Mr. Tuckett." He and Edward shook hands.

"Tweeds for shooting, the Colonel said. Shall we get on with measuring you up? If you'll come this way."

"You'll be okay, Judith?"

"Yes. I'll wait." She found a chair and settled down.

Eventually Edward and Mr. Tuckett reappeared from beyond the curtain, Edward hauling his sweater back over his head. Now came the choice of tweed, and thick books of samples were produced. Was it to be Harris Tweed or Yorkshire tweed, dogtooth or herringbone? Finally Edward made his choice, a Scottish thornproof in a sludgy green, with a faint red-and-fawn overcheck.

Mr. Tuckett said, "I shall order it immediately," and he saw them to the door with as much flourish as Nettlebed himself.

On the pavement, Edward let out a sigh of relief. "Phew. That's over. Let's go and find a drink and something to eat." And he put a hand beneath her elbow and steered her across the road.

What he found was a pub with a small garden, so Judith didn't need to go into the bar. There were tables dotted about, and over a low stone wall a good view of the harbor. Judith said she would have Orange Corona to drink, and he laughed and went indoors, ducking his head under the low doorway. Presently he came out again, with her orange and a tankard of beer and a luncheon menu.

"It's not quite as upmarket as the Mitre, but at least we're spared that deathly hush, broken only by the mouselike scrape of cutlery on china." He frowned at the bill of fare in an exaggerated grimace. "Sausages and mash. Homemade Cornish pasties. Let's go for the pasties."

"All right."

"And for afters you can have trifle, jelly, or an ice cream."

A woman in a pinafore came out to take their order. Edward gave it, his lordly manner belying his sixteen years. He was really, Judith marveled, extraordinarily sophisticated.

She sipped her drink. It was a good place to be. Better than the Mitre. Fun to sit in the open air, with the wheeling, gliding gulls making their endless racket around the fishing boats.

"I didn't realize that you were back from school already."

He smiled. "Why should you?"

"I thought Loveday might have told me."

"Some hope. She thinks of nothing but that wretched pony."

Across the wooden table his smile faded. Suddenly serious, he said, "Ma told me about your aunt being killed. Ghastly. I'm sorry. It must have been the hell of a shock."

"Yes, it was. But I'm afraid she never drove very carefully."

He said, "I went to her house. Palmer and I were detailed to take the farm truck over and bring back your stuff. Mary Millyway has probably unpacked your clothes by now. Ma told me very firmly that the pink bedroom is yours."

"She's been so kind. Everybody has been."

"No skin off her nose. And she likes a mass of people around." He looked up. "Oh, hurray, here come our pasties. I was beginning to feel faint with hunger."

The pasties were enormous, steaming, and fragrant. When Judith cut hers in two, bubbling morsels of steak and potato slipped out. A breeze gusted from the sea and blew her hair over her face. She pushed it back and smiled at her companion.

"I'm so glad," she told him in a burst of contentment, "that we didn't go to the Mitre."

BACK at Nancherrow, Judith settled into the pink bedroom, feeling it was really hers now because all her things were there. Mary Millyway had made space for her desk and her books and had unpacked all her clothes. It was six o'clock and a beautiful evening, and beyond the window Judith could hear the doves in the courtyard. Loveday and Diana weren't back from the pony club yet, so Judith sat down to finish the letter to her parents.

Please write soon and tell me everything you are doing. Or tell Dad to take some snaps so that I can see if Jess is growing.

Everything is changing so quickly that sometimes it is quite difficult to keep up. I wish I could be with you and talk about it all. I suppose growing up is always a bit lonely.

Lots of love, and please don't worry. I'm all right.

❧❧ *1938* ❧❧

*I*N SINGAPORE, in her Orchard Road bungalow, Molly Dunbar awoke with a start, in a sweat of panic, consumed by some nameless fear. Ridiculous, she said to herself, because it was not even dark, but midafternoon. Siesta. No ghouls, snakes, or intruders. A nightmare perhaps.

After a little the terror evaporated. So nothing. Just her own imaginings flying in all directions, as usual, even as she rested next to her husband, safe in her own bed.

She looked at her watch. Three o'clock on an April afternoon and the heat almost unbearable. On the far side of the bed Bruce was snoring lightly. She envied his ability to sleep away the tropical afternoon. Cautiously, so as not to wake him, she got up, drawing a thin wrapper about her. Treading softly, she went through the slatted doors onto the wide, shady veranda. Beyond it the garden simmered under a bleached sky.

It was immensely quiet. Jess, servants, dogs still slept. Molly sank into a long rattan chair. Alongside was a cane table, with all the small necessities of her sedentary life: her book, her sewing box, magazines. Today it also bore Bruce's three-week-old copy of the London *Times.*

Molly picked up the newspaper. The date was March the fifteenth, and the headlines leaped at her, for on the twelfth of March, Nazi Germany had occupied Austria.

Old news now, of course. They had heard it on the wireless almost as soon as the shocking event had taken place. Bruce, though grim-faced, had not talked about it very much, and Molly had simply pushed it out of her mind. There was a photograph.

Hitler, driving in state through the streets of Vienna, his car flanked by German troops. If this, she asked herself, had been allowed to happen, then what on earth was going to happen next?

In London, in Parliament, the mood was grave. Winston Churchill had stood to speak, and his warnings tolled like a death knell. "Europe is confronted with a program of aggression . . . only choice open . . . to submit or take effective measures."

She folded the newspaper and dropped it to the floor. Effective measures meant war. If there was a war in Europe, if England was involved, then what would happen to Judith? Should they not send for her right away? Forget about school, jettison the plans they had made for her, and bring her out to Singapore. War would never touch them here.

But even as the idea occurred to her, she was sure that Bruce would not agree to it. He could not imagine England in mortal danger. Judith would be perfectly safe. Ridiculous to panic.

She knew this because she had heard it all before. When Louise had been killed, and Molly was all for getting the first passage home, Bruce had insisted that there was no point in taking impulsive action. Judith was at boarding school, Miss Catto was in command, and Biddy Somerville close to hand if needed. "But she has no *home*," Molly had wept. "I could be *with* her." But Bruce was adamant. And because Molly had no money of her own with which to travel, there was nothing she could do.

Molly did her best to come to terms with the situation. And in the end Bruce had been maddeningly right. All the problems had sorted themselves out, and the void left by the death of Louise was filled by this benevolent family called Carey-Lewis.

She remembered that day in Medways when she had seen Diana Carey-Lewis for the first and only time. Their lives had touched only for a moment, but she still retained a vivid image of the beautiful youthful mother and the bright-faced ragamuffin child. Molly was grateful that Mrs. Carey-Lewis had taken Judith into her home. Now it was two years later—Judith would be seventeen in June—and in all that time scarcely a week had passed without the arrival of a long, loving, dear letter, with all the news a mother would want to hear. The earliest letters were of school, of life at Windyridge, the shock of Louise's death, and Judith's astonishing inheritance. Then the visits to Nancherrow and Judith's gradual absorption into the Carey-Lewis clan. Later there was news of a Christmas with Biddy and Bob in their new house in Devon; a half term with Heather and the Warrens in Porthkerris; a trip to London with Diana Carey-Lewis and Loveday to stay with Athena at Cadogan Mews and to go on a round of shopping and luncheons, culminating in an evening at Covent Garden to see the Russian Ballet.

All the trials and treats of a girl growing up. And Molly, her mother, was missing it all. It was so unfair, she told herself on a surge of resentment. It was all wrong. And yet she knew that she was not alone in this. Her anguish was shared by thousands of other British wives and mothers.

She sighed. Behind her, indoors, the bungalow was stirring. Amah's soft voice from Jess's bedroom, rousing the child from sleep. Jess, now six, had grown tall and slender. Soon Bruce would emerge, neatly turned out for the office, and later it would be time for afternoon tea: the silver teapot, the cucumber sandwiches. She must pull herself together, shower and dress, and then present herself once more as a respectable memsahib.

AT SEVENTEEN Judith was as excited about Christmas as a small child, counting the days until the end of term. From Loveday she had gleaned scraps of information concerning plans laid and guests to be invited to Nancherrow.

"We're going to be the most enormous houseful. Mary Millyway is counting sheets like a maniac, and Mrs. Nettlebed is up to the eyes in mincemeat. Athena's coming from London, and Edward's going to Arosa to ski, but he's promised he'll be back in time."

Which caused Judith a tremor of anxiety. It sounded as though it was going to be the best Christmas ever. But how awful if Edward didn't make it home. He was grown now, had left Harrow and done his first term at Cambridge, and seeing him again was part of her excitement. In fact, a big part. She wasn't in love with him, of course. Being in love was something that you fell into with film stars or other beings safely unattainable. But his presence added such life to any occasion that it was hard to imagine any celebration being complete without him.

At last the final morning of term, the annual carol service in the chapel, and then home. Judith and Loveday escaped out into the bitter cold. Palmer was there, and they were soon away.

At Nancherrow, they found a huge spruce erected in the hall. As they came in through the front door, Diana hurried down the stairs to meet them with a garland of holly in one hand and a long festoon of tinsel in the other.

"Oh, darlings, there you are. Judith, heaven to see you."

"Who's here?" Loveday asked.

"Only Athena so far, and not a cheep yet from Edward. Pops and Walter Mudge have taken the tractor and gone to find me masses more holly. And Athena's writing Christmas cards."

"Now, what was I doing?" Diana gazed, as though for inspiration, at her tinsel and her holly. "Decking halls, I think. Why don't you go and find Mary." Already she was drifting off in the direction of the drawing room. "See you at lunch."

Alone in her pink bedroom, the first thing Judith did was to change out of her uniform and put on proper, comfortable clothes. She was rummaging in her suitcase for a hairbrush when she heard Athena calling her name. "I'm here," Judith said.

The next instant Athena was there. "Just popped along to say hello and season's greetings and all the rest." She flopped languidly down on Judith's bed and smiled. "How's everything?"

Judith sat back on her heels. "Fine."

Of all the Carey-Lewis family Athena was the one she knew least well, and consequently, Judith was always a bit shy. It wasn't that Athena wasn't friendly or funny or easygoing, because she was all those things. She was just so sensationally glamorous and sophisticated that the impact of her presence was apt to stun. She didn't have a proper job, and done with Switzerland, she now spent most of her time in London, roosting in her mother's little house and leading a life of pleasure. Men buzzed about her, and whenever she was at Nancherrow, she spent much time on the telephone, placating lovelorn swains.

But Judith was sympathetic. In a way it must be a terrible responsibility to be possessed of such beauty. Long blond hair, flawless skin, and enormous blue eyes fringed with black lashes. Athena was as tall as her mother, slender and long-legged, and she wore very red lipstick and red nails and was always dressed in the height of fashion. Despite all this, she was sweet and generous and not in the least swollen-headed.

Now she curled up her legs and settled herself comfortably for a chat. "How's school? Aren't you getting utterly sick of it? I nearly went mad with boredom when I was seventeen. All those ghastly rules. Edward said he never realized how stultifying Harrow was until he left. I think Cambridge has opened up a whole new world for him."

"Have—have you seen him lately?"

"Yes. He spent a night in London with me before setting off for Arosa. We had a lovely time, lots of catching up on news. He's joined the University Flying Club, and he's learning to fly an airplane. Don't you think that's frightfully brave?"

"Yes, I do," Judith said with total truthfulness.

"What are you going to wear for Christmas feasties? Have you got something new?"

"Well, yes. It's made out of a sari. Mummy sent me a sari for my birthday, and your mother helped me draw a picture, and her dressmaker made it." It felt very companionable, discussing clothes with Athena. Loveday never talked about clothes, because she didn't care how she looked.

"Sounds sensational. Can I see it?"

Judith went to open the wardrobe and to reach for the padded hanger on which hung the precious dress. She held it in front of her, spreading the skirts to reveal their width. So fine was the silk that it all felt light as air. Around the deep hem the gold key pattern of the sari's border glittered with reflected light.

Athena's jaw dropped. "It's divine. And what a color. Not turquoise and not blue. Utterly perfect." Judith felt warm with delight. It was reassuring to have Athena, of all people, so genuinely enthusiastic. "And you must wear gold earrings. I'll lend them to you."

She watched Judith replace the dress in the wardrobe and then looked at her wristwatch. "Goodie. It's a quarter to one. I'm starving. Let's go down before Nettlebed starts banging his gong." She rose from the bed. "Isn't it heavenly to know it's holidays and you've got days and days? All the time in the world."

JUDITH was awakened by the wind, a gale which had risen during the night, howling in from the sea, clouting at the window. The morning had not yet started to lighten, so she lay in bed thinking of the day ahead.

Although parcels were already piling up under the tree, Judith had not yet got a single present for anybody. She brooded about this for a bit, then got up, sat at her desk, and made a list. Only three days in hand. Swiftly she got dressed and went downstairs.

It was now eight o'clock. Breakfast at Nancherrow started at half past eight, but she knew that Colonel Carey-Lewis was always early. She opened the dining-room door, and he lowered his paper and looked up.

"I know I'm interrupting you," she said, "but I've got a problem," and she explained about the Christmas presents. "So if there was a car going to Penzance, I could go too and shop."

He smiled and immediately offered her a ride into town. He planned to go to the bank there anyway and then on to his club. Then at about twelve thirty they could rendezvous for lunch at the Mitre.

"Oh, I am so grateful," she told him.

IN PENZANCE that morning the streets ran with water, and gutters overflowed, and beleaguered shoppers struggled with umbrellas, only to have them blown inside out. Bundled up in boots, a black oilskin, and a woolen hat, Judith fought her way from shop to shop, gradually becoming laden with parcels.

At half past eleven she found herself in the stationer's, having bought presents for everybody except Edward. She thought about it, then plunged once more out into the rain and set off for Medways.

Even this old-fashioned shop was touched by seasonal cheer. Paper bells hung from the lights, and there were more customers than usual. An elderly salesmen approached her, and Judith said, "A scarf. Something bright. Not navy or gray. Red perhaps."

"We've got some lovely tartan scarves. They're cashmere, though, and quite pricey."

Cashmere. A tartan cashmere scarf. She imagined Edward with such a luxury knotted casually around his neck. She said, "I don't mind if it's a bit expensive."

"Well, let's have a look, then, shall we?"

She chose the brightest—red and green with a dash of yellow—and the salesman retreated to wrap it. Standing there, waiting, she looked about her with affection, for this fuddy-duddy old shop had been the unlikely venue for momentous memories.

"There you are now, miss." He had wrapped the scarf in holly paper. "And this is your bill."

Judith wrote her check, and as she handed it over, somewhere from behind her a voice said her name. She turned and found herself face to face with Edward.

The shock lasted an instant, to be replaced by a joyous leaping of her heart. "*Edward!* What are you *doing* here?"

"Came looking for you."

"I thought you were still in Arosa."

"Got back this morning, on the night train from London." He laid a hand on her arm. "We can't talk here. Let's get out." He looked down at the parcels. "Is this all yours?" He sounded disbelieving.

"Christmas shopping."

"Have you finished?"

"I have now."

"Then let's go." He was already gathering up her packages, making his way towards the door, and she hurried after him. Then they were out in the rain-driven streets, heads down against the wind, crossing the road for the shelter of the Mitre Hotel.

In the lounge, there was a welcome fire and no other people to disturb them. Edward piled her packages on the floor, and Judith took off her oilskin and hat and tried to do something about her hair. There was a mirror over the mantelpiece, and she saw her face, cheeks rosy from the wind and eyes bright as stars. Happiness shows, she thought, and she turned to face him.

He looked wonderful. Very tanned and hard and fit. He had divested himself of the sodden ski jacket and beneath it wore corduroys and a navy-blue roll-necked sweater. She said, "You look great."

"So do you."

"We didn't know when you were coming home."

"I wouldn't miss Christmas for all the skiing in the world." He smiled at her. "Got in at seven o'clock. It seemed a bit early to start ringing home and demanding transport, so I left my stuff at the station and walked up to Pops's club and beat on the door until somebody let me in. I spun a sob story. Told them I'd been traveling for two days. So they let me have a bath, and then some kind lady cooked me breakfast."

228

"Edward, what nerve you've got."

He grinned mischievously. "And just as I was finishing breakfast, who should walk in but Pops."

"Was he as astonished as I was?"

"Just about. And he told me he'd brought you into town and was meeting you here at twelve thirty. So I came to look for you."

"What made you think of Medways?"

"Well, you weren't in any other shop, so I finally ended up there." He grinned again.

The very thought of him, in this appalling weather trudging around Penzance in search of her, filled Judith with a warm glow.

He said, "What have you been doing with yourself?"

"Nothing much. Just school. I only got back from St. Ursula's yesterday. But tell me about Arosa."

"Terrific," he told her. "Fantastic snow. We skied all day and danced most of the night. There's a new bar, Die Drei Husaren, where everybody goes. We were usually swept out at four in the morning."

We. Judith suppressed an unworthy pang of envy. "Athena told me you're learning to fly."

"I've learned. I've got my pilot's license. It's bliss. Easy as driving a car and a million times more fascinating."

"I think you're dreadfully brave."

"Of course," he teased her, "the original intrepid birdman." He checked his watch. "It's a quarter past twelve. Pops will be here before long. The sun's over the yardarm, so let's have a glass of bubbly."

"Champagne?"

"Why not? You don't hate it, do you?"

"I've never drunk it."

"Then now is a good time to start." And he called for the waiter.

"But . . . in the middle of the *day*, Edward?"

"Of course. Champagne can be drunk at any hour of the day or night; that's one of its charms. Besides, what better way is there for you and me to start Christmas?"

JUDITH sat at her dressing table, leaned anxiously towards the mirror, and for the first time applied mascara to her eyelashes. Athena's Christmas present to her had been a beautiful casket of

cosmetics, and the least she could do was to try them. She checked her reflection now; it was wonderfully improved.

It was seven o'clock on Christmas evening, and she was dressing for the climax of the holiday, Christmas dinner. Beyond her door the house was filled with small sounds. A clatter of dishes. Mrs. Nettlebed calling to her husband. The faint strains of a waltz— probably Edward trying out the gramophone, should they want to dance after dinner.

Judith brushed out her hair and coaxed the ends under into a gleaming pageboy. Now, the dress. She went to her bed, where she had laid out the butterfly-blue concoction. She lifted it, weightless as gossamer, over her head, felt the thin silk settle over her body. Next the gold earrings which Athena had lent her. The new lipstick—Coral Rose—the new scent, and she was ready.

She surveyed herself in the long mirror. It was marvelous. She looked really grown up. Eighteen at least. And the dress was a dream. She turned, and the skirts floated out around her, just like

Ginger Rogers's, just the way they would float if Edward asked her to dance. She prayed that he would.

She turned off the lights and went down the back stairs, and so to the drawing-room door. She took a deep breath and went through, and it felt a bit like walking onto the stage in a school play. The huge room danced with firelight and glittering Christmas baubles. She saw Aunt Lavinia, majestic in black velvet, ensconced in an armchair by the fireside, with the Colonel and Tommy Mortimer and Edward standing grouped about her. Aunt Lavinia raised her hand in a little gesture of welcome, and the three men turned.

For an instant there was silence. "Judith!" The Colonel shook his head in wonderment. "My dear, I hardly recognized you."

"What a gorgeous apparition!" That was Tommy Mortimer.

"I don't know why you're all so surprised," Aunt Lavinia scolded them. "Of course she looks beautiful. . . . And that color, Judith! Just like a kingfisher."

But Edward didn't say anything. He crossed the room and took

Judith's hand in his own. She looked up into his face and knew that he didn't have to say anything, because his eyes said it all.

At last he spoke. "We're drinking champagne," he told her.

"Again?" she teased him, and he laughed.

AFTERWARDS, in the years to come, whenever Judith recalled that Christmas dinner at Nancherrow in 1938, it was a bit like looking at an Impressionist painting: all the sharp edges blurred by the softness of candlelight and the muzziness of a little too much champagne. The fire flamed, but the paneled walls and dark portraits retreated to become no more than a shadowed backdrop for the festive table. Silver candelabra marched down the center of this, with, all about, sprigs of holly, scarlet crackers, dishes of nuts and chocolates. The dark mahogany was set with white linen place mats and napkins, the most elaborate of the family silver, and crystal glasses fine and clear as soap bubbles.

The men were dressed in formal evening wear—dinner jackets, white shirts, and black bow ties. Edward sat opposite Judith, and from time to time she looked up and caught his eye, and he would smile as though they shared some splendid secret, and raise his wineglass to her.

Alongside Edward was his younger sister. Loveday at sixteen was still on the cusp of becoming an adult. Clothes were still unimportant to her. She still lived for her riding and spent much of her days down at the stables, mucking out in the company of Walter Mudge. Tonight her dark curls were artless, as always, and her vivid face, with those amazing violet eyes, shone, innocent of makeup. But her dress—her first long dress, chosen by Diana—was sheer enchantment: green organdy cut low over Loveday's shoulders and deeply ruffled at neck and hem. Even Loveday had been seduced by it, and dressed herself up without a complaint.

At the far end of the table Diana's slinky satin dress was the color of steel. With it she wore pearls and diamonds, the only dash of color her scarlet nails and lipstick. Beside her sat Tommy Mortimer and Athena, looking like a summer goddess in white.

Conversation buzzed as the delicious feast went down. First paper-thin slices of smoked salmon, then turkey, roast potatoes, buttered sprouts and carrots, cranberry jelly, dark gravy rich with wine. There followed Mrs. Nettlebed's Christmas pudding, mince pies, and dishes of thick Cornish cream. Then nuts to be shelled and little tangerines to be peeled.

Finally the ladies rose from the table and withdrew, headed for the drawing room and coffee. As Diana led the way, she paused to stoop and kiss her husband. "Ten minutes," she told him. "That's all the time you're allowed to drink your port."

And by the time the men did join the ladies, Diana had the sofas and chairs pushed aside, the rugs rolled back, and the gramophone stacked with her favorite dance records.

The music was another thing Judith was always to remember, the tunes of that year: "Smoke Gets in Your Eyes" and "You're the Cream in My Coffee" and "Deep Purple." She danced that one with Tommy Mortimer, who was so expert that she didn't even have to think about what her feet were doing. Then there was a waltz, and Aunt Lavinia and the Colonel showed them all up, Lavinia's diamond-buckled shoes twinkling as she turned with all the lightness of a young girl.

Waltzing was thirsty business. Judith went to pour herself an orange juice and turned from the table to find Edward at her side. "I've left the best till the last," he told her. "Now come and dance with me."

She laid down the glass and went into his arms.

> *I took one look at you,*
> *That's all I had to do*
> *And then my heart stood still.*

But her heart wasn't standing still. It was thumping so hard she was sure that he must feel its beat. He held her very close and sang the words of the song softly into her ear, and she wished the music would never end. But finally it did, and they drew apart.

There was a bit of a lull, and everybody was grateful for a breather. Aunt Lavinia was preparing to go home and saying good night to everybody. And when she was gone, Diana waited for a moment, then turned to her guests. "What shall we do now?" She smiled. "I know. Let's play sardines."

Athena let out a groan. "Oh, *Mummy*. Grow up!"

"Why not sardines? We haven't played for ages. Everybody knows how to play, don't they?"

Edward explained. "We turn off all the lights. One person hides.

233

The others wait here. We count a hundred and then all go off in search. If you find the hider, don't say anything. Just sneak in and hide alongside, until everybody's crammed into a laundry basket or a wardrobe or wherever. Last one in is the booby."

They drew cards to see who would hide first. "Spades are high," Diana explained. Judith turned her card over. The ace of spades. She said, "It's me."

Loveday was dispatched by Diana to switch off all the lights. "But not the upstairs landing. Otherwise there'll be people falling downstairs. Quickly, off you run."

"Now"—Edward took charge—"we'll give you a count of a hundred, Judith, and then we'll come after you."

"Anywhere out of bounds?"

"The kitchen, I think. I don't suppose the Nettlebeds are finished in there yet. Otherwise you've got a free rein."

Loveday returned. "It's really dark and spooky," she announced with some satisfaction. "You can scarcely see a *thing*."

Judith was gripped by a tremor of fear. Ridiculous, but she wished that the high card had been picked by one of the others. However, there was nothing to be done except to brave it out.

They had started counting before she was even through the door. "One, two, three . . ." She closed the door behind her and was overwhelmed by inky blackness. She shivered, searching in her mind for some bolt-hole. Behind the door they were still counting. "Thirteen, fourteen." Her eyes were becoming used to the dark, and she was able to see, at the far end of the hall, the faint gleam from the light upstairs.

She went forward uncertainly. On the right the small sitting room and then, farther on, the dining room. She moved to the left, bumped into a table, felt the cold brush of leaves against her bare arm, then the upright of a doorway. Fingers fumbled across the paneling, found the handle, and she slipped inside.

The billiard room. Black-dark now. Softly she shut the door behind her. Her feet made no sound on the thick rug.

The tall windows in this room had a deep sill, where sometimes she and Loveday perched, watching a game in progress. Not a very imaginative hiding place, but she could think of no other. She gathered her long skirts and scrambled up onto the sill, then swiftly drew the curtains closed.

It was dreadfully cold because the glass of the windows was icy. Far off a door opened. A raised voice. "We're *coming!* Ready or not!" They were on the hunt. She hoped they would all find her before she died of cold.

The wait seemed to last forever. More voices. Footsteps. Laughter. Minutes passed. And then, very softly, the billiard-room door opened and was closed again. She held her breath. Then a curtain was gently drawn back, and Edward whispered, "Judith?"

"Oh," an involuntary sigh of relief that the waiting and the tension were over. "I'm here," she whispered back.

He vaulted lightly up onto the deep windowsill and drew the curtain behind him. He stood there, tall and very close. And warm.

"Do you know how I found you?"

"You mustn't talk. They'll hear."

"I smelt you."

She stifled a nervous giggle. "How horrible."

"No. Lovely. Your scent."

"I'm freezing."

"Here." He drew her towards him, and began to rub her arms briskly. "You *are* frozen. How's that? Is that better?"

"Yes. Better."

And with that, he put his arms around her, pulled her close, and kissed her. She had always imagined that being kissed for the first time, properly, would be terrifying and strange, but Edward's kiss was not strange in the least, just wonderfully comforting and, obscurely, what she had been dreaming of for months.

He stopped kissing her, but continued to hold her, pressed to his shirtfront, nuzzling her ear. "I've been wanting to do this all evening. Ever since you came through the door looking like—what was it Aunt Lavinia said?—a beautiful kingfisher."

He drew away and looked down at her. "How could such a funny little cygnet grow into such a beautiful swan?" There was enough light to see his smile. She felt his warm hand move from her shoulder, down her back, caressing her waist and her hips through the thin folds of the dress. He kissed her again, and now his hand was kneading her soft flesh. . . .

And it all came back. The horror returned. She was in the dark, grubby little cinema, and Billy Fawcett's hand was on her knee, groping, violating. . . .

Her panic was totally instinctive. What had been pleasurable became all at once menacing, and it was no good telling herself that this was *Edward,* because it didn't matter. She could not have stopped herself had she wanted to, but sharply brought up her arms and shoved hard against Edward's chest.

"No!"

"Judith?" She heard the bewilderment in his voice as he let her go. For a moment neither of them spoke. Gradually Judith's panic died away, and she felt her racing heart settle down to its normal beat. What have I done? she asked herself, and was filled with shame because she had behaved like a flustered idiot. Billy Fawcett. She suddenly wanted to scream with rage at herself. Thought about trying to explain it all to Edward, and knew that she could not.

She said at last, "I'm sorry." It sounded pathetically inadequate.

"Don't you like being kissed?" Clearly, Edward was confused. Edward Carey-Lewis, that privileged, gilded youth, had probably never in all his life had any person say no to him. "I thought that was what you wanted."

"I did . . . I mean . . . It's *nothing* to do with you."

"But—" He stopped. Turned his head to listen. Beyond the curtains the billiard-room door was opened and gently closed. Discovery was close at hand. Too late now to make amends. In some despair Judith gazed up at Edward's profile and told herself that she had lost him forever.

The curtain twitched aside. "I thought you might be here," whispered Loveday, and Edward stooped to hoist her up to join them.

THAT night the old dream returned. The nightmare that she had thought buried forever. Her bedroom at Windyridge and Billy Fawcett climbing up his ladder. And then she was jerking awake in a sweat of fear, her mouth open in a silent scream.

It was as though he had won. He had spoiled everything, because in some ghastly, gruesome way Edward's hands had become Billy Fawcett's hands, and all her inhibitions had leaped into life. She lay in her darkened bedroom and wept into the pillow, because she loved Edward so much and she had ruined everything.

But in the morning she heard a soft knock and her door open. "Judith?" She sat up, blinking and confused.

Edward. She stared at him stupidly. Saw him shaved, dressed, and looking not at all as though he had climbed into bed at three o'clock in the morning.

"What is it?"

"Don't look so alarmed." Then he came to settle himself on the side of the bed. He said, "We have to talk."

"Oh, Edward." She felt as though she were about to cry.

"Here." He stooped and retrieved her dressing gown from the rug. "Put this on, or you'll die of cold." She took it, shoving her arms into the sleeves, bundling it around her. "Now look, I've thought everything through. What happened last night—"

"It was my fault."

"It wasn't anybody's fault. Perhaps I misjudged the situation, but I'm not going to apologize because, by my reckoning, I didn't do anything to apologize for. Except perhaps to forget how young you still are. Dressed up and looking so glamorous, it seemed to me that you'd grown up in a minute. But of course, nobody can do that."

"No." Judith looked down at her fingers pleating the edge of the sheet. She said painfully, "I did want you to kiss me. And then I spoilt it all."

"But you don't hate me?"

She looked up into his blue eyes. "No," she told him. "I'm much too fond of you to hate you."

"In that case, we can wipe the slate clean. I just wanted to be certain that we understood each other. We're all going to be together for a few days, and nothing would be more uncomfortable than any tension between us. Do you understand what I'm saying?"

"Yes, Edward."

"My mother is as sharp as a needle when it comes to other people's relationships. I don't want her sending you quizzical looks or asking me loaded questions. So you won't droop around, will you, doing an imitation of the Lady of Shalott?"

"No, Edward." But Judith was churning with mixed emotions. Relief was uppermost. Relief that Edward wasn't going to despise her. And she found herself touched by Edward's good sense, prompted by concern for his mother and her house party, but surely, too, he had been thinking a little bit of her.

"So"—he smiled—"family loyalties?"

Which filled her with love for him. She pulled him close and

237

kissed his smooth cheek. The nightmare of Billy Fawcett had flown again, chased off by Edward and the clear light of morning.

He got off the bed. "I'll go down to breakfast. How long will you be?"

"Ten minutes."

"I shall wait for you."

❧ *1939* ❧

S PEECH Day at St. Ursula's took place during the last week of July, the end of the school year. It was an occasion of great ceremony, following a time-honored pattern—assembly of parents and girls in the Great Hall, a prayer, a speech or two, prize giving, the school hymn, a blessing from the bishop, and then afternoon tea.

By ten to two the hall was packed with humanity and extremely warm, for outdoors bloomed a perfect summer day. Mothers sported garden-party hats and white gloves and flowered silk frocks. Fathers were in dark suits, except that here and there stood a man in service uniform. Edgar and Diana Carey-Lewis were part of this throng, as were the solicitor Mr. Baines and his wife.

The front of the hall was filled with girls in their regulation party frocks of long-sleeved heavy cream silk, and black silk stockings. Judith, sitting in the very back row of the school party, looked at her watch. Speech Day was always an ordeal, and being eighteen and knowing that this was the very end of school somehow didn't make it any more bearable. To divert her thoughts from her discomfort, she began to make a mental list of cheering events that were about to happen.

The most important was that Miss Catto had started to make arrangements for Judith to go to Oxford. But that wouldn't be for another year, because passage had already been booked for October on a P&O boat bound for Singapore. She was going to spend ten months, at least, reunited with her family. She could hardly wait to see Jess, who was eight now. She could hardly wait to see them all.

More immediately, there were the summer holidays. Two weeks in August to be spent with Heather Warren and her parents and, later on, a visit to Aunt Biddy. Uncle Bob was at sea, and her cousin,

Ned, had joined the *Royal Oak,* so she would be happy to have a bit of company.

Otherwise, Nancherrow. Which meant Edward.

She sat in the stuffy hall suffused with blissful anticipation. The events of Christmas had tipped the scales in Judith's relationship with Edward, and she had fallen totally in love. Because of him the incident at the party had slipped away unnoticed, and she could not imagine how any man so attractive and desirable could be, as well, so understanding.

Judith had not seen Edward since January. He had spent his Easter vacation on a ranch in Colorado, invited by a fellow Cambridge undergraduate, a young American. Edward had sent Judith a couple of postcards, with pictures of the Rocky Mountains. These treasured mementos she kept. Now he was in the south of France with a party of friends, staying in somebody's aunt's villa. But he'd be home for a bit later in the summer. Anticipation—looking forward to seeing Edward again—was all part of the joy.

Another exciting thing was that Mr. Baines had said that Judith could buy a little car. She had learned how to drive and had passed her test first go. But it was difficult at Nancherrow to find something to drive. Diana's Bentley and the Colonel's Daimler were so grand as to be out of the question.

When she explained her predicament to Mr. Baines, he had been most understanding, but said he would first have a word with Captain Somerville. And there the matter had rested. But Judith was full of hope because, at the end of the day, she couldn't imagine Uncle Bob saying no.

It occurred to Judith that with luck she would get the car before she went to stay with the Warrens and would be able to drive herself to Porthkerris. Loveday had been invited as well to join the cheerful household over the grocer's shop for a few days. Loveday, at seventeen, was also leaving St. Ursula's forever, having made it perfectly clear to her long-suffering parents that without Judith, St. Ursula's would be unbearable.

Two o'clock, and at last the ceremony was under way. The bishop delivered his short prayer, followed by speeches, prize giving. For Judith the English Prize, and also the History Prize—a bonus because that had not been remotely expected. Then, finally, the school hymn. The music mistress crashed out a chord on her piano, everybody rose to their feet, and eight hundred voices just about raised the roof.

The power of the music affected Judith deeply. Now she had come to the end of an era, and knew that she would remember every detail of the moment. The hot summer afternoon, the great surge of voices. It was hard to decide whether she felt happy or sad.

Happy. She was happy. As she sang, her spirits soared.

AUGUST now, and a wet Monday morning. Summer rain, soft and drenching, streamed down upon Nancherrow. Loveday, with Tiger, the big black Lab, at her heels, emerged into the outdoors by way of the scullery. She wore gum boots and an old raincoat, and as she set off in the direction of Lidgey Farm, the rain caused her dark locks to curl more tightly than ever.

She took the road up onto the moors. Tiger ran ahead, and she quickened her pace to keep up. She couldn't see much, but it didn't matter, because she knew all of Nancherrow, the farm and the estate, like the back of her hand.

At last Lidgey farmhouse loomed out of the murk, solid and squat, with farm buildings and stables and piggeries all about it. Loveday climbed the gate and crossed slippery cobbles to the door. Here she toed off her boots and let herself in.

The ceiling was low, the little hall dim. She pushed open the kitchen door to be assailed by the warm smell of cooking. Vegetable broth and warm bread. "Mrs. Mudge?"

Mrs. Mudge was standing at her sink peeling potatoes. Because the kitchen was living room as well, one end of the table was piled with newspapers, seed catalogues, and bills waiting to be paid. Uncleaned boots stood by the range. There was a dresser, painted blue, its shelves crammed not only with mismatched china but curling postcards, an old-fashioned telephone, dog leads, and a basket of eggs waiting to be washed.

The Lidgey kitchen always looked this way, and Loveday liked it. It was somehow cozy. And Mrs. Mudge was comfortably grubby as well, standing there flanked by all the unwashed crocks and bowls of her morning's labor. The flagged floor and the worn rugs were distinctly dirty, but Mr. Mudge and Walter saw nothing to complain about, so well fed and cared for were they.

Mrs. Mudge turned from her sink. "Loveday!" As always, she

looked delighted. There was nothing she enjoyed so much as an excuse to put the kettle on, make a pot of tea, and gossip. "Well, this is some nice surprise. Walked up, did you, in this weather?"

Mrs. Mudge's being toothless made her look quite old, but she was, in fact, quite young, in her early forties. Her hair was straight and lank, and on her head was a brown beret, which she wore as constantly as her rubber boots.

"I've got Tiger. Do you mind if he comes in?" Which was a silly question because Tiger was already in and sniffing at Mrs. Mudge's pig bucket.

She cheerfully shooed him away. "Want a cup of tea, do you?"

Loveday said yes, because drinking tea with Mrs. Mudge was part of tradition. "Where's Walter?"

"Up the top field with his father." Mrs. Mudge abandoned her potatoes and filled her kettle. "What did you want him for?"

"Would you tell him I'm going away tomorrow to Porthkerris for a week, so he'll have to see to everything for the horses. But there's plenty of hay, and I cleaned all the tack last night."

"I'll make sure he don't forget." Mrs. Mudge took her tea caddy from a shelf. "Why are you off to Porthkerris?"

"I'm going to stay with the Warrens, with Judith. And you'll never believe this, Mrs. Mudge. Judith and I are going to drive ourselves! Judith's gone off today with Mr. Baines, the solicitor, and he's going to help her buy a car for herself."

Mrs. Mudge, clattering cups and saucers, paused. "A car of her own! You can hardly believe it, can you? What else is going on down at the house? Full up yet, are you?"

"The very opposite. Pops and Judith and I are the only ones there. Athena's in London, and Edward's in the south of France."

"What about your mother?"

Loveday made a face. "She went off yesterday to London."

"To London? With you all coming home and the middle of the holidays?" Indeed, Diana Carey-Lewis had never done such a thing before. But Loveday, despite feeling a bit put out at her mother's defection, thought that she understood.

"Between you and me, Mrs. Mudge, I think she got a bit depressed. She needed to get away. I suppose she wanted a change."

Mrs. Mudge poured the tea and settled down in her chair. "What does she want a change for, then?"

"Well, everything is a bit depressing, isn't it? I mean, everybody talking about war, and Edward's joined the Royal Air Force Reserve, and I think that frightens her. And Pops is a bit down in the mouth as well and insists on listening to all the news bulletins full blast. They're digging up Hyde Park for air-raid shelters, and he seems to think we're all going to be gassed. Not much fun to live with reality. So she just packed a suitcase and went."

"It's not a good time for any of us, really. Except I don't suppose Walter will have to go. Farming's a reserved occupation, his dad says."

When Loveday had finished her tea, she looked at her watch. "I'd better be getting back. Come on, Tiger. We've got to go home."

The rain had eased off a little. She went back across the farmyard and climbed the gate, then sat for a bit on the top rail.

Walter. She thought of Walter and the coming war, and felt grateful that he would not be leaving Nancherrow to be a soldier. She was very fond of him. For all his wild ways she found him enormously attractive. He was rough and foulmouthed, and rumor had it that he was beginning to spend far too many evenings in the Rosemullion pub, but still, he was a constant in her existence and one of the few young men with whom she felt at ease. Ever since prep school Edward had been bringing friends home to stay, but they seemed to come from a different world. While Loveday mucked out the stables or rode with Walter, they lay about in deck chairs or played not very energetic tennis.

Walter. She thought about war. Every evening they all listened to the nine-o'clock news, and every evening world events seemed to be worsening. Loveday could not begin to imagine war. Would there be bombs dropping? Would the German army land somewhere and march across the country? If they came, what would happen?

Tiger, impatient, was whining at her. She sighed and climbed down from the gate and set off. To cheer herself up, she thought about tomorrow and going to Porthkerris. And by the time she reached home, her spirits were quite restored.

August 9th, 1939

Dear Mummy and Dad,

I am sorry I have not written for such a long time. I am at Porthkerris with the Warrens, and Loveday has come too. The weather is absolutely gorgeous. Heather has left school, and she's going to do a secretarial course and then maybe go to London and get herself a job.

Mr. Baines and Uncle Bob have let me buy a car of my very own. It is a little dark blue Morris with four seats, and too sweet. It meant that Loveday and I were able to come here under our own steam. I can't tell you what fun it was, driving ourselves, and just as soon as I can, I'm off to see Phyllis. She is married now and is living in Pendeen and even has a baby.

I must go. Loveday and Heather want to go to the beach, and Mrs. Warren has packed us a picnic.

My love to you as always.

LOVEDAY stayed a week, and it was a constant source of wonder to Judith the way she fitted in to life in the crowded house over the grocer's shop. Loveday was entranced by the Warrens and by the novelty of living bang in the middle of a busy little town and of stepping out the door straight into the narrow cobbled street that led down to the harbor. Most of all she enjoyed the beach, the sands bright with striped tents and cheerful holidaymakers. And so slender and tanned and dazzlingly pretty was Loveday that she inevitably drew admiring glances.

But the time flew by, and soon Palmer, the chauffeur, turned up from Nancherrow, and Loveday's suitcases were loaded, and everybody emerged onto the pavement to see her off with kisses and hugs and promises that she would come again.

At first it felt a bit strange without Loveday. Like all the Carey-Lewis family, she had that gift of adding unexpected glamour to almost any gathering. But it was nice, too, to have just Heather for company and to talk about the old days.

They sat at the kitchen table and drank tea and discussed how they would spend the day. They decided to go off to Treen to swim and to picnic. The cliffs would be lovely on a day like this.

And so they went by way of the Lands End Road. At Treen, with picnics in haversacks on their backs, they made the descent from the high cliffs to the sandy cove and found that there was not another person to be seen.

Sunbathing on the rocks, they talked. Heather confessed that she now had a boyfriend, one Charlie Lanyon, the son of a prosperous timber merchant. Judith deliberated as to whether to tell Heather about Edward, but decided against it. What she felt for Edward was too precious, too tenuous to share with anyone, even Heather.

"Are you going to get engaged?"

"No. What's the point? If there's a war, he'll be called up, and we shan't see each other for years. Besides, I don't want to get married and be lumbered with kids. Not yet."

"So what do you want? A job in London?"

"Eventually. Have my own little flat, a proper salary. I want to see the world. I'd like to go abroad."

They spent all that day on the rocks and the sand, and in the water. When it was time to go, Heather turned to look at the sea, a deep aquamarine blue. She said, "You know, it won't ever be like this again. Not ever. Just you and me, and this place and this time."

Judith understood. "I know. It can never be quite the same."

By six they were back in Porthkerris, sunburned and exhausted. The shop was closed, but Mr. Warren was in his little office and had a message for Judith. "You had a phone call, about an hour ago." He searched around on his desk and handed a scrap of paper over. On it were two words: "Ring Edward."

Heather was agog, but Judith hesitated. The telephone on the desk was the only one in the house. Mr. Warren caught her hesitation. "I'm going upstairs to have a beer."

Heather, her black eyes sparkling, said, "I'll come and pour."

Judith watched them go, then took Mr. Warren's seat behind his desk, lifted the receiver of the old-fashioned telephone, and gave the operator the Nancherrow number.

"Hello." It was Edward.

She said, "It's me. Mr. Warren gave me your message. I thought you were still in France."

"No. I got home, to a practically empty house. No Ma, no Judith. Pops and I have been leading a bachelor existence."

"Did you have a good time in France?"

"Amazing. I want to tell you about it. How about this evening? I thought I might drive over to Porthkerris and take you out for a drink. Would the Warrens mind?"

"No, of course they wouldn't mind."

"Well, say eight o'clock. How do I find you?"

"It's just behind the old Market Place—Warren's Grocery. A bright blue door with a brass handle."

"Unmissable." She could hear the smile in his voice. "Eight o'clock. I'll see you." And he rang off.

She sat for a little, dreamy and smiling. He was coming. He wanted to see her. She must change, bathe, wash her hair. She sprang from the chair and ran up the stairs two at a time.

AT EIGHT o'clock she was in her bedroom applying lipstick when she heard a car draw to a halt outside the grocery. She went to the open window and saw a dark blue Triumph, Edward clambering out of it. "Edward! I won't be a moment."

She collected her shoulder bag, took a last glance at her reflection, then ran downstairs. Edward held out his arms, and she went to him and they kissed on the cheek. He was very brown, his hair bleached by the Mediterranean sun.

She said, "You look wonderful."

"You too," he said. "So where shall we go? Which is the fashionable nightspot this season?"

"I suppose we could try the Sliding Tackle."

"What a good idea." So they set off, strolling down the narrow street to the water, and turned along the harbor road. It was a fine and golden evening, and summer visitors were ambling along the quay. Outside the Sliding Tackle a noisy young group sat at a wooden table downing their beer.

Edward led the way inside, ducking beneath the crooked lintel of the doorway. Judith stepped into semidarkness and was assailed by the reek of beer and cigarette smoke, and the din of convivial voices. "Dreadfully crowded," Edward observed. "You stand here and grab a table if one comes free. I'll get you a shandy." He left her, shouldering his way towards the bar.

With startling luck a party sitting at a table under the tiny window got up to depart. As soon as they were out of the way, Judith eased herself onto the narrow wooden bench and put her handbag beside her, laying claim to a space for Edward.

He returned, carrying a tankard for himself and a glass for her. "Brilliant girl. Murder having to stand all evening." He set down their drinks and slid onto the bench.

"I never realized the Sliding Tackle was so small."

245

"Tiny." Edward reached for a cigarette and lit it. "Anyway"—he raised his glass—"cheers. It's so good to see you again. It's been so long."

"Tell me about France. Where did you go?"

"To a villa up in the hills behind Cannes. Very rural. Surrounded by vineyards and olive groves. And the villa had a terrace wreathed in vines where we had all our meals. Heaven."

"Whom did the villa belong to?"

"A rather nice older couple called Beath. I think he was something to do with the Foreign Office."

"So you didn't know them? Then how—"

"I went to London to some party with Athena. And I met this jolly girl, and she told me her aunt and uncle had this villa in France, and she had been invited out to stay, and the invitation included a chum or two."

"Edward, you are the—"

"Why are you laughing?"

"Because only you could go to a party in London and end up spending two weeks in the south of France. She must have been frightfully pretty."

"Villas in France tend to make girls pretty. Just as a socking bank balance renders the most hideous of women attractive."

He was teasing. She smiled. "So what happened next? You said the invitation included a chum or two."

"Yes. She'd fixed things up with a girlfriend, but all the chaps they fancied were committed to other arrangements. So"—he shrugged—"she asked me. And said, 'Bring a friend,' and off the top of my head I suggested Gus Callender."

It was the first time Judith had heard the name. "Who's he?"

"A dour Scot from the wild Highlands. He's at Cambridge, doing engineering. Quite a shy, reserved sort of fellow, but terribly nice. One of the girls fell wildly in love with his brooding, Heathcliff looks. As well, he's something of an artist, which added an extra dimension."

He sounded, Judith decided, an interesting character. "An engineer and an artist. Funny mixture."

"As it happens, there's every chance you'll meet him. After we'd arrived in Dover, I suggested he come back to Nancherrow with me, but he had to return to darkest Scotland and spend a bit of time with his mum and dad. He'll maybe come later on. He seemed quite tempted by the idea."

But Judith had talked enough about Gus Callender. "Tell me more about France. Was it beautiful?"

"It was great going south, but it wasn't so much fun coming back. After Paris the roads to Calais became choked with traffic. Panic. War nerves. All the British families on holiday suddenly deciding to scuttle for home."

"What did they think was going to happen?"

"I don't know. I suppose the German army suddenly bursting through the Maginot Line and invading France. Or something."

"Are things *really* as bad as that, Edward?"

"Pretty bad, I reckon. Poor Pops is racked with apprehension."

"I know. I think that's why your mother ran away to London."

"She's never been much use at facing up to cruel facts. She telephoned last night, just to make sure we were all surviving without her and to give us the London news. Athena's got a new boyfriend. He's called Rupert Rycroft, and he's in the Royal Dragoon Guards."

"Goodness, how smart."

"Pops and I have got bets on how long it will last. A fiver each way. I'm going to get another beer. How about you?"

"I'm all right. I've not finished this yet."

He left her to fight his way back to the bar, and Judith looked about her. Two old men, clearly locals, sat firmly established on the benches which flanked the fireplace. And there was a rather grand group of people, probably staying at one of the big hotels up on the hill, making this foray to see how the natives lived. They were finishing their drinks and preparing to leave.

Their going created a gap, and Judith was left with a clear view across the room to the far end. A man sat there alone, a half-filled tumbler on the table before him. He was watching her. Staring. She saw the pale unblinking eyes; the drooping, nicotine-stained mustache; the tweed cap low on his brow. She reached for her shandy, then quickly laid the glass down because her hand had started to shake.

Billy Fawcett.

She had neither seen him nor heard news of him since the day of Aunt Louise's funeral. As the years passed, her girlhood trauma had gradually faded. But never totally disappeared. Older and better informed, she had even tried to find some sympathy for his pathetic sexual aberrations, but it was impossible. The memory of him had almost destroyed her relationship with Edward.

And he was here, in the Sliding Tackle. Staring at her, his eyes like two pebbles in his florid face. She looked for Edward, but he was jammed in at the bar, and she could scarcely scream for help. Oh, Edward, she begged silently, come back quickly.

Now Billy Fawcett was picking up his tumbler and making his way across the flagged floor to where she sat, petrified. His cheeks were flushed and netted with purple veins.

"Judith." He was there, steadying himself with his knotted old hand on the back of a chair. "Mind if I join you?" He pulled the chair from the table and cautiously lowered himself onto it. "Saw you," he told her. "Recognized you the moment you came through the door." His breath stank of old tobacco and whisky.

Edward was on his way. She looked up, her eyes a mute appeal for help, and Edward, in some confusion, visibly bucked at finding the broken-down old stranger sitting at their table. He said politely, "Hello there," but there was not much friendliness in his voice, and his expression was wary.

"My dear boy, I apologize . . ." The word took a bit of saying, so Billy Fawcett tried again. "Apologize for interrupting, but Judith and I are old friends. Had to have a word. Fawcett's the name. Billy Fawcett. Ex-colonel, Indian army. I don't think we've had the pleasure. . . ." His voice trailed away.

"Edward Carey-Lewis." Edward did not put out his hand.

"Delighted to meet you." Billy Fawcett took a great slug of his whisky, then slapped the glass back on the table. His eyes narrowed. "I suppose, Edward, you wouldn't have a cigarette on you? Seem to have run out."

Silently Edward reached for his packet of Players and offered it to Billy Fawcett. With some difficulty Fawcett extricated one and lit up. He took a long drag, coughed, slurped another mouthful of whisky, and settled his elbows on the table, as though he intended to stay forever.

"Judith used to live next door to me," he told Edward. "With her aunt Louise. Wonderful woman, Louise. My best friend. You know, Judith, if you hadn't turned up, I'd have probably married Louise.

She had a lot of time for me before you turned up. Good friends. Miss her like hell. Never felt so alone. Abandoned."

His voice shook. With a mottled hand he wiped away a dribbling tear. He had reached the maudlin stage of drunkenness, wallowing in self-pity. Judith stared into her shandy. She did not want to look at the man and was too appalled to look at Edward.

Billy Fawcett rambled on. "Different for you, though, eh, Judith? You didn't do too badly, did you? Scooped the lot. Louise always said she'd look after me, but she didn't leave me a bloody thing." He brooded on this injustice for a bit and then fired his broadside at Judith. "Conniving little bitch."

Edward rose unhurriedly to his feet, towering over the old drunk. "I think you'd better go," he told him quietly.

Fawcett's apoplectic face, wearing an expression of disbelief, stared up. "Go? Young whippersnapper, I'll go when I'm ready, and I've not done yet."

"Yes, you are. You're finished. Finished with drinking and finished with insulting Judith."

"Go to hell," said Billy Fawcett.

Edward's response was to take hold of the collar of Billy Fawcett's sagging jacket and yank him to his feet. By the time he had done protesting—"Don't you dare lay your hands on me"—Edward had propelled him away from the table, across the threshold, and out the door. He dumped him on the cobbled pavement, where Billy Fawcett collapsed into the gutter. There were a good many people around, and all of them witnessed his humiliation.

"Don't come back here," Edward told him. "Don't ever show your face in this place again."

Edward strode back into the bar. Judith was white as a sheet. She took a deep breath, determined not to shake or cry.

Sitting down at the table, Edward said, "Tell me, was that old toad really a friend of your aunt's?"

"Yes."

"She must have been mad."

"No, not really. Just kindhearted. I hated him."

"Poor Judith. How horrible."

"And he . . ." She thought about Billy Fawcett's hand creeping up her leg and wondered how on earth she could possibly explain to Edward and make him understand.

For a bit nothing was said. Edward lit a cigarette. "I think you need to talk, don't you?" he said at last. She simply sat, staring at her hands. "You hated him. Why?"

She began to tell him about the cinema, and once she had started, it wasn't as difficult as she thought it was going to be. At the end she said, "I was fourteen, Edward. I hadn't got the faintest idea what he was up to. I panicked."

"Did you tell Aunt Louise?"

"I couldn't. I just couldn't. Afterwards I had nightmares about him. I still have sometimes. I know it's childish, but my psyche jumps every time I'm reminded of him."

"Is that what happened at Christmas when I kissed you?"

She was so embarrassed by Edward's even mentioning the incident that she could feel the blush, like fire, creeping into her cheeks. "It wasn't a bit like Billy Fawcett, Edward. It was just that when you . . . touched me . . . it all went wrong."

"I think you have a trauma."

She turned to him, almost in tears of despair. "But why can't I be shed of it? I'm still frightened of him, because he hates me so much. At Aunt Louise's funeral he looked as though he would like to kill me."

"If looks could kill, we'd all be dead." Now Edward smiled and bent to kiss her cheek. "Darling Judith. Do you know what I think? I think you need a catalyst of some sort. Don't ask me what, but something will happen. You mustn't let one unhappy memory come between you and love. You are far too sweet for that."

"Oh, Edward, I'm so sorry."

"There's nothing to be sorry about. And now I think I should take you home. It's been something of an evening."

"The best bit was just having you here."

"When are you coming back to us at Nancherrow?"

"Sunday, next week."

"We'll be waiting for you." He got to his feet and stood until she had extricated herself from the bench. Outside, the sun had slipped behind the sea. There were a few people still around, relishing the twilit warmth, but Billy Fawcett had gone.

EDWARD telephoned the next morning. "Judith, good morning. I wanted to ask if you'd slept well."

251

"I did. And I'm sorry about last night."

He hesitated. "This is the other reason I phoned. There's a slight panic on here. Aunt Lavinia took ill last night. Apparently she's got pneumonia, and everybody's a bit worried."

"Oh, Edward, I can't bear it." Aunt Lavinia, so seemingly indestructible. "Is your mother home?"

"Pops phoned her last night. She's driving back today. But Athena took off for Scotland with Rupert Rycroft at the beginning of the week. Pops put a call through to some remote glen or other, but all he could do was leave a message."

"And Loveday? Is she all right?"

"A bit tearful, but Mary Millyway's a motherly comfort."

"I'll come back to Nancherrow today if it would help."

"That's what you mustn't do. I only told you because I thought you'd be upset if you weren't told. But don't cut short your holiday. We'll see you next Sunday. And incidentally, Gus'll be here as well. There was a message when I got back last night. He's driving down from Scotland, on his way already."

"Oh, *Edward.* What an inopportune time. Can you put him off?"

"I don't know where he is. It'll be all right. He's an easy guest."

"Well, send my love to everybody. And love to you."

"The same, by return." She could hear the smile in his voice. "Bye, Judith."

Gus Callender, behind the wheel of his dark green Lagonda, had finally reached Cornwall, the last leg of his journey. After Scotland the changing colors of the sun-washed landscape had caught his painter's eye, and he longed to stop then and there to capture on his sketch pad this place and this light forever. But he was expected at Nancherrow, and painting must wait. He had come a long way, he thought as he entered Truro. Perhaps longer than anyone realized.

It was Edward Carey-Lewis who had first started to call him Gus. Before that, he had been Angus, the only child of two elderly parents. His mother, a simple soul, was devoted to her son and husband. His father, Duncan Callender, was an astute Aberdeen businessman who had pulled himself up from humble beginnings and had amassed a tidy fortune. Accordingly, when Angus was seven, the family moved from a town house in Aberdeen, where the boy was perfectly content, to an enormous Victorian mansion on the banks of the river Dee, where the neighbors were old noble families who occupied huge estates. Duncan was determined to raise his son a gentleman.

Angus was dispatched to an expensive preparatory school. He came top of his class, and very soon his Aberdeen accent was a thing of the past. Duncan Callender was delighted.

Finished with prep school, Angus went on to Rugby School, where he discovered the joys of the art room and his ability to draw and paint. With the encouragement of a sympathetic art master he began filling a sketchbook with pencil drawings, tinted by a pale wash of color. Then one day, leafing through a copy of *The Studio,* he read an article on the Cornish painters—the Newlyn School. Illustrating this was a colored plate of a work by Laura Knight: a girl standing on a rock and watching the sea. The sea was peacock blue, and the girl's hair was copper red, in a single plait which fell across one shoulder. For some reason it set his imagination ablaze. Cornwall. Perhaps he would become a professional artist, settle in Cornwall, wear bizarre paint-stained clothes, grow his hair; and there would always be some beautiful, devoted girl to live with him in his fisherman's cottage, or perhaps a converted barn.

The illusion was so real that he almost felt the warmth of the sun, smelled the sea wind scented with wildflowers. A schoolboy's fantasy. He could never be a professional painter; he was already mainstreamed for Cambridge and a degree in engineering. But he carefully removed the colorplate and, suppressing his conscience, spirited it away. Later he framed it, and the unknown girl by the Cornish sea was hung on the wall of his study.

In other directions as well, Rugby widened his experience. Too self-contained to make close friends, he was nevertheless popular, and from time to time invitations were proffered to spend part of the holidays in country houses in Yorkshire or Wiltshire or Hampshire. These he accepted, and was kindly received. But it all seemed a bit like playacting, and the thought occurred to him that since he was seven and the family had left Aberdeen, he could remember no place where he'd felt comfortably at home. Not his father's house. Not school. Not the hospitable country establishments in Yorkshire, Wiltshire, and Hampshire. However much he enjoyed himself, he always felt that he was standing apart and watching others. And he wanted to belong.

Cambridge, for Angus, came as a revelation and a release. From the first moment, he thought it the loveliest city he had ever seen, and the college buildings a dream of architecture. Before long his sketchbook was filled with swift, penciled impressions—punts on the willow-fringed river, the Bridge of Sighs, the twin towers of King's College silhouetted against the sky.

His college was Pembroke, as was Edward Carey-Lewis's. They had arrived as freshmen at the same time, in 1937, but it was not until their second year that they got to know each other. Almost immediately Edward had begun to call him Gus. And such was Edward's influence that he was never again called anything else.

Gus had planned his route on a map: Truro to Penzance and then the coast road to Lands End and Rosemullion. There Nancherrow was written in italics, with a dotted line for the approach road.

Driving down the coast, he was rewarded by a sighting of the Atlantic, the green rollers pouring in over a sandbar. The road turned inland, and there were narrow lanes, fields bounded by irregular drystone walls, houses with the chalky patina of limewash. All slumbered in the sunshine, in an air of timelessness, as though here it would always be summer.

Presently, ahead, shimmering in the light, Gus saw the great sweep of Mounts Bay, a shout of blue, the horizon blurred. And it was all piercingly familiar, as though he were returning to a place long known and deeply loved.

Yes. There it all is. Just the way I knew it would be.

The sheltering harbor, the tall-masted boats, the scream of gulls. And over all, the cool, salty smell of open sea. He felt like a man returning to his roots. Coming home.

Loveday was picking raspberries. It was good to have something to do outside, because anxiety for Aunt Lavinia pervaded the house like a cloud. For her father it had even taken priority over the news on the wireless, and he now spent his time on the telephone, talking to the doctor and arranging for nurses to be at the Dower House. It was Loveday's first experience of possibly mortal illness. People died, of course. But not Aunt Lavinia.

She moved down the line of canes, picking the sweet red fruit and dropping them into a basket which she had slung, by a piece of string, around her waist. It was a bright afternoon, but a nippy wind blew in from the sea. She had pulled on an old yellow cricket sweater of Edward's. It was far too long, drooping down over her cotton skirt, but she was grateful for its brotherly comfort.

She was on her own because after lunch her father and Edward and Mary Millyway had all gone up to the Dower House. They would see the doctor, then sit in Isobel's kitchen and drink tea. Isobel, perhaps, needed comforting more than any of them.

"How about you, my darling?" her father had said to Loveday. "Do you want to come as well?"

And she had put her arms around him and, weeping, told him no. If the worst happened, she wanted to remember Aunt Lavinia the way she was, not as an aged and sickly lady, slipping away from them.

So Loveday stayed home and picked raspberries for Mrs. Nettlebed, who wanted to make jam. Now, carrying the heavy basket, she made her way along to the kitchen. She found Mrs. Nettlebed icing a cake and dumped the basket onto the table. "Do you want me to help you make jam?"

"Haven't time now. Do it later, I will. And you've better things to do, because the visitor's arrived."

"The visitor?" Loveday had forgotten about Edward's wretched friend. "Is he here already? What's he like?"

"No idea. Nettlebed let him in, took him up to his room. You'd better go up and say how do you do. It's Mr. Callender."

Reluctantly Loveday went. Up the back stairs and down the guest-room passage. His door stood open. He was standing with his back to her, staring out the open window, and she realized that he was unaware of her presence. She said, "Hello."

Startled, he swung around. For an instant they faced each other across the room, and then he smiled. "Hello."

Loveday found herself disconcerted. What she had expected was a clone of the various youths Edward had brought home during his school days. But here was a different breed altogether. He looked older than Edward, more mature. Dark and thin, rather serious. Interesting. Up to now Walter Mudge had been her yardstick for the sort of man she found attractive. Gus Callender had the same dark hair and dark eyes, but he was taller, less stockily built, and when he smiled, his whole face changed and he didn't look serious any longer.

"You're Gus Callender."

"That's right. And you must be Loveday."

"I'm sorry there's nobody here but me." She advanced into the room and perched herself on the high bed.

"That's all right. Your butler made me welcome."

Loveday looked at his luggage, still standing at the foot of the bed. "You don't seem to have done much unpacking."

"No. To be truthful, I was wondering whether I should. Mr. Nettlebed led me to believe that there are some problems. An illness in the family. Perhaps I should tactfully take myself off."

"Oh, you *mustn't* do that. Edward would be so upset and disappointed. Everybody will be back for tea, so you'll see him then. What time is it now?"

He looked at his wristwatch, heavy gold and leather-strapped to his sinewy wrist. "Just on three o'clock."

"Well." She considered. "What would you like to do?" She was not very good at being hostessy. "We could go down to the cove." She slid off the bed. "It's rather a steep path to the sea, so have you got rubbery shoes on? And a pullover? It might be a bit nippy on the cliffs."

He smiled at her bossiness. "Okay on both counts." He slipped on a dark blue Shetland sweater. "Lead the way."

She took him down the stairs and out the front door. The wind pounced upon them, chill and salty, as they went across the terraced lawns and onto the path, down towards the sea. Loveday went speeding ahead, so that it took Gus a good deal of effort to keep up with her. But he cantered along, ducking beneath the tunnel of gunnera, slipping and sliding down the precipitous steps to the quarry. Then across the quarry and over the gate; a farm lane, a stone stile, and, finally, the cliffs.

She was waiting for him, standing on grassy turf. The wind tore at her cotton skirt and sent it ballooning about her long tanned legs, and her violet eyes were brimming with laughter.

"I thought I was going for a walk, not a marathon run."

"But worth it. You must admit, worth it."

And Gus looked, and saw the dark turquoise sea, the scrap of beach, and the mammoth breakers hurling themselves against rocks at the foot of the cliffs. Spray, in rainbow-shot explosions, sprang twenty feet into the air. It was spectacular.

They found shelter from the wind behind a huge boulder, yellow with lichen and stonecrop. Loveday settled herself, snuggling into her sweater for warmth. Gus lay beside her, legs outstretched, his weight supported by his elbows.

She turned her face up to the sun. After a bit, "That's better," she said. "Warmer now. You live in Scotland, don't you?"

"Yes. Aberdeenshire. On Deeside."

"Are you near the sea?"

"No. Just the river."

Loveday thought about this. "I don't think I could live away from the sea. It's torture."

He smiled. "As bad as that?"

"Yes. And I know, because when I was twelve, I was sent off to boarding school in Hampshire, and I nearly expired. I lasted half a term, and then I came home. I've been here ever since."

"I see."

She brooded for a bit, and then, "Do you think there's going to be a war?" she asked.

"Probably."

"What will happen to you?"

"I'll be called up. I'm in the Territorial Army. The Gordon Highlanders. It's like being a part-time soldier. I joined in 1938, after Hitler walked into Czechoslovakia."

"Edward's going into the Royal Air Force."

"I know. I suppose we both saw the writing on the wall."

"What about Cambridge?"

"If the balloon does go up, our final exams will have to wait."

Loveday sighed. "What a waste." She fell silent for a time, then said, "What time is it?"

"Half past four. Someone should buy you a watch."

"They do, but I always lose them. Perhaps we should go back." She unfolded her long legs and abruptly stood up, impatient to be off. "The others should be home before long."

He pulled himself to his feet and felt the smack of the wind. "This time how about keeping to a reasonable pace?" He spoke lightheartedly, knowing that it wasn't much of a joke. Not that it mattered, because Loveday was not listening. She had paused,

257

turned away from him, as though reluctant to leave the sea. And in that moment Gus saw not Loveday, but the Laura Knight girl, the picture that he had stealthily removed, so long ago, from the pages of *The Studio*. Even her clothes—the worn tennis shoes, the striped cotton skirt, the aged cricket sweater—were the same. Only the hair was different. No russet plait lying like a heavy rope over one shoulder. Instead, Loveday's mop of dark, shining curls, ruffled by the wind.

They retraced their steps, and by the time the house appeared above them, Gus was warm with exertion. He stopped to shed his sweater, and Loveday smiled. "On a really hot day, by the time you've got this far, all you want is another swim."

Just then, Gus heard the sound of an approaching car. Looking, he saw a stately Daimler cross the gravel to halt by the side of the house.

"They're back." Loveday seemed filled with apprehension. "Pops and Edward. . . ." And she raced across the grass, calling to them. "What's happening? Is everything all right?"

Gus followed at a deliberately slow pace, all at once wishing that he were anyplace but here. This was not the time to be an unknown guest.

But it was too late now. He climbed the wide stone stairway which bisected the top terrace and stepped onto level ground. The Daimler stood there, its occupants forming a little group. Edward, seeing Gus, detached himself and came forward. "Gus! Great to see you." And so warm was his welcome that all reservations vanished. Gus was filled with gratitude.

THE following morning Edward rang Judith at the store.

"Hello?" Her voice was thin with anxiety. "Edward? What is it?"

"It's okay. Good news."

"Aunt Lavinia?"

"She seems to have pulled through. Apparently she woke up this morning, asked the night nurse what on earth she was doing sitting by her bed, and demanded a cup of tea. If she's fit for visitors, I'll take you to see her Sunday. Meanwhile, everybody's flying back from all points of the compass to be here. Ma arrived last night, and Athena and Rupert are on their way from Scotland. The whole thing has turned into a complete circus."

"Wish I was with you all."

"Don't wish too hard. It's a bit like living in the middle of Piccadilly. But I miss you. There's a hole in the house without you."

"Oh, Edward."

"See you Sunday morning."

It was not until the final day of her stay in Porthkerris that Judith set off to see Phyllis. Just beyond Pendeen she drove past the tin mine where Phyllis's husband, Cyril, was working a weekend shift. The countryside was bleak, primeval, forbidding.

As Judith pulled up to the cottage, Phyllis came running to greet her with the baby in her arms. "Judith!" she cried, and they hugged.

She had changed. Not aged exactly, but lost weight and, with it, some of her bloom. But nothing could stop her smile.

The cottage was dismal, a two-room affair with a washhouse tacked on the back. It had one cold-water tap. All was clean as a bleached bone, of course, but just about as cheerful.

Judith had brought small presents, and Phyllis was thrilled with them. Some lavender soap and a coat for little Anna. After Phyllis put the baby in her pram, they settled down to tea.

There was much to talk about, and Judith began by filling in the details of life with the Carey-Lewises at Nancherrow.

"Sounds lovely," Phyllis said. "By this time it must feel like they're your own family. How's that young doctor you met on the train? The one you wrote me about. Still around, is he?"

"You mean Jeremy Wells? We scarcely see him now. When he left St. Thomas's, he went into practice with his father in Truro, so now he's a busy country doctor with little time for socializing."

Judith had brought with her a wallet of recent snapshots of Singapore taken by her father. "It must be a wonderful place," Phyllis said, leafing through the pictures. "And now you've finished school, you'll be joining them. When are you going?"

"I've got passage booked in October." Judith sighed. "But I really don't know what I'll do if there's a war."

"Terrible, isn't it?" said Phyllis. "Everything so uncertain. Why can't that Hitler leave people alone?"

All at once she sounded desolate, and Judith tried to cheer her. "But *you'll* be all right, Phyllis. Mining's bound to be a reserved occupation. Cyril won't have to go and be a soldier."

"Some hope," Phyllis told her. "Made up his mind, he has. Reserved occupation or not, if war breaks out, he's going to join the navy. Truth is, he's fed up with tin mining. He's wanted to go to sea ever since he was a little boy."

"But what about you? And the baby?"

"I dunno. The mine company owns this house. We don't have to pay rent; it's like a tied cottage. But if Cyril goes in the navy, we'd have to get out. I'd go back to Mum's, I suppose."

It was late in the afternoon before Judith said her good-byes and set off on the drive back to Porthkerris. She found it painful to tear herself away and leave Phyllis in that unlovely cottage which spoke of little money and hard times.

And if there was a war, then Cyril was going, leaving Phyllis and her baby behind. *I'd go back to Mum's, I suppose.* Dispossessed. If only there was some way of helping. But it would just be interfering. Phyllis had her dignity. All Judith could do was keep in touch and visit as often as she could.

THE Nancherrow kitchen on Sunday mornings was a cauldron of furious activity. Nine in the dining room to feed. No, Mrs. Nettlebed corrected herself, eight, because Mrs. Carey-Lewis had taken to her bed and would probably have to be taken a tray. Mrs. Nettlebed stood at her kitchen table and rubbed flour, sugar, and butter briskly through her fingers into a large earthenware bowl. In the oven a twelve-pound sirloin of beef on the bone was simmering away, and the aroma was of rich meaty juices mingled with the scent of onion.

The kitchen door opened. Mrs. Nettlebed, imagining that it was her husband, did not raise her head but said, "Do you think we should have whipped cream with the soufflé?"

"Sounds delicious," said a man who was not Mr. Nettlebed. She jerked around and saw none other than Jeremy Wells.

"Dr. Wells!" She stood there, her hands all floury, and beamed. "You're some stranger. Did the Colonel send for you?"

Jeremy closed the door. "Why should he send for me?"

"Mrs. Carey-Lewis. She's poorly." She frowned. "If the Colonel didn't send for you, then why are you here?"

"Just to see you all. Where is everybody?"

"All gone to church. Except Mrs. Carey-Lewis."

"Perhaps I should pop up and see her. Have you got a houseful?"

"Bulging, we are. Athena brought her young man, Captain Rycroft, and Edward's got a friend staying too. And Judith's coming back from Porthkerris this morning."

"Is there enough lunch for me?"

"Enough and over, I would say. Now why don't you go up and see Mrs. Carey-Lewis."

JEREMY found Diana propped up on downy pillows and wearing a lace-trimmed voile bed jacket. Beside her, Pekoe lay curled into a ball and fast asleep.

"Jeremy, what are you doing here? Oh, Edgar didn't bother you with a summons, did he?"

"No, he didn't call." He came to sit on the edge of the bed. She looked washed out, pale as paper. "So what have you been up to, to get yourself in this state?"

"Oh, Lavinia's been so ill, and there's too much to do. Mary and I have got to buy thousands of yards of horrible black cotton and somehow make curtains for every window in the house. The truth is, I've run out of energy. So I came to bed."

"Are you worrying about Mrs. Boscawen?"

"Yes, a bit. Lavinia's not out of the wood yet. And I was frazzled anyway, after London and strings of late nights, and then I had to come bolting home to find everybody bringing people to stay." She smiled at him wryly. "This young man of Athena's wants to marry her. He's called Rupert. Terribly sweet. Royal Dragoons. Rather conventional and totally unexpected."

"That sounds rather cheering news."

"Well, it is, in a way, but how can anything be joyful when the papers are full of such gloom and doom, and everything gets worse every day? Edgar makes me listen to the nine-o'clock news each night with him, and sometimes I think I'm going to be sick with terror."

Her voice shook, and Jeremy felt real concern. He laid his hand over hers. "You mustn't be afraid, Diana. You're never afraid of anything."

"I've been like an ostrich all this year, burying my head in the sand and pretending that it's not going to happen. But it isn't any good any longer. Deceiving oneself, I mean. There isn't going to be

261

a miracle. Just another terrible war." To his horror Jeremy saw her eyes well with tears, and she made no effort to brush them away. "After the Armistice in 1918, we told ourselves that it would never happen again. A whole generation of young men wiped out in the trenches. All my friends. Gone. And do you know what I did? I stopped thinking about it. I stopped remembering. I simply put it all out of my mind. But now, only twenty years later, it's all starting again, and I can't help remembering. Dreadful things. Going to Victoria Station to say good-bye, and all the boys in khaki, and then the pages and pages of casualty lists."

She was weeping now, dabbing at her streaming cheeks with a scrap of handkerchief. "I'm talking too much, aren't I?"

"Not at all. It seems to me you need to talk, and I am here to listen."

"Oh, darling Jeremy, you are the dearest man. And actually, I know there has to be a war. I know we can't go on letting dreadful things happen in Europe. Somebody has to stop Hitler, and I suppose it has to be us." She smiled at him wryly, and it was like a watery beam of sunshine on a wet day. "Now, I'm not going to moan anymore. It's so lovely to see you. But I still can't think why you're here. Why aren't you mixing potions and telling people to say 'Aah'? Or perhaps your father's given you the day off?"

"No. As a matter of fact, I am no longer my father's partner. I volunteered to join the navy. Surgeon Lieutenant Commander Jeremy Wells, RNVR. How does that sound to you?"

"Oh, Jeremy. Terribly impressive but frightfully frightening and brave. Do you really have to do this?"

"I've done it. I even went ahead and bought my uniform. I have to report to Devonport Barracks next Thursday. I wanted to see you all. Say good-bye."

"You'll stay, of course."

"If there's a bed."

"Oh, darling boy, there's always a bed for you. Did Mrs. Nettlebed tell you about Gus Callender, Edward's chum? He's rather interesting. Loveday, I fear, is besotted."

"*Loveday?*"

"Isn't it astonishing? You know how offhand she's always been with Edward's friends. Giving them dreadful nicknames and mimicking their voices. Well, this is quite a different cup of tea."

Jeremy found himself amused. "Why is he so interesting?"

"I don't know. Reserved, I suppose. And he's an artist. Amazingly good. Anyway, we all seem to have entered a tacit agreement not to tease. Even Edward's being tactful. After all, we sometimes forget that our wicked baby is nearly eighteen. Perhaps it's time she fell in love with something that doesn't have four legs and a tail. And I must say, he's very sweet with her."

Suddenly she yawned and settled back on her pillows. "I wish I didn't feel so tired. All I really want to do is sleep."

"Then sleep."

"It's made me feel so much better, just talking to you. Tell Mary you're staying. She'll find a room for you."

"Right." He stood. "I'll come and see you later on."

HE LEFT her, closing the door behind him. For a moment he hesitated, hearing the sound of music coming from the far end of the guest wing. Judith's room. She was here. She had returned from Porthkerris. Was probably unpacking. And had put a record on her gramophone for companionship.

Bach. "Jesu, Joy of Man's Desiring."

He stood there and listened. After a bit he went down the passage, his footsteps muffled by the thick carpet. Judith's door stood ajar. He pushed it gently open. Suitcases and bags stood about the floor, apparently abandoned, for she sat at her desk writing a letter. Her profile was framed by the open window, and he remembered the little girl in the railway carriage. Now, with her honey-colored hair falling across one cheek, he saw that she was in the full flower of womanhood. Her concentration, her unawareness of his presence rendered her so vulnerable, so lovely, that all at once Jeremy found himself wishing that time could be stopped. He wanted the moment to last forever.

The music of Bach came to its stately conclusion. "Judith."

She looked up and saw him, and he watched her face pale with apprehension. She said, "Diana's ill."

"Not a bit," he told her instantly. "Just tired out."

"Oh." She dropped her pen and leaned back in her chair. "What a *relief.* Come and sit down. I haven't seen you for months."

So he stepped into the room and lowered himself into a little armchair. "Did you have a good time in Porthkerris?"

"Yes. It's always fun there." Then she smiled. "You know, Jeremy, you are extraordinary. You never change. You look just the same as you did when I first saw you, in the train from Plymouth."

"I don't know quite how to take that. I always thought there was room for improvement."

She laughed. "It was meant as a compliment. Have you got the day off or something?"

He said, "I'm on leave. Embarkation leave, I suppose you call it. I've joined the navy. I report to Devonport next Thursday."

"Oh, *Jeremy*. We'll miss you. Will you go to sea?"

"With a bit of luck. Now"—he heaved himself out of the little chair—"I must go and find Mary and be given a billet."

Standing in the open doorway, he paused, listening. From downstairs could be heard voices, footsteps, slamming doors, and Tiger's joyous barking. "The church party would appear to have returned. See you later."

THEY had all come back, flooding into the house: the family and the two strangers whom Judith had yet to meet. And Edward. Downstairs. Her heart began to beat with scarcely suppressed excitement. As she put on a splash of scent, Loveday appeared in the doorway.

"Judith! What are you doing? You've got to come down and see everybody. . . . Gosh, you look super."

"So do you! Where did you get that heavenly jacket?"

"It's Athena's. She lent it to me. It's Schiaparelli. Isn't it divine? Oh, Judith, I have to tell you about Gus before you meet him. He's simply the most wonderful person I've ever met in my life, and we've done lots and lots together, and he never seems to be the least bit bored with me or anything like that."

Her face, as she imparted this riveting information, shone with a sort of inner happiness that Judith had never seen before. She had always been pretty, but now she looked sensational. Falling in love, Judith decided, suited Loveday well.

"Oh, Loveday, why should he be bored with you? Nobody's ever been bored with you in all your life. Tell me, what sort of things have you been doing together?"

"Oh, *everything*. Swimming, and showing him the farm, and taking him places so that he can do his painting. He's a frightfully clever artist. But do come down now. Everybody's having drinks in the garden."

Following Loveday down, stepping outdoors, Judith was dazzled by light. The garden shimmered and flickered in noonday sun reflected from the sea. In the breeze the leaves of the eucalyptus shivered, and the thick white fringe of Diana's garden umbrella, speared through the center hole of an ornate cast-iron table, jigged in the wind.

Beyond the dark shadow of the umbrella, canvas chairs had been set up, tartan car rugs spread upon the grass. Judith looked for Edward, but he was not there. Only three figures waited for them, gracefully arranged, as though they had been posed. This impression of a canvas was so strong that Judith found herself regarding the scene as though appraising a painting, a brilliant oil, importantly framed in gold: *Before Lunch, Nancherrow, 1939.* A work that one would long to own, be impelled to buy, however costly, and keep forever.

Three figures. Athena lay on a rug, propped up on her elbows. Two men had drawn up chairs facing her. One was very dark, the other fair. They had shucked off their jackets and ties and rolled up their shirtsleeves. Gus Callender and Rupert Rycroft. So which of them had captured the wayward Loveday's heart?

Loveday ran to join them. "Where is everybody?" she demanded as the two young men rose from their chairs. Judith followed her across the grass, momentarily suffused with shyness. Both men, she saw, were tall, but the fair one was exceptionally lanky and thin.

Athena turned her dark glasses onto Judith. "Hello, darling. Heaven to see you. You haven't met Gus and Rupert. Chaps, this is Judith, our surrogate sister. The house always seems half empty when she isn't here." They all shook hands.

Rupert was the very tall one, Athena's friend, unmistakably army, with his neat mustache and his relentless haircut. But Gus was not unmistakably anything. His eyes were as black as coffee, his skin was olive, and he had a deep cleft in his chin. His demeanor was one of a man strangely contained, even shy perhaps.

"Where is everybody?" Loveday asked again.

Athena told her as they all settled down. "Pops has gone up to see Mummy, and Edward's hunting up something to drink."

Gus had laid his jacket on the grass beside him. Now he reached

265

to pick it up, feeling in his pocket for his cigarettes. As he did this, an object slipped from an inner pocket and fell upon the grass alongside Judith's chair. She saw a small, thick sketchbook, secured with a rubber band. Loveday, sitting at his feet, pounced upon it. "Your sketch pad. You mustn't lose that."

He looked embarrassed. "Sorry." He put out a hand to take it, but Loveday hung on. "Oh, do let me show Judith. You wouldn't mind. I want her to see. Please."

Judith felt a pang of pity for Gus, who clearly did not want his essentially private work put on display. She said, "Loveday, perhaps he doesn't want us all gawping." She looked at Gus. "Do you carry a sketchbook with you always?"

"Yes." Suddenly he smiled at her, perhaps grateful for her championship, and the smile transformed his solemn features. "Some people take photographs, but I'm better at drawing."

He took the book from Loveday and tossed it into Judith's lap. "Feel free. Just pencil sketches—nothing very good."

But Loveday intervened, coming to kneel at Judith's side, turning the pages, and keeping up a running commentary. "And this is the cove. Isn't it lovely? Gus did it in a moment. Here's Mrs. Mudge's barn, with the hens on the steps."

As the pages were slowly turned, Judith found herself filled with wonder. Each small sketch had been set down with the detail of an architect's drawing, and he had tinted them with pale washes of watercolor. The colors were totally original, observed by a true artist's eye, so that an old tin-mine stack stood lilac in the evening light; a slated roof was blue as hyacinths.

Halfway through the book, Loveday announced, "This is the last. The rest is blank." She turned the final page with a flourish. "Ta-ra ta-ra, it's me. Gus did a painting of *me.*"

But there was no need to be told. Loveday, sitting on some cliff top and silhouetted against the sea, wearing a faded pink cotton dress, the wind ruffling her dark curls. And Judith saw that Gus had captured the very essence of Loveday, at her most vulnerable, her sweetest. This was a miniature portrait painted with love.

She looked up and saw that Gus was watching her. For a split second she experienced an intense rapport with him. *You under-stand. I know that you know. Don't say anything.* He had said nothing, but the words came through like a telepathic message. She smiled at him and tossed the sketchbook over. "Really brilliant. Thank you for letting me look."

"Not at all." He turned to reach for his jacket, and the spell was broken, the moment over. "It's just a hobby."

Now, from the open French windows, Edward and Jeremy emerged, both bearing trays of bottles and glasses. Judith watched them, treading across the sunlit summer lawn, laughing together over some unheard joke, and just seeing Edward made her heart lift. She knew that this was the instant of total certainty, that she loved him beyond all else, had always loved him and always would.

The trays were set down with a thankful thump. Edward came to stand between Judith and the sun. She looked up into his face, saw his blue eyes and his lock of fair hair. He stooped, supporting himself on the struts of her deck chair, to give her a kiss. He said, "You got home safely."

"About an hour ago."

He smiled and straightened up. And it was enough.

The drinks were dispensed, and with everybody finally settled, they discussed plans for after lunch.

"We're definitely going to the cove," Loveday announced. "Anyway, Gus and I are going, whatever anybody else wants. The tide's high at five o'clock, and it'll be quite perfect."

"I wouldn't miss it for anything," said Athena. "We'll all go. And we must have a picnic—tea and lemonade and biscuits."

"It sounds a bit like a military expedition," said Rupert.

Athena slapped his knee playfully. "Oh, don't be silly."

Edward frowned. "Judith and I aren't coming."

"Of course you must come. Why not?"

"We have a previous engagement. We're going up to the Dower House to see Aunt Lavinia. Just for a little while. She hasn't seen Judith since she was ill."

"Oh, well." Athena shrugged. "If it's only for a while, you can join us later. We'll leave one of the tea baskets for you to lug down, so don't not come or we'll be short of food. Talking of which . . ."

At that point Colonel Carey-Lewis made his appearance, stalking across the lawn towards them. "How very comfortable you all look," he said. "But Nettlebed asks me to tell you that luncheon is served."

And with that, the small procession straggled indoors.

RIGHT AFTER LUNCH EDWARD drove with Judith to the Dower House. Aunt Lavinia, her bedroom filled with sunshine and flowers, lay in bed, propped up by snowy pillows, her shoulders wrapped in a Shetland shawl, her white hair neatly dressed.

"Oh, my darlings, I've been so looking forward to this. Judith, I haven't seen you for far too long."

She had lost a lot of weight, but those eyes were as bright as ever. Judith stooped to kiss her.

"And Edward, dear boy. Come and sit down. Now"—Judith had drawn up a chair, and Aunt Lavinia reached for her hand—"how was Porthkerris? And tell me all about Athena's young man."

They stayed for half an hour, and they talked and laughed and brought Aunt Lavinia up to date on every single thing that had happened. They told her about Rupert and Jeremy and Gus.

But finally, discreetly, Edward glanced at his watch. "I think perhaps we should be on our way, Aunt Lavinia. We don't want to tire you out. Is there anything you want?"

"No. I have everything." And then she remembered. "Yes. There is something you can do for me."

Aunt Lavinia let go of Judith's hand and turned to the drawer of her bedside table. She groped inside and withdrew, attached to a crumpled label, a key. She said, "The Hut," and held it out to Edward. "It has been sadly neglected since I fell ill. Before you go, will you and Judith check that everything is all right?"

Edward, standing, laughed. "Aunt Lavinia, you're a constant surprise. The last thing you need to worry about is the Hut. But rest assured, if there is so much as a mouse or a beetle, we will send it on its way."

Outside, Edward led the way along the path, through the rose garden, and down to the orchard. The Hut, tucked into its sheltered corner, basked in sunshine. Edward fitted the key in the lock, and Judith followed him inside.

They stood, very close, in the small space between the two bunks. It still smelled pleasantly of creosote but was musty with imprisoned heat. A huge bluebottle buzzed around the hurricane lamp, and in a corner was an enormous cobweb studded with dead flies.

Edward went to open the windows, and the bluebottle buzzed away into the open air. He delved into a cupboard and came up with a small brush and dustpan. She watched while he neatly dis-

posed of the cobweb and its victims, then went out and shook
contents onto the grass. Returning, "What else?" he asked her.

"I think that's all. Perhaps the windows need cleaning."

"That'll be a nice job for you, one day when you've nothing bet
to do." He stowed the dustpan and brush, then settled himself
the edge of one of the bunks. "You can play house."

She sat too, on the other bunk, facing him. He was so close sh
could have reached out and touched his cheek. Their eyes met. He
said, "Dear Judith. You've become so lovely. Did you know that?
And I did miss you."

"Oh, Edward."

He put his hands on her shoulders, and leaned forward across
the little space and kissed her. A gentle kiss that swiftly became
passionate, but this time she neither drew away nor rejected him,
because her entire body seemed to leap into life.

He stood and lifted her, and laid her down on the bunk. He sat
at her side and stroked her hair from her face, and then, gently,
began to undo the small pearl buttons of her cotton dress.

"Edward. . . ." Her voice was a whisper. "I've never—"

"I know you haven't. I shall show you the way." He gently pushed
her dress down from her shoulders. And she wasn't frightened, just
peaceful and excited all at the same time. She took his head between her hands and gazed into his face. "I love you, Edward." And
after that there was no need to say anything more.

A BUZZING sound. Not the bluebottle, but an enormous, droning
bumblebee. Judith opened her eyes and watched it settle on one of
the dusty windowpanes.

Beside her, on the narrow bunk, Edward lay, his arm beneath
her. She turned her head, and his brilliant eyes were open and
startlingly close. He said very quietly, "All right?"

She smiled and nodded. "What time is it?"

He raised his arm to look at his watch. "Half past three." He
sighed deeply. "Perhaps we should stir ourselves. We have to show
up at the picnic; otherwise a thousand questions will be asked."

"Yes. I suppose."

He kissed her. Then he sat up and, with his back to her, pulled
on his shirt and trousers. Beyond the opened door the breeze
stirred the apple trees. Edward left her then and went through the

269

door, reaching in his pocket for cigarettes. Judith watched him lean a shoulder against the wooden post of the small veranda. A bit disheveled and deliciously decadent, with his bare feet and his tousled hair.

Edward. She could feel the smile creep into her face. Now they had taken the final step, and he had been wonderfully sweet, claiming Judith for his own in the most complete of ways. They were a pair. A couple. Sometime, somewhere, they would be married and together forever.

She yawned and sat up, and reached for her own clothes, then slipped on her dress. Edward, finished with his cigarette, came back to her and sat down once more. They faced each other, just as they had done before, an hour ago, an age ago, a world ago.

She did not speak. After a bit he said, "We really should go."

But there was so much to say. "I do love you, Edward." That was the most important. "I suppose I always have." It was wonderful to be able to say the words, not to have to be secretive any longer. "I can't imagine, ever, loving anybody else."

He said, "But you will."

"Oh, no. I never could."

He repeated himself. "Yes. You will." He spoke very kindly. "You're grown up now. Eighteen. With the whole of your life ahead of you. This is just the beginning."

"I know. Of being with you. Belonging with you."

He shook his head. "No. Not with me."

Confusion. "But—"

"Just listen. What I'm saying doesn't mean I'm not enormously, intensely fond of you. Protective. Tender. All these things. All the right emotions. But they belong to now. This moment, this afternoon. Not for always."

She listened and was stunned with disbelief. He didn't know what he was saying. She felt the warm certainty of being loved drain slowly from her heart. How could he not realize what she knew beyond all doubt? That they belonged to each other.

She searched frantically for reasons for his excuses. "I know what it is. It's the war. You're going to have to go fight with the RAF, and you might be killed, and you don't want to leave me all alone—"

He interrupted her. "The war has nothing to do with it. Whether or not there is a war, I have a whole life to live before I commit

myself, settle down. I'm not twenty-one yet. I couldn't begin to make a long-term decision if somebody put a gun to my head. Maybe I will marry someday, but not until I'm at least thirty-five, and by then you will have gone your own way and made your own decisions, and be living happily ever after."

He sounded like a grown-up trying to coax a sulky child into a good humor. She lost her patience and rounded on him. "Edward, what you're saying is that you don't love me."

"I do."

"Not the way I love you."

"Perhaps not. Like I said, I feel ridiculously protective about you, as though I were in some way responsible for your happiness. I've watched you growing up, and you've been part of Nancherrow all these years. That incident with the wretched Billy Fawcett brought it all home to me. It made my flesh creep to think of you being traumatized by that bloody old man. I couldn't stand thinking of it happening again."

She began to understand. "So you made love to me. *You* did it."

"I wanted to lay his ghost to rest forever. It had to be me, not some lusty lout giving you a miserable time, destroying all the joy."

"You were doing me a kindness. You were sorry for me." Her head was starting to ache. She could feel the pain throbbing in her temples. "A good turn," she finished bitterly.

"Darling Judith, never think that. Give me the benefit at least of loving you with the best of intentions."

But that wasn't enough. She looked down, away from his eyes. She said, "I seem to have made a terrible fool of myself."

"Never. It's not foolish to love. It's just that I'm not right for you. You need somebody quite different—an older man who'll give you all the wonderful things you deserve."

"I wish you'd said all this before."

"You're angry."

"Well, what do you *expect* me to be?" Her aching eyes were hot with unshed tears. "So what happens now?"

He shrugged. "We're friends. Nothing changes that."

"We just carry on? Like we did before? Being tactful and not upsetting Diana. I don't know if I can do that, Edward."

He stayed silent. After a bit he stood and went to close the windows. The bumblebee had flown. He went to the door, waiting for her to go out before him. As she did so, he stopped her and turned her to face him. "Try to understand. Nothing's changed."

Which Judith thought was perhaps the most stupid, untrue thing she had ever heard any man say. She pulled away and plunged out into the orchard, running, willing herself not to burst into tears.

They returned to Nancherrow in silence. Judith's headache had reached proportions which rendered her incapable of any conversation. She thought, with sinking heart, of the picnic down at the cove. Seeing the others. All too much. As they approached the house, she took a deep breath. "I don't think I want to come to the cove. I've got a headache."

"Oh, *Judith*." He clearly thought this was some excuse, and he turned to look at her. "I say, you do look pale. I am sorry. When we get in, why don't you lie down for a bit. We can go down to the cove later."

"Yes." She thought with longing of her own quiet room, the curtains drawn against the unforgiving light, the cool soft linen beneath her throbbing head. Peace. Solitude. A space of time in which to gather up her dignity and lick her wounds. "Perhaps I will. You mustn't wait for me."

When they got out of the car and went into the house, there on the table in the hall stood the picnic basket. Beside it was a note: "Come right away. No hanging about. X. Athena."

Judith said, "You'd better go."

But he clearly felt guilty about leaving her. He gazed down into her face. "Are you sure you'll be all right?"

"Of course. Just go, Edward."

Still he lingered. "Am I forgiven?" He was like a small boy, needing reassurance that all was right with his world.

"Oh, Edward. It was just as much my fault as yours." Which was true, but so shame-making, it was unpleasant to think about.

It was, however, enough for Edward. He smiled. "I couldn't bear the thought of us not being friends." He lifted the heavy basket and turned. "I shall be waiting for you," he told her.

Judith could feel the tears again swimming up into her eyes, and it was not possible to speak. So she nodded, and he walked away through the open door, was silhouetted for an instant against the sunlight, and then gone.

She went towards the staircase, sank down at the bottom, and leaned her forehead against the cool wood of the banister. The tears now were flowing, and she was weeping like a child. It didn't matter, because there was no person to hear, and it was a relief just to give way to her misery and let it all pour out.

At that moment she heard footsteps at the top of the staircase. "Judith?" It was Mary Millyway. But Judith, frantically mopping at tears, was not capable of speaking.

Mary was coming downstairs. "I thought you'd gone to the cove." Judith shook her head. "No."

"So what are all the tears about?" Mary sat beside Judith and laid an arm around her shoulders. "Tell Mary. What is it?"

"Nothing. I've—I've just got a headache. I didn't want to go to the cove." Only then did she turn her face to Mary. "You haven't got a handkerchief, have you?"

One was produced, and Judith blew her nose.

"Now, what are we to do about this headache? How about coming up with me, and I'll find something in my medicine cupboard."

The comfort of her presence, her aura of normality and good sense were like a balm. She helped Judith to her feet and led her upstairs to the nursery, settled her in a corner of the sofa. Then she disappeared and returned with a glass of water and a couple of tablets. "Take those now and just sit quiet, and I'll make tea."

Judith dutifully took the tablets. She lay back and, with her hand clenched around Mary's handkerchief, closed her eyes.

Presently Mary returned, bearing teapot and cups on a little tray. "There's nothing like a cup of tea when you're feeling a bit down."

Judith took the steaming tea from Mary, and the cup rattled in her hand. "Thank you, Mary. You are a saint. I don't know what I'd have done if you hadn't been here."

"I don't think," said Mary, "that I've ever seen you cry like that before. Something happened, didn't it?"

Judith glanced up, but Mary was concentrating on pouring tea for herself. "Why do you say that?"

"Because I'm not a fool. I know you children like I know the back of my hand. You wouldn't be in tears for nothing, sobbing your heart out as though you'd lost the world. It's Edward, isn't it?"

Judith saw in Mary's face neither curiosity nor disapproval. She was simply stating a fact. She would neither judge nor blame.

She said, "Yes, it's Edward." The relief of admitting it, saying it out loud, was immense.

"Fallen in love with him, have you?"

"It was almost impossible not to."

"Had a row?"

"No. Just a sort of misunderstanding. You see, I thought it was all right to tell him how I felt. But I was wrong, and at the end of it all, I made a complete fool of myself."

Mary said, "Gone a bit too far, has it?"

"You could say that."

"Well, it's happened before, and it'll happen again. But I feel some vexed with Edward. He's a lovely man, and he'd charm the birds out of the trees, but he's no thought for others, nor for the future. Skims over life like a dragonfly."

"I know. I suppose I've always known. . . . I told Edward I'd go down to the cove later. But I don't want to face them all, asking questions, wondering. I wish I could just disappear."

She waited for Mary to say, "Don't be so silly; no point in running away." Instead, she said, "I don't think that's such a bad idea."

Judith looked at her in amazement.

"Where's Mrs. Somerville now?" Mary asked.

"Aunt Biddy? In Devon. In her house there."

"You're going to stay with her?"

"Yes. Later."

"I think you should go now. This very afternoon."

"But I couldn't just go."

"Now listen, my dear. Someone has to say this, and there's nobody but me to do it. I've watched you growing up, seen you being absorbed by this family, and a wonderful thing it's been. But it's dangerous too. Because they're *not* your family, and if you're not very careful, you're in danger of losing your own identity. You're eighteen. It's time to break loose and go your own way."

"How long have you thought this, Mary?"

"Since last Christmas. I guessed then that you were getting involved with Edward. I prayed you wouldn't, because I knew how it would end. You've landed yourself in a bit of an emotional mess, but the best thing to do is to grasp the nettle. Take the initiative. If for no other reason, to shore up your own dignity."

Judith knew that she was right, but the complications of departure were numerous. "How can I just leave, without any sort of excuse? It would be *too* ill mannered."

"Well, the first thing to do is to telephone your aunt. Ask if she'd mind if you turned up this evening. And then we'll make *her* the reason for your going. Say she's unwell, all alone, needs nursing. When the others get back, I'll say she rang you, and it sounded so urgent you just got into your car and went."

"So you mean—"

"You don't need to see anyone, not until you're strong enough, and ready. Now it's time to get moving."

JUDITH had fetched her car from the garage, and Mary stowed her suitcase in the back. Then they hugged. "So. That's it. Don't grieve for Edward," Mary said. "Don't look back, nor let your heart be broken. You're too young and too lovely for that."

"I'll be all right."

Judith got in behind the wheel and started the engine. It was agony not crying, but she managed not to. She told herself, "It's not forever," but it felt like that. The car rolled forward across the gravel. In her side-view mirror she saw the reflection of Nancherrow, washed in sunlight, receding away. And she knew that she would come back, but Nancherrow, as she'd known it, would never, ever be quite the same again.

PART II
🎔 *1939* 🎔

*B*IDDY Somerville's house, perched on the hill above the little town of Bovey Tracey, was called Upper Bickley. It was quite old, solidly built of plastered and whitewashed stone. On the ground floor were kitchen, dining room, sitting room, and hall. Upstairs were three bedrooms and a bath, and up again, a musty loft packed with sea chests, old photographs, and Ned's long-abandoned toys.

The house was reached by a steep, winding Devon lane, and the entrance was a farm gate which always stood open. Behind the house was a garden with a stone boundary wall, and beyond that was the beginning of Dartmoor—a sweep of turf and heather crowned by brooding tors. On clear summer days there was a spectacular view over the town to the twinkling waters of the English Channel.

It was the first house the Somervilles had ever owned, and very different from living in naval quarters, but they had a wide circle of friends and were invited to attend dinner parties, race meetings, and cheerful tennis afternoons.

August 1939, and Biddy was content. The only cloud on the horizon, and it was a great one, was the darkening threat of war.

On Sunday evening at nine Biddy was at the window of her sitting room waiting for Judith. Bob had been home for the weekend but after tea had set off back to the base at Devonport. In these tense times he was never away from his office for more than a day.

Biddy was not alone, because a dog was lying at her feet—a Border collie, with a thick coat and an engaging face, that Ned had found wandering around the dockside at Scapa Flow. Ned had brought her home two months before, and now Biddy could scarcely imagine life without Morag.

Still at the window and beginning to be anxious, Biddy heard the car coming up the hill. She hurried to the hall, switching on the light that hung over the front door. Standing with Morag at her heels, she saw the little Morris come through the open gate. The car door opened, and Judith emerged.

"Oh, darling, what a relief." They hugged. "Did you have a dreadful journey?"

"Not too bad. Just long. I'm sorry for springing myself on you."

"Oh, don't be ridiculous. We always love it when you come."

Judith looked down. "Who's this?"

"Morag. She's Ned's."

"What a sweet dog. Hello, Morag."

Biddy carried Judith's case inside and dumped it on the bottom stair. In the glare of the hallway light they stood and looked at each other. Judith seemed a bit pale and much thinner than when Biddy had last seen her.

"Where's Uncle Bob?"

"Went back to Devonport after tea. You'll see him next weekend. Now, what would you like? Food? Drink?"

Judith shook her head. "Just bed. I'm exhausted."

"Up you go, then. And in the morning I'll bring you a cup of tea."

AT NINE O'CLOCK BIDDY WOKE Judith, bearing the promised cup of tea. My first day without Edward, Judith thought, and wished that it hadn't had to start so soon.

"It's a bit misty, but I think it's going to be fine. How did you sleep?"

One step at a time. That was the only way to get through such an unbearably miserable vacuum. Judith made a huge effort and sat up. "Like a log," she said as she reached for her tea.

"Such a drive. You looked drained." Biddy came to sit on the bed. She wore linen trousers and a checked shirt, and though she had put on a bit of weight, her face was just the same—lipstick and laughter lines and bright eyes.

She waited for a moment and then said, "Do you want to talk?"

Judith's heart sank. She tried stalling. "What about?"

Biddy became impatient. "Oh, darling, I'm not a dimwit. Something's happened. Nervous silences are not in character for you, nor making impulsive decisions. So tell. My own life was never unblemished. Whatever it is, I shall understand."

Judith, trying to marshal her thoughts, met Biddy's eyes. Biddy was really family, not just pretend. Being here with her felt right. She put down the teacup and said, "It's just that I've made the most awful fool of myself."

"How?"

Judith told her just about everything, starting at the beginning, when Edward came to pick her up from school for those first spring holidays, and ending yesterday, when she had told him she loved him, only to suffer the terrible humiliation of his rejection. "It was Mary Millyway who suggested that I come to you. I'd like to stay. Just till I've had time to pull myself together."

"I hope it takes ages, because I love to have you here." And Biddy put her arms around Judith, and hugged and patted, and rocked her to and fro.

"And don't feel you have to be cheerful all the time. The great thing is to keep busy. I've got blackout curtains to cut out and sew, and a great list of stuff that Bob says we've got to lay in, in case the war starts and there's an instant shortage. So lots of shopping. Why don't you have a bath and get dressed."

Biddy was right. Occupation was all-important. After breakfast they sat at the kitchen table and made shopping lists. Candles and

277

electric lightbulbs. Petrol. Tins of soup. Spools of black thread for making the curtains. Then everyday items. Food for Morag, butter, a fresh chicken, potatoes, and biscuits. Biddy gathered up her purse, and they drove down the hill into the little town.

That afternoon they started in on the blackout curtains. While Judith set up the old sewing machine on the dining-room table, Biddy measured the windows and cut the lengths of cloth. As soon as the first curtain was finished, they hung it and stood back to survey the result. Biddy sighed. "I've never made anything so unattractive or so disagreeable. All afternoon, and we've only made *one*. The whole house is going to take us forever."

"Well, just be grateful you don't live at Nancherrow."

Over supper they talked about Molly and Jess and going to Singapore. Afterwards it was time for the nine-o'clock news: Nazi troops on the march; Anthony Eden flying somewhere with a fresh missive from the British government; mobilization of reservists imminent. Biddy, unable to bear this gloom, turned the knob of the wireless to Radio Luxembourg, and all at once the room was filled with music.

And Judith was back with Edward, dancing, and it was last Christmas at Nancherrow. I've survived one day, she told herself. One day without him. It felt like the first step of a thousand-mile journey.

By the time Bob Somerville returned to Upper Bickley on the following Saturday morning, a number of events—some quite alarming—had taken place. Herr Hitler, orating at his generals, announced that the destruction of Poland would commence within days. Then the sinister news broke upon the world that the Nazis and the Russians had signed a nonaggression pact. It seemed that nothing now could avert war. Then local people had to present themselves at the school hall and were duly issued gas masks. Biddy and Judith carried theirs home, stowed them under the hall table, and devoutly prayed that they would never have cause to wear them.

By the weekend Judith had completed the mammoth task of stitching the curtains. Now Bob had driven from Devonport, arriving just before midday. His cap, with its golden oak leaves, was jammed down over his brow. His jacket was an old one, and the four stripes of gold braid, set with the purple of an engineer officer, had become tarnished.

Biddy went out to meet him. "I feared you mightn't make it," she told him. "I thought there might be some panic on."

"There is. It's nonstop. But I did want to see you both."

On Sunday, Judith and Bob, with Morag bounding at their heels, climbed five miles up a moorland track, then paused to sit in a grassy hollow. The morning quiet was filled with country sounds. The lowing of sheep, a dog barking, church bells ringing.

Judith plucked a blade of grass and began to shred it with her thumbnail. She said, "Uncle Bob, do you think we could talk?"

He had taken out his pipe and was filling the bowl. "Of course. You can always talk to me."

"It's about something rather difficult. I've decided not to go to Singapore. More than anything I want to see Mummy and Dad and Jess again." Judith took a deep breath. "But it's the war. Everybody's going to be in the thick of it. Everybody I really love. If I go to Singapore, I'll feel like a rat deserting a sinking ship. I mean, it would feel like running away."

Bob was puffing on his pipe. He said, "If you join your parents, no one will think the worse of you. If you don't go, I shall feel you are displaying boundless patriotism. But what about university?"

"Well, Oxford would have to wait. What I'd like to do is join one of the services, but there's not much point joining up unless I've got some sort of a qualification. Heather Warren, my friend in Porthkerris—she's going to learn shorthand and typing. Perhaps I could go back to Porthkerris and do it with her."

"But why not do that from here? Go to Exeter or Plymouth. Biddy misses Ned, and she likes having you around. You'll be able to keep each other company."

"But you've said yourself that the first thing to be rationed is petrol. I wouldn't be able to use my car, and there's only one bus a day out of Bovey Tracey."

Uncle Bob began to laugh. "What a girl you are for details. You'll make an excellent petty officer. I'll work something out. Just be with Biddy for a bit."

She was suddenly filled with love for him. She said, "All right," and leaned forward and kissed his weather-beaten cheek.

It was nearly half past two before they started home. As they made their way through the garden, they heard a car climbing the hill. They stood waiting until the car appeared, a dark Royal Navy staff vehicle with an officer at the wheel. Bob frowned. "My signal officer," and he went to meet him.

The young man, a lieutenant, stepped out of the car and saluted. "Captain Somerville, sir. A signal. It came through an hour ago." He handed it over.

Bob Somerville read the message. After a bit he looked up. "Yes," he said. "Well done, Whitaker. I'll need fifteen minutes. I must have a word with my wife, and pack."

"Right, sir."

Uncle Bob went indoors, and Judith knew that he wanted to be alone with Biddy. She felt fearfully apprehensive, her imagination leaping ahead to imminent invasion or dire news of Ned. "What is happening?" she asked.

"It's a special appointment," Lieutenant Whitaker told her. "The Commander-in-Chief, Home Fleet, has requested Captain Somerville to join his staff at Scapa Flow. With all convenient speed."

Exactly fifteen minutes later Bob reappeared, with Biddy at his side. Back in uniform, back in charge, he looked distinguished.

Lieutenant Whitaker relieved him of his luggage, and Bob turned to embrace his wife. "Send Ned my love," she said.

It was Judith's turn. "Good-bye, Uncle Bob," and they hugged.

He got into the passenger seat, and then he was gone. Biddy and Judith listened until they could hear the car no longer.

Afterwards Judith was always to think of that August Sunday afternoon, and Uncle Bob's going, as the moment when the war really started. The events of the following week—the German invasion of Poland and Mr. Chamberlain's speech declaring war—became in retrospect simply the final formalities preceding a mortal struggle that was to continue for nearly six years.

September 13th, 1939
Dear Diana,

I am so sorry I haven't written to you before, but somehow there hasn't been time. It was horrid leaving you all at such short notice, but I know that you understood.

Aunt Biddy is much better now. But Uncle Bob has gone to Scapa Flow to take up the post of engineer captain on the staff of the Commander-in-Chief, Home Fleet. Biddy can't go with him, and for the time being I am staying here with her.

I decided, before Uncle Bob left us, that I must learn shorthand and typing. It turns out that Biddy has a friend called Hester Lang, a retired civil servant in Bovey Tracey. She came for bridge the other afternoon, and we got talking and she said she would teach me. Once I've got that under my belt, I think I might join the services. The Women's Royal Naval Service, probably.

I do hope all is well. Please give my love to Colonel Carey-Lewis and everybody.

THE reply to Judith's missive arrived at Upper Bickley in an envelope addressed in Loveday's childish scrawl. Judith curled up on the sitting-room sofa and slit the envelope.

September 22nd
Darling Judith,

We loved getting your letter and Mummy's asked me to write.

Tremendous news about your uncle. He must be frightfully efficient and clever. I had to look Scapa Flow up in the atlas. It's practically in the Arctic Circle.

Here things are happening. Palmer, the gardener-chauffeur, has gone off to join the infantry. Mary's been making blackout curtains. Mummy held a Red Cross meeting here, and Pops is putting buckets of water everywhere in case we catch fire. When winter comes we are going to dust-sheet the drawing room and live in the little sitting room. Pops says we must conserve fuel.

After you went, we all missed you dreadfully, but the others followed pretty sharpish. Jeremy was the first to go, and then Rupert shot off to Edinburgh. Edward is at some training base, but we don't know where, because his address is Somewhere in England. I expect he's having the time of his life, flying around and drinking beer in the mess.

And Gus went to Aberdeen, the HQ of the Gordon Highlanders. It was simply ghastly saying good-bye to him. It's so mean, meeting the only man one could ever possibly fall in love with and then having him whisked away. I cried buckets.

Three days after Rupert left, Athena announced that she was going to Edinburgh too, and she got into a train and went. Isn't she

281

the *end?* She's living in the Caledonian Hotel. She says that Edinburgh is bitterly cold, but it doesn't matter, because every now and then she can see Rupert. As for me, I am staying put. Mummy is going to get masses of hens and they will be my war work, and Walter Mudge says he'll teach me how I can help on the farm.

Longing to see you again. Come back as soon as you can.

Lots of love, love, love,

Loveday

P.S.—STOP PRESS! Too exciting. A moment ago, a telephone call from Edinburgh. Athena and Rupert got *married* in a registry office there. Mummy and Pops are torn between delight and fury that they missed the ceremony. It can't be much fun being married and living all by yourself in the Caledonian Hotel.

Judith folded the letter and put it back in its envelope. She gazed from the window and thought about Nancherrow. And Edward. Somewhere in England. Training. *He's having the time of his life, flying around and drinking beer.*

It was still impossible to remember him dispassionately. The way he looked and the sound of his voice. But remembering him did not make her want to cry any longer, so perhaps things were getting a little better.

MID-OCTOBER, six weeks into the war, and nothing very much had happened: no invasion, nor bombing, nor battles in France. But the horrors of the destruction of Poland kept everybody glued to the wireless. It was now beginning to get cold. Judith looked forward to the long, dark months without enthusiasm. At least she had her typing and shorthand lessons to keep her occupied.

On Saturday, the fourteenth of October, Judith and Biddy were in the kitchen, discussing how they were going to spend their day. Judith had to go down to Bovey Tracey to return a book borrowed from Hester Lang, and so she would do the shopping. As Biddy began to compose the inevitable list, the phone rang.

It was Uncle Bob. Last night a German submarine had breached the defenses of Scapa Flow. The *Royal Oak* was in the harbor. She'd been torpedoed, lost.

Ned's ship. Ned Somerville was dead.

AFTER THE *ROYAL OAK* WAS SUNK, Uncle Bob got home for a couple of days, trying to comfort Biddy, feeling all the time just as lost and bereft as she. Then he'd gone back to Scapa Flow, and Judith and Biddy were on their own again.

It was a shattering time, but Biddy was grateful for letters, including a kind note from Colonel Carey-Lewis. And Judith had another letter from Loveday, with news of Nancherrow. Athena was home and was going to have a baby. Rupert had gone to Palestine with his regiment and their horses. Gus was in France with the Highland Division, and Edward had one of the new planes called Spitfires. Jeremy Wells was bucketing to and fro across the Atlantic in a destroyer. Merchant-ship convoys. It sounded pretty rough. Mr. Nettlebed had become an air-raid warden, as had Tommy Mortimer in London. And they were all so terribly sad about Judith's cousin, Ned.

Towards the end of the year it got bitterly cold, and there was snow all over Dartmoor and down the road in Bovey Tracey. Uncle Bob got home for four days over Christmas, then was gone again. Without Ned they tried to treat Christmas just like an ordinary day.

Now Judith sat in the kitchen writing to her parents. She paused and blew on her chilled fingers, then went on with her letter:

> Biddy is still not able to cope with much. She doesn't want to do anything or see anybody yet. It will be better when she gets interested in Red Cross work or something. She is too energetic a person to be doing nothing for the war effort.
>
> I miss you all dreadfully, and sometimes wish I were with you, but now I know I made the right decision. How worried we would have been to think of Biddy on her own.

❧ *1940* ❧

BY THE end of March, after the coldest winter that people could remember, the worst of the snow had finally disappeared. The warm west wind brought a softness to the air, and in the garden of Upper Bickley the first of the daffodils tossed their yellow heads in the breeze.

At Nancherrow, guests from London arrived to stay for Easter. Tommy Mortimer stole a week's leave from his civil defense and brought a store of prewar delicacies from Fortnum & Mason: pheasant in aspic, chocolate-covered cashew nuts, scented tea, and tiny jars of beluga caviar. Mrs. Nettlebed, eyeing these assorted gifts placed upon her kitchen table, was heard to remark that it was a pity that Mr. Mortimer couldn't lay his hands on a decent leg of pork.

Meals at Nancherrow were still served in certain formality in the dining room, but the best of the silver had been stowed away in chamois bags for the duration of the war, and Nettlebed, relieved of the tedious chore of polishing silver, put himself in charge of a vegetable garden. Gradually his grave and pallid features became quite sunburned, and Athena swore that Nettlebed had found his true vocation.

It was in the middle of these Easter holidays, on the night of the eighth of April, that Lavinia Boscawen died. She had simply gone to bed as usual, fallen asleep, and never awaked. It was Isobel who found her. Old Isobel, treading upstairs with Mrs. Boscawen's early morning drink of hot lemon water.

AT UPPER Bickley, the telephone rang, and Judith went to answer it. "Judith, it's Athena. Mummy wanted me to call you. I'm afraid it's very sad news. Aunt Lavinia died."

Judith, stunned, said, "I am so dreadfully sorry. You must all feel devastated."

"Yes. Oh, Judith, would you come to the funeral? Next Tuesday, the sixteenth. It would mean a lot to us all if you did."

Judith hesitated. "Will—will you all be there?"

"Of course. Not Edward, though. He's incarcerated on his airfield. Do come. Everything's ready for you. We never allow anybody into *your* bedroom."

"I'll—I'll have to have a word with Biddy."

"Surely she'll be all right. Besides, it's time we all saw you again. Come on Sunday. Jump on the train. I'll meet you at Penzance. Must fly, darling. See you then."

Judith sought out Biddy and explained the situation.

"Of course you must go. What a sadness." Biddy eyed Judith, standing there chewing her lip. "Will Edward be there?"

Judith shook her head. "No. He can't get leave. If he was going, I'd probably make some excuse."

"Darling, all that happened half a year ago. You can't languish over him for the rest of your life. So off you go."

But Judith remained doubtful. To all outward appearances Biddy was recovered. Prompted by Hester, she had joined the Red Cross and had started seeing friends again. But Judith knew that with Ned's death something of Biddy had died as well. Some days a flicker of her old liveliness returned; other days a depression fell upon her, and she lay in bed and refused to get up.

Judith said, "I just don't like to leave you alone."

"I shall have Hester down the road and all my nice Red Cross ladies. Besides, now that you have finished with the shorthand and typing, there's really no reason for you to stay. I don't want you to go, of course, but let's face it—I must be independent. A few days without you will give me practice."

So Judith said, "All right," and all at once looked forward to returning to Nancherrow. It was going to be dreadfully sad, but she would be *there*, returned to her own pink bedroom, her loved possessions: her desk and her gramophone and her cedarwood box. She thought of being with Loveday and Athena and Mary and Diana and the Colonel, and she knew that it was the next best thing to coming home.

AFTERWARDS, when it was all over, everybody decided that Lavinia Boscawen's funeral was so exactly right that she might have arranged it herself: a sweet spring afternoon, Rosemullion Church filled with flowers. Isobel was there and the solicitor Mr. Baines and Jeremy's parents, Dr. and Mrs. Wells. The Nancherrow party occupied the first two pews. All of them had managed to deck themselves out in black. All except Athena, who wore a flowing maternity dress of cream crepe and looked like a serene angel.

They sang a hymn or two, and Colonel Carey-Lewis read a suitable passage from the Bible, and then there was a prayer. The coffin was borne out into the sunlit graveyard, and the congregation followed.

Judith, tactfully distanced from the family, watched the ritual of burial. "Dust to dust and ashes to ashes." And then she found herself wishing that Edward, for his sake, could have been here to help send Aunt Lavinia on her way.

The wake took place in the Nancherrow dining room. The great

285

table had been set out with Mrs. Nettlebed's tarts and scones, tiny cucumber sandwiches, and iced fairy cakes.

Judith helped Loveday hand around cakes, pausing now and then to chat. She was headed for the sideboard when she found herself, midpassage, face to face with the solicitor.

"Mr. Baines. How good of you to come."

"Judith, I want to talk to you. Could we remove ourselves for five minutes or so? The Colonel says we may use his study."

"Of course." She eased her way from the room, and with Mr. Baines she went down the passage to the study. She sank into a sagging leather armchair. "What did you want to talk to me about?"

"A number of things. How are you?"

She shrugged. "All right."

"Colonel Carey-Lewis told me of your cousin's death. Tragic."

"Yes. He was only twenty. It's terribly young to die, isn't it?" She explained about the shorthand and typing lessons that had helped to fill the long, cold, bereaved winter at Upper Bickley. "I've got my speeds now, so I suppose I can leave Biddy and get a job, but I feel reluctant just to walk out and leave her alone."

"Perhaps the time will come sooner than you think." Mr. Baines sat down, crossing one leg over the other. Judith watched as he took off his spectacles and gave them a polish with his silk handkerchief. "Now, it is perhaps a little precipitant, but I wanted to have a word before you departed for Devon. It's about Mrs. Boscawen's house."

"The Dower House?"

"Exactly so. I wonder what your response would be if I suggested that you should buy it."

Judith stared at him as if he had taken leave of his senses. "The last thing in the world that I need just now is a *house*. There's a war on, and I'll probably join the services and be away for years. Besides, isn't it part of the Nancherrow estate? Won't Colonel Carey-Lewis want it?"

"I have discussed it with him, and apparently not. Let me explain. As one of your trustees, I consider that property probably the best investment you can make. And this is a good time to buy because house prices have dropped, as they always do in wartime. I know the future is filled with uncertainties, but we must look ahead. Whatever happens, you would have a home. Another consideration is your family. Owning the Dower House would mean a base for your mother and father and Jess to return to when their time in Singapore is over."

"That isn't going to happen for years."

"No. But it will happen."

Judith fell silent. All at once there was a great deal to think about. The Dower House. Her own home. Roots. Leaning back in the armchair, she gazed at the empty fireplace and let her imagination lead her through the quiet old house. The drawing room, sparkling with sunlight and firelight, and always the scent of flowers. She thought of the time-stopped atmosphere that never failed to enchant. She saw the terraces down to the orchard, Edward's hut. Would it be possible to deal with so many memories?

She said, "You have to understand—I've always dreamt of having a house of my own. But if I can't live in it, what is the point? The Dower House can't be left standing empty."

"It needn't stand empty," Mr. Baines pointed out. "Isobel will go, of course. She's made plans to live with her brother and his wife. The house could be rented, perhaps to some London family anxious to evacuate to the country. Or we could find some person grateful for a roof over their head who would care for it. . . ." He talked on, but Judith had stopped listening.

A person grateful for a roof over their head, a person who would care for the house. She said, "Phyllis."

Halted midstream, Mr. Baines frowned. "Sorry?"

"Phyllis could caretake." Alight with excitement, she sat up, leaning forward. "She used to work for us at Riverview. She married a miner, but he's joined the navy."

And she went on to explain about Phyllis, who had had to return to her mother's overcrowded house in St. Just. "Phyllis could bring her baby, and *she* could look after the Dower House for us. Wouldn't that be the most perfect arrangement?"

"Judith, you're not buying a home for Phyllis. You're making an investment for yourself."

"But it's *you* who wants me to buy it, and *you* suggested a caretaker. And I've come up with the perfect answer."

He accepted this. "Fair enough, but we seem to have gone from one extreme to the other. I think we must slow down a bit. This is a big step we're considering, and an expensive one. So you have to be certain."

"How much will we have to pay?"

"I would guess in the region of two thousand pounds. There will be repairs and renovations, but the bulk of these will have to wait until the war is over."

"Two thousand pounds. It seems a lot of money."

Mr. Baines allowed himself a small smile. "But a sum that the trust can easily afford."

"Is there really so much? In that case, let's go ahead."

So for a little they talked, laying plans. Mr. Baines would be in touch with Uncle Bob and would contact an engineer. "I'll call you in Devon when I have any news. Then you should come back to Cornwall, and we'll finalize the arrangements."

"I can't wait. Is it wrong to feel so excited on Aunt Lavinia's funeral day?"

"I think," said Mr. Baines, "that the reason for your excitement would afford her nothing but pleasure."

A MONTH had passed at Upper Bickley before the telephone call came through from Mr. Baines. A Thursday morning. Biddy had taken herself off to her Red Cross ladies and Judith was in the garden gathering the first of the lily of the valley when the telephone rang, and she hurried to answer. "Upper Bickley."

"Judith, Roger Baines here. The Dower House has all been arranged. All we need is your presence and a few signatures. Unfortunately, the engineer's report is not that good."

"Never mind," she said. "Someday we'll mend the defects. The most important thing is that we've got it. I'll come to Cornwall on Monday, probably lunchtime. Good-bye. And thank you."

She hung up the receiver and stood there, smiling in an idiotic fashion for a moment or two. She thought, the weather was getting nicer, and Cornwall would be lovely. She'd take Biddy with her. Time she had a change. They'd book rooms at the Mitre Hotel.

By noon on Monday they were in Penzance. Judith came out of the Mitre just as the bank clock chimed half past twelve. The newsagent's placards were black with the morning's news— GERMANS REACH THE BELGIAN COAST.

She walked to the offices of Tregarthen, Opie & Baines. Inside, Mr. Baines stood up from behind the desk. "Judith! Right on time too. Is Mrs. Somerville with you?"

288

"Yes, and the dog. We're all settled in at the Mitre. She's taken Morag for a run on the beach, but I said I'd be back for a late lunch. I hope you can join us."

"What a nice idea. Well, let's not waste any time."

It didn't take very long. Some papers to be signed and the check to be written. When the check was filled out, Judith pushed it across the desk, and Mr. Baines attached it neatly to the rest of the documents.

He leaned back in his chair. "The Dower House is, actually, ready for habitation. Mrs. Carey-Lewis and Isobel have disposed of Mrs. Boscawen's clothes and her personal effects. Isobel leaves this afternoon. At five o'clock her brother is coming to pick her up."

"Is she terribly distressed?"

"In truth, I think she's quite excited starting out on her new life. And she has spent the last two weeks scouring every nook and cranny so that you will find no speck of dust." He smiled. "We'll go to Rosemullion after lunch. Then she can hand over the keys."

"What about the furniture?"

"The Carey-Lewises want you to have it."

"Oh, but—"

Mr. Baines overrode Judith's protestations. "None of it is particularly valuable, but it is perfectly usable and will do splendidly until you acquire some bits and pieces for yourself."

AFTER a cheerful luncheon with Biddy they all got into Mr. Baines's car and set off for Rosemullion. Isobel was waiting at the Dower House when they arrived, dressed in her best black coat and skirt. She was ready for departure, but she took them around, basking modestly in their admiration for the labor she had put in washing curtains, polishing floors, cleaning windows.

Upstairs they went, and up again to the attic bedroom where Isobel had slept. Opposite this another loft, where were stacked old boxes, and bundles of magazines. Isobel said, "It's a nice room. I always thought it would make a lovely bedroom, but then where would we have put all of this?"

Biddy crossed over to the dormer window and gazed out at the view. She said, "You're right, Isobel. It would make a perfect bedroom. You can see the sea."

They went downstairs again as a car rattled up to the front door.

Isobel's brother. Her luggage was loaded; then Isobel shook hands with all three of them and was driven away without, as Mr. Baines observed, so much as a backward glance.

"I'm glad," said Judith. "Wouldn't it have been awful if she'd got all emotional? I'd have felt as though I was throwing her out. Let's put the kettle on, and we can have a cup of tea."

Because it was a warm afternoon, they took their tea on the sheltered veranda. A breeze rustled the branches of a deep-pink prunus, and somewhere a thrush sang. While they drank from Aunt Lavinia's rose-entwined bone-china cups, Morag disappeared on a tour of exploration.

Presently Biddy lay back in her chair and closed her eyes. Mr. Baines and Judith left her for another tour of the house, this time with a beady eye for defects that needed attention—a damp patch in Isobel's attic, a dripping kitchen tap. Mr. Baines then went outside to eye gutters and downpipes. Judith, her presence now unnecessary, returned to Biddy. On her way through the kitchen she took, from its hook, the key of the garden house.

Biddy turned to her. "Mrs. Boscawen must have been a very tranquil lady."

"Why do you say that?"

"Because I don't remember ever having been in such a tranquil place. It's like another country. Already Devon seems so far away."

"Is that a good thing?"

"Yes. Upper Bickley is too full of memories. I wake in the night and think I hear Ned. I go into his bedroom and bury my face in his blanket and weep with desolation. It's been such a terrible winter. Without you I couldn't have endured it."

Judith said, "It's over now."

"I still have to go back. Face up to reality. I know that."

"You don't have to go back. We can move in here tomorrow."

"But my poor little house in Devon! I can't just *abandon* it."

"You can let it, furnished. Some naval family would jump at it, so handy to Plymouth. Staying here will be a lovely holiday for you, and you can help me clear out all those boxes in the attic."

Biddy laughed. "That won't be much of a holiday." But Judith could see the growing excitement in her expression.

"Come on, Biddy, say yes. I'm going to ask Phyllis and her baby to live here, so even if I do go off to be a Wren or something, the three of you can be here together. And I'll take you to Nancherrow, and once you've met all of them, you won't feel a bit lonely. Don't you see? It all works out perfectly."

"But how about Bob? I must be there if he has leave."

"It's only a little farther than Devon. Please don't think of any more objections."

Finally Biddy succumbed. "All right. We'll give it a try."

"Now come and let me show you the garden."

So together they stepped out across the grass to the garden, and then to the orchard; tiny buds of new fruit had already formed on the trees.

Biddy breathed the scented air. "What's that little house?"

"Oh. That's the Hut. It was built for Athena and Edward."

She went ahead of Biddy, climbed the wooden steps, and smelled the warm odor of creosote. She unlocked the door. Saw the bunk where she had found and lost her love. And her eyes filled with tears.

"Judith." Biddy, behind her.

She brushed the tears away and turned. She said, "So stupid."

"You and Edward?"

"I haven't been here since. I had to come today."

Biddy said, "This is yours now. You can fill it with new memories. And failing all, you can always use it as an extra spare room. For, possibly, guests who snore?"

All at once the tears receded, and they were laughing. Biddy gave Judith a hug and shooed her out through the door. And they hurried back through the orchard and up through the garden to tell Mr. Baines of the plans that they had laid.

The Dower House
Rosemullion, Cornwall
Saturday, 25th May
Dear Mummy and Dad,

Once more, ages since I have written. I am so sorry, but so much is happening. As you can see, we've moved in. Biddy and her dog and me, and Biddy loves it.

On Thursday, Biddy and I drove to Saint Just to see Phyllis, and we invited her to bring Anna and come live here. Phyllis burst into tears, she was so overcome with delight. Phyllis will sleep in our attic, where Isobel used to sleep, and we're clearing out the second room for Anna.

On Friday I took Biddy for lunch at Nancherrow. She and Diana were gassing away in no time and shrieking with laughter at silly jokes, and Biddy is going to join Diana's Red Cross group.

I really want to go and join up with the Wrens. The war news is ghastly. The Allies have fallen back to Dunkirk. It has all happened with such terrible speed. But Mr. Baines is utterly certain that we're going to win the war, so I have decided to be certain, too.

Lots of love,

Judith

THE nine days' wonder—the evacuation of the British troops trapped at Dunkirk—began. The first men were brought home on the night of May 26, but Dunkirk was ablaze, and the jetties and harbors destroyed. And so what was left of the British Expeditionary Force gathered on the beaches to wait for rescue, lined up in long, winding queues.

Troopships and naval destroyers, under constant gunfire and air attack, lay offshore, but there was no way that the beleaguered troops could reach them. Word went out, and the following night, from Dover, a fleet of small boats began to flow across the English Channel: yachts and barges, tugs and dinghies. The men who skippered these crafts were old men and young boys, bank managers and fishermen—any person, sufficiently resolute, who had spent his peacetime summers in boats.

Their brief was to get as close to the beaches as they could, load up with troops, and deliver them to the offshore ships which lay waiting. Unarmed, raked by enemy fire, they kept this up for nine days. On June 3 the operation ceased. Over three hundred thousand troops had been ferried home to England. The entire country gave thanks, but forty thousand men had been left behind, to spend the next five years as prisoners of war.

The Fifty-first Highland was not at Dunkirk. This division remained in France to fight on alongside a disheartened French army. It was a losing battle. The German advance continued until this last courageous remnant of the British army was driven to the coast. Finally, at St.-Valéry-en-Caux, they were surrounded by the German divisions, and all that remained of the Highlanders were marched into captivity. The Black Watch, the Argylls, the Seaforths, the Camerons, the Gordons. Gus.

During those dark days Judith existed on tenterhooks of anxiety and suspense. At the Dower House the wireless was kept on from morning to night in order that no bulletin should be missed. Gradually, in dribs and drabs, came news of who had been rescued and who had been left behind. Palmer, the Nancherrow gardener-cum-chauffeur, had made it. As had Edward Carey-Lewis, his fighter squadron having flown successive patrols over the mayhem of Dunkirk, driving German bombers away from the beaches. Mrs. Mudge's nephew, from St. Veryan, was posted missing, presumed killed.

After St.-Valéry all hope was lost for Gus. He was gone, with his regiment, into eclipse. They all prayed that he was alive and had been taken prisoner, but so many had been killed during the ferocious fighting that it seemed unlikely. For Loveday's sake, brave faces were worn, but she refused to be comforted.

"THE thing to do," said Mrs. Mudge, "is to keep busy. Least that's what people say, but how can I say that to my poor sister, worrying herself sick over whether her boy's dead or alive?"

Loveday had never seen Mrs. Mudge so down.

"I feel I should go to St. Veryan and be with her for a few days. For company there isn't nothing like a sister, is there?"

"Then why don't you go, Mrs. Mudge?"

"How can I? Got the cows to milk and the dairy to see to."

It was half past ten in the morning, and they were sitting at the kitchen table at Lidgey and drinking tea. Helping Walter and his father on the farm, learning to cope with the balky tractor, feeding poultry and pigs, Loveday spent much of her day at Lidgey. Lately, since the black tidings of St.-Valéry, she had taken to escaping here on the smallest excuse. For some reason she found the down-to-earth company of Mrs. Mudge comforting. While trying to come to terms with the idea that Gus was dead, all she wanted to do was talk about him as though he were still alive. Mrs. Mudge was good at this. Over and over she would say, "Mind you, he might have been taken prisoner."

Mrs. Mudge pulled herself wearily to her feet and went to the range to pour herself another cup of tea. Loveday looked at her and thought that something must be done. By the time Mrs. Mudge sat down again, Loveday had made up her mind. She said firmly, "You must go to St. Veryan. Today. For a week if necessary. Walter can help me, and I'll do the milking."

MRS. Mudge, who had been away for a week, was returning to Lidgey. In a way Loveday felt rather sorry. Coping with the milking, a marathon task that she had taken on so impetuously, had proved to be tremendously hard work. At first she had been slow and clumsy, but Walter, alternately swearing at her or handing out a bit of foulmouthed encouragement, had been uncharacteristically co-operative and had seen her through.

Without a lot of chat. Walter was a taciturn fellow. Loveday was not sure if he had been told about Gus. Whatever, Walter said nothing. When Gus was staying at Nancherrow, the two young men had met one morning down at the stables and Loveday had introduced them, but Walter had been at his most offhand and mannerless. It had occurred to Loveday at the time that perhaps he was jealous, but the idea was so preposterous that she put it out of her mind.

The last cow had been milked and the little herd turned out into the fields again. Loveday had hosed and scrubbed the parlor, taking pride in shining cobbles and milk pails, determined that Mrs. Mudge would find no fault. Then she crossed the farmyard and climbed the gate that led into the lane, and sat there on top of the rail. This was one of her favorite views, and this morning the distant moors and fields looked particularly bright and sparkling.

Her mind, curiously, emptied. She hadn't thought about *nothing* for ages, and it felt rather pleasant, like floating in space. And then, gradually, mindlessness was filled with the image of Gus, striding up the lane towards her, with his painting gear slung in a knapsack over his shoulder. His presence came across so strongly that all at once she was consumed with the irrefutable conviction that he was still alive and thinking about her. She closed her eyes and sat clinging to the rail. And when she opened her eyes again, everything was different, and the world was brimful with the old possibilities of happiness.

She jumped off the gate and ran all the way to the house and through the back door.

"Take your boots off, Loveday. They're caked with dirt."

"Sorry, Mrs. Nettlebed." In socked feet she came into the kitchen. She wanted to ask if there had been any news. But until there came some confirmation of Gus's safety, Loveday was not going to whisper a word of her new hope.

She said, "What's for breakfast? I'm ravenous."

"Fried eggs and tomatoes. On the hot plate in the dining room. Everyone else has finished already. You'd better hurry along."

So Loveday washed her hands in the scullery, then went down the passage to the dining room. She was about to go in when the telephone began to ring. She stopped dead and waited, and when nobody answered, went into her father's study and picked up the telephone on his desk.

"Nancherrow." For some reason her mouth had gone dry.

Click, click went the telephone. "Hello?" *Click, click.* "Who's that?" A man's voice, blurred and distant.

"Loveday," she said.

"Loveday, it's me. It's Gus."

Her legs, literally, turned to water. She collapsed onto the floor, taking the telephone with her. "Gus, where are you?"

"In hospital. Southampton. I'm okay. Being shipped home tomorrow. I tried to ring before, but there aren't enough telephones."

"What—what happened? Are you badly hurt?"

"Just my leg. I'm on crutches, but all right. There's no time for more. I just wanted to speak to you. I'll write."

"I'll write too. What's your address?"

But the line went dead. "Gus? Gus?" She jiggled the hook on the receiver and tried again. "Gus?" He was gone.

Still sitting on the carpet, she laid her head against the cool dark wood of her father's desk, and tears streamed quietly down her cheeks. She said aloud, "I knew you were alive."

And after a bit she got up, calling for her mother, and she fled up the stairs to share in joy the incredible news.

LOVEDAY received two letters from Gus at the end of June. They came in the same envelope. One was a long account of his escape from France, the other a little note on a single sheet. The note said, "I thought your father might like to read the enclosed account, but this little note is just for you. It was so wonderful to hear your voice answering the telephone. I thought about you all the time I was waiting to get on that hell-hole of a beach, determined that I was going to make it. It is such a beautiful day here, and the hills are all bloomy in the morning light, and the sunshine sparkling on the river. When I am able to walk a bit better, I shall go down to the bank and try to catch a fish. Write to me and tell me everything you are doing. With all my love, Gus."

ON THE twenty-fourth of July, at two o'clock in the morning, Athena had her baby at Nancherrow, with old Dr. Wells in attendance. She was called Clementina Lavinia Rycroft. The Colonel immediately sent a cable to Palestine letting Rupert know that she had come.

That evening Judith went to Nancherrow to see the new arrival. Old Dr. Wells dropped in again to check on mother and child, and also to tell them that Jeremy was in a naval hospital near Liverpool. His destroyer had been sunk by a U-boat in the Atlantic, and he and three other men were in the sea, hanging on to a raft for a day and a night before they were picked up by a merchantman. He was suffering from exposure as well as burns from the explosion, and Mrs. Wells had gone up to Liverpool to sit at his bedside. Eventually Jeremy would be given sick leave and come home.

Meanwhile, invasion fever had swept the country. Aluminum pots and pans were being collected and melted down and made into Spitfires. The Colonel was back in uniform, now as commanding officer of Rosemullion's defense volunteers—the Home Guard—with Nettlebed as his sergeant. They had already been issued guns. All church bells were silenced and would ring out only to warn that the Germans had landed. In the air battles over the Channel young fighter pilots were doing brilliantly.

At the Dower House, little Anna was thriving. Cyril was in the Mediterranean and had been made a leading seaman. He'd sent Phyllis a photograph of himself, looking very brown and well.

Phyllis thought she was in heaven, for after the dismal little house in Pendeen and then her mother's overcrowded cottage, the domestic arrangements of the Dower House seemed the very height of luxury. Especially the boiling-hot water streaming from a tap into sink or bath.

It was a Monday in July, washday, and outside in the washing green, a space between the garage and the back door, Judith and Phyllis were pegging out the laundry to dry. They paused as a car came up the gravel approach to the house and stopped. "Know who it is?" said Phyllis.

"Yes." Judith could feel the smile spread across her face. "It's Jeremy Wells." And she went across the grass to meet him.

Jeremy Wells. Over the washing line Phyllis watched. She'd waited a long time to set eyes on the young doctor Judith had met all those years ago on the train. Only fourteen she'd been then, but she'd fancied him. No doubt about that. Then she'd met him again at Nancherrow, and Phyllis decided that it was written in the stars.

Judith, of course, pretended that there was nothing in it. But she'd been distressed enough when she heard that he'd been blown up in his ship. And now here he was, looking right as rain as far as Phyllis could see, and they were talking away nineteen to the dozen, grinning like Cheshire cats.

She might have stood there gawping forever, but Judith suddenly called to her, and she crossed the crunchy gravel.

"This is Phyllis Eddy, Jeremy. Her husband's in the navy too."

"Leading seaman," Phyllis was able to tell him proudly.

"That's terrific. He must be doing well."

Judith said, "Jeremy's on his way to stay at Nancherrow."

"Lovely," said Phyllis. He wasn't actually good-looking, and he wore spectacles, but he had the nicest smile she'd ever seen.

He said, "I'm not expected until lunchtime, and I couldn't drive through Rosemullion without coming to see you all, and see the old house, and what you've done to it."

Phyllis smiled to herself. He had come calling. "Why don't you take Dr. Wells inside, Judith. I'll get the last of the washing on the line and then bring you a cup of coffee."

THERE was a great deal to talk about, news to catch up on. It was eleven months since they had been together—that hot August Sunday that had ended so disastrously with Judith's precipitous flight from Nancherrow. Now, she thought, the months of war at sea had hardened Jeremy, honed him down, and there were lines on his face that had never been there before.

They talked about Athena and Rupert and baby Clementina. "We all thought Athena would hand her straight over to Mary Millyway, but in fact, she's frightfully maternal. And Loveday's become a total land girl. She works like a beaver and has dozens of hens."

Jeremy had heard the story of Gus Callender's miraculous escape from St.-Valéry. Judith told him of Gus's seconding to the Gordon Highlanders overseas. "Gus and Loveday write to each other a lot." Then Jeremy asked after her friend Heather, and she was touched by his interest, because he knew her only by hearsay.

"Biddy and I went over to Porthkerris and had tea with Heather's parents one day, and got all their news. Heather's working with the Foreign Office, somewhere terribly secret."

And then Judith told him the tragic details of Ned Somerville's death and about Biddy's coming to live at the Dower House. "She got a lift into Penzance this morning. I don't know when she'll be back."

He asked about her family in Singapore, and she was telling him their latest news when Phyllis appeared with a coffee tray. She set it down and with a faintly coy smile went on her way. Judith, hoping that Jeremy had not noticed, handed him a cup of coffee. She said, "We've talked about everybody but you. Your ship being torpedoed and everything." She saw the expression on his face and added quickly, "But perhaps you don't want to talk about it."

"It doesn't matter."

"Your father said you had burns."

"Yes. My shoulder and back. Not too gruesome. No skin grafts."

"What happens next? Another ship?"

"I devoutly hope so."

"But aren't you frightened at the thought of going back?"

"Of course. But you learn to pretend you're not afraid."

It was all very depressing. Judith sighed. "So many battles."

"And Edward's in the thick of it. Have you heard from him?"

"Only family news."

"Doesn't he write to you?"

Judith shook her head. "No."

"What happened?"

She looked at him. "Nothing." But she was useless at lying.

"You loved Edward."

Judith dropped her eyes. When she stayed silent, he spoke again.

"I know how it was. I knew, that last Sunday, when you were all in the garden at Nancherrow before lunch. Edward and I brought the drinks out. Then he went over to speak to you, and it was as if some magic, glittering ring enclosed the pair of you . . . held you apart from the rest of us."

She found it almost unbearable to be reminded. She said, "Perhaps that's what I wanted you all to think."

"In the afternoon you left Nancherrow abruptly. Something happened, didn't it?"

There was little point in denial. "Yes. I always loved Edward, Jeremy, right from the moment I met him. I imagined that he felt the same about me. But, of course, he didn't. He was not taken with the idea of a permanent commitment."

"And you let that end all friendship?"

"I'd gone too far, said too much. I had to back away."

"And leave Nancherrow?"

"I couldn't stay. Not with seeing him every day."

"Are you still in love with Edward?"

"I try not to be. But I suppose you never fall out of love with the man who was the first love of your life."

"How old are you?"

"Nineteen. Just."

"So young." Jeremy smiled, understanding. "I'm sorry to have pried. I didn't intend to invade your privacy. It's just that I know Edward so well, his good points and his faults, and I was concerned. Afraid that he'd hurt you."

"It's over now. And I don't mind *you* knowing."

"Good." He finished his coffee. "Now, before I have to be on my way, will you show me around your property?"

So they embarked on a tour of inspection, starting at the top with the new attic nursery and ending in the kitchen. And after a bit more chat Judith went with him to his car. "Will I see you at Nancherrow?" she asked.

"Of course. Tell you what, why don't you come down this afternoon, about three, and we'll walk down to the cove. With whoever wants to come. We could swim."

It was an inviting idea. She hadn't been to the cove for too long. "All right. I'll bike over."

THE LONG DRIVEWAY OF Nancherrow was lined with hydrangeas in full flower. Judith had changed into shorts, and in her bicycle basket was her bathing suit rolled in a towel. As she cycled out of the trees, the windows of Nancherrow blinked in the sunshine. There didn't seem to be anybody about, but the front door stood open. Judith parked her bike, leaning it against the house, and turned to go indoors. But she suddenly jumped nearly out of her skin because Jeremy had appeared from nowhere and was standing right behind her.

"Oh! You brute. What a fright! I never heard you!"

He put his hands on her arms, holding her still. "Don't go in."

His face was taut and, under his tan, very pale. Judith stood bewildered. "Why?"

"A telephone call. Half an hour ago. Edward's dead."

She was grateful that he held her so steadily, for her knees were trembling and she felt a terrible panic. She shook her head in passionate denial. "No. Not *Edward.*"

"He was killed this morning. His commanding officer rang up to break the news. He spoke to the Colonel."

Edward. She looked up into Jeremy's face and saw, behind the spectacles, that his eyes shone with unshed tears. And she thought, We all loved Edward, in different ways. Each one of us, every person who ever knew him, is going to be left with a great hole in his life.

"How did it happen?" she wanted to know.

"There was a tremendous enemy raid on the shipping in the harbor at Dover. Stukas and Messerschmitts. The RAF fighters got twelve German planes but lost three of their own. Edward's Spitfire was one of them."

Shock had drained her. Now she found herself suffused with rage. "How do they *know* he's dead? How can they be *sure?*"

"Another Spitfire pilot saw it happen. A direct hit from one of the Stukas. His plane exploded. No ejection. No parachute."

She listened in silence, and hope died. Then Jeremy took her in his arms. She put her arms around his waist, and thus they did their best to comfort each other, her cheek pressed against his shoulder, feeling the warmth of his body. She thought of the family, some-where indoors, and the grief that had invaded the lovely, happy, sun-filled house. How were they going to come to terms with the

agonizing loss? All that was certain was that she, Judith, had no part in this private desolation.

She drew away from Jeremy. "We shouldn't be here, you and I."

Jeremy understood. "You go if you want to. But I must stay. The Colonel's anxious for Diana. There might be something I can do to help."

"Oh, Jeremy, I wish I could be like you—strong. But at the moment I just want to escape. Go home. Is that awful?"

"No. Not awful at all. If you like, I'll drive you."

"I've got my bicycle."

"Ride carefully. You've had a shock."

"Tell Diana I'll be back. Give her my love. Explain."

He nodded. She got on her bicycle and pedaled slowly away.

Afterwards Judith had little recollection of that journey from Nancherrow to the Dower House. Her brain felt numb. She went inside, into the flagged hall, where the only sound was the slow ticktock of the grandfather clock.

"Phyllis!"

Silence. She went out onto the veranda. In the garden she saw Phyllis, sitting on a rug with Anna and Morag and some toys. Morag, hearing her, woofed, and Phyllis looked around.

"Judith! We weren't expecting you back so soon. Didn't you go swimming?"

"No." Reaching Phyllis's side, Judith sank down on the rug beside her. "Phyllis, I have to ask you something. If I go away, will you stay here and take care of Aunt Biddy for me?"

Phyllis frowned. "What are you talking about?"

"I'm going tomorrow to Devonport. I'll sign on there, in the Women's Royal Naval Service. Of course, I'll come home again; I shouldn't get my orders for at least two weeks. And then I'll go for good. But you won't leave Biddy, will you, Phyllis? Promise me."

She was, Phyllis realized, working herself into a state. But why? She laid a hand on Judith's shoulder. "Of course I shan't leave her. Now, let's talk quietly. I know you've been thinking for months about joining up. But why all at once? What made up your mind? Has something happened?"

"Yes."

"Tell Phyllis, then."

Tell Phyllis. She sounded just the way she used to, in the old days at Riverview. Judith took a deep breath and said it. "Edward Carey-Lewis has been killed."

"Oh, God."

"Jeremy just told me. That's why I came home. I just wanted you so badly." Suddenly her face crumpled like a child's, and Phyllis pulled her roughly into her arms and rocked her as though she were a baby. "I don't think I can bear it, Phyllis."

"Shh. . . . There now." Then all at once Phyllis understood. It was young Carey-Lewis to whom Judith had given her heart.

Life was so cruel, she thought, and war was worse.

THREE days passed before Judith returned to Nancherrow. She propped her bicycle by the front door and went in. The old Nancherrow perambulator was parked in the hall, waiting for Clementina, and on the table was the usual pile of letters. Down the passage, the door of the small sitting room stood open, and she saw Diana at her desk.

The desk was littered with correspondence, but Diana was simply gazing out the window. She looked thin and pale.

Judith said her name, and she turned. She held out an arm. "Darling, you've come." Judith swiftly crossed the room and stooped to embrace her.

"Oh, Diana. I'm so sorry."

"Darling, you mustn't say things like that; otherwise I go to pieces. You've just got to talk ordinarily to me. Did you bike over? Sit down for a moment."

"I'm not disturbing you?"

"Yes, you are, but I want to be disturbed; writing letters was never my strong point, and so many people have written us about Edward, and I simply have to answer them. And when I read the letters, even the most banal of condolences fill me with pride and comfort."

"How is the Colonel holding up?"

"Shattered, lost. But trying not to show it too much. I keep thinking of Biddy, when her Ned was killed. How perfectly terrible for her to have no other children to keep her going. *You* must have saved her life."

"Diana, I'm going away. I've signed on with the Wrens."

"Oh, darling."

303

"I knew I had to go sometime. Biddy and Phyllis and Anna are settled at the Dower House, and there, I imagine, they'll stay for the duration. Perhaps you can keep an eye on them."

"Of course. What are you going to do in the Wrens? Something frightfully glamorous?"

"No. Shorthand and typing. They call it being a writer."

Diana sighed deeply. "I can't bear the thought of you going, but I suppose you must. I couldn't bear saying good-bye to Jeremy either, when he had to leave us. And that reminds me." She turned to her desk, opened a tiny drawer. "If you're going to leave us, you must have a key."

"A key?"

"Yes. To my house in Cadogan Mews. When war broke out, I had half a dozen spares cut. Rupert's got one. Athena, of course. And Gus. And Jeremy. And Edward had one. . . . Oh, here it is." She tossed it across and Judith caught it.

A small brass latchkey. "But why are you giving me this?"

"Oh, darling, you never know. In wartime everybody goes to and fro through London, and it could be a place to lay your head for a night. Are you going to stay for lunch? It's rabbit pie."

"No. I think another day. I only wanted to see you."

Diana understood. "All right." She smiled. "Another day."

EACH morning Edgar Carey-Lewis made it his business to collect the post from the hall table, take it into the privacy of his study, and go through all the condolence letters before handing them over to Diana. He read each one, filtering out well-meant but clumsy efforts which might upset his wife. These he answered himself.

This morning there was a large buff envelope, with an Aberdeen postmark. He sat at his desk and slit the envelope with his paper knife. From it he withdrew a letter and a sheet of cardboard folded in two. The letter was signed "Gus," and he felt touched that another of Edward's Cambridge friends had taken the trouble to write.

Gus wrote of Edward's charm, his boundless capacity for friendship, and his generosity of spirit. And then,

Looking through my Cambridge sketchbook I came upon this drawing I did of him. At a college cricket match, as he stood by the pavilion, padded up and waiting to go in. If you wish, toss it into the wastebasket, but I thought that you might like to have it.

Edgar laid the letter aside and took up the makeshift folder. Inside was a sheet of paper, the top edge rough where it had been torn from Gus's sketchbook.

His son. Sketched in pencil, later washed in color. Edward, dressed for cricket, in white shirt and flannels. Face half turned, smiling, that stubborn lock of hair falling across his forehead. In a moment he was going to put up a hand and push it aside.

Edward.

All at once he couldn't see it properly because his vision was blurred by tears. Caught unawares, disarmed, he was weeping.

❧ *1942* ❧

THE Wrens' quarters, where Judith had lived for eighteen months, was an uncomfortable block of flats in the North End of Portsmouth. Ten girls occupied each small flat, sleeping in double-deck naval-issue bunks. There was no heating, for reasons of fuel economy, and the cold of winter was so extreme as to be painful.

And so it was a relief to be going to London, even for a single night. Judith was looking forward to meeting Heather Warren, whom she hadn't seen since the beginning of the war. Bundled up in her greatcoat and carrying her overnight bag, she checked out at the Regulating Office, then stepped forth into the bitter January morning to catch a bus to the railway station.

The train when she boarded was blissfully overheated. She took off her coat and hat and settled by the grimy window with her newspaper. She scarcely registered the bomb damage to the station, because it had all become so familiar.

It was then that she became aware of an uncomfortable tickle at the back of her throat, the classic start to one of her miserable colds. Since joining the Wrens, she had endured at least three. I shall ignore you, she told the tickle. I've got two days' leave, and you're not going to ruin it for me.

The train would soon be on its way. She unfolded her *Daily Telegraph*. JAPANESE ADVANCE THREATENS SINGAPORE was the headline. Filled with apprehension, she thought of her family. And of Gus Callender, now with the 2nd Gordons in Singapore. Judith had heard nothing from her family for weeks, and she prayed that by now they had left Singapore. Gone to Sumatra or Java. Anywhere. Somewhere safe.

DIANA's property in London had been converted, years earlier, from two coachman's dwellings with stabling for horses beneath. The front door stood in the middle, with garage on one side and kitchen on the other. A narrow staircase led straight to a spacious upper floor, with a sitting room, a large bedroom, a bathroom, a small lavatory, and a small bedroom.

Miraculously, the house had survived the blitz. Judith took out her key and let herself in. She glanced into the kitchen, saw the fridge, empty and open, so closed its door and turned on the switch. Before the corner shop closed, she would buy some rations.

Carrying her grip, she went up the stairs to the sitting room. She had been to Cadogan Mews several times and was always assailed by the comforting sensation of coming home. It was a bit like a miniature Nancherrow. Comfortably appointed: cream curtains and thick beige carpeting, relieved here and there by Persian rugs. There were pictures and mirrors, fat cushions on sofas, and even family photographs.

Judith looked at her watch. Half past twelve. No time to change. Now her throat felt rough as emery boards, and she went into the bathroom to take a couple of aspirin. Then she fixed her hair, put on some makeup, and left. Already she was running late for her rendezvous with Heather.

In Sloane Street she got a bus to Piccadilly Circus. The streets of London were battered and dirty, houses bombed and store windows boarded up. It was a city at war, and every other person seemed to be in uniform.

She got off the bus and walked to Swan & Edgar's. Heather was there, instantly visible with her dark, shining hair, and wearing an enviable scarlet overcoat and long suede boots.

"Heather! I'm sorry. Ten minutes late. No, don't hug me. I'm getting a cold, and I don't want to pass on any germs."

"Oh, I don't give a darn for germs." So they hugged anyway, laughing, because it was so wonderful to be together again.

"You're looking terrific, Heather."

"You too. I like the uniform. It suits you."

"How long have you got?" Judith asked.

"Just today. I've got to be back this evening. I'm starving. Let's eat lunch. Now, where to?"

Judith suggested the Berkeley, which was frightfully grand, and they set off to walk the short distance. Going inside, they were injected into a world of comfort. There were a great many people about—elegant women, staff colonels, Free French officers, all talking and drinking and laughing. When they were seated, a porter took their overcoats, and then a waiter came forward. Heather ordered champagne.

Judith muttered, "Shades of Porthkerris Council School," and they began to giggle.

The champagne was poured, and they raised their glasses and drank. Almost at once Judith felt better. She said, "I must remember, champagne is the remedy for colds."

It was a lovely lunch, the restaurant so pretty, so different from the battered streets beyond. They ate oysters and chicken and ice cream, catching up on the long months since they had seen each other.

"Are there any nice chaps where you're working, Heather?"

She laughed. "Most of them are so bright they're just about barmy. They're interesting, very cultured. But weird."

"What do you do with the Foreign Office? What's your job?"

Heather shrugged, reached for a cigarette, and Judith knew that she had clammed up. "Let's talk about you," Heather said. "What's your job?"

"Not very exciting. I'm at Whale Island, the gunnery school. I work for the training-development officer."

"Got a boyfriend?"

Judith smiled. "Lots."

"Not one in particular?"

"No. Not after Edward. I'm not going through that again."

"I read about Singapore in the paper this morning."

"So did I."

"Have you heard from your family?"

"Not for too long. I just hope they've been evacuated. But I wish I could find out what's happening." She looked at Heather. "You—you couldn't find anything out, could you?"

Heather stubbed out her cigarette. "No. We only deal with Europe." She sighed. "It's a bloody war, isn't it?"

So they drank coffee, and paid the bill, collected their coats, and plunged out into the bitter cold.

Heather said, "It's been great. A wonderful day."

"I adored every moment."

"Good-bye, love." A quick hug and a kiss, and she was gone.

JUDITH proceeded back to Cadogan Mews, stopping at the corner store for groceries. Armed with her emergency ration card, she bought bread and eggs, margarine and milk, and a jar of raspberry jam. Back at the house, she put the groceries in the fridge. She found a hot-water bottle, filled it, went upstairs, and put the bottle between the bedsheets.

She took more aspirin and looked in the bathroom mirror. Her face seemed peaky and pinched, and she drew a deep scalding bath and soaked in scented steam. Dried, she put on her nightgown and an old Shetland sweater. Then she climbed into the downy double bed in Diana's bedroom. Within moments she succumbed to exhaustion and closed her eyes. Almost at once, or so it seemed, she opened them again.

A sound. Downstairs. The front door opening, and softly being closed. An intruder. Some person had come into the house. Petrified, she lay rigid, unable to move, and then flung herself out of the bed and ran to the head of the stairs, determined that if the newcomer was foe rather than friend, to bash him over the head with any heavy object that came to hand.

He was halfway up already, muffled in a heavy overcoat, gold lace gleaming on epaulettes. He carried an overnight grip and a sturdy canvas sailing bag. She saw him and felt weak with relief. Not an intruder breaking in. Instead, the one person—had she been given the choice—she would have really wanted it to be.

"*Jeremy.*"

He paused and looked up. "Good heavens, it's Judith."

"I thought you were at sea. What are you doing here?"

"I could ask the same question." He came on up the stairs, dumped his luggage, and stooped to kiss her cheek. "And why are you receiving gentlemen in your nightgown?"

"I was in bed, of course. I've got a rotten cold."

"Then get back into bed right away."

"No. I want to talk to you. How long are you staying?"

"Just till morning." He placed his cap on the top of the newel-post and unbuttoned his greatcoat. "I had a couple of days' leave and went to Cornwall to spend them with my parents."

"I haven't seen you for ages. Years." She suddenly thought of something. "There's nothing much to eat here. Are you starving?"

He was laughing. "Don't worry. My mother helped me pack a nose bag." He draped the greatcoat over the banister and heaved up the canvas sailing bag. "Come on, and I'll show you."

He led the way downstairs to the little kitchen to unload the bag. Judith sat on the end of the table, and it was like watching somebody open a Christmas stocking. A bottle of whisky. Gordon's gin. Two lemons. An orange. Packets of potato crisps and a pound of farm butter. Last of all, a sinister bloodstained parcel.

"What's in there?" Judith asked. "A severed head?"

"Steaks."

"Where did you get steaks from? And farm butter? Your mother isn't dabbling in the black market, is she?"

"Grateful patients." He opened the fridge and laid the butter and the bloody parcel alongside the meager rations Judith had placed there. "A whisky would do that cold good. Whisky and soda?"

He found a siphon stowed away in an obscure cupboard. He poured two whiskies, squirted in the soda. The drinks fizzed deliciously, and he handed Judith one of the tall tumblers.

So they went upstairs and made themselves comfortable by the gas fire, Jeremy settling in one of the armchairs and Judith curling up on the hearthrug. She said, "Tell me about you. What's been happening?"

"I had to come to London to see Their Lordships at the Admiralty. I'm getting a promotion. Surgeon commander."

"Oh, Jeremy." She was delighted. "Well done. You'll get your brass hat. What else?"

"I'm joining a new ship. A cruiser, H.M.S. *Sutherland*."

"Still in the Atlantic?"

He shrugged. He was being cagey. He said, "Have you heard from your family?"

"Not since the beginning of the month. All at once they are in so

309

much danger. I wish now I'd gone to Singapore when I finished school. At least we'd all be together."

To her horror her voice had started to shake. She took another sip of whisky. "I'm all right. It's just that this evening I'm not feeling well. I'm sorry. I'm not very good company."

"I like you just the way you are. However you are. My only regret is that I have to leave early in the morning. Now"—he got to his feet—"what we both need is a good hot meal and perhaps a little music. You get back into bed, and I'll take charge of the galley." He switched on the wireless. Dance music. The distinctive strains of Carroll Gibbons relayed live from the Savoy Hotel. "Begin the Beguine." She imagined the diners crowding onto the floor.

He held out his hand, pulled her to her feet. "Bed," he said, and propelled her gently towards the bedroom. She went through the door and heard him go downstairs. She sat at the dressing table and gazed at her pallid reflection in the mirror. She combed her hair and put on a bit of lipstick and wished that she had a beautiful frilly bed jacket—the kind Diana wore. The old sweater was scarcely romantic. But this was Jeremy, so did she want to look romantic? The question caught her unawares, but there didn't seem to be any answer, and so she got into bed again, savoring the delicious smells emanating from downstairs.

"Begin the Beguine" ended, and Carroll Gibbons, at his piano, played "All the Things You Are." Presently Jeremy appeared at the door, carrying a tray. He had taken off his jacket and wore an apron over his dark blue sweater. He set the tray on the bed beside her. The steaks were still sizzling, served with potato crisps and tinned peas—even gravy. There were, as well, two replenished drinks.

"Eat the steak before it gets cold," he said.

It was all delicious and immediately restoring. And her steak was so tender that it slipped easily down her painful throat.

Finally she told him, "I'm completely stuffed," and she lay back on the pillows in total satisfaction. "Thank you, Jeremy. You never cease to surprise me. I didn't know you could cook."

"Any man who's ever sailed a boat can cook, even if only to fry a mackerel." Then all at once he became professional. "When did you start this cold?"

"This morning, in the train. My throat began to be sore."

"In my suitcase I have a magic pill. I got them in America,

310

brought some back. They look like small bombs, but they usually do the trick. I'll give you one."

Carroll Gibbons and his orchestra were playing their sign-off tune. A second or two of silence, and then the chimes of Big Ben tolled out, slow and sonorous. "This is London. The nine-o'clock news." Jeremy looked at Judith inquiringly, and she nodded. However dire or grave, she must listen, and she would be able to cope, simply because Jeremy was there, strong and companionable.

The news was bad. The Japanese were closing in. Singapore had suffered its second day of bombing . . . trenches and fortifications being dug . . . fierce fighting on the Muar River.

Jeremy went to the sitting room and switched the wireless off. Presently he returned. "Doesn't sound too good, does it?"

"Gus Callender's there. With the Second Gordons. Poor Loveday. Poor Gus."

"Poor you." He leaned down and kissed her cheek. "I'll take the tray away and tidy up the kitchen. Then I'll bring you your pill. You'll be all right in the morning."

He went, and Judith was left alone in the warm, downy bed. It was strangely quiet. Quite suddenly, without meaning to, she started to think about her mother. Not as she was now, half a world away, in mortal danger and probably terrified, but as she *had* been. As Judith remembered her last, at Riverview.

Riverview. She remembered getting off the train after school and climbing the path to the house, bursting in through the door, calling "Mummy!" And she was always there. In her sitting room, with tea ready on the table, surrounded by her pretty bits and pieces. She heard her voice, reading to Jess before bedtime. Day had slipped into day without much excitement. But nothing bad had ever happened either.

There was, of course, the other side of the coin. Molly Dunbar, sweet and pliant, had been an ineffectual mother. Nervous about driving, shy of making new friends. Change had always alarmed her. A gentle nature; not Molly's fault. War, disaster, upheaval brought out the best in some women—steadfast courage, enterprise, determination to survive. But Molly Dunbar was barren of such resources. She would be defeated. Destroyed.

"No." Judith heard herself speak the word, an anguished refutation of her own fears. As though it were possible to shut out despair, she turned and buried her face in the pillow. She heard Jeremy coming back up the staircase, across the sitting room.

His voice. "Did you call me?"

Still muffled in pillows, she shook her head.

"I've brought the magic pill. And a glass of water." He sat on the edge of the bed beside her. "Judith!"

She flung herself onto her back and stared up at him with tear-sodden eyes. "I don't want pills," she told him. "I just want to be with my mother. I *hate* myself for not being with her."

He said nothing to this. Just held out the pill, which did indeed look like a tiny bomb. "Swallow this, and then we'll talk."

With an effort she raised herself onto one elbow, took the pill, and sank gratefully back onto the pillows. Jeremy smiled. "Do you want to try to sleep?"

"No." She sighed. "It's so *stupid,* not to be able to stop thinking. So *stupid.* I'm twenty years old and I want my mother. I want to hold her and touch her and know she's safe."

Tears filled her eyes again, and she felt too weak to control them. "It's six years since we were together. And now I just want a letter. Something. So that I know where they *are.*"

"You mustn't give up hope. Even now they may be en route to someplace safer. Communications at a time like this are bound to fall apart. Try not to be too despondent."

Judith thought about this for a bit. Then she said, "My mother isn't strong. She has no confidence, and I fear for her."

The tears returned, streaming down her cheeks. Jeremy could scarcely bear it. She seemed so despairing that he did what he'd been longing to do all evening. He took her into his arms and drew her near. She lay passive, grateful. Her hand came up to touch the thick wool of his sweater, and her fingers closed upon it, clinging to him.

He said, "You know, when I was a small boy and despairing about something, my mother used to say, 'This will pass. One day you will look back and it will all be over.' "

"Did that make things any better?"

"Not much. But it helped."

She took a long breath. "Jeremy, when you were clinging to that raft in the middle of the Atlantic, what did you think about?"

"Staying afloat. Staying alive."

"Didn't you remember things? Lovely places? Good times?"

"I tried to."

"What in particular?"

It was clearly important to her, and so Jeremy, trying to ignore the physical arousal of his body, dug into his memory for the images that still had the power to delight him. "Autumn Sundays in Truro, and the bells of the cathedral ringing out for evensong. Being at Nancherrow. Early morning swims with Edward and, walking back, knowing that we'd be eating the most tremendous breakfast. Music. 'Jesu, Joy of Man's Desiring,' and knowing that you had come back to Nancherrow."

"Music's good, isn't it? It lifts you up, away from the world."

He said, "That's me. It's your turn now."

She sighed. "All right. My house. My own home. The way it feels, and the clock ticking in the hall, and the view of the sea. Knowing that I can go back one day and never leave it again."

He smiled. "You hang on to that," he told her. She closed her eyes. He looked down at her face, at the long lashes against the pale cheeks, at the shape of her mouth. He leaned down and kissed her forehead. "You're tired, and I've got an early start. I think we should call it a day."

At once her eyes flew open in alarm, and her grip on his sweater tightened. Jeremy, telling himself to be resolute, began to ease away. "You mustn't go," she said. "Please. Don't leave me. I want you to be with me."

"Judith—"

"No, don't go." And she added, "It's a double bed. There's masses of space. I'll be all right if you stay. Please."

Torn between desire and his inbred good sense, Jeremy hesitated. "Is that a good idea?" he asked. "If I spend the night with you, I shall, in all probability, make love to you."

She was neither shocked nor seemed particularly surprised. "That doesn't matter."

"What do you mean, it doesn't *matter?*"

"I mean, if you want to, I would like you to make love to me." Suddenly she smiled. He had scarcely seen her smile all evening, and he felt his heart turn over. "It's all right, Jeremy. I want you to hold me and make me feel safe."

"I can't make love to you with all my clothes on."

"Then go and take them off."

"I can't. You've got hold of my sweater."

She smiled again, and her hold on him loosened.

"JUDITH."

She stirred. Put out a hand to touch him, but the bed was empty. She dragged open her eyes. Jeremy was sitting beside her, dressed and shaved. "I've brought you a cup of tea."

A cup of tea. "What time is it?"

"Half past five in the morning. I'm on my way."

She stretched and yawned and pulled herself into a sitting position, and he handed her the steaming cup. "I just wanted to say good-bye. I wanted to say thank you."

"Oh, Jeremy, I'm the one who should be grateful."

"It was lovely. Perfect. A memory."

Suddenly Judith felt shy. She lowered her eyes.

"Try not to worry too much," he said. "And take care of yourself. I'll write. I'll write and try to say all the things that I wish I'd said last night. On paper I'll probably make a much better job of it."

"You didn't do too badly last night. But I'd love a letter."

"Good-bye, darling Judith."

"If you take this tea away from me, I'll say good-bye properly."

And he laughed and relieved her of the cup and saucer, and they embraced and kissed like the friends they had always been, but now like lovers too.

"Don't get blown up again, Jeremy."

"I'll do my best not to." Then he drew away from her, and Judith heard him close the door behind him. Almost instantly she was asleep.

It was ten o'clock before she awoke again. She thought of Jeremy, smiling to herself, remembering last night. An interlude of magic unexpectedness, and even joy. Jeremy Wells. Everything was changed now.

Meantime, she realized that she was recovered. The cold was gone. How much of this was due to Jeremy, rather than his professional medications, it was impossible to say. Whatever, she was herself again, filled with energy.

She didn't have to report back to quarters until evening, but at the back of her mind there lurked the possibility of a letter from

Singapore, and all at once it became important to return without delay. She flung back the covers and sprang out of bed.

By two o'clock in the afternoon she was back at the Wrens' quarters, signing herself in. She went to the wooden grid of mailboxes, and under "D" there was a thin blue envelope with her mother's writing. Judith took it to her flat. Because it was Sunday, there was nobody around. She sat on a bunk, still in her greatcoat, and slit the envelope.

Orchard Road, Singapore
16th January 1942
Dearest Judith,

I haven't much time, so this will be rather short. Tomorrow Jess and I sail on the *Rajah of Sarawak* for Australia. Kuala Lumpur fell to the Japanese four days ago, and they are advancing like a tide towards Singapore. Dad has to stay here, as he is responsible for the company office and the staff, and if it wasn't for Jess, I would stay and take my chance, but what can I do?

When we get to Australia, I shall send you a cable to let you know that we have arrived. Please tell Biddy, as I haven't time to write to her.

If anything should happen to Dad and me, you will look after Jess, won't you? I love you so much. I think about you all the time, darling Judith.

Mummy

It was the last letter from her mother. Four weeks later, on Sunday, February 15, Singapore was surrendered to the Japanese.

IT WAS nearly a month since Jeremy had said good-bye to Judith. He was in New York, where H.M.S. *Sutherland* was having a refit in the Brooklyn Navy Yard. For the Royal Navy, New York was open house, and Jeremy had never experienced such hospitality. At a cocktail party on the East Side, near Central Park, a delightful couple called Eliza and Dave Barmann had invited him to "weekend" with them on Long Island. Now, in their large old clapboard house on the water's edge, he sat at a desk writing to Judith.

Jeremy laid down his pen, his eye deflected by the sight of a ferryboat chugging across Long Island Sound. It occurred to him that he had been putting this letter off because it was so personal, and so important, that he feared that he would not be able to find the right words. He watched the boat until it disappeared from view; then he picked up his pen again.

Finding you at Diana's house was one of the best and most unexpected of bonuses. I am so grateful that I was there when you were feeling unwell and so worried. Being with you that night, and letting me share and, I hope, comfort, has become, in retrospect, like a small miracle, and I shall never forget your sweetness.

The truth is that I love you very much. I suppose always have done. But I didn't realize it until that day you came back to Nancherrow, and I heard "Jesu, Joy of Man's Desiring" from your room, and knew that you were home again. In that moment I finally understood how important you were to me.

One day the war will end, and with a bit of luck we'll all come through it, and we'll go back to Cornwall and pick up the threads of our lives. When that happens, I would like for us to be together again, because I cannot contemplate a future without you.

Here he stopped once more, assailed by self-doubt. He wanted, more than anything, to marry Judith, but was it fair even to suggest such a thing? At thirty-four, so much older than she, he wasn't much of a catch—a country G.P. short on worldly goods. While Judith, thanks to her late aunt, was a girl of wealth and property. The life of a rural doctor's wife was ruled by endless telephone calls, broken nights, canceled holidays. Perhaps she deserved more than that, a man who would give her a secure family life and an income that matched her own. She had grown so lovely, so desirable that it was obvious that men were going to fall in love with her. Was it being desperately selfish, at this moment in time, to ask her to marry him?

He simply didn't know, but he plowed on.

We have always been friends, and I don't want to say anything that might spoil our good relationship forever. But please write to me as soon as you can, and let me know whether in time you might consider our spending the rest of our lives together.

I love you so deeply. *Please* write and set my mind at rest.

Finished. He threw down his pen for the last time, then sat gazing despondently at the pages which had taken him all morning to compose. Perhaps he shouldn't have wasted his time. Perhaps he should tear them up, forget it all.

"Jeremy."

His hostess appeared through the open door. She said, "We're taking you to the club for lunch. Did you get your letter finished?"

"Just about."

"Do you want to mail it?"

"No. No, I might want to add something. Later. I'll mail it when I get back to the ship. I'll just go and tidy myself up."

AT THE end of April, at the end of a long day, Judith finished typing a final letter for Lieutenant Commander Crombie. It was nearly six. The two Wrens who shared the office had already packed up and gone, and now Judith left too. It was a golden spring evening, and she cycled out onto the main road, heading back to quarters. She was tired. Pedaling along, she thought about putting in for leave, going back to Cornwall. Just for a few days; that was all she needed. A long weekend.

A terrible void had been left by the loss of contact with her family. For nearly seven years she had lived with the pleasurable anticipation of a regular envelope filled with trivial, precious news from Singapore. But now each time she returned to quarters, she had to remind herself that there would be nothing to look for in the pigeonhole labeled "D."

Not even a letter from Jeremy. Over two months had passed since they had said good-bye in London. *I'll write,* he had promised. *So much to say.* And nothing had come. As the weeks slipped by, there dawned the uncomfortable suspicion that Jeremy had made love to her for much the same reason that Edward had. After all, it had been she, unwell and deeply upset, who had begged him to stay with her. *Darling Judith,* he had called her. All that she could imagine was that he had had second thoughts. Their love in London had simply been an interlude, charming but lightweight. She told herself that she understood. But the truth was that she felt dreadfully hurt.

These not very cheerful reflections lasted her all the way back to quarters. As she went inside, the duty officer said, "Dunbar, there was a telephone call for you. I put a note in your pigeonhole."

She went to the mailboxes and found the scrap of signal pad:

317

"Wren Dunbar. 1630 hours. Call from Loveday Carey-Lewis. Please ring back."

Loveday. What was Loveday wanting?

She went in search of a free telephone, dialed the number for Nancherrow, and dropped some coins in. Loveday answered.

"*Judith!* Sweet of you to ring back. Look, I'll be terribly quick. Mummy and I are coming to London this weekend, staying at the Mews. Please come up too. Can you?" She sounded frantic.

"Well, I could try for a short weekend."

"Oh, do. Say it's dreadfully important. Life and death. Mummy and I are going up in the train. How soon can you be with us?"

"I don't know. Saturday at the earliest."

"Perfect. Make any old excuse. Anything." *Pip-pip-pip* went the telephone. "Byeee." *Click.*

Judith, in some puzzlement, replaced the receiver. What on earth was Loveday up to now? The only thing that was perfectly clear was that tomorrow morning somehow she must persuade First Officer to sign a weekend pass.

SATURDAY was a beautiful April morning, without a cloud in the sky. In the warm spring sunshine London looked surprisingly lovely. Trees were in fresh green leaf. Carrying her overnight bag, Judith walked the cobbled length of the Mews to Diana's house and opened the door.

"Hello!" Loveday was at the head of the stairs. "I was terrified you wouldn't make it. Did you have to tell frightful lies to get permission?"

"No. Just bow and scrape a bit." Judith climbed the staircase. She dumped her bag, and they hugged. "Where's Diana?"

"Shopping, needless to say. We're meeting her at a quarter to one at the Ritz. Tommy Mortimer's giving us all lunch."

"Heavens, how smart."

Judith looked about her. The pretty room was bright and filled with flowers. Nancherrow flowers, brought from Cornwall. She flopped down on one of the ample sofas and sighed with pleasure. "When did you get here?"

"Thursday, on the train. And Tommy met us with a car." Loveday giggled. "Did you know, he got a medal for being frightfully brave in the blitz? He rescued some old girl from her burning

318

house. Turned out she was livid because he hadn't rescued her canary as well."

Loveday was laughing now. She looked, thought Judith, prettier than ever, charmingly sophisticated in a dress of hyacinth blue. Black patent high heels, bright lipstick, violet eyes sparkling.

She had curled up in one of the big armchairs. "Everybody sends their love—Pops, Athena, Mary Millyway, the Nettlebeds."

"What news of Rupert?"

"Battling it out in North Africa. But he writes long letters to Athena." She fell silent. Across the room they faced each other, and the laughter died from Loveday's face. "At least she hears from him. Nothing, I suppose, from your family?"

Judith shook her head. "Not a word. It's like a shutter's come down. But the boat Mummy and Jess were on never got to Australia. The *Rajah of Sarawak* was probably torpedoed, but there's been no official confirmation."

"And your father?"

She shook her head again. "Nothing." Then, "And Gus?"

For a moment Loveday sat, eyes downcast, her fingers picking at the braid of the armchair. Then abruptly she sprang to her feet and went to stare out the window. After a bit she said, "Gus is dead."

Judith felt cold with shock. "Then you've had news."

"No. But I know."

"*How* can you know he's dead?"

Loveday shrugged. "I just know." And then she turned to face Judith. "I would know if he was alive. Like I did after St.-Valéry. Then, it was like a message, but without any words. And I was right. He was safe. But after Singapore fell, every day I sat on the gate by the Lidgey farmyard and thought and thought about Gus, and tried to get a message to him, and to get him to send one to me. There's nothing there but darkness and silence. He's gone."

Judith was horrified. "But Loveday, you mustn't give up hope. Just because it happened once, that telepathy thing, it doesn't mean it's bound to happen again."

Loveday was immovable, stubborn as she had always been once she had set her mind on something. "I would know if he was alive. And I know, I *know,* that he's been killed."

"Oh, Loveday." Judith sighed. "Is this what you had to tell me? Is this why you wanted me to come to London?"

"That. And other things." Then Loveday dropped her bomb-shell. "I'm going to get married. I'm going to marry Walter."

"*Walter*. Walter Mudge?" The whole idea was inconceivable. "But what has got into you that you want to marry Walter?"

Loveday shrugged. "I like him. I always have."

"I like him too, but that's no reason to spend the rest of your life with him. You love Gus—"

Loveday rounded on her. "Gus is dead," she shouted. "So I'll never marry Gus. And don't tell me to wait for him, because what is the use of waiting for a man who's never coming back to me?"

Judith, prudently, made no answer to this. She thought, I have to be very cool; otherwise we're going to have the most resounding row and say terrible things that can never be unsaid. She changed her tack. "Look, you're only nineteen. Even if you're right about Gus, there are thousands of other men in the world just waiting to come into your life. I understand about you and Walter. You work together, and you see him all the time. But Loveday, what have you got in common with Walter Mudge?"

Loveday threw her eyes to heaven. "Oh, Lord, we're onto that. Lower-class, ill-educated farmworker. Marrying beneath me—"

"I don't think that."

"I've heard it all, particularly from Mary Millyway. But Walter's my friend, Judith. I like working with him. We're the same sort of people. Besides, he's masculine, attractive. I thought you'd under-stand. Back me up."

Judith shook her head. "You know I'd back you up to the ends of the earth. It's just that I'm not able to sit and watch you making such a mess of your life. After all, you don't *have* to marry him."

"Yes, I do."

"What?"

"I'm going to have a baby."

"Oh, *Loveday*. When . . . I mean—"

"Don't try to put it delicately. If you're asking when was the baby conceived, I'm happy to tell you. At the end of February, in the hayloft over the stables, and I'm not in the least ashamed."

"You thought Gus was dead?"

"I knew he was. I was so lonely, so unhappy. And Walter and I were seeing to the horses, and suddenly I started to cry, and I told him about Gus, and he took me in his arms and kissed away my tears, and I never knew him to be so gentle and so strong, and it was the most comforting thing that had ever happened to me." She was silent for a little and then said, "It didn't seem wrong at all."

"Does your mother know?"

"Of course. I told her as soon as I was sure. And Pops too."

"What did they say?"

"A bit astonished, but sweet. Said I didn't have to marry him if I didn't want to. Another baby in the nursery wouldn't make any difference. And when I said I *did* want to marry Walter, they bucked slightly but said that it was my decision. Besides, with Edward gone, at least they know I'll always be around."

All of which, knowing the Carey-Lewises, was perfectly understandable. In their charmed, upper-class fashion they had always been a law unto themselves. Their children's happiness came before everything else, and their loyalty to those children would always override social mores or the problems of what people would say. Diana and the Colonel, shoulder to shoulder, were clearly making the best of the situation. The most sensible thing that Judith could do was join their ranks and gracefully accept the inevitable. This was an enormous relief, because now she could stop being indignant and start being pleased and excited instead.

She said, "They have to be the best. Parents, I mean." Suddenly she was smiling, despite the prick of tears behind her eyes. She pulled herself off the sofa. "Oh, Loveday, I'm sorry. I had no right to be so difficult." And Loveday came to her, and they were both laughing and hugging. "I was just a bit surprised. Forget everything I said. You and Walter will be fine. When's the wedding?"

"Next month. You'll come, won't you?"

"I wouldn't miss it for anything. I'll fix a week's leave right away. Where are you going to live, you and Walter?"

"There's an old cottage on Lidgey. Pops is going to do it up for us, add on a proper bathroom. It's only two rooms, but it'll do for now."

"A real little love nest. What about a honeymoon?"

"Haven't really thought about it. Look"—Loveday peered at her watch—"it's midday. We'll have to set off for the Ritz in a moment. Let's have a drink to celebrate." She headed for the stairs and then turned. She was grinning like the wicked little girl Judith remembered from school days. "Thank heavens we're grown up. I never thought it would be much fun, but it is fun, isn't it?"

Fun. Loveday's high spirits were infectious, and Judith felt the lift of her own heart. The dark tides of war receded, and she was filled with the reasonless happiness of childhood. After all, they were young, the sun was shining, Loveday was going to be married, and she herself would be going home on leave for the wedding. She smiled. "Yes. Yes, it's fun."

The Dower House
Sunday, 31st May
My darling Bob,

Well, the wedding is over, and the happy pair are on a three-day honeymoon at the Castle Hotel in Porthkerris. Goodness, I wished you had been there. But I said a little prayer for you, stuck up there in Scapa Flow. Today I'm on my own. Judith, Phyllis, and Anna have taken a picnic down to Nancherrow Cove, so I am able to sit down and write you all about the wedding while it is still fresh in my mind.

On Thursday, Judith arrived home, and she behaved exactly like a small girl back for the school holidays, i.e., tore off her uniform and put on old clothes, and then went from room to room, checking every detail of her little domain. Afterwards we sat and talked for hours. Mostly about Molly and Bruce and Jess. She is determined to remain hopeful, but I don't imagine we shall get word of them until the end of hostilities. Then I asked about her love life, but she doesn't seem to have one and, for the time being, doesn't even seem to want one. Wary, I think. Once bitten, twice shy. Which is understandable.

On Friday she went off on her bike to Nancherrow to inspect Loveday's new house, which is now just about finished. The afternoon was spent gathering wildflowers with which to decorate the church, and we spent Friday evening decorating—Athena and Diana and Mary Millyway and myself.

Saturday was the most perfect day for a wedding. We all got into our rather outworn finery and walked down the hill to the church. I have to admit the church looked really lovely, lacy with cow parsley and garlands of honeysuckle. The place was packed. Diana looked a dream in pale turquoise silk, and the Colonel immensely distinguished in a gray frock coat. Little Clementina Rycroft was a fairly inefficient bridesmaid, removing her shoes and socks before she walked down the aisle, and ending up on Mary Millyway's knee sucking jujubes.

As for the bride and groom, they made an extraordinarily attractive couple. Loveday looked enchanting in white voile, white stockings, and white ballet slippers. No veil. Just a wreath of marguerite daisies on her shining dark head.

Then we piled into carts the Colonel had hired. Nancherrow was looking suitably festive, with flowers everywhere, and long tables, with white damask tablecloths, all set for luncheon in the courtyard. Even with rationing, it really was a feast. There was cold salmon and roast pork, and wonderful puddings coated with cream. I sat between Mr. Baines, Judith's solicitor, and Mr. Warren, from Porthkerris. Heather Warren had been asked, but she couldn't get away.

The meal took quite a long time, but by five o'clock the bride and groom were on their way. Loveday flung her bouquet at Judith, and then they got into Mr. Mudge's old car and rattled off to Porthkerris.

It's been such a special time. I think it's done us all good to put depressing news out of our minds, just for a little, and simply enjoy ourselves. As well, it has given me cause to think ahead. If the worst happens, and Molly and Bruce and Jess never return to us, then I think that you and I and Judith must make every effort to stay together after the war. Perhaps it would be a good idea for us to find somewhere near Rosemullion, where you could keep a little boat, and we could have a garden. In truth, I don't want to go back to Upper Bickley. The house is too full of memories. Here I have made a new life. This is a place where I would like to stay. Would you mind, my darling Bob?

My love. Take care of yourself.
Biddy

❧ 1945 ❧

TRINCOMALEE, Ceylon. H.M.S. *Adelaide,* her steel decks simmering in the heat, was the depot ship for the Fourth Submarine Flotilla. Her permanent berth was Smeaton's Cove, a deep inlet enclosed by two jungly promontories. The commanding officer was Captain Spiros, and each day two Wren writers were ferried on board the ship to work in his office. One of these was a languid girl called Penny Wailes. The other was Judith Dunbar.

Because of the apparent glamour of their job, they were much envied by their fellow Wrens, who made their way each morning to humdrum jobs ashore: the Pay Office or the Supply Office. But in fact, Judith and Penny found their day very long. They came on board at half past seven in the morning and did not return to quarters until evening.

Judith had been here about a year. In September 1944, after D-day, she had volunteered to go overseas, and the next thing she knew, she was on a troopship sailing through the Indian Ocean with a small detachment of Wrens towards Trincomalee. Now, with the war in Europe over, more ships of the Royal Navy arrived daily, bringing sailors starved of female company. They found no pubs, no picture houses, no girls.

At the end of another broiling day Judith and Penny stood on deck, waiting for the ship's boat to take them ashore.

When the boat drew alongside, the officer of the watch gave the signal, and Judith and Penny, being the lowest rank, ran down the gangway and boarded first. A few officers followed, the deckhands pushed off, and the boat swept away in a great curve.

Judith sat and turned her face into the fresh ocean breeze, and she could taste the salt on her lips. They rounded the promontory which guarded Smeaton's Cove, and the harbor opened up before them. In its haven lay battleships, cruisers, destroyers, and frigates—sufficient might to strike terror into the most aggressive of enemies.

In minutes they were approaching the Naval Headquarters jetty, busy with the coming and going of boats, the loading of personnel and stores. Onshore, caught in the curve of the beach, lay the complex of NHQ buildings, all square and white as sugar cubes, towered over by graceful palm trees.

The boat was berthed, and the officers stepped ashore in order of seniority. Judith and Penny were the last, and they set off to walk wearily up the dusty white road. They passed through a gate, guarded by sentries, and presently they came to another pair of guarded gates—the entry to the Wrens' quarters. A long palm-thatched building was the mess and the recreation room, its verandas smothered in bougainvillea.

In the mess hall Sinhalese stewards were serving an early supper, and Judith helped herself to a glass of lime juice, then went out onto the terrace. A path led to the far side of the camp, where sleeping bandas—thatched huts—were grouped beneath trees for shade.

At this time of day there were always a good many Wrens about. Those who worked ashore finished at four o'clock and so had plenty of time for a game of tennis or a swim. They wandered about in bathing suits, pegged underwear to washing lines, or had already changed into the khaki slacks and long-sleeved shirts which were regulation evening wear in this area of malarial mosquitoes.

Judith reached her own banda and went in. Twelve beds stood on either side, not unlike a school dormitory, and wooden fans, high in the palm-thatched ceiling, stirred the air into some semblance of coolness. Over each bed hung a white mosquito net.

Girls lay reading books, perusing mail, blancoing shoes. One had put a Bing Crosby record on her portable gramophone: *"When the deep purple falls,/ Over sleepy garden walls . . ."*

Judith flopped down on her bed, her hands linked beneath her head. It was strange how things happened. Days passed when she didn't even think of Cornwall, the Dower House, and Nancherrow. There was little opportunity for brooding, and old times, old friends were all an age away. But now "Deep Purple," which was inextricably entwined with those last days before the war. . . .

She thought of the group. The picture that had remained in her imagination: *Before Lunch, Nancherrow, 1939.* The green lawns, the blue sky, the sea, the breeze skittering the fringe of Diana's sun umbrella, the dark shadow cast upon the grass. And the figures who sat about in deck chairs or on tartan rugs.

Edward, the golden charmer, loved by all. Shot out of the sky during the Battle of Britain.

Athena, shining blond head, bare arms the color of dark honey. Then not even engaged to Rupert Rycroft. Now she was twenty-seven and Clementina was five, and Clementina had scarcely ever seen her father.

Rupert, the archetypal Guards officer. He had survived the North African Campaign and then Sicily, only to be nigh mortally wounded in Germany. The doctors had amputated his right leg. This news had come in a letter from Diana, who, though much dismayed, could scarcely conceal her relief that her son-in-law had not lost his life.

Gus Callender, the dark, reserved young Scot. The engineering student, the artist, the soldier, who had slipped so briefly into their lives, only to disappear in the mayhem of Singapore. *He is dead,* Loveday had insisted. And Loveday was now a farmer's wife and the mother of Nathaniel. Gus's name was no longer mentioned.

Finally, Jeremy Wells. News of him had filtered out to Judith via letters from home. He had come through the Battle of the Atlantic and had been posted to the Mediterranean, but that was all she knew. Since the night with him in London, she had received no message, no letter. She told herself that he was out of her life, but sometimes she yearned to see his face again, to be in his reassuring presence, to talk. And yet, what would they have to say to each other after all the years? Time had healed the hurt that he had inflicted, but the wound had left her wary.

"Is Judith Dunbar in here?" A Wren was making her way down the banda towards Judith's bed.

"Yes, I'm here." She sat up.

"Sorry to burst in, but I just looked through my mail and I got one of your letters by mistake. Thought I'd better bring it."

She handed it over. Judith saw Loveday's writing and experienced a spooky nudge of coincidence. "Deep Purple," and now a letter from Loveday. She hadn't had one from her in months. She leaned back, slitting the envelope with her thumbnail.

Lidgey
22nd July 1945
Darling Judith,

Nat and I have just been for tea at the Dower House, and I missed you so much that I thought I would write. Nat is asleep and Walter's gone to the pub to have a jar with his mates. Nat's two and a half now, and the biggest thing you've ever seen. The only time he behaves is when he's at Nancherrow, because of Mary Millyway, who doesn't let him get away with a thing.

Biddy told me that your uncle Bob has been posted to Colombo. Funny that you have both ended up there. I wonder if you've seen him yet. I looked on the map, and it's the other side of the island from Trincomalee.

News of Nancherrow. About two months ago Athena and Clementina left, to go and live in Gloucestershire with Rupert. He was brought home, and was in hospital for yonks, and then in a rehabilitation place learning to walk with a tin leg. So he has been invalided out, and he and Athena are living in a farmhouse on his father's estate, and he's going to learn all about running the place.

The war being over is a great relief, but everyday life hasn't changed much, still only a trickle of petrol, and food as tight as ever. But we can always slay a hen, and there are still eggs. One of the bottom fields of Lidgey is now a vegetable garden, and Walter's father and Nettlebed work it together. Mrs. Mudge is still slaving away in the dairy. She adores Nat and spoils him rotten.

Now I suppose I must wash up supper things, which are all over the place. Do write back. It seems funny walking down to Nancherrow and having to tell myself that you aren't there.

Love, love,
Loveday

ON A Monday in August over the wireless came news bulletins about the bomb dropped on Hiroshima. Then three days later the news of Nagasaki. A few more tense days and the Japanese finally surrendered.

All the ships of the fleet held thanksgiving services, and the Royal Marine Buglers played the last post in memory of all the men who had been killed. There were great celebrations that night, the whole East Indies Fleet lit up with flares and searchlights, rockets exploding and hooters hooting. On the quarterdeck of the flagship the Royal Marine band played—not ceremonial marches, but "Little Brown Jug" and "In the Mood."

It was wonderful, but at the same time Judith felt a bit scared. Because she knew that sooner or later somebody would tell her what had become of Mummy and Dad and Jess.

SHE waited for news. Life continued. Traveling each morning to H.M.S. *Adelaide*. Long, sweltering hours spent typing. Back to quarters each evening.

Perhaps now, she would tell herself. Perhaps today.

Nothing.

Her anxieties were compounded by the driblets of information trickling in from the first of the Japanese prison camps—atrocities, slave labor, starvation, disease. Everyone in the captain's office was thoughtful and kind, and each evening as they made the return journey Penny Wailes remained at Judith's side until they had passed through the Regulating Office and confirmed that there was still no news.

And then at six o'clock one evening Judith was in her banda after a swim, combing her wet hair, when one of the leading Wrens from the Regulating Office came in search of her.

"Dunbar. Message for you. You're to go and see First Officer tomorrow morning. Ten thirty. She's fixed it with Captain Spiros."

"Fine. Thanks," she heard herself say quite calmly.

The next morning she blancoed her shoes and her cap, put on a fresh white uniform, and walked out into the dazzling sun, down the road that led to NHQ.

THE morning was almost unbearably hot. Even the fan churning overhead did little to cool the air, and First Officer Beresford's cotton shirt was already damp and sticking to her neck.

The relevant papers lay on her desk, and she began to read, although, already, she knew them by heart. A knock at the door. Outwardly composed, she raised her head as Judith entered. "Dunbar. Thank you for coming. Pull up a chair and make yourself comfortable."

"Thank you, ma'am." Judith sat facing First Officer across the desk.

Their eyes met. First Officer looked down, busying herself by neatening the papers. Then, "I'm afraid it's not very good news, Dunbar. I am sorry."

"It's about my family, isn't it?"

"Yes. We heard through the Red Cross. I—I have to tell you that your father is dead. He died in Changi Prison, of dysentery, a year after the fall of Singapore. Others with him did all they could to care for him, but there were no medicines and little food. But he had friends around him. Try not to think of him dying alone."

"I see." Judith's mouth was suddenly so dry that she could scarcely speak the words, and they came out in a sort of whisper. "And my mother? And Jess?"

"So far we only know that their ship, the *Rajah of Sarawak*, was torpedoed in the Java Sea a few days out of Singapore. She was grossly overcrowded in the first place, and she went down almost instantly. The official verdict seems to be that if there were survivors, there could have been no more than a handful."

"Have they found anyone who did survive?"

First Officer shook her head. "No. I think, my dear, that you shouldn't hold out any hope."

The fans circled overhead. From beyond the open window came the sound of a boat's engine approaching the jetty. Somewhere a man was hammering. They were gone. They were all dead. Years of waiting and hoping, and now this.

Out of the long silence she heard First Officer say, "Dunbar? Are you all right?"

"Yes, I'm all right," she said, and was astonished to hear her voice so expressionless and calm. "I knew something happened to the ship. But still, I told myself they would have got themselves into a lifeboat, been picked up. . . . But I don't suppose they had a chance. Jess was little. And my mother had never been much of a swimmer."

First Officer again glanced down at the papers on her desk, which Judith now realized were her own service record. "I see that Captain and Mrs. Somerville are your next of kin."

"Yes. He's Rear Admiral Somerville now, over in Colombo. Biddy Somerville is my mother's sister. I must send her a cable."

"You can write what you want to say, and we'll put it through. I think you should take some leave. Get away from Trincomalee. Why not go to Colombo and spend some time with Rear Admiral Somerville?"

Uncle Bob. At this bleak watershed of her life Judith knew that there was no man in the world she would rather be with. "When could I go?"

"Right away. You're due two weeks' leave, but we'll add compassionate leave on to that. Which would give you a month."

A month. A whole month with Uncle Bob. Colombo again. She remembered the house where she had lived, and her mother sitting on the veranda sewing, and the cool winds blowing in from the Indian Ocean.

First Officer was waiting patiently. Judith looked up, and all she could say was, "You've been so kind to me."

326 Galle Road
Colombo
Tuesday, August 28th, 1945
Darling Biddy,

Thank you for the cable in response to mine. It made me feel much better, knowing that, although we are worlds apart, we are thinking the same sad thoughts, perhaps comforting each other. The worst is knowing that they died so long ago and we never knew. The conditions in Changi were unspeakable. Poor Dad. As for Mummy and Jess, I simply pray they were killed instantly when the *Rajah of Sarawak* was torpedoed.

As for me, I am safely here with Bob. (Not Uncle anymore; he says I am too old.) When I first arrived in Colombo, Bob was waiting for me. As I clambered out of the car, he simply took me in his arms and hugged me, and didn't say a word. It was at that moment that I fell to pieces and bawled like a baby. It was such a relief to know that I didn't have to be brave on my own any longer.

His house is a bungalow but enormous. The butler is a lovely man, a Tamil called Thomas. He is tall and has a lot of gold teeth, and always wears a flower behind one ear. Bob also has his own car with a driver called Azid.

I didn't do anything for days, just slept a lot and lay on the veranda. In the evenings we talked a lot. Bob told me that he's laying plans to leave the navy and that you've been thinking of selling up in Devon and moving to Cornwall. I can think of nothing that would be more wonderful for me.

On my third evening Bob took me to a cocktail party on board a visiting cruiser. Lots of new faces, civilians and military, and in the midst of socializing, Bob introduced me to a man called Hugo Halley, a lieutenant commander, RN, who works in the C-in-C's office. About eight of us, including Hugo, went ashore and had dinner. Last Sunday, Hugo and I drove down to Mount Lavinia to swim. He has asked me out again, so I am going to *have* to do something about my wardrobe. Colombo ladies are very chic, and my washed-out garments make me look like a poor relation.

It's funny, but I'm just beginning to realize how heavy was that load of uncertainty, never knowing what had happened to Dad and Mummy and Jess. Now, at least, I don't have to lug it around anymore. The void left by their going is unfillable, but some sort of a future is starting to be possible again. Getting back to England and picking up the threads will be a bit like starting all over, at the beginning. The beginning of what, I haven't worked out. However, I suppose I will.

SEVEN in the morning—pearly and still, the coolest hour of the day. Barefoot, wrapped in a thin robe, Judith emerged from her bedroom and made her way out onto the veranda. She found Bob breakfasting in peaceful solitude and asked if she could borrow the car. "Of course," he said. "I'll tell Azid."

That morning she asked Azid to take her to Whiteaway & Laidlaw, the store that Molly used to patronize. Judith found her way to the ladies' department, where she was confronted by an overwhelming profusion of clothes.

In a curtained changing room she slipped on dress after dress. Silks and cottons and fine voiles, peacock shades and pastels. It was agony to have to choose. In the end she bought a ball gown of pink sari silk, and three cocktail dresses, including an irresistible black dress of mousseline de soie, with a huge white organza collar. Then accessories: sandals and pumps and handbags. And finally, a luxurious assortment of cosmetics.

That evening she donned the irresistible black dress and went dancing with Hugo. After that, the days slipped by so fast that they turned into a week and then another. Swimming, tennis, and sightseeing; cocktails, dinner, and dancing. Now it was mid-September, and it would soon be time to journey back to Trincomalee.

AT HALF past five in the evening Bob Somerville, still in uniform, was on the veranda having afternoon tea when Judith appeared. "Pull up a chair," he said. "Thomas has conjured up some cucumber sandwiches. How was tennis?" he asked.

"Good game. With Hugo and another couple. Serious stuff."

"Before I forget, I've fixed that lift for you. A car, next Saturday morning. They'll pick you up at eight o'clock."

Judith screwed up her face like a child. "I don't want to go."

"Don't want you to go. But there it is. Duty calls. And talking of duty, Chief Officer Wrens rang me this afternoon. Asked if you'd be available to help tomorrow morning."

"Help do what?" Judith asked cautiously.

"There's a ship stopping off en route for England. The *Orion*. A hospital ship. The first batch of prisoners of war from the Burma Railway. They've been in hospital in Rangoon. They're being allowed ashore here for a few hours, their first step back to civilization. There's going to be a reception for them at the fort. Chief Officer's rounding up some Wrens to act as hostesses."

"What did you tell her?"

"Told her I'd have to discuss it with you. I explained that your father died in Changi and perhaps meeting up with a lot of emaciated prisoners would be a bit close to home."

Judith nodded. From the Burma Railway. At the end of the war the labor camps had been opened and their horrors exposed. Thousands of men had died. Those who survived had labored in the steaming jungle for as long as eighteen hours a day. Brutal guards had kept them working despite hunger, exhaustion, malaria. Now they were coming home.

She sighed. "I'll *have* to go. If I don't, I shan't be able to look myself in the eye for the rest of my life. What do I have to do?"

"Muster at nine a.m., the Galle Road Wrennery."

"Right."

THE next morning, in uniform and feeling apprehensive, Judith reported to the Wrens' quarters. A lorry was parked outside, and when the Wrens had all assembled, they trooped aboard. A moment later they were lurching up the Galle Road.

Judith and another Wren sat side by side at the back. The girl looked at Judith. "I don't know you, do I? I'm Sarah Sudlow."

"Judith Dunbar."

Behind them the Galle Road, wide and busy with traffic, streamed dustily away between tall palm trees. Judith thought of her father, living in Colombo, driving this way day after day to and from the offices of Wilson-McKinnon. She thought of him dying in the filth and hopeless misery that had been Changi. Dad, I'm doing this for you, she thought. Don't let me be too useless.

Beside her Sarah Sudlow shifted on the seat. "It's a bit of a facer, isn't it? I mean, drumming up things to *say*." She considered the problem. "Tell you what, much easier if we do it in pairs. Then if one of us runs out of chat, the other can chip in. What do you say? Shall we stick together?"

"Yes, please," said Judith instantly, and at once felt better.

The lorry rumbled across a bridge, then past the fort and on to the harbor. And in position at a jetty, immaculately ranked, was a Sikh pipe band in khaki shorts and tunics, and magnificent turbans.

The Wrens climbed down from the lorry. Others were there before them: officers from the garrison and Naval Headquarters, two ambulances, and some naval nursing sisters. On the grassy expanse of Gordon's Green could be seen army tents strung with bunting, and at the head of a tall flagpole flew the Union Jack.

Orion lay at anchor about a mile offshore. "Looks a bit like a prewar liner on a pleasure cruise," Sarah observed. "Ironic to know that most of her passengers are too sick to make the trip ashore. Oh, goodness, they're actually coming."

Judith looked and saw three tenders headed for the jetty, each packed with men. Suddenly the drums rolled and the Sikh pipers hoisted their instruments, and they began to play an old Scottish air: *Speed, bonnie boat, like a bird on the wing . . .*.

"Oh, no," said Sarah. "I hope I'm not going to blub."

The tenders drew closer, and the men who had survived hell were returning to the world again. What a way to make their landfall, greeted by the sound of the pipes. Some person, Judith decided, had been inspired. The wild music streaming out into the wind sent shivers down her back, and she, like Sarah, felt tears behind her eyes.

Judith said in as steady a voice as possible, "Why are they playing Scottish tunes?"

"Most of the prisoners are Durham Light Infantry, but I think there are some Gordon Highlanders as well."

All Judith's senses pricked. "I once knew a Gordon Highlander. He was killed at Singapore."

"Maybe you'll meet up with some of his chums."

The first tender had come alongside, and her passengers, in orderly fashion, began to climb up onto the jetty. Sarah squared her shoulders. "Come on. Nice smiles and a cheerful manner."

But after all their apprehension it wasn't difficult at all. Ordinary young men, and as soon as Judith heard them speak, in the accents of Northumberland, Cumberland, and Tyneside, she lost all her reservations. Bone-thin, still wearing the pallor of sickness and malnutrition, they all came down the jetty looking neat and clean, kitted out in jungle-green battle dress. They approached slowly, as though not certain what to expect, but as the white-clad Wrens mingled amongst them, their shyness melted away.

"Hello. I'm Judith."

"I'm Sarah. Welcome to Colombo."

Soon each girl had gathered about her a number of men, all of them clearly relieved to be told what they had to do.

"We're going to take you up to Gordon's Green, where the tents are. We've plenty of transport if anyone wants a ride."

But Judith's group, now swelled to about twenty men, said that they would walk, and they set off at an unhurried pace, up the gentle slope that rose from the shore.

Long afterwards Judith remembered the official reception for the returned prisoners of war. The Royal Marine band playing out on the green. The visiting dignitaries come to pay their respects. Under the tent, trestle tables were loaded with sandwiches and cakes, iced coffee and lemonade. Having safely delivered their charges, Judith and Sarah were pressed into duty loading trays and making sure that every man got his share of the feast. At last the assembled company, sated, drifted out to lie on the grass, smoke cigarettes, and listen to the band.

By half past eleven Sarah was nowhere to be seen, and the stewards had begun clearing away the detritus of the party. So Judith left the tent and stood observing the peaceful scene of random groups of relaxing men. And then her eye was caught by a single man, who stood with his back to her, apparently intent upon the music. She noticed him because he was different. Lanky and fleshless as the others, but not wearing the anonymous jungle-green uniform and canvas gym shoes. Instead, a pair of battered desert boots. On his dark head was a Gordon glengarry, ribbons fluttering in the breeze. A worn khaki shirt, the sleeves rolled up to his elbows. And a Gordon kilt—ragged and faded, the pleats stitched down with twine. But still, a kilt.

For an instant she thought it might be Gus, and then saw at once that it wasn't, because Gus was dead. Lost, killed in Singapore. But perhaps he had *known* Gus.

She walked across the grass towards him. She said, "Hello."

Startled, he swung around, and she was looking up into his face: dark eyes, thick brows, cheeks cadaverous. She experienced an extraordinary sensation, as though for an instant she had been frozen in time.

It was he who broke the silence. "Good God. Judith."

Oh, Loveday. You were wrong. You were wrong all the time.

"Gus."

He isn't dead. He's here. With me. Alive.

She said, "You're alive."

"Did you think I wasn't?"

"Yes. I've thought for years you were dead. Ever since Singapore. We all did."

"Do I look like a corpse?"

"No. You look wonderful." And she meant it. "The boots and the kilt and the glengarry. How on earth did you hang on to them?"

"Only the kilt and the bonnet. I stole the boots."

"Oh, Gus." She took a step towards him, put her arms around his waist, and pressed her face into the worn cotton of the shirt. She could feel his ribs and could hear the beating of his heart. His arms came around her, and they simply stood there, very close. After a bit they drew apart. "I never saw you in the tent," she told him.

"I was only there for a little while."

"When do you have to be back on board?"

"Tenders at three o'clock."

"We could go back to the Galle Road, where I'm staying. Have a drink or some lunch. There's time."

"What I would really like," said Gus, "is to go to the Galle Face Hotel. I've got a sort of date there. But I couldn't go on my own, because I haven't any money."

"I've got money. I'll come with you. We'll get a taxi up on the road." So they slipped away. Nobody noticed or, if they did, said nothing.

In the taxi, she said, "My parents were in Singapore, about the same time as you. And my little sister. They didn't survive."

"I *am* sorry."

The taxi was driving along the edge of the Galle Face Green. Gus was saying, "It's not exactly in the same league, but my parents have died as well." He turned to face her. "They were elderly. I was the only child. Perhaps they too thought I was dead."

"Who told you this?"

"A social worker in the hospital in Rangoon."

"At Singapore couldn't you send word to *anyone*?"

"I tried to smuggle a letter out, but I don't suppose it worked."

The taxi turned into the forecourt of the hotel. Judith paid the driver, and they went inside.

"Gus, you said you had a date. Who with?"

"Wait and see." Behind the reception desk stood a Sinhalese clerk. "Does Kuttan still work here?"

"But of course, sir. He is in charge of the restaurant."

"I wonder if I could have a word. I'm Captain Callender. A friend of Colonel Cameron's. Gordon Highlanders."

"Very good, sir. Would you like to wait out on the terrace?"

They walked out, Gus choosing a table, arranging the cane chairs. She wondered at his coolness, his detachment, his air of authority despite his rags of uniform. There was an inner strength that was palpable. She found this a little daunting. Sooner or later she was going to have to tell him about Loveday.

Drinks were brought to them on the terrace. Children, with amahs in attendance, were swimming in the pool. The breeze rattled the palms. Gus said, "It's just the same. It hasn't changed."

"You were here?"

"Yes, on our way out to Singapore. Our troopship stopped off here for four days. It was a particularly riotous time. Parties and pretty girls." He said again, "A good time."

"Captain Callender."

They had not heard him come, but now Gus rose to his feet. "Kuttan." The man stood, beaming, his white tunic embellished with red silk epaulettes. He held a silver tray on which stood a bottle of Black & White whisky.

"I could not believe my ears when I was told that you were here. God is very good. This is Colonel Cameron's bottle of Black and White that he asked me to keep for him." He looked about him. "Colonel Cameron is not with you?"

"He died, Kuttan."

The old man stared with sad dark eyes. "A fine gentleman." He looked at the whisky bottle. "He paid for this that last night. He said, 'Kuttan, we will celebrate on our way home.' And now he is not coming." He set the bottle on the table. "So you must take it."

Gus held out his hand in thanks. "Good-bye, old friend." They shook hands. And then Kuttan stepped back, placed his palms together, and salaamed with affection and respect.

When he had gone, Gus sat down and looked at the bottle. He said, "I shall have to find some sort of bag to put it in. I can scarcely be observed carrying it on board."

"We'll find something," Judith promised him. "You can take it back to Scotland. What will happen when you get home?"

"Report to HQ in Aberdeen, I suppose. Medical checkups."

"Were you very ill?"

"No more than anyone else. Beriberi. Dysentery. They reckon about sixteen thousand Brits died."

"Do you hate to talk?"

"What about?"

"Singapore. I had a last letter from my mother . . . but it didn't really tell me anything, except confusion and chaos."

"That was pretty much it. After the Japanese invaded Malaya, Singapore was doomed. We were sent to do rearguard action at the causeway onto the island. We held our positions for three or four days. Then the Japanese reached the reservoirs that supplied all the freshwater. They turned off the taps. That was it. Capitulation."

"What happened to you then?"

"We were put into Changi. I got put in a working party, sent out into the streets to repair bomb damage. I got quite good at scrounging supplies. I even sold my watch for Singapore dollars and used them to bribe one of the guards into posting a letter to my mother and father, but I don't know if he did. As well, he brought me paper and pencils, a drawing block, and I managed to keep them filled and hidden for the next three and a half years. A sort of record. But not one for human consumption."

"What happened next, Gus?"

"Well, we stayed in Changi for about six months, and then we were all put in steel cattle trucks, traveling north to Bangkok for five days and nights. Thirty to a truck, no space to lie down. It was ghastly. We had one cupful of rice each and one cup of water a day. At Bangkok we all fell out of the cattle trucks, weak with relief that the ordeal was over. What we didn't know was that it was only just beginning."

Gus downed the last of his drink. "That's all," he said. "No more about me." Across the table he sent her the ghost of a smile. "I want to hear about you. When did you join the Wrens?"

"The day after Edward was killed."

337

"That was grim. I wrote to the Carey-Lewises. I was in Aberdeen then, after St.-Valéry." He frowned, remembering. "You bought Mrs. Boscawen's house, didn't you?"

"Yes. After she died."

She waited. He said, "And Nancherrow? Diana, the Colonel?"

"Just the same."

"And Loveday?"

He was watching her. She said, "Loveday's married, Gus."

"Married?" His expression became one of total incredulity. "Loveday? Whom did she marry?"

"Walter Mudge."

"But . . . *why?*"

"She thought you were dead. She was utterly convinced that you'd been killed. I don't know if I can explain. But after St.-Valéry she had this premonition that you were alive. And you were. It made her believe that there was some sort of telepathy between the two of you. After Singapore she tried again, thinking about you, waiting for some sign, or message, from you. And none came."

"I could scarcely ring up on the telephone."

"Oh, Gus, you know what Loveday's like. Once she's got an idea in her head, she's immovable. In some strange way she convinced us all."

"Is she happy?"

"I think so, though I haven't seen her for quite a long time. Oh, Gus, I'm sorry. I've been dreading telling you. But—"

He said, "I thought she would wait for me."

All at once he looked desperately worn and tired. He rubbed a hand over his eyes. She thought of him going home, back to Scotland, to nothing. No family. No Loveday.

She said, "Gus, whatever happens, we *must* keep in touch. You must give me your address so that I can write to you. I'll go and get some paper and a pen. And something to hide your whisky in. I shan't be a moment."

She went back indoors, paid the bar bill, and was given a hefty brown paper bag in which to conceal the Black & White. After that, she found writing paper and a pencil. When she returned to Gus, he sat as she had left him, his eyes fixed on the horizon.

"Here." She handed over the paper and pencil. "Your address." He wrote, then pushed them back to her. "Gus, if I write, will you promise to answer? We haven't, either of us, got much left. So we must sustain each other. It's important."

"Yes. Important. Judith . . . I must go. I mustn't miss the boat."

"I'll come with you."

"No. I'd rather go alone."

"We'll find a taxi. Here. . . . Money for the fare."

"I feel like a kept man."

"No, not kept. Just pretty special."

They went out through the foyer, and the doorman called a taxi. "Good-bye, Judith." And then he said, "Just one thing. When you tell them, at Nancherrow, about today, tell them I'm okay."

"Oh, Gus." She reached up and kissed him on both cheeks. He got into the taxi and was driven away. Judith watched him go. Then, Keep in touch, she thought. You mustn't disappear again.

"Can I get a taxi for you?"

She turned and looked at the doorman. No point in returning to the fort. She would go home now. "Yes. Thank you."

On the Galle Road once more, she thought about Loveday and the marriage that should never have taken place. The child who should never have been conceived. The bleak homecoming that awaited Gus.

Now the taxi was slowing down. She saw the familiar gates, the sentry. She got out and paid the driver. And then, on this day of extraordinary events, the last extraordinary thing occurred. The doors of Bob's bungalow stood open, and he was running down the wide steps to meet her.

"Where have you *been?*" He sounded distraught.

"I—I—" Completely knocked off course by his outburst, she could scarcely find the words to explain. "I met someone. I'm sorry."

"Don't be sorry." He put his hands on her shoulders. "Just listen. I got a telephone call from Trincomalee. A signal's come through. Jess . . . Java . . . the *Rajah of Sarawak* . . . a lifeboat . . . a young Australian nurse . . . internment camp . . ."

She watched his craggy face, his eyes keen with excitement, his mouth making words that she scarcely understood. "Tomorrow. RAF . . . Jakarta to Ratmalana. She'll be here."

It finally sank in. He was telling her that little Jess was alive. Safe.

"Jess?" It took an enormous effort even to say her name.

Abruptly Bob pulled her into his arms. "Yes," and there was a break in his voice. "She's coming back to you!"

"Pretty exciting day for you. Your sister, isn't it?"
"Yes."
"How old is she?"
"Fourteen."

It was five o'clock in the afternoon. Judith and Bob had presented themselves at the RAF station, Ratmalana. The plane from Jakarta would be landing soon. They walked across the dusty parade ground towards the control tower—Bob Somerville and Judith, a group captain and an aide. Outwardly cool, Judith was trembling inside with nerves. Shading her eyes, she stared into the sky.

And then she saw the plane, heard its engines as it floated out of the southwest. It touched down in a blast of thundering noise, then came taxiing back to the control tower. At last the doors opened and steps were trundled up. The passengers alighted: a group of American pilots, two soldiers . . .

Finally she was there, clambering down the steps. Skinny and brown, wearing shorts and a faded green shirt, with sun-bleached hair clipped in a crop. Clumsy leather sandals sizes too big, a small canvas rucksack slung over one shoulder. She paused, clearly a bit lost, apprehensive. Then bravely she set out after the others.

Jess. At that moment they might have been the only two people in the world. Judith moved to meet her, searching that bony little face for some trace of the chubby child, the sweetly weeping four-year-old to whom she had said good-bye all those years ago. Jess saw her and stopped dead.

"Judith?" She had to ask, because she couldn't be sure.
"Yes. Judith."

She held out her arms. Jess hesitated for an instant, then flung herself forward into Judith's embrace. She was so tall now that the top of her head reached Judith's chin, and holding her felt like grasping something very brittle, like a starved bird. Judith buried her face in Jess's rough hair, and it smelled of disinfectant, and she felt Jess's skinny arms latch tight around her waist.

When they joined the three men, they were met with great kindness and tact. Bob did not kiss Jess, simply rumpled her hair with a gentle hand. She didn't say much, didn't smile. But she was all right.

340

The group captain walked with them to where the car waited, then saluted smartly as the car moved away. "Now"—Bob smiled down at his small niece—"you're *really* on your way."

She sat between them in the back of the huge car. Judith couldn't stop looking at her. There were scars on her right leg, and her hair looked as though it had been chopped off with a carving knife. But she was beautiful. "When you saw Uncle Bob, did you recognize him?" she asked.

Jess shook her head. "No."

Bob laughed. "How could you, Jess? You were only four years old. We were together for such a little while. In Plymouth. It was Christmas."

"I remember Christmas. I remember the silvery tree."

"You know something, Jess? You talk like an Australian."

"Ruth was Australian." She pronounced it "Austrylian."

"Was she the girl who looked after you?" Judith asked.

"Yeah. She was great. In my bag I've got a letter for you from her. She wrote it yesterday."

They left Ratmalana behind them and were bowling north, along the wide road to the city. Jess gazed with some interest from the windows. "Where are we going?"

"To my house," Bob told her. "Judith's been staying with me."

"Is it a big house?"

"Big enough."

"Will I have a room by myself?"

"If that's what you'd like."

Judith said, "I've got two beds in my room. You could sleep with me if you'd rather."

But Jess did not commit herself. "I'll think about it." And then, "Could I change places with you so I can see out of the window?"

After that, she simply sat with her back to Bob and Judith, intent on all that passed them by. Little farms, then wayside shops and filling stations. Finally they entered the Galle Road, and it was only when the car swung in through the gate that she spoke again.

"There's a guard on the gate." She sounded alarmed.

"Yes. A sentry," Bob said. "He's not there to stop us getting out, just to make certain no unwelcome guests come in. I have a gardener too, and a cook, and a butler called Thomas. He cannot wait to meet you." The car drew up and stopped. "In fact, there he is."

341

Thomas was down the steps and opening the car door, a hibiscus blossom tucked behind his ear. Beaming with delight, he helped Jess out. He gathered up her rucksack and led her indoors, with an arm about her thin shoulders. "You have had a good journey? You are hungry, yes? You would like refreshment?"

But Jess, looking a bit overwhelmed, said that what she really wanted was to go to the lavatory, so Judith retrieved the rucksack and led her down the passage to the quiet of her bedroom.

"You mustn't mind Thomas. He's been so excited ever since we knew you were coming. The bathroom's in here."

Jess stood in the open door and simply looked at the polished taps, the gleaming white porcelain. "Is this all for you?" she asked.

"You and me."

"There were only two lavs in the whole camp at Asulu. They stank. Ruth used to clean them."

"That can't have been very nice." Which was inadequate but the only comment she could think of. "Why don't you go on in."

Which Jess did. Judith sat at her dressing table to wait. Then Jess returned and perched herself on one of the beds. Through the mirror their eyes met. "Have you made up your mind?" Judith asked. "Do you want to sleep in here with me?"

"Okay. I thought you'd look like Mummy, but you don't."

Judith turned. "I'm sorry."

"No. Just different. She never wore lipstick. When I got out of the airplane, I thought you mightn't be there to meet me. The rehabilitation officers at Asulu couldn't find anybody for me. We had to stay in the camp until they'd found out where you were."

"Like looking for a needle in a haystack. What happened was that I was told that both Mummy and Dad had died. You too, for that matter. And I came here on compassionate leave."

Jess looked at her. "Will we stay together? You and me?"

"Yes. Together. No more being apart."

"Where shall we go?"

"Cornwall. To my house. Now"—she looked at her watch—"it's time to shower and change for dinner. It's early tonight. We thought you might be tired."

"I only have these clothes."

"I'll lend you something of mine. Another pair of shorts and a pretty shirt. And I've got a pair of thong sandals you can have."

Jess looked with distaste at her feet. "These are horrible. I haven't worn shoes since forever. It was all they could find."

"Tomorrow we'll go buy a whole new wardrobe for you, and warm clothes for England. Proper shoes and socks. Now why not take a shower. There's everything you need in the bathroom."

Jess reached for her rucksack and from its depths produced a toothbrush and a comb. Then she withdrew a wad of yellow lined paper. "This is for you. From Ruth."

Judith took it. "Do you want me to read it now?"

Jess shrugged her shoulders. "Doesn't matter."

"I'll keep it for later." And she put it on her dressing table.

She showed Jess how to work the shower and left her to it. When Jess emerged again, she smelled of rose-geranium soap. They spent time choosing clothes, deciding on white tennis shorts and a blue silk shirt. When the sleeves had been rolled up over her spiky elbows, Jess took up her comb and flattened her damp hair.

"You look perfect. Feel comfortable?"

"Yeah. I'd forgotten about silk. Mummy used to wear silk dresses. I'm going to go and find Uncle Bob."

"You do that."

It was good, for a moment, just to be alone. Judith was exhausted by emotion. Ten years was too long for love to survive; too much had happened to Jess. But it would be all right if they took their time rebuilding a relationship. Jess was back. A beginning.

She showered and dressed in thin trousers and a sleeveless shirt, then picked up the yellow pages of the Australian girl's letter.

Jakarta
September 19th, 1945
Dear Judith,

My name is Ruth Mulaney. I am twenty-five years old. I am an Australian. In 1941 I finished my nurses training in Sydney and went to Singapore to stay with friends of my mother and father. When the Japs invaded Malaya, I managed to get a passage on the *Rajah of Sarawak*.

We were torpedoed six days out in the Java Sea at about five in the evening. Jess's mother had gone below for a moment and asked me to keep an eye on Jess. The ship sank very quickly. There was a lot of screaming and confusion. I grabbed Jess and a life jacket, and we jumped overboard. I was able to hang on to her, and then a lifeboat came and we managed to get into it.

We were adrift the next day and another night. The next morning we were sighted by an Indonesian fishing boat and taken in tow to their village in Java. I wanted to go to Jakarta to try to get another boat to take us to Australia, but Jess was ill. She had cut her leg somehow, and it was septic and she ran a fever. So the other survivors went on, but we stayed in the village. I thought Jess was going to die, but she's a strong little tyke and managed to pull through. By the time she was fit to be moved, Japanese planes were appearing in the sky. Finally we got a ride in a bullock cart to Jakarta. But the Japanese were there, and they picked us up and put us in a camp at Bandung with other women and children.

Bandung was the first of four camps. The last, at Asulu, was the worst of all. A labor camp, and all of us women were made to work in the rice fields or clean latrines. We were always hungry and sometimes starving. We ate rice and soup made of vegetable scraps. Sometimes the Indonesians threw a bit of fruit over the wire, or I was able to barter for an egg. Jess was never really ill again, but suffered boils, which have left some scars.

Around the end of August we were told that Allied forces would be landing in Java. After that, the guards disappeared, but we stayed in the camp because there wasn't anywhere else to go.

Finally the British came. I think they were pretty shocked when they saw the state we were in.

Over these three and a half years Jess has witnessed some terrible events, atrocities, and deaths. All of these she seems to have learned to accept. She's a very courageous little person. During this time we have become very close to each other. She is miserable about saying good-bye. To make things easier, I've said that one day she must come to Australia and stay with me and my family. I'd be grateful if, when she is a bit older, you'd let her make the trip. Take care of our little sister.

Regards,
Ruth Mulaney

Take care of our little sister. For three and a half years Ruth had been Jess's security, however tenuous. This was where her love and her loyalty lay. And she had had to leave it all behind.

Judith got up and went out in search of Jess. She found her alone on the lamplit veranda, turning the pages of Bob's old photograph album. Jess glanced up. "Come and see these. They're so funny. Mummy and Dad. Ages ago. Looking so young."

Judith settled herself beside Jess on the cane settee and laid an arm around her shoulders. "Where's Uncle Bob?"

"He's gone to change. He gave me this to look at. This is when they lived right here in Colombo. And here's one of you in a terrible hat." She turned another page.

Judith said, "I read the letter. Ruth sounds a special person."

"She was. And she was brave. Never frightened, not of anything."

"She says you were pretty brave too." Jess elaborately shrugged. "She says when you're a bit older, she wants you to go to Australia and stay with her. I think it's a great idea."

Jess's head shot up, and she looked into Judith's face. "*Could* I? Could I go?"

"Of course. Absolutely. Say, when you're about seventeen? That's only three years away."

"Three *years!*"

"You'll have to go to school, Jess, when we get back. You'll have a lot of catching up to do."

But Jess was not interested in talking about school. "That was the worst about saying good-bye. Thinking I'd never, ever see her again. Can I write to her and tell her?"

"Certainly. Then you can both start looking forward to it." She hesitated, "Meanwhile, I think it's time we went home."

JUDITH was packing. Four items of baggage. The great shopping expedition had taken most of a day, and Judith had cast prudence aside. She knew that in England, clothes rationing was tighter than ever, and once they got home, there wouldn't be a hope of buying anything very much. So for Jess a complete wardrobe: shirts, sweaters, skirts, woolen knee stockings, pajamas, shoes, a thick dressing gown, and a sensible raincoat. All this lay on Jess's bed in neat folded bundles.

It helped having a rear admiral as a relation. Bob had pulled strings and fixed them berths on a troopship heading home, and Judith was now on indefinite leave pending a compassionate discharge. In three weeks' time she and Jess would be in England.

345

> The Dower House
> Rosemullion, Cornwall
> Sunday, 21st October
>
> My darling Bob,
>
> They're home. Safe and sound. I hired a huge taxi and went on
> Friday to scoop them off the train at Penzance. I don't think I've
> ever been more excited. Both are looking well, if tired. Jess has
> talked a lot about you and the time she spent in Colombo.
>
> The most touching was when she saw Phyllis again. As the taxi
> arrived at the Dower House, Phyllis and little Anna, with Morag in
> tow, came out to meet us. Jess took one look and was out of the taxi
> before it had even stopped, to cast herself into Phyllis's arms.
>
> This morning I went to church and said *thank you*.
>
> I think the time has come for me to fly this nest. I saw a lovely
> house in Portscatho, looking over the sea. It's in good nick, so I
> shall put in an offer. I want to be all settled in for when you come
> home again.
>
> As for Phyllis, the great news is that Cyril has decided to stay in
> the navy. He is now a petty officer, with a D.S.M. for gallantry. I
> think they must have a home of their own, somewhere for Cyril to
> come for his leaves. Perhaps a little terrace house in Penzance.
>
> So that's about it. Darling Bob, how lucky we are.
>
> > My love as forever,
> > Biddy

As THEY trudged up the Nancherrow drive, it looked a bit unkempt, with potholes and puddles. The hydrangeas were long over,
their flower heads browned and sagging with the rain.

Around the last curve of the drive, and the house stood before
them. They stopped for a moment. Jess said, "It's really big."

"They needed a big house," said Judith. "They had three children and lots of friends always coming to stay."

They reached the sanctuary of the front door. There they shed
raincoats, toed off their boots, then went into the hall.

Unchanged. Flowers stood on the round table, where still lay the
dog leads, the visitors book, the stack of mail.

"Judith." Mary Millyway, a bit grayer now, came down the stairs.
"I can't believe you're really here. And this is Jess? Lovely to meet
you. Oh, you're both soaking. Walk down, did you?"

"Yes. I don't yet have a petrol ration for my car, and we've only one bike. Where's Loveday?"

"She'll be here directly. Walking down from Lidgey with Nat. Let's go and tell Mrs. Carey-Lewis you're here." She led them to the small sitting room.

And there they were, sitting on either side of the fireplace—Diana with a tapestry and the Colonel with the Sunday *Times*. At his feet old Tiger lay asleep, but Pekoe, who had been dozing on the sofa, let loose a cacophony of barks. Diana sprang to her feet.

"It's Judith. Oh, darling, it's been a thousand years. Come let me hug you." She was as lovely as ever, despite the fact that her corn-colored hair had faded to silver. "You're looking utterly wonderful! And Jess. We've heard so much about you."

Released from Diana's embrace, Judith turned to the Colonel, who was now standing, awaiting his turn.

"My dear." Formal; as always, a little shy. She took his hands in hers, and they kissed. "How pleased we are to have you home again." Then he smiled at Jess. "What do you think of Cornwall, eh? Doesn't rain like this *all* the time."

Jess said, "I actually remember Cornwall."

"Do you, by Jove? Why don't we sit down, and you can tell me about it. . . . Here, on this stool by the fire."

Diana sank back into her chair. Judith sat on the end of the sofa.

"Darling, what a time you've had. You look thin. And little Jess! Such experiences. Biddy telephoned the moment she got the cable from Bob. And so dreadfully sad about your parents. The Nettlebeds send their love; they have Sundays off now. Was it heaven to get back to the Dower House?"

Brittle with excitement, she chattered on, and Judith tried to listen, but she was thinking about Gus Callender. Was now the moment to tell them that Gus was alive? No, she decided. The first person to be told, and in private, was Loveday.

"And what plans have you made for Jess?"

"First a bicycle." Judith smiled. "Then I suppose I'll go and see if Miss Catto will take her at St. Ursula's."

"But, my darling, of course she will. Oh, isn't it too extraordinary how life goes full circle. Oh, I haven't told you about Athena. She's going to have another baby. In the spring. I can't tell you how we missed them when they went. The house was empty without a child."

No sooner were the words out of her mouth than could be heard the piercing tones of Nathaniel Mudge, on his way from the kitchen and in full spate of argument with his mother.

"I don't want to take my boots off."

"You've got to. They're covered in mud. Now come here."

"No."

"Nat!"

A howl. Loveday had clearly caught him and was forcibly removing his boots. Diana said faintly, "Oh, dear."

A moment later the door burst open and her grandson catapulted into the room, his cheeks scarlet with indignation.

Judith got up from the sofa as Loveday appeared in the open doorway. Looking exactly the way she always had—a ragamuffin teenager in trousers and an old pullover.

They simply stood there, grinning at each other. Then, "Well, look who's here," said Loveday. They met and hugged and kissed perfunctorily, just the way they always used to. "Sorry we're late, but— Nat, don't put your fingers near Pekoe's eye."

Nat glared at his mother, and Judith, for all her good intentions, dissolved into laughter. "You seem to have met your match."

"Oh, he's a horror. Aren't you, Nat? Very sweet but a horror."

He set about clambering onto the sofa and commencing to bounce, but then Mary bustled in to tell them that tea was on the table and scooped Nathaniel out of the air mid-bounce to bear him, shrieking with what one hoped was glee, in the direction of the dining room.

"She's the only person," said Loveday with a sort of hopeless pride, "who can do a thing with him. Come on. Let's eat."

So they trooped through to the dining room, where the tea table had been set with all the remembered nursery treats—jam sandwiches, chocolate biscuits, and a fruitcake baked in a ring. It was a much diminished table from the old days. All the leaves had been removed, and what remained looked strangely small in the middle of the huge, formal room.

By the time tea was finished, the afternoon had faded into darkness. Yet nobody stood to draw the heavy curtains. "Such bliss," said Diana. "No blackout. I still haven't got used to it. Mary, don't start clattering about with the teacups; we'll wash them up. Take Nat up to the nursery and give Loveday a few moments to herself."

She turned to Jess. "Perhaps Jess would like to go too. There are lots of books and jigsaw puzzles."

"What a sweet girl," Diana said when they had gone. "No tears? No nightmares? No ill effects?"

"I don't think so."

"Perhaps a check-over by a doctor might be a good idea. Talking of which, old Dr. Wells popped in the other day. Jeremy is hoping to come home for a bit. He hasn't had leave for about two years."

Judith said, "I should think he'd be demobbed soon," and was delighted with the casualness of her voice.

Loveday helped herself to a slice of cake. "I can't see him settling down in Truro after all that bobbing about on the high seas."

"I can," said Diana. "The perfect country G.P." She surveyed the shambles of the table. "I suppose we'd better wash up."

"Don't worry, Mummy," Loveday said. "Judith and I will do it."

And they went to the kitchen, where Judith tied an apron around her waist and filled the old clay sink with scalding water from the brass tap. "What's happened to Heather?" she asked Loveday. "I haven't heard from her in years."

"She's gone to America on some mission with her boss at the Foreign Office. Last we heard, she was in Washington."

"How about Tommy Mortimer?"

"Oh, he pops down from London from time to time. With other old chums. Keeps Mummy amused."

Judith squirted washing-up liquid into the water, then put in the first pile of plates. She said, "How's Walter?"

"He's all right."

"How's the farm going?"

"Fine."

Her answers were so laconic, so disinterested that Judith's heart chilled. She said, "What do you do when he's not working? I mean, do you go to the cinema or picnics or down to the pub?"

"I used to go to the pub sometimes, but to be truthful, I'm not all that keen on pubs. So Walter goes alone."

"Oh, *Loveday,* it doesn't sound much fun. What about the horses? Do you still ride together?"

"Not much." She had found a tea towel and was taking the plates from a rack and drying them very slowly, then setting them down in a stack on the scullery table.

"Are you happy, Loveday?"

Loveday took another plate out of the rack. "Who was it who said that marriage was a summer birdcage set out in a garden? All the birds of the air wanted to get in, and all the caged birds wanted to get out. You're a bird of the air. Free. You can fly anywhere."

"No, I can't. I've got Jess."

"Not wanting to get into the summer birdcage? No lovelorn sailor? I can't believe it." She wiped another plate. "I always thought that Jeremy was in love with you."

Judith said, "I think you were probably wrong."

The last plate and Judith pulled out the plug, and the suds seeped away. She turned, leaning against the sink. "Loveday—"

"You will come and see me, won't you? At Lidgey." Loveday put the plate on the stack. "You never saw my funny little house when it was finished. I love the farm and the animals. And I love Nat too, even though he's such a holy terror." She looked at her watch. "I must go. My kitchen's a mess, and I've got to get Walter's tea and get Nat to bed."

Judith said, "Don't go. I have something to tell you."

Loveday looked a bit taken aback. "What?"

"You promise you'll listen and not interrupt and hear me out?"

"All right." Loveday hitched herself up onto the table and sat there, shoulders hunched and trousered legs dangling. "Fire away."

"It's about Gus."

Loveday froze. The only sound was the hum of the refrigerator. "What about Gus?"

Judith told her.

"So then he said it was time he went back to the hospital ship, and we got a taxi for him and said good-bye. And he went. End of story."

Loveday had kept her word. Made no comment and asked no questions. Simply sat, motionless as a statue, and listened to the story. At the end she said, "Is he all right?"

"I don't know. He looked amazing, considering all he'd gone through. Thin and a bit worn."

"I was so certain he was dead. It was like being certain with every bone of my body. A sort of emptiness. A void."

"I know, Loveday. You mustn't blame yourself."

"Did he believe that I would wait for him?"

"Yes." There wasn't any other answer.

"Oh, God." Sitting under the cold overhead light, her face was shadowed and pinched, her violet eyes empty of expression.

"I'm sorry, Loveday. I hated telling you."

"He's alive. I should be rejoicing. Not sitting here looking like a wet weekend." She fell silent for a moment and then said, "Do Mummy and Pops know?"

"No. I wanted to tell you first. If you like, I'll go tell them now."

"No. I will. It's better that way. Then I must go home."

THE next morning Diana came to the Dower House. The little household had dispersed after breakfast. Anna first, trudging down the hill to the Rosemullion Primary School. Then Biddy had departed for the Red Cross in Penzance. Jess, who had discovered the Hut, had gone down to do a bit of cleaning.

Now eleven o'clock, and Phyllis was pegging out the washing, while Judith, in the kitchen, made soup. The carcass of yesterday's chicken had been boiled up for stock, and she was at the sink peeling onions. She heard a car draw up outside the house. Expecting nobody, she looked and saw Diana getting out of a battered little fishmonger's van, which had been bought to conserve petrol at the beginning of the war. Judith went to the door.

Diana carried a large, old-fashioned marketing basket on her arm. "Oh, darling, not interrupting, am I? I've brought you some vegetables and fresh eggs. And I wanted to have a word."

"Come in. I'll make you a cup of coffee."

In the kitchen, Diana put the basket on the table and sat down. Judith went to fill the kettle and then set it on the range. "Do you mind if I go on chopping?"

"Not a bit." She loosened the knot of the silk scarf draped about her throat. "Loveday told us about Gus."

"Yes. She said she was going to."

"It sounds as though he's going to need a little help. I feel we should all rally round. Do you think I should write and ask him to come and stay at Nancherrow?"

"No. I don't think that would be a good idea. Later perhaps. But not now. If you asked him, I don't think he'd come."

"So what are we to *do*?"

351

"I wrote to him. I'll write again in a little while. If only I could get some reaction, we'd at least know how he was faring."

"We were so fond of him, Edgar and I. . . ." Her voice trailed away. She sighed. "Do you blame me?"

"Blame you?"

"For letting her marry Walter?"

"You could scarcely stop her. She wanted to marry him."

"Yes. And we didn't just *let* her; in a way we encouraged her. Our baby. Edward was gone, and I couldn't face losing Loveday as well. Marrying Walter meant she stayed near us. And we'd always liked him, despite his lack of polish and rough ways. He'd always been so caring of Loveday, keeping an eye on her on hunting days and helping her when she started working on the farm. He was her friend. I've always thought that the most important thing when you get married is to marry a friend. Passionate love cools down after a time, but friendship lasts forever. I believed they were right for each other."

"Is there any reason to suppose that they're not?"

Diana sighed again. "No. Not really, I suppose. But she was only nineteen. Perhaps we should have told her to wait."

"Diana, if you'd argued, she'd have just become more determined to get her own way. That's the way she's made. I tried to argue when she told me, and I got my head bitten off."

The coffee was ready, and Judith poured two mugs. Diana said, "I really thought it would work. It worked for me."

"I don't understand."

"Edgar was always my friend. I knew him from when I was a little girl. He was a friend of my parents'. He used to take me to the park, and we'd feed the ducks. And then the war started—the First War. I was sixteen and wildly in love with a young man I'd met. He was in the Coldstream Guards, and he went off to France. And then he came home on leave. But of course he had to go back to France, and he was killed in the trenches. By now I was seventeen. And I was pregnant."

Diana's voice never changed. She said all these things, evoking who knew what memories, and continued to sound as inconsequential as though she were describing a ravishing new hat.

"Pregnant?"

"Yes. Too careless, darling, but we weren't very worldly-wise in those days. I couldn't tell my parents, so I told Edgar. And Edgar said that he was going to marry me and be the father of my little baby, and that I would never, ever have to be worried or troubled for the rest of my life."

"And the baby?"

"Athena."

"But . . ." But there was nothing to say.

"Oh, darling, you're not shocked, are you? It was just another sort of love. I never felt I was *using* Edgar. And after all the turmoil and passion and despair, being with him was like slipping into a peaceful harbor, knowing that nothing could ever harm one again. And that's how it's stayed."

"Does Athena know?"

"No, of course she doesn't. Why should she? Edgar's her father. He always has been. It's odd. I haven't thought about it all for years. In fact, I'm not quite sure why I'm telling you now."

"Loveday."

"Of course. History repeating itself. Another hateful war, and a baby on the way, and the man one turns to. One's friend." She drank her coffee. "I've never told anyone else."

"I would never breathe a word."

"I know you wouldn't. What I'm trying to say is, Edgar is my life. I expect you used to wonder about Tommy Mortimer, but he was never my lover. Just a person I needed. And Edgar let me have him. Because Edgar is the dearest, most generous man in the world. And has made me so happy. You see, it really *worked* for me. That's why I thought it was right for Loveday."

"Diana, it was Loveday's decision. Not yours."

At this moment, perhaps fortuitously, they were interrupted. The door burst open and Jess appeared, looking tousled and cobwebby. She caught sight of Diana. "I'm sorry. I didn't know you were here."

"Oh, darling Jess, don't be sorry. What *have* you been doing?"

"Cleaning the Hut. When the summer comes, I'm going to sleep out there. All the time."

Diana smiled. "Won't you be lonely?"

"I shall take Morag with me for company." To Judith she said, "Did you ring St. Ursula's?"

"Yes. And we've got an appointment with Miss Catto tomorrow."

IT WAS FOUR O'CLOCK IN THE afternoon, and Judith sat in Miss Catto's study. In outward appearance the school had changed. The war years had left their mark. Even the neat little study looked a bit battered, and the carpet threadbare and worn.

Miss Catto, now in her forties, looked a good deal older. But her eyes were just the same, wise and kindly.

Jess, clearly, had taken to Miss Catto. At first a bit overawed and nervous, she had answered questions with no more than monosyllables, but it hadn't taken long for her to lose her shyness, and the interview had turned into a chatty conversation. After a bit a senior girl called Elizabeth had come to show Jess around the school. They had not yet returned.

"I suppose we'll have to have a clothes list?" said Judith.

Miss Catto smiled. "You'll be delighted to know that it has been considerably reduced. The girls all go about in their own cheerful clothes. Now each one is very much her own person."

Across the desk they looked at each other. "I promise you, my dear, that I will do my best to make sure that Jess is happy. Now, how about a cup of tea?"

"I DON'T want you to come in, Judith. I want to say good-bye on the front doorstep. If you come in, it will just go on for longer."

"You'll be all right?"

Judith recalled saying exactly the same thing to her mother on their way to St. Ursula's.

"Yes. That nice girl, Elizabeth, said she'd be there to show me my dormitory and everything."

"That was kind of her."

They were nearly there. Judith turned the car up the hill and through the school gates. It was half past two and raining, a steady mizzle of a sea mist gently drenching the bare trees.

As she had promised, the senior girl was at the main door, waiting for them. "Hello. I'll take your suitcase and your hockey stick. Can you manage the rest?"

Everything was duly carted indoors. On the step, in the drizzling rain, Judith and Jess faced each other. Given the smallest encouragement, Judith knew she might behave like the most sentimental of mothers and start brimming at the eyes.

"Bye, Jess. Love you."

They kissed. Jess gave her a grin, turned away, and was gone.

Judith wept a bit in the car going home. It was hard not to feel rather empty and bereft. Trundling back across the mist-driven moor, she decided that what she needed was contemporary company, and so would go and see Loveday. She hadn't been to Lidgey yet, simply because all her time lately had been taken up with Jess.

She drove past the gates of Nancherrow to the turning to the farm. The lane was a bumpy, winding mile to the main farmhouse, but halfway down, on the left, stood the low stone cottage that the Colonel had had renovated when Loveday and Walter were married. She came to the gate, which stood open, propped by a boulder, beyond which led a grassy track, melding into what should have been a garden but wasn't. Just the washing line, and a few gorse bushes, and some toys lying around. She got out of the car, walked up the path, and opened a paint-scarred door.

"Loveday!" Judith was in a tiny hall hung with old coats and mud-stained waterproofs. She opened a second door.

Kitchen, living room, all in one. Almost a replica of Mrs. Mudge's. A Cornish range, clothes hung on a pulley high overhead, flagged floors, a few rugs; the clay sink, the pig bucket, piles of old newspapers, the dresser laden with odds and ends. Nat lay on the sagging sofa, fast asleep. The wireless, perched on the dresser, burbled away to itself: *"We'll meet again, don't know where, don't know when. . . ."* Loveday was ironing.

"Well, where have you turned up from?"

"St. Ursula's. Just left Jess there."

"Is she all right?"

"She was amazing. No tears. The one who's feeling really blue is me, so I've come for a bit of cheering."

"I'm not sure if you've come to the right place. But take your coat off. Sling it down somewhere."

Which Judith did. She went over to the sofa and gazed down at Nat. His cheeks were bright red, and he clutched an old blanket. "Does he always sleep in the afternoon?"

"Not usually. But he didn't get to sleep till two this morning." Loveday filled the kettle and put it on the range. *"But I know we'll meet again some sunny day,"* mooned the wireless. She went to the dresser and switched it off. "Soppy tune."

She dumped herself down on the sofa beside her sleeping son.

"Hey, Nat. Wake up. We're going to have tea." She laid a hand on his round stomach and bent to kiss him. Judith thought she looked terrible. She seemed tired out, with dark rings under her eyes.

Nat's eyes opened. Loveday set him on her knee and cuddled him, talking to him until he was properly awake. Staring about, he spied Judith. "Who that lady?"

"That's Judith. You met her at Granny's. And she's come to see you." She set him down on the floor, found a little truck for him to play with, and left him to his own devices.

The kettle was boiling. She reached for the teapot. "If you want to help, you can lay the table. There's saffron cake in the bread bin."

Between them they pushed some of the papers to one side to make space at the table. Loveday said, "I'm sorry about the mess."

"Don't be silly."

"I'll give it a spring-clean and then send you a formal invitation. It's actually very sweet, and the new bathroom's lovely. Tiled and everything. Pops was really generous." She poured Judith's tea.

"Where's Walter?"

"Oh, somewhere. Up the top field, I think. He'll be back soon for the milking."

"You're looking tired, Loveday."

"So would you if you hadn't got to sleep until two."

Loveday fell silent, sitting with her bony elbows propped on the table, her hands wrapped around the hot mug, eyes downcast. The long dark lashes lay on her pale cheeks, and Judith saw to her dismay that they shone with seeping tears.

"Oh, Loveday."

Loveday shook her head. "I'm just tired." A tear dribbled down her cheek. She put up a hand and roughly brushed it away.

"Is it you and Walter?" It took some courage to say, because Judith knew she was liable to have her head bitten off. But Loveday hadn't flown at her. "Is there something wrong between you?"

Loveday muttered, "Another woman. He's got another woman."

Judith felt herself go weak. Carefully she laid her mug on the table. "How do you know?"

"I know. He's been seeing her. Evenings, at the pub. Mrs. Mudge told me."

"*Mrs. Mudge?*"

"Yes. The word got through to her from the village. She told me because, she said, I ought to know. Have it out with Walter."

"Who *is* this woman?"

"She's a mess. She came down to Porthkerris during the summer. Turned up with some phony painter or other. From London. She lived with him for a bit and then moved out. She's in a caravan up the back of Veglos Hill."

"What's her name?"

"You're not going to believe this—Arabella Lumb."

"It can't be true." And suddenly, incredibly, they were both laughing.

"Arabella Lumb." The name, on repetition, sounded even more unlikely. "Have you ever seen her?" Judith asked.

"Yes, once, when I went for a beer with Walter. She sat in the corner by the bar all evening eyeing him. She looks like a great bosomy tinker. You know, mother earth stuff. Bangles and beads and sandals and green varnish on her toenails."

"She sounds ghastly."

"I have a horrid feeling that Walter is besotted." Loveday sat back in her chair. "And I don't know what to do."

"Take Mrs. Mudge's advice. Have it out with him."

"I tried last night." Loveday's voice was despondent. "I was fed up. Walter got home at eleven o'clock, and he'd been drinking whisky. I could smell it. We had the most terrible row, and we woke Nat up, shouting at each other. And he said he'd do what he bloody pleased and see who he bloody wanted. And he said it was my fault anyway, because I was such a bloody useless wife and mother."

"That's unkind and unfair."

"And there's another thing. He doesn't like me taking Nat down to Nancherrow. He resents it, I think. Says I'm trying to turn Nat into a little sissy. He wants him to be a Mudge, not a Carey-Lewis."

It was all understandable, but bewildering too. "I'm not being much help, am I?" said Judith.

"Yes, you are. Just being able to talk about it helps. Mummy and Pops would"—she searched for the word—"*explode* if they knew."

Nat had been lying on his stomach, intent on his toy. Now he scrambled to his feet. "I want somefin to eat."

Loveday hoisted him up onto her knee. She pressed a kiss on the top of his thick dark hair and, with her arms encircling him, buttered a slice of bread and gave it to him.

By the time tea was over, it was past five o'clock. Judith said, "I must go. Biddy and Phyllis will be wondering what's happened to me, imagining terrible dramas with Jess."

"It was lovely seeing you. Judith, you won't say anything, will you? About what I've told you."

"Of course not. But you must keep talking to me."

"I'll do that."

They came to the door to see Judith away. Outside, the mist had thickened. Judith turned up the collar of her coat and prepared to dash for the car, but Loveday said, "Have you heard from Gus?"

Judith shook her head. "Not a word."

And she drove home through the dark, dismal evening.

By now she had written to Gus three times. As the days went by with no message from him, her anxiety grew. Instincts told her loud and clear that all was not well.

As CHRISTMAS loomed, the weather deteriorated. So now, Monday, it was raining. Judith, battling with a recipe for a wartime Christmas pudding, broke an egg into the flour mixture and began to stir. In the hall the telephone rang. Phyllis, cleaning in the attic, clearly did not hear it, so Judith went to take the call.

"Dower House."

"Judith, it's Diana. Darling, I've got such exciting news. Jeremy Wells is home. On leave. And the best is, he's going to be demobbed and come home for good. Isn't it unbelievable? They're letting him go. . . . Judith? Are you there?"

"Yes. Yes, I'm here. It's wonderful. When—when did you hear?"

"He rang me this morning. He's coming to Nancherrow to spend a few days. So we thought we'd have a coming-home party Wednesday evening. Loveday and Walter and Jeremy and you. You will come, won't you?"

"Of course. I'd love to."

"About a quarter to eight? Such heaven to have you all with me again. Good news of Jess?"

"Yes, good news. She's a star at hockey, and she's doing well in her studies."

"Clever little thing. And Biddy?"

"Biddy's in Devon. She phoned on Saturday. Sold the house, so now she can pay for the new one. But she'll be here for Christmas."

"Send her my love when she rings again. See you Wednesday."

Judith put down the telephone. Jeremy. Back. Demobbed. Home for good. She told herself that she was neither sorry nor glad. She only knew that before they could resume any sort of an easy relationship, she must face him with the hurt and disappointment that he caused her. Jeremy had given a promise and broken it. So, a confrontation. . . .

"What are you doing standing there staring into space?"

Phyllis, descending the stairs with her dusters, had paused halfway in some puzzlement, a hand on her pinafored hip.

"Sorry?"

"Got a face on like a bulldog, you have." She came on down. "Was that someone on the telephone?"

"Yes. Mrs. Carey-Lewis. Just asking me to dinner on Wednesday. Jeremy Wells is back."

"Jeremy." Phyllis's jaw dropped in delight. "That's lovely. So what's the face for? I'd have thought you'd be over the moon."

"Oh, *Phyllis.*"

"Well, why not? He's a lovely man. And a good friend to you."

"I *know,* Phyllis."

"He always fancied you, Jeremy did. Any fool could tell. And it's about time you had a man about the place. A bit of fun."

Somehow this was the last straw. Judith lost her patience.

"You don't know anything about it. And I've got a Christmas pudding to make." On that exit line she marched back to the kitchen.

IT WAS Rupert Rycroft, ex-major, the Royals, who found Gus Callender again. Rupert had stepped from the portals of Harrods and paused, debating his next move. It was twelve thirty on a bitterly cold December day, and after his foray into Harrods, which had produced a silk scarf, a gift for his wife, he could call the rest of the day his own. He decided to hail a taxi and go to his club for lunch.

Rupert, a tall and personable figure, carried not the mandatory umbrella, but a walking stick. When a taxi appeared at last, he hailed it by raising his walking stick like a flag. The driver drew alongside. "Where to, sir?"

"Cavalry Club, please."

As Rupert stooped to open the door, he noticed, amongst the stream of oncoming pedestrians, a young man walking towards him—tall, vaguely familiar, unshaven and gaunt, painfully thin, in a battered leather jacket. Rupert called to him. "Gus!" The young man stopped dead and turned.

"Gus. Rupert Rycroft."

"I know. I remember." Close up, his appearance was even less encouraging. He looked like a down-and-out.

At this moment the taxi driver chipped in. "Do you want to take this cab, sir, or don't you?"

"Yes, I do." And Rupert suddenly knew that if he let Gus out of his sight, he would never find him again. He turned back to Gus. "How about lunch?"

"Thanks, but no. I'd disgrace you. Haven't shaved."

So Rupert persisted. "I've all day. Why don't we go back to your place, and you can clean up and then we'll go to a pub."

Still Gus hesitated. "It's a pretty crummy place."

"No matter." Rupert opened the taxi door and stood aside. "Come on, old boy. Get in."

AT HOME that night Rupert told the story to Athena. Gus's flat on the Fulham Road was cold and dreary, with peeling wallpaper, and newspapers and magazines piled everywhere. Rupert waited while Gus shaved and combed his hair, and then they went down the road to an old pub. There, over beer, Rupert asked Gus straight off how he had got himself into this situation. Gus explained that it had not been much of a homecoming when he got back to Aberdeen. He had expected to have enough family money to start life over again. But with the hospital costs for his elderly parents and the drop in the property market, the capital had dribbled away.

Even worse, the desire to draw seemed to have left him. In fact, he'd been in a psychiatric hospital in Dumfries for the past seven weeks. The doctors had put him there because he'd fallen to bits—nightmares, the shakes, floods of tears. A sort of breakdown.

Listening to all this, Rupert was appalled. He urged Gus to return home with him, but Gus firmly refused. After that, there didn't seem to be much else to say. They finished the beer, and each went on his separate way.

That evening, after talking it over with Athena, Rupert put

through a call to the Dower House to give Judith the alarming news.

Judith was surprised by the call, all the way from Rupert's home in Gloucestershire. As she listened, she realized she was shivering. Her worst fears about Gus had been confirmed, and when Rupert asked if she'd help, she said, "Give me his address." She would make the long drive to London tomorrow, spend the night at the Mews, and find Gus the next morning. Perhaps she could convince him to return to Cornwall with her.

She suddenly realized she would miss the party for Jeremy. With a sigh she dialed Nancherrow. Once more, explanations. From time to time Diana made little cries of horror, but Judith plowed on. "If Gus agrees to come to the Dower House, I don't think we should tell Loveday."

"But she's bound to find out sooner or later."

"Yes, but not immediately. From what Rupert said, it doesn't sound as if Gus is in any state for emotional confrontations."

For a moment Diana was silent. Judith held her breath. Then Diana said, "Yes. You're right, of course."

"I'm sorry about spoiling your party."

"I think darling Jeremy will be sorry too."

JEREMY had found his own way upstairs, lugging the battered green naval-issue suitcase. It was so long since he had been at Nancherrow that he didn't immediately unpack, but went to open the window and gaze out at the courtyard and the dovecote there. He found he had to remind himself that the war was over and he was really back in Cornwall. And he felt enormously grateful that he had been allowed to live, to return.

Presently he heard swift footsteps in the passage outside and the voice of his hostess.

"Jeremy!" She was there, wearing gray flannel trousers and a pale blue mohair sweater. "Goodness, you look wonderful. Mediterranean tan. Now listen. I've got so much to tell you I don't know where to start."

She told him all that had happened to Gus and how Rupert had found him. And Judith had gone to London today to see if she could do anything to help.

"It's all a bit depressing, because this evening I'd planned a lovely

361

coming-home party for *you,* and Nettlebed had plucked pheasants, and Edgar was blissful, down in the cellar choosing a wine. But then Judith rang last night, and Loveday telephoned to say that Walter couldn't make it either, so we've decided to forget about it for the time being. It's too disappointing."

"Don't worry," Jeremy assured her bravely. "It was sweet of you even to think of it."

She left him with his mind in something of a turmoil. This new, peacetime life seemed to be beset by problems, decisions to be made. A colleague in the navy had approached him with an idea that Jeremy found attractive. He could not commit himself, however, until he had spoken to Judith.

He longed to see her again and, at the same time, dreaded a confrontation that might end forever his long-cherished dreams. Over the years since that night in London he had constantly thought of her. From the mid-Atlantic, Gibraltar, Malta, he had started letters that were never finished. He had, time after time, run out of words, crumpled up the pages. Telling himself that by now she would have found someone else.

But she wasn't married. He knew that much. Now Diana's revelations about Gus Callender filled him with disquiet. The fact that she had opted out of the coming-home party and gone to be with Gus did not bode well for him. Perhaps her compassion had turned to a deeper emotion. Love. He didn't know. He had not known anything for far too long.

IT WAS nine o'clock Thursday morning and still only half-light. In Cadogan Mews lights still burned inside the little houses. Judith heaved her overnight bag into the car and got in behind the wheel.

She followed Rupert's directions and without trouble found the building on the Fulham Road. She got out of the car and rang the bell. When the door finally opened, there, unbelievably, was Gus.

He didn't look nearly as awful as she had feared. Dreadfully thin and pale, of course, but shaved and neatly dressed. Using all her powers of persuasion, she tried to convince him to come back to Cornwall, to the Dower House, with her. Politely he refused.

She argued, begged, cajoled—all with no result. At last, exasperated, she said, "I'm not *asking* you to come with me. I'm *telling* you. And I shall stay here and nag at you until you do."

For the first time Gus smiled. "Just give me five minutes."

It was a long drive, and by the time they reached the Dower House, it was dark. Gus rolled down the window, and he took a huge breath of fresh air. He said, "You know, I can smell the sea."

"Me too."

He closed the window. "Judith."

"What is it?"

"Thank you."

The next morning she let Gus sleep late while she went into Penzance. There she bought a range of art supplies, hoping that in time he would feel like painting again.

Eleven o'clock on Friday night, and still Walter had not returned. Loveday, curled up on the sofa, sat and watched the face of the clock, the slow minutes ticking by. He had gone at seven. Finished the milking, washed up, and was away, not stopping even to eat the shepherd's pie she had made. She had held a sulky silence, because if she said anything, she knew that there would be yet another blowup, concluded by the ear-stopping slamming of the door.

Since the afternoon that Judith had come for tea, relations between Loveday and Walter had deteriorated at an alarming rate. She was beginning to believe that he actually hated her. He hadn't spoken kindly to Nat for days, and if they did all sit down to a meal together, Walter endured it in silence. Lately she hadn't even tried to break through his sullen antipathy.

A quarter past eleven. Restless, Loveday got off the sofa and switched on the wireless. It was always good for a bit of music.

She thought about Gus. Most of the time she didn't think about him, because memories of what she had done filled her with such anguish and regret. She now realized that at nineteen she had been childishly set on getting her own way. Refusing to countenance the fact that perhaps she was mistaken in her conviction that Gus had died in Singapore; grabbing at the first straw which came her drowning way, which happened to be Walter. She knew now that if it hadn't been Arabella Lumb, it would have been something, or someone, else bringing everything to a head.

From the bedroom she heard Nat crying. She went through and picked him up out of his cot, bundled in a big blanket, and brought

363

him back to the sofa. Presently he quieted, and she switched off the wireless and lay down beside him.

When she woke at seven, the electric light was still on, and she knew at once that Walter had never come back. Nat was slumbering peacefully, and cautiously she slid off the sofa.

Outside, it was dark and stormy. She went to the range and riddled out the ashes and made up the fire. The range, simmering gently, was set for another day. That was all she was going to do. Her husband's welfare was no longer of any concern.

In the hall, she took her thick raincoat from its peg and tied a woolen scarf around her head. Then she gathered Nat into her arms, swaddling him into his blanket. Carrying Nat, Loveday set out on the long walk home to Nancherrow.

In the morning Nettlebed was the first down, and his routine was changeless. Drawing back curtains, opening windows a chink to let the fresh air in. Then a kettle on the Aga for the Colonel's tea. After that, down the passage to the gun room to take old Tiger out.

Nettlebed was chilled to the bone by the time they returned indoors. With Tiger waddling at his heels, he went back to the kitchen, where the dog settled down on his blanket. The clock said half past seven. As Nettlebed reached for the tea caddy, he heard the scullery door fly open. Startled, he called, "Who's there?"

"Only me, Nettlebed." Loveday kicked the door shut behind her, her arms filled with a blanketed bundle that could only be young Nat. "I just walked down from Lidgey."

He was horrified. "Carrying Nat?"

"Yes. I'm exhausted." She laid Nat carefully on the huge scrubbed table, making a pillow with a corner of the blanket.

Nettlebed watched, heavyhearted. He feared, and guessed, the very worst. He had known for some time that there was trouble afoot at Lidgey. It was his custom a couple of evenings a week to take himself down to the Rosemullion pub. He had noticed Walter with that woman, Arabella Lumb. It was obvious that they had not met by chance.

Loveday asked, "Where's Mrs. Nettlebed?"

"Upstairs in the flat. She's taking the morning off. Everything all right, Loveday?"

"No, Nettlebed. Not all right. All wrong. Walter never came

home last night." Biting her lip, she met his sad gaze. "You know, don't you? Arabella Lumb."

"Yes." He sighed. "I guessed."

"It's all over. Me and Walter, I mean. Right from the beginning it was one huge, horrible mistake. And I'm not going back."

"What about young Nat? He's Walter's boy."

"I don't know. I haven't had time to think it through." She frowned. "I have to get it all clear in my head before I face them all—Pops and Mummy and Mary. What I would really like is to be on my own for a bit. Go for a walk."

As he listened to her steady voice, watched her, it occurred to Nettlebed that this was a Loveday he had never known before. No tears, no tantrums. Simply a stoic acceptance of a miserable situation. Perhaps, he told himself, she has finally grown up.

He said, "I could take young Nat up to our flat. Mrs. Nettlebed will keep an eye on him for the time being."

"Oh, Nettlebed, you are kind. You won't say anything, will you?"

"Breakfast's at half past eight. I'll keep mum till you're back."

"Thank you." She gathered up the sleeping Nat and handed him over. Nettlebed carried the child up the back stairs to his quarters. When he returned, having left Nat in the care of his astounded wife, Loveday had gone, and taken Tiger with her.

Gus opened his eyes. From downstairs he heard the gentle chimes of the grandfather clock softly striking seven o'clock. He could not remember when he had last slept so soundly.

He thought back to yesterday, a day of ordered tranquillity, exercise, and fresh air. In the evening he and Judith had played piquet, and there had been a Brahms concert on the wireless. When it was time for bed, Phyllis had made him hot milk and honey, laced with a teaspoonful of whisky. Perhaps this potion had knocked him out; more likely it was the extraordinary healing quality of Lavinia Boscawen's old house. A sanctuary.

He was now filled with a long-forgotten energy. He got up, went to open the window and lean out, smelling the cold air and the tang of the sea. He thought of the new day ahead, the first rays of dawn streaking the skies with pink. And he was once again obsessed by the old desire to set it all down, to capture it with brushstrokes and washes of color.

He stepped back. On the dressing table were the drawing book, pencils, paints, and brushes Judith had bought for him. He looked at them and told them, Later. When there is light in the sky and shadows on grass; then we shall get to work.

He swiftly dressed in his cords, a heavy sweater, his leather jacket. Quietly he made his way down the stairs, through the kitchen, then out into the cold.

He remembered the length of the Nancherrow drive. It was too far to walk, and he was impatient to be there. So he opened the door of the garage. Judith's bicycle. He wheeled this out onto the gravel.

The bicycle was far too small for him, but he swung his leg over it and set off, spinning down the hill and through Rosemullion. Then up the hill and through the Nancherrow gates.

Out of the trees, and the house loomed—a pale bulk. By the front door he propped the bicycle against the wall. He cautiously made his way around the house and finally stepped onto the grass.

The sky was lightening. There was the smell of damp earth, and all was clean, newly washed, pristine and pure. He went down the slope of the lawns and plunged down the path through the woods and to the cliff.

The tide was out, and the beach, a gray sickle of sand, was rimmed by seaweed. The sun was up now, and long shadows lay across the turf. And he remembered that August afternoon, the summer before the war, when Loveday had brought him to the cove. They had sat, sheltered from the wind, and it had felt like being with a person whom he had known for the whole of his life.

He looked for that rock where they had been together. And then he saw her, and screwed up his eyes in disbelief. She sat with her back to him, crouched against the rock, the dog close against her side. For a second he thought that he had gone mad again. But then, sensing his presence, Tiger raised his head, heaved himself to his feet, and came lumbering up over the boulder-strewn grass. He barked and came on, tail thumping, as fast as his arthriticky legs would carry him.

He reached Gus's side, and Gus stooped to fondle his head. "Hello, Tiger. Hello, old boy."

And then he straightened, and she was standing there with her back to the sea. The woolen muffler had slipped off her head, and he saw her dark curls, lit from behind by the sun, like an aureole.

Loveday. He had found her again. And it was almost as though she had known he would come and had been waiting for him.

He heard her call his name. "Gus," and the wind caught the word and sent it flying inland, over the winter fields. "Oh, *Gus.*" And she was running up the slope, and he went to meet her.

SATURDAY morning, and Jeremy Wells had overslept. Not by much, but breakfast at eight thirty was a Nancherrow rule, and he didn't get downstairs until a quarter to nine. In the dining room he found Diana and the Colonel now onto second cups of coffee.

He apologized. "I am sorry."

"Oh, darling, it doesn't matter a bit." Diana was opening her mail, and the Colonel was deep in *The Times*. At Nancherrow, conversation at breakfast had never been encouraged. Jeremy took a boiled egg from the sideboard and went to sit at the table.

In the kitchen, Nettlebed was starting to get edgy because Loveday still had not returned. He now regretted his collusion and simply wished that she would come back before he was forced to break the news to the Colonel. Preoccupied, he wandered to the window. Not a sign of the wretched girl.

At ten to nine he let himself out of the scullery door and walked out to the back drive, where he looked down the length of the garden towards the sea. There was nobody on the path from the woods. From his vantage point, however, he could see the big garage, and one of the doors stood open. The little van was gone. The implications of this were ominous. In something of a state he returned to the house. In the gun room, he found Tiger, fast asleep in his basket. And then as Nettlebed went back to the kitchen, he heard, from his own flat upstairs, the unmistakable roars of rage from Nathaniel Mudge.

Time's come, he told himself.

He went into the dining room, cleared his throat. The Colonel looked up from his paper. "What is it, Nettlebed?"

"Could I have a word, sir?"

"Of course."

Now both Mrs. Carey-Lewis and the young doctor were paying attention. "It's . . . rather delicate, sir. It's Loveday."

"What about Loveday?" The Colonel's voice was sharp.

"She turned up in my kitchen this morning, sir, at half past seven. With young Nat." He cleared his throat again. "There seems to have been some trouble. Between Walter and her."

A long pause. And then Mrs. Carey-Lewis said, "But what's *happened?*"

"I think, madam, that Walter's eye has been caught by another young woman he has been meeting in the pub. He never came home last night."

The three of them were staring at him in apparent total astonishment. The Colonel spoke. "Where is she now?"

"That's it, sir. She went off for a walk, to be on her own. Said she'd be back for breakfast. And she's not back, sir. And the small van has gone from the garage."

"The poor precious." Mrs. Carey-Lewis sounded despairing.

Then Jeremy Wells spoke. "You're certain she's not down on the cliff? Do you think I should go and look?"

The Colonel considered this. "Just to set our minds at rest." He stood up, folded his newspaper, and laid it neatly by his plate. "And *I* must make my way to Lidgey and find out what the hell is going on."

WITHIN half an hour Jeremy had jogged down to the cliff and back. He found them all in the kitchen—Diana and Mary Millyway, Nettlebed, and young Nat, finally placated by a serious breakfast. As Jeremy went into the room, they all turned to look at him. He shook his head. "Not a sign."

Diana gazed forlornly at him. "I do wish Edgar were back."

Just then they heard a door slam, and the next moment he was there, his expression as angry as Jeremy had ever seen it. "Mary, take the boy away," the Colonel said. And when she had whisked Nat out of the kitchen, he told them the sorry saga as Mrs. Mudge had vociferously given it to him.

Walter had not returned in time to see to the milking, and his parents had finally done it themselves. Not until they were finished did their errant son appear, looking much the worse for wear. He had shown no remorse. He had told the Mudges that he had had it up to here with Nancherrow, with Lidgey, with serfdom. He was getting out. He'd been offered a job in a garage, and he was going to live up Veglos Hill with Arabella Lumb.

"So that's the situation. The first person to be enlightened must be our solicitor, Roger Baines." The Colonel reached into his breast pocket and took out his gold watch. "Ten o'clock. I shall telephone him from my study." He looked about him, from one grave face to another. Then his gaze alighted on his wife, and his steely expression softened. "My darling Diana, you were about to say something."

"It's just that . . . Loveday might have gone to Judith. Judith would be just the person she would turn to."

"It's an idea. Do you want to ring up the Dower House?"

"No," said Diana. "Telephone calls can be distressing. I think somebody should go to her and explain the situation." She smiled persuasively. "Jeremy would go for us, I'm sure."

"Of course." He wondered if she knew what she was doing to him. Or, perhaps, for him. He said, "I'll go now."

JUDITH, for once, was on her own. It being a Saturday, there was no school for Anna, and Phyllis had taken her to St. Just for the day. Now it was past ten o'clock, and the other occupant of the Dower House, Gus, had not appeared. The door of his bedroom remained firmly closed, and Judith was pleased, because that meant that he was having a good rest.

She had decided that this was a good opportunity to do what she had been meaning to for ages—measure the drawing-room windows for new curtains. And so she had found the stepladder and the yardstick and tape measure, and balanced on top of the ladder, she measured the pelmet. She was just deciding that it might look better two inches longer when she heard the front door open and shut. Footsteps across the hall, and then Jeremy walked into the room.

He was wearing a thick, tweedy sweater and had a scarlet muffler around his neck. Her first thought was that he looked so exactly the same that the years that had flown by since their last encounter might never have happened. And the second thought was identical to her reaction that night in London: Had she been given the choice, he was the only person she would have really wanted to see.

Which was unexpected and rather annoying, because it left her defenseless, and she had intended being quite cool with him.

He said, "What are you doing?"

"Measuring the window. I'm going to have new curtains."

He smiled. "Can you come down? I want to talk to you, and if you stay up there, I'll get a crick in my neck."

So she descended, and he came to give her a hand. When she reached the floor, he kissed her cheek and said, "It's wonderful to see you again. Are you on your own? Loveday's not here?"

"Loveday?" Judith looked into his face and realized then that something was amiss. "Why should Loveday be here?"

"She's disappeared. She's left Walter. Or rather, Walter's walked out on her. Look, why don't we sit down and I'll explain."

They sat on the wide window seat, and Jeremy told her all that had happened. Judith listened in growing dismay, unable to think of anything to say. "Oh, dear." Which was fairly inadequate, given the circumstances. "Poor Loveday."

"Is Gus about?"

"Yes. He's upstairs. He's still asleep."

"Are you sure?"

Judith frowned. "Perhaps I'd better go and look." She got up and went up the staircase.

"Gus?" No response. She opened the door of Biddy's bedroom, to be met with the sight of the empty bed. His pajamas had been flung across a chair, and his clothes were gone.

Bewildered, she went downstairs again. "He's not there," she told Jeremy. "He must have got up early."

Jeremy said, "I have a feeling he's with Loveday. We must call Nancherrow."

As he said this, the telephone started to ring. Judith went out into the hall, and Jeremy followed so that he was by her side when she picked up the receiver. "Dower House."

"Judith." It was Gus.

"Gus. Where are you?"

"I'm in Porthkerris. Telephoning from your friends, the Warrens. Loveday wants to talk to you."

"She's with you? Has she spoken to her mother and father?"

"Yes. Just this moment. Look, before I put her on, there are three things I have to say. One is that I stole your bicycle, and it's at Nancherrow, sitting by the front door. The second thing is that I'm taking your advice, and I'm going to be a painter. Or try to be."

It was almost too much to begin to understand. "But—"

"There's a last thing. I've said it once, but I have to say it again. Thank you."

"Oh, Gus . . ."

But he was gone and, instead, Loveday was on the line. Loveday's voice, high with excitement, gabbling away as she used to, when they were children. And Judith was so relieved to be speaking to her that she forgot all about being cross.

"Loveday, you are the *end.*"

"Oh, Judith, don't fuss. You don't need to worry anymore. I went down to the cliffs, just to work out what to say to everybody, and I took darling Tiger with me, and we were sitting brooding and watching the sun come up, and the next thing I knew there was Gus. And I didn't even know he'd come *back* to Cornwall. I didn't even know he was with *you.* And suddenly he was *there,* exactly at the moment when I was wanting him most."

"Loveday, I'm so happy for you. So what did you do?"

"We talked and talked. And then we went back to the house, and I put Tiger back into the gun room, and Gus started up the fishmonger's van, and we drove over the moor to Porthkerris."

"Why Porthkerris?"

"Because we knew here we could find a studio for darling Gus. To work in and live in, and never go back to Scotland. I knew Mr. Warren would be able to tell us who to go and see. So we came here. And they were utterly adorable, as always, and Mr. Warren's been blasting away on the telephone, and we're all going to look at a flat on the North Beach. It's got what's known as a kitchenette."

She might have wittered on forever, but Judith decided that the time had come to interrupt. "When are you coming home?"

"Oh, this evening. We haven't *eloped* or anything like that. We're just being together. Planning things."

"What about Walter?"

"Walter's gone. Arabella Lumb has won the day, and good luck to her. Pops spoke to Mr. Baines, and they reckon I can keep Nat. And Gus says he thinks it's quite a good idea to start married life with a ready-made family." She fell silent for a moment, then said in an entirely different voice, "I always loved him, Judith. Even when I was sure he was dead. When you said he'd come back from Burma, it was the worst and the best thing I'd ever been told. I know I've been impossible."

371

"Oh, Loveday, if you weren't impossible, you wouldn't be you. That's why we all love you so much."

"Come tonight," said Loveday. "Come to Nancherrow. Let's all be together. Just like it used to be. Only Edward gone. But I think he'll be there too, don't you? He'll be around somewhere, drinking our health."

Judith said, through her tears, "He wouldn't miss it for all the world. Good luck, Loveday." She put down the receiver and was in floods. "I'm crying because it's all so happy. Have you got a handkerchief?"

Jeremy fished one from his pocket and gave it to her, and she wiped away the tears. "I gather," said Jeremy, "that all is well."

"Blissful. They're together. He's going to paint and live in a studio at Porthkerris. With a kitchenette."

She smiled at him, and all at once there were just the two of them. No other diversions. And for the first time a certain shyness. "Would you like a cup of coffee?" Judith asked.

"No, I don't want coffee. I want you and me. It's time to talk."

They went back into the drawing room, and the deep window seat, and now the low sun was shining onto the old-fashioned furniture and the faded rugs, sparking rainbow lights from the drops of Lavinia Boscawen's crystal chandelier.

Judith said, "Where do we start?"

"At the beginning. Why did you never answer my letter?"

She frowned. "But you never wrote."

"I did. From Long Island."

"I never got a letter. I waited and waited. And I decided you'd simply changed your mind, got cold feet; decided that you didn't want to keep in touch."

"Oh, Judith." He let out a sigh that sounded more like a groan. "All these years." He took her hand in his. "I did write. I was staying in a house in Long Island, and I just about tore myself to pieces trying to get the right words down. And then I took the letter back with me to New York and set it off by service mail."

"So what happened?"

"I imagine a ship was sunk. The Battle of the Atlantic was at its peak. The mail, and my letter, may have ended up at the bottom of the ocean."

She shook her head. "What did the letter say?"

"It said a lot of things. It said that I would never forget that night we spent together in London. And it told you how much I loved you. How much I'd always loved you, from the moment of finding you again at Nancherrow and hearing the sound of 'Jesu, Joy of Man's Desiring' come from your bedroom. And at the end I asked you to marry me. Because I couldn't imagine a future without you. I asked you to write. To say yes or no and to set my mind at rest."

"But you got no answer. Didn't that strike you as odd?"

"Not really. I never considered myself much of a catch. And you had youth and beauty and financial independence. So when I received no reply from you, I didn't think it was odd. Just the end of everything."

Judith said, "Edward made love to me because he was sorry for me. I was so afraid that your motives were the same."

"Never that, my darling."

"I see now. But I was younger then. Not all that sure of myself." She looked at him. "There's something we haven't talked about— Jess. She's part of me now. My responsibility. Whatever happens to me happens to Jess as well."

"Would she mind if I happened to you? Because I would like very much for all three of us to be together. I always remember her in the train, being terribly naughty. I can't wait to see her again."

"She's fourteen now. And when we get married—"

"Did you really say that? *When* we get married?"

"I believe I did."

"I've got gray hairs now."

"I know. I've seen them, but I'm much too polite to remark."

Suddenly she was laughing, and he kissed her, and the thought flashed through his mind that it would be a brilliant idea to gather her in his arms and make long and passionate love to her. But common sense told him that now was not the right moment.

Gently he let her go, putting up a hand to smooth honey-colored hair away from her face. He said, "Shall we, for the moment, pull ourselves together and try to plan for our future? Except that I haven't decided anything for myself yet, let alone you and Jess."

"Are you going back to Truro and take over from your father?"

"Is that what you would like?"

Judith was honest. She said, "No. I'm sorry, but I never want to leave this house. I know one shouldn't let bricks and mortar rule

373

one's life, but this place is so special. It's been a haven, a sanctuary, for so many people. Do you understand?"

"Completely. So cross Truro off the list. I have an old naval colleague, a good friend. A surgeon commander, RNVR, called Bill Whatley. He put an idea to me a couple of months ago, when we were both in Malta. Supposing the two of us started up a new practice right here? In Penzance."

Judith, scarcely daring to hope, stared at Jeremy. "Could you?"

"Why not? Bill's a Londoner, but he wants to settle his family in the country, preferably by the sea. We talked it over, but I didn't want to commit myself. I didn't want to come blundering back into your life if you didn't want me around. A bit embarrassing, having a lovesick old flame on your doorstep."

"Penzance is scarcely my doorstep. And if you're a G.P. in Penzance, it's too far away to live *here.* Night calls and things like that."

"There'll be two of us in the practice together. I can commute. We shall build a beautiful modern surgery, with a useful flat for night shifts."

"With kitchenette?"

"Of course." Jeremy was laughing. "You know something, my darling? We are crossing bridges we haven't even come to." He looked at his watch. "It's a quarter to twelve. I suppose I ought to get back to Nancherrow, or Diana will think that I've joined the club and eloped as well. Will you come with me, my darling Judith?"

"If you want."

"I do."

"Shall we tell them all? About you and me?"

"Why not?"

For some reason the prospect was a bit daunting. "What *are* they going to say?"

"Why don't we go and find out."

ROSAMUNDE PILCHER

"My books are not autobiographical," says Rosamunde Pilcher, but facets of her own experience enrich her sweeping sagas. Like the heroine of *Coming Home,* Pilcher grew up on the sunny coast of Cornwall in a tiny village near St. Ives, which is the model for her fictional Porthkerris. And she, too, experienced family separation. Her father worked in the far reaches of the British Empire as a civil servant in Burma, but he returned home to enter the navy before the outbreak of World War II.

The war changed her life. Pilcher joined the Wrens at eighteen and served as a submarine spotter in Trincomalee, Ceylon—now known as Sri Lanka. One evening, curled up on her bunk in her quarters, she tapped out a short story on a borrowed typewriter. It was her first story accepted for publication, and a career was born. After her post-war marriage to Scottish businessman Graham Pilcher, she continued to write while raising their four children. Years of carefully crafting short stories and romances culminated in her international best sellers *The Shell Seekers* and *September.*

Today the author lives outside Dundee in the Pilchers' longtime family home, which is filled with flowers, dogs, guests, and visiting grandchildren—fertile ground, her many fans hope, for another memorable novel.

OSCAR
The True Story of a Husky
Commander Nils Lied

OSCAR

THE TRUE STORY OF A HUSKY

By Commander Nils Lied

*B*orn on Heard Island in
1951 during the worst blizzard
of the Antarctic year, Oscar grew to be an
outstanding sled dog and a true hero.
Strong, intelligent, and dignified, he showed
an uncanny ability to follow old trails and
to sense the dangers in unknown terrain,
winning the respect of the men who
worked with him. Yet unlike many huskies
Oscar never cringed or fawned before
men, and Nils Lied, his trainer, never
took his loyalty for granted.
A fearsome fighter, Oscar became the
undisputed leader of any pack, and he took
his teams over more than six thousand
kilometers of exploratory treks. His
remarkable spirit is recalled with
affection by the master and companion who
journeyed with him across the frozen
frontiers of an untamed land.

1
Birth of a Husky

THE pregnant husky bitch was restless. Her time was near, and anxiously she ran back and forth over the Australian National Antarctic Research Expedition's camp at Atlas Cove. She could sense the hurricane approaching, and she had to find some sort of shelter in which to throw her litter. We had built a small lean-to for her close to the big dog-pens, with dry sacking on the floor, and a small pup-pen in front. The bitch had inspected it, but as it smelled strange and unfamiliar she had only circled, warily, sniffing at the pen-door.

And she was hungry. Part of her lot lately had been to suffer repeated attacks from the other bitches in the teams, which had prevented her from eating her share. Instinct had kept her away from the vicious husky fights in order to protect her swelling teats.

From a distance I watched her restless prowling, and turned to study my well-thumbed, grubby notebook.

"Yes," I grumbled to myself, "gestation period is sixty-five days, so she'll pup some time tonight, or tomorrow, at the height of the hurricane." Replacing the book, I lit my pipe and went outside.

From the carcass of a seal, I cut three handfuls of meat, which I carried to the new pup-pen. Cautiously I peered into the cookhouse. The door was open and the cook's back turned. I grabbed a jug of milk and retreated soundlessly with a triumphant grin. The milk, too, went into the pup-pen. I whistled piercingly, and the pregnant bitch loped heavily across the snow. She had no fear.

I had all the right smells, and my familiar hands were firm, but gentle. She let herself be led to the new pup-pen, and while I held the door open, I thrust her inside with my knee.

"You'll be all right," I reassured her gently.

Satisfied that I had done everything possible, I hurried over to one of the huts, glancing over my shoulder at the low, scudding clouds rolling up from the southwest, now hiding the mighty ice cone called Big Ben: I knew very bad weather was to come.

In her shelter the bitch whined softly, knowing the great blizzard would strike at any moment. She sniffed the sacking on the floor, the walls and the low pitched roof. She was very unsure of her new surroundings, but before long she gulped down some of the seal meat and milk. Her hunger satisfied, she began circling in the same spot; then, flopping her heavy hindquarters down, she lowered her head on her outstretched front paws and slept. In her sleep she whimpered and twitched, while under the tightly stretched skin across her belly there was constant movement.

IN THE "met hut"—the weather station—all the machines were showing a sudden drop in pressure. The wind, already gusting at over one hundred kilometers an hour, was still building up.

Frank Hannan, senior weatherman and leader of the expedition, straightened as I entered the met hut. He wore his outdoor parka, and all that was visible of his face was a tremendous red-black beard and mustache, worried blue eyes, a nose, and a quick flash of white teeth as he spoke. A violent gust shook the hut, and he flinched as a large map crashed down from the wall.

"Nils," he said, "this could be the worst hurricane that you and I will ever live through."

"I've never heard such a wind," I agreed. "And I'm on duty in the radio station tonight, too. It'll be a long, cold night."

"Before you start duty, Nils, can you help batten down the camp?" Frank asked.

"Of course," I replied. "I'll get a couple more men to give me a hand lashing down the loose gear, and we'll have to haul the cutter above the high tide. And you know the bitch is going to throw her litter tonight," I added. "I fear the pups won't survive."

"We can't worry about that now," Frank said. "First things first. We have about an hour before the hurricane hits."

I noticed the barometer take another dive as we both buttoned up, pulled on gloves and went outside. The strength of the wind was steadily increasing, and the perforated steel radio masts, antennae and guy-wires on the huts sounded like a deep-throated orchestra, adding to the fury and menace of the oncoming hurricane. We had to grab at any support as we struggled from hut to hut, rousing the other men, leaning into the wind to keep upright.

Already the big wind pushed water into the Atlas Roads, and great, crested waves attacked the beaches around Atlas Cove below the camp. Moving as fast as we could, our hands and faces numb with cold, and deafened by the shrieking wind and crashing ocean, we strapped and weighted every hut and piece of machinery before towing the heavy, diesel-driven cutter across the beach and up among the tussocks of coarse grass. Frozen and exhausted, we fought our way back to the mess hut while sheets of snow, sleet and black lava sand flung across the camp.

After a hot meal Frank, diesel engineer Pete Lawson and I returned to the met hut to follow the progress of the blizzard. Already all was pitch-black, and land, sea and sky were indistinguishable. The hut, in spite of being weighted down with rocks and earth and secured with steel wires, shook like a baby's rattle, and objects kept crashing down from the shelves.

Pete stood at one of the small windows, looking out. He said, "It's times like this I feel that Heard Island is beyond the edge of the earth."

Which in a sense was quite true. Heard Island was for us the gateway to Antarctica, the last continent on earth to be explored, separated from inhabited lands by the world's loneliest oceans. Nearly twice the size of Australia, it's a vast wilderness of snow, of mountains, glaciers, fjords and rare wildlife. For millions of years almost the whole surface of that land has lain beneath ice, thousands of meters thick.

From the study of Antarctica, scientists have been able to discover more about the nature of the earth and its atmosphere. Four years before, in 1947, Australians had set up a base on Heard Island, dominated by the three-thousand-metre-high sentinel of the southern Indian Ocean, Big Ben. We were there to learn about Antarctica, and we were involved in scientific investigations of all sorts from biology to earthquakes.

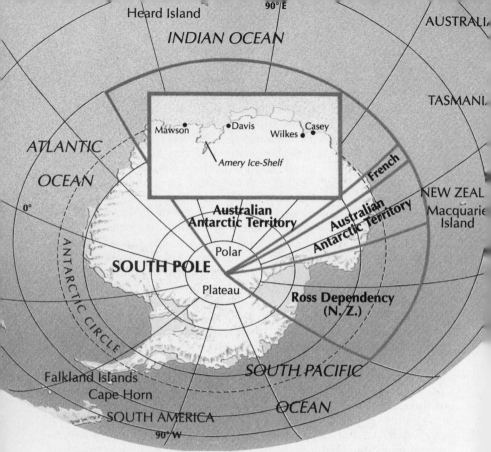

My thoughts returned to the bitch in labor. Although the puppen was only forty paces away, I wouldn't have been able to walk half that distance in safety. "We might have to dig the husky bitch out later on," I said, "but she'll be all right for now. She'll be too worried to have her pups with the blizzard winding up like this."

My fears were interrupted by the ringing of the field telephone which connected the met hut with the radio shack.

"I can't receive a damned thing anymore," the duty operator shouted in the telephone. "I've a feeling we've lost our antennae."

"In that case, you'd better join us in here," Frank shouted back.

As the radio operator crashed through the door a few moments

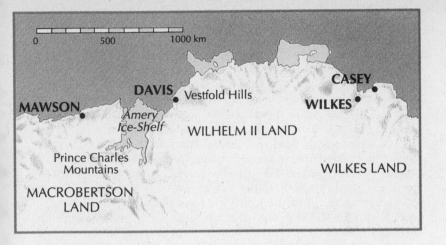

later, Frank pointed to the wind recorder: "Now, that *is* unusual," he said with mixed fear and admiration. The latest gust, with a wind-speed of over two hundred kilometers per hour, had pushed the recording pen completely off the chart-drum. The great blizzard was now at full force. We felt as if the whole island was being attacked by all the most evil and powerful forces of nature.

Suddenly the wind whipped around and blew with renewed vigor from the opposite direction. And this time it brought snow: buckets and sheets of it, swirling from the lower slopes of the glaciers, and snow-laden sand from the beaches. In minutes enormous drifts had formed, some right to the roof of the huts, while other places were scoured down to the black, frozen ground.

Frank kept checking the met instruments. "The main center has passed," he reported tensely. "It will start to ease off shortly."

And so we waited while the hurricane blew itself out, and spent its force against the steep slopes of Big Ben.

THE bitch slept through the early stages of the blizzard. She was used to hurricanes. Heard Island rises out of the Southern Ocean right in the path of deep Antarctic depressions, and the great winds often blow across it.

As the lean-to shook in the increasingly violent gusts, the bitch

385

lifted her head and whimpered. The sacking in front of her low door flapped, and eddies of wind entered the lean-to and ruffled her fur. Hungry again, she finished the last of the seal meat. The first birth pangs made her arch her back, while she waited with twitching hindquarters for the pain to subside. She was worried. Although she was sheltered she did not feel secure. There was no snow to deaden the sound of the hurricane, or to keep the lean-to steady. To her, snow meant shelter, warmth and drinking water: in a blizzard she always let herself get snowed right under, curled up with her back to the wind, nose resting on her back paws, her bushy tail draped across her snout. But now she had no such conditions to reassure her. Silently she fought against giving birth to her pups, while the life within her became more insistent.

When the center of the hurricane passed and the wind turned, bringing snow, she was very near. Gradually a huge drift built up around the lean-to, and soon no more drafts invaded the shelter.

Her restless twitching ceased. Only a muffled roar could be heard, just as if she had made herself a cave in the snow like her Arctic ancestors. She gratefully licked at the snow around her.

With the muscles of her belly contracting regularly, and her back arched high, she turned around and around in the same spot. Her hind legs bent low, and a small, wet, bloody bundle fell from her body. Quickly she turned, and carefully bit through the umbilical cord. Now the tiny pup was bound to her only by that strong instinct which makes all newborn life seek its mother. The bitch relaxed, knowing this was her only pup. She licked him clean, then gently picked him up in her mouth. In the far corner of the lean-to she curled up with her back against the door and pushed the pup against her belly with her nose. There he lay, covered by her bushy tail, warm and secure. He struggled feebly, guided by instinct, until his toothless gums found her milk-swollen teat and he began to suck, oblivious to the raging blizzard.

2
Oscar, a Husky Pup

WE CALLED him Oscar.

He grew very quickly, and benefited greatly from the unusual undivided attention given him by his mother. From a blind, rat-like, whimpering newborn pup, he soon developed into a small, fat, roly-poly bundle on four very inadequate legs, exploring the camp, playing under the huts and treating any open door as a personal invitation to enter. With the other pups born that spring he roamed all over the camp, and sought constant handling and attention from all the men of the expedition.

The back door of the galley was his favorite haunt, and it was here the pups displayed their inherited fighting instinct. The young dogs operated in packs, like street-gangs of young hoodlums, and were destructive if not watched closely. Whenever the cook appeared at the door, he would be mobbed by dozens of eager pups led by Oscar, who watched his every move.

"I've tried changing my clothes, my boots and my times of movement," the cook complained. "I've sprinkled kerosene on my boots, even thrown my voice like a ventriloquist, but the little rascal still finds me and follows me around. I can't shake him off."

Oscar soon learned to fend for himself, and even as a pup seemed more wolf than husky. He had great intelligence, and smelled danger of any sort with an uncanny sureness. His eyes were slanted and watchful, with a pale mark above each one, and he had a distinctive hackle that ran the length of his back. He was always hungry and would eat almost anything.

One day in late August, one of the men left a pair of freshly-oiled boots drying on the doorstep of his hut. The fleece lining and the buckles gave five-month-old Oscar slight indigestion; otherwise there was nothing left to remind the owner of his animal-skin boots. As the men gradually became accustomed to the pups, nothing even remotely edible was left lying within their reach.

Often rival gangs of pups clashed, led and provoked by Oscar, and fur flew all around, accompanied by the agonized yelps of the wounded and vanquished. Our dogs were crossbreeds, with the best characteristics of both the Greenlander and the Labrador. Thousands of years ago, there was a land bridge between Asia and Alaska across the Bering Strait. It is thought that the Siberians occasionally crossed the land bridge and brought their dogs, Samoyeds, with them. The Samoyeds mated with Arctic wolves, and the resulting crossbreed is what is now known as the Arctic Husky. There are two strains: a squat, deep-chested dog with short legs—the Greenlander; and a big, long-legged rangy dog, more like a wolf—the Labrador.

Jack Walsh, our dog trainer, was constantly occupied with making special sled traces, harnesses and other gear, and keeping track of the ever-growing Heard Island dog population. As the pups reached six or seven months, they were harnessed into teams for trial, to be trained as sled dogs. Oscar emerged as outstanding; he soon understood the purpose of his harness, and from that moment held himself apart from his playmates. He grew into an exceptionally large, strong and rangy dog, with a proud bearing. After the first couple of punishments for disobedience, he recognized his driver as supreme master, knowing he could not better a man with a whip. But he didn't become cringing or fawning as other dogs often did. His attitude seemed to be that there was a job to be done, with as little fuss as possible.

Just as Oscar had followed the cook around the camp months before, so he took to some of the older huskies, and he made overtures of friendliness to one bad-tempered, seasoned Heard Island sled dog. As Oscar confidently approached, sniffing, his tail curled up over his back, the old dog snarled menacingly, and moved his great bulk forward.

Undeterred, Oscar plowed on. With unexpected suddenness and fury, the old husky hurled the full weight of his heavy body at the young dog, bringing his great shoulders down over Oscar's still grinning face, knocking him off his feet. With a savagery unknown in domestic dogs, he snarled and twisted his head around, ready to sink his sharp fangs into Oscar's neck. Aroused by the unnatural quiet of the other dogs, I rushed to the dog lines, and was horrified at the sight that met my eyes. Grabbing the whip from its hook on the stake, I cracked it, forcing my way through the pack crowded around in a bloodthirsty ring, and beat the old dog with the whip handle, forcing him off the pup. Another ten seconds and Oscar would have been torn to pieces. Oscar never forgot that lesson.

As Oscar grew older he became an outstanding fighter. He developed his own style, which grew in efficiency with his increasing weight and stamina. He would crouch low, fangs bared, feet gathered for the customary rush. But it was always the other dog who rushed first. Oscar would duck his opponent's vicious slash, then with a lightning forward and upward thrust sink his fangs in his opponent's throat or chest; and with a tremendous heave his great body would rise from his hind legs, throwing the other dog onto his back. As wolves and huskies do, he attacked the throat, the legs and the soft parts of the belly, until his victim's snarls and roars changed to whimpers and whines, acknowledging defeat.

With such a large dog population, Jack had to allow a certain amount of fighting among the packs. The king dogs helped him to keep discipline in the pens, and once a king had established himself, it was merely a matter of his occasionally giving a young and misguided dog a lesson in behavior. Oscar was one of many high-spirited young dogs, but I often heard Jack say in admiration, "He has the makings of a king. He'll lead the pack one day."

Some dogs were stupid, some were clowns, some were workers, others were loafers, but only one was king. The king kept his whole team in order, and would snarl at any dog who was making the work harder. Just like antelope bulls and wolves, a dog became king by fighting the ruling leader and winning, and the pack accepted the authority of the king husky absolutely.

Because he showed such promise, because he was born during a great blizzard and because of his indomitable spirit, I was drawn to Oscar. Even when he was a pup there seemed to be a mutual attraction between us, although he always kept his proud, slightly remote manner. He appreciated a pat, and rough play, but hated to be petted. He remained suspicious of hand-feeding, even from me, and preferred his meat tossed to him on the snow. His temper was even and his courage unequaled.

When I left Heard Island in March 1952, Oscar was not quite a year old, but his size, and the beauty of his coat, as well as his wolflike appearance, made him stand out. Before my ship sailed, I paid a visit to the dog lines to say good-bye. Oscar had become so much part of my life that I found it difficult to imagine what it would be like without him.

3
Dog Training

ON HEARD Island, the dogs had not been of much use to us because of the steep terrain. But teams were being trained nevertheless, ready for the push further south into the heart of Antarctica.

Several years passed before I returned to that part of the world.

Main photograph: A penguin rookery on Heard Island.
Right: A Nansen hickory sled.
Center: A husky sleeps out a blizzard curled up in the snow.
Bottom: Husky team on a training run.

Amid great excitement, a new base had been established in the Antarctic in 1954: Mawson Station, named after Sir Douglas Mawson, Australia's first great Antarctic explorer.

Jack Walsh came back to Australia while I was still in Melbourne. He had continued training the huskies, sending teams of the best dogs down to Mawson on the *Kista Dan*, a newly chartered Danish polar ship.

"Ah, Nils," he sighed as we sat over a beer one hot day in the late spring. "Oscar is such a beauty. One of the biggest dogs I have seen, and strong as a horse."

I asked what work he had had the dogs doing.

"It's more a question of what they haven't been involved in," he began. "During the first year on Mawson, the fieldwork couldn't have been done without them. The research team made one exciting journey along the coast from Mawson, a round-trip of about a thousand kilometers, living off the land and hunting seals to feed the dogs. They had to make sure the dogs were at full strength because they were so dependent on them: in fact, first thing every night when they stopped to make camp, they fed the dogs and patted and praised the ones who expected it. And each morning, no sooner had the dogs got into their harnesses than they'd be straining and stretching, eager to set out on another day's run. Your old friend Oscar came on every journey from the new base. He's so strong and even-tempered. I'd never consider going out on a journey without him in the pack."

It warmed my heart to hear of Oscar, and with each passing day my nostalgia for the days on the ice grew. I made inquiries about the next expedition to Antarctica, unable to resist the lure of unknown territory, the splendor and terror of an Antarctic blizzard, and the breathtaking beauty of the shimmering icebergs, the fjords and glaciers in every shade of blue and dazzling white.

During the last days of December 1955, the *Kista Dan* sailed from Melbourne, and I was a member of the 1956 wintering party bound for Mawson. This time I was in the weather team, and to my delight, in charge of the dogs. Ours was the third wintering party to Mawson, the biggest one so far. Twenty men, several extra huts, a huge hangar, two aircraft (a de Havilland Beaver and an Auster) and tons of extra equipment swelled the holds of the small polar ship.

Several times during the voyage we were beset by pack ice, and these floating masses slowed us down. Once we were stuck in the grinding pack for eleven days, and time began to hang heavily on my hands. I was sitting listlessly in the mess when the expedition leader walked in with a sheet of paper in his hand. We all crowded around him as he tacked the paper onto the notice board and said: "Well, chaps, here's some excitement. We have decided to establish a second base, a small one with no more than five men somewhere in the Vestfold Hills area in Princess Elizabeth Land. This is just a preliminary plan but I think you'll like the idea." With that he left us.

I cast my mind back to all I knew of the Vestfold Hills—the vast area was almost completely unexplored, and was extraordinary for its lack of snow and ice-cover, one of the rare pieces of land that was brown and showed earth. Curious, I elbowed my way up to the notice board to study the plan more closely. Just one sleeping hut, one living hut, one engine hut and workshop, one store hut. Electric heating and cooking. A small tractor for jobs around the camp, dogs for field transport. Of the five men, one would be weatherman, one weatherman and radioman combined, one radioman-in-charge, one diesel engineer and one geologist.

"What an opportunity!" I breathed. "I'd give my next year's wages just to spend a year establishing the new base."

"You're mad, you big mug!" one of the others retorted. "It'll be nothing but hard work, and no fun at all. No way would I take it on."

"Nils, you're an incurable romantic," said Bill Bewsher, an old friend and the officer in charge of our party. "After a year at Mawson you'll be thinking of nothing but getting back to civilization!"

I turned to Bill, smiling at his tall, lanky frame, crowned by an old balaclava and with a tattered scarf slung around his neck. "After a year at Mawson, I know I'll still want to spend another year at the new base in the Vestfolds. You don't appreciate my quest for adventure and knowledge," I replied. Accompanied by a sally of laughter I dashed up the companionway and headed for the leader's cabin.

Five minutes later I slammed the door cheerfully behind me, full of the assurance that the job I wanted was mine.

THE *KISTA DAN* SLOWLY nosed her way at last through the narrow entrance into Horseshoe Harbour and Mawson Station. "Up there on the hill is your met hut, and down in the hollow you can see the mess and the sleeping huts." One of the old hands pointed everything out to the newcomers.

We could see men walking around ashore, no doubt eagerly waiting for the first batch of mail, fresh fruit, vegetables and meat for many months. To the right of the camp an unholy din had started up as soon as the ship hove in sight of the base. It was, of course, the howling of the irrepressible huskies, leaping about on their chains.

"Harry, look," I pointed. "Dogs to spare for you to take back."

"We could do with twice that number," he replied.

Harry Ayres had come with us as an observer on behalf of the New Zealand Antarctic Expedition, led by Sir Edmund Hillary, and to take over most of our huskies as a gift from the Australian government to the New Zealanders. One team with a couple of spare dogs and bitches would be left for me to look after, and from these we intended to breed more dogs, of the toughest possible kind. They would be born, trained and brought up at Mawson, acclimatized from birth.

Cheery greetings and the roar of the amphibious landing-craft engines almost drowned the din from the dogs as we came ashore. Together, Harry and I strolled across the uneven rocks below the camp, and were soon surrounded by a mob of howling, excited huskies.

"Ah, what a beauty, that's the sort of husky we want," said Harry admiringly. Following his gaze, I saw, with mixed pride and apprehension, the object of his admiration.

"That," I told him, "is Oscar. The only dog that I couldn't bear to part with."

As I approached, Oscar stopped his excited leaps. He came down on all fours, and slowly retreated the length of his chain. There he stood, looking at me, and the years of absence yawned between us. He drew further back, doubtful, slightly suspicious. Unable to bear the thought that he'd forgotten me, I removed my gloves and held out my bare hands to him.

"Here, Oscar, here. Don't you remember me?" Trying to keep the disappointment out of my voice, I kept my hands in front of me and let him sniff while I talked to him in just the same way I had so often done before on Heard Island. Oscar sniffed. At last his hanging tail curled up across his back and began to swing from side to side, and he poked his great muzzle into the palm of my hand.

"Dear God," said Harry. "He remembers you after all this time. Four years, isn't it?"

"Yes," I replied with relief. "Now you've seen what sort of dog he is, you'll understand why I want him to stay here."

The dog trainer from the previous year wandered over. "I hear you and Oscar are old friends," he said to me. "Oscar is not the king yet, but I certainly think he will be before too long. At present, there are two brothers, Butch and Mac, who operate as co-leaders of the pack. No single dog can hope to beat that combination.

"It's a very rare thing, a shared kingship," he continued. "I'd only read about it before, and at first it confused the other dogs almost as much as it did me. There have been some savage and bloody battles here. Once I was almost too late."

"Tell me more about it," I said, fascinated.

"It was that one over there, Gus, who took Mac on," he said. "I swear it was confusion about who was the leader that made him do it. For some reason, I didn't notice the fight was on at first. There had been one of those thick fogs for days—the dogs had been chained up, getting more and more restless, so I started letting them off their chains a few at a time to give them a run. I didn't hear the snarling when the fight began, but in no time at all, Mac and Butch had Gus on the ground, ripping at his belly and head with their claws. Gus was just fending them off, but he was bleeding badly from the throat and getting weaker every second. I separated them as quickly as I could, but old Gus has never been the same since. Almost as if he lost his pride for ever. He's docile, even abject, and often seems dull-witted compared with the dog he was a year ago. And I reckon that Oscar will take them on next."

With that, he swept Harry and me off to his workbench to admire his straps and traces. A few days later, Harry sailed away with all the youngest dogs, pups and bitches, taking with him a good assortment of sturdy gear for dog handling.

I was left mainly the older dogs, as most of the men believed that aircraft and weasels—large tracked vehicles designed to travel over snow and ice, and capable of towing sleds—would replace dogs before long. I seemed to be the only one who believed that the polar husky was irreplaceable. Butch and Mac were left, and so were Oscar, Horace, Streaky, Brownie, and the two team bitches, Dee and Denny—nearly all old friends from Heard Island days—plus a couple of misfits.

I set about retraining and mating the dogs. Over the years, they had had so many different drivers and trainers that there was no one system they understood and responded to instinctively. Day after day we repeated our rigorous training program, and bit by bit they learned how to pull a sled driven from behind, instead of being led.

The huskies had a keen sense of justice, and respected me more when I was just, and harsh, than if they'd been treated with nothing but kindness. The tool of my trade was a braided, ox-hide leather whip, about five meters long. Each day I spent the first few hours practicing with the whip, until I could stand back five meters and knock a box of matches off the top of a 44-gallon drum. If the dogs misbehaved, I used the folded whip across their rumps. If they fought, I used the butt end anywhere that I could get it in, but only if I was sure which one of them had started the fight—to offend their sense of justice was to lose their respect for ever. Riding the sled, I could flick the rump of even the farthest dog with perfect accuracy.

I had one problem dog—Dee. Successive parties at Mawson had found her impossible to train for sledding. She seemed to hold everyone in abject fear, and would run off to the full length of her chain, lie down and shiver whenever anyone approached. I had tried once before to train her, but whenever I approached with a harness she went silly with fright, dribbling and howling like a motherless baby. A rifle-bullet seemed to be the most sensible thing for her, but I was determined to try one last time to make her useful.

My campaign started by spending most of my spare time sitting on a rock down by the dog lines. I puffed contentedly on my old pipe, and I didn't even look at Dee for the first week or so, but talked to her quietly. The rest of the team stood on their hind legs whenever I appeared, begging for a pat and a rough-and-tumble. Except Oscar. He mostly kept his distance, and only very rarely when I sat down would he come up and put his great shaggy head and nose into my hand, then burrow his head under my arm. He never, never showed any affection to any other expedition member; only to his master. And even I knew never to expect it.

Gradually I started to win Dee's confidence. I placed small bits of seal meat close by my feet. At first she was far too timid to come near, but as soon as I moved a few meters away she rushed in and snatched up the meat. I always handled it first with my bare hands, so that she got used to my smell.

For weeks on end, I didn't even attempt to pat her, but finally she overcame her fear and snatched a piece of soft seal meat from my hand. She became less and less timid, and one day I placed my bare hand on her head. She stood quite still and shivered violently, but did not run away. Gently I stroked her head and scratched her behind the ears. She endured it, her tail between her legs. That was the turning point in our relationship. Soon after, she behaved like a normal dog and let me feed her, pat her and handle her generally.

To make a sled dog of her was more difficult, but finally I managed by starting to walk her on a lead. The most difficult test was to come—making her accept a harness. The first few tries were dismal failures, but my patience was rewarded when she decided that to accept a harness only meant another walk with me. Finally, one day Denny was left at home, while Dee took her place in the team. The base doctor came with us for the run, full of doubt.

"Well, I never thought I'd see that!" he exclaimed. Dee was running flat out with the leaders, legs spread wide, her small powerful body straining forward, while her pulling trace was kept as tight as a violin string.

As the weeks passed I spent more and more time with the dogs, training them to a perfect pitch so they'd be ready for pulling heavy sleds when our exploration and surveying program got under way. One morning, just as I began my whip practice for the day, a meeting was called. Tired of too much talk, I had begun to stay away from meetings; if there was anything I needed to know, my old friend Bill Bewsher would always tell me.

That morning I put the dogs through all their paces, and we all worked up a sweat, the dogs and me alike. By midday I was more than ready for a big meal, and with a sense of great satisfaction made my weary way over to the mess hut. I was met on the steps by Bill.

"Nils, there was a meeting this morning," he began hesitantly. "And there are one or two things you should know."

"Tell me while I eat, Bill," I said. "I'm famished," and I tried to lead him into the mess hut. To my surprise, Bill resisted, stepping backward and pulling me with him.

"The fact is, Nils, I couldn't bear to eat with you. And neither can anyone else. You smell. You smell just like a stinking husky after a run. A combination of ripe seal meat, blubber, and just plain wolf-flavored dog smell.

"We made a new rule this morning," he continued, shifting uneasily from one foot to another. "All outer clothing is to be removed in the cold porch, before you enter the mess. And the only person this applies to is you."

I looked at him in amazement. "Well, I'll be damned!" I said and burst into laughter.

With relief, Bill began to laugh with me. "You mean you didn't know?" he asked. "You really are the complete dog-man!"

Only a week later, the dogs were the center of camp controversy again. A couple of the men claimed that it was unfair that I was the only driver. When I heard about it, I simply said, "Go ahead! Saddle the dogs, and go off and do a seal count if you like." I couldn't help smiling to myself, as I knew they were in for a surprise.

Gleefully, a few of the men went down to the dog lines, put the harnesses on the team, and maneuvered the sled down to the sea-ice—the ocean which had frozen hard. Watching the performance through the mess window, we heard the cry of "Mush!" as, with a great flourish, they flew out over the sea-ice. Then Oscar looked back over his shoulder and discovered that a completely strange driver was in charge. Though I was too far away to see, I could just imagine the look of incredulity that came over his face as he thought "Blow this! I'm not going to pull for an amateur!" He turned around and headed straight back for the dog lines, ignoring the shouted instructions and strenuous efforts from the drivers to prevent it. Oscar and his team shot across the ice, and without a pause he brought the team up to the dog lines and sat down. I never heard another whisper of complaint from the men.

4
Castles of Ice

BY MID-July, after months of preparation, we were ready for our first expedition. This was to search for the Douglas Islands, reportedly sighted in 1912 by Sir Douglas Mawson, and never seen since. A Norwegian whaler had tried to find them in the 1930s but, unable to trace them, decided that all Mawson had seen was icebergs.

On July 15, so close to midwinter that it was still pitch-dark at 10 a.m., I harnessed the dogs, preparing to head roughly fifty kilometers northeast. A bleak wind whistled off the plateau and out over the sea-ice. The thermometer showed forty-two degrees below freezing, yet the three of us were keyed up with excitement and didn't even feel the cold. There was Syd Kirkby, the surveyor; Peter Crohn, the geologist; and me: radio and weatherman and, of course, dog driver.

The dogs' blood was running hot. Denny, the team bitch, was in full heat, and all three of us were kept busy preventing a free-for-all. Fortunately, she had been trained to run in the lead position, and I clipped on an extra length of trace to increase the inducement for the dogs behind her.

"Don't you think we'd better leave her behind, Nils?" asked Peter. "She'll cause us more trouble than she's worth."

"Not on your life," I replied. "She'll add another five knots to our speed. You just watch! With the team behind her, she'll be too frightened not to run like blazes, and the rest of them will spend all day trying to catch up. All we have to do is to grab her whenever we stop, to keep her away from the dogs, except Oscar. His and Denny's pups should be prizewinning sled dogs."

With that, I roared "Mush", and we were off.

We all hung on to the bucking sled as we drove out of the harbor and the dogs ran off their early morning exuberance. The heavy load settled them down, and soon we had cleared all the local islands, and started to cross the frozen sea to the east.

As we traveled, the wind off the plateau dropped, and the next group of coastal islands loomed up among frozen-in icebergs ahead. We steered for the northernmost island in the group, and started looking for a campsite. We always avoided camping on the open sea-ice, just in case it broke up and floated away, taking us with it. Many times during the year, often for no apparent reason at all, the sea-ice would break up, and vast areas of it float away to join the moving pack ice further out to sea. So we usually looked for an island, a rocky outcrop on the shore, or tried to get up on the polar plateau itself.

"Hey, look at that!" shouted Peter. "Up ahead there, the perfect campsite, in that little bay." Then his face fell as he realized that the flat, snow-covered site he'd chosen was at the top of a steep slope, and surrounded by a treacherous tide-crack, where the stable land-ice meets the constantly shifting sea-ice. "Oh, no," Peter said, "we'd never get the dogs to cross the tide-crack, and even if we did that slope is far too steep with this heavy load."

"Not for my dogs," I said, without even thinking.

Peter turned and looked at me speculatively, and his face took on a crafty look. "Well, prove it to us, Nils," he said. "I'll bet you five thousand dollars they can't do it."

Five thousand dollars, I thought to myself. That was more than my life's savings. I had great faith in my dogs, but to ask this of them might be too much. But the alternative was to lose face, and to give in to the new belief that the dogs' days on the ice were numbered. With the blood pounding in my temples, I made up my mind.

"You're on," I said quietly.

I turned and surveyed the terrain ahead of us. To get to the plateau, I had to get the dogs and sled across the jumbled tide-crack, a sort of hinge formed as the sea-ice rises and falls with the tides and the swell of the ocean. Then we had to negotiate a very steep, slippery ascent with ice blocks and floes overriding rock outcrops. As I looked up the slope, Oscar turned his big shaggy head to me, as if understanding all that hung on the bet I'd made. Then his attention was distracted by Denny, and he began straining forward toward the tantalizing bitch.

It was the inspiration I needed. Taking Oscar's cue, I went to the front of the sled, untied Denny, staked the sled into the ice and led her to the top of the slope, where I put in her stake and chained her firmly. I tramped back down to the sled and the waiting dogs, and repositioned Oscar in the lead.

"Okay, Oscar," I whispered to him. "This is your test. Take us up to Denny." With that I unstaked the sled, jumped on the platform and roared the familiar command: "Mush! Mush!"

With an almighty heave, Oscar whipped the heavily-loaded sled away, and it bounced clean over the tide-crack. Without so much as a pause to gather his strength, Oscar came at the steep slope from an angle, working out how to reduce the steepness as much as possible. Denny was howling with excitement, spurring Oscar's determination, and as if driven by an engine the dogs pulled the sled straight up the slope and onto the smooth, flat plateau. My heart was pounding as I jumped off the platform and rounded the sled to see how Oscar was. His chest was heaving and his mouth flecked with foam, but the look in his eyes showed his triumph was as great as my own.

Soon the tent was up, and a pot of pemmican hooch, a high protein beef stew, was bubbling on the portable cookstove. The dogs had already received their ration of special dog pemmican made of fat and dried meat, and I had tied Oscar and Denny up together for the night.

"About that five thousand, Peter," I began. "I don't want it, you know. I just wanted to prove to you that you can't manage on the ice without dogs, and as dogs go, Oscar is the best."

Peter turned to me shamefacedly, and I realized there was nothing more to be said. We lit our smokes and relaxed on our sleeping bags, listening to the gentle creaking of the great ice as it rose and fell to the almost imperceptible breathing of the sea.

THE following day, in clear, calm weather, we drove off on the next leg of our search for the Douglas Islands. Somewhere to the north, out on the frozen sea, the icebergs might be hiding two lonely specks of rocks. Although it was bitterly cold, sixty degrees below freezing, we hardly felt it as there was no wind, and we ran at an energetic pace. Denny's trace was stretched tight, with the two brothers Butch and Mac in hot pursuit behind. Then came Oscar, running with his old mate Streaky, and, as the last pair, Horace and Brownie. Oscar obviously felt Denny was his girl, as he had been tied up with her overnight, and panting and snarling he tried to overtake Butch and Mac. Even Brownie, the dumbest dog in the team, seemed to have gained new vigor: he acquired an almost alert look, and I laughed aloud at the thought of the strain it must have caused him.

In every dog team there are certain types of dog: the bright ones, the bullies, the lazy and cunning ones and the idiot dogs. Brownie was an idiot dog. If it was at all possible Brownie tangled his traces, even on a straight run. If there was a crack in the ice, he was the one who fell in. If we sledded on blue slippery ice, Brownie's legs flew out in all directions, and he ended up under the sled. Other dogs had no trouble in stealing his food. But I was fond of the old idiot, especially when he greeted me with a stupid grin on his face.

Streaky was the bully who originated every vicious fight among the dogs. He was battle-scarred, one ear half bitten off and blind in one eye. In harness he was good, strong and consistent.

Horace was lazy and cunning, always pulling with the trace just tight enough to deceive the driver. But a slight tug at his trace revealed the deception, and over and over again I would flick the whip out and remind him of his duties. He always got enough food, even when rations were short, and looked big and healthy, with an impressive lionlike head.

Of the Butch-Mac combination, Butch was the lovable, hardworking affectionate clown. Both he and Mac, his powerful coleader, bore the scars of many battles. Their leadership had been won the hard way, and this unique combination was unbeatable. Once, back in the autumn, Oscar had contested their leadership: combined, they gave him the lesson of his life. Now Oscar was biding his time, filling the role of title contender. He had grown to a great size, weighing sixty kilos, and his wolfish hackle became more pronounced all the time. His paws were almost the size of my hands and when he stood up on his hind legs he towered over me. Physically and mentally, I thought, he was equipped to take the leadership when the time came.

My daydreaming was interrupted by the appearance of hundreds of icebergs ahead of us, locked in the sea-ice. They looked like a medieval city, with cottages and low buildings, churches with spires and domes, all dominated by the most beautifully

401

designed castles of ice, complete with buttresses, towers, steep ramparts and darkened gates, a vast conglomeration. Some of them had recently moved with tides and currents, and wide refrozen channels frequently crossed our course.

Searching for the lost islands, we drove on reluctantly, leaving behind us the majestic city of ice. By then we were far out from the coast, still on a northeasterly course, and we took frequent compass bearings to compare them with our map. We kept a short lookout, taking it in turns to ride on the sled, sweeping in all directions with the field glasses. The surface of the sea-ice became jumbled and broken; big icebergs had sailed through the area like attacking battleships, leaving broad rivers of crushed floes in their wake. Some huge cracks had water in them and were very dangerous. I was anxious about our passage, but my worries were constantly relieved by the comedy provided by Brownie, who managed to put his feet into every crack, floundering around looking more like a rag doll than a sled dog.

"Halt!" cried Syd. "According to our map reference, we should now be standing on top of the Douglas Islands."

The three of us looked at each other in despair. For as far as the eye could see, we were surrounded by nothing but sea-ice and icebergs. Huddling together for warmth, we held a conference and decided to turn back to the city of icebergs we had passed earlier, and have a closer look in the last two hours of daylight.

The long whip lashed forward, the team turned in a wide arc, and we began wearily to retrace our steps. From the speed with which the vapor from our breath formed into ice on our beards, we knew the temperature was falling rapidly. We watched each other's faces for telltale white spots, the first sign of frostbite, and over and over I pressed my bare hand over my nose and cheek-bones to restore circulation.

Before long we were back at the icebergs, meandering around with no real direction. Then, with no warning, the dogs increased their pace, suddenly running full tilt, whining eagerly at something we could not see.

"It's either a seal, a seal-hole, or land," I told Syd and Peter with a mounting sense of excitement. "They only behave like this when they think the run is nearing the end, or if they smell a seal.

And if they think they are nearly home, then they smell land!"

With the dogs running strongly, we all three rode the sled. And as we rounded a large grounded iceberg we saw dead ahead two small snow-covered islands, almost completely hemmed in by castles of ice. The dogs had found the Douglas Islands.

After making camp on one of the rediscovered islands, we set to work to confirm our position. Syd took bearings of several widely spaced stars, measuring angles with his theodolite, and our subsequent calculations pinpointed our position to within a meter. By midnight, we had finished these astrofixes and our scientific work was done. We had a last brew of coffee, crawled into our double-thickness sleeping bags and fell immediately asleep, twitching and tossing as life returned to our cold hands and feet. Outside, the lovelorn dogs howled for Denny, tied up out of their reach.

Syd had managed to get the middle spot in the tent to sleep in, much sought after in a polar tent because it's so much warmer with the body heat of one man on each side. But the man in the middle also had to serve as breakfast table for the duty cook, supporting at least two wooden lids from the ration boxes, the portable cookstove, kettle and cooking pot, as well as an assortment of cups, plates and cutlery.

Next morning it was my turn to cook. I boiled the kettle and served up a mixture of leftovers and extra: a tin of "Trim", a sort of meat compound, with a squeeze of marmite and a bit of onion powder to hide the taste of last night's pemmican.

The dogs rose and shook themselves as I crawled out of the tent. Several of them were lifting their paws off the ice, as if they were marching on the spot. When I checked the thermometers I realized the reason: during the night the air temperature had dropped to more than sixty below freezing, and on the ice it would have been even less.

Oscar and Denny had been tied up separately overnight, but when I appeared, Oscar thought he was about to be reunited with her. He rushed forward to the full length of his chain, howling like a lost soul. Denny, on the other hand, was indifferent. She had conceived and was fast losing interest in Oscar, although his ardor was undiminished, and his disappointment as I retreated into the tent was heartbreaking.

403

Clutching a block of ice to make a fresh pot of coffee, I wormed my way back in.

"Lovely day outside, gentlemen," I announced cheerfully. "Birds singing in the trees, not a cloud in the sky. The baker and milkman have been, but a parking attendant has put a ticket on our sled!"

"Sometimes I think you're half mad, Nils," said Syd, grumpy, as he was most mornings. "Let's get to work then."

All day we collected geological samples, took astrofixes, made maps and explored. By next morning, the temperature had risen to forty below, but a low drift of snow could be seen in the Mawson area to the west—a sure sign of very bad weather just hours away. Frantically we began to pull down the tent and pack up, anxious to be on our way back to the safety of Mawson as soon as possible, for a blizzard could whip waves up at sea, breaking the ice and leaving us stranded on an island only we knew existed. We put extra lashings on the sled and drove off after a large breakfast, unsure when we would be able to have our next meal.

Racing against time and the blizzard we knew would soon come hurtling down from the polar plateau, one man rode the sled and the other two held on to the handlebars, running alongside to lighten the load. We kept up a cracking pace. Again and again the long whip whistled forward. "Hi! Hi! Mush!" Every hour we rested the dogs, and were grateful ourselves for a few minutes rest while we munched chocolate and high-protein biscuits, trying to keep up our energy.

The wind was increasing steadily, and before long snow started to hurtle across the ice. At first it was only waist high, but enough to worry the dogs. Instinctively they started to turn away from the set course to keep their heads out of the wind. Constant correction became necessary, and our pace was getting slower and slower.

Suddenly, a solid wall of snow approached us from the coast. The blizzard. A violent gust nearly turned the heavy sled over, and quickly we drew tight the strings on our parka hoods, till only a small opening was left. The whole dog team flopped down on the ice with their backs to the wind, ready to sit it out, preparing to be snowed in snugly.

"I'll have to lead them," I yelled into the wind. "They won't be able to see a thing in this, but they'll pull blind if we stay with them."

"We'll take it in turns," Peter yelled back. "You start us off, Nils."

Bent double, I struggled up to Denny. "Come on! Mush!" I shouted hoarsely. The team rose in their traces, and we began a weary slog through the blizzard, anxiety prodding us across the wide sweep of frozen sea which separated us from shelter and safety.

Leaning on the wind, with my face half averted from the icy blast, I trudged on, trying to keep a steady course. It became more and more difficult as the strength of the blizzard increased, and the big wind forced the snow-filled air back into our lungs every time we tried to face it.

I was roused by a shout from the rear where Peter was looking at the compass, constantly wiping its face to read it. "Nils, keep more to your left, more into the weather."

Reluctantly, I turned into the wind again, keeping my gloved hand over my face to allow me to breathe behind it. Now and again I turned and looked at the dogs. They had bunched together and were pulling almost as one, their heads turned partly away from the blast. The weather sides of their coats were completely iced up, like white suits of armor. Oscar frequently ran a paw across his face to rub off the ice which had formed in thick crusts around his eyes and nose. He was the only dog to realize the danger of that blinding, choking layer of ice.

"Hold it!" I yelled back to the others. "We'll have to get rid of the ice round the dogs' eyes and nostrils."

"Let's do it with our bare hands, then," said Peter. "That will be the quickest." Within minutes the dogs were gratefully licking their deiced chops, and we struggled on. As I walked I could feel a gentle touch on my knee. Looking down, I discovered old Butch had maneuvered himself so close to me that he was able to keep his nose free of ice by occasionally rubbing it across the back of my knee. I quickly bent down and patted his grizzled old head, and he nudged me in reply. The rest of the team dragged along behind with their noses only centimeters above the heavy imprints of my mukluks. Slowly and tortuously we made our way across the treacherous stretch of open sea-ice.

It felt as if whole lifetimes had passed by the time Peter came up and took the lead, and I gratefully dropped to the rear of the sled. But there was no respite. Heavily loaded as it was, the sled was blown sideways like a ship under sail, and the bows kept running up into the wind. Syd and I walked alongside, half leaning on the sled, trying to keep it on an even keel. Now and then we completely lost sight of Peter and the lead dogs, blotted out by swirling eddies of snow.

Tiring more every minute, we slogged along. The temperature was not really low, but in that violent wind the cold gripped our faces and hands like icy steel bands. I could no longer feel the left side of my face, and my left eye felt as if it would drop out at any moment, like a piece of rock-hard marble. Each time I removed my glove to put my bare hand on my frostbitten face, my hand lost all feeling. It became a vicious circle. The howling wind drowned all other sound. We were in a world apart, suffering a horrible, lonely nightmare, and each step became a separate effort of will.

We rested our exhausted dogs each hour, crouching behind the sled, sharing our chocolate and biscuits with them and rotating the task of leader.

"Should be nearly there," Syd said encouragingly at last. "Another mile or two. We can't afford any more stops, though. Come on, let's get going."

Again I took my turn at the head of the team. Faithfully the dogs rose to each occasion. Butch regained his position by my knee, and nudged me as I patted him. He and Mac, the old leaders, seemed to be more tired than the rest. They had been breaking trail all day, often through drifts of loose, heavy snow, and both dogs were stumbling. Oscar was less affected. His trace was tight, and his was the only tail in the team still curled over his back. He knew how to keep himself free from ice, and his gaze was firmly fixed on Denny, laboring just ahead of him. I envied him his spirit.

The only contact with reality came through the soles of my mukluks as they left their faint prints on the hard-packed snow covering the sea-ice, which separated us from the black Antarctic Ocean by less than a meter. I found the words of an ancient prayer for sled dogs running through my head like a refrain:

Look kindly, Oh Lord, on these Thy Creatures
for We are dependent on Them
and They, with Us, are utterly dependent on Thee.

WITHOUT warning, I stumbled across a deep crack in the ice. It looked like one of those tidal cracks which we always found near solid land. With mounting hope, I tried to follow where it led, and nearly walked straight into a large opening in the ice— a seal's blow-hole, and big enough for a seal to haul out. That meant land! This *must* be one of the coastal islands, I thought.

Then we saw it! A rift in the curtain of swirling snow gave us a quick glimpse of black rock, and a few more steps brought us up short in front of a high, steep island.

At last, a shelter where we could sit out the worst of the blizzard. Breathing a sigh of relief, I was startled by a shout from Peter. Fearing he'd slipped, I jerked around toward him. But Peter was pointing ahead at the team, where Oscar, on pleasure bent, was sidling up to Denny, harness and all. "What a dog!" laughed Syd, with undisguised admiration. "After a day like this!"

While I watched over the team Syd and Peter searched along the island for a spot to get up. They soon returned, and confirmed that the only place where we had any hope of getting ashore was right in front of us. We would have to leave the sled below and carry all our gear to the top of the island, where the only flat snow-covered area gave us enough room for the tent. Where to stake the dogs was our most pressing problem, but we finally decided to peg them out along the narrow ice foot, a rim running right round the bottom of the island. Despite our exhaustion, we would have to keep regular watch to ensure they were all right.

We cut steps where the rock was covered with ice, then bundle by bundle carried all our gear to the top. First we dug a square in the snow big enough for our tent-base, then we fought against the violently flapping tent-cloth before we finally managed to raise it, guy it, and steady it down with walls of snow-blocks. Gratefully we crawled inside and got the portable cookstove going. After a meal we checked our supplies and agreed to ration our fuel, just in case the blizzard lasted for several days.

"The first break we get in this we'll make a run for it," I suggested. "We may possibly be in for a series of depressions, but often we get a lull in between. It shouldn't matter much what time we take off from here, anyway. The moon is full, and the dogs will find their old tracks."

"I agree," said Syd. "Let's get some sleep while we can."

Fully clothed we wormed into our sleeping bags, our outer boots within easy reach. Half sitting up we dropped off to an uneasy sleep.

Shortly before midnight we were awakened by a thunderous crash. The guy ropes on the weather side of the tent had snapped, and the gale had set the tent flapping like a giant sail. Syd, who had been whacked across the back of his head by the tent wall, was out of his sleeping bag and through the entrance sock of the tent in one movement, completely forgetting to put his boots on. Peter and I grabbed a tent-pole each from the inside, and held the tent down while Syd fixed the ropes outside.

"Hell!" said Syd despondently, as his head came back through the entrance, "either of you blokes got a dry pair of socks?"

Several hours later, when we woke again, it sounded as if someone were standing outside the tent shoveling gravel onto it. With terrible reluctance, I struggled into my frozen mukluks, windproof outer clothing, black felt blizzard-mask and two pairs of heavy, greasy wool mittens, covered with a large over-mitt of windproof material with a leather palm.

Outside I gathered seven half-kilo cakes of dog-pemmican and made my way down to the ice foot. Things had changed for the worse. The main ice sheet was moving before my eyes, and the wide tide-crack had filled with water to a depth of about a meter. Broken bits of ice floated around in it, moved by the big wind, which whipped ice-cold salt spray across the dog lines. More than a meter of the ice foot had been ground away, and it looked like more ice would break off at any time.

The dogs had moved as far in on the ice foot as their chains would allow, then curled up with their backs against the wind and spray. Old Mac and Butch already had thick coatings of ice across their backs, and seemed impervious to the weather. The other dogs were also apparently asleep; only Oscar prowled back and forth unhappily, growling every time the spray hit him.

Scrambling back up the slope, I thrust my head through the

entrance sock of the tent. "Afraid your urgent assistance is required," I panted. In a few minutes we were all down on the crumbling ice foot.

"It's going to waste too much time if we take the dogs up one by one," I ventured. "We shall have to drag the whole lot up, moored as they are. One man in front, one in the middle, and one astern."

We knocked the mooring stakes loose, and I grabbed the front end of the dog line next to Denny, and started to climb. Slipping and scrambling, we made our way to the top, using every possible crack and outcrop for handholds and footholds. An hour later we finally staked the dogs, retrieved the sled and crawled, spent, into our tent once again.

WE SLEPT through the death-throes of the blizzard. When we woke late in the afternoon the wind had dropped, the drifting snow whispering lightly across the rocks and among the crevices on the island. The short span of fitful daylight had faded into night, and through the thin snow flurries we could see the sky, where a full moon cast a broad, silvery band across the frozen sea.

The exhausted dogs didn't stir as we started to move around our makeshift camp. They had attained the maximum degree of comfort, snowed right under, curled up for warmth.

Peering around, at long last we were able to see exactly where we had made camp in the blizzard. Our island was the northernmost of the Spjotoy group, well apart from the rest, about twenty kilometers northeast of Mawson, and way off our course. Had we passed it we would have continued veering away and eventually bypassed Mawson altogether, heading for the wide open spaces.

While there was a lull, we set off on the final leg of our homerun. The blizzard had died down almost completely, and the full moon had created an icy fairyland of towering blue-black icebergs, dark-smudged islands and an endless, shimmering mirror on the petrified sea, stretching away beyond the horizon.

At a full run the dogs brought us into the harbor, and we could hear the exhaust from the diesels mingle with the excited howls from the dogs left back in camp. Several of the huts had lights at their small windows. We were greeted with relief by the men on base, and within minutes had collapsed into our beds.

EXHILARATED by our discoveries and the night run, Peter, Syd and I were up at first light. The blizzard had passed, and it was an unexpectedly fine day. A down-slope plateau wind was blowing at a steady thirty knots, gusting occasionally up to fifty knots. In the hope of just such a day, we had brought from Australia a number-one wood to do a bit of golfing on the sea-ice.

The three of us set off for the harbor, our pockets bulging with golf balls dipped in black enamel. Peter had collected some large wood-screws to serve as tees; he countersank them on an emery wheel and screwed them into the ice. Gingerly I placed one of our valuable golf balls on the ice and lined up the flight path, feeling absurd in full polar gear.

Pete was behind me with a pair of binoculars. I waited for a lull in the wind, then let her have it. Just as I drove off, a tremendous gust hit, nearly blowing us over. The drive was a good one, and the wind took the ball and propelled it right across the Mawson harbor, through the harbor mouth and out over the ice. Pete yelled, "I can still see the ball! It's heading for Flatoy Island!"

That island is four kilometers from the harbor mouth, and the ball hurtled across the expanse of sea-ice, finishing up somewhere in the tide-crack. We saddled up Oscar and went after the ball without much hope of finding it. But with his uncanny knack of sensing excitement, Oscar bounded off to the tidal crack, his nose quivering. And sure enough he found the ball nestled into the edge of the island.

Over a year later, I was back in Melbourne having a drink with a journalist when the talk came around to golf and exceptionally long drives. I told my story amid roars of incredulous laughter. Near us in the pub happened to be *The Herald's* golfing writer, and overhearing our conversation he asked, "Was that fair dinkum?" The following day *The Herald* ran the story. When I next visited the library of the Antarctic Division in Melbourne, the librarian gave me a hug, and said: "At last we have cracked it. Nils, you are our first explorer in *The Guinness Book of Records*. And of all things, for a golf drive!" There it was, the longest golf drive on record, and it still is, as far as I know.

The Southern Journey

AFTER that exciting and terrifying journey into the city of ice-bergs, Oscar became a father for the first time. The four pups grew very quickly, and as the long winter waned they played happily around the caravan and tractor sleds below the camp.

Oscar accepted the pups with a somewhat grudging patience. I often smiled to myself when I saw him playing with them, completely out of character for him. When they became too enthusiastic he simply shook them off and walked away.

Unusually for a husky, he seemed to know he was their father. The only normal attachment among huskies is a brief one between a bitch and her very young pups; as soon as the pups are old enough to live on a diet of seal meat, their ways part and any further attachment is extremely rare. Unlike domestic dogs, huskies operate in packs, yet are sufficient unto themselves. Should a half-grown pup in his ignorance approach his mother while she was eating, he would receive short shrift.

So came the spring and summer with long days of brilliant sunlight, interspersed with blizzards. The need for more young dogs became pressing as our Heard Island veterans grew older. The year before, several litters had arrived during prolonged blizzards and only five pups out of twenty-five survived. It was then we hit on the idea of a permanent maternity shelter for the bitches. We spent a day or so making the camp doctor's porch "dog-proof", and lining the walls and floor with insulating material.

One bitch, Dinah, was used only for breeding. We had tried to sled her, but a combination of low morals and a complete disregard of the driver's wishes made her an impossible sled dog. However she was beautifully built and quite a good mother, so we kept her.

Dinah, about to whelp, was introduced to her new surroundings and immediately settled down, much to our relief. Sometimes a bitch would insist on choosing her own place to throw her pups, and no power on earth would induce her to accept a man-made "maternity ward." Dinah realized she was onto a good thing and produced six perfect, healthy pups. They all survived, and after a few weeks completely ruled the doctor's hut until the base doctor begged us to find somewhere else. So we fitted out a caravan the same way, just in time for the next litter, which was Denny's. But our good luck wasn't to continue.

Denny chose a night of howling September blizzard to throw her litter. The first pup was born dead, but she produced another seven in quick succession. The fierce blizzard made it impossible to have a heater inside the caravan, as the gusty drafts would either have put it out or possibly started a fire. But the pups had to be kept warm during those first, critical hours of life. While Denny gave birth to the last few, the first-born pups were left without protection, and several of them looked completely lifeless. I desperately tried to keep the early arrivals warm, while Denny calmly dropped one steaming bundle after another on the ice-cold floor. Denny and I then tried to keep the feeble life in the tiny, helpless pups going, but we were losing the battle.

Taking my courage in my hands, I decided to rouse the base

Oscar accepted his pups with a somewhat grudging patience.

doctor. Gathering up all the pups and piling them like sausages inside my parka, I called out to Denny, and we staggered off into the black, howling night.

"Gentle massage and artificial respiration, like this," the doctor said, sitting up in his bed and kneading one small pup in his warm hands.

The rest of the pups he tucked around him under his blankets. "They'll be all right," he assured Denny and me. "It's just these last two we've got to help. Nils, get me two bowls of water, one hot, the other cold, and that old bit of towel."

By now the little pup I had been kneading for ten minutes had started to show signs of life. He squeaked and wriggled, and his body temperature was almost equal to that of my hands.

"Under the blankets with him," the doctor ordered. Then he proceeded to dip the last pup alternately in hot and cold water. He gently blew down its open mouth while squeezing its chest like a small bellows. For several minutes nothing happened, and then the pup slowly jackknifed its body, and a very feeble squeak, like a mouse, was heard over the doctor's breathing. We had won.

PLANNING for a new major expedition—the Southern Journey—was well under way, and it was decided that a major base for the exploring party should be established in the Prince Charles Mountains, four hundred kilometers south of Mawson. In the months of longer daylight the unexplored ranges were to be surveyed, astrofixes made, and the rocks studied in what was our most important project for the whole year.

Initially the journey to the ranges was to be undertaken by two weasels, or tractors, towing special weasel-sleds with gear, food and spares for the base camp in the field. We were to keep flying in supplies for as long as the sea-ice in Mawson Harbour was firm enough for the Beaver aircraft to take off on skis.

As part of the preparation for the big expedition, we made several trips on sea-ice along the coast using both weasels and dog teams. These runs raised the question of taking the dog team on the Southern Journey. Opinion at the base was divided. There were strong supporters for weasels only, while others thought the dogs might work if they were a lot younger, and did not have to travel so far. Driving techniques would be slightly different on the

413

Continental icecap, with the menace of the deep fissures called crevasses. There was also the danger of losing control of dogs and sled down a long slope of slippery blue ice. Ropes around the runners were necessary, the driver had to wear crampons—spikes to dig into the ice—and the dogs' traces had to be considerably longer to enable the team to fan out in crevassed areas. However, the preparatory runs with dogs had been successful, and that seemed to clinch it in the minds of the Southern Journey party. We began to plan for the addition of a dog team.

"Well, Nils, what do you think?" asked Bill Bewsher, the officer in charge. Bill was the only man I felt I could trust with the dogs.

"I think you should take six dogs," I replied, "provided you remember that these dogs are well past their prime; you could lose some. The only two I am certain will return are Oscar and Horace—Oscar, because he's stronger than the rest, and Horace because he's lazy and cunning and won't extend himself completely. So don't let them pull a heavy load right into the ranges, save them till you really need them in more difficult country among those mountains. I'll make new traces, assemble a new sled, and cut seal meat in easy feeds for transport. I'll fix up some dog boots for when you strike needle-ice, and have special ropes cut to make braking easier. The rest is up to you."

The next day I broke out new, tarred rope from the store, and spliced a complete new set of pulling traces. Several new harnesses were made, so that each dog had a spare. Finally, the whole team got a brand-new set of dog boots. I made them from stout, windproof tent-cloth material with soft leather soles. Prolonged contact with what we called "needle-ice," blue ice covered with tiny, needle-sharp ice-crystals, often gave the dogs sore pads, and could put them out of action.

Our two pilots finished their depot-supply flights, the final preparations were made and the men's personal gear loaded on the weasel sleds. The dogs were in fine condition, and we could feel their tension and excitement. We who were left behind watched the weasel-train head south, the blue smoke from the exhaust being whipped away by the keen plateau wind. As they got under way, the dog team swung out to the left to pass the laboring weasels with their heavy cargo sleds in tow.

414

IN THE WEEKS THAT followed I haunted the radio-hut. At appointed times each day we made contact with the field-party, and Bill Bewsher sent me almost daily reports of the progress and condition of the dogs. Sometimes he asked for advice, but mostly the field-party reported back on distance traveled, weather conditions and other scientific data.

More and more frequently, Bill's short messages included, "Weasels unable to keep up with dogs." I could imagine the dogs making easy going of the sastrugi, which is hard-packed snow blown by prevailing winds into waves from a few centimeters high up to two or three meters. Whereas the flexible Nansen-type dog sled, bound together with rawhide lashing, would snake across the rough sastrugi, the rigid vehicles and cargo sleds took an awful pounding. At last came a red-letter day when we heard that the field-party had managed to push through the last difficult stretch of crevassed country to reach the main depot, four hundred kilometers to the south.

My dogs were called on to perform an almost impossible task. They were to pull as never before, and support three men in the field for many weeks on end, without even a day's rest. With the dog team the men completed three separate journeys from the depot, traveling a total of six hundred kilometers in and around the mountains.

Poor old Mac, the leader, was the first to go. He was the oldest, and had only one thought in his brain—to pull; and pull he did till he dropped in the traces, still going forward. The men tried to revive him and pitched a temporary camp, but the poor dog could not even lift his head. Finally his dwindling life was ended with a bullet.

With the remaining five dogs, the party pushed through the first set of ranges to a second series of mountains. They drove in among an imposing array of jagged peaks which they fixed with astro-shots and surveyed. Running low on supplies, they returned to the depot for a refit and set out again the next day.

The second dog trip went as far as a third set of ranges, and here they found a mighty glacier running down to the Amery Lowland, which seemed to be the beginning of the vast, floating Amery Ice-Shelf pushing out to the coast between Mawson and the Vestfold Hills. They established a depot on top of the glacier, then descended almost three thousand meters over dangerously crevassed terrain. In the rugged mountains pushing their dark peaks through the inland ice, geologist Peter Crohn found deposits of coal, and several large frozen lakes, perfect for aircraft landings.

Having completed their survey they struggled back up the glacier with their heavy load, the men pulling alongside their five dogs. Crevasses blocked their progress on all sides, and only by probing every step, the dogs sniffing for danger, did they find their way through.

Determined to complete their program, they allowed themselves only a day's rest before setting out on the last field trip to the far ranges. And this time it was too much for Brownie, who died from exhaustion. Syd Kirby said afterward that it was Brownie's stupidity that killed him: he was willing enough, but always managed to fall into every crack and crevasse en route, just as he had done when we were looking for the Douglas Islands. When a crevasse had to be crossed, the other dogs made sure they had enough slack in their pulling traces before making the leap, and rarely had any trouble. Brownie never quite succeeded, although the men could feel the agonized concentration of his brain as he endeavored to calculate the exact length of trace needed to clear the crack. He would leap and, with a howl of fright, disappear down the crack, to be pulled up again by his harness. Although he was not as old as the rest of the team, Brownie became more and more exhausted by his repeated mishaps, and finally collapsed in his traces.

The loss of another dog was a severe blow, but the remaining four dogs did a magnificent job. To make things more difficult, on the return journey they had to plow through four days of softly falling snow. Again the men harnessed themselves alongside their dogs, until they reached the main depot.

Syd had completed eight astrofixes and Peter had made the first extensive geological survey of the Prince Charles Mountains. They had kept up their weather reports, and also charted the flow of the glaciers through the ranges and down to the coast, as well as collecting information on prevailing winds, snow-waves and glaciers. Their job was done.

The last few weeks of grueling work had taken their toll on the four dogs. Every ounce of spare flesh had been wasted from their bodies, and they looked like a pack of ravenous wolves. On the journey back to Mawson Oscar led the team, with Dee, the bitch I had spent so long training, pulling alongside him, sorely in need of a rest. The day came when there was a radio message to tell me that Dee was sick, and asking for advice. She had started passing blood, and I knew with an overpowering feeling of sadness there would be little hope of saving her. The following morning she was dead.

That camp was marked by a two-metre-high snow cairn built over Dee's body. Her never-failing willingness to work had endeared her to all the men. They decided to take the three remaining dogs on board the weasel-sleds, and let them ride the last hundred and fifty kilometers back to Mawson in relative comfort.

As the Southern Journey party straggled in to Mawson, confirmation arrived of my transfer to the new base in the Vestfold Hills. I had been accepted as weatherman and radioman, with charge of the dogs. The last few days of my year at Mawson sped by as the men who'd been on the Southern Journey filled us in with details of their adventure.

Then once again I boarded the *Kista Dan,* this time headed for the new base, Davis. With me were five dogs. Four of them were half-grown pups, six months old. The fifth was Oscar.

6
The Smallest Base

FOR the next three days the little red ship steamed east. We made the most of the fresh Danish food, canned beer and clean sheets on our bunks, which were made up by the ship's stewards every morning. After a year "on ice," the small luxuries felt wonderful.

To Oscar, a journey by sea was familiar enough and he spent most of his time dozing. But the young dogs were fascinated by the water rushing past, and they stood for hours with their paws on the rail, looking intently down at the sea.

While the *Kista Dan* steadily plowed through the long swell, I wrote letters and reorganized my gear. Most of the men with whom I'd spent the year on Mawson were also on board, but they were heading home, dreaming of fresh roast turkey, home-baked

Main photograph: The front of the Amery Ice-Shelf south of Mawson.
Top: Mawson Station in summer 1958, with the supply ship *Thala Dan* in harbor.
Below: The tide-crack, where the land-ice meets the shifting sea-ice, presents a daunting barrier to a sled.

Top: A weasel threads its way through large sastrugi.
Middle: Two newborn husky pups.
Bottom: Sledding on sea-ice with the edge of a glacier behind.

scones and fresh fruit. They thought I was odd. Only geologist Peter Crohn, from experience, reassured me about staying on for two years running, and building a new base from scratch.

"The second year is the best," he said simply.

At last the ship turned south again and approached the coast. One more night at sea, then we would be near enough to see the Vestfold Hills.

After an early breakfast of crusty bread, herrings and coffee with cream, we made our way up to the bridge. Ahead of us a barrier of ice appeared to block our path, but the little ship merely slowed down, then steamed steadily on. The flared bows rose steeply, then sank, as the first wide ice floe in front of the ship split with a crack like a rifle shot. Slowly, a few meters at a time, the *Kista Dan* forced her way all day through the heavy pack. Around us giant icebergs glittered blue-green and iridescent in the low night-sun.

With the dogs tethered around me on the forecastle, I gazed in the gathering darkness toward the distant smudge on the horizon which was the Vestfold Hills—over seven hundred and fifty square kilometers of bare rock. It looked like a lunar landscape, with low, rocky hills undulating like a boulder-strewn desert from the coast to the polar plateau forty-five kilometers inland.

The captain decided not to negotiate the field of giant icebergs skirting the base, and through the night we stayed in open water, steaming up and down and waiting for daylight. A brilliant moon cast a silvery, probing lance across the pack making the bergs look ghostly, while the rocky land stood out in sharp relief: blue-black shadows in gullies and crevices, the peaks and ridges highlighted by the pale moon glow.

A wet nose thrust itself into my hand, and two sturdy paws came to rest on the bulwark beside me. It was Nel, the little team bitch, who was studying the terrain with as much curiosity as I was, her eager nose twitching toward the shore. Then a great shaggy head rubbed against me as Oscar joined us at the rail. I reached across and scratched him behind the ears. At that moment, the wind picked up and an unmistakable smell wafted across on the offshore breeze—the terrible stink of elephant seals.

At dawn the ship turned and cautiously threaded her way among the great bergs toward the coast. Soon we pushed in among some of the outlying islands, broke through into open water and dropped anchor in a wide bay. The ship's hands swung two amphibious army landing boats called Duwks overboard, and I heard the leader's crisp order: "Get the dogs ashore in the first load."

Each dog was slung in his harness, and protesting strongly they were lowered into the waiting Duwk. As I joined them we cast off and steered for the cluster of newly erected huts above the beach. With a gentle bump the wheels hit the sand, and the amphibian rose out of the icy water and crawled ashore.

Above the beach, the huts had been erected on a rocky flat shelf. From there down to the beach was a rough track cleared through the boulder-strewn sandy slope. The landing beach itself was two hundred meters long, with the rocky land sloping upward on all sides, then leveling off in an undulating plateau which rose higher as it stretched in toward the polar icecap.

I was met by my four companions for the coming year: Bob Dingle, officer in charge and principal weatherman; Bruce Stinear, geologist; Alan Hawker, senior radioman; and Bill Lucas, diesel engineer.

Together we pegged the dogs and then walked up to the camp. There were three main huts for living quarters, which would all be joined by passages later, and two smaller ones to be used for stores and balloon-filling for meteorological work, as well as a tiny hut housing the auroral all-sky camera. The huts were made of panels with aluminum sheeting on the outside and plywood underneath, then, as insulation, a kind of cork compound pressed into blocks, and on the inside, plywood again. The whole structure was bolted together with long tie rods to keep each hut waterproof, snow-proof and airtight.

The sleeping hut was built specially to house five men. It was about seven meters by five, with five separate cubicles and a porch at one end leading into the adjacent mess hut and working quarters. Thermostatically controlled warm air was circulated at floor level through the center of the hut. Each sleeping cubicle was partitioned off by plywood walls and contained a bunk, a cupboard, a chest of drawers and a writing table with a small window above it. The door was just a curtained opening.

The community hut was much larger, and it was here that we

421

were to cook, eat and entertain ourselves in the long nights when work was over. One side, about a third of the area, was sectioned off into two rooms, one for the radio station and the other for the meteorological office. On the opposite side of the hut was a small storeroom where we kept food intended for immediate use. We jokingly called it "the music room" because it also housed our record player and records. Storage was very important in a small camp like ours, and every available space was taken up with shelves or cupboards. We had enough food for two years, in case the relief ship should fail to get through the ice the following summer.

The main living space in the community hut had a bright red linoleum floor, a table just big enough to seat half a dozen people comfortably, and tubular steel chairs. The other end of that room was occupied by a long kitchen work top, an electric cooking stove, a stainless steel sink and a fuel stove for emergency heating and cooking. Washup water simply ran through the plughole in the sink into a large red bucket. Plumbing to dispose of water beyond the hut walls would be useless, as any pipes brought out into the air would freeze solid.

The third large hut housed two diesel engines and a workshop, and the far end was partitioned off into a small porch, our back entrance, and a bathroom. Before emerging through the hut wall the exhaust pipes from the two diesels were brought through a large snow-melting tank to provide hot water, while the power from the engines gave our camp electricity for heating, cooking, lighting and radio communications. In the engineroom were two workbenches with vices, welding equipment and countless tools for carpentry and engineering.

Two smaller huts were apart from the rest. One was purely for storage, while the other was used for filling our weather balloons with hydrogen gas. The balloon filler stood in the center, and the rest of the space was crammed with bottles of hydrogen and more shelves.

Finally, there was the tiny hut which contained the all-sky camera, with a special lens that could take in the entire sky when photographing aurora. We had batteries and instruments for synchronization with similar cameras at other bases in Antarctica.

WE DIDN'T WASTE A second that first day. There were stores to be unloaded from the *Kista Dan* and stacked away, and there was a lot to be done inside the huts, which hadn't yet been wired for electricity. We worked till ten o'clock that night, then crawled into our bunks, dead tired.

Next morning we were up again at dawn. There were still more stores to be unloaded before the *Kista Dan* could sail, and it was not until three-thirty that afternoon that she weighed anchor and crawled out of the harbor. Slowly her red hull disappeared among the great icebergs floating majestically beyond the bay—a tiny speck in the vast expanse of ice and foam-flecked sea.

On the smallest base ever established in Antarctica, we had a huge job ahead to make everything operational before the onset of winter. The huts were not properly secured against wind and snow; one diesel badly needed an overhaul; our main transmitter was still in its crate; stores were stacked loosely all over the camp. Meanwhile weather observations and radio schedules had to be carried out, and a general routine kept going as we all got to know each other.

Bob Dingle and I were old Antarctic friends; this was his fourth expedition. Sandy-haired Bob was a good organizer, quietly capable of a tremendous amount of work—a sort of one-man expeditionary force. He was lean and muscular, of average height, and could walk the legs off anyone. He never seemed to relax, and never said much about himself, or much in criticism of anyone else.

Bruce Stinear, the geologist, at forty-one was the oldest of our party, with lots of experience in roughing it. He had served in the air force during the war and, like Bob, was not inclined to talk much. He was thin, wiry and dark-haired with a black mustache under a high-bridged, hooked nose.

Alan Hawker, senior radio officer, was twenty-six and the youngest in our party, although he had already spent a year at the Macquarie Island base. He came from Dimboola, Victoria, and was ardently interested in anything to do with radio. He was short, thickset and placid. Nothing worried him, and often he would sit and twiddle radio knobs till all hours of the night, talking to other "radio-hams" all over the world.

Of the five of us, our engineer Bill Lucas, who had never been to Antarctica before, was by far the jolliest. Nearly all the time he was laughing at, or with, someone. He was an unending source of amusement. We were sure his pants were lined with quicksilver as he could not sit still for two minutes, and always had some project or other which had to be done immediately. He seemed to be able to make almost anything from scrap materials and was a master at improvisation. He was tall, lantern-jawed, and grew a pointed beard. The effect was rather startling, because Bill was never able to do anything with his hair, which just sprouted all over his head. The happy-go-lucky effect was enhanced by two missing front teeth.

He hated politicians and parking attendants, followed by car dealers, "big business" and police. Many were the nights when we sat around the dinner table, quietly reading, when Bill would suddenly shout, "Knock 'em off!" or "We should blow the whole joint sky-high!" followed by a long tirade about the people or institutions that had offended his sense of balance in the world.

THIS then was Davis in January 1957. Our first day alone began at 7 o'clock.

"Our immediate task," said Bob at breakfast, "is to establish the station for the coming year. Then we can get on with the real work. I've listed our five main objectives." He began to read. "One—meteorology; two—to carry out as complete a geological survey as possible of the Vestfold Hills; three—synchronizing the all-sky camera with all other stations in Antarctica; four—biological survey, defining what wildlife exists on Antarctica at the various times of the year; and five—astrofixes."

We spent the first few months establishing the camp, but with the arrival of the sea-ice I was able to devote most of my time to exercising and training our young dog team. Every morning after an early breakfast the struggle was on. To train six-month-old dogs is the most exasperating, patience-testing work anyone could undertake.

By the time Oscar arrived at Davis he had done nearly six thousand five hundred kilometers of sled-hauling. He had kept his distant manner and, since becoming team leader, was jealous of his position: any attempt by another dog to challenge his privileges met with swift and merciless punishment. His willpower was stronger than ever, and with advancing years his cunning had increased. If he was not in the mood for sledding he would hare out onto the sea-ice at the beginning of a sledding run, look back over his shoulder and, if my attention seemed to be distracted, veer around, and lead the team straight back to camp. It became a battle of wits and will between driver and dog, and on a few occasions it was necessary to use the whip as punishment. Had I given way to Oscar he would have been my boss in no time at all. After his first few attempts at this trick, however, we reached an understanding, and he would lead the team as straight as an arrow.

To TEACH the team the difference between right and left I used the Eskimo words "illi" for right, and "eeouk" for left, commands learned in my youth from Ajungilak, my Eskimo friend. On one of his trips to Greenland my seafaring father, who was a great friend and admirer of the Eskimos, telegraphed my mother to say he was bringing a surprise home to Norway. No details. Just that cryptic message.

A couple of weeks later my father's ship docked in the river below us. I thought he would bring me another husky pup, which he had done on a previous trip, but as he came down the gangway he had in tow a young lad with a broad brown face, stockily built, and wearing a fur anorak. Father came down onto the wharf and pushed the young Eskimo before him. "This is Ajungilak, which means happy in Eskimo," he said. The broad face with slightly slanted eyes cracked in an enormous smile. He shook hands, and announced he was happy to be with us, although "it is so very 'ot here." He spoke a rough sort of Danish, interspersed with a few Eskimo words, close enough to our native Norwegian.

Father explained that he was to stay with us for a while, share my room, and go to school with me. He was about twelve years old, but might have been older—he never seemed too sure about his age.

Ajungilak had an unholy respect for my father, the captain of a big "umiak," or ship. We became firm friends, as I helped him with his schoolwork. The other pupils left him strictly alone after he flattened the school bully, much to my delight, and the teachers took an interest in such an unusual student.

425

We were encouraged to go camping, hunting and fishing, and also skiing as winter came on. I taught him all I knew. Ajungilak was absolutely tireless, as all the Eskimos are, and when the snow-falls got heavier he made a harness for my dog, a Greenland husky called Bjorn, as well as a Greenland-type sled. With this equipment we went off camping in the snow, often in the high country. We never carried a tent—Ajungilak was always able to find a big snowdrift into which we would tunnel a cave, or, if the snow was suitable, he would make an igloo, the most comfortable and snug shelter one could wish for. It was he who trained me (and Bjorn) in the finer points of dog-sledding. After some time of consistent effort the dog responded to the Eskimo commands for right and left. Ajungilak also taught me to make Eskimo-type harnesses from lampwick. His sled had no metal screws or nails in it, but was lashed together with rawhide, so it would "work" in uneven terrain.

As summer approached, Ajungilak became very restless. He was obviously homesick, missing the vast glaciers and fields of sea-ice of his native Greenland. Father sat us down one evening, and told us he was doing a run up to Greenland again. Would Ajungilak like to go home? The brown face split in that huge smile that we'd come to expect, and I knew I would lose my friend, probably for good. The next day the ship set sail with Ajungilak. I never saw him again.

AT DAVIS, if I wanted my young dogs to turn right, I ran on the left side of the team, brandishing the whip, and shouting, quickly and sharply: "Illi, Illi!" remembering my training all those years ago. The word for left, "eeouk", was a long, drawn-out sound, entirely different from the other command. The dogs soon learned to associate the two distinctive sounds with right and left, and knew that if they failed to turn I would come running up with the dreaded whip in my hand. For very sharp turns I would also lash the snow to either side, but after some time of intensive training I could sit on the sled and merely shout the commands, and the team, led by Oscar, would turn off in the required direction. To stop the sled, I would shout "whoa!" and stand back on the brake. To start them off, we used the tried and trusted "mush!"

426

Oscar had a remarkable sense of direction and an ability to follow old tracks. Without difficulty he could go straight back to the previous day's sledding, and instinctively knew when he was in dangerous country. When the going was easy the crafty old veteran would let his team do most of the work, his trace taut, but only just. But when the going was hard, Oscar's trace would be as tight as a violin string.

One cold, blustery morning, three of us harnessed the dogs for a trip on the plateau. We hoped to be able to mark out a safe route inland from the coast for future traverses by tracked vehicles in the following year. Oscar, as usual, was in the lead, this time on an extra long trace. We expected to strike crevasses, so he was put well out ahead.

The team climbed well, and we had covered some forty kilometers when we approached what we called "domed country", areas of icy domes with valleys snaking in between them. From long experience we knew this was a badly crevassed area. Bob decided that he should go out in front with a long probe to check for slots, so we tied a ten-metre nylon climbing rope to secure him to the sled in case he dropped through, and away he went with the dogs in hot pursuit.

Bob gradually led us further and further through the domed country, all the while probing with his ice spear for the telltale brittle crust hiding a deep crevasse. I sensed that Oscar was far from happy in these surroundings. He always displayed a keen "crevasse-sense," and now his head was moving from side to side, while he was continuously sniffing.

Suddenly, there was a great "whoosh" and Bob disappeared.

I stopped the sled, and secured it with ice spikes driven into the hard-packed snow. Then while Bruce kept the dogs quiet I did a very cautious belly-crawl up to the crevasse. Peering over the edge I spotted our pathfinder swinging on the end of his rope about ten meters down what appeared to be a bottomless chasm. I shouted to him to hang on, and retreated backward to the sled. There I grabbed two ice axes and crawled back to the crevasse, where I managed to slide them under the rope on the lip of the hole. The idea was to provide a smooth surface for the rope to run over, and also to prevent the rope from cracking the ice under the sled and landing us all in the crevasse.

427

From there on it was largely up to Oscar and his team. Gingerly we turned the dogs and sled around and slipped the ice spikes. Oscar knew what was expected of him. He turned that great shaggy head and looked at me with complete under-standing.

"Mush, Oscar!" I yelled, and with that he threw himself into the traces with all his tremendous power, the other dogs follow-ing his example. We were all rigid with fear, knowing one move-ment in the wrong direction meant the end.

It was a bit like drawing a cork out of a champagne bottle, even to the last "pop!" as Bob suddenly appeared out of the hole, unceremoniously dragged by Oscar and his team.

THE youngsters pulled extremely well considering they were only six months old at the start of the sledding season, and grad-ually I instilled some discipline into their unruly heads. The small team all came from one of Oscar's litters: Nel, the little team bitch; Nils, a heavy, nuggety young dog; Peter, of finer build, but without doubt the most consistent and hardest worker of them all; and Phil, a big shambling clown, always with a grin on his face. Oscar too kept discipline among his small family: either on the run or at camp he stood no nonsense from the pups.

Lovable, friendly, affectionate, yes—but, oh, how hopelessly tangled they could get in the traces, and how they taxed my patience and strength in the beginning. I would run, ride for a while, run again, stop, disentangle traces, heave aside eager youngsters trying to lick my face after they'd received a hiding; I would curse, yell, pat, crack the whip, kick bottoms and nearly burst into tears. Then with a shout of "Mush! Mush!" we would be off again—heads down, tails curled over backs, taut traces, and perfect formation in a steady trot, while I would sit exhausted on the sled, sweat streaming into my eyes and beard, feebly fishing out my pipe and tobacco.

Apart from the training, the dogs were not much trouble to look after. So long as they had their food they were quite happy, whether in good or bad weather. Traveling in the field, their fuel consumption was about two kilos of seal meat a day, or less than one kilo of special dog-pemmican. On this they were able to keep going all day at a cruising speed of about ten kilometers an hour with a fully loaded sled. In good weather, on good ice, and with a lighter load they could easily reach a speed of sixteen kilometers an hour.

At Davis during the better weather we tied them up along a strong chain that was held steady by two big drums, one at each end, sunk into the ground and filled with rocks. In this way, spaced along the chain, they could move freely without getting at each other and starting a fight. When the weather worsened we gave each of them an empty packing case for shelter, but usually the blizzards didn't worry the huskies very much, and they used their packing cases to store their meat, or lift their legs against. They were quite happy and warm as long as they could burrow into the snow.

After a while Bruce joined me and the dog team, and we began an early exploration program. With Bruce weighing down the sled and riding the brake when necessary, I was able to concentrate entirely on training the youngsters as a team. I tried several combinations, but finally adapted a sort of elongated fan-system, where the first three dogs were fanned out in front, and the others paired behind. Oscar's trace was the longest, then came Nils and Nel slightly behind him, then Peter and Phil beside each other.

Within a week we achieved wonders. Discipline, stamina and speed developed, and Oscar responded to whip and word alike. During the first few days of April, we completed eighty kilometers of local reconnaissance trips, just getting familiar with the territory. We surveyed the track inland up a long, hook-shaped fjord running along the Sorsdal Glacier at the extreme south-southwest end of the Vestfold Hills landmass. With the team improving daily, we ranged far and wide, through islands, beaches, bays and fjords, doing geological and biological surveys and map checking. We were ready for our first serious journey.

7
The Edge of the Land

WE WERE nearing the end of autumn, and the Antarctic winter was about to put its icy grip on the great continent. As soon as I had finished my next rostered week's cooking duty, Bruce and I were to set out on our first overnight sledding journey to establish a food and fuel depot along the coast on the northeastern extremity of the Vestfold Hills. We hoped to take only three days, but in case the weather and ice surfaces were poor, we had to be prepared to be away longer. It was April 15 when we set out for our first depot run from Davis.

The sled was a three-and-a-half-metre hickory Nansen-sled, made in Norway. Its runners were covered in plastic, and it was lashed together with rawhide to make it flexible. The driver, standing on the platform behind the handlebars at the back, could operate a very efficient brake, a long spike which dug into the ice. There were three light boxes on the sled for provisions, while the polar tent, axe, shovel, marker poles and other odds and ends were lashed on with rope.

Amid their usual excited howls the team was harnessed, I cracked the whip, and despite the heavy load, the youngsters took off like a rocket. Soon we were past the last point previously covered in our training runs, heading seaward around the far side of the coastal islands. The morning breeze had dropped, and it was sufficiently calm to allow us to keep the map case open on top of the load.

Presently we came to an area of "tombstone" country, where the sea-ice had been forced shoreward by great pressure over shallow water. The ice was pushed up to form rough, man-high masses—very difficult terrain to cross.

There were, however, narrow jumbled channels between the broken ice, and we urged the dogs through them, Oscar carefully leading the way. A few kilometers further on we came to a stop in front of an awesome spectacle. Hundreds of icebergs of the most fantastic shapes blocked our path. They had moved inshore during summer and now extended in an almost unbroken line from the coast to the open sea. It looked discouraging, but then we spotted a slight thinning in the number of bergs further out to sea. The ice was very young, and around the tide-cracks at the foot of the bergs water could be seen.

We swung the team toward a narrow opening to seaward, and shortly after we were in a different world of silent, brooding, eerie giants—the guardians of the coastal ramparts of ice. The stillness was threatening, and the dogs too seemed to fear this spectacle of towering ice all around. Now Oscar came into his own. His shaggy head moved from side to side, discarding blind alleys that led only into blue walls of ice. His instinct made him plunge ahead through narrow passages just wide enough for us. We passed between a split berg nearly eighty meters high, with two cathedral-size pinnacles pointing accusing fingers to the sky.

It was terrifying. I knew that at any moment these pinnacles could crash down and pulverize everything beneath them. But gradually the narrow passages became wider and we emerged on the other side. As we looked back we saw a seemingly impenetrable wall of ice, beautiful but frightening in its blending of light and shadow.

We were still on the new black ice, thin enough for the dark water to be visible through it, but now we headed back toward the coast. Far ahead we could see the northeastern end of the Vestfold Hills, our destination, where the last of this enormous rock area was swallowed up by the continental ice sheet. Before long the ice sheet and its nunataks, or mountain-heads, rose immediately in front of us, blocked by a fair-sized island straddling the bottom of the fjord. The sun was about to set, and our luck was in: the lee side of the island offered a likely campsite— a low saddle between two high points, and a wide, snow-covered slope leading up to it.

The dogs sensed the end of a long pull. Their tails curled up and, with a last burst, we crossed a mushy, waterlogged tide-crack. While Bruce unloaded the sled and carried the gear up to our campsite, I unharnessed the dogs and staked them out along our mooring wire. Then they received their ration of pemmican, and were soon curled up in the snow like balls of fur.

Not long after we had the tent pitched, darkness settled over the ice. Like flickering fireflies, four snow petrels flitted across the rocks, giving the only touch of movement to the awesome stillness of the landscape. Snuggled into our sleeping bags, warm and weary, we fell to reminiscing, telling each other stories from our pasts.

Over the next few days we explored and collected samples. We established a depot, weighed down with rocks and marked with a bamboo pole and red pennant. Our final job was to build a marked cairn on top of the island for a future fixed point. As the last day of our expedition died in a blaze of color to the west, I fed the dogs and we retired to the tent. We fell asleep to the gentle chatter of our small neighbors, the snow petrels, nesting under the boulders nearby.

AFTER this trip we settled back into camp life at Davis for a short time. We had plenty to do with the daily chores, radio schedules and weather observations. I overhauled traces, harnesses, sled and camping gear in preparation for the next journey.

On April 21, we circumnavigated the outer islands again to do a fauna count. During the trip we saw hundreds of elephant seals on the move toward the open sea. In a small area we counted ninety-eight seals, some lumbering clumsily toward the open water, others just resting on the sea-ice. We went across to Magnetic Island and found a blowhole where we saw the only Weddell seal of that trip. He was a rather incongruous sight, suddenly popping his head up through his breathing hole, viewing the approaching dog team with an unblinking stare from his round, saucerlike eyes. Perhaps he knew that we had no harpoon with us, because it was not until he saw Oscar's slavering jaws that he disappeared with a contemptuous splash.

On May 1, in the afternoon, the first of three Beaver flights from Mawson landed at Davis, bringing as visitors the pilot, a radio operator, a surveyor, as well as Wombat, an extra dog. We tried out Wombat with my team, and he proved completely useless, although I had been assured that he pulled well. Wombat pulled, certainly—but backward. This got too much for young Nils, who promptly got stuck into Wombat and gave him a thorough thrashing, later helped with enthusiasm by Phil and Peter before I stepped in and separated them. Order restored, we proceeded on our way, with Wombat still pulling strongly, backward.

Finally I tied him to the rear of the sled, where he trotted along quite happily. This was a great disappointment, as time was too short to train him before our next longer journey. So we asked for old Horace, who was flown across on the following flight. He appeared to be as fit as a fiddle, despite having done no work since his return from the Southern Journey the previous season at Mawson. Unlike Wombat he assimilated right away and pulled in his customary position just in front of the sled. Now we had a strong team of six dogs, and for emergencies we had Wombat.

But it wasn't long before trouble broke out. Continuing our survey work, I had been on a reconnaissance trip in the Beaver. As we touched down on the sea-ice back at the camp, Bill, one of the visitors, rushed out to greet us.

"Oscar and Horace have had a fight," he shouted. "Horace got loose and attacked Oscar, and they had a fair set-to before we could separate them. Looks like Horace is making a bid for leadership."

"Any damage?" I asked.

"Horace is covered in blood around the head, but I think it is Oscar's. He got a good grip on Oscar's ear and ripped it half off," Bill replied.

"Well," I said, "this means trouble on the next trip unless they sort it out before we leave. If they clash again, let them finish it."

The other dogs were restless, and leapt around on their chains. They sensed a battle for supremacy, and their blood-lust was up. Oscar kept shaking his head, glaring down at Horace, who, full of confidence after drawing blood, stood on his hind legs and howled defiance. Wombat, chained at the far end of the dog line for his own protection, had retreated the full length of his chain, trying to appear as inconspicuous as possible. Poor Wombat, none of the others ever missed an opportunity to bite or slash at him.

"I'll have a bet on Horace," said Bill. "These Mawson dogs are surely superior to your Davis ones."

"Nonsense!" I said hotly. "Oscar will belt the hide off him. It's just a shame for Horace's sake that he is dumb enough to challenge Oscar. You wait and see. But we won't have any peace in the team until they settle it one way or the other."

We picked up our gear and went up for dinner.

Washing up afterward, we were rudely interrupted by a sudden terrible din from the dog lines. Bill took a quick look through the window. "It's on!" he shouted, and we rushed out, the dishes left floating in the grimy water.

This time both Oscar and Horace had managed to get off their chains at the same time, and had joined battle on the long smooth snowdrift below the dog lines.

"Let them fight," I yelled, as some of the men tried to rush in to separate the dogs. I had the long dog-whip in my hand, ready to subdue the victor before he killed his adversary. "Now,

433

just watch the work of an expert," I added, pointing at Oscar.

We watched the preliminaries—the stiff-legged strutting, deep-throated growls, fangs bared. Both dogs were old and battle-wise. Both weighed nearly sixty kilos. Oscar was the big, rangy dog; Horace was deep-chested, squat and powerful. He had a shorter muzzle, almost like a bear, and a manelike ruff round his thick neck. Oscar, in battle, looked like one of his wolfish ancestors, every muscle in his powerful body tensed, the hackle along his back bristling, his wounded ear flat against his head and his slanting eyes bloodshot with rage.

The two dogs made several false rushes at each other, then Horace came in low, making a bid for Oscar's bleeding ear. Oscar leapt aside, spun in mid-air, and with a lightning slash opened a long gash in Horace's shoulder. Roaring with rage, Horace blindly charged again, but this time Oscar did not leap aside. He crouched and met the charge low down.

"This is it," I thought.

Oscar's fangs closed on Horace's chest, and both dogs rose in the air as Oscar lifted his adversary to throw him on his back. This normally would have determined the winner, but Horace was tough: he let himself be felled, but at the same time somersaulted backward. Oscar lost his grip, leaving a bloody gash in the other dog's chest. Growling and panting the two huskies circled again.

"Second round," said Bill. "I wish you'd stop them, Nils, they'll kill each other."

"No," I replied. "Don't worry, I won't let Horace get killed."

Again and again Horace charged, each time suffering cruel slashes from Oscar, who obviously was saving his strength for the final onslaught. Oscar too had received several vicious bites and thrusts, and the other dogs were wild with excitement, the smell of fresh blood driving them to a frenzy. I had witnessed fights to the death where, as soon as one dog was felled, the pack would rush in and pull the loser to pieces.

At last Horace seemed to tire. His charges were less frequent, and delivered with more caution. The dogs met in a head-on charge and, like bears, fought on their hind legs, each having hold of the other's ear. The snow around looked like a plowed field, with blood spattered on its pure white. Then, as if by mutual agreement, both dogs let go again and circled.

"Round three," breathed Bill.

Again the false rushes, then Oscar met Horace's charge almost flat on the ground. With a furious roar he sank his fangs in Horace's throat, rose on his hind legs, and with a vicious twist threw the other dog on his back, straddling him. With cruel slashings Oscar raked his soft belly, the complete master.

It was the end of the battle. Feebly Horace struggled, and his growls of defiance turned into howls and whimpers. Before Horace's spirit could be broken, I let the long whip whistle over Oscar, and each dog was grabbed by the men and put back in place along the chain.

The victor and the vanquished licked their wounds, and the other dogs soon quieted down. The dogs on either side of Oscar tried to reach him in order to pay homage, but the old leader was in no mood for frivolities. A deep growl was enough to send them cowering back.

Oscar had become king of the huskies. No dog would ever challenge his supremacy again.

8
Walkabout Rocks

TWO DAYS LATER, we had another visit from the Beaver, this time with two physicists aboard. Blizzards at Mawson delayed their departure for home, and we decided that Dave Gallow, who was in charge of the auroral program, should help us check the operation of our all-sky camera. The next few days were spent exercising the dog team, building survey-cairns up and down the coast, and preparing for a much longer journey into the far northeast of the Vestfold Hills. Even with the depot already established, our load would be close to four hundred kilos, but with old Horace added to the team, and the sledding surfaces on the sea-ice greatly improved, we felt we could confidently expect each dog to pull about seventy kilos. The night before departure we packed the sled and gave the dogs a mighty feed of fresh seal meat.

After an early breakfast, we harnessed the team and set off north along the coast. It felt good to be on the move again, and Bruce grinned at me as we ran beside the sled. Soon we plunged in among the enormous field of icebergs, this time taking the inshore route. On smooth blue ice we headed toward Depot Island, where we could see the small red pennant fluttering above our cache of food and fuel.

Morris, one of the men from Mawson, had come out with Bruce and me, and we could hear his breath rasping in his throat. "Never," said Morris, as he sat exhausted on the sled, "did I realize that driving dogs could be so tiring!"

We arrived at our depot camp in record time, and had the best part of the afternoon to prepare for the coming evening's astro-fix. As we erected our tent, Morris unpacked his survey-gear and set up theodolite and chronometer. By 9 p.m. Morris had his fix, and after a huge meal we all collapsed into our bags. Outside, our dogs were curled up in a big snowdrift.

While Morris spent the next day in camp trying to get a time-signal for his chronometer, Bruce and I set off on foot to find a possible route through the ice-choked entrance to Tryne Fjord. Bruce, as always, carried his geological hammer and sample bags. When we returned to the friendly-looking camp after a twenty-kilometer walk, Morris had a hot drink and dinner ready.

The following day we hoped to locate records left by the explorer Sir George Hubert Wilkins in an area further north. Bruce carried the available information in his map-case, and that evening we studied it over our strong black coffee. We had to make an early start because the round-trip would be about twenty-five kilometers through rough ice, and we also needed time to look for the records. Mid-May was rather late in the year for traveling, as daylight was less than five hours and growing progressively shorter.

We had our breakfast in darkness, and left with a light load on the sled in the gray Antarctic dawn. As the light slowly increased, the faintly luminous icebergs served as landmarks on our north-easterly course. A tortuous winding track led us out onto the big, frozen fjord, and we all rode the sled for a while. Presently we encountered areas of refrozen sea-ice where small sharp floes jutted up in all directions. Time after time the dogs' traces became stuck until finally I ran with the team, holding the traces off the ice. Often during the crossing the sled capsized, but at last we were free, and could see a giant, dark bluff ahead, its dome lit by the dawn.

By the time we reached the foot of the bluff, and had the dogs pegged out on the ice below, it was midday, and full daylight. Seams of black basalt ran from the top to the bottom of the big bluff, and to the left were several smaller bluffs. We had to investigate every one of them.

"We'd better spread out," said Bruce. He and Morris started to climb the main bluff, while I tackled one to the left. While I was struggling for hand- and footholds near the top, an exultant yell from Morris distracted my attention, and I landed in a heap at the foot of the bluff. He and Bruce, atop the other bluff, were performing a sort of Indian war dance, a small flag fluttering gaily from Morris's outstretched hand. They had found the records. Forgetting my bruises, I scrambled up to join them.

While Bruce had been busy knocking specimens off a large rock formation, Morris had poked around and found a small crevice under the rock. He stuck his hand in and hauled out an ordinary brown paper parcel, tied with string. The parcel contained an enamel cylinder with a typewritten statement by Sir George Hubert Wilkins, in which he claimed the land for the King, dated January 11, 1939. With the records was a small Australian flag, and an issue of the Australian geographical magazine *Walkabout*, dated October 1, 1938.

Reverently, we sat down and inspected the contents. We were looking at a piece of history, proof that men of vision and enterprise had laid claim before us to that great slice of frozen continent, which since had been established as Australian Antarctic Territory.

Bruce wrote a note, stating that the records had been found by us, May 10, 1957, as representatives of the Australian National Antarctic Research Expedition, based at Davis, and ended with our names. Then we resealed the package and put it back into the crevice.

Exactly twenty years later, I was approached by the Antarctic Division and asked to provide guidelines for the men at Davis to find the documents. I sent them a map and my diary with a description of the approach and the bluff, and now, to my delight, they are stored as historical documents in Canberra. The men who found the records, still wrapped in the old issue of *Walkabout*, named the surrounding bluffs "Walkabout Rocks."

9
The Long Night

ON MAY 27, the glowing disk of the sun rose briefly for the last time at Davis, and for many months we were to walk in darkness. The winter was the worst time of the year in Antarctica. It was always dark, always night, and there were frequent blizzards. And it was bitterly cold; the temperature often dropped as low as sixty degrees below freezing on the coast. Inland on the icecap it was very much colder; no life could exist.

Until July 16, the sun disappeared completely from our sight, and we were left with barely an hour of dusky twilight in the middle of the day. The rest of the time it was completely dark.

As the long night fell, snow gradually built up around the camp area. We kept shoveling it from the windward side of the huts, where an enormous drift had built up, almost reaching to roof height. We had another blizzard, and from then on we entered and left the living hut through a tunnel. We merely had to open the door to enter a dark cavern in the solid wall of snow, and gradually the cavern was enlarged until it provided us with an extra storeroom, and a source of drinking and cooking water.

Each day, as soon as the darkness lifted to a murky twilight, I put on a parka and mukluks and walked across the hard-packed drifts to the dog lines. Nel and Oscar spotted me first with excited howls, followed by all the rest. I recognized each dog's voice, and I grinned to myself as Oscar's full-throated, bass roar almost drowned the high-pitched howls of Nel and the younger dogs. Except for Wombat, who lived in terror of attracting any attention, they ran in circles, stood on their hind legs, pawed the air and kept up an incessant din while I dragged out a seal carcass. The din grew even greater as I chopped off large chunks and threw one to each dog; as the last dog was fed there was utter silence, broken only by the cracking of bones and frozen meat.

I would walk along and pat each dog in turn, but they never paused in their savage wolfing down of the frozen meat. Only Phil, an enormous dog, would get off his haunches and give me a lick. He was always hungry and looking for extra meat, practically turning himself inside out with gratitude and wanting me to stay and play with him. Often I let good-natured Nel off the chain for a run, confident that she would not go far or come to any harm. She raced delightedly up and down, flirting with the dogs and investigating the whole camp.

But for long, long hours each day of that endless winter, we stayed in the hut breathing the stale air, simply awaiting the sun's return, unable to break the tedious monotony. All we had to do were routine jobs such as cooking—each taking a turn to do a week of it, beginning at lunchtime on Sunday and ending the following Saturday night.

It is difficult to say who was the best cook, because we each had our own way of going about it, and we each liked different things. As soon as Bob's week came around we feasted on Cornish pasties . Bob took his pasties very seriously, and nobody dared to compete with him. Alan was good at tasty rissoles and stews, and colossal sandwiches in which the ingredients seemed to come from every food packet in the entire store. Bruce concentrated on macaroni, while I used to serve seal-meat steaks, and marinated seal liver.

Bill had a passion for sweet things and during his turn as cook he seemed to make nothing but ice cream. One day, close to midwinter, he made up a huge quantity and as usual put the mixture out in the snow to set. Nel found it. Through the windows we were entertained by the sight of an enraged cook floundering through deep snow trying vainly to catch Nel, from whose mouth the tea towel that had covered the bowl fluttered gaily. Traces of ice cream were smeared all over her muzzle. At last Bill admitted defeat and returned, giving me a baleful glare.

"You and your damned dogs," he shouted furiously. "I'll never make ice cream again!"

When we were fed up with listening to records or the short-wave radio, we often read. Books on Antarctica and the Arctic were very popular; we enjoyed the works of famous Antarctic explorers such as Shackleton, Amundsen, Scott, Nansen and Mawson. We also had a chess set, Scrabble and cards. But it became progressively harder to fill in the long nights which seemed to us to be getting longer, rather than shorter.

DURING the midwinter the dogs had very little exercise and put on a good deal of weight. The pups grew into big dogs, chesty and well muscled, and they were all fighting fit. None of the harnesses fitted the young ones anymore, and I had to make new sets. At last, on July 8, the morning dawned fine and cloudless with a temperature of forty-six degrees below freezing. The team was harnessed at dawn, about 9:30, and I had a team of howling, leaping huskies raring to go. Even Oscar lost all his decorum and was standing on his hind legs, mad with excitement. I slipped the moorings, yelled "Mush!" and hurled myself on the sled. From the dog lines down to the sea-ice, where there was now a long, hard-packed snow slope, we hurtled along at breakneck speed. We hit the sea-ice with the speed of an express train, the dogs running flat out and in perfect formation.

Out over the sea-ice the frantic pace continued, and I felt a savage joy at being free. Forgotten in an instant was the long winter, the gloom and the stale air in the living quarters. I felt alive again, and the dogs seemed to feel the same release from the weeks spent chained up in darkness. We set course for Mule Island, a short run southwest of Davis. The day was beautiful, with sparkling cold air, and fantastic red and orange colors from the sun below the horizon. And on a tiny islet northwest of Mule Island I was amazed to find twenty-one huge elephant seals, proof for the first time that sea elephants wintered in the Antarctic.

After five carefree, golden days, the weather closed in again. Imprisoned once more in the cabin, we fell to talking about the dogs, their individual traits and characters, and in particular, whether they could think. I believed that they could, or that at least our huskies could, and that they could even plan ahead, particularly Oscar. That week he proved it.

When in base camp, the dogs were staked out on a long solid chain with short chains holding each individual dog's collar. These were horse-chains, absolutely necessary to contain the combined power of a whole mob of excited huskies. But then one evening, Oscar got loose. He had a marvelous time for a dog, settling old scores, eating everything in sight, scouring the whole camp. I thought it was just an accident, and after securing him on the chain again, I checked the clip, but it was fine.

The next day Oscar was loose again. Four times that week he got loose, plainly more than coincidence, and I had to listen to rude remarks about a dog's intelligence being greater than my own. Stung, I decided to keep watch. As long as we had any light, I stood out of sight, observing the dog lines. Oscar picked a time when the camp was quiet; then as I watched in amazement, he turned round and round in the same spot, twisting his short chain until it was only as long as my thumb. The rest was easy. With a sharp jerk, using his tremendous strength, he made the clip fly open. That was all the proof I needed. Oscar could think.

Blizzards howled across the camp and the polar winds drove snow into every crack and crevice, packing it as hard as concrete. And we waited once again. But in the few calmer periods we could feel a new lightness—a vague promise that the long night was coming to an end.

10
Life Returns

As I had calculated, we ran out of our stored-up seal meat in mid-September, and from then on we depended entirely on meat hunted with the dog team, far out among the icebergs. Our first kill for the new season was a huge old Weddell bull, which took three men to load on the sled, and the dogs were stretched to the utmost pulling it home.

September merged into October, and each clear day I went out hunting. Odd days of snow, drift and strong wind reminded me that summer was still far off, but signs of spring were all around us. In singles, pairs, groups and regiments the Adélie penguins were on the march across the great ice. With a terrible urgency, driven by an instinctive, compelling force, the small black white-breasted birds hurried toward the coast to breed and rear their young during the short Antarctic spring and summer. Sometimes waddling upright with their comical drunken sailorlike gait, sometimes propelling themselves on their smooth shirtfronts using their back legs, they steered a straight course across the sea-ice to their old individual nesting sites on the islands or the coast.

Out on the dogsled, I drove around the outer islands through small armies of scattered penguins. The young dogs were frantic with excitement, particularly Nel, who simply could not pass a penguin without trying to grab it. Oscar knew that an attack on a wandering penguin while sledding would bring swift punishment, and it was enough to shout a command to him whenever

441

any of his team could no longer control the killer instinct. If Nel dashed off to the left after a penguin, Oscar would simply wait till her trace was tight, then give a sudden jerk to the right. Nel would be pulled clean off her feet, and a growl from the leader would quickly bring her back in line.

The penguins had come from ice floes that moved freely in the open water, far from the Antarctic coast. Every year it was the same, the birds returning by instinct to the same nest, if possible with the same mate. We watched them for hours, fascinated by their humorous antics and their devotion to their mates. They were like proud little old men, waddling among the rocks with their backs straight and their chests thrown out.

First they built their nests—a neat ring of small stones or pebbles. They dashed here and there among the rookeries, picking up walnut-sized pieces of rock in their beaks and carrying them carefully back to the nests. Each stone was examined by their mate, who either accepted it and added it to the collection, or rejected it out of hand. A lot of stealing went on by the more enterprising birds: as soon as one penguin's back was turned, another would rush in and steal one of its stones, more often than not while the first penguin was doing the same to the thief's nest.

Their courting was a ritual, held in daylight among the rocks and snow. In their thousands they paired off, male and female, making a peculiar squawking, cawing cry. They looked as if they were kissing, with their beaks touching, and their calls could be heard all along the coast, reverberating from the steep cliffs of the islands.

They were brave little birds, guarding their eggs and young against marauding birds, and from traitors among themselves. They resolutely attacked me if I came too close to their nests. Both males and females took turns sitting on the nest, and during the incubation period of about thirty days it was never left unguarded. Usually two eggs were laid—single ones were an exception.

To do a complete check on the rookeries, I skirted all the coastal islands to seaward right down to the Sorsdal Glacier, where I landed on the southernmost outcrop of the Vestfold Hills. Some of the penguins were already occupying their old nests, while others were still arriving, springing straight up out of the water in an arc and landing on their two feet on firm ground.

Luckily I got back to Davis before the weather broke once again. Dark heavy clouds rolled up while the barometer took an ominous dive, and the wind gradually rose to screaming fury. Soon the land and the ice were obliterated in swirling, blinding snow, heavy and clogging, building up colossal drifts within minutes. It was a typical spring blizzard. For three solid days it blew with undiminished force, the hurricane gusts moaning and shrieking through guy ropes and antennae. A couple of empty fuel drums disappeared from the stack on the beach, the wind lifting them clean over the top of two of the islands offshore.

Confined to the living quarters again, we began to dream of all sorts of freedom, hating the restricted space and the weather that kept us there. One night, when the hut filled with cooking aromas, my mouth watered as I thought of all the foods I missed. As if he'd read my thoughts, Alan, who was at the stove thoughtfully stirring a bubbling pemmican stew, looked at Bruce and said: "What would you like for your first big meal when you get home?"

Bruce heaved a big sigh and said, "A whopping big fresh garden salad, I think. A glass of fresh milk, or better still a vanilla milk shake, and bags of fresh mangoes, pineapple, oranges and crisp apples."

Alan grinned. "I'm going to book into the best hotel I can find, and have fried chicken and champagne for breakfast—in bed. Pork chops and whisky for lunch, still in bed. Then I'll slowly get up, dawdling as much as I like and have a long hot bath. Then down to the bar for cocktails and nuts, and then I'll entertain all my friends to the best dinner money can buy!"

By this time, Bill was bursting with ideas. "Here's my menu," he announced. "Pheasant cooked in wine, and stuffed with bacon and mushrooms; around it there'll be french fried potatoes, fresh garden peas, tomatoes, and rich brown gravy made with wine. For sweets, just two huge peaches, perfectly ripened, taken from the tree that evening. Turkish coffee, Drambuie and a really good cigar. And as for the company, none of you!"

At that moment, the stew bubbled up to the top of the pot, dribbling all down the sides and making a sloppy brown stain on the stove top. We all groaned; pemmican had never tasted so horrible as it did that night.

443

Main photograph: Setting up for an evening astrofix.
Above left: A young elephant seal.
Above right: Adélie penguins diving into the sea.
Far right: (top) Icebergs in the light of the midnight sun.
(Center) Oscar with friend at Davis in January 1958.
(Bottom) Davis base in summer.

After the blizzard, we found that a small group of Adélie penguins had sheltered at the bottom of the snow slope below the dog lines. Squatting with their backs to the wind, they let the tempest rage over and around them. When the wind dropped they all set off again on their journey to the rookeries, leaning sideways into the gusts like sailors on a heaving deck.

Two days later, the dogs' main mooring chain broke at one end, and the team grabbed this golden opportunity to attack Wombat. His terror of the other dogs had grown daily, and he simply didn't have the will to defend himself. By the time I arrived on the scene, lengths of chain were wrapped around him and vicious bite marks were all over his body. Wombat was dead.

FROM the last few days of November to the middle of January, I reveled in the continuous light of the short Antarctic summer. At midnight the low disk of a golden sun brought out the offshore icebergs in sharp relief, casting long blue-black shadows behind them. The south and west sides of islands and bergs glittered in the night-sun, and the clouds above were changed into fairy-tale gossamer veils of the most beautiful pastels. The South Land was a place of great beauty and infinite peace.

Late one such night with Alan I headed to base at a terrific pace on evening frost with a seal on the sled. I glanced at the meter on the sled and gave an exultant yell, startling Alan.

"What's the matter?" he cried. "What's gone wrong?"

"A thousand miles of sledding," I shouted, hardly able to believe it. We both looked ahead at the running dogs, fanned out in perfect formation, hauling the two of us and a big Weddell seal with nonchalant ease, every pulling trace taut.

"Yes," said Alan, reading my thoughts. "They've come a long way in the last year. When they first started training we never thought you'd be able to knock them into this kind of shape."

I thought of the many short and long trips we had made, of our ambitious desire to visit the entire Vestfold Hills area, to explore the reach of the fjords, the island guard, the land behind, all of which we had achieved. More than sixteen hundred kilometers: a thousand miles of sea-ice travel. A thousand miles of sun and wind, of darkness and light, of violent blustery days with wind-driven snow and stinging numbing cold, and of better days and nights with a slight breeze ruffling the dogs' fur and a brilliant sun glittering on ice-crystals under a cloudless sky. A thousand miles of living.

Day after day the sun beat down on the great ice and the rocky land. The snowdrifts around the camp grew smaller, and out on the sea-ice the measuring stakes planted when we arrived quietly emerged. Lookout Lake, Station Lake and Camp Lake finally appeared as the ice melted. Large deep cracks and pools of water lay around the frozen-in icebergs, and the open sea sent long probing fingers from the ice edge toward the coast. Hungrily the sea pressed inshore, gradually breaking off more and more of the outer edge, which was swept away to join the moving pack ice.

Day and night the birds were feeding along the ice edge: cape pigeons, storm petrels, giant petrels, penguins, and skuas. Often as we drove along, Adélie penguins would shoot out of the water and land with a plop and a flutter on the ice to stare at the odd caravan driving past only a few meters away. On our trips south along the coast we were gradually forced further and further inshore by the receding ice. The big bergs around which we had cheerfully driven during the dark winter months could now be seen as floating castles glittering on the far western horizon.

We made our last geological journey in December, to Bluff Island, where we climbed the steep cliff face to observe the cape pigeons. The birds were sitting tight on their first eggs, squirting a stinking reddish spit on any intruder with amazing accuracy over a distance of two meters. From Bluff Island we circumnavigated the outer islands then steered toward the coast again.

Soon after, we entered a subsidiary fjord system on beautiful, fast surfaces. The Weddell seal pups there had grown into "porkers", snoozing peacefully in the sun, many of them already independent of their mothers. We left the sea-ice and drove ashore at the end of a fjord arm, where Alan stayed to look after the dogs while I tramped a short distance inland.

An hour or so later as I was walking back to the sled I heard a terrible ruckus, and topping a ridge saw my beloved, well-trained team trying to climb the rocks, sled and all, to find out where I had gone. The dogs completely ignored Alan who, helplessly tangled up in dogs and traces, was being dragged along the ground like a sack of potatoes, trying to shout commands, stop

447

the team and get back on his feet. Finally, before he was dragged onto hard rock, I roared at the top of my voice from about a hundred meters away: "Sit!" Six bottoms immediately plonked down on the ground, six tails wagged in unison, six pairs of pricked ears and bright eyes listened and looked in all innocence as I clambered down to be greeted by a bruised and red-faced Alan.

"I had my arms wrapped around Oscar," he shouted in fury, "but the old devil just walked off with me!" Trying not to let my amusement show, I untangled the traces and freed Alan, turning the sled homeward as I did so. With relief we sat on the box soaking up the warm sun, relaxing while the docile dog team ran us back to base.

As the days passed well into December the temperature rose to above freezing, at least in the daytime, and soon we could hear and see water running everywhere. The big snowdrifts melted before our eyes, and finally our snow tunnel collapsed: for the first time since the middle of May we could open our entrance door, and let the sun and fresh air stream into the mess hut. The dogs had a wonderful time digging great holes in the soft, mushy snow, and as the drifts melted I moved them around to keep them on clean snow as long as possible.

On December 17, I made the last sledding run on sea-ice for the year. With Alan, I set off in lovely sunny weather with my team of eager dogs. Keeping well in from the outer edge we were gradually forced inshore by the open water, which now extended far into the Mule Island Group, leaving most of Elephant Island, Hawker Island and big Mule Island in open water.

During the first two weeks of December, sun and wind had wreaked havoc on the sea-ice. Just south of Elephant Island we came to a rather wide lead, a crack with black water swirling along its sharp edges. The lead was three meters across at the narrowest part. Our sled was four meters long, so we knew we would just make it. But the dogs balked at the open water, and started to run back and forth in front of the lead. There was only one thing to do. I told Alan to sit with his feet up on the sled boxes, pushed the sled to the edge of the lead, and with a smart crack of the whip I drove Oscar in.

He shot across the lead and scrambled out on the other side with such speed and power that he pulled the rest of the team in after him. With a violent jerk, a splash and a shudder we sailed across.

We came across lead after lead, doggedly crossing each one in the same way, and soon found ourselves in very watery "tombstone" country inside the Mule Group. In the hollows among upended floes, deep pools had formed, and I needed all my skill to prevent the heavy sled from side-slipping into the sea.

To get ashore on Mule Island, I had to cross an expanse of ice that had the blue look of old, rotten and insecure sea-ice. Shouting encouragement to the dogs, I drove them at a full run toward the island. Several times the runners broke through with a sickening crunch, while spouts of water, like small geysers, shot up alongside and behind. Oscar seemed to realize the urgency and kept up the cracking pace. With a mighty bound he flew across the tide-crack on Mule Island, dragging the sled right up among the rocks on shore. We pegged the dogs and trotted off to count the sea elephants. As the thaw advanced their wallows had become deeper, more slushy and far more smelly.

To get away from the island was even more difficult than the landing. Again I steered for the open ice, riding roughly across floes, rocky cracks and water-filled pools. In brilliant sunshine we went back along our tracks, following the edge of the fast ice. Open pack ice, seemingly motionless, floated on the tranquil black sea to the west, and soon we could see the camp's steel radio masts like silver probes silhouetted against the blue sky.

For the last time, Oscar responded to my sharp call, "Illi! Illi!" With tails curled jauntily in the air the dogs swung in toward base, and in long loping bounds on broad pads brought us home.

Sadly I unharnessed my friends and clipped them on the mooring chain, and sadly I stowed away traces, harnesses and sled. Our fieldwork was finished.

From now on till their transfer to Mawson, the dogs would have several weeks' rest, sleeping in the sun on their snowdrift, or walking with us over the bare, rocky land during the Antarctic summer days.

DRIFTING ice filled the bay on the morning of February 4, 1958, and it was only during her final approach that we spotted the *Thala Dan,* slowly nosing and probing her way into our harbor. The new season's party had arrived.

After the last of the stores for the newcomers had been stacked on the campsite, I wandered away from the others down to the dog lines. Thoughtfully I sat on a large rock with Oscar at my feet, gently scratching his ears. Quick steps across the snowdrift disturbed my thoughts. The expedition leader looked down at me with his keen gaze, and in his clipped, decisive voice he asked: "Anything wrong?"

"I hate leaving this bunch of ruffians here," I replied. "I wonder if it would be possible to bring Oscar home to Melbourne with us and retire him." Hardly stopping to think, I began to invent excuses to prolong his life. "He is getting a bit old now for sledding, and his teeth are wearing down from chewing frozen seal meat." I knew that there was no justification for my request. Old huskies either die a natural death on the ice, or they're shot. I knew I was being sentimental, but I couldn't bear to think of Oscar in trouble or unloved, knowing I couldn't get to him.

The leader looked from me to the dogs, and back again. Then he smiled; he understood. "Very well. I suppose we owe him that much after all he has done. I shall get in touch with the zoo authorities as soon as we are at sea."

Early next morning, we picked our way out among the icebergs, and as the small station glinted in the morning sun, the ship gently lifted her flared bows to the first swell from the open sea, and set course for Mawson. On the forecastle were tethered our dogs, all sniffing the offshore breeze.

Now we steamed in open water, where a few months earlier the Great Ice had subdued the sea with its frozen mantle, and where so many times our dogs had raced homeward among the majestic icebergs. A snow petrel shot across our bows, then soared, the sun glinting on its spread wings of pure white—a last farewell.

11
The End of a Polar Legend

MELBOURNE lay sweltering under the late summer sun. The air was still and the forty-degree heat had sapped the life of the city, reducing the Sunday crowds to a few listless and irritable people. Passing through the zoo gates I made my way between enclosures until I arrived at a large, shaded pen with a wading pool and a roofed shelter. In the shadows the big dog lay inert in the heat, dozing fitfully with his legs stretched out from under him.

With the key which the keeper had lent me, I unlocked the door and let myself into the pen.

"Oscar," I called.

His head lifted, cocked to one side, and his battle-scarred ears pricked up. I squatted just inside the gate, and with his tail wagging slowly from side to side, he loped across to me and put his big head under my arm. I buried my fingers in his thick pelt and could feel the sweat moistening the roots of his woolly coat. I led him into the shade and sat alongside him.

Oscar was getting old. In man-years he'd be close to sixty. He was panting, his tongue hanging out; still not acclimatized, he hadn't molted his coat, and his discomfort tore at my heart. His keeper had told me of his placid good nature, his patience and endurance, but somehow the idea of keeping him in the zoo seemed just as terrible as shooting him. I knew neither was a fitting way for such a hero to end his days.

In his old age, he had become pure wolf, in looks at least: the slanted eyes, the hackle along his back ending in his long bushy tail, his huge pads with strong nails—so strong that they had scratched footholds in hard, blue ice—and his heavy double-layered coat which kept out the bitter cold of the polar waste. Sitting there with Oscar, I was reminded of moonlit nights when he let out long, mournful howls, gradually joined by the whole team. It was the sound of the ice desert, the vast loneliness of Antarctica.

Slowly Oscar got to his feet, stretched and yawned in my face, then he walked sedately across the sunlit ground in front of us to cock his leg against his greatest asset—a tree.

Again we sat companionably, his muzzle pushed affectionately into my hand, and my mind drifted back to our days together, tearing across the sparkling ice. Immersed in my thoughts, I lost track of time altogether, and when I next looked up, the sun had fallen low in the sky, and the first welcome evening breezes were ruffling Oscar's heavy coat. Sadly I left the enclosure, the haunting memory of Oscar's howls following me down the paths of the Melbourne Zoo.

451

THERE WAS A CRISIS on the ice. Not only at the Australian base: the Norwegians, the Argentineans, the New Zealanders, the Russians, the British were all suffering. The dogs were dying out. Season after season, the men of the Antarctic had been mating the dogs, but with no results. The weasels and Sno-Cats had become far more efficient than before, planes were being used more and more frequently, but no base could run without dogs.

A priority message was dispatched to the Melbourne Zoo. They were recalling Oscar. Some of the old hands remembered his enthusiasm for Denny while he was still just a young dog, and in a flash, an idea became reality.

So Oscar went home. Home to the vast areas of ice and snow, to the howling blizzards, to the silences, to the cold and to the eternal sunlight in summer.

Although the expedition leaders planned to use him to sire pups and do no work, Oscar had other ideas. The team he joined was small, three bitches and one other dog. While he did set about his duty mating with the bitches, each morning he rushed to his old spot in front of the sled, waiting for the lead harness to be attached. He shed his years and took on the eager look of a young dog again, chivying and snapping at the team when they slouched or made errors of judgment. The Eskimo commands had stayed with him, and he responded to his new masters as if I myself had been behind him. As his offspring grew into usable sled dogs, Oscar trained them to negotiate the doubtful sea-ice, to bridge crevasses, even to find their way back to base camp when the driver was lost. Before long, he was the father of more than fifty pups, and defying tradition and history, Oscar decided to retire.

He dozed in the sun, and at night he slept inside one of the huts. He was fed like a king and had the freedom of the camp, visiting his favorites and moving about as he pleased. His fame was such that nothing was denied him.

One spring evening, when Oscar was over twelve years old, a wild shrieking blizzard blew up. That night, he got stiffly up and indicated, as so often before, that he wanted to be let out, and he disappeared into the swirling eddies of snow and sleet. This time he did not come back. Just like the great Arctic wolves, his ancestors, he simply disappeared.

Born in Norway in 1920, Nils Lied was the son of an adventurous ship-owner who often captained his own vessels across the Atlantic. When Nils was still a child, his parents gave him a boat and taught him to sail, and thus began his lifelong passion for seafaring.

At the age of eighteen, Nils first shipped out from his homeland to work for his father. He later served in the merchant navy and in the Royal Norwegian Navy during World War II, sailing virtually all over the world. He distinguished himself as one of the leaders in the raid on Telemark in southern Norway, destroying vital parts of a German heavy-water production plant. At twenty-six he had attained the rank of Lieutenant Commander and was skippering his own corvette.

Commander Nils Lied

After the war Lied returned to Norway to become a radio-operator and navigator for an airline. In 1948 he emigrated to Australia and was soon intrigued by reports of parties setting out to explore Antarctica. He joined seven expeditions to the great frozen continent between 1951 and 1968 and was always in charge of the dog teams, practicing the skills learned from Ajungilak, a boyhood Eskimo friend. Several geographical features of Antarctica have been named after him. These include Mount Lied, Lied Bluff, Lied Glacier, Lied Island, Lied Lake and Mount Nils.

Nils Lied spent the last years of his life in retirement with his wife, Erika, on the east coast of Tasmania. He enjoyed looking back on his 8500 kilometers of Antarctic sledding, nearly all of it in the company of Oscar. The great husky was, Lied would recall, "a unique and incredible animal. He had a 99-centimeter chest and weighed 52 kilos, and standing on his hind legs he could put his paws on my shoulders and look over my head." Nils Lied felt fortunate to have been part of the Antarctic exploration—and he was especially grateful for having shared it with the legend that was Oscar.

The quiet war hero and Antarctic explorer drowned in a flash flood at St. Helens, Tasmania, in December 1993. He was seventy-three.

THAT CAMDEN SUMMER
LaVyrle Spencer

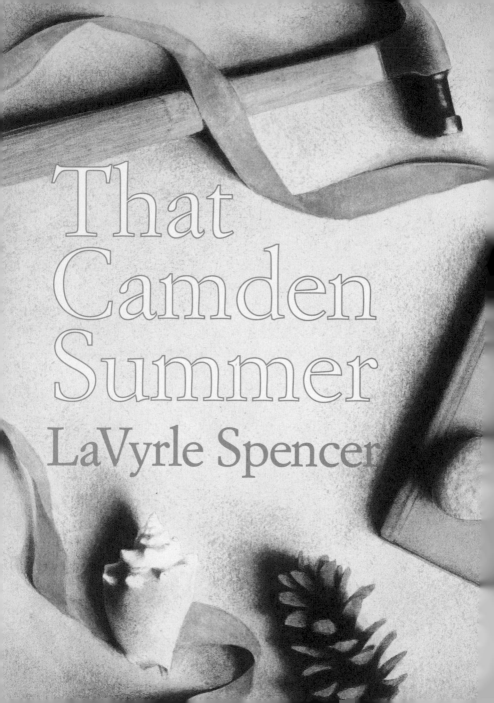

That Camden Summer

LaVyrle Spencer

*I*t was a romance neither of them was looking for. Roberta Jewett was having enough trouble just finding her footing in a town scandalized by the very sight of her.

Gabe Farley was more than content to live out his quiet life in the home he had shared with his late wife.

One life in an uproar. The other at peace. And both destined to change forever during that extraordinary Camden summer.

CHAPTER 1

ROBERTA Jewett had hoped for fair weather the day she moved her children back to Camden, Maine. Instead, a brew of needly rain and thready fog had followed the Boston boat all the way up the coastline. The water, tumbled to a smart chop by a persistent southwest wind, made for a hellish voyage. Poor Lydia had been sick all night.

The ten-year-old lay on the hard wooden bench with her head in Roberta's lap, her complexion greenish, her French braid shredded at the edges like an old piece of rigging. "How much longer, Mother?"

Roberta looked down at her youngest and pushed the disheveled hair back from her face. Lydia had never been a sailor like the other two. "Not long now. Let me see if I can tell where we are." She eased Lydia's head from her lap. "Be right back."

She glanced at her other two girls, Susan and Rebecca, asleep nearby with their cheeks and arms flattened on a varnished tabletop. Around them, other passengers dozed on the uncomfortable seating provided for those with the cheapest tickets.

No panoramic views here, only minuscule portholes. Roberta made her way to one and found it beaten by rain. The glass was fogged. She cleared it with her coat sleeve and peered through.

Going on seven a.m., and the sky was becoming murkily light. A bell buoy clanged. Yes, there was Negro Island light. Almost home. Camden was smudged by the downpour but visible. She studied it pragmatically, stirred less by nostalgia than by defensiveness.

Inside the protected harbor the featureless huddle on the shore took on identity: Mount Battie, which rose behind Camden like a great black breaching whale; the wharf where the *Belfast* would land; the skeins of streets climbing the eastern skirt of the mountain; the spires of familiar churches—the Episcopal, the Baptist, and the Congregational, where she had gone until she married and moved away; the omnipresent smokestack of the Knox Woolen Mill, which supported most of the town and where she'd probably still be working today if Mother had had her way.

Somewhere out there the morning shift was heading toward the mill. Some of those workers Roberta had known when they were schoolmates. What would they think of her now, returning as a divorced woman? Probably the same thing Mother did. "No decent woman sunders a marriage, Roberta," her letter had said.

Mother would not have come down to the wharf this early—her lumbago or some other convenient complaint would be keeping her in bed—but Roberta's sister, Grace, would be waiting when the steamer landed, along with Grace's husband, Elfred, whom Roberta remembered only vaguely.

The lights of the little seaside village poked through the blur, and she returned to her children. "Rebecca, Susan, wake up." She shook each of them, then went to the bench to tip Lydia upright. As Roberta sat down, she tucked her youngest beneath an arm. "We're just entering Camden harbor. How're you feeling?"

"Terrible. I never want to ride on this barnacle breeder again."

"You shouldn't have to. The house is bought, the job is mine and nothing short of a hurricane will force us to move again—agreed?"

Nobody answered. Roberta appealed to the pair at the table. "Girls, come here."

They rose with limp resignation and sat down at Roberta's right, fourteen-year-old Susan resting against her mother's arm.

"Listen, all of you. I'm sorry I couldn't rent a stateroom. I know it's been an awful ride, but we need every penny to get started here. You understand, don't you?"

"It's all right, Mother," Rebecca reassured her. Sixteen-year-old Becky never complained about anything. Instead, when the younger ones did, she chastised them.

"Now," Roberta said, "straighten your skirts, fix your hair and gather up your things, because we'll be at the landing soon."

They shook their skirts and buttoned their coats, but little repair was done on hair, and they looked as unkempt as ever. Then they gathered up their belongings and moved to the companionway that emptied onto the first-floor deck. Here the windows were more generous, and other passengers were peering out, waiting to disembark.

"I wonder if the children will be with Grace and Elfred," Roberta said.

"How old are they again?" Lydia asked.

"Very nearly the same as the three of you. Marcelyn is sixteen, Trudy's thirteen and Corinda, I believe, is ten."

"I hope they're not as weird as their names, and I hope they're not stuck-up because they've lived here all their lives and we've never been here before." In general, Lydia was the negative one.

Rebecca played the peacemaker. "For all we know, they think our names are weird. Besides, *I* think their names are dramatic."

"You think everything is dramatic," Lydia said.

"Everything but you. You're just a little naysayer."

"Girls," Roberta said, and they quieted down. She turned her attention to the people on the wharf, which was sliding into view.

Roberta had ambivalent feelings about returning here, but the girls needed stability, and a little shot of family wouldn't hurt. They had never known their grandmother, aunt, uncle or cousins, and it was high time they did. Let my family be tolerant, she thought. That's all I ask. I'll provide for my girls, but when I can't be there for them, I'll need my family to be.

The boat whistle blasted, and the *Belfast* hove up against the wharf. For better or worse, after eighteen years Roberta was home again.

THE four Jewetts descended the gangway huddled beneath two umbrellas. A well-dressed man, hunched beneath his own umbrella, hurried forward, coattails flapping.

"Birdy?" he called above the wind.

"Elfred?" she called back. "Is that you?"

"It's me all right. And these must be your girls." He came so close that their umbrellas bumped, and she could see he was the man she remembered, though he now sported a mustache.

"Yes, these three. Girls, this is your uncle Elfred."

"Come inside. Grace is waiting where it's drier."

461

He herded them along to the steamship office. New electric lighting sent a glow through the windows. Inside, a heavyset woman wearing a fruit-trimmed hat opened her arms and rushed forward.

"Birdy, oh, Birdy, you're really here."

"Oh, Gracie, it's so good to see you!"

They hugged hard, blocking the doorway and the other passengers streaming around them.

"Our little Birdy has flown home at last."

"Heavens, I haven't been called that for a while." In the first few years of her marriage Roberta had returned home occasionally, without her husband. But as his philandering had escalated, she had stayed away, unwilling to face questions.

The embrace ended, and the two women stood back to take stock of one another. Grace was only a shade over five feet tall, a firmly packed matron shaped like a cracker barrel, with a pudgy face. Her hair was tidily dressed, and her clothing expensive. Behind wire-rimmed spectacles, there were tears in her blue eyes.

By contrast, Roberta's gray-blue eyes were dry and held, perhaps, a touch of reserve. She was a head taller than her older sister. Her clothes were cheap and wrinkled. She flouted convention by not wearing a hat, and her thick mahogany hair had drifted from its rat and straggled along her neck. There were age lines sprouting at the corners of her eyes and a bit of girth developing at her midsection. Everything about her said, "I'm heading for forty and not ashamed to show it, and here are my three reasons why."

"Come on, Gracie, meet my girls." The pride in her voice was unmistakable. "Girls, introduce yourselves."

They did so with impressive elocution and bearing, as if they had no idea they looked like ragamuffins. During the introductions Grace hugged them all, and Elfred bent over each of their hands in turn. He then turned to their mother to make up for the abrupt greeting outside in the rain.

"Well, Birdy, hello. Gracious, how you've changed."

"Haven't we all, Elfred."

He was nattily dressed, with a gorgeous silvering mustache that tilted up at the corners. He had grown stocky and developed some silver at the temples, too, but at middle age it became him. He seemed to know it, though, which spoiled the whole effect. His smile released the power of a surprising pair of dimples and long-lashed brown eyes that were true heartbreakers. Some sixth sense warned Roberta that he used them for that purpose whenever it suited him, and she suffered his gloved hand on her shoulder for a moment longer than it needed to be there.

"Welcome back to Camden," he said.

"Thank you. Is the house ready?" Elfred sold real estate and had arranged the purchase of her house.

"Now, Roberta, 'ready' is a relative word. It needs work."

"Work I'm used to. When can we see it?"

"As soon as you'd like, but Grace was hoping you'd stop by our house first for breakfast."

"We're all ravenous. We ate last night about six o'clock."

Grace grew radiant. "Then you'll come! Wonderful! We've given the children permission to be late for school so they could meet your girls. Elfred, what about Roberta's trunks? Will you speak to the station agent about them? I imagine she'll want—"

"I'll speak to the station agent myself," Roberta interrupted.

"Oh, well, of course," Grace said, her eyes flitting to her husband as if expecting to be told whose side to take.

"Mornin', Elfred, Mrs. Spear," a man said as he brushed around them on his way inside. He was dressed in dripping brown oilskins, Wellington boots and a plaid wool newsboy's cap, his brown hair shaggy beneath it. He looked to be about Elfred's age.

"Hey, Gabriel, not so fast," Elfred called. "Meet Grace's sister, Roberta Jewett. Birdy, maybe you remember Gabriel Farley?"

"No, I'm afraid I don't. How do you do, Mr. Farley."

He touched his cap. "Mrs. Jewett," he said. "You're moving back to stay, I hear."

"Yes, I am," she replied, surprised that he knew.

"Into the Breckenridge house," Elfred put in.

"The Breckenridge house!" Farley cocked an eyebrow the color of old rope. It was very untamed and made him look grumpy when he scowled. "Does she know what she's getting into?"

"Don't scare her, Gabe. She hasn't seen it yet."

Farley leaned closer to Roberta and murmured, "You've got to watch this fellow." Without elaborating, he tossed a teasing grin at Elfred and bade them farewell.

When he had moved on, Roberta accosted her brother-in-law. "All right, Elfred, just exactly what are you getting me into?"

463

"The best house I could manage with property as scarce as hens' teeth these days. Since the trolley line came in, the town is booming. Now, are you sure you don't want me to speak to the station agent about your trunks?"

"Quite sure. I spent seventeen years with a negligent husband who was rarely around, and I have no intention of starting to rely on a man at this late date. All I need is the address."

"Tell him it's the old Breckenridge place, on Alden Street."

As she turned away to make the arrangements, Grace's eyes swung to Elfred with an expression that said quite clearly, "You see? I told you what she was like!"

Cartage drays were hired to deliver her freight. Then, much to the amazement of the Jewetts, Elfred boarded the entire troop into a shiny black touring car.

"This is really yours?" Becky exclaimed, awestruck.

Elfred laughed. "That it is."

"Gosh! I've never been in one before."

Neither had Roberta, but she immediately preferred it to a jolting, smelly horse and carriage.

Elfred drove them to a lovely three-story Queen Anne on Elm Street. The house was stately and large, its fish scales and gingerbread painted in five colors. Inside, it was decked out with a plethora of polished wood, leaded glass and elaborate wallpaper. The furnishings were rich, the carpets imported, the light fixtures already converted to electricity. But so painfully neat, Roberta thought, glancing into the parlor from the foyer. I wonder where they do their living.

"It's beautiful, Grace," Roberta said as Elfred stepped behind her to take her coat.

Mercy! she thought. Was that his body bumping me from behind while Grace wasn't looking? Roberta turned, but so did Elfred— away from her to hang her coat on a brass tree and to see to the girls' coats. Perhaps it was accidental, she thought.

"Sophie has breakfast all ready," Grace said. She tilted over the ornate banister and bugled up the stairs, "Girls, are you there?"

Three prim young darlings came down, all dressed in starched layers with oversize grosgrain bows in their hair. The oldest, Marcelyn, acted as spokesperson. "How do you do. Mother has set a special table for us in the solarium. Would you like to see it?"

464

The Jewett trio followed, mesmerized, their eyes lifting as they passed beneath the novel electric lights, which burned away the April gloom. In the solarium, a hexagonal room situated at the rear of the home, fine china was laid on a filigreed iron table. Ferns, palms and orchids flourished on metal racks, while rain pecked at the windows.

"Holy Moses!" Rebecca exclaimed. "You must be filthy rich."

A couple of dubious glances flashed among the Spear girls, followed by a hint of giggling.

"What's so funny?" Rebecca asked.

"Do you always say exactly what you think?" Marcelyn replied.

Rebecca shrugged. "Pretty much."

"Mother would have dyspepsia if we talked like that."

"We can say anything we want in front of our mother. If she doesn't like it, we discuss it. She believes in living your life the way you see fit."

"Oh, dear," Marcelyn breathed.

"Why do you say that?"

"Well, our mother would— I mean, well, goodness."

A buxom gray-haired woman waddled in bearing a tray that dented her ample stomach. "Here you are. Some nice, piping kedgeree," said Sophie as she placed steaming plates before them.

Lydia peered at the glob on her plate. "What is it?"

"What is it? Why, it's fish and rice in egg sauce. Every Mainer knows what kedgeree is."

"Well, we're not Mainers."

"But your mother was."

"Yes, but our mother doesn't cook much," Lydia said.

"Doesn't cook much!" Sophie stopped in her tracks. "Why, that can't be so."

Under the table Rebecca nudged Lydia's leg, shutting her up. Sophie placed hot biscuits, butter and blueberry jam on the table, and left the room, saying, "Now you clean your plates."

The moment she disappeared, Susan and Lydia set out to do just that, with manners leaving much to be desired. While they ate, Rebecca observed, "Marcelyn is an interesting name."

"It comes from my great-great-grandmother on Father's side," Marcelyn explained. "It is said that when she was thirteen she gave birth to her first child in the snow beside the Megunticook River,

465

wrapped it in a fur robe and carried it down to the trading post, where her husband was stone drunk in bed with an Indian woman. She sliced off her husband's left ear and said, 'There. Now maybe the ladies won't find you so pretty and you'll stay home where you belong.' Have you ever heard of anything so sad and romantic in your life?"

"What a drama it would make!" Rebecca exclaimed. "We should write and perform it sometime."

"You write plays?" Marcelyn asked.

"We write them all the time. And perform them, too."

"For whom?"

"Why, for Mother, of course, and for our friends and our teachers—anyone who'll sit still long enough to watch, actually."

"Your mother sits and watches you put on plays?"

"Oh, she'd stop to watch us do anything—act, sing, play the piano. Do you *never* put on plays?" Rebecca seemed amazed.

"We, uh, um . . . no. I mean, we never thought about it."

"What do you do for fun?"

"Well," said Marcelyn, glancing at her sisters, "we stitch."

"Stitch! I said *fun*."

"Well, sometimes we go rowing."

"Not sailing?"

"Gracious, no. Mother would never allow us. It's too dangerous. But we had a clambake once out on the beach at Sherman's Cove."

"Once?"

"Well, Mother didn't like us getting our hems dirty."

Rebecca thought that over, chewing some kedgeree, discovering it was very tasty. "My mother doesn't care much about hems, clean or dirty. She cares more about our minds. The imagination, she says, is a priceless gift, and we must cultivate it at every opportunity. The next time we put on a play, would you like to try it with us?"

Marcelyn Spear beamed at her newfound cousin. She had inherited her daddy's pretty brown eyes, and they positively gleamed as she said, "Oh, Rebecca, do you really mean it?"

"Of course. And call me Becky. For our first play we'll do your great-great-grandmother's story. We'll start working on it right away!"

Marcelyn leaned forward. "Listen, everybody. Anything that's been said this morning is not to be reported to Mother—agreed?" She aimed a warning gaze at Trudy and Corinda.

"But she'll ask," Corinda said.

"Then tell her we had a lovely chat and nothing more. You want to put on plays, don't you?"

MEANWHILE, in the formal dining room the adults had finished their breakfast and were enjoying hot coffee. Elfred sat back, playing with a toothpick and sending some unsettling grins to Roberta whenever Grace wasn't looking.

Grace was getting down to brass tacks. "Well, Birdy," she said officiously, "I've been waiting for you to mention—*it.*"

"It?"

"The . . . well, you know. The divorce," she whispered.

"Why are you whispering, Grace?"

Grace stiffened. "Don't be obtuse, Birdy. Did you really do it?"

"Yes, I did it."

"Oh, Roberta, how could you?"

"What should I have done? Stayed with him for another seventeen years, and let him chase women and gamble away what little money he made and come back to me when his funds ran dry or when his other woman threw him out? Because that's what he did, Grace, time and time again. I just couldn't tolerate it anymore."

"But George was so charming."

Roberta scarcely stopped herself from rolling her eyes. Like your own charmer, Elfred here, she thought, who's sending flirtatious messages to me at this very moment? "You barely met the man," she replied. "But you're right about that. He charmed one woman after another."

"Nevertheless, Mother and I are both dead set against this divorce. What will people say, Birdy?"

"I don't give a hoot what they say, Grace."

"And you really plan to take this job as the county nurse and go flitting off across the countryside?"

"I've already taken it. I start as soon as we're settled."

"Roberta, don't be outrageous. A divorced woman going from town to town—it just isn't done." Grace leaned forward earnestly. "Listen to me, Birdy. Take a job in the mill. That way the townspeople won't have as much reason to question your motives."

"Question my motives!" Roberta leaped to her feet. "Listen to yourself, Grace! You're telling me *I'm* the one who has to vindicate

467

myself, just because I'm the *female*. You'll wait till hell freezes over before you get any apologies from me."

"All right. . . . I'm sorry." Grace pressed the air with both palms. "It was just an idea, that's all. Sit down, Birdy."

"I'm done sitting. Actually, I'm anxious to see my house, so Elfred, if you'd be so kind . . ."

Elfred wiped his mustache and rose. "Anytime you say. Let's collect your children."

At the door, when coats were donned, Grace gripped Birdy's hand. "Don't be angry. I'll come over soon, and we can talk some more."

"Yes, do that," she replied. "Girls, say good-bye to your cousins."

The girls exchanged friendly good-byes. In the commotion of departure Elfred made sure his hand was hidden from view when he touched Roberta's waist with a suggestive squeeze.

CHAPTER 2

"ELFRED, stop it!"

She had let the girls run ahead through the rain while she and Elfred readied their umbrellas on the stoop.

"I beg your pardon?"

"You know perfectly well what I mean! Just keep your hands to yourself and we'll get along fine, Elfred."

Rendering a grin that would have charmed the scowl off a Quaker matron, he doffed his bowler and motioned her ahead of him down the walk. "As you wish. Shall we join the children?"

He drove them through the rain in his shiny black touring car. The girls sat in the back while Roberta kept to her corner of the front seat and looked out her window.

"So many motorcars," she said. After watching one pass, she turned to question her brother-in-law. "Do you like yours, Elfred?"

"I do, but some of my customers refuse to get into it. People still think the horse is more reliable."

"Do you?" she asked.

"No."

"So if you were a woman, you'd get a motorcar instead?"

"Oh, now wait a minute, Birdy. Don't tell me *you're* thinking of buying a motorcar!"

"Why not?"

"But you're a woman!"

She snorted. "With plans of my own. Now take me down Main Street, would you? I want to see what it looks like."

"It looks the same as always."

"It does not. Grace has written about all kinds of changes."

"Very well. One quick trip, then it's up the hill to Alden Street."

"All right, Elfred," she said with mock servitude, and sat back to enjoy the ride through the town where she'd grown up.

Even in the rain Camden appealed. The mountains rose behind it in gentle curves, the little village looped at their throat like a necklace. Camden's shape was dictated by the horseshoe crescent of rocky coastline that formed a calm natural harbor, made all the more calm by dozens of islands that dotted Penobscot Bay.

Main Street curved like an eel and climbed at the north end. The white wooden structures of the business section that Roberta remembered from childhood were gone, destroyed by fire in 1892. In their place were two- and three-story buildings of red Maine brick. Though the buildings were different, the character of the town remained the same. Its roots had been put down by Calvinists, who valued hard work, Sunday worship and a sheltered seaport. If that port was of exceptional beauty, so much the better.

Roberta searched for familiar landmarks. On the white spire of the Baptist church the town clock still set the pace of daily life. Beside it, the village green remained unchanged, but progress had come to Camden. Telephone poles trimmed the length of Main Street. Concrete sidewalks followed the poles. There were electric trolleys and streetlights and a new, expensive YMCA building. But the sign that snapped Roberta's head around swung from a building at the north end of Main.

"Elfred, does that sign say Garage?"

"Roberta, don't even think it. Women simply cannot own cars. They cannot operate them. You can break your arm cranking them."

"Pull over," she said. And after a beat, "Pull over, Elfred!"

He did so, grumbling. "How you and Grace can be sisters is beyond me."

Roberta put her face closer to the rain-spattered window and squinted at the sign hanging outside. " 'Boynton's Motor Car Company,' " she read aloud. "How much does a motorcar cost, Elfred?"

He refused to answer.

"I can find out quite easily."

"All right," he said, exasperated. "This one cost eight hundred and fifty dollars. A roadster would be about six hundred."

"I don't have that much, but I'll get the money somehow. Where does one buy gasoline?"

"Birdy, please, your sister is going to be very upset with me if she thinks I assisted you with this crazy idea."

"Don't worry, Elfred, I'll make sure Grace knows that anything disgraceful was clearly my idea."

Elfred was beginning to realize this woman had a tongue like a double-bit axe. But he liked women, and this one in particular whetted his interest, with her single state and her sassiness. As a distraction from a boring, overweight wife, Mrs. Birdy Jewett would do very well.

"One buys gas at the hardware store. Now may I take you home?"

Roberta grinned smugly. "Please do."

ALDEN Street was a mere stone's throw above downtown. The Breckenridge house was as old as Camden itself and during the last two decades had been owned by the final survivor of the clan, one Sebastian Dougal Breckenridge.

People around town remembered the days when Sebastian had kept his place shipshape. But many years had passed since his creaky old joints could endure the torture of kneeling to weed a garden, or his arthritic arms support a paintbrush, or his feeble mind remind him that the house needed care if it was not to tumble down the hill into Camden harbor.

Roberta gaped at the place and felt her stomach drop. "This is it?" There was only silent disbelief from the back seat.

"Elfred, you can't be serious. You spent my money on *that!*"

"Two hundred dollars isn't much, Birdy. I could have gotten you a much nicer place for four, but you said two was your limit."

Two hundred for the house, two hundred for the motorcar—that was what she had planned. Now she owned a hovel and could afford one third of a car, and had no way of getting the rest quickly.

"Oh, Elfred, how could you? Why, it's a . . . . a derelict!"

"It's got a good sturdy foundation and windows that close."

"Without glass," she said, looking up. On the second floor one pane had been covered with a sheet of wood. Surely the place had not been painted in a decade.

"Glass can be replaced," Elfred said of the upstairs window.

"Not by me, it can't. I'm no glazier, Elfred." Roberta's disillusionment was fast growing into blazing anger.

"You said you wanted to save money on a structure that could be fixed up. I assumed you had set aside some money for that purpose."

"Not this much! I said fix up, Elfred, not rebuild."

Roberta sat glaring at her new domicile.

"Do you want to go in and look?" Elfred asked.

"No. I want to suspend you from the tallest tree in Camden."

Elfred smiled behind his hand while she stewed in tight-lipped anger. "Oh, come on, Birdy, at least go in and have a look."

She was so distraught she got out of the car without an umbrella and marched up the weedy yard without waiting for anyone.

Elfred grabbed his umbrella and rushed to catch up with her. He did so at the bottom of the porch steps, where she had come up short. Upon closer scrutiny it appeared the porch itself was ready to rot off. The floor had holes in it where feet had gone right through. She stood with her hands on her hips.

"This is deplorable. Just deplorable."

Elfred urged her up the steps, picked his way across the good boards and opened the front door. She preceded him into what she supposed was a living room. Wonder of wonders—it had electricity! But the wires were strung outside the walls, and the bulbs hung bare. There were newspapers everywhere. The walls had been papered with them. Soot stained the ceiling above a heater stove, and trash littered the floors. The place stank of decay.

Roberta announced, "I want my money back."

"I can't get it back," Elfred told her. "The sale is conclusive."

Roberta marched up to him, grabbed his folded umbrella and jabbed it smartly into his belly. Elfred doubled forward.

"Oof! Ro-Roberta, what in the—"

"How are we supposed to live in this? How, Elfred!"

Elfred hugged his belly and stared at her, aghast. The girls had come onto the front porch and stood looking in dubiously. Rebecca stepped over the threshold and the others followed, picking their way carefully. Susan peered up a creaky-looking stairway that divided the two downstairs rooms. Rebecca walked over to a wall and peeled a strip of newspaper off, revealing ancient wallpaper behind it. "It won't be so bad, Mother. Once we paint the walls."

A kitchen adjoined the living room. Lydia ventured into it, followed by the others. She opened a door beneath a dry sink, releasing a fetid odor.

"Close that door, Lydia!" Roberta ordered. To Elfred she snapped, "I suppose there's no bathroom."

"No. Just an outhouse."

She turned away, too angry to face him.

"Listen, Birdy. This is what you get for two hundred dollars. I figured it could be repaired with a little help."

She spun on him. "You repair it, then, Elfred, because I don't have time! I've got to go out and earn a living for my girls. And while I do it, am I supposed to leave them in this?" She was shouting by this time. "*You* stuck us with this skunk's nest! *You pay* to make it livable! Lord help me, I trusted you, Elfred."

Elfred was backing away because Birdy was brandishing the umbrella again. He spread both hands as if to ward her off. "All right, Birdy, all right. I will. I'll see Gabriel Farley right away."

"Yes sir, you will," said a deep voice from the front room, and Gabriel Farley himself materialized. He stepped through the doorway into the kitchen and said, "Hello again."

"Well, where did you come from?" Elfred asked.

"Figured you could use me. If these ladies were going to live in old Sebastian's wake, it'd have to be fixed up some." He crossed his arms, cinched his hands beneath his armpits and scanned the tops of the walls. "Wouldn't mind giving you an estimate."

Roberta shot him an acid glance. "Well, that was fast," she remarked dryly.

"Lucky thing we met at the wharf, or I wouldn't have known this place was going to be lived in again."

Roberta wondered just how lucky. "So you're a carpenter?"

"Carpenter, painter, general tradesman—all rolled into one."

Her glance shifted from one man to the other. "Couldn't be you two are in cahoots now, could it? Like maybe Elfred just *happened* to purchase this wreck for me, and now Mr. Farley just *happens* to have the time to repair this piece of junk."

Gabe Farley, unruffled, studied Roberta Jewett from beneath his wiry eyebrows. First divorced woman he'd ever seen, and he wasn't sure what to make of her. There she stood, confronting him and Elfred with her suspicions, just the way a man would. Stood there with her hair looking like a patch of swamp grass and her coat all crinkled and hanging unbuttoned. He thought, Whew! Are the women going to talk about this one behind her back! The men, too.

"Well now, Mrs. Jewett, you could be right," he said, removing his cap to scratch his skull, then replacing the cap. "Could be wrong, though, too. So I guess it's up to you to decide if you want my help."

"Answer me straight, Mr. Farley. Are you in cahoots with my brother-in-law?"

"Nope."

She turned away and wandered the room. "Well, even if you are, I guess there's no problem, because Elfred just agreed to finance the repairs on this house. Didn't you, Elfred?"

Elfred cleared his throat. "Go ahead, Gabe. Work up an estimate and bring it to me. We'll work it out somehow between Roberta and me. She's got to live somewhere, and this—I'm afraid—is it."

"All right. I'll look around. Excuse me," he said to Roberta, touching his cap and leaving the room.

The girls had gone exploring, and two of them called from the front porch. "Mother, come out here."

She went to join Rebecca and Susan, who were standing at the porch rail looking out through the rain. "Look, Mother," Becky said enthusiastically, "we'll be able to see the harbor from here and all the boats and the islands. I'm sure we'll be able to see them once the rain clears. And the sunrises! Oh, they'll be stunning, Mother!" She turned to her mother in appeal. "I know it looks bad now, but we don't care. We love it. We want to stay."

"We've already picked out our room," Susan put in.

Roberta studied her two oldest daughters a moment. If there was one force that could stop Roberta on a dime, it was her girls. Suddenly she laughed. "Who says I'm poor when I have riches like you? Come here, girls." She opened her arms. They came and nestled up against her and linked their arms around her waist. There they stood, like three fisherman's knots in the same rope, watching the rain skim off the porch roof and peck into the sodden earth below.

"I'll need some help from you if we stay," Roberta said.

"Of course, Mother."

"You'll be alone a lot. Do you mind?"

"Who's the one who taught us, 'When you have imagination, you're never alone'?" asked Rebecca.

"That's my girl." She jostled Rebecca. "Where's Lydia?"

"Upstairs exploring."

"Shall we go find her?"

Smiling, the three went to do just that.

LYDIA was indeed exploring the house. She had culled some colorful glass floats from fishing nets left behind by Sebastian. They were scarlet and aqua blue and saffron yellow and would look just dandy hanging on the porch rail. Then, daydreaming, she hummed a song from *H.M.S. Pinafore* as she climbed the stairs. At her school in Boston she had played the part of Josephine, and was transported now to a ship on the briny sea. She idled her way into the rear bedroom, which looked out at Mount Battie. Its ceiling followed the steep roofline, and at one end it had a pair of long, skinny windows. Mr. Farley was on one knee, examining the wall around them.

"Hello," she said.

He looked back over his shoulder. "Oh, hello."

"I'm Lydia."

He pivoted on the balls of his feet. "It's nice to meet you, Lydia. I'm Mr. Farley."

"I know. Are you going to fix this house for us?"

"I think so."

"It's quite a mess, isn't it?"

He let his gaze rove around. "Oh, it's not so bad. That window in the other bedroom needs replacing, and it'll need a new porch, but the roof is slate, and she's good for another hundred years."

"This is going to be my room," Lydia told him. "Mine and Becky's and Susan's. Mother will take that one." She pointed behind her.

"Have you talked it over already?"

"No. But Mother pretty much always lets us have our way. Unless it would hurt somebody or be bad for our minds. We want to stay, so I know she'll say yes."

"Why do you want to stay?"

"Because we have a grandmother here and cousins and Aunt Grace and Uncle Elfred, and because there's an opera house here, which Mother says we'll frequent, and exceptionally fine schools, and if you attend high school here, you don't even have to be tested to go into college—they just let you in. Did you know that?"

Amazed, Gabriel cleared his throat. "No, I didn't."

"Mother says education is paramount."

Mother does, does she? Gabriel thought. He studied the precocious child. She was no higher than his armpit and rather the ragamuffin, in scuffed brown high-top shoes and a sacky brown dress. Her sandy braid was in disrepair. But her cheeks were rosy, and her eyes as bright as a tern's. "How old are you?"

"Ten."

"You speak awfully well for a ten-year-old."

"Mother reads to us a lot and encourages us to create."

"Create what?"

"Anything. Music, poetry, plays, essays, paintings, even botanical exhibits. Once we wrote an opera."

"An opera," he repeated in undisguised surprise. "My goodness."

"Do you have children?"

"Yes. I have one daughter, Isobel. She's fourteen."

"Susan is fourteen. Maybe we'll all be friends."

"I'm sure Isobel would like that."

"And Rebecca is sixteen. Susan and Rebecca do everything together, but I'm the baby and sometimes they won't let me. At least they let me put on plays. Well, I'd better go now."

She raced out and collided with her uncle Elfred, who had just reached the top of the stairs. She looked up. "I'm sorry, Uncle Elfred. I was just going to find Mother."

"She's downstairs on the front porch with your sisters."

Lydia clattered off down the steps, and Elfred joined his friend in the rear bedroom. "Well, what do you think?" he asked as he reached into his pocket for a cigar.

Farley rose. "About the house or about her?"

"Take your pick," Elfred said, striking a match and puffing to light the stogie.

At that moment Roberta had climbed halfway up the stairs and was being followed by her three girls. She shushed them with a finger to her lips and motioned them to stay where they were. Then she tiptoed to the top and strained to hear what she could.

Farley said in a lowered voice, "She doesn't care much what she says, does she?"

"Or how she looks," Elfred added. "She's got plenty of what a man

475

likes to get his hands on, though, and that's what matters, eh, Gabe?"

Farley chuckled. "Well, I did get over here pretty fast, didn't I? But heck, I never met a divorced woman before. I was curious."

"So was I. So I . . . tested her a little bit."

"Tested her? Why, Elfred"—this with teasing approval—"and you a married man."

"It was just in fun."

"What'd she do?" Farley was nearly whispering.

Though Roberta heard no answer from Elfred, she imagined an off-kilter grin, implying whatever a randy mind wanted to imagine, before Farley replied, "Elfred, you devil."

Both men laughed.

"A word of advice," Elfred went on in the confidential tone of one worldly stud helping out another. "Warm her up a little first. She's got a belligerent side."

"Thought you said you only tested her."

"She blew a cork when she saw the house, and jabbed me in the gut with my own umbrella. Damnable temper on her."

Farley laughed. "My guess is you deserved it. And I'm not talking about the condition of any house."

Roberta had heard enough. With her face afire she stomped into the room and confronted the two men. During that moment, when everyone knew what the whispering and snickering had been about, she fixed her glacial eyes on Farley. "When can you begin work?"

Farley hadn't even the grace to blush. "Tomorrow."

"And Elfred, *you shall pay.*" Her manner gave a second meaning to the statement that nobody could mistake. "And make sure Grace knows about it, so there's no trouble between her and me."

"I'll make sure."

"And *you*"—she skewered Farley with contempt in her eyes—"make sure you complete the job and get out of here in the shortest time possible. Is that clear?"

"Yes, ma'am," he said. "Anything you say."

She executed an about-face as regally as if dressed in hooped taffeta, and headed for the door. "The drays are here with my belongings. Would you please help the teamsters unload." It was an order, issued with her back turned on them.

When she was gone, Gabe and Elfred exchanged silent messages with their eyebrows, then snickered once again.

CHAPTER 3

ROBERTA'S furniture was as ill-kempt as she, a lackluster collection that would do nothing aesthetically to enhance their lives.

"Oh, don't worry about the rain," she told the draymen, "just bring it right in here. Well, don't just stand there, Farley, make yourself useful! You, too, Elfred."

Elfred quite disliked being put upon to do such physical labor and left for his office the moment he could conveniently scramble off. After helping the draymen carry the heaviest pieces, including an upright piano, Farley went, too.

Roberta sent the girls upstairs to unpack some cartons of clothing and bedding. She went into the living room and perused the collection of crates and trunks, wondering where she might find kitchen equipment in all those boxes. It was nearly midday, and the girls would be getting hungry. Suddenly it seemed too overwhelming to face. Besides, the air coming in the open front door brought the smell of the ocean and of the earth greening. So she located the claw-footed piano stool in the mountain of crates, opened the cover to the piano keys, sat down and played "Art Is Calling for Me," from *Naughty Marietta*. She lit into it with energy and heard the girls begin to sing upstairs.

Suddenly Roberta Jewett felt incredibly happy. She had her girls and a place to keep them and a job waiting. There was no husband to make a fool of her anymore. She and her girls had made a new start. With a nimble arpeggio she finished the song, spun around on the piano stool . . .

And found herself face to face with Gabriel Farley.

He was relaxed against the doorjamb, with his hands tucked under his armpits, as if he'd been there awhile.

Her face soured. "I thought you were gone."

"I was. I came back."

Farley had been standing in the doorway for a full minute, wondering what kind of woman sat at the piano and ignored a mountain of crates that needed unpacking. "Your girls sing well," he said.

From upstairs Rebecca called, "Mother, who's here?"

"It's Mr. Farley," she called back.

"What does he want?"

"I don't know." Then to him, "What *do* you want, Mr. Farley?"

He boosted off the doorframe and came in. "Thought you could use a little help with the heavier boxes."

"No, thank you." She marched over to the mountain, selected a box and hefted it down. "We'll manage."

He came and lifted it out of her hands, his height advantage making it effortless for him to pluck it from her.

She gave him a dirty look. "Haven't you got work to do somewhere?"

"Ayup."

"Then why aren't you there?"

"Got my own business—me and my brother. He's working at a job out by the Lily Pond, and he'll get along fine till I get there. Where do you want this?"

The carton held her cast-iron frying pans. He handled it as if it contained nothing more than a thimble.

"In the kitchen." She followed him, watching as he set it on the floor beside the iron cookstove.

"Look, Mr. Farley." She lowered her voice. "I heard you whispering with my brother-in-law upstairs. You're not going to gain any advantage by hanging around here acting indispensable."

"Why, Mrs. Jewett, you do me an injustice," he said, brushing his palms together.

"No, Mr. Farley, *you* do *me* an injustice. I'm bright enough to have figured out what you and Elfred were whispering about."

Farley considered her for some time. He decided an admission of his first mistake would put them on friendlier terms.

"Very well. Please accept my apology."

"No, I will not."

Farley couldn't decide whether to chuckle or gape. Never having had an apology flung back at him before, he gaped. "You won't?"

"No, I won't. Because it was rude and embarrassing what you did, and since I have no wish to further our acquaintance, I choose not to accept your apology."

A few beats passed before he muttered, "Well, I'll be damned."

"Good," she said. "That would please me very much."

She disappeared into the living room, leaving him to gape further. He felt his curiosity about her gather steam, and followed her.

From the doorway he watched her clamber onto a packing crate and reach for a bandbox from high on a stack. The back of her skirt was a wrinkled mess, and the back of her hair was just plain awful.

"So do you not want me to do the work on the house, then?"

"Suit yourself. That's between you and Elfred. But if you do it, knock before you enter, and stop staring at my hindside the way you're doing right now. I'm not interested, Mr. Farley. Not in you or any man, is that understood?" She stepped down with the bandbox and faced him.

Off came his cap, and he scratched his head in a frenzy of astonishment. "Good Lord, woman, you carry a big stick, don't you?"

"Yes, I do. But you haven't lived in my shoes, so don't judge me, Mr. Farley."

"You'd better get one thing straight." He reset his stance and pointed at her. "Women around here don't talk like that. And if you want to have any friends, you better not either."

"Talk like what?"

"You know what I mean. Like—like *that!* Like you were!"

"Oh, you mean women around here pretend that men aren't whispering about them behind their backs?"

"Look, I apologized for that!" He pointed again but was beginning to get rosy in the face.

"And then you added insult to injury by standing in the doorway staring at me as if I were Lady Godiva. Shame on you, Mr. Farley. What would your wife think?" She put the bandbox on the piano stool, lifted off the lid and pulled out a stack of folded scarves.

He stood behind her, prodded by her chastising into actually wondering what his wife would have thought. He shifted his weight before defending himself with the most paltry excuse.

"I don't have a wife."

"I'm not surprised," she replied while tying a scarf on her head backward. She turned to find him looking as though he'd like to clunk her a good one. "What are you still doing here, Mr. Farley?"

"Darned if I know!" he spouted, and clumped through her living room and down the rickety porch steps, into the rain.

"Good riddance," she mumbled, and went to work.

GABRIEL Farley and his younger brother, Seth, were building a garage for one of the rich summer families who had homes in

Boston and cottages here. Gabe had been glowering most of the afternoon, before Seth finally asked, "What's eating you today?"

"Nothing."

"Something with Isobel?"

"Nope."

"Ma?"

"Nope. Mind your own business, Seth."

Seth knew Gabe. Best way to get it out of him was to quit asking.

Pretty soon Gabe said, "I'm going to be starting a job for Elfred Spear tomorrow, so I'll leave you to finish this one."

"What's Elfred got going?"

"Well, it's not exactly Elfred's job. He's just the one who's paying me to do it. It's the old Breckenridge house."

"You're kidding! That old wreck?"

"Ayup, it's a mess all right, but nothing that can't be fixed with some soap and water and plenty of paint. I'll be putting a whole new front porch on, though. Might need you when I get to that."

"Just let me know when."

They worked awhile before Seth asked, "So who's Elfred carrying on with these days?"

Gabriel kept on sawing. "He didn't say."

"I feel sorry for that wife of his."

"What she doesn't know won't hurt her."

"Listen to yourself, Gabe. The man makes a fool of her—and him with three daughters, to boot."

"You saying you never stepped out on Aurelia?"

"Y' darned right. I wouldn't do that to her. You aren't saying you stepped out on Caroline, are you?"

"Good Lord, no. Not as long as she drew breath."

"Then how can you excuse it in a rounder like Spear?"

Gabe dropped his tools, rubbed his eyes hard and sighed. He'd been unhappy with himself all day long, and darned uncomfortable about what had happened up at the old Breckenridge house. "I don't know, Seth. I guess I'm in a state right now. I'm just so sick and tired of living alone."

"You're not living alone. You've got Isobel."

Gabe walked to the unfinished doorway and stared out at the rain. Caroline had never minded the rain like most people do. She often worked right out in it.

"Yes, I know. I've got Isobel. And the older she gets, the more she reminds me of her mother."

Seth crossed over to stand near his brother and give his shoulder a squeeze. "Comin' close to the time Caroline died. Is that it?"

"Ayup. Every year at this time it gets bad." Spring—heartless spring—it was always difficult to get through spring without Caroline. "You want to know how bad it got today?"

Seth dropped his hand from Gabe's shoulder and waited.

"I ran into Elfred Spear at the wharf, and this woman was with him—his sister-in-law, actually. She's divorced, she's got three kids and she's moving into Breckenridge's mess. I heard that, and I went hotfootin' it up there to see if she could use a carpenter." Gabe shook his head, a little abashed. "But she caught on to me, and let me tell you, Seth, she put me in my place. It was embarrassing."

"So that's why you're in this puckered-up mood." Seth went back to work, hammering a diagonal onto the crossbuck door. "What's she like?" he inquired offhandedly.

Gabriel turned from the doorway. "Heck, she's a mess." He resumed work, too. "Clothes, hair, house—you name it, everything a mess. Even her kids. They look like a bunch of orphans."

"So what are you standing here fussing about her for?"

"I don't know. Because I've got to go back there tomorrow and face her again, I suppose."

"Well, maybe she won't be there if the house is that bad."

"Oh, she'll be there all right. Probably playing her piano. I tell you, Seth, it was the darnedest thing you ever saw. There she sat, playing the piano in the middle of all that filth. And her kids were singing upstairs! You'd have thought they were living in the Taj Mahal. But you know what? They're a happy bunch. And one of those little girls, the youngest one, well, I want to tell you, that one's got a head on her shoulders. The way she talked, her mother teaches them a lot."

"That'd be the, ah, the woman with the tacky clothes."

Gabriel bent a wry glance at Seth. "What're you gettin' at?"

"This's the most you've talked about any woman since Caroline died, you know that?"

"You're demented, man. She's about as lovable as a water moccasin, so don't go spreading any rumors, you got me?"

"Yes sir!" Seth squelched a grin. "Gotcha!"

THE RAIN LET UP TOWARD evening. Gabriel stowed his tool caddy in his Ford C-Cab and lifted a hand in farewell to his brother. He headed downtown to their shop to pick up some price lists and catalogues before going home.

He lived on Belmont Street in a tall, narrow white house with a shed out back where he parked his truck. He passed beneath a white pergola on his way through the yard, glancing at the canes of the climbing roses. They were all he'd kept of Caroline's flowers, and for seven years he'd carefully pruned and fertilized them each summer. The rest of the garden he'd allowed to fall victim to the grass. This saddened him, for when he thought of Caroline, he thought of her in a sunbonnet, caring for the flowers she'd loved so much.

He stepped into the kitchen and was met by a reedy girl who had inherited his height, but little more of him. She was all Caroline's— from the buggy-whip thinness to the paprika hair. Though not classically pretty, she had her points. Her skin was fair and unflawed, and her green eyes tilted up at the corners.

"Hi, Daddy. I thought you'd never get here. I'm starving."

"You're always starving. What's for supper?"

"Fish cakes and boiled potatoes."

Mercy, he got so tired of fish cakes. But Isobel did the best she could. Often he felt guilty that she had to spend so much of her time on duties that a wife and mother should have handled.

He washed up while she put the fish cakes on two plates, dumped potatoes into a bowl, poured milk for herself and coffee for him.

"I met some new girls today," he said as the two sat down.

"Girls? You mean my age?"

"One of them. The other two are sixteen and ten. They just moved into town, and they're cousins of the Spear girls."

"What were they like?"

"The youngest one was smart as a whip. I talked to her the most. I don't know much about them, except they looked rather like ragamuffins. I found out they were moving into the old Breckenridge house, so I went there to scare up a little business."

"They must be awfully poor if they have a house like that."

"I think they are."

"Is their dad going to work at the mill?"

Gabriel took a swig of coffee. "Ah, no. Actually, there is no dad. Just a mother."

"Oh." Isobel grew somber. Because she had been reared primarily by Gabriel, it was difficult for her to imagine growing up without a dad. "Poor kids."

"I think they do all right. They certainly don't lack for imagination, and they seem to be a rather happy troop—singing, playing the piano, writing operas." He pushed back his plate.

"Writing operas!"

"Ayup. That's what the little one said. Her name is Lydia."

"My gosh! They must be brains!"

"I thought the same thing." He stood, picking up his stacked plate and cup. "Well, I've got an estimate to work on, so you get your schoolbooks and I'll leave half of the table for you."

They spent the next two hours sitting in their white-painted kitchen. It was a comfortable room with a pressed-tin ceiling and a curious combination of outdated and modernized equipment. The lights were electric, the range wood burning. The sink had a drainpipe but no faucet, only a pump.

Night pressed its dark face to the windows. When Isobel had finished studying, she looked up to find her father staring into space, his pencil idle. "Daddy?"

"Hm?" Gabriel started from his reverie. For some odd reason he'd been thinking about that Jewett woman. "What?"

"Maybe you should give up and go to bed. You're staring."

"Am I? Well, I'm not tired. Just woolgathering. Listen. I have to give this estimate to Elfred Spear. You don't mind if I take it over there now, do you?"

"Tonight?" she said in surprise. "It's kind of late, isn't it?"

Gabriel checked his pocket watch. "Nine. That's not too late." He pushed back his chair and tamped his estimate together. "Rain's stopped. Guess I don't need my oilskins. I won't be long."

She stretched, bending backward on her chair, both arms raised. "Okay. Good night, Daddy."

"See you in the morning." He went out without touching or kissing her, thinking how grateful he was to have her and worrying about the day when she'd probably get married and leave his house.

Disturbed by the prospect of loneliness, he put it from his mind.

HE PULLED up in Elfred's yard and left the truck's engine running as he approached the front door.

Elfred, in a smoking jacket, answered the bell himself. "Well, for heaven's sake, Gabe, what are you doing here at this hour?"

"Brought that estimate."

Elfred removed a cigar from his mouth and looked down at the papers in some surprise. "At nine o'clock at night? You *are* in a hurry, aren't you, Gabe?" He chuckled conspiratorially.

Gabriel scratched his left sideburn. "Well, I can use the work."

"Sure, Gabe. I know how it is." Elfred glanced at the estimate and said, "I don't know why I even bothered to have you write it up. She's not the kind of woman a man says no to, is she?"

Gabriel put his hand on the doorknob, eager to be away. It was useless to protest that he had no ulterior motives in hurrying with the estimate after the wisecracking he and Elfred had done at the woman's expense.

With a wicked grin Elfred said, "Go ahead, Gabe. Give 'er hell."

Gabe stalked back out to his truck, thinking, That Elfred is one repugnant man.

He drove home, where he walked into the kitchen and wearily pulled off his jacket. Then he washed and dried the dishes, wiped off the table and put a neat little doily in the middle, just as Caroline had always done. On it he put her philodendron plant. With his dish towel he wiped some fingerprints off a cabinet door, then folded the towel neatly.

Gabe looked the room over. Rugs aligned, cupboard neat, chairs pushed in. Just as Caroline would have liked it.

Near eleven o'clock he plodded upstairs to his lonely bed.

Chapter 4

THE Jewetts awakened late and ate boiled macaroni in hot buttered milk for breakfast—the fastest thing Roberta could devise to slam on the table. Things were in such chaos that the girls couldn't find their combs, and their dresses were wrinkled from traveling, but nobody seemed to care.

Late heading off for school their first day, neither Roberta nor the girls made an issue of it as they set out together.

"Would you look at that," Roberta remarked, catching sight of the harbor below. "Like one of Lydia's glass floats." The weather had cleared overnight. The water took on so intense a blue it appeared as if the sun were lighting it from below rather than above. The earth, washed by the previous day's rains, smelled brash and black. Late or not, the Jewetts were enraptured by their new surroundings.

They walked beneath an eddy of gulls who scolded continuously. Susan eyed them and scolded back. "*Cree cree* yourselves!*"

"Are they ring-billed?" Lydia asked.

"No, they're herring gulls," Susan replied.

Rebecca began reciting Swinburne:

> *The lark knows no such rapture,*
> *Such joy no nightingale,*
> *As sways the songless measure*
> *Wherein thy wings take pleasure. . . ."*

" 'To a Seamew.' " Roberta cocked her head and watched the birds. "A lovely choice, though these can't be mews, not on this coast. I agree with Susan. I think they're herrings."

Rebecca said, "I hope I like my English teacher."

"And my music teacher," added Susan.

"I like this town," Lydia, the pessimist, put in, surprising them all. "It's pretty."

At the school, the principal, Miss Abernathy, an overfed woman around forty, welcomed them, but noted that it was nearly nine thirty. "School begins at eight, Mrs. Jewett."

"Yes, I know," Roberta replied, unruffled, "but we were reciting Swinburne on our way."

"Swinburne?" repeated Miss Abernathy. "It's not common for our students to be familiar with his works."

"Oh, my girls are familiar with as many poets as I can get them to experience. And composers and authors as well."

"So we have a trio of scholars here. They should do very well."

Roberta left them at school without the slightest doubt that that's exactly what they'd do.

When she got back home, Gabriel Farley was sitting on her front step. "What do you want?" she asked ungraciously.

He lumbered to his feet. "I'm repairing your house."

"Hmph." She went into the house without even slowing.

His gaze followed her through the open doorway until she disappeared into the kitchen. He'd cooked his goose with her yesterday, that was for sure. Not that it mattered, because he really didn't like her much.

Resigned to the fact, he got his tool caddy from the truck. After examining the outside of the house, he decided he'd better get the porch torn off and rebuilt first. It was dangerous with the floor half rotted.

From the porch he heard Roberta dragging boxes around in the kitchen, unpacking things. "Mrs. Jewett?" he called.

She came to the doorway wearing a dish towel tied backward around her skirt. "What?"

"I'll start with the front porch if that's okay with you."

"I don't care where you start. Just don't bother me." Abruptly she hied herself out of sight again.

He got a ladder, climbed up to the porch roof and started ripping off the wooden shakes. The yard became littered with nails and broken pieces of wood. By late morning he had the rafters exposed and was beating on one with a hammer when he heard shouting.

"Mr. Farley?"

Gabe looked down from the ladder and saw Mrs. Jewett standing below, shading her eyes with one hand, squinting up. Her hair was a fright and the armpit of her blouse was damp.

"Ayup?" he said.

"May I ask you a few questions about your motorcar?"

"Ayup. Watch out." She stepped back, and he dropped a length of discolored wood. "It's not a car. It's a truck. A Ford C-Cab."

She glanced at it, then back up at him. "Do you like it?"

"Ayup, I do."

"Better than a horse?"

"You mind if I come down there and talk?" He'd been balancing his hips against the ladder and twisting to look down at her.

"No, of course not. Come ahead."

He backed down the ladder, and they stood their distance. "Truck's much easier than a horse. You don't have to feed it or clean up after it," Gabe said.

"Elfred says a woman couldn't own a motorcar, because she couldn't start it. Do you agree?"

Gabriel glanced at the truck. It was an odd-looking thing—doorless, with a black leather top. "That's hard to say. I've never seen a woman start one. Want to find out for sure?"

Her eyebrows twitched while she decided. "Yes, I suppose so."

"All right, then, come on. Let's see what you can do."

As he let her pass before him through the break in the bridal wreath shrubs that edged the yard, he noticed she wore the same scuffed, run-over shoes as the day before. They made their way to the far side of his truck.

"Get in." He motioned her up. "You might as well do it all, right from the start."

She stepped onto the running board, wrestled her skirt around the brake lever and sat down on the patent-leather seat.

"I'll take you through it step by step." He propped one foot on the running board and pointed as he spoke. "Now, that lever right there on the steering column is your spark. It's got to be on RETARD. If you accidentally leave it on ADVANCE, she'll kick back when you try to crank 'er, and chances are you'll get hurt."

"Spark on RETARD," she repeated, gingerly touching the lever.

Again he pointed to the steering column. "This right here is the throttle, and it should be halfway up when you start 'er. That gives 'er the gas."

"Throttle halfway up."

"And this"—he dropped a hand over the brake handle—"is the emergency brake, but it's got a lot to do with shifting, so make sure it's pulled all the way back." He moved his hand and let her give it a try.

"Good," he said. "Now get out. We've got to go up front."

If she were any other woman, he would have offered her a hand down. But the tongue-lashing she'd given him yesterday made him wary.

He led her to the front of the vehicle and pointed to a loop of wire protruding from the radiator. "That's the choke wire. Pull it out." She did, making no comment. "Now back inside again." She followed him to the driver's side. "Just reach in and turn the key to the battery position. Now let's see if you can crank 'er."

The crank had a wooden handle. When she reached for it, he pulled her arm back sharply. "Wait a minute. This is the most dangerous part. Always remember, you have to pull up. And one more thing. Don't wrap your thumb around the crank. Fold it along the top; that way, if she ever decides to kick back, your hand will fly free a little easier. Like this, see?"

487

He demonstrated, then moved aside and let her take over.

Gripping the crank handle, Roberta felt her heart dancing with apprehension. She glanced up and met Farley's eyes.

"It'll be okay," he said. "Everything is set right. Go ahead."

She set her jaw and pulled up so powerfully that a muscle wrenched in her shoulder. The engine fired, and Roberta leaped back with a hand over her heart. "I did it!"

"Go on!" he yelled above the noise. "Get back in!"

They both got in, and the racket was awful, the engine rocking the machine till the two of them looked palsied.

"Okay, your spark goes back down to ADVANCE so the engine'll run smoother, and the throttle goes back up."

She put the spark and then the throttle where he said.

"You want to drive 'er?" he asked.

"You mean you'd let me?" she replied, amazed. "Thank you, Mr. Farley. Yes, I'd appreciate it."

"Hands on the wheel, then."

She gripped the wooden steering wheel and sat tensely on the edge of the seat.

"Relax some."

"Relax? Doing this? You cannot be serious!"

He smiled to himself and pointed down at her feet. "Okay, those three pedals plus the emergency brake are what make it run. The left one puts it in neutral, the middle one is reverse and the right one is the brake. First put your emergency brake halfway up and push the neutral pedal all the way down. Don't be scared—halfway up."

She followed orders with far less assurance than she'd shown when she'd told Elfred she wanted to own one of these things. Her knuckles had turned white on the steering wheel.

"Now push the emergency brake full forward and your foot all the way down, and that puts 'er in first gear."

She shifted cautiously, and the car lurched forward, then began rolling down the boulevard, half on people's grass, half on the street.

"All right. Here we go. Use the throttle."

"Where's the throttle?" she shouted.

He took her right hand and guided it to the throttle lever. "Right there. Give 'er some gas now, slowly."

They accelerated and bumped along Alden Street.

"Good heavens, I hope I don't kill us both!"

"You'll get used to it. Turn left and go up the hill."

He helped her steer around the corner. "You're doing very well," he told her. "Do you think you'll want one of your own?"

"Please, Mr. Farley, I can't talk and drive at the same time."

"All right, I'll shut up." He sat back and watched her. She had gumption, and he couldn't deny a hint of admiration. He didn't know any other female who'd have gotten behind that steering wheel.

"Are you ready to try reversing now?"

"Oh, dear," she said.

"You'll do fine." He guided her through the process of slowing, turning around in a driveway and heading back down the mountain.

Halfway down, they encountered a car coming up.

"Mr. Farley!" she shouted. "What should I do?"

He resisted reaching for the steering wheel. "Just steer to the right."

She did, chanting, "Oh, my soul. Oh, my soul." He smiled to himself and waved at Seba Poole, who gaped as the two cars passed.

"You're lucky I didn't kill us both, Farley! I never knew roads were so narrow!"

"You did fine. Seba's still on the road and so are you."

She relaxed a little and asked, "Who was that?"

"Seba Poole. Runs the fish hatchery at Lake Megunticook. He likes to gossip, so word'll get around you've been driving my truck."

"Too bad for you," she remarked.

They rumbled the remainder of the way without conversing, but a grudging respect had been set in motion during the drive. She found him patient and good at explaining; he found her plucky and admired her grit in spite of her occasional shriek for help.

In front of her house she stopped, heaved a sigh of relief and let her fingers slide from the wheel. No sooner had her shoulders wilted than they squared again resolutely. "May I run through it one more time to make sure I remember?"

"Of course."

"Spark on RETARD," she said, and repeated what she'd learned without a slip. She met his eyes directly. "How did I do?"

"Perfectly."

As they stood in the street beside the vehicle, she studied it and finally said, "So tell me, Mr. Farley—you can be honest—do you think I'm crazy to want to own my own motorcar?"

"Well, you certainly can drive one. You've proven that today."

"There's a garage downtown where I could have it repaired, right?"

"Well, yes, if the trouble conveniently develops when you're in town. What do you want the car for?"

"I've got a job as a public nurse."

"Traveling all by yourself?" He acted surprised.

"Yes."

"In that case . . ." He clamped his hands beneath his armpits. She was beginning to see that the pose covered a range of responses.

"In that case, forget about the motorcar?"

"Well, let me put it this way. I wouldn't want any woman of mine driving all over these mountains in one of these things."

"Yes, well, you see, Mr. Farley, it's my good fortune that I no longer have to answer to any man for what I do."

"You asked my opinion and I gave it."

"Thank you, Mr. Farley," she said. "Now I'd best get back to work." She marched off to the house. He went back to work, wondering why she'd asked his opinion if she didn't want it.

Sometimes, from up on the ladder, he'd see junk come flying out the front door. Once she flung out some scrub water. Right afterward he heard the piano start up and stopped working to listen.

Strange woman, playing the piano between bouts of scrubbing.

SHORTLY after noon Roberta's mother arrived on foot.

"Mr. Farley," she hailed, "is that you up there?"

"Hello, Mrs. Halburton." She was tilted back, eyeing him with a grouchy expression—a jowly, overweight woman dressed in a pail-shaped hat, pressing a black purse against her diaphragm.

"I can't believe she hired you to fix up this old wreck. Why, it's hardly worth the match it would take to send the place up."

To the best of his recollection he'd never heard Myra Halburton greet anyone with anything but complaints. It gave him a twinge of pleasure to disagree with her. "Oh, I don't know. You might be surprised when I get all done."

She picked her way to the door, complaining nonstop about the construction mess. "Roberta," she called, "you in there?"

Gabe heard Roberta answer, "Mother?" She appeared at the door and her voice lost all color. "Hello, Mother. Come in."

Inside, Myra Halburton gave the place the once-over, grievance written all over her face. "This is all so unnecessary, Roberta. This is what comes of getting divorced. You had a decent home and a husband, and now you've got this."

"How do you know I had a decent home, Mother? You never came to see it."

"Oh, yes, blame me. You're the one who moved off, the minute you got old enough, as if your family meant nothing to you."

"I moved because I had to, to go to college. And I stayed with George because I had to. What else can a wife do? Well, now I can do as I please."

"But the disgrace, Roberta. It's all over town that you've divorced him. How's a mother supposed to hold her head up?"

"You might try telling people that I've got three lovely children I intend to support on my own with my job as a public nurse."

"Traveling all around the countryside unescorted? Oh, that'll really impress my friends. How do you intend to get around?"

"I'm buying a motorcar."

"A motorcar! There's no getting through to you, is there? Why can't you just take a job in the mill like the other women do?"

"The mill again! We were arguing about that when I left."

"You were always too good for the mill, weren't you?"

"It isn't a question of being too good for the mill. It's a question of what I wanted out of life."

"All I see is that you defied me years ago and went off to spend money your grandparents had left you—to study nursing, of all things. And look what it got you. This pathetic house." Myra touched her forehead. "You've given me a monstrous headache, Roberta. I need to go home and lie down."

"Very well, Mother. I'll tell the girls their grandmother stopped by and would like to meet them soon."

Her tone was acid enough to send Myra toward the door without a good-bye. Watching her go, Roberta thought sadly, Why should there be a good-bye when there was no hello? No hug. Only Myra sailing in on a billow of complaints, as always.

CHAPTER 5

W<small>HEN</small> Myra stormed out of the house, Gabe was sitting under a tree, finishing up a cheese sandwich.

"That girl has always had the power to exasperate me. Now I have to walk all the way back down, and what do I get for my trouble but her disrespect!"

Gabe sprang to his feet. "I can give you a ride, Mrs. Halburton."

"I'd be obliged, Mr. Farley. At least *some* young people know how to treat their elders!" She tramped straight to the truck, and he leaped forward to give her a hand up.

Gabe had heard enough of the argument to realize Roberta and her mother got along like a pair of hens tied over a clothesline. He thought of his own mother, a kind woman with loving ways, and felt a twinge of compassion for Roberta.

Myra complained all the way down—so much so that Gabe was ready to kick her out at ten miles an hour and watch her roll.

W<small>ATCHING</small> Myra climb into Farley's truck, Roberta indulged in a rare moment of heavyheartedness. Part of the reason Roberta had left Camden was to escape her mother. How misguided she'd been to believe the years might have tempered her.

Grace—the favorite had always been Grace. Grace, who walked, talked, postured the way Mama told her to; who stayed in Camden, married Elfred, gave him her inheritance to start his business, bore his children and turned a blind eye to his extramarital forays. Obviously, Elfred had the wool pulled over Myra's eyes as well.

Ten minutes after Farley's truck rolled away, Roberta was standing on a chair pulling some rotting curtains off a kitchen window when Elfred suddenly gripped her waist with both hands and said, "My-my-my. This is too tempting to resist."

She let out a screech. "Elfred, let me go!"

"What if I don't? What'll you do?"

She shoved at his arms, but he was surprisingly strong. "Elfred, I'm warning you! I'll tell Grace what a philandering goat you are."

Elfred only laughed. "You wouldn't do that to your sister."

"I will. So help me, I will. Elfred, stop that!"

"Ooo, Birdy, why don't you and me just slide up those stairs and make a few bedsprings twang?"

"Elfred, you're the most despicable heathen God ever put on this earth. Now let me go!" She kicked backward.

Elfred laughed once more and slid his hand up her calf.

From behind him Gabe Farley said quietly, "Hello, Elfred."

Elfred craned around, startled. "Oh, Gabe, it's just you! Whoo, you scared me. Didn't know who it was." Elfred let his hands trail off Roberta.

Gabe stood foursquare in the kitchen doorway feigning nonchalance when, in truth, he was feeling a faint twinge of revulsion.

Roberta scrambled down off the chair. Her face was scarlet.

"Something I'd like to show you out here, Elfred. You mind coming outside with me?" Gabe turned, and Elfred followed.

There was nothing he wanted to show Elfred, but they stood in the yard talking about the house. Eventually Elfred explained, "I was just having a little fun with her, Gabe. You know how it is."

"I don't think she was having as much fun as you were."

Elfred's eyebrows arched. "Oh, what's this? A different song than you were singing yesterday, isn't it, Gabe?"

"Come on, Elfred, use your head. You can't manhandle a woman that way. Why, I could hear her objecting clear across the yard. Suppose it had been Grace coming toward the house instead of me."

"You staking your claim on her, Gabe?"

Gabe raised his palms and let them drop. "That's *not* why I got you out of her kitchen. When a woman puts up a fight, you back off, Elfred. I shouldn't have to explain that to you."

"Well, Gabe, I won't horn in on your territory, but I'm going to keep an eye on you. After all, she's my sister-in-law, and I have to look out for her." Giving a wicked chuckle, Elfred departed.

Gabe eyed his touring car as it pulled away. What a jerk Elfred was! Was it only yesterday he himself had been abetting the man?

In the kitchen Roberta found herself grinding a bristle brush into the filthy floor as if it were her brother-in-law's liver.

THOUGH Roberta and Gabe kept out of each other's way as the day wore on, the scene in the kitchen remained in their minds. Finally, at three thirty, Roberta wiped her brow with the back of a wrist and listened. Nothing but silence. It was darned uncomfortable having Farley working around here, thinking who-knew-what about her run-in with Elfred.

What was he doing out there anyway? She untied the dish towel from her waist, tossed it onto a kitchen chair and went to the door. Farley was standing in the littered yard with his back to her, drinking water from a fruit jar. She watched for some time, trying to figure him out. He backhanded his mouth and capped the jar. Then he bent to start collecting the discarded shingles. He loaded a bunch of them on his arm, turned and saw her in the doorway.

And stalled, as if encountering a bear in the woods.

She did the same. They faced off, distrustful and staring. Finally she spoke. "I suppose you think I encouraged him."

"No, I don't." He carried the shingles off and dropped them.

"But isn't that what divorced women do?"

"Elfred is notorious around this town for chasing women. Everybody knows it but his wife."

"He is pathetic."

Still stinging from Elfred's taunts, Gabe felt obliged to put up some argument. "That may be, but when a man runs around, there's usually some pretty good reason at home."

"Oh, that's a typical reaction from a man," she said disdainfully. "Naturally, you'd blame my sister."

"I'm not blaming your sister. I was just making a generalization."

"Well, make your generalizations somewhere else! He's a family man. How do you think his daughters will feel if they find out their father is bedding any woman he takes a fancy to?"

He flashed the palms of two dirty gloves. "Look, I'm sorry I said what I did, all right?"

"Well, you should be, because you men don't consider what wives and children suffer when you have your innocent affairs. I know because I had a husband exactly like Elfred!"

She spun and disappeared into the house. Like many men in town, Gabe had often laughed about Elfred's adulteries and disparaged his wife for her ignorance. But watching him use his wiles on Birdy Jewett left Gabe questioning how funny it actually was.

Stacking shingles for a bonfire and intent on his thoughts, he was unaware of the children's return from school until one of them spoke—the little one he'd enjoyed so much yesterday.

"Hi, Mr. Farley. Look who's here!"

495

"Hi, Daddy!"

"Isobel! Well, for heaven's sake!"

"Susan and I met at recess," Isobel explained, "and I told her you were working for her mother, so she asked me if I wanted to come home and see where they're going to live."

Rebecca exclaimed, "Our porch is gone!"

"I'm just about to burn it up."

"Mother, we're home!" The four girls started to boost each other over the doorjamb while Roberta came to stand above them.

"How was school? And who is this?"

"This is Isobel!" they chorused.

Gabe picked up a plank and strode across the yard. "Girls, wait!" He angled it like a gangway, and they climbed it like sailors and bounced on it, babbling about school. Somehow amidst the chatter Isobel's full name got through to Birdy.

"Isobel Farley?" she repeated.

"He's my dad," Isobel confirmed.

Roberta met Gabe's glance from her high vantage point. "Oh, yes, of course. Well, hello, Isobel."

Lydia said, "He's going to build a bonfire to burn the shingles. Can we help him, Mother?"

"Yes, please! Can we?"

The girls trooped down the gangplank as Gabe ignited the stack of shingles. They collected more and fed the fire while Gabe stood back and tended it with a rake.

Without preamble Rebecca began reciting: " *'By the shores of Gitche Gumee,/ By the shining Big-Sea-Water—'* "

"What's that?" Isobel said.

"That's *Hiawatha*. Don't you know *Hiawatha?*" She paused and struck a dramatic pose. "I am Hiawatha, courageous Indian brave, fasting in the forest *'in the blithe and pleasant Spring-time. . . .'* " Without the slightest compunction she began to chant and dance, as if she were wearing buckskin and eagle feathers. Her sisters picked up the cue and danced, too, round and round the fire, while Isobel, as inhibited as her father, stared in fascination.

Abruptly Rebecca broke off her chant. "I know!" she exclaimed. Her sisters stopped as well. "Lobsters!" She bounded toward the gangplank. "Mother, can we go collect lobsters and cook them on the bonfire?"

"The bushel basket's in my bedroom, full of towels." Roberta turned away, and her three girls scampered after her. Momentarily they returned with Lydia in the lead, carrying the basket.

"Come on, Isobel!" she cried. "You have to show us where Sherman's Cove is. That's where Mother says the lobsters are."

Isobel stood rooted and dazed. "May I?" She looked up at Gabe.

"Lobsters?" Nobody ate lobsters. They washed up on the rocks at high tide and made nuisances of themselves. Those who bothered to pick them up buried them for fertilizer. He murmured at her ear, "Are you sure you want to eat lobsters?"

"I want to go along. Please, Daddy."

He had his doubts about this wild trio, but Isobel had an eagerness in her eye that had been absent for a long time. "Go ahead," he said, "but change your dress first."

"But Daddy, if I do that, it'll be too late!"

"Oh, all right, go ahead. But tomorrow you change immediately after school, as usual." Isobel scurried after the other three.

In their wake the yard grew silent except for the snapping fire. Gabe finished raking up the trash and burned up most of the remaining shingles. His tools were in the truck and he was squatting beside a brilliant bed of coals by the time the girls came lugging the bushel basket with their cache covered with seaweed. Their dresses were filthy, and their shoes wet. Isobel's hair was hanging like sea grass. Everybody was talking at once.

"Look, they're positively huge!"

"Oh, the fire is just right!"

"Mother, where's the lobster pot?"

"Come and see them, Daddy! Rebecca knew how to put sticks in their claws so we didn't get pinched."

There followed an admiring of lobsters, with four disheveled girls trotting all over the yard, into the house, back out. Roberta called, "You may stay if you'd like, Mr. Farley, and eat with us."

Lobsters? He shuddered. Moreover, he remembered Elfred's innuendo. "No, thanks. I'll be going home now."

HE WENT home and ate alone. Sardines and soda crackers. Some tinned peaches. Two cups of hot coffee. Three cinnamon jumble cookies his mother had made. He washed his fork and cup, watered Caroline's houseplant, swept the kitchen floor, shook the rugs, and

Isobel hadn't shown up yet. He bathed and shaved, and still she hadn't come home. Gabe had decided to get in the truck and go back there to fetch her, when she arrived, breathless and flushed.

"Daddy," she called from downstairs. "Daddy, where are you?"

"Isobel?"

She came bounding up the stairs to his bedroom.

"What in the world have you been doing out this late?"

"Oh, the Jewetts are so much fun! We were sitting around the fire, and Mrs. Jewett got out a copy of Longfellow, and she read us the first verse of *The Song of Hiawatha*. Then everybody took turns reading a verse. They know some of them by heart! We're going to read the next five verses tomorrow."

From a girl who was easily bored by everything, from school to family visits, such exuberance impressed her father.

He asked, "How was the lobster?"

"Messy, but pretty tasty. Mrs. Jewett melted butter and fried rice cakes, and we ate them with our fingers."

"Isobel," he said gently, "I know you had a good time with the Jewetts, but their mother lets them run pretty wild. You can't be staying out after dark and traipsing off after school without changing your dress and eating around a fire like some savage Indian."

"Why, the Indians aren't savage! Have you read *Hiawatha?*"

"No, I haven't. I'm only asking you to remember the manners you've always been taught and the rules we've had in this house."

"I will, Father. May I go to their house tomorrow, then?"

He had no logical excuse to refuse. "If you change your dress first and act like a lady. And you'll ride home to supper with me."

"I will."

Later, after he had come to her room to say good night, Isobel tried to remember if he'd ever hugged her the way Mrs. Jewett hugged her girls. Once, when Lydia was reading, Mrs. Jewett had reached over and rubbed her head, and Lydia had gone on as if she didn't even notice. I'd notice if my dad ever rubbed my head, Isobel thought. Or if he ever hugged me good night.

Suddenly, drawing up her covers, Isobel felt the sharp stab of loneliness she always hid from her father. The image of her mother was fading. "Mother," she whispered. "Mother."

She whispered it that way sometimes, because she never got a chance to say it aloud the way other children did.

CHAPTER 6

As soon as the girls were off to school the following morning, Roberta set out for Boynton's Motor Car Company toting her umbrella. Clouds, heavy with mist, skulked at sea level and dampened everything that moved through them.

Inside Boynton's, it smelled like rubber but was blessedly dry. Roberta stamped her feet on the horsehair mat.

"Good morning. May I help you?"

She looked up and encountered the bespectacled face of a heavyset man in his forties. He wore a mustache and a pin-striped suit.

"I hope so. I'd like to buy a motorcar."

It took a beat before he replied, placing his palms flat together and rubbing them twice. "Certainly, madam. Hamlin Young at your service. And you are?"

"Roberta Jewett."

"Jewett. The sister-in-law of Elfred Spear?"

"Yes. Grace's sister."

"Ahh," he crooned, tipping his chin up. "Someone told me you were moving to Camden."

Elfred, undoubtedly. He must have happened to mention Roberta was divorced, too, the way Hamlin Young's eyes glinted with new speculation. She predicted what would happen next: He'd take the liberty of touching her somewhere.

"The motorcar, Mr. Young," she reminded him.

"Yes, of course. Have you ridden in one yet?"

"Yes, a couple of times."

"Have you driven one?"

"Just once."

"You have! Well! That's amazing. I must admit I haven't sold one to a woman yet."

"Then I'll be the first. I have some questions for you, Mr. Young, about the cost and the maintenance."

"We'll get to that later. First let me show you what we've got." There it was: He touched her elbow with the tips of his fingers. He touched her again while presenting the Oldsmobile Runabout, and again as he directed her to an Overland Touring Car. By the time they came to an ordinary Model T, she adroitly kept plenty of space between them.

"How much would this one cost?"

"Three hundred and sixty dollars, brand spanking new."

Only three hundred sixty. Elfred had said six hundred.

"If I buy this and it needs repair, will you do it here?"

"Yes, ma'am. But I wouldn't be doing my job unless I warned you about some of the things you'll have to know how to do."

She was informed about the tires needing patching, the carburetor needing frequent adjustment, the fan belts needing replacing.

"But I thought you did repairs."

"These are all things that can happen out on the road."

"Oh," she said, showing her first hint of dismay.

He could tell she was disappointed and touched her on the shoulder with an open hand that lingered. "I'll be glad to show you how to do some of these things."

His presumption snapped her out of her funk. "If a man can do it, I can do it. I'll be back, Mr. Young."

She went next to the Camden Bank. Mr. Tunstill, the vice president, gave her run-down shoes and threadbare jacket the once-over and informed her that his bank could not authorize one-hundred-and-fifty-dollar loans to women. He suggested she marry a man with an automobile if she wanted to drive.

She was back out in the drizzle in less than ten minutes, so angry she was unaware of the fact that her shoes were getting soaked.

Back at Boynton's she asked Mr. Young what arrangements could be made if she didn't have enough cash. He was sorry, he said, but without a bank loan his hands were tied.

She had only one other possibility, and loathe though she was, she decided to give it a try.

Elfred's real estate company was housed in one of the new brick structures on Main. When Roberta walked in, he spied her through his glass-walled office and came at her with arms extended. "Birdy! What an unexpected surprise!" He herded her into his office while they were followed by inquisitive eyes. He stationed her on an oak chair beside his rolltop desk and swiveled his own chair to face her. "What brings you down here, Birdy?" His eyes glinted wickedly. "You change your mind about what I suggested yesterday?"

"Stop it, Elfred!"

He grinned and leaned back comfortably, extending a foot so it got lost inside the folds of her skirt.

"Your employees are watching," she reminded him.

"All they can see is our heads and shoulders. What do you want?"

"A loan."

"Ooo, a loan," he singsonged. "For that car you want?"

"That's right."

"What'll you put up?"

"Nothing. I'll sign a promissory note."

"Mmm, you'll have to do better than that, Birdy." He began to run his shoe up and down her shin. She rammed her heel into his kneecap and thrust him backward, chair and all. He gasped.

"A hundred and fifty, please, Elfred, and make it quick before I decide to tell Grace what you suggested within twenty-four hours of my moving into town."

He said, nursing his knee, "Don't try to bamboozle me, Birdy. I'm a bigger bamboozler than you are."

"You don't think I'd tell her? Try me."

Her threat began to sink in, and Elfred lost his cockiness. "That's blackmail, Birdy, and you know it."

"Yes. And if you wish to prosecute me for it, go ahead. Of course, you'll have to weigh whether it's worth losing the respect of your wife and children, because I *will* tell Grace."

"You've got a lot of nerve, Birdy, you know that?"

"Don't put me to the test. I can sign a promissory note or I can put a serious crimp in your life. Now which will it be?"

He scooted his chair to a black safe and started spinning its dial. She watched his shoulders, and when he turned, he handed her a wad of bills. She stuffed them into her jacket pocket while rising. "Have a note prepared, and I'll sign it, dear brother-in-law."

She left him with a sour expression on his handsome face.

WHEN she got back home, there was a stack of lumber in her yard, and Gabe Farley was hammering down a brand-new porch floor. His brother was with him; both were dressed in slickers.

"I didn't think you'd be working in the rain," Roberta said.

"Wait for a sunny day in Maine, you'll never get any work done," Gabe answered. "This is my brother, Seth. This is Mrs. Jewett."

They exchanged hellos—hers cool, his curious.

Since the plank was gone, Roberta struck off for the back door, but Gabe's voice stopped her. "Thank you for letting Isobel stay last night. She couldn't quit talking about it when she got home."

"You're welcome." She headed away again.

"She likes your girls," he called.

"They like her, too," she replied without slowing or turning as she disappeared around the house.

Seth watched her go. "She doesn't like you much, does she?"

"No, not much."

"But Isobel stayed over last night?"

"Just for supper. I don't want her hanging around here too often, though. I get the feeling Roberta lets her girls run wild."

"Which you and I never did."

Gabe grinned at Seth over his handsaw, and they both got busy.

At four o'clock the girls, including Isobel, returned from school. All four girls yammered at once. "Wow! A new porch floor! It can be our stage." They clumped around on the fresh boards, getting them wet and dirty. Rebecca spread her arms like a thunderbird and recited a few lines of *Hiawatha* to the front yard. The others applauded raucously, and then they all tramped inside.

Gabe and Seth—one on the roof, one on a ladder—exchanged glances. Gabe shrugged. "See what I mean?"

Inside, the girls' voices could be heard as they charged through the house, into the kitchen, up the stairs. The men could hear Roberta calling, "Hey! Come down here and tell me about school."

After a while they all piled outside, still in their school dresses, eating cold rice cakes. "Daddy, I'm taking the girls home to show them our house!" Isobel shouted.

He stopped hammering and peered over the edge of the roof. What could he say? His daughter had been a guest here yesterday. "Change your dress when you get there. And don't make a mess."

"We won't!" Off they galloped through the mist.

On the roof, Gabe watched them. From the front door, with her hands on her waist, so did Roberta.

WHEN the three Jewett girls saw Isobel's kitchen, they came up short. "Golly, it's so clean," they said in awe.

"We keep it just the way Mother kept it," said Isobel.

"How long has she been dead?"

502

"Seven years."

"How did she die?"

"Our horse kicked her."

"Oh, how awful."

"Then you know what my dad did?" The Jewetts waited, rapt. "He shot the horse. I saw him crying after he did it, and I was only seven years old, but I remember it just as clear as a bell."

"Gosh," someone said, breathless.

"I'll tell you a secret," said Isobel. "Her clothes are still in the bureau."

It was Lydia who asked in a whisper, "Could we see them?"

"Only if you promise not to touch them. He's real funny about her things. You can only look, okay?"

They tiptoed through the spotless parlor and up the narrow stairs. Just inside the bedroom door, the girls stood respectfully silent. Isobel went to the bureau, which had drawers along the right and a tall door on the left. She opened the door and said, "See? This was her nightgown, and these were her dresses."

"Golly, doesn't it give you the willies?"

"No, silly. She was my mother." Isobel closed the door.

Susan spotted a photograph in an oval frame. "Is that her?"

"Yes. Daddy has kept it here forever."

"Gee, she was beautiful." Susan picked it up and gazed.

"Don't touch, Susan, remember?"

"Oh, sorry." She replaced the picture.

"Now I'll show you my room."

After the tour of her room Isobel obediently changed clothes, then offered them cinnamon jumble cookies. "My grandma fills the cookie jar every week, just like my mother did." The four of them cleaned up the cinnamon jumbles, leaving an empty jar.

ROBERTA'S girls returned home bursting with the story of the dead woman whose clothing still hung in her husband's bureau.

"Mother, guess what."

"I couldn't guess. What?"

Rebecca did the honors. "Mr. Farley's wife was kicked by his horse and she died. Then he shot the horse himself and killed it. Isobel saw him crying afterward! Isn't that romantic?"

A shudder went through Roberta. "That's not romantic. That's

503

tragic." She set aside her ironing and sat at the kitchen table with her girls.

"And listen to this! He keeps the house just the way she left it, and she's been dead *seven years,* and her clothing is still hanging beside his in their bureau. We saw it."

"And her picture is on his dresser, and she's just beautiful. She had on a white dress, and her hair was just like Lillian Russell's."

Roberta's gaze drifted toward the front porch, where Farley had been working. She imagined him keeping a shrine to his beautiful dead wife, this carpenter who could irritate her so, and her expression softened. "That's very pitiful."

"We ate up all the cinnamon jumble cookies," Lydia divulged.

"All?"

Lydia nodded.

"Well, he won't be too pleased about that. I don't think he wanted you over there in the first place."

"Why not?"

"He's not used to having a tribe of hooligans traipsing through the place, like I am. Now listen"—Roberta cheered up—"I have something to tell you. We're getting our new motorcar tomorrow."

There were a lot of questions and rejoicing then, and the subject of the Farley household was dropped.

But across town, when Gabe finished his supper and reached into the cookie jar, he found it empty and swore under his breath.

CHAPTER 7

THE girls had gone to school the next morning when Roberta heard the first hammerblows on the porch. What had happened to her animosity toward Gabriel Farley? Since the girls had come home with their story about his wife, her negative feelings seemed to have dissipated like clouds from the sky.

He kept popping into her thoughts, and whenever he did, she always pictured him in a doorway, which is where he'd been when he'd so fortuitously interrupted Elfred. She had seen two sides of Farley: One considered divorced women fair game; the other rescued them from unwanted attention. One held that all marital troubles started with the woman; the other was a husband who had kept a shrine to his wife for seven years. What kind of man was capable of such devotion? Roberta admitted she was mystified by him.

She headed out her back door and around the house. She could hear the hammers in syncopation, ringing through the foggy day with an eerie bell-like tone. In the front she encountered Farley constructing a new set of steps. Whereas yesterday she had all but snubbed him, today she paused. "Good morning, Mr. Farley."

He straightened slowly. "Morning, Mrs. Jewett."

At the far end of the porch his brother was putting up a railing. "Morning, Mr. Farley," she offered.

"Ma'am," he replied, remembering her snub and continuing to work, leaving Roberta to face Gabriel.

"I hear my girls emptied your cookie jar last night."

He dropped his chin and drawled, "Waaal . . ."

"I'm not very domestic," she admitted. "When they get around good food, they sometimes lose their manners."

"My mother fills it every week. She'll load it up again."

Why would a man keep his wife's clothing? she wondered. Did he take it out and touch it? This disconcerting picture made him more human than Roberta wanted him to be. She shored up her wayward thoughts and said, "Well, I'm off to Boynton's to get myself a motorcar."

"You're buying one, then."

"Yes, a Model T Ford."

"It's for sure you'll know how to drive it." He ventured a grin.

"Yes, I will, won't I?" She nodded. "Well, see you later."

When she was gone, Seth remarked dryly, "Oh, she's talking to you today."

"Seems to be a moody woman," Gabe replied, returning to work.

SHE drove her spanking new Model T Ford away from Boynton's, feeling sassy and free, with the side curtains rolled up in spite of the drizzle. Her own motorcar, completely paid for! And nobody to tell her where she could go with it!

Such elation demanded company, so she stopped at Grace's and gave several bleats on her Klaxon.

Grace stuck her head out the front door and slapped her cheek. "Oh, merciful heavens, what will she do next?"

"Grace, come on out and take a ride with me."

"Are you insane, Roberta?"

"Not at all! Come on, we'll go show Mother."

"Mother will be furious."

"Mother is always furious. Come with me anyway!"

"Oh, Birdy." Grace flapped a hand, but this innocent collusion became more than she could resist. When they were girls, it was always Birdy who got them in trouble, and as she grabbed her coat, Grace realized she was letting herself in for more of the same.

Their mother lived in a sturdy two-story Colonial on Elm Street. In the few short blocks it took to get there, the sisters reverted to giggles, driving along, ringing the brass bell beside the Klaxon, feeling smart and worldly in this man's contraption that drew open-mouthed stares from all the drivers they passed.

Grace went to her mother's door. "Look, Mother, Birdy's done it. She bought the motorcar!"

"Oh, that girl, she'll be the persecution of me yet! And you shouldn't be riding in it. People will be calling you loose women."

"But Mother, what harm can come of a little ride?"

"Does Elfred know you're running around alone?" asked Myra.

"No." Grace's enthusiasm was fading fast.

"You tell your sister to take you straight back home before Elfred finds out!" Myra raised her voice and screeched at Roberta, "You might think it's just fine to go out and buy yourself a car, but this is a small town, and women don't do things like that. Now you take your sister home!" She slammed the door.

Grace returned to the car somewhat glum. "Mother's probably right. I knew it before I came with you."

By the time she had returned Grace to her house, Roberta's own spirits were dampened. She should have known better. Grace was not only under Elfred's thumb, she was under Mother's as well.

When Roberta pulled up at home, the reaction she received was far different. Farley and his brother stopped pounding and moved toward the car like children toward a circus.

"Well, there she is!" Farley called. "And isn't she pretty!"

Roberta got out and met them at the bridal wreath hedge. Seth started circling the car, but Gabe stayed by Roberta. "Did you leave the spark lever up so you don't break an arm next time?" he asked.

"I did."

"And the throttle up, too?"

"The throttle, too."

"You learn quickly, Mrs. Jewett."

"I'll have to. I've a whole mess of repair tools that Hamlin Young assured me I *had* to have—a tire-patching kit, a spare fan belt, and screwdrivers and wrenches for the carburetor."

"And don't forget the transmission bands."

"Oh, dear," she said, touching her lips melodramatically like a maiden in distress, putting them both in danger of laughing. The moment held a beat of disquiet while they stood in the rain enjoying each other, taken off guard by the realization that they were becoming friends.

Her voice held a teasing note as she spoke again. "What is this new nuisance, transmission bands?"

"Something that can be adjusted pretty simply with a screwdriver. You'll know when they need it, because the pedals will go all the way to the floor."

"And then will I crash into the next fixed object?"

He did laugh this time. "It won't happen suddenly. You'll feel it for a while. The car will start running jerky."

Seth returned from circling the car. "There's nothing like a Ford," he said, then added, "Well, I got a porch to finish." He went off to do so, leaving Gabe with Roberta, studying the Model T.

She grinned at Gabe. "You know, I couldn't afford a car, so I blackmailed Elfred over that incident in the kitchen."

Gabe's surprised eyes flashed her way. "You didn't."

"Yes, I did. I told him I'd tell Grace if he didn't lend me one hundred and fifty dollars."

Amusement put crow's-feet at the corners of Gabe's eyes. "So old Elfred's finally come up against one woman he can't charm."

"That's right. By the way, I never said thank you for rescuing me from him," Roberta said quietly. "I'm grateful you did."

"Oh." He crossed his arms and nudged at the gravel with the toe of his Wellington. Then he looked at her squarely and said, "This is a mighty uncomfortable subject, Mrs. Jewett, after the remarks I made about you. You know, I'm real sorry about that."

"Are you? Well, you're forgiven, Mr. Farley."

He stood a moment, meeting her eyes, his face lighting with color; then he cleared his throat. "I'd better get back to work, too. You let me know if there's anything I can teach you about the car."

"I will. Thanks."

They walked toward the house separately, as if uncomfortable with the turn their friendship had taken.

ROBERTA loved having the girls around the house. That afternoon she picked them up at school along with her three nieces and Isobel. The clan had grown until she hadn't enough chairs in the front room for them. They had decided to do a dramatization of *Hiawatha* instead of the infamous sketch about the earless great-great-grandfather, and were choosing stanzas and talking about costumes.

Roberta learned a lot about the Farley household by listening to their chatter. Like all children getting to know one another, they asked questions, and Isobel answered, editing nothing.

"My dad hates going to school for programs. He probably wouldn't come even if we did do *Hiawatha* there."

"Sundays we eat at Grandma's, but mostly I cook for my dad."

"In the evenings? Oh, I don't know. We do dishes, and I study. Sometimes I have to help him clean the house."

What Roberta pieced together was the picture of a lonely girl with a very boring existence. She began to notice Isobel's overt response to any sign of affection. When Roberta hugged the girl farewell that night, Isobel hugged her back hard and exclaimed, "Oh, Mrs. Jewett, I love it at your house! It's so much fun here."

"Well, you're welcome anytime, Isobel."

Roberta tried to remember if she'd ever seen Gabriel hug his daughter, but she didn't think so.

CHAPTER 8

ON FRIDAY morning Roberta went to the regional office of public nursing in Rockland, seven miles from Camden. There she got her orders from a sweet-faced woman named Eleanor Balfour, who issued her white uniforms, caps and medical supplies; gave her assignments for the coming week; and advised her she would need to get a telephone wire into her home, for which the state would pay.

"A reminder about our service," Miss Balfour concluded. "It's as much teaching as it is nursing—in homes, in the schools, wherever you go, be prepared to preach cleanliness and hygiene." She pushed back her chair. "A major portion of our fight is against ignorance. And," she added with a smile, "muddy roads in the spring. They don't call us nurses on horseback for nothing."

"I won't be on horseback, Miss Balfour. I own a motorcar."

"You do! And you've mastered driving it?"

"If not mastered, at least minored."

Miss Balfour laughed. "Well, good luck, Mrs. Jewett."

ROBERTA found herself excited and needing someone with whom to share her exhilaration. Almost naturally, it seemed, she hurried home to Gabe, who had showed up earlier without his brother.

"Hey, Mr. Farley, I got my first assignment!" Roberta crowed as she barreled across the yard.

Gabe came down the ladder. "Which is . . ."

"Inoculating schoolchildren against diphtheria. I'll start right here in Camden. Have you ever been inoculated, Mr. Farley?"

"Nope."

"I'll do that for you if you like."

"Oh, you'd relish the idea of making me howl, wouldn't you?"

Roberta wasn't above a little teasing. "Come on. You've probably hit yourself with a hammer that hurt more than this little shot will."

Suddenly, down below, the mill whistle blasted. "Well, it's noon," she remarked. "I'm hungry. Have you eaten yet?"

"Nope. Still in the truck."

"I'll make us some coffee if you want to eat with me."

"Sounds like a good idea. I'm ready to take a break."

Ten minutes later they sat in her kitchen at a scarred wooden table eating sandwiches. The room was far from neat, but he could see she had scrubbed it down and washed the windows.

"Guess what," Roberta said. "The state of Maine is going to pay for a telephone wire for me."

"Well, congratulations." He reached for his coffee cup. "Just watch what you say on it."

"Why?"

"Party lines. My mother likes to listen in on them."

She sat back comfortably. "What is your mother like?"

"My mother?" He thought awhile. "Oh, she's a nice woman. She does a lot of housework for Isobel and me. She's a widow, so washing our clothes and filling our cookie jar gives her something to do."

"My mother and I never got along. That's pretty much why I left Camden," said Roberta.

"How old were you then?"

"Eighteen. Right after high school. She wanted me to go to work in that infernal mill, and I absolutely refused. She thought I'd settle down here and wait on her, just like Grace. But my grandmother had died and left Grace and me each a small inheritance. Grace gave hers to Elfred to start his business. I took mine and went away to college, which upset my mother a lot.

"Now, with my college education and my worldly ways, I have disgraced myself by throwing off a husband and returning to Camden with little more than the clothes on my back. My mother fails to see that if I hadn't pursued my nursing career, my children would have starved. Their father would have seen to *that*."

"He wasn't from Camden?"

"No, from Boston. From everywhere, really. Wherever there was a roving card game or a woman who'd come running when he'd crook his finger at her. The last time I saw him I told him he was free to live with any woman he wanted. All he had to do was sign the divorce agreement. He refused, so I bribed him by offering him one last stake. Do you know how much it was?"

She met Gabriel's eyes while he sat waiting.

"Twenty-five dollars," she said quietly. "He got rid of a wife and three daughters for a measly twenty-five dollars."

He noted the hurt in her eyes as she looked away. The room grew very quiet. Gabe's attention was riveted on the woman whose face had suddenly lost its toughness. It lasted only seconds before her gaze returned to him.

"And you know what?" In place of the hurt a touch of pride lit her eyes. "I've never been happier in my life. I don't have much, but I don't need much. And I certainly don't need a husband, nor do I want one. What's kept me going are my children."

Their eyes locked, but neither said a word for a long stretch.

Finally he asked, "Why did you marry him, then?"

"I don't know. He was a charmer. He talked a fancy game, and I fell for it, just like a dozen other women after me."

It was rare for Roberta to let her vulnerabilities show. Gabriel guessed as much and once again said nothing, only waited for her to go on. But suddenly the spell seemed to have broken.

"Goodness, I've bent your ear," she said. "Now it's your turn. What about your wife?"

"My wife?"

She could see he would take some drawing out. "Your marriage was a lot different from mine," she prompted.

"Oh, yes." He reached for a salt shaker and absently toyed with it. "As night and day." He sat ruminating for so long she wished he had a crank, like her Model T, so she could get him started. Finally he said, "She was pretty 'bout perfect." He sat up a little straighter, keeping his eyes on the shaker. "She was kind and gentle and pretty as a rosebud. I was a carpenter. What could I give her? Why, when she said she'd marry me, I was so . . ." Roberta waited, just as he had during her story. "I thought I was the luckiest man since the birth of time. We had a mighty good life together. Bought that little house on Belmont Street. Then Isobel came along, and Caroline wanted more babies, but, well, none came." He cleared his throat.

"Anyway, one day—it was seven years ago next Tuesday, April eighteenth—she stopped downtown for something, and just as she was getting back in the carriage, the mill whistle blew and scared the horse." He paused, swallowed. "It reared, and . . ."

His story faded into silence as Roberta glanced at the telltale shine in his eyes, and he stared out the window. Her throat had closed, and her heart tumbled along like a stone in the rapids.

When he spoke again, his broken voice said as much as his words. "It's hard to lose somebody when you aren't done with them yet."

She didn't know what to say.

"Well"—he pushed back his chair and got to his feet—"that porch isn't going to paint itself." Turning his back, he tried to hide the fact that he was swiping at his eyes with the side of his hand.

She tried to remember if she had ever seen a man this close to tears, but nothing came to mind. She had not intended to wrench his heart so, and she could tell that he was chagrined at having shown her more than he intended.

"It's all right, Mr. Farley," she said kindly, rising, too. "There's no need to feel ashamed of a few tears."

He nodded, hanging his head, and she studied the back of his hair as it lifted from his collar in sandy brown spikes.

"Listen." He half glanced over his shoulder. "Thanks for the coffee." He walked out, giving her a view of nothing but his back.

FROM THE STORIES THEY HAD told, each knew that the other was suffering from a past that left no room for new love. She was done with men for good. He still loved his dead wife. But every noise that they heard through the walls served as a reminder that they had created a bond between them, and nothing would ever change it.

Later that afternoon Roberta was pressing one of her uniforms when Gabe called, "Mrs. Jewett?"

How odd. The sound of his voice suddenly put a flutter beneath her ribs. She set down the iron and went to the doorway. "Yes?"

He was standing just inside the threshold. "I finished up out here, so I'm going to call it a day. I'll be back on Monday morning, but if you're gone before I get here, well, you have a good first day."

"Yes, thank you. I'll be working at the girls' school."

"Well, you take it easy on those kids, then."

She smiled guardedly. They stood for a moment; then he shifted his weight to the opposite foot. "About earlier," he said self-consciously. "I'm sorry. I shouldn't have told you all that."

"It's all right. I'm glad you did."

"No. I got a little carried away. I could see it made you . . . Well, that wasn't—" He ran out of words and ended by clearing his throat. "Well, you know what I mean." Only now did he meet her eyes. "I imagine Isobel will be showing up here with your girls, so tell her to be home by six, will you?"

"Certainly. She'll be there."

He nodded once—and stood there. So did she. Each recognized a faint reluctance to face two days without seeing the other.

"Better go," he said.

"Have a nice weekend."

"Ayup. You, too."

ROBERTA had trouble keeping her word about getting Isobel home by six. The girls had brought home another new friend, Shelby DuMoss, as well as Grace's girls. All eight had headed up the mountain to look for birch bark, and came back lugging a dead tree. They were unrolling the bark to make the shell of a canoe for their play when Roberta announced it was time for guests to go home.

"Oh, nooo!" they chorused. "Just a few minutes longer? Please?"

"No. I promised Isobel's father."

Isobel went, but she was back the next day and so were all the others. Roberta took them on a hike up Mount Battie, and they identified birds and explored the budding dogwoods and the willows and a pond where frogs sang.

Later they tramped downhill all the way to the shore and came upon some boys cleaning flounder and got a bucketful in exchange for free admission to the first performance of *Hiawatha*.

Roberta fried the flounder and took them outside, where she sat with the girls on the porch floor with their legs hanging over the edge. It was there Gabriel found them as he came on foot across the front yard. Though they all saw him coming, none spoke as he approached, only chewed their fish and licked their fingers.

"Evening," he said lazily.

"Evening," they all replied in unison.

"Figured I'd find you here, Isobel."

"I've had my supper if that's what you're worried about."

"So I see." He shifted his gaze to Roberta and let it stay.

"Would you like some flounder, Mr. Farley?" she said levelly.

"No, thank you. I've had my supper."

"Too bad." She swung her heels like the girls, and he could tell from the thumps that they were marking his new latticework.

"I like Isobel home by six," he told Roberta pleasantly.

"It's Saturday. I didn't think you'd mind."

"She's got her hair to wash and shoes to polish for church."

"Oh, that's right. Well then, Isobel, time to go." Roberta leaned back to see Isobel down the line.

Isobel reluctantly got up. "Night, dear," Roberta said softly.

"Night. And thank you."

Roberta watched to see if Gabe would drape an arm around his daughter's shoulders as they turned and headed across the yard, but he didn't. They just walked off into the growing dark.

ON SUNDAY afternoon Grace showed up, driven by Elfred in their black touring car. She barged right into the house, braying, "Roberta, I've got to talk to you. It's about these girls and the hours you've got them keeping! Elizabeth DuMoss called me to ask what kind of a place you're running over here. She demands to know just what was going on last night, and so do I!"

Elfred came in, too, and hung back just far enough to give his nasty glances room to sail.

Grace carped on. "You had my girls eating fried fish with their fingers! And you took them tramping up that mountain and let them get their dresses filthy!"

Roberta suddenly grew tired of her sister. "Yes, Grace, and they loved it. As a matter of fact, they didn't want to go home."

"Oh, Roberta," Grace gasped melodramatically, "how you do wound me. Elfred and I had decided to give a small party at our house to introduce you to some of our friends, but now I don't know. You're attempting to undermine me with my own children." Her voice broke as she fished out a hanky.

Roberta folded her sister in a hug. "Oh, Grace, I'm sorry. Forgive me. I'd love it if you'd give a party for me. Truly I would."

Grace made a big show of deciding. "Well, I guess we could. Next Saturday. Maybe dinner and a little music afterward."

"That would be just grand."

Then Grace spoiled it all. "We thought that if we were to show our support for you, let everybody see that we're still willing to have you in the house, then others in town will overlook your being divorced and will follow suit."

It took all Roberta's civility to keep from shoving Grace's fat face clear to the back of her fat neck. Willing to have her in the house! Jumping Judas. If it weren't so hypocritical, it might have been funny: Grace, with her philandering husband, willing to play the moral leader of the town while all of it was laughing at her behind her back.

After they left, Roberta's anger remained. Even playing the piano failed to wipe out the hurt she felt. She was still agitated when she climbed into bed. *If we're still willing to have you in the house, then others will overlook your being divorced.* As Roberta grew drowsy, her last thought was that she couldn't wait to rant about it to Gabriel Farley. He was the only one who'd understand.

CHAPTER 9

O N MONDAY morning Gabe arrived before Roberta left for work. She was upstairs when the girls came bombarding her with good-byes, then clattered down the steps on the run, late as usual. She went down seconds later in her starched white uniform and peaked white cap to find him in the living room, wearing leather gloves and holding a pane of glass.

"Oh! I didn't know you were here," she said, startled.

Gabe stared as if he'd never seen her before. Her hair was coiled up, with the cap nestled at the back. Her starched uniform nearly reached her ankles and was covered by a white apron with a bib.

He'd never paid much notice to her shape before, but looking at her in that uniform was like looking at the Maine shoreline from the top of Mount Battie: The curves showed up, plain and plentiful. And she looked so tidy! Why, even her run-over shoes were gone; in their place, immaculate white oxfords.

He'd been gaping for some time before he realized it and got his mouth moving. "Gonna get that window replaced today."

"Yes, good."

Still he didn't move.

After a beat Roberta said, puzzled, "Mr. Farley?"

He motioned at her. "The uniform."

She looked down. "Is something wrong with it?"

"Um, no. It's . . . ah . . . No, it's . . ."

She waited, hiding her amusement.

"Nice," he finally finished, setting the pane of glass on his boots.

"The state issues them. Well, I've got to go. I'll see you between five and six, I imagine."

"Ayup."

He watched her go outside. When she reached the porch steps, he called, "Oh, Mrs. Jewett?" She returned to the door and looked in. "You want I should crank that flivver so you don't get dirty?"

"No, thank you, Mr. Farley. I can manage."

He remained in the shadows so she couldn't see him watching her. She made a sight, cranking that car in her starched white uniform. When the engine fired, a big smile bloomed on her face and she glanced up at the house as if to win his approval.

He smiled, too, and then carried the pane upstairs, thinking it would be much lonelier around here today.

THE time went slowly without her. In only a week he'd grown used to the noises she made—clattering things, humming, playing the piano at ridiculous times, coming out to talk to him.

At noon Gabe ate his sandwich alone, remembering how they'd

sat together last Friday. But she's so different from Caroline, he thought, little realizing the implication of his musing.

His mother found him there, eating the last of his cookies. Maude Farley was of medium height and stocky, with fleshy arms whose undersides waggled when she moved.

"Gabriel!" she called as she came across the yard.

"Well, what are you doing here?" he asked, brushing the cookie crumbs off his palms.

"Came to see what you're doing to old Breckenridge's place," Maude said. "I heard she's over at school giving shots, so I figured it was okay. Besides, I want to talk with you about Isobel."

"What about her?"

"Everybody says she's running with this woman's girls. And I hear you've been spending a lot of time up here yourself."

"Ma, you've been on that party line too much."

"All I'm saying is, this here is a divorced woman, and you'd better mind your p's and q's around her, because the entire town knows it. And I don't want my granddaughter around these wild hooligans, getting a bad reputation."

"You know what, Ma?" He forced his voice to remain calm. "I'm getting a little mad here. I'm a grown man. I don't have to explain my comings and goings to you or to a town full of gossips who don't know Roberta Jewett from Adam. This is the happiest Isobel's been since Caroline died. I've never seen a mother who spends so much time with her children or one who enjoys them more. They laugh together, and she's in there playing the piano with them and having fun. Now what's wrong with that?"

"Just get your work done and get out of here, Gabriel."

He said it quietly, without rancor, but she knew he meant it: "Maybe the one who should get out of here right now is you, Ma."

He had a bad afternoon after that, worrying about what his mother was going to tell the other women on the party line, wondering why he hadn't just come right out and claimed there was nothing between him and Roberta Jewett.

At midafternoon Seth showed up. "Boy, is Ma steaming," he said. "She says she's all done filling your cookie jar."

Gabe angled his brother an amused glance. "Well, that'll sure fix me, won't it?" They both laughed, and Seth thumped Gabe between the shoulder blades.

"So you gettin' along pretty good with Mrs. Jewett?"

"No, nothing like that. We just talk a lot, that's all."

"Didn't think you ever talked a lot."

"About the people we were married to."

"Ohhhh," Seth said, tilting back his head sagely. "About the people you were married to. Isn't *that* interesting?"

"Not you, too! Damn it, Seth, you're as bad as Ma!"

"No, I'm not. I'm just teasing, and I don't gossip either."

"Go on," Gabe said with affection. "Get out of here."

AT FIVE Roberta came home and found Gabe down on one knee, washing off his tools by the pump. She stopped behind him and said, "I'm glad you're still here."

He whipped around, caught unawares. Then he settled back on one heel, and asked, "So how was your first day?"

"Not bad. Only three children fainted." She reached up to remove a hatpin and her white cap. "Where are the girls?"

"At your sister's, looking at her old dresses for costumes." They had announced they were going to perform *Hiawatha* on Sunday afternoon.

He rose, taking in details. Her apron was dotted with blood, and her uniform was wrinkled. She tucked a wisp of hair behind her ear.

"May I talk to you about something?" she asked.

"Sure," he said, carrying his tools, walking with her to the back step, where she sat with her elbows on her knees, monkeying with her cap while she spoke. He sat beside her, leaving a discreet distance between them.

"Would you be completely truthful with me?" she said.

"Depends on what you're going to ask."

She drew a deep breath. "Elfred and Grace told me yesterday they were going to have a party for me. Grace said that they wanted to show the good citizens of Camden that even though I'm a social outcast, they're willing to have me in their house in the hopes that others will be equally as magnanimous." She gave up fiddling with her cap and looked at him. "Is it really that bad? Is everybody in this town talking about me just because I'm divorced?"

"I don't gossip much myself, so I wouldn't know." He shifted his gaze to the pump. "What do you care what they say?"

"These people don't even know me."

517

"No, they don't. So you'll just have to face them down and show them you're a good person."

"You think I'm a good person?"

"Yes, I do. Now that I've come to know you, I certainly do." He thought it best not to look at her while divulging, "My family thinks there's something going on between you and me, and they're giving me the raspberries."

"What exactly does that mean—the raspberries?"

"Nothing. Forget I said it."

"What? Are they teasing you? Warning you off? What?"

"Forget it." He got to his feet. "I'd better go."

Her temper spiked because she wanted whole honesty and he pulled back, afraid of it. "All right. Be stubborn!" she snapped, rising, too, and marching inside.

He watched her go, upset by her show of temper. After standing awhile, trying to decide how to handle it, he followed her inside. He felt as if there were a brick in his belly, knowing he'd displeased her. She was staring out a window, with her arms crossed.

"Roberta," he said, "it doesn't matter what they say."

She spun angrily and tapped her chest. "Not to you, but to me it does! My own sister! Your family! Everybody thinking the worst of me when none of it is true. None of it! Just because I'm divorced doesn't mean I don't have morals."

"I know that," he said quietly. "I shouldn't have said that about my family. I'm—I'm sorry."

Her expression was flat and cold. "Maybe you should have your brother finish the work around here." She brushed past him and headed up the stairs.

He shouted up, "I don't want him to!"

"Well, I do!" She disappeared around the upstairs corner.

"I started it, I'll finish it!" he yelled. Then even louder, "Roberta, get back here!"

She reappeared at the top of the steps. "Stop yelling, Farley. Pack up your tools and go, because I don't know what's going on between us, but whatever it is, I don't need the aggravation in my life." *Wham!* Her bedroom door slammed.

He braced an arm on the wall and hung his head, wondering why he was arguing with her—a bullheaded, know-it-all smarty who set about proving at every turn that she could get along without a man.

After all, she had *told* him she didn't want anything to do with men. Why was he hanging around here?

In her room Roberta had slammed the door, but it was warped and swung open again. She pressed her spine against it, letting her temper settle. Silence from him. A long silence while she wondered what he was doing down there. Then at last she heard his footsteps clunk away and the sound of his truck driving off.

Gabe did not send Seth to finish the job for the remainder of that week. Instead, he made sure he got there after Roberta left in the morning and finished before she returned. She didn't know who was doing the work and told herself she didn't care. Each day she saw progress—the walls sanded and painted, the woodwork revarnished. A new doorknob on the back door. Her bedroom door adjusted so it would close properly. And that's when she knew.

ON SATURDAY, Roberta commandeered one of Grace's old dresses from the costume stack, took it in severely, polished up her run-over black shoes and drove over to the Spears' house for their party.

Who should be there but Gabriel Farley. When their eyes collided across the room, he raised his punch cup. She flashed him a dismissing smile, then avoided him while everybody else was being introduced. The women offered sterile hellos, and the men held her hand too long. Elfred touched her every chance he got, always under the guise of being the polite host.

By nine o'clock Roberta was ready to take a hatchet to him. That's when the music started and Farley came up to her.

"I'm not going to let you get by without speaking to me."

She glanced at him coolly. "Hello, Gabriel."

"You look very nice this evening."

"Thank you. So do you." He'd had a haircut and was wearing a suit and tie. His face was lightly burnished from outdoor work. Though his eyebrows would never lie neatly, their unruliness added to his appeal. He was, in fact, a sturdy, handsome man.

"Are you still mad at me?"

"Yes. Are you still doing the work in my house?"

"Yes."

"I thought so. Thank you for fixing my bedroom door."

"That's so it'll work the next time you slam it in my face."

"You deserved it. You made me very mad that day."

"Well, I'll be out of your hair for good on Monday."

"Ah," she said. She glanced over the crowd. "I thought maybe your mother would be here. I wanted to meet her."

"She and the Spears are not particular friends."

"Oh. I thought maybe she avoided coming because of her objections to me."

He refused to comment. "Roberta . . . could I walk you home?"

"No, you can't, Gabriel. I drove my car."

"Then, could I drive you home? Because I walked."

"Why on earth would you want to drive me home?'"

"Honest, Roberta, sometimes I really don't *know* why! Do you know what an exasperating woman you are?"

She laughed aloud. Several people turned around to look.

"Oh, all right, then," Roberta conceded. "What the heck."

When the party ended, she expected him to slip up to her car secretly after she was safely inside it. Instead, Gabe fell in beside her in the vestibule as she was thanking Grace and Elfred.

"Maybe I should see you home, Birdy," Elfred offered.

"I'm seeing Roberta home, Elfred. No need for you to worry about her." At least a half-dozen people overheard and saw Elfred's gaze drop to Gabe's hand as it commandeered Roberta's elbow.

When they reached her house, Gabe walked her to the porch. "I think we threw Elfred a curveball, leaving together," he remarked.

"I wanted to throw him a lot more than that. He invites me to his house, then paws me in front of his wife. Thanks for rescuing me."

"You're welcome."

"So I take it you're not coming to see the play tomorrow."

"Oh, of course I'm coming. If I didn't, I'd look like a degenerate next to you."

His irony put a smile on her face. "Well, I'll see you then," she said as they reached the steps. He stopped and let her ascend them alone. "Thanks for bringing me home."

He should have turned and left. She should have gone directly inside. Instead, he remained, looking up at her dim form above him. She said, "Do we know what we're doing, Gabriel?"

Her near frankness took him by surprise, but he stood relaxed, in place. "I don't think so, Roberta," he replied.

There was no question they were thinking about kissing. The setting and situation were classic—a shadowed porch, moonlight white on the lawn, the smell of spring lilacs blossoming nearby. But the idea was folly. Claims had been made that warned them that any intimacy would be capricious at best, misguided at worst. If they gave in to their whim, they would undoubtedly regret it later. So they said good night and she closed the door between them.

THEY were perhaps a little too proper with each other the next day when he came to her house for the play. Anyone who knew them could have sensed undercurrents. But the girls were the only ones who'd seen them together much, and they were too busy to notice.

The production was poorly attended. Elfred and Grace found it beneath their dignity to sit on the grass. Sophie, their maid, came in their place. Myra had begged off with a headache, and Isobel's grandmother withheld her presence on the off chance it might be misconstrued as a nod of acceptance for the divorced woman.

But one set of parents came—the DuMosses, who, Roberta suspected, wanted to check out the place where their daughter, Shelby, was spending a lot of time. They were polite but reserved, and brought their own blanket to sit on.

Some of the kids from school came as well, including the boys who had given Roberta the fish. And, surprisingly, Rebecca's and Susan's English teachers, Mrs. Roberson and Miss Werm.

The girls had been truly inventive, having set some stanzas to music and constructed their birch-bark canoe as a stage prop. Each of them had chosen a section of the legend to recite in costume. Rebecca, wearing the *moccasins enchanted whose stride measured a mile*, recited the stanza about Hiawatha's wooing of Minnehaha:

> *"As unto the bow the cord is,*
> *So unto the man is woman,*
> *Though she bends him, she obeys him,*
> *Though she draws him, yet she follows,*
> *Useless each without the other!"*

Roberta leaned back on her hands on the grass and moved her lips silently with the familiar words. She felt Gabriel's regard like one feels sunlight, and when she turned her head, he was studying her in somber reflection, as if unable to help himself.

Bow and cord, man and woman.

But I am not useless without Gabriel Farley, Roberta thought.

I've proved that. I can provide for my girls, love them enough for two. I have a house, a motorcar and a job that gives me security and dignity. Why would I want to jeopardize any of that by succumbing to any paltry attraction I might feel toward the man?

Neither did Gabe feel useless without Roberta. He had a daughter he loved, a clean, smoothly run house, a family who cared for him, a thriving trade and the respect of the town. Why would he want to risk any of that by taking up with this divorced woman?

When the play ended, they remained distant, applauding with the others. But while Roberta hugged her daughters unreservedly, Gabriel gave Isobel little more than an awkward pat.

When her guests dispersed, Roberta bade him a good-bye kept intentionally impersonal. Isobel got the customary loving send-off that meant, Come back anytime.

ON MONDAY afternoon Gabriel was already finished and loaded up when Roberta brought her car careening to a halt behind his truck. "Gabriel! Wait!"

He strolled forward to meet her. "Something wrong?"

"No. I just promised I'd give you that inoculation, that's all."

"Oh, you don't have to bother."

"It's no bother. Come on in."

He had little choice but to follow, or look like a fraidycat. She led him to the kitchen and ordered, "Roll up your sleeve."

She was soon holding what looked like a knitting needle, and the idea of having it jammed into his hide made Gabe blanch. When the needle pierced his skin, he flinched.

"You all right?" Roberta asked.

He sucked air through his teeth and nodded. "That hurts."

"It will for a while, and tomorrow you may run a little fe—" She looked up. His eyes were closed, and he was weaving.

"Sit down, Gabriel," she ordered, guiding him to a chair. She put her hand on the back of his head and forced it down. "Take big, deep breaths," she said. "It'll pass."

While he followed orders, she watched the rise and fall of his shoulder blades inside a tightly stretched red-plaid shirt. She did what she would have done for any woozy child in school: put her hand there and lightly rubbed, making small, comforting circles on Gabriel Farley's muscular back.

Slowly Gabriel's light-headedness faded and he became aware of her rhythmic stroking. It had been a long, long time since any human being had comforted him in any way. He remained doubled forward, enjoying the touch of her gentle fingertips. Being touched, soothed, was something he hadn't realized he'd missed. "That feels good," he mumbled.

After a while she bent toward his right ear. "Feel better now?"

"Mm-hmm."

As her hand slid away from his shoulder, he lifted his head. His eyes were unguarded and steady on her. Then his fingers closed over her hand.

"Gabriel, I don't think—"

"Don't say anything," he said, and pulled her onto his lap.

"I'm not starting anything with you, Gabriel."

"I'm not starting anything with you either. I've just been thinking about kissing you. I got the idea you'd been thinking about it, too."

"It's a stupid idea."

"You talk too much, you know that?"

When he kissed her, she stopped resisting. His skin was cool and rough around his lips from the day's growth of whiskers. It had been years since she'd kissed a man, and she certainly wasn't going to let herself be unduly swayed by the first, thus becoming what all divorcées were rumored to be. So she let him do the work and remained merely amenable. By the time Roberta got up, she was in full control of her emotions. "This is a very bad idea," she said.

"I told myself the same thing."

"It was just that poem yesterday and all that claptrap about bows and cords." She took several steps and found something to keep her hands busy—washing some greasy knives the girls had left on the butter dish. "The girls will be home soon. Maybe you'd better go."

"Sure," he said, pushing up from the chair.

"Are you all right now? Is the dizziness gone?"

"Fine. Sorry I was such a baby."

"No, you weren't. That just happens to some people." He would not have guessed he'd just kissed her from her businesslike manner. "Did you finish everything here? I mean, your work is all done?"

"All done. I won't be bothering you anymore."

She didn't know whether to walk him to the door or stay where she was. In the end, she stayed, and he left without another word.

CHAPTER 10

A<small>T HIS</small> house, evenings were lonelier for Gabe. Isobel spent every spare minute at the Jewetts'. The housework was left to him. His mother—stubborn to a fault—had been as good as her word and refused to refill his cookie jar, or even to change the sheets.

On a Friday night in early May, Gabe had made a kettle of oyster stew for supper and was waiting for Isobel when the telephone rang.

He lifted the earpiece from the prongs. "Hello?"

"Hello, Mr. Farley? This is Susan Jewett. We just got our new telephone!"

"You did? Well now, isn't that exciting." In the background he could hear the piano playing.

"Mother said we could each make one call, and I said I wanted to call you because I was wondering if it would be okay if Isobel stays for supper. We're trying to talk Mother into a clambake!"

"I've already made supper for Isobel and me."

"But can't she stay anyway?" Susan's voice got whiny and trailed away from the phone. "Mom, he won't let her. . . ."

The piano ceased, and a moment later Roberta's voice came on. "Gabriel? We really do want Isobel to stay. Do you mind?"

It's lonely here, he wanted to say, but of course could not. "She's there so much."

"Because we enjoy her. The girls talked me into a shore picnic. They want to dig some clams."

"Well, in that case, I guess it'll be okay."

"Good. Thanks, Gabriel."

A lull fell, and he imagined her impatient to get their outing under way. He knew he should release her, but he wanted to keep her on the line. "Listen, Roberta." He cleared his throat and polished the edge of the oak telephone box with a thumb. "About what happened that day. I know you weren't too pleased with me, and I just wanted to say I'm sorry. I shouldn't have pressed the issue."

"It's okay, Gabriel. I have to be more careful than most. So let's just forget it, because it didn't amount to anything."

It didn't? Funny, but Gabe thought it had.

"Gabriel? Isobel says your mother has stopped coming over with cookies and to help with the housework. Is that because of me?"

He cleared his throat again. "No, it's not because of you."

The line went quiet while Gabriel suspected she figured out he was lying. Then she surprised him by asking, "Well, in that case, would you be interested in digging clams with the girls and me?"

He forgot about rubbing the phone box with his thumb. "Well, that sounds mighty tempting, but you sure about this?"

"I could use a little help."

"I'll be right over."

He showed up in fifteen minutes, dressed in tan duck trousers, canvas shoes and a roomy Norfolk jacket. His step was animated, and he was whistling. He bounded up the porch steps in two giant leaps and called through the open front door, "Anybody here?"

The racket inside was laughable: clattering kitchenware, slamming doors, girls' giddy voices and Roberta shouting orders.

He walked right in and stopped in her kitchen doorway. She was back to the Roberta he first knew. The dress needed pressing, the shoes needed replacing and the hair needed tidying, but as he stood there observing the commotion, he felt alive, as he had not in days—being with her and the kids again.

" 'Lo, Roberta," he said, low-key.

Roberta spun around and smiled brightly. "Oh, Gabriel, you're here! That didn't take you long."

"Daddy, hi! I can't believe you're going with us!" Isobel hugged his waist. He dropped his hands to her shoulders, but Roberta saw he was out of his element with spontaneous affection.

"Oh, this is going to be so much fun!" said Isobel.

Roberta got busy again, putting butter and lemon and sweet potatoes into an open hamper on the table. When the hamper was packed, Gabe took it from her hands. "Here, I'll carry that."

"Hey," she teased, "you're a good man to have around."

They were both in glad moods as they herded the children outside like a regular family of six. Gabe cranked Roberta's car, and she drove, with all four girls stacked in the back seat, singing tunes from *H.M.S. Pinafore*.

Roberta parked on the hill above the Glen Cove clam flats, and the girls tumbled out and went clambering over the rocks that had been nudged by a million tides to form a rim around the cove. The shadows of the mountains sloped down to the sea and stained the evening blue. Before them were the flats—mushroom brown and dull except where the surf lazily licked the sand silver.

Gabriel studied the peaceful scene and said, "I haven't been back here since Caroline died. She wasn't particularly crazy about clams, but she loved to go clamming. Sometimes she'd talk me into bringing her out early so she wouldn't miss the sunrise."

Roberta turned to study his profile. A faint puff of wind fluttered the hair against his forehead. Twilight painted shadows beside his straight nose and somber mouth. "I envy you your happy memories. I wish I had more of them."

He dragged himself from his reverie and rejoined her in the present. "I'll start digging the pit if you'll gather some seaweed." He stepped out onto the rocks.

For the next half hour everybody kept busy. While Gabe built the fire and Roberta collected kelp, the girls searched the flats for tiny sand spouts, where they dug. The sun slipped behind the mountain. When the fire had subsided to coals, Roberta knelt beside Gabriel and helped him layer the rocks, seaweed, foods and canvas cover.

"There," Gabe said, sitting back on his heels. "In an hour we'll have a meal fit for a king."

"I'm starved," Lydia said.

"Yeah, me, too," Isobel added.

The girls moved off into the growing shadows, leaving their parents behind. Gabriel stretched to his feet. "I'll build us another fire so we've got something to poke at."

He did, and they sat on turtle-shaped rocks while the dusk and the dampness lowered upon the shore. The clam bed seethed and sent out a soft, warm hiss that kept them company.

Roberta glanced up at the sky and recited:

> *"Lo! comes the evening, purply soft*
> *To lift the glowing stars aloft."*

Gabriel glanced over. "Who wrote that?"

"I did."

He pondered a moment. "You know so much that I don't know."

"Perhaps I do, but I cannot build a porch."

Sometimes she could really put him at ease, this woman in the wrinkled dress, with tumbledown hair. He'd come to prize spending time with her, and he was beginning to admit it wasn't only because of the children. "I hadn't thought of that," he said. Now that he did, however, he felt less ignorant.

He appreciated her silently for a while before speaking again. "You're really something, Roberta, you know that?"

They sat side by side with their ankles crossed. The moon had risen and spread a beaten-gold path across the water. In the distance one of the girls shrieked, followed by a chorus of muffled laughter.

Finally Roberta asked quietly, "So how is it, being back here where you used to bring Caroline?"

"Not as bad as I thought. Quite enjoyable, actually."

"Once before, you mentioned a day you thought was going to be bad for you. April eighteenth."

"Oh, that."

"Am I treading on hallowed ground?"

"Surprisingly, no. A month ago you would have been, but—I don't know—maybe I'm healing at last."

"So what did you do on April eighteenth?"

"Fed her roses for her, same as I do every year."

"Does Isobel do it with you?"

"No. It's my special time with Caroline. I, well, talk to her then."

He was studying the fire. She was studying him. "Be careful, Gabriel."

He looked over. "Of what?"

"Shutting out your daughter too long."

He bristled. "I haven't shut out my daughter."

"She talks at our house. She tells us things."

"Like what? If she said I shut her out, it's not true."

Roberta could tell this was touchy ground. "I'm not saying you do it consciously."

"If it wasn't for Isobel, I'd have lost my mind when Caroline died!"

"Have you ever told her that?"

"I don't have to tell her. She knows."

"Funny. She thinks she's in your way sometimes."

"In my way? Why would she think she's in my way?"

"You never hug her, Gabriel. You never touch her. I've watched you, and I can see that you don't know how. I imagine when Caroline was alive, she did that for both of you. That's often how it is: The mother does the overt loving. But you're her only parent now, and she needs to know you love her." She could see Gabe's jaw was clamped hard. "Showing it is hard for some people," she told him. "If you don't know how, watch me." He turned away. "It's the little things that count. We say I love you in a thousand ways."

Roberta was in too deep to withdraw now. There were things on her mind that she simply had to say on Isobel's behalf.

"She's told me that she's not allowed to touch her mother's dresses. What would you have felt like if you'd been told you could not touch any of Caroline's things after she died? You would have been so hurt, Gabriel."

He spoke at last, and she could hear his banked anger. "But it was hard after Caroline died. You don't know how hard!"

"No, I don't. What I'm asking you to understand is that it was equally hard for Isobel. You handled your grief separately from hers, and by doing so, you made her believe she was in your way. You're angry with me for being so blunt, I can tell."

"Y' darned right I am. You're accusing me of a lot of things here that I don't think I deserve."

"I'm not accusing you."

"The hell you're not!" He leaped to his feet. "You're telling me I haven't been a good father to Isobel. Who appointed you judge!"

"I never said that."

"You've said plenty! Behind my back at your house—you just admitted it!"

"Look what we found!" The girls were back, bearing a starfish.

"Not now, girls!" Gabriel snapped. "Roberta and I are talking about something important."

Isobel looked nonplussed. "What's wrong, Daddy?"

What could he reply? He was being a boor and he knew it.

Roberta stepped in. "I think our food's done. Let's uncover it."

"I'll uncover it," Gabriel said.

Their outing was ruined. Though jerky conversations were attempted while they ate, none were between Roberta and Gabriel. It was nearly ten o'clock when they repacked the hamper. He shoveled sand into the fire pit, and Roberta sent the girls on to the car.

She had to speak. "You're really mad at me. I mean *really*."

He leaned over to whisk something up off the sand to escape facing her. "Yes, I am, Roberta." Suddenly he turned on her. "You know, things ran pretty smoothly at my house before you came to town. I took care of my daughter and we got along fine. Maybe you'd better take a look at that junk hole you live in and see if your own mothering could use a little improvement. And for heaven's sake, why don't you ever iron your dresses!"

In the following silence they glared each other down and felt their blood race. Then he spun and strode across the flats.

She yelled, "You bullheaded, closed-minded dunce!" Then she kicked a spray of sand before heading after him.

When she reached him, he was cranking the car as if he wanted to lift it and drag it home.

"I'll do it myself," she insisted. "Give me that!"

"Gladly," he said, and stormed around to the passenger side. It irritated him that he didn't have his own truck. She was too damned independent for her own good, and it was the last straw that tonight of all nights *she* was driving *him!*

In the back seat the girls sat motionless, wary. Roberta put the car in gear, and a timid voice from the rear asked, "What's wrong?"

They answered simultaneously.

Gabriel: "Nothing."

Roberta: "We had a fight."

"About what?" Rebecca asked.

Gabriel: "Nothing."

Roberta: "About what kind of parents we are."

"Roberta, shut up!"

"I don't shut up around my kids, Farley!" she yelled. "You shut up! Shut up all your feelings and all your wife's old dresses and the truth about what your mother and the respectable citizens of Camden think of Roberta Jewett and her girls!"

Gabriel clammed up and glared outside. The back-seat passengers rode silently. Into Camden they rumbled, past the mill and up the hill to Alden Street. Roberta stopped the car, catapulting them all forward in their seats. In grim silence they started dividing property. Isobel hovered behind, near tears.

"Thanks for the picnic," she told Roberta, then whispered, "Aren't you and my dad going to talk to each other anymore?"

Roberta touched Isobel's jaw. "I don't think so, honey."

"But"—Isobel glanced at her father waiting by his truck—"can I still be your friend?"

Roberta took Isobel in her arms. "Of course, sweetheart. We'll always be your friends." Isobel clung, and tears stung Roberta's eyes.

529

Gabriel's engine fired, and he shouted, "Isobel, come on!"

"Bye," she whispered, and Roberta heard tears in her voice.

Her own three said good-bye and watched while Farley chugged away. Roberta carried the hamper to the house.

CHAPTER 11

ROBERTA and Gabriel had spent too much time together to shrug off their fight as if it didn't matter. Their friendship had ended on a note of bitterness that carried through the days that followed. Whenever they recalled the clambake, they remembered the unfair criticism each had suffered at the hands of the other.

Roberta thought, My house might be messy, but how dare he intimate that I don't give my children proper care? I won't have them living in some *museum* where nothing is touchable. And if he doesn't like the way I keep myself, too bad. Let him find some fluffy pink pea brain who lives and breathes only to please him.

Gabriel thought, For her to think I don't love my daughter— well, that's just rubbish! The idea of Isobel growing up and leaving me scares me half to death. So maybe I don't fawn over my girl like Roberta does, but that's a woman's way. And if I ever again have any dumb ideas about going over there and spooning with that woman, I hope somebody will knock my brains out for me.

One night about a week after the clambake Isobel was waiting when Gabriel came home from the shop.

"Daddy, guess what!" Her face was aglow with excitement. "We've been asked to put on *Hiawatha* for the whole school!"

"That's wonderful, Isobel."

"By the principal herself! Mrs. Roberson and Miss Werm told her about it, and Miss Abernathy said the student body should see it, because it's an American classic. I'm *so* excited! You'll come, won't you, Daddy?"

He began to say, But I've already seen it.

Roberta's admonition flashed past, stopping him. *We say I love you in a thousand ways. If you don't know how, watch me.*

He found himself answering as she would. "Of course I'll go."

"You will?" Overcome, Isobel flung her arms around him. "Oh, Daddy, I never thought you'd agree to see it twice."

Suddenly it seemed as if Roberta were there, like some guardian angel. When instinct told Gabe to draw back, the specter of Roberta ordered him, "Don't miss this chance."

He curled his arms around Isobel and touched his cheek to her hair. He sensed her surprise, and he wondered why it had taken him so long. They remained close while he felt some sentimental cog slipping into place. Then she drew back and looked up at him with a smile of wondrous amazement.

THE school performance of *Hiawatha* was held at two o'clock on the last Thursday in May. Gabriel had worked all morning in the shop and had gone home at one o'clock to freshen up. Roberta had been working on the other side of Bald Mountain, and she had had little time to think of clothes and combs. He arrived with ten minutes to spare. She arrived ten minutes late.

The girls put on a splendid performance and, when it was over, were rousingly applauded. Miss Abernathy thanked and praised them, and the audience rose and shuffled out of the auditorium.

Gabriel went straight outside. Roberta headed for the stage steps, where she met the cast coming down. He was waiting in the sun when Roberta came out with one arm around Susan, the other around Isobel, and surrounded by young people. As she came down the schoolhouse steps, their gazes collided, bringing a mix of good memories and bad. If their hearts sent up faint flutters, neither of them revealed it.

The young people buffeted her along toward Gabe, and Isobel rushed forward to hug him. "Daddy"—she looked up into his face, radiant—"everyone is getting together at the Jewetts' for lemonade. May I go, please?"

Gabe simply couldn't find the heart to refuse her. "All right. Home by supper though, huh?"

"I promise." She scampered off.

Roberta had observed the exchange with some surprise as Gabe heartily returned Isobel's embrace. When he raised his head, their eyes met, but coolness emanated from them both.

As the group moved away, a stab of loneliness caught Gabe. While Roberta cranked her car, he thought she paused to glance over at him. But someone walked between them and cut off his line of vision, and when it cleared, the car was rolling away.

THE SCHOOL YEAR ENDED ON Memorial Day, and summer was officially launched with a grand parade and picnic at which Roberta once again fended off advances from Elfred when Grace and Myra were not looking. Then he cornered her at her car, where she'd gone to get a blanket. His attack this time was more audacious, and she ended up slapping him hard enough to leave a red welt on his cheek before he finally backed off, flinging a threat over his shoulder. "I'll get you yet, you little slut. You're giving plenty of it to Farley—you can spare a little for me!" He never returned to the picnic after that, and though Roberta wondered how he'd explain the bruise, she never asked, nor did Grace mention it.

JUNE arrived, spilling thick green down the mountainside and silvering Penobscot Bay. All the berries—blue, straw and choke—bloomed in sheltered patches, while columbine waved, wild and sweet, in the soft summer breeze. Summer changed the harbor and the busy quay around it. Racks of salt codfish appeared near the wharves. The summer people came, filling the cove with sails and occupying the cottages out along Dillingham's Point. At Laite's Public Beach swimmers donned their woolen bathing outfits and took to the water by the dozens. The gang from Roberta Jewett's front porch swam there, too, and spent time rowing and fishing and taking picnics up on Mount Battie. Isobel was often with them, for Gabe had hired a widow to do his housekeeping.

As summer advanced, Roberta grew to love her work more and more. Crisscrossing the countryside, she learned through the grapevine who was expecting, then called at those homes to give prenatal advice and assign midwives. She initiated a program aimed at the prevention of typhoid fever and other communicable diseases. She gave eye and ear examinations and visited the sick who were newly released from the hospital. She also learned more about running a Model T motorcar than she cared to.

One day in late June she had been sent out to do a checkup on a mother and six-week-old infant, and had climbed some of the worst roads Knox County had to offer. It was a hot, hazy day. The wooden steering wheel felt greasy beneath Roberta's hands as she hurtled down the washed-out roadbed. She hit a rock and bounced high and hard, and when she landed, the engine stopped running. She coasted to a halt at the intersection of Howe Hill and Hope Road.

"Blasted machine!" Roberta thumped the steering wheel, opened the door and stood on the gravel road with her hands on her hips, disgusted. She looked around at the wild mustard blooming tiredly in the dry-wash ditch and heard the incessant note of the katydids hidden in the weeds and grasses. The sun baked the top of her head while she wondered what to check first. Fan belt? Not likely, since the radiator wasn't hissing. As she peered under the hood and jiggled the spark-plug wires, she thought about checking the gas. Using the wooden dipstick, she found her problem—bone-dry. Hauling the Valvoline gas can out, she heard an oncoming engine. A black touring car appeared at the crest of the hill from the east. Even before he pulled to a stop, she recognized Elfred.

He was smoking a cigar and smirking as he got out, leaving his jacket behind. "Well, what have we here—a damsel in distress?"

"Not at all," she answered. "I'm just refilling my gas tank."

"Well, allow me, Mrs. Jewett," he said, handing her his cigar. "Here, hold that, will you?"

As Elfred poured, she studied him from the rear. Finally she asked, "What are you doing out here?"

"Looking at the Mullens' place. She's decided to sell rather than run it by herself. What are you doing?"

"I had a case up there." She motioned. "A new mother."

He half glanced over his shoulder. "I haven't seen you since the picnic." He quit pouring. "You know, I didn't like how you treated me that day." He put the wooden plug in the can and stored it on the back seat. "You put a mark on my face that I had trouble explaining to Grace."

Roberta scrabbled through her mind for something to say while Elfred sauntered toward her, wiping his hands on a white linen hanky. He stored the hanky in a rear pocket, then reached her way. She took one quick step backward.

"You're a little jumpy, Birdy," he said, reclaiming his cigar.

"I'd better get going. The girls are expecting me at five."

"Not so fast there." His hand lashed out and grabbed her arm. "Don't I get any thanks for helping you out?"

She pulled back, but he hung on. "Thank you, Elfred. Now may I go?"

"That's not much of a thanks, Roberta. I was thinking of something a little more personal."

533

"Let me go, Elfred." She pried at his fingers, but he threw his other arm around her and hauled her up hard against him, his mustache an inch from her lips.

"Not this time, Birdy. This time nobody's here to stop me." He lowered his face, but she whipped hers aside. "Elfred, please. Don't!" Her rising panic seemed to add to his fire.

"Come on, Roberta, don't be so stingy." The struggle intensified. So did her fear.

"Stop it, Elfred!" He hauled one way, she strained the other, and their combat stirred up dust on the road.

Then Elfred grabbed her hair, yanked her head back and kissed her. Her white cap fell to the road. The smell of cigar smoke rose from behind her, filling her nostrils as he grappled for control. She kept pushing at his chest while his mouth bruised her lips, until he shifted for a new grip and her chance came. One hard shove and she tripped him—spinning, breaking free, running.

She took five steps before he brought her down on one hip, screaming, against the running board. Pain ripped through her hip and her right shoulder. "Ow!" she cried. "Elfred, my arm!"

It was wrenched beneath her as he flung her over with surprisingly little difficulty and straddled her thighs. She struck him in the face with her left fist so hard that he yelped and rocked to one side, and she got free. Up she scuttled, but he grabbed her skirt and sent her sprawling on her back again.

She was pinned by the neck by one of his strong hands while he loomed above her, enraged now, a scarlet bulge blossoming near his eye. "Damn it, Birdy! You're gonna put out, and you're gonna do it now!" Her nails dug uselessly at his hand, scratching her own throat instead.

I can't breathe, she tried to say, but could not.

He shook her head against the gravel. "You think you're too good for me, don't you, Birdy? Well, I got women all over this county can't wait to pull their pants down for me. So why not you, Birdy Jewett?" He released her throat just enough to give her breath and spoke through crimped lips. "Now you're gonna do it, Birdy."

"You'll have to kill me first," she whispered raspingly.

"No, I won't." The coal of his cigar came up close beneath her chin. "Don't make me burn you, Birdy. You got to learn to do what a man says. Now unbutton me."

Wild with fear, she strained to lift her chin free of the heat. "Please, Elfred. . . ." Tears leaked down her temples.

"Do it." He touched her with the cigar, and she screamed.

And unbuttoned his trousers. Then she felt him shrug off his suspenders. With a knee to her stomach, he flipped up her skirts. He flung the cigar into the weeds. She bucked then and tried to throw him off, but it was useless. He pinned her wrists above her head, grinding gravel into them as he forced himself on her.

She felt the hot tears seep from between her quivering eyelids as her brother-in-law defiled her. She endured it by placing herself beyond what was happening . . . beyond his bestiality and the smell of his cigar smoke, beyond the pain of the rocks grinding into her from below and the ignominy of being treated as less than human. She withdrew into the singing of the katydids and the promise of cool water and the sounds of her children's voices on the front porch in the evening twilight, marveling at fireflies.

When it was over, she flung an arm over her eyes and remained motionless. Elfred boosted himself up. "That damn gravel is hard on the knees," he said. "Come on, Birdy, you better get up."

She felt his hand on her arm. "Don't touch me," she said, jerking free of his detestable touch. With her eyes still covered, she threw down her skirt. She spoke in a dead calm. "You touch me again and I swear I'll murder you, Elfred."

The certainty in her voice made Elfred hesitate.

"Look, Birdy, it wouldn't have had to be so rough if you'd have given in weeks ago. I tried it nice, but you just wouldn't listen."

"Is that how you rationalize the crime you've just committed?" She refused to move her arm and look at him. "Get away from this place before I get in my motorcar and run you down."

When he left, she was still lying in the road where he'd raped her, her arm still across her eyes.

CHAPTER 12

ONLY when he'd driven off did Roberta roll to her side, coil tightly and hug her belly. The delayed shock rattled her body against the sharks'-teeth gravel, but she wept quietly, letting the tears roll onto the stones.

"Get up. Go for help." She heard the inner voice, but rising, she would have buckled, so instead lay waiting out the shakes. Meanwhile, the katydids went on caroling. She was aware of them subliminally—and of some puny chickory weeds poking up against the horizon, and of the horizon itself, brilliant green meeting brilliant blue—while uncaring nature forged on with its summer schedule and left a ravaged woman to gather her forces in the road.

Time passed, five minutes or ten, before the voice got through. "Get up. Go for help." She pushed to her feet unsteadily, the gravel embedded in her palms. She shuffled to the car, leaving her white cap in the road. She cranked the Ford and drove off.

The voice in her head told her where she must go. She didn't want her children to see her in this condition, nor her mother—and Grace was out of the question. But why inflict her troubles on Gabriel Farley? Sheer instinct drove her to seek refuge at his door.

There, she heard the voice again. "Let him be home. . . ." She knocked and he came, holding a dish towel.

"Roberta?"

"Gabriel . . . I didn't know where else to come."

"What happened?" He gripped her arms and felt her shuddering deep within.

"The girls are home . . . and . . . I don't want them— Oh, Gabriel, I'm sorry to be such a nuisance."

"You're not a nuisance, Roberta. Now tell me what happened."

She turned her head away and told him, "Elfred raped me."

"Oh, no," he whispered as her knees gave. He plucked her up and carried her through his house—up the stairs, into a bedroom—and laid her on a soft, chenille-covered bed. "He *raped* you?"

"I tried to stop him, but it was no use. He was so strong, Gabe, and I—" A sob interrupted. She flung an arm over her eyes and felt Gabriel touch her sleeve. He saw flagrant evidence—the gravel ground into her wrist, her dirty clothes, the bruises on her throat.

From behind her arm she said, "I didn't do anything to encourage him, Gabriel. Honest. You've got to believe me."

"I believe you, Roberta."

"I fought and I screamed, but there was nothing I could do. First he held me down, and when I wouldn't stop fighting, he burned me with his ci-cigar."

"Oh, Lord." Gabriel drew her up and gathered her close as she wept, while pity and rage created a maelstrom of emotions within him. He forced himself to ask, "Where?"

She pulled back some. "Under my chin."

"Lie down, Roberta. Let me see." When he saw the red-rimmed blister, his rage trebled. But he forced himself to think of her first and vengeance second.

"I've got to put something on that."

He moved to rise, but she clutched his sleeve. "No, Gabe, please. Isobel will be coming home for supper, and she can't find me here, looking this way. I don't want my girls to find out."

He covered her hand with his own, squeezing hard. "Isobel's at your house. I'll call there and tell her to stay awhile, and say you'll be late." He rose from the bed, extending his hand to prolong his touch as he moved away. "I'll only be a minute, Roberta."

She rested, fanning her hands over the soothing nap of the soft bedspread that had probably been selected and washed and tucked beneath the pillows countless times by his wife. Odd, but the thought of that dead woman whom she had never known brought courage and strength to Roberta.

When Gabe returned, he found her sitting up. "I brought some boric acid and pineoline jelly, but you should see a doctor."

"No," she said with surprising vehemence. "No doctor! It'll be all over town. The burn is nothing." She took the tin and tried to open it, but her shaky hands couldn't manage.

He retrieved the tin and opened it. "Lie back. I'll do it."

She did as ordered, lifting her chin while he dusted the burn with boric acid, then dabbed it with pineoline. She winced, and he asked, "You're sure about the doctor?"

She nodded, her eyes downcast.

"Then what do you want me to do?"

"A bath," Roberta said quietly. "I'd like a bath."

Her answer jolted him with unwanted images and a keener realization of the sordidness remaining, even after the act was over.

"Of course," he said, opening a dresser drawer.

"I'm so much trouble to you," she said.

"Yes, but not in the way you think. Not today." He laid some clothing beside Roberta. "These are some things of Caroline's. She was a lot thinner than you, but that's a dress she wore while she carried Isobel, so it should do. I'll bring up some water."

He went off, leaving her with his wife's precious, untouchable clothing. She picked up the violet-sprigged muslin maternity dress. The evidence of his generosity released her tears once more. She put her face into Caroline Farley's dress and silently told her, "I love your husband. I don't want to, but I do, and he doesn't want to love me either, but I believe he does. He's a good man, and you were lucky. Thank you for letting me borrow your clothes."

Gabe stopped in the doorway, holding a dishpan of hot water, with a towel slung over his shoulder. Roberta raised her face from Caroline's dress, which she held bunched up in both hands. There was a prayerfulness to her pose that caught at his heart.

"Brought you some soap and a washcloth and towel, too." He laid them on a chair, then turned to find her watching him.

"Thank you, Gabriel," she said. "You're very thoughtful." She sent him a weak smile, and he headed for the door.

"Listen. I've got to leave for a little while. Will you be all right?"

"I'll be fine."

"You wait here for me. Don't walk home, understand?"

"I won't. But Gabriel? Where are you going?"

"To my shop," he lied.

"Wait! Gabriel, could I ask you one more favor?"

"Anything."

"My nurse's cap . . . I must have left it up there on the road where it happened. I don't want anyone to find it, and I need it for tomorrow morning. Would you mind getting it for me?"

"Just tell me where."

"At the bottom of Howe Hill, where it meets Hope Road."

"I know where it is. Won't take me long. I'll be right back."

Gabe didn't think twice about taking her car. He motored to Elfred's, his adrenaline pumping sweet vengeance through his blood.

The Spears' front door was open, and voices came from the rear of the house. The family was probably just finishing up supper.

Gabe pounded on the screen and shouted, "Elfred, get out here! I want to talk to you!"

In the depths of the house the voices silenced.

Gabe beat the door again. "Elfred, get out here now or I'll come in there and drag you out. You know what this is about." He stepped inside and let the door slam loudly.

Elfred peered around the dining-room archway and saw Gabe.

"Farley, are you crazy?" he said. Visibly frightened, he wiped his mouth with a linen dinner napkin. Then he pointed a finger and said, "You get out of here, Farley, or I'll have the police on you."

Gabe marched down the hall to the dining room. "I'll get out of here when I've finished my business with you, you bastard." He collared the surprised diner and hauled him back down the hall in a headlock, opening the screen door with the top of Elfred's head.

"Elfred! Oh, dear Lord!" Grace cried, following.

Gabe hauled Elfred down four steps. Every word Gabe spoke came out in a clear baritone bellow. "Now, this is for the woman you raped, Elfred, cause she can't do it herself."

He landed the first blows—four of them—while Elfred's head was couched at his hip. They broke Elfred's pretty little nose and put a matching strawberry on the eye Roberta had missed. Elfred's children and wife were standing in the doorway crying, but Gabe worked on him for another minute or so, until Elfred's legs would no longer support him. Then Gabe dropped him like a used saddle.

He stood over Elfred, his adrenaline still pumping, scarcely taxed by pulverizing the man who had preyed on women for years. "You had this coming for a long time, Elfred, and I'm happy to be the one to do it. Anybody wants to know where to find me, I'll be at home, waiting to testify as to why I ground you into chicken mash." He touched the brim of his cap, and bid, "Evenin', Elfred," before turning to Roberta's car, whose engine was still running.

IN GABE'S bedroom after he left, Roberta bathed herself, scrubbing her flesh until it hurt. Don't let me be pregnant, she begged in silence. Once, she said aloud, "Elfred, you'll pay! Mark my words, you'll pay!" little realizing Elfred already had.

When she had toweled dry, she donned Caroline Farley's maternity dress. It smelled of lavender from her bureau drawer. While Roberta combed her hair, she studied Caroline's picture on the dresser: a dainty rose of a woman, with every delicate feature a man could desire. In the mirror Roberta's own reflection showed bold features with little to recommend them save strength. When she'd finished combing, she said to the picture, "Thank you, Caroline. I'll do something nice for your daughter. How will that be?"

Then she sat on the chair to wait for Caroline's husband. When Gabe finally knocked, she was dozing, her chin on her chest.

"Roberta?" he called quietly. "May I come in?"

Her head bobbed up. "Oh, Gabriel, yes, come in."

He entered the shadowed room, where the smell of soap still lingered. "I hated leaving you alone, but I had to."

"You've been very kind to me tonight, Gabriel, especially considering how badly it ended the last time we were together."

"Here's your cap," he said.

She reached for it and paused. "Your hand, Gabriel. What have you done?"

"I beat the living daylights out of Elfred Spear."

"Oh, Gabriel." Her eyes filled again. She dropped her head and put a hand to her face, trying to hide her feelings for him. This was not the time or the place to reveal them.

He settled into a squat at her knees. "I'm sorry, Roberta. Everybody's going to know now. But a jerk like that has got to be stopped sometime, and if I didn't do it, who would?"

She nodded and said, "I know. It's just so unexpected, your fighting for me. I've always had to fight for myself."

He reached out and put a big, bluff hand on her hair. He felt her silent weeping and went up onto his knees, drawing her forward till his mouth rested on her mahogany hair. They remained that way a long while.

Then Gabriel whispered, "I went out there to get your cap, and I saw the scuff marks in the gravel. So help me God, I wanted to go back to Elfred's house and finish him off. In all my life I've never wanted to harm anyone, but tonight I want to kill Elfred."

Roberta pulled up her head and made out only the dim outline of Gabe's features. "How badly did you beat him?"

"Bad. I broke some bones."

"Oh, Gabe. Do you think they will arrest you for it?"

"I don't know. Either way the whole town is gonna know."

"You know what everyone's going to say about me, don't you? I'm divorced. I must have asked for it."

He thought for a while, then said, "I'm sorry if I made it worse by beating him up. I shouldn't have done it in front of his family."

She took pity on him and touched his collar. "It's all right, Gabriel." She lifted her face. "I'm very tired and I want to go home."

"You've been through a lot, so hang on, Mrs. Jewett," he said.

A second later she was in his arms.

"Gabriel, put me down. I'm not Caroline."

"I know you're not Caroline. I've known that for quite some time," he declared as he carried her down the stairs.

"You don't listen very well," she said, circling his neck with both arms, for any other way was awkward. "I said put me down."

"Heard you." He took her through the kitchen and went out into the starlight through the strong scent of roses.

"You just carried me under Caroline's rose arbor."

"Ayup," he said.

"And if you drive my motorcar, you'll have to walk back home."

"Ayup," he said. "Done it before." He dropped her feet when they reached the car, and opened the passenger door for her. Then he did the cranking and got in, putting the automobile in motion.

As they approached her house, he said, "All right, now what are you going to tell the girls about tonight?"

"I don't know. All four of those girls are innocents. They don't deserve to learn that the world has cruelty like Elfred's, and when I think about them finding out it makes me detest him all the more."

Gabe braked and shut off the engine. Then he sighed. "Well, let's just go in there and see what they say. I'll take my cue from you."

"Thank you, Gabriel," she said. They got out of the car and walked to her house to face their children, together.

CHAPTER 13

THE house smelled strongly of chocolate. Through the lighted kitchen doorway Roberta glimpsed all four girls gathered around the table, eating something from a flat pan. They were talking loudly and laughing as Roberta and Gabriel entered the room.

"Hello, girls. We're here," she announced.

They all glanced at the doorway, and their faces lit at the sight of Roberta and Gabriel together.

"What's in the pan?" Roberta asked.

"Fudge. Becky made it for supper."

"Fudge? For *supper?*"

"Well, you weren't here, so we didn't know what else to have."

Isobel had been eyeing Roberta curiously. "Why are you wearing my mother's dress?" she asked.

Roberta looked down at the worn garment. "Because I had an emergency, and Gabriel offered to lend me this."

"He did?" Isobel turned her wide eyes on her dad. "You told her she could wear Mother's clothes?"

"That's right," he said, feigning nonchalance, helping himself to a piece of fudge.

"What happened to *your* dress?" Rebecca asked suspiciously.

"It got soiled."

Gabe bit into his piece of fudge, and Isobel asked, "What happened to your hand?"

"Fistfight."

All four girls spoke at once. "What!" "A fistfight!" "Over Mother?" Rebecca's demand rang out at the end. "What's going on here?"

Roberta's eyes sought Gabe's. "I think we'd better tell them."

"All right, whatever you say," he said. "Susan, get your mother a chair. She's been through a lot tonight."

Susan retrieved the piano stool, and Roberta sat, holding Lydia's and Susan's hands. She told her story, searching for veiled language.

It was apparent that only Rebecca understood the full import of what Roberta was telling them. Becky asked no questions, but Roberta knew they were rampaging through her head.

Before any of the youngsters could ask for details, Roberta steered the conversation on another tack. "Gabriel beat up your uncle Elfred for attacking me. Now listen. Your cousins were there when it happened, so I'm not sure they'll want to come over here anymore. And as for going over to their house, I'm afraid that's going to be against the rules from now on."

Roberta took a deep breath and sat up straighter. "Gabriel and I thought you should know what happened, but I'm all right now, so you don't have to worry. He took good care of me."

On that note the evening broke up. They all wandered out to the porch, where Isobel gave Roberta a good-bye hug and said, "I'm sorry Mr. Spear was so mean to you."

"Thank you, Isobel. But don't worry about me." Fireflies were glimmering in the shrubs as the girls went ahead. Gabriel lingered on the porch with Roberta, feeling protective. He took her hand. "You're quite a woman, Roberta, you know that?" he said quietly.

"Actually, I think I'm pretty ordinary, but it's nice to hear you say that anyway. Thank you, Gabe."

"Well, good night," he said. "I'll try to stop by tomorrow night and see how you are."

"I'll be here," she said as he descended the steps.

"Night, Mr. Farley," her girls chorused.

"Good night, girls. Take good care of your mother now."

IN HER bedroom, where her own discarded clothes were strewn around, Roberta hung Caroline Farley's worn maternity dress, carefully centered on a hanger, on a hook behind the door.

As she donned her faded summer nightgown, two opposing wills urged her. One said cry. The other said don't cry. She was struggling between the two, straightening out her unmade bed, when Rebecca knocked and said, "Mother, may I come in?"

"Sure." Roberta sat on her bed, trying to appear unemotional.

Becky slipped across the room and sat on the opposite side of the bed. She found the courage to speak first. "You didn't tell Susan and Lydia everything, did you?"

A terrible lump formed in Roberta's throat. Her lips shaped the word no, but it failed to emerge as she wagged her head sorrowfully from side to side.

It took a while before Rebecca could say, "You don't think I know about it, but I do. About what Uncle Elfred did to you." Her eyes were big with the certainty of it. "He did, didn't he?"

Forever after, Rebecca would never be the innocent girl she had been, but Roberta would not lie. She nodded slowly twice.

"I know what it's called. I've heard the boys say it. How could Uncle Elfred do that to you? It's so horrible."

"Yes, it is. Elfred's been making innuendos to me ever since I got here. Always when Grace's back is turned. Poor Grace."

"Will she divorce him, like you did our dad?"

"I don't know, Becky. My suspicion is that she'll think I lured her poor beleaguered husband on, that it was all my fault, just because I'm divorced. She and Grandma are in cahoots on that."

"But how could she think that?" Rebecca grew indignant.

"Ah, Becky." Roberta slumped back. "Women get blamed— that's just how it is. Especially divorced women. But you and I know the truth, and Gabriel knows, and that's all that really matters to me. I'm only sorry if it hurts you girls." Her hand lifted and fell. "Oh, Becky, I wish I could undo it for you."

At her mother's surge of emotionalism Becky hurried around the bed and kissed her. "Don't you worry, Mother. I'm going to take extra good care of you from now on, and I think Mr. Farley will, too."

ROBERTA was still asleep the following morning when the telephone rang downstairs. Bolting up, she felt her pulse clamoring as the phone rang again.

"Oh, my," she mumbled, scrambling out of bed, noting the alarm clock said seven thirty. She plunged down the stairs and grabbed the receiver as the bell jangled for the fifth time. "Hello?"

"Morning, Roberta."

"Oh, Gabe." She rumpled her hair and squinted at the bright kitchen window. "What are you doing calling at this hour?"

"Wondering how you're doing today."

"I just woke up, and I'm going to be late for work, but other than that I'm doing all right, Gabe. Really I am."

"Well, good. Something I want to talk to you about. You suppose you could meet me around noon at Lily Pond?" He gave her directions and they agreed on eleven thirty. She stood for a few seconds after she'd hung up, wondering what he wanted.

WHEN she arrived at their meeting place, his truck was pulled off the road into the shade beside a clearing that led down to the pond. Around the edge of it, water lilies spread the surface with plate-size leaves dotted with big yellow blooms. Across the water, houses were visible, but on the near side residences were secluded in the woods.

Gabe was propped against a waist-high boulder forty feet away, wearing a straw hat. When she waved, he boosted himself up and walked toward her. She enjoyed watching his lanky movements, the relaxed stride of his legs in his blue denim pants, and the slight ruffle of breeze against the rolled-up sleeves of his white shirt.

"Come on," he said, "let's go sit in the shade by the truck."

"All right." She turned and walked beside him through the stubble of clover and meadow grass.

"I brought us sandwiches, and I thought we could sit here and eat," Gabe said. In the truck he found a brush and swept off the running board.

She sat, and he sat, putting a sandwich tin between them. He took out a fruit jar full of iced tea and uncapped it.

They began eating, companionably quiet for a spell before Gabriel said his piece, looking off across the meadow at the woods. "What happened to you yesterday—that bothers me something terrible. I couldn't sleep last night for worrying about you."

"But I'm not your worry, Gabriel."

"May not be, but I worry just the same. What if, well, what if you were pregnant? If that happened, I'd marry you, Roberta. That's what I came here to tell you."

She nearly dropped her sandwich. "If I were pregnant?"

Turning his face to her, he nodded. His eyes were the gray-blue of new smoke, and serious. "That's right."

"To protect me from gossip."

"Something like that." He finished his sandwich and took a long drink of iced tea, studying the woods again. "I figured it was a way out of a fix for you."

She was quiet for so long he finally looked over and found her packing away the uneaten portion of her sandwich in the tin.

"What's the matter?"

Roberta put her feet flat on the ground. "A marriage of convenience isn't exactly my style. If a man wanted me, I'd expect him to show it by doing some serious courting. The thing is, Gabriel, I think you're scared. I think you love me, and you're scared to death to say so, so instead you use this trumped-up excuse for suggesting we should get married. I'd rather not tie myself to a man who's still in love with his first wife. So I appreciate the thought, but no thank you, Gabriel. Not unless you love me." She rose and strode toward her car while he leaped to his feet.

"That's a fine way to fling a man's offer in his face!" he shouted at her back.

"I thanked you, Gabe, didn't I?" She tossed a half glance over her shoulder, and he grew angrier. He stomped across the mixed weeds and caught up with her at her car.

"Roberta, we're middle-aged people, for cryin' out loud!"

"Which precludes courtship? Emotion? Don't get me wrong, Gabriel. I'd never ask you to give up your memories of Caroline. But you'd have to love me as much as you did her, otherwise it would never work." She began cranking up the car.

"Roberta!" he yelled above the noise of the sputtering engine. "All of our children want us to marry, can't you see that?"

She yelled back, "Of course I can! Examine your motives, Gabriel, and when they're the right ones, ask me again."

The car backed away and turned around and left him standing in the shade wondering what he'd done wrong.

CHAPTER 14

MYRA Halburton belonged to an organization called the Greater Camden Ladies' Tea, Quilting and Benevolent Society. One of its members was Maude Boynton, whose husband owned the motorcar company. Another was Jocelyn Duerr, a neighbor of Gabriel's. Niella Wince lived near the Spears. And the roster twined on and on.

Two days after Elfred Spear's beating, the Benevolent Society gathered for its biggest event of the year, a garden luncheon beneath the elms in the backyard of its president, Wanda Libardi.

Maude Boynton brought up what everybody was wondering about. "Myra, is it true that Gabriel Farley beat up Elfred?"

"I guess there's no sense in trying to hide it. But Gabriel Farley will pay for what he's done!"

Jocelyn Duerr asked, "Your divorced daughter has been seeing a lot of Gabriel, hasn't she?"

Myra fended off the question. "I don't keep tabs on what Roberta does. Running all over the country in that car." The other women exchanged pointed glances that said, "Later." Sensing the undercurrents, Myra made her excuses and left early.

Once Myra's skirts rustled off through the garden gate, the hostess opened the gossip herself. "She's always got so much to brag about, but now that the gossip's going the other direction, she's certainly clammed up, hasn't she?"

"Whatever Myra says, that younger daughter of hers is behind this rivalry between Gabriel and Elfred. Why else would two grown men who've been friends for years get into a fight that way?"

"And right out in the yard where everyone could see it!"

"I saw that Jewett woman over at Gabriel's house the night he beat up Elfred. Parked her car there, just as bold as brass."

"Well, I haven't spoken up till now—out of respect for Myra— but I actually *saw* the fight." Niella Wince's lips were pruned up with self-importance.

"You didn't!"

"Out my bedroom window. A person couldn't help but look, with all that yelling going on. It didn't leave any question that that woman thinks every man is fair game, married or not."

They all chewed on that; then someone said, "Poor Grace."

"Poor Caroline. What would she think if she were alive?"

"Gabriel Farley's been at Roberta Jewett's place plenty, let me tell you. He and Elfred both have been running up there to her house like a pair of regular tomcats."

"What about those Jewett children? Shouldn't somebody see that they're removed from their home if it's being run like a bordello?"

"Who?"

"Well, aren't we the Benevolent Society? Doesn't that make it our duty?"

"Now hold on. She's been seen at Gabriel Farley's house, but that doesn't make her an unfit parent."

"Then what does? She's a hussy. Married, divorced, twitching her tail before the nicest single man in town, then trying to break up the marriage of her very own sister. Furthermore, she leaves her children untended at all hours, and they say her house looks like a pigsty. I say we speak to someone in authority and have them go over there and see what's what."

One Benevolent member had remained silent throughout this exchange. Elizabeth DuMoss, normally genteel, spoke up with a ferocity that startled her peers.

"Now just a minute, all of you! I've been sitting here listening while you planned your little war against a woman who is not here to defend herself, so I'm going to do it for her. You call yourselves a benevolent society, but I'm afraid today you've made a mockery of the very word.

"Every woman in this yard has conveniently overlooked the fact that Elfred Spear is a shameless debaucher. He mocks his wife while her back is turned, and makes a joke of his marriage with his countless adulteries. We all know he does it. He's embarrassed many of us at public and private gatherings by touching us, and any of you who'll deny it are outright liars.

"Well, he's gotten away with it long enough. This is our chance to stop Elfred Spear. All we have to do is stand behind Mrs. Jewett and stop the rumors rather than spread them. And what is her greatest crime? Is it that she's divorced or that she's living her life the way many of us wish we could live ours?"

As Elizabeth DuMoss stopped speaking, the women beneath the elms kept still. Some faces were red with embarrassment, others white with rage, but none were impassive.

Elizabeth gathered up her gloves and parasol. "At this time I submit my resignation from the club. I find I cannot be affiliated with an institution that would put undeserved duress upon a woman like Mrs. Jewett. I bid you good-bye." Before Elizabeth DuMoss reached the garden gate, she heard the furor burst forth behind her.

SHE went straight to the shop of Gabriel Farley. Finding him out on a job, she dropped off a note for him. It said:

> Mr. Farley,
> The Benevolent Society is going to try to undermine the reputation of Roberta Jewett and get her children taken away from her. We cannot let that happen. Please come by my house this evening.
> Elizabeth DuMoss

ELIZABETH DuMoss was a pretty woman with soft brown eyes, gentle manners and an exceedingly rich husband. She loved her husband in countless ways, and they had a faithful marriage. But she had never forgotten her grade-school crush on Gabriel Farley.

When he rang her bell at six fifteen that evening, she rose from the dinner table and told the maid, "I'll get it, Rosetta. Please, go on serving dinner." She approached the front door with the assurance of one who is the unassailable head of a small-town society.

"Hello, Gabriel," she said, opening the screen door.

"Hello, Elizabeth." He extended his hand. "I got your note."

She held up a finger and said, "One moment, Gabriel." She moved down the hall to the dining room. "Excuse me, Aloysius, Gabriel is here now. Children, continue with your supper."

A chair scraped back and Aloysius DuMoss brought his considerable girth and walrus mustache into the hall. He extended a hand to Gabriel and said, "Let's step into the morning room."

What was said among the three of them drove Gabriel straight to Roberta's door. The girls were on the front porch when he arrived, slung into hammocks, reading and shooing away mosquitoes.

"Your mother home?" he asked as he mounted the stairs.

"She's in the kitchen. Mom!" Susan yelled over her shoulder, "Mr. Farley's coming in."

Roberta met him in the kitchen doorway. "Well, back so soon?" she said. "You come a-courtin'?"

He whisked her into the kitchen. "If it's courting you demand, you're going to get it, Roberta, because I want to marry you."

"Goodness, that's quite a change from this afternoon—"

Gabe shut her up with a kiss. It was fiery and insistent and tinged with the awareness that a porchful of young people could come slamming into the house at any moment.

And deuced if they didn't.

They heard Susan whisper, "My mom is kissing your dad," then giggles that brought Gabe's head around as he ordered over his shoulder, "Out, you two!" and added belatedly, "Hello, Isobel."

"Yes, out," Roberta seconded. "And don't come back till we tell you to."

Gabe resumed his stance, and Roberta brazenly pulled his head down for more. Some time later they came up for air, and she looped her arms loosely over his shoulders. "Oh, Gabriel," she said, gazing into his eyes, "what took you so long?"

"What do you mean, what took me so long? Do you remember the first time I kissed you? You just sat there like a lump of dough. It takes a man a while to get up his courage after that."

"I don't remember it that way. I just thought it was a bad idea."

He grinned. "Obviously, you don't anymore."

"No, Mr. Farley, I don't anymore."

"Good, because you've got to listen to me. You've got to marry me because the Ladies' Benevolent Society is making noises about trying to force your kids away from you somehow. And it's my fault, because I bashed in Elfred's face, and they figured we were fighting over you because you were probably carrying on with both of us."

She stared at him. "Who told you this?"

"Elizabeth DuMoss. She belongs to that society. Belonged. Actually, she quit today when they started raising these preposterous issues. Gave 'em a piece of her mind, too. Then she warned me what they were planning to do."

Roberta said, "My mother is a member of the Benevolent Society."

He closed his eyes and breathed, "Oh. I'm sorry, Roberta."

She walked toward the dry sink, turning her back on him. "Why would Elizabeth DuMoss stand up for me?"

"Because she knows what kind of a snake Elfred is."

She snapped him a look. "You told her what he did to me?"

"I didn't tell her. I think she just guessed from what she heard about me beating him up. Roberta, look"—he moved up close behind her and pulled her back against him—"this is all my fault. If I'd cornered Elfred out in the country, someplace where nobody would have known, this wouldn't have happened. I'm sorry. Please don't throw me out again. Let us fight this thing together."

"Why would you want to, Gabriel?" she asked, gripping his arm with both her hands. "Why? I've got to know."

His heart was pounding against her back. But he took the plunge and whispered, "Because I love you, Roberta."

The grip of her hands on his arm tightened. "I love you, too, Gabriel. I hope you'll believe that. But if I married you now, anything they'd say about me would go unchallenged. And I'm a good mother. A good one! I won't let anybody say different!"

"But if you'd marry me, they wouldn't challenge you at all, so why put yourself through that?" He turned her to face him.

"We don't know that I'll have to. So far it's just a rumor."

He could see he wasn't going to convince her tonight, so he pulled her loosely into his arms. She rested against his sturdy bulk, and it felt good to be there.

"Gabriel?" she said after a while, getting back to reality.

"What, love?"

"I've made a decision."

"Which is?"

"To talk to my mother and see what she knows about the Benevolent Society." Roberta drew back and looked into Gabriel's eyes. "Because if she's a party to this, I can't remain in this town, Gabe."

He gripped her arms. "Don't scare me that way. Roberta, Camden is my home. This is where I want to stay."

She pulled back slowly until she was standing free. "Then we'd better wait and see, hadn't we, Gabe?"

He sighed and felt heavy with foreboding. "Yes, I suppose," he finally agreed. "We'd better wait and see."

And on that forlorn note they went out to face the glowing eyes of their children, for whom they had no answers yet.

CHAPTER 15

GOING home should have been more inviting, Roberta thought as she approached Myra's house. But stepping up to the back door brought only dread.

Roberta knocked, and instead of "Roberta, dear, come in," she heard, "Oh, it's you." She entered the moss-green kitchen uninvited.

Displeasure corrugated Myra's face.

"Hello, Mother," Roberta said resignedly. "May I sit down?"

"Have you been to Grace's?"

"No, Mother. Why would I have been to Grace's?" She sat, taking the chair she had not been asked to take.

"She's been crying for three days!" Myra's eyes bulged as she seated herself on the farthest chair from Roberta. "May God forgive you for what you've done to your sister."

"What have I done to my sister?"

"Made a fool of her before this whole town, that's what!"

"Would you like to hear my side of it, Mother? Just this once? Because I think you should. Today. Now. Get it all out in the open. I can't live this way anymore, wondering why you dislike me so much!"

Myra's mouth snapped shut. "Don't be silly. I don't dislike you."

"No? Well, you could have fooled me! Mothers stand behind their children. You never did. It was always Grace, Grace, Grace! I couldn't please you if I had married the King of Siam! So why not?"

"Roberta, you're overwrought."

"Y' darn right I am." Roberta rose and bent over the table as her ire elevated. "That gang of hypocrites you have tea with has decided I'm not a fit mother, and they're going to try to get my children taken away from me. And if you're a part of it, Mother, you'd better hear the whole story first!"

Myra gasped. "How could you believe—"

"I could believe it because you've never once in your life spoken up for me. They say I've been having an affair with Gabriel. I'm not. They say I'm having another one with Elfred. I'm not. But let me tell you about your precious Elfred. From the time I set foot in this town, he's been trying. After all, I'm just a loose divorced woman, right? He has seduced woman after woman while his wife was right in the room. The whole town jokes about it, but Grace pretends it isn't happening. Only this woman"—Roberta tapped her chest—"wouldn't fall for it." Her voice began losing its fight. "This woman said no and forbid him in her house. Until—until three days ago when my car ran out of gas out in the country and Elfred came along and found me." Very softly she asked, "And what do you suppose he did, Mother?" A beat passed. "He raped me."

Myra covered her mouth and whispered, "Oh, no."

"That's why Gabriel beat him up, and that's why my car was seen at Gabriel's house late that night. I couldn't come to you, because you'd have blamed me. You're probably thinking now that I must have done something to tempt Elfred, aren't you?"

Behind her hand Myra's mouth quivered.

"Well, I didn't. So he gave me this." Roberta tipped back her head. "It's a cigar burn. It's how he made me stop fighting."

Tears had actually formed in Myra's eyes as Roberta sat down tiredly in her chair. "Now I have to know, Mother. Are you one of the Benevolent Society who wants to see my children taken away?"

Myra whispered, "No. I didn't know a thing about it till now."

Roberta breathed a hidden sigh. "Well, that's one good thing." She waited for her mother to express concern about her condition, but instead Myra was gazing past her, perhaps mourning the end of her delusions about Elfred and Grace.

"Maybe I did favor Grace," Myra said. "But there was a reason." She paused, and heaved an overburdened sigh. "My parents arranged my marriage to Carl Halburton. He was a good man. Never very outgoing or warm, but a hard worker and a good provider. When Grace was born, he was very proud.

"But Carl and I, we . . . it wasn't . . ." Myra cleared her throat and began again. "Well, let me tell it this way. A train spur came through town, and a crew came to lay it. They ran those tracks right behind our backyard, and this one young fellow used to see me out there hanging clothes. He'd come over and ask to get a drink from the pump. Then he started coming to visit me even after the crew moved up the line. He was a handsome, smiling fellow, very different from Carl. He made me laugh, and he told me I was pretty."

Roberta knew, even before the story continued. "What was his name, Mother?"

Dreamily Myra answered, "His name was Robert Coyle."

"He was my father, wasn't he?"

"Yes."

It was a peculiar moment in which to feel close to her mother, that moment in which Roberta was told she'd been lied to her whole life. Yet she had never seen softness in Myra before.

"He left, of course, with the crew," Myra continued. "And Carl knew right away that the baby wasn't his. When you were born, he announced that your name was to be Roberta, as a constant reminder of the sin I'd committed. He never let me forget it, so I suppose I wanted to pass down some of my regret to you."

"But Mother, I was still yours."

Myra shifted in her chair and said, "Yes. Well, it was hard."

There was little dignity in begging for crumbs at this point. It seemed Myra was not going to confess any love for her daughter or apologize for withholding it. What was done was done.

Roberta sat back and glanced around the room, as if coming awake from a séance. "Well, you taught me one thing, Mother."

"What's that?"

"Never to cheat my own children on love."

Myra's mouth got stubborn. "I tried very hard with you, Roberta, but you were always so headstrong . . . and different."

Some people can never admit they're wrong, Roberta realized. "So what about this Benevolent Society taking my children—you say you don't know anything about it?"

"No. Nothing. Roberta, you aren't going to go kicking up a fuss over there, are you?"

"Mother, listen to yourself! These are my children I'm fighting for." By now Roberta had become inured to Myra's callousness, but Myra hadn't offered a single word of commiseration about the rape, no word of blame for Elfred.

"Mother, you do believe me about the rape, don't you?"

"Oh, please, Roberta."

"Why would I make up such a story? And where do you think I got the burn if I was lying?"

"You and Grace are both my daughters. What can I do?"

Open your arms and close them around me, Roberta thought.

"Nothing," Roberta finally answered, accepting within herself that she truly meant it. Surprisingly, now that she had expunged her anger, she felt more amicable toward Myra.

"I really mean that, Mother. I don't expect anything from you. I guess if you continue being good to Grace, she needs it more than I do anyway. Well"—Roberta pushed back from the table and rose—"I'd better get going. I took time off work to come here, and I'll have to make it up."

Myra looked relieved that the visit was over. Roberta couldn't wait to get away. At thirty-six years old she had done a lot of growing up today, and it felt good to have it behind her.

SHE was late getting home, and the others were already there. Gabe's truck was parked on the boulevard, and a new swing hung on the front porch; the girls were crowded onto it. Gabriel was sitting on the front step reading a newspaper.

As she slammed the car door, he walked across the yard to meet her. A fine and unexpected leap lifted her heart at his approach.

"Hello," she said. "Where did the swing come from?"

"Made it for you."

"Thank you. It's very nice."

They had stopped in the break of the bridal wreath bushes. "I wish that I could kiss you," he said.

"I wish you could, too. I found myself thinking about kissing you a lot today."

"That's a good sign. Does that mean you'll marry me?"

"Not necessarily. But I thought about that, too, especially after I talked to my mother. She said she didn't know anything about the Benevolent Society taking my kids away from me."

He nodded and a half smile narrowed his eyes, which roved over her hair and face. "I've never told you before, but I really like you in your uniform."

"Do you? Why's that?"

"The way you roll up your hair, neat and tidy. The way your apron straps cross in the back. Your clean white shoes."

"You'd like me neat all the time, wouldn't you?"

"I guess so."

She took a turn assessing him and liked what she saw. "If we were married, where would we live?" Roberta asked.

"Your house is too small."

"And your house is too Caroline's."

"Are you going to be jealous of her?"

"I doubt it. I actually spoke to her picture when I was alone in your room."

"What did you say?"

"I said, 'I love your husband, Caroline Farley.' And I do, Gabriel." She saw clearly how she had stunned him with her declaration.

He got slightly breathless, and his lips dropped open. "Roberta, I don't understand. You love me, yet you won't say you'll marry me."

"Come on, you two!" Isobel yelled. "It's almost seven thirty and the meat loaf is done!"

Roberta glanced at the porch. "Let's take this up on the new swing at eleven o'clock or so," she suggested, and he let her lead the way to the house.

THAT supper seemed to take forever. By the time Gabriel had driven Isobel home and walked back up the hill, it was after eleven.

Roberta was waiting inside the living-room screen door in the dark when he came up the porch steps.

"Hi," she whispered, opening the door stealthily. "I didn't think they'd ever go to bed."

"Me either."

"I can't believe I'm sneaking around like this at my age."

"Me either, but it's kind of fun."

"All except for the mosquitoes."

"Maybe they'll leave us alone. Come on." He took her hand, and they tiptoed to the swing. "Now what were we talking about when the girls called us in for supper?"

This was what they'd been waiting for all day, this moment of reaching, touching, tasting once again. It was immediate, that first kiss, and earned by a long day's wait. The kisses Roberta had missed during the waning years of her marriage she received over and over in a roundelay of sweet repetition.

A mosquito came and bit her ankle, and she tucked her legs up, covering her feet with her skirt. Then two mosquitoes bit Gabe at once. He said against her lips, "Let's go in, Roberta."

"I can't, Gabriel. If I weren't divorced, it would be different, but that's just what the town expects me to do—take men into my house at night when my girls are sleeping."

Another stinger sank into his jaw. "Then go get a blanket."

"Oh, Gabriel, you can't be serious." He could hear the makings of a chuckle in her tone. But just then she killed a mosquito on her face. "All right, I will."

When Roberta returned with the blanket, Gabriel got them situated to his liking, leaning back on the swing and dragging her with him until their limbs were aligned. Then he flipped the blanket over their heads. Roberta scolded, "Gabriel!" And giggled.

Five minutes later a voice outside their blanket said, "Mother? Is that you under there?"

Gabe and Roberta turned to a couple of pillars of clay. Finally Roberta lifted the blanket far enough to peep out.

"Yes, Rebecca?" her thirty-six-year-old mother said, striving for dignity where there was none.

"Mother? What in the world are you doing under there?"

Gabriel jumped in. "Ah, the mosquitoes," he explained lamely, folding back the blanket. When Roberta started laughing, he couldn't help himself and started, too.

Rebecca planted her fists on her hips. "Mother, for heaven's sake, come in before the neighbors see you out here with that ridiculous blanket over your heads!"

She slammed into the house, cranked off the light and left the two on the porch laughing, with the blanket pressed to their mouths.

Finally Roberta said, "Let's say good night. We're too old for this anyway." She rose, taking a tail end of the blanket along.

He grabbed it, towing her back to him, and his wide hands caught her high around the ribs. "Marry me, Roberta," he said seriously, lifting his face as she looked down on him.

He had come a-courtin' as she'd said she wanted. But courtship was one thing and everyday life was another—with mothers, and brothers-in-law, and ladies' societies.

"Maybe," she replied, and kissed him good night.

CHAPTER 16

TOWARD dawn the next morning Roberta had a nightmare about the rape. She awakened herself with a scream, her heart driving like a ramrod in her chest.

Rebecca came tearing in. "Mother, what's wrong?" She flew to the bed and held Roberta fast. "Were you dreaming?"

"It was terrible." Roberta's voice shook as she clutched her daughter. "It was Elfred again, doing that awful thing to me, only he lifted his head, and it was Gabriel, and I kept trying to fight him off, pushing at him and telling him he was a liar. Oh, Becky."

Becky petted Roberta's hair and kept her close. "It was just a dream, Mother. Don't be afraid."

"Why would I dream such a thing about Gabriel?"

Becky sat back, capturing her mother's hands. "I don't know, but last night it didn't look like you were trying to fight him off at all."

"Oh, goodness." Roberta glanced at the window. Remembering last night, her terror subsided. "You were very displeased with us."

"Not really. I'm happy you've got Mr. Farley."

"Really?"

"He's given you a wonderful summer, given us all a wonderful summer, actually—our first Camden summer, filled with so many good memories. I think you should marry him, Mother."

"He asked me again last night."

"I keep thinking about how safe you'll be with him. And pretty soon Susan and Lydia and I will be all grown up, and when we find husbands and move away from home, you'll be so lonely. I'd love knowing that you were with Mr. Farley. And at holidays we'd all come home—Isobel, too—and what a good time we'll have."

Roberta kissed her daughter's cheek. "I love you, Becky, light of my life. The older you get, the dearer you get."

Becky looked into her mother's eyes and said very simply, "Marry Mr. Farley, Mother. I think you love him more than you know, and sometimes you can be too independent for your own good."

"Can I now?" Roberta chided good-naturedly, tipping her head.

"Yes, you can. So think about it." Becky got up and padded barefoot toward the doorway. She said over her shoulder, "Besides, if you marry him, you two won't have to kiss under a blanket on the porch swing. You can come in the house, where you belong."

LESS than one hour later, Roberta called Gabe on the telephone. "Good morning, Gabriel," she greeted.

"Why, this is a surprise," he said.

"Did you sleep well?"

He cleared his throat. "Actually, no, I didn't, Roberta."

"Oh?" she said, with a flirtatious undertone. "Why's that?"

He chuckled deep in his throat, and the sound prompted pleasant shivers up her trunk.

"I've been thinking," Roberta went on. "They're doing an Oscar Wilde play at the opera house tonight, and I promised the girls I'd take them. Would you and Isobel want to come?"

"To a play? I'm willing to give it a try."

She smiled and felt young. And impatient! "Gabriel?" she said.

"What, Roberta?"

"Tonight seems a very long time away."

SHE had a hectic schedule at work that day, with plenty of medical tasks to occupy her mind. But Gabriel occupied it, too. She planned how, at the end of the afternoon, she would wash her hair and pin it up the way he liked. This night she intended to accept his proposal of marriage. "Gabriel," she would say, "I accept your proposal. I'd be very proud to be your wife."

But when she got home, a strange woman was sitting on her new porch swing, dressed in a hat ringed with cabbage roses. Beneath it her straight summer suit and brown oxfords looked severe.

"Mrs. Jewett?" she said, rising at Roberta's approach.

"Yes?"

"My name is Alda Quimby. I'm a member of the Camden school board, and I've been asked to speak to you by our chairman, Mr. Boynton."

Both women remained standing as Roberta said, "What can I do for you, Mrs. Quimby?"

"I may as well warn you, it isn't pleasant."

Roberta knew exactly what it was, and exhibited no patience. "Well, spit it out then. That bunch of dried-up hussies known as the Benevolent Society thinks I'm not a fit mother, right?"

Mrs. Quimby's mouth dropped open, then snapped shut tight. The flowers on her hat fairly trembled on her self-righteous head.

"Mr. Boynton's wife is a member of that society. Through her, it's come to our attention that your children are left to fend for themselves five days a week, and that in your absence other town children have taken to gathering at your house without any adult supervision. Is that correct?"

"I work to support my children—*that's* correct!" Roberta snapped.

Mrs. Quimby's mouth puckered. "You're divorced, I believe."

"Yes, thank goodness. And I'm a licensed nurse and the owner of this house and the owner of that motorcar and quite capable of raising my children on my own."

"Mrs. Jewett, I'll make this as plain as possible. Complaints have been waged about your causing a fistfight between two men in this town, one of whom is married and is—to add to the shamefulness of the incident—your own brother-in-law. And *today* there's a rumor that you and the other man were seen spooning on this very swing at midnight last night!

"Mrs. Jewett, I'm sure you'll understand that the school board must concern itself with the welfare of any child whose well-being is threatened by lack of normal daily parental care and whose home is being run like a bordello."

Roberta scarcely trusted herself to remain on the porch lest she send highfalutin Alda Quimby bouncing down its steps.

"You don't know the first thing about what makes a good parent!" Roberta shouted. "If you did, you'd be at Elfred Spear's door right now. I'll ask you to leave, Mrs. Quimby. And if you want to question my morals or the care I give my children, you'd better be prepared to do so through legal channels, because I shall fight you until I'm dead before I'll let you take my girls away. Now get off my porch!"

"Mrs. Jewett, at the next school board meeting—"

"Off!" Roberta gave Mrs. Quimby a little push, and the woman scuttled off with her cabbage roses trembling.

WHEN Gabriel arrived that evening, he found Roberta in a state of extreme agitation, still in her uniform. She filled him in on what had happened, then raved, "How dare they!"

The girls were all hovering, as incensed as their mother.

Rebecca said, "I'll tell that school board a thing or two!"

"Yeah, our mother is the best!" added Susan.

Isobel said, "I'll tell them, too, the idiots!"

"Could they really take us away from her?" Lydia asked, at ten still young enough to be more fearful than angry.

"I don't think so," Gabe said. "Roberta, I'm so sorry."

Then something wonderful happened: Gabriel took Roberta in his arms with all four girls looking on. "Don't you worry, Roberta. I won't let anybody take *anything* away from you—ever."

He opened the circle of two, and it became a circle of six as their

daughters closed in around them. If there was ever a moment when the two families bonded, this was it.

"Now listen," Gabe said. "We're not going to let this keep us from going to the theater, are we?"

Alda Quimby had ruined Roberta's wonderful day; now here was Gabriel trying valiantly to rescue the mood—a true reversal of roles for him and Roberta.

"Oh, all right," she said, and hurried upstairs to get ready.

THE Jewett-Farley clan attracted plenty of gawkers at the opera house that night. During intermission they stood in the lobby sipping lemonade, watching people's glances carom away, as if everyone in the place weren't whispering about them.

One couple came to greet them: Elizabeth and Aloysius Du-Moss. Elizabeth said, "Mrs. Jewett, may I have a word with you?"

She led Roberta aside. "Forgive me for intruding on your evening, but I thought you should know. There's a movement afoot to bring up this unpleasantness about you at the school board meeting Monday night."

Elizabeth gripped Roberta's arm imploringly with her gloved hand. "Listen to me. Don't let them cow you. They've got no power to do this. They've got no right! No right at all!"

Roberta was stunned by Mrs. DuMoss's ferocity. "Perhaps not, but they're doing it anyway, and no matter what I might have threatened, I don't have the money to hire a lawyer."

"You don't need money. If it should come to that, I have money, and I would be the first one to come to your aid."

"You? Why, Mrs. DuMoss?"

"Please . . . Elizabeth."

"Elizabeth. But why? You scarcely even know me."

Elizabeth squeezed Roberta's arm harder, then released it. "I know enough. And we won't let them get away with it."

The last act of the play was lost on Roberta as she kept remembering Elizabeth DuMoss's words to her. When the play was over, they all rode home in Roberta's motorcar. The girls were starving, so Roberta made popcorn, then said, "We'll be in the backyard. Come on, Gabriel."

Outside, she told him that Elizabeth had offered to help. "But Gabe, she hardly knows me. Why would she do such a thing?"

"I don't know."

He drew on her hand, and she fell against him. "Oh, Gabe, this has been the most mixed-up day. All day at work I was planning to come home and get cleaned up the way you like me; then I was going to tell you I'd marry you. Only, when I got home, that Quimby woman was on my porch, and now all of this talk about the school board—"

"Hold it a minute. Back up to the part about you marrying me. Did you mean that?"

"Yes, I do. But I don't want that darned school board to know it. If anything comes of this inquiry, I want to fight it on my own merit as a mother."

He sighed and said, "All right, Roberta, we'll do it your way." His hands dropped from her waist.

"Gabriel," she whispered, "come on. Don't be mad. Aren't you even going to kiss me?"

"We wouldn't want the school board to find out," he said.

She grinned. "If you won't kiss me, I'll kiss you." Putting her lips near his, she said, "Right now I want to give them something to talk about."

CHAPTER 17

SEVERAL days later, when the school board convened at seven thirty p.m. in the auditorium of the high school, Roberta was present. So were Gabriel and his brother, Seth, and Seth's wife, Aurelia, as well as most of the members of the Benevolent Society, a number of teachers, and Elizabeth and Aloysius DuMoss. Other nosy townspeople came also, hoping for additional fodder for gossip.

After Mr. Boynton had called the meeting to order and the six-member board had discussed some mundane school business, the chairman deferred to Alda Quimby.

"Mrs. Jewett, now if we might ask you a few questions." Alda cleared her throat, and Gabriel squeezed Roberta's hand.

"Ask anything you want," Roberta replied from the second row.

In the back of the hall a group of young people who had been expressly forbidden by their parents to attend the meeting slipped inside to stand quietly along the rear wall. Roberta's children were there, and Isobel, of course; Shelby DuMoss; and a cross section of others. The last to enter were Marcelyn, Trudy and Corinda Spear.

Alda Quimby noted their arrival, pruned her lips and began again. "Mrs. Jewett, you moved here, I believe, this past spring, following your divorce."

"That's right," Roberta said loud and clear, so everyone in the hall could hear.

"You secured work as a nurse, employed by the state, and you travel around the countyside in an automobile—"

"Which I purchased from Mr. Boynton here. Hello, Mr. Boynton. It's nice to see you."

Boynton turned as red as a boiled lobster while Alda Quimby went on. "So your job takes you away from home from early morning until late at night."

"Some days."

"During which time your children fend for themselves."

"My children are sixteen, fourteen and ten and have been taught to be self-reliant. Yes, they fend for themselves when necessary."

"Your house, Mrs. Jewett, has become rather a gathering spot for other young people of Camden, has it not?"

"I guess you could say that."

"Where they are allowed to stay past suppertime and into the late hours of the night, whether there is any supervision or not."

From the back a young voice called, "Why don't you ask us?"

Roberta's head snapped around; then she whispered to Gabe, "I told them they were not to come here."

"It's their lives, too, Roberta," Gabe replied low.

"Children are not allowed at school board meetings!" Mrs. Quimby shouted above the clatter as the children headed straight for the front of the hall.

"At our house we're allowed to speak. Why shouldn't we here, when it's my mother you're accusing?" Becky fearlessly led her legion to battle. "Don't think we don't know what kind of things you whisper behind her back just because she's divorced. Well, the best part of our lives began when she got rid of our father. And she has a job that we're all very proud of, too."

Lydia chimed in. "She's a nurse, and she helps people."

"And she owns her own motorcar, and she runs it herself, which most women would be afraid to do." That was Susan.

"But our mother's not afraid of anything," Lydia said.

"Not even of you. She wouldn't have *had* to come here tonight, and neither would we"—Rebecca's glance took in her cohorts—"but we thought you should know what we do at our house."

Isobel stepped forward. "Before Mrs. Jewett came, I was really lonely. You all know my mother is dead, so I didn't have anyone at home after school either. Then I met Susan and Becky and Lydia and their mother, and everything changed. The first thing we did together was *Hiawatha*. Mrs. Jewett let us use her front porch and—"

"And make any costumes we wanted." Shelby DuMoss led a round of remarks from the children. Even the Spear girls chimed in.

"And props. Gee, my mother wouldn't let us make a mess like that on our front porch!"

"Then she let us put on the play for our parents."

"And then we put it on at school, didn't we, Mrs. Roberson?" Becky turned to find her teacher in the crowd.

In row four, Mrs. Roberson stood up. "They certainly did. If any of you thought the performance was originated and rehearsed at school, you stand corrected. Miss Werm and I attended the performance on Mrs. Jewett's front porch and saw how the children were encouraged to take part in some very healthy activities there."

Miss Werm stood up. "Not only drama but music as well. And I heard something about nature walks that she conducted."

"Oh, yeah! She took us up Mount Battie, and we identified trees and collected insects, and she'd recite poetry."

"It's always fun at her house because everybody laughs there."

"And nobody tells us to be seen and not heard."

"And there's always something to do." These remarks were made by the Spear girls.

"I'm reading a book by Robert Louis Stevenson—"

"And we're probably going to make it our next play."

Silence fell across the hall, a vast, memorable silence in which the gilding of Roberta Jewett's reputation began. In the midst of that silence Gabriel rose calmly to his feet. He looked straight at Alda Quimby and spoke in a deep, sure voice.

"I have watched my daughter blossom this summer. Mrs. Jewett opened her heart and her home and took Isobel in as if she were one of her own." He looked down at Roberta. "And for that I am eternally grateful."

Without histrionics, Gabriel resumed his seat.

"Mr. Farley," Alda Quimby pursued, "there is another issue—a, well, a delicate matter. But in the presence of these children . . ."

Elizabeth DuMoss stood up, radiating social grace. "I believe I can shed light on that issue. You all know me and my husband, Aloysius. And this is our lawyer from Bangor, Mr. Harvey. If the children have finished, a private session might be in order. Mr. Chairman, would the board mind repairing to another room?"

"Of course, Mrs. DuMoss."

"I believe Mrs. Jewett and Mr. Farley should be present, too."

When they had gathered in a classroom down the hall, Aloysius introduced Mr. Daniel Harvey, a tall, courtly fellow with an affable mien. Mr. Harvey suggested that everyone seat themselves at the school desks. Then he stood in front, by the teacher's desk, addressing them in a voice calculated to soothe.

"Mr. and Mrs. DuMoss have asked me to be present tonight to represent them and you, Mrs. Jewett—should the need arise—in what they hope shall be the immediate silencing of the allegations regarding licentious conduct on the part of Mrs. Jewett. Mrs. Du-Moss informs me that since what she has to say involves Mr. Spear, she felt his children should be protected from hearing it at all costs. To that end, she has requested that each member of the board sign a confidentiality agreement."

The board had never come up against such a request before. However, given Aloysius DuMoss's largesse to the school district, they had little choice but to sign. With the signatures completed, Mr. Harvey said, "I shall let Mrs. DuMoss proceed."

Elizabeth rose and, followed by her husband, ascended the podium and sat at the teacher's desk. Aloysius stood at his wife's shoulder as she spoke in a reserved, cultured voice.

"I recently heard a rumor about a fistfight between Gabe Farley and Elfred Spear. The night of that fight Gabe yelled something in Elfred's front yard that nobody in this room has had the courage to say and that I believe must be said. The word was rape, and I know about it because it happened to me."

Aloysius gripped his wife's shoulder as her throat worked and the knuckles on her linked hands turned white.

"When I was seventeen years old, Elfred Spear raped me." Tears suddenly glittered in Elizabeth's eyes. Her husband dipped his head near hers and fortified her with a whispered word.

566

She cleared her throat and continued. "The ramifications of that night have affected me the rest of my life. My marriage to Aloysius began in fear. Only his patient love has seen me through the nightmares that took years to go away. Since the Benevolent Society's attack on Mrs. Jewett, my nightmares have returned."

Elizabeth's eyes sought and found Roberta's, and their kindred pasts brought the glisten of tears to the eyes of both of them.

To the room at large, Elizabeth stated in the most ladylike tone, "I damn Elfred Spear all over again for what he did to me. I did nothing to encourage him—nothing! The women Elfred preys upon are sentenced to eternal silence because if they were to speak up, *they* would be accused, just as you've accused Mrs. Jewett.

"I wish to confront you tonight with a plea to stop persecuting her. If you don't, you should know that our estimable fortune will be behind Mr. Harvey in defending Mrs. Jewett in whatever way is necessary. There will be newspaper reporters here, too, challenging your motives. In the process, Elfred Spear's wife and children will be dragged through the trail of evildoing he's left behind. Gentlemen and lady, I leave you to decide where to go from here."

Elizabeth sat back and relaxed her hands. Her husband patted her shoulder as she looked up at him.

Mr. Boynton said, "We need a few minutes to talk this over."

The DuMosses, their lawyer, Roberta and Gabe left the room. Out in the hall, when the schoolroom door closed behind them, Roberta and Elizabeth stood before one another in a moment of poignant silence before hugging.

"How can I ever thank you, Elizabeth?"

"Perhaps you already have. I've let it out at last, and it feels so good. I wouldn't have done that but for your own misfortune."

"You spoke for both of us," said Roberta.

"I'll tell you one thing," Elizabeth said, putting on a more cheerful face. "Alda Quimby will pay the price for spearheading this inquiry. It'll drive her crazy that she can't tell this to every woman in that Benevolent Society."

The door opened and Mr. Boynton stood before them. "The inquiry is dropped," he said simply. "Sorry, Mrs. Jewett."

The six school board members silently filed away.

Gabriel hugged Roberta, then Elizabeth. Roberta thanked Mr. Harvey and Mr. DuMoss also. Finally Elizabeth suggested, "Why don't we all gather at our house to celebrate? What do you say?"

"That sounds wonderful," Roberta said. "But do I dare leave my girls alone?" They were all laughing even before Elizabeth replied, "The school board will probably call an inquiry."

Outside they encountered their children, who all spoke at once. "We did it!" "We saved you!" "Mother, I was so proud."

"Oh, Mrs. Jewett, you won! You won!"

Amid the celebrating, there was a somber moment when Roberta went up to her three nieces and hugged them. "Thank you for what you said tonight," she told them. She wondered what they knew about their father and hoped they were ignorant of his gravest faults. "Give your mother my love. And tell her I'm getting married soon."

Corinda's eyes widened in excitement. "You are, Aunt Birdy?"

"To Mr. Farley. But shh! Don't spread it around here tonight. We haven't told the girls yet."

Corinda giggled as they parted company, with Roberta's hand slipping from her nieces' shoulders with a lingering melancholy. Gabriel came up behind Roberta and sensed her sadness over the irreparable rift between her and her sister. He touched her waist and said, "There's someone here I want you to meet."

It was his sister-in-law, Aurelia, who, along with her husband, Seth, was invited to join the group heading over to the DuMosses'. From Aurelia and Seth, Roberta felt only open friendliness.

The children strayed away to their various homes as the adults drove to the DuMoss home. It was there, after their first toast to Roberta's victory, that Gabriel proposed a second toast.

"To my future wife," he said. "Roberta has agreed to marry me."

Felicitations poured forth, accompanied by hugs. Elizabeth lifted her glass. "To the future Mr. and Mrs. Gabriel Farley!"

And as many glasses touched, Roberta realized she would have her first true Camden friend in Elizabeth DuMoss.

CHAPTER 18

WHEN Roberta and Gabe got back to her house, the kitchen light was on and all four girls were eating divinity with spoons.

"We tried to get it thick, but our arms got tired beating it," Isobel explained. "But it's really yummy. Want some?"

"What are you still doing here?" Gabe asked breezily.

"I live here, didn't you know?" she replied cheekily, licking a spoon.

Gabe slung an arm loosely around Roberta's neck and said, "Know something? You're going to. Tell 'em, Roberta."

"Your father and I are going to get married."

"Heck, we knew that," Isobel replied, still licking.

"Sure, we knew that," Becky seconded.

"When, Mother?" Lydia asked.

Roberta deferred to Gabe. "When, Gabe?"

"When do you want to?"

Isobel answered, "Sooner the better, so we can all live together."

Roberta turned to Gabe again. "Where we going to live?"

"Here," he replied, as if he'd known all along. "Gonna knock a hole in that wall over there and add on a bedroom for us, and the girls can share the two rooms upstairs."

"I get Isobel in my room!" declared Susan.

"Who's going to stand up for you, Mother?" asked Rebecca.

"Who wants to?"

Three hands went up. "I do!" "I do!" "I do!"

"I know. We'll draw straws," Roberta declared.

Rebecca won the drawing, and Roberta felt a secret spark of pleasure: It was right that Becky stand up for her. After all, she'd been encouraging this union for some time.

Minutes later Gabe and Roberta were back out on the front porch in the dark, saying good night.

It was different, kissing as an engaged couple. Betrothal removed certain restrictions. Gabe got more and more reckless, until Roberta pushed him away and whispered, "Stop, Gabe."

He freed her abruptly, sensing her rising fear. "I'm not Elfred, Roberta. I won't hurt you."

"I know," she whispered.

"But he's scared you, hasn't he?"

"Some. Maybe."

He thought awhile, damning Elfred and fearing for the blight the man might have left on their future. Necking with all their buttons closed was one thing; facing a marriage bed was another. He wondered if she'd delay their wedding to avoid her fears.

"So when can we get married?" he asked.

"Oh"—she let out a puff of breath—"I don't know. How long will it take you to get an addition on the house?"

He thought about his schedule. "I can't start for a few weeks."

"Well . . ." She thought a moment. "What about November?"

It seemed light-years away, but Gabe hid his disappointment and said, "Guess that's all right." He realized that as a groom, he had been given a more delicate second bride than the first. Roberta would need an inordinate amount of patience and understanding on their wedding night and perhaps for many nights to follow.

THE girls had something to say about waiting until November. They wanted the wedding to be held on the front porch, and there was a good chance that by then it could be covered with snow.

So the date was moved up to October fourteenth, and Gabriel got busy with the addition. The bedroom wing was weatherproof but still shy of being finished when their wedding day arrived.

Roberta awakened early, rolling her face to the window, where a flawless roseate dawn was ascending. A perfect day for a wedding, she thought. Nevertheless, she curled deeper into her rumpled double bed, realizing that tonight she'd be sharing a bed with Gabe. She pressed a hand to her trembling stomach.

How could a person want something and fear it, too?

Sometimes the day seemed to crawl, sometimes fly toward four o'clock. When she was dressing, with the girls traipsing in and out of her bedroom asking for last-minute items, her nerves were as on edge as if she were seventeen and a virgin.

The girls had new dresses, and though they all looked adorable, Rebecca, in an ankle-length dress of apricot satin, looked quite breathtaking. And so grown up! Roberta thought.

Shortly before four Lydia called, "Gabe and Isobel are here!"

When Roberta saw Gabe on the porch, wearing a new black wool suit, she could tell he was far from calm. His freshly shaved cheeks were rosy as the dawn as he said, "Hello, Roberta."

She said, "Hello, Gabriel," very formally. Then they both laughed nervously as she pushed open the screen door.

Isobel said, "Gosh, Roberta, you look so pretty!"

Belatedly he said, "Yes . . . yes, you certainly do."

She was decked out in ivory, an Austrian-draped dress that fell in layers from beneath her breast and showed her high-topped shoes.

Her hair was swept up in back around a white silk rose, much as she wore it with her nurse's cap.

"And you look very elegant. You bought a new suit."

He cleared his throat and glanced down briefly. "Ah . . . yes."

"I thought we'd wait outside on the porch," Roberta said.

"Oh, certainly!" Gabe replied nervously.

Some guests began arriving: Seth, who would stand up for Gabe, with Aurelia and their children; Gabe's mother, Maude, with whom Roberta had forged an uneasy peace; the DuMosses and their children; Mrs. Roberson and Miss Werm; and Eleanor Balfour, from the regional nursing office. And, of course, Myra.

Grace was conspicuously absent, though Roberta really hadn't expected her to attend. Elfred wasn't at the wedding either, of course. Word had it that his business wasn't doing well.

The Reverend Davis, the minister from the Congregational church, suggested they get started.

The ceremony was ordinary by any standards, except for the fact that the bride accompanied her daughters on the piano while the trio sang "Oh Promise Me" in three-part harmony, and Rebecca recited the *Hiawatha* bow-and-cord verse.

The Reverend Davis then asked the groom, "Do you take this woman?" and when Gabe answered, "I do," the four girls mouthed the words along with him. They did the same when Roberta gave her response. When Gabriel kissed his bride, the kiss was brief and self-conscious. An audience definitely rattled him. When he lifted his head, the girls swarmed around them, and the guests came forward, too, with hugs and congratulations.

The wedding feast was all finger food, passed around by the four new stepsisters, who had helped their mother make it. Among the refreshments were cold sandwiches, fudge and snow-white divinity—no spoons required this time—and Gabe's favorite sour-cream cookies, which his mother had volunteered to make.

Soon it was after six p.m. and their guests were leaving. The girls were going off to sleep at Gabe's house with Grandma Maude, and Gabe had no idea how to approach the next couple of hours.

The yard emptied. Gabe and Roberta stood on the front-porch steps listening to the autumn silence. Beyond the rooftops the sea looked like a plate of sky-blue enamel broken by the distant, jutting islands that burned up out of the water like small fires. Vibrant or-

ange and blue—the entire vista—with occasional spires of ever-
greens poking through and white boats coming home at day's end.

"I remember when you built this porch," Roberta said.

"Six months ago."

"Is that all?"

"Whoa, did you hate me."

Roberta chuckled. "I did, didn't I?"

He had been waiting for her head to turn so he could read her
eyes. She turned it, and if there was anxiety within her, she hid it well.

"Are you tired?" he asked.

"Yes, I am."

"Want to go in?"

In answer she turned, and her footsteps slurred across the hollow porch floor. They crossed the living room and stood in the
doorway to the kitchen. The girls had left the room cleaner than it
had ever been. On the table sat Caroline's philodendron plant.

As Roberta's eyes paused on it, Gabe asked, "Do you mind?"

"No, of course not. Isobel asked if she could bring it over. Actually, it dresses up the room. There are things Isobel can teach me."

He had never met another human being like Roberta, so unsus-
ceptible to jealousy, so open to change. "I love you, Roberta," he
said. "I've been standing here realizing just how much."

"Why, Gabe," she said as he curled her into his embrace.

She would have said, "I love you, too," but he kissed her with a
tenderness so exquisite that it made her heart hurt. Then he embraced her full length, and she knew the next step was up to her.

She leaned back, hands coming to rest on his chest, and said, "If
you don't mind, I think I'll use the new bathtub."

"I don't mind," he said, releasing her.

While she went inside and closed the bathroom door, he
removed his shoes, his tie, his collar and jacket. He then sat on a
chair in their new bedroom, waiting.

Finally the bathroom door opened, emitting a billow of moist air
and the scent of powder. Roberta stood in the doorway in a blue
cotton nightgown. She glanced at Gabe's bare feet, his unbuttoned
shirt. It was obvious he'd been sitting there waiting.

"Do you want to . . ." She motioned behind her, leaving the
invitation unfinished.

"Oh, sure." He went in and brushed his teeth and washed his

face. When he came back out, she was sitting on the edge of the bed facing him. He went around to the other side and, with his back to her, removed all but his short-legged union suit and got in.

When he lay down, she lay down. It was still shy of seven o'clock and far from dark. He turned on his side and looked over at her. She was looking at him.

"This is unlike me," she said. "I am no cowering wallflower."

He took her hand, watching his thumb as it played over hers. "Roberta," he said, "tell me what scares you most."

"The memories come back. I can only go so far, and then it's as if I'm on that gravel road again. I don't know how to get over it."

He continued rubbing her hand with his thumb, letting her get used to seeing him on the other half of her bed. His eyes kept steady on hers as he wondered how to proceed.

Finally he whispered, "Come here," and rolled to his back. "We've both done this before," he said. "Do what you want."

She lay above him, looking down, while he flung his wrists back and let them lie pulse up on the pillow. She studied his eyes for a long moment. Her right hand lay on his chest where he'd released it, over his heart, which she could feel beating as fast as her own.

A tress of her hair fell from behind her ear across his chin. He did not move, only met her gaze with his steady one. She threaded the stray hair behind her ear and slowly leaned to kiss him.

After she ended the kiss, they opened their eyes, so close they could feel the radiant warmth of each other's skin.

She whispered, "Gabriel, your heart is racing. I can feel it."

"Is yours?"

"Yes," she whispered, kissing him again. Midway through the kiss she found his upturned wrists and circled them with her hands, squeezing as if to pinion him in place and keep him from lunging up, though he was only lying as before, posing no threat at all. His pulse beat up against her palms. Then desire came as a gift, an onslaught free of fear or memory. Roberta smiled, let her eyes close, and claimed her victory over Elfred Spear.

SHE would see Elfred intermittently in the years that followed. But they never spoke, nor did she and her sister, Grace. The Spear girls, though forbidden, found ways to come to Roberta's house and take part in plays and musicales with their cousins.

573

Myra came, too, when invited, but never stayed long and always left in a huff over some disagreement with her younger daughter.

"What makes Grandma so ornery?" the girls would ask.

And Roberta would reply, "Who knows?"

And then one day they asked, and Gabriel replied, "Jealousy."

Roberta snapped her head around to gape at him. "What?"

"She's jealous of you. Don't you know that? So is Grace. Because you're always so happy and you've made your happiness yourself."

"Really?" She considered his opinion for some time, then kissed him. "Why, thank you. I never would have figured that out."

"That's because you don't have an ounce of jealousy in you, so you can't see it in others."

"Hm," she said thoughtfully.

They walked to the kitchen, where the supper dishes were waiting to be washed. He called over his shoulder, "Whose turn is it?"

Someone called back, "Not ours!"

Someone else called back, "Not ours!"

It was nice having teams—when they did their work. But there were always so many more inventive things to do!

Gabe looked down at Roberta and said, "Should we do 'em?"

"Naw, let's leave 'em."

"They'll be all dried on tomorrow."

"But tomorrow it'll be somebody else's turn."

He laughed, then cocked an eyebrow suggestively. "So what else should we do instead?"

She went up on tiptoe and whispered something in his ear.

He faked a gasp and said, "Mis-sus Farley!"

Then they snagged jackets from the hooks by the door and called, "Hey, girls! Be right back. Gotta take a run over to the shop real quick!"

And ran out into the twilight, giggling.

LAVYRLE SPENCER

The author by a 1916 Ford at the Owls Head Transportation Museum, Owls Head, Maine

LaVyrle Spencer recently fell in love—with the charming seaside village of Camden, Maine, that is. When she and Dan, her husband of more than thirty years, arrived there to research her latest novel, the townspeople, as she puts it, "rolled out red carpets for us."

One of the highlights of Spencer's stay was a visit to the library to see the papers of the poet Edna St. Vincent Millay, whose fond writings about her Camden childhood and her independent mother inspired the book. While in Camden, Spencer also cranked and rode in a vintage 1916 Model T Ford, took in the local flora and fauna, and made the scenic trek up Millay's beloved Mount Battie—all experiences the novelist from Stillwater, Minnesota, put to good use in her evocative story. "Reality is a premier goal of mine," Spencer says. "I constantly research, and work to titillate the five senses of my readers. I have a list on my wall that says 'See, Hear, Feel, Taste, and Smell,' which, even after nineteen years of writing, I refer to often."

Readers obviously appreciate the attention LaVyrle Spencer pays to detail in her down-to-earth romances. *That Camden Summer* is nothing less than her eleventh best seller in eleven years.

The original editions of the books in this volume are published and copyrighted as follows:

Come to Grief
Published by Michael Joseph Limited
distributed by Penguin Books Canada Limited at $29.99
© 1995 by Dick Francis

Coming Home
Published by St. Martin's Press
distributed by McClelland & Stewart Inc. at $35.00
© 1995 by Robin Pilcher, Fiona Pilcher, Mark Pilcher, and the Trustees of Rosamunde Pilcher's 1988 Trust

OSCAR: The True Story of a Husky
Published by Kerr Publishing Pty Ltd.
© 1987 by Nils Lied

That Camden Summer
Published by G. P. Putnam's Sons
distributed by BeJo Sales Inc. at $32.50
© 1996 by LaVyrle Spencer

ILLUSTRATORS
Todd Doney: *Come to Grief,* title spread
Robert Hunt: *Come to Grief,* interior art
James Griffin: *Coming Home,* interior art
Donna Diamond: *That Camden Summer*

ACKNOWLEDGMENTS
Pages 6-7: Todd Doney/The Image Bank.
Page 142: Painting by Laura Knight.
Pages 142-143, 144 (background): courtesy of the Board of Trustees of the Victoria and Albert Museum.
Page 233, lines 23-25: from "My Heart Stood Still," By Lorenz Hart and Richard Rodgers. © 1927 Warner Bros. Inc. (renewed). Rights for the extended renewal term in the United States controlled by The Estate of Lorenz Hart (WB Music Corp., administrator) and Williamson Music (ASCAP). All rights reserved. Reprinted by permission of Warner Bros. Publications U.S. Inc. & Williamson Music.
Page 325, lines 17-18 from "Deep Purple," Lyric by Mitchell Parish. © 1934, 1939 (renewed 1962, 1967) EMI Robbins Catalog Inc. All rights reserved. Reprinted by permission of Warner Bros. Publications U.S. Inc.
Pages 378-379 (main photograph); 390 (main photograph): Paul Raffaele. Page 378 (inset): W.R.J. Dingle. Pages 380; 390 (top right); 418-419 (main photograph, top left); 444-445 (main photograph, right center and bottom): I.R. McLeod. Pages 384-385: map by David Carroll. Pages 390 (center, bottom); 418 (bottom); 419 (bottom); 444 (top left and right): Colin Monteath. Pages 5 (left); 412; 419 (top, middle); 445 (top right): Harry Black.
Page 453: Jack Walsh.

203 241 9607